FINAL
GAME

FINAL GAME

Shawan Lewis

URBAN BOOKS

http://www.urbanbooks.net

501470470

URBAN SOUL is published by

Urban Books
1199 Straight Path
West Babylon, NY 11704

ISBN-13: 978-1-59983-034-6
ISBN-10: 1-59983-034-5

First Printing: November 2008

10 9 8 7 6 5 4 3 2 1

Printed in the United States of America

For Sevalyn—I wanna be like you when I grow up.

Acknowledgments

Favor. The one word that chronicles how I got to this point in the game of life. I thank You, Father, for the wins, losses, sidelines, and slam dunks. Despite my flagrant fouls, You guard me still. There is no better coach, and I wouldn't trade You for the world.

To my team: Mom, Nia, Nana, Aunt Becky, David, Sandra, Shawnda, and Karen—thanks for continuously doing what you do to make me better.

To my agent, AB: Thanks for working hard to make deals happen.

Urban Soul: Thanks for seeing my potential and for offering a chance to show my stuff.

Special thanks to: Carl Weber, Roy Glenn, Nicole Peters, Urban Books, Karibu Books, Mejah Books, Lushena Books, Expressions, Sepia, Sand & Sable, Robilyn, Azarel, Life Changing Books, Enoch Pratt Free Library, Brother Nati, Masamba, Dexter, Carvellus, Michael J. Burt, Jonathan Luckett, Tina McElroy Ansa, Annika, Benita, Sabirah, and all of the book clubs, book distributors, media outlets, and organizations that have supported me.

Family and friends—too many to mention but never forgotten. Thanks for standing by me.

To the readers, particularly those who have been patient for book two, here it is. I appreciate your support. Enjoy!

Prologue:
Forgotten Promises

*September 11, 2006, Tavern on the Green,
Manhattan, New York*

Darin

Under a dark velvet sky, I saw the sun, even though it was night. I'd been to hell and back, and never thought I'd live to share my life story. Only God could break down the walls I'd constructed around my heart to bring me to the sacred place where I stood. Ribbons of washed white silk swayed under the moonlight. A harp and violins serenaded an angel my way. Her brilliance outshined the prettiest star in the sky. I was mesmerized more by her beautiful spirit than by her outward glamour. Why she took a chance on me, and accepted my faults, I'll never know. I do know that God spared me so I could help others. He knew I'd fall short on this journey. He sent me a soul mate to guide me to my best life. A life far different from how I came into the world, and how I handled my first marriage.

In the midst of this joyous event, full of garden splendor and well-wishers, I pictured the blessings ahead. As a professional athlete, I got paid to slam-dunk basketballs. I became a franchise player by studying the game endlessly, building my technique from the heroes that had preceded me . . . Magic, Jordan, and Byrd. I was a talented ball player, but I'd never built anything solid in my personal life. My relationships with family and lovers had collapsed, like a frame structure hit by a hurricane. It was my survival at the World Trade Center that made me realize that God was the architect of my foundation. He pieced me back together, and discarded the infidelity, greed, and bitterness that had plagued my spirit.

I smiled at my bride as she arrived at the gazebo. The cathedral ivory train that flowed from her gown was stunning. In this precious moment of time, she reached for me and clasped her hand in mine. I wanted to say something, but my emotions had me numb. The tears flowing down my face were my reaction to true love shining down on me, erasing the pain. I squeezed my bride's baby-soft hand as I reflected on my past.

Five years ago, I wasn't afraid of anything in life. Nothing unnerved me, not even cheating on my first wife . . . until September 11th. On that day, the magnitude of my sins came crashing down. Trapped on the fifteenth floor of the South Tower, I'd tried to find solace in prayer, but I couldn't. The screams and cries surrounding me were deafening. I hadn't attended church in years. The only verse I could remember was from Psalm 23 . . . I repeated the verse over and over, blocking out the agony from a crushed leg due to fallen cement. Terrified people were dying at my feet. It felt like the Apocalypse . . .

I wasn't even supposed to be at work that morning. I had scheduled a marriage-counseling session for me and my wife, Serena. We'd separated after she found out about my affair with an insurance broker, named Carmen. But our marriage had been deteriorating long before I cheated. When we lost our daughter, Hope, at birth in 1999, our sadness affected our relationship. Serena was either distraught or had an attitude all the time. I stayed out of the house to avoid her accusations about my whereabouts. We put energy into our jobs instead of our marriage. I shared my problems with Carmen, whose office was eight floors above the sportswear firm I headed. I couldn't express my feelings with my wife, but I confided in another woman who was practically a stranger.

Serena had a travel agency in the North Tower. We had attempted to salvage the marriage by starting counseling sessions. I missed the first session. Serena caught Carmen and me the same day at Starbucks, only a few blocks from the counselor's office. Serena saw me saying sweet nothings to a woman that should have been her. I noticed my wife staring, and ran after her as she left the coffee shop.

I followed her all the way to our penthouse in Manhattan. When we arrived, I came clean about the affair. She told me to pack my bags. I didn't put up a fight, which made her question whether I wanted to remain married.

The morning of September 11th, for whatever reason, I couldn't get Serena off my mind. I called her at 8:20 AM—she always arrived early at her office to review paperwork. She had answered on the first ring.

"Good morning, this is Serena Simms."

I gripped the phone with my sweaty palm, pausing before I spoke. "Morning, babe, it's me." She didn't reply. "I was thinking about you, wondering how you're doing."

"Oh, it's so nice to know I was on your mind after you sexed Carmen."

"Serena, it's not like that."

"Darin, stop trying to convince yourself that what you do is right. I don't know why you are wasting my time. I work. Do you remember what that is? Or are you still too busy having love lattes at Starbucks?"

I clenched my jaw as I stood up from my executive office chair, frustrated. I glanced at the smog from my window. "I'm at the office. See, Serena, I didn't even want to get into it with you today. I called because I thought we could get together and talk. I spoke to Dr. Collins yesterday. She said we could come in this morning for a counseling session at nine o'clock. Do you wanna go?"

She sucked her teeth. "We tried that already, and you never showed up. No, I don't wanna go to counseling, and you can go to hell for all I care."

"Forget about it, Serena."

"Forget you, Darin!" she screamed. "I'm tired of being your afterthought. I tolerated you playing doctor to your baby mama, Paige, and now I gotta deal with you cheating on me? No, I don't think so."

I sighed heavily into the phone. "Serena, first of all, Paige had pneumonia, and I had to help take care of Darin Jr." I bit my lip as I thought about the drama I'd caused in my marriage. "And the situation with Carmen . . . I made a mistake."

There was a long pause before Serena said, "Darin,

I'm done stressing over us. Good-bye." She hung up on me.

A proud man, I brushed the hurt off my shoulder as if it were lint on my tailored Italian suit. Known for my taut physique, I never took the elevators when I was at the office. I opted to get a decent workout by using the stairwell in the Tower. My diamond-crusted Rolex watch lit the way as my cobalt-colored alligator shoes marched up the steps to Carmen's office. From the projects to a penthouse suite, I'd climbed my way up the ladder to success. The Mercedes 500 AMG, the one-carat diamond stud in my ear, and Carmen had been my rewards for working hard. Once I got to her private office, she wasted no time soothing my ego.

Carmen sauntered over to me, sexily clad in a black satin and lace push-up bra. "Mornin' love," she said, touching my freshly trimmed mustache. She loosened the red tie that rested on top of my crisp white shirt. "You don't look so happy to see me." Her eyebrows rose slightly as she fingered the edge of my tightened jawline.

I closed my eyes and rubbed the side of my neck, trying to release tension. "Every day, I gotta deal with the same shit," I huffed as I removed my suit jacket.

"What, wifey givin' you grief again?" she asked in her strong Bronx accent. She took off my shirt, tossing the garment on her leather office chair.

I smirked as I unbuckled my pants, allowing them to fall in one smooth swoop. "What you think?" I asked, pulling her body close to mine.

She licked her lips as she hiked up her Ann Taylor pleated skirt, exposing a curvaceous bare bottom with a honey-tone, hair-free love triangle. "Well, I think you need a mini vacation," she whispered in my ear on her tiptoes. I playfully smacked her butt as I pulled off my boxers. Our smiles merged into a passionate kiss. In between moans, I backed Carmen up against her desk. She reclined against the antique bronze work area, elevating her legs in the air like an agile gymnast. We continued to kiss as my fingers massaged her wet folds. She arched her back as I licked down the middle of her body, all the way down to where my fingers teased her swollen clit.

"Darin, fuck me!" she cried as her hands gripped my waist.

I plunged into Carmen as she gasped in pleasure, her face contoured in a sexy scowl. She contracted her muscles around my manhood as I thrust deeper into her. The sensation was beyond belief.

"Damn, Carmen," I breathed in a husky voice against her neck. "This pussy is fittin' me like a glove." I pressed her legs back farther as her nails dug into my sweaty back. Our pelvises beat like a drum until lust erupted. We melted into one another, spent from another erotic episode.

Finally, we unlinked our bodies and got dressed. "Hopefully, your day will be better," she laughed, hugging me.

I ran my fingers through her short silky curls. "I hope so. You wanna do lunch?"

Carmen tapped my nose. "Only if you don't cancel on me again. I hate when you keep me waiting."

I kissed her swiftly on the cheek. "I always make it up to you, don't I?" I asked, giving her a sly look as I swaggered toward her office door.

She crossed her arms, saying nothing.

"I'll see ya soon. I promise," I said, giving her a wink. She smiled. "You better."

I sprinted down the stairwell, headed to my office. One instant was all it took. A thunderous bang and the roar of concrete moving sent my world into a fog. It felt like an earthquake. Someone called my name in a piercing scream. I sensed Carmen was calling for me, but all I could think of was Serena. I had been with someone else, but she was still my heart. Blinded by dust and smoke, I ran down the steps. I tried to get to Serena. Her building was right next to mine. I wanted to make sure she was all right. I reached for my cell phone but realized I'd left it in Carmen's office. I ran, despite the chaos of those being trampled around me. I kept going until heavy debris fell on me and I couldn't go anymore.

At that moment, I cried a river. Deep moans of regret echoed from my soul. All I knew was that things were not right in my life. Blood from a head wound, mixed with sweat and tears, trickled down my face. All the material possessions, the women, and the success . . . none of that mattered. I'd placed emphasis on fleeting desires, instead of battling the storms of life through faith. If I'd believed in my marriage more, maybe I wouldn't have been trapped in a building that day. Maybe Serena and I wouldn't have even come to work, opting to go to counseling, or perhaps a carriage ride through Central Park. Serena had lost faith in me when I missed the first counseling session. It seemed as if the tragedy taking place would keep us apart forever.

I remembered praying, "I accept Jesus Christ as my Lord and Savior. Father, please forgive me." I thought, *If only I had another chance.*

I was ready to give up, when a strong hand took hold of mine. A courageous firefighter rescued me from the building. I was in pretty bad shape, but I made it.

In the hospital, I vowed to be a better man. I asked God to forgive me for being a terrible husband. Serena Yvette Simms perished in the North Tower of the World Trade Center on September 11, 2001.

Rekindling the Past

September 11, 2002

Darin

On the first anniversary of the tragedy, survivors and loved ones of fallen heroes came together at Ground Zero. My high school sweetheart, Paige, attended the ceremony with me. When we were growing up in Goode, Virginia, I never paid her much attention. She was part of the "churchie" crew, always going to some revival or Bible study. I really cared for Paige, but I gravitated toward the girls that were not on their best behavior. Paige had been determined to capture my heart, and after a while it became difficult to resist her charms. We dabbled in and out of love over the years without thinking about the consequences. When she got pregnant, I freaked. Parenthood was not an easy adjustment for me. My immaturity caused her a lot of pain. We decided it was best to be friends and focus on raising our son.

I landed an opportunity to play professional

basketball in New York. I married Serena, a former model, in 1998 after a whirlwind courtship. Paige went to real estate school, moved from Goode, and began a career in Long Island, New York. Eventually, Paige found love again. She met her fiancé at a community car seat check. His name was Malcolm Davis, and he was a firefighter. The same firefighter that saved me from the Tower. After he'd pulled me from the rubble, and brought me to safety, he'd gone back to rescue others. He didn't make it back out the second time.

During the memorial, Paige and I cried among the brokenhearted, mourning the loved ones we lost. When the ceremony ended, I suggested we walk to Starbucks. Tired of being depressed, Paige and I reminisced about our childhood days. Conversation over coffee rekindled romantic feelings.

We began dating again. Ironically, we both relocated near Washington, D.C. I got traded to the Washington Warriors, and Paige found a better opportunity with a real estate firm in Alexandria, Virginia. Committed to having a blessed relationship, we abstained from sex. Honestly, this was no easy task. I was used to having my way, and Paige was too beautiful to ignore. However, I was no longer in control. The Holy Spirit had a hold on my heart, and I didn't want to lose everything again. So, we waited, building our future on mutual respect and friendship. On the Sunday that we got baptized at the church we'd joined, I proposed.

Karma

Darin

Fast-forward four years, and you'll see a new Darin Simms. Tonight, I was ready to pledge my love to Paige. Tomorrow is never promised. My life is not my own. Though I began on sinking sand, I stood proud on my wedding day, a changed man. No bling. No news cameras or reporters. No bodyguards or entourage. Just a man and a woman ready to release the past and become one among a private gathering of family and friends.

Paige and I prepared to recite our vows. There were doves in an ornate white cage, waiting to be released into the air.

The minister smiled as he looked at the guests gathered. "Is there anyone here who knows why these two should not be joined in marriage?" he asked. "Speak now, or forever hold your peace."

I wiped my brow in a joking gesture, relieved that no one said anything. Paige squeezed my hand as she chuckled softly.

The minister cleared his throat to continue when a female voice cried out, "Darin, wait!"

The music stopped. Everyone gasped in surprise. There was loud chatter among the guests as the woman, under a veil of tears, walked down the aisle toward me. Paige looked at me, confused. I looked at the woman, shocked. This was supposed to be the day that the Lord had made, but as the woman in the red satin gown stretched out her hand to touch mine, I felt a familiar storm brewing.

Carmen stood inches away from me, crying in my face. When my hand retreated, refusing to grasp hers, creases in her forehead formed. The flawless skin on her face now flushed from anger.

"Carmen, what are you doing here?" I asked as I put my arm around Paige's waist. Beads of sweat collected at my temple as I tried to battle the embarrassment and irritation of Carmen showing up at my wedding.

"Darin, what's going on?" Paige whispered under trembling lips. Hers eyes blinked fresh tears as she looked up at me.

I didn't say anything. I kissed Paige's brow, glanced at my ex-lover, and then shook my head. A beautiful day was suddenly turning into a nightmare.

"Miss, do you have something to say?" the minister asked.

Carmen wrung her hands as tears fell between her lips. "Darin, you broke your promise. You never checked on me after September 11th." Carmen hiccupped on her own sorrow. "My calls and e-mails were unreturned. You treated me like I was dead. Like you and I never happened. You brushed me off like I was some trick!"

I let go of Paige. "Carmen, please . . . now is not the time."

She scowled as her right hand pulled a small pistol from the confines of her strapless dress. In a matter of seconds, that black steel she'd lifted from her cleavage was aimed at my chest.

"Perfect timing, motherfucker!" Carmen screamed.

During the next few moments I felt as if I were watching a horror film at the scariest part. Screams soared to the sky. People ran for cover. The minister jumped in front of me, taking the first bullet. His Bible and lifeless body fell to the ground. I grabbed Paige and shielded her with my body. My best men, Harper and Eli, had managed to get the gun from Carmen, but not before a second shot rang out. I felt a burning sensation in my back. The last thing I remember before I blacked out was Paige holding me on the ground.

The Aftermath

Darin

Passion can be dangerous, especially when you take pleasure from the wrong woman. In the heat of the moment, everything felt like fireworks. However, when I deposited seed into Carmen and moved onto greener pastures, I left her betrayed. Maybe she felt like passion had ripped out her heart, threw it in the gutter, then pissed on it. Unsettled pleasure turned deadly. Carmen got revenge. A man of God was killed, and a foolish baller got shot. On my wedding day, when bullets scattered dreams into cold-ass reality, the only remarkable gift that remained was Paige. My past indiscretions had put her life in danger, yet she sat by my hospital bed and prayed. She held my hand, forgiving me once again. Loving me despite the uncertain future that lay ahead.

I swallowed hard as I stared at her. Her eyes were slightly puffy from lack of sleep. Her hand smoothed my brow as she smiled at me. "You want some water, babe?"

I slightly shook my head *no*. "Not right now." I closed my eyes for a second. "Where's Darin Jr.?" I asked, squeezing her hand as I looked around the dimly lit room.

Paige placed her hand over mine. "Don't worry. He's still at our condo with Mama. I guess what they say is true. God watches over children and fools. His chicken pox kept him from being a junior grooms-man at our wedding. He doesn't even know what hap-pened. I made Mama promise to stop worrying and keep her emotions in check. He'll find out soon enough." She got up to open the blinds, allowing sun-light into the room. "I think we need some light up in here," she said, sitting back down.

I turned my head away from the window and her. "We need more than light up in here. We need a mir-acle."

Paige sighed as she ran her fingers through her spiral curls. "Darin, you lived through September 11th, and a bullet to the spine. What more do you want?"

I slowly turned my head toward her. "Paige, I can't feel my legs," I said softly.

She sat down and nuzzled her head against mine. "Darin, you just woke up from a ten-hour surgery. There's swelling around your spine. You gotta give yourself time to recover. The doctors say it's too early to tell whether the paralysis is permanent or some-thing that will resolve over time."

"I need to know what's going to happen to me. What about my basketball career? What if I can't walk?" I bit my lip. "I won't be able to do what a hus-band needs to do for his wife."

Paige raised her head, looking totally disgusted with me. "Darin, I can't believe this. After what went down, it's still all about you!" she cried. "You're worried about a damn job, as if no one else has to think about how this accident will change their lives. I have a career, too, Darin." She got up and walked over to the window. "But I'm willing to give all that up to take care of you, if that's what it takes." She crossed her arms as she leaned against the window ledge. "God spared your life. You worryin' about walking, instead of thanking Him for keeping you here to see your son grow up."

"That's easy for you to say. You ain't in a hospital bed wondering if you can be the same man you used to be!" I spat.

Paige walked over to the edge of the bed, her hands planted on her hips. "Yeah? Well, if the tables were turned, you can best believe I'd have more to worry about than you. See, I'm not shallow to think that sex will save a marriage. Hold me. Compliment me. Write me a love letter. Most importantly, appreciate what I do for your ass. That's the best kinda love a man can give to his woman. Sex is the easy part. We can work through that. Keeping me happy is where the real work comes in."

I leaned my head farther into the pillow and closed my eyes, frustrated.

Paige sat back down and grabbed my hand. "Darin, look at me."

I slowly opened my eyes.

"I understand you're hurting," she said. "What happened at our wedding was devastating, but we can't give up now. We've gone through too much, and waited a long time to be together. We don't need to figure everything out in one day." She clasped my hand tighter, resting her chin on top. "Let's just try to stay faithful. That's all we gotta do right now."

I cracked a smile at Paige as I kissed her hand. "Sorry I raised my voice."

She leaned over and kissed my cheek. "I'm sorry I got upset, too. You need to rest."

The nurse came in to administer more medication in my IV catheter. "Mr. Simms, the doctor will be in to speak to you in about a half hour. Can I get you anything?"

Paige and I looked at each other, concerned. I shook my head as the nurse finished adjusting the levels on the IV monitor and left. "I won't be resting now. I'm nervous about what this doctor has to say."

Paige folded down the hospital blanket, then rested her arms on the edge of the bed. "Let's try to think of something else for right now, okay?"

I nodded yes, then tapped her nose. "All the heartache I caused you, and you still hangin' in there with me," I said. "Remember how I was back in the day?"

"*Was,*" she said with a smirk. "The more things change, the more they stay the same."

We laughed as we remembered how our journey of being together began.

Growing Pains

Spring 1988

Darin

Sweat forming on my skin from steam fog, I pulled Paige into the shower with me. She shrieked, complaining that the water was too hot. I didn't even flinch when the spray hit my body. Hot water is soothing to me. I lowered the temperature and guided her into the tub. The water beat hard against my back as I sucked all over her neck.

"Is the water okay now?" I asked, wrapping my arms around her waist.

"Much better," she moaned as she smoothed her hands over my chiseled chest.

We kissed passionately while our bodies moved under the pounding shower. My erect flesh pulsated against her soft love triangle. I was ready to make love to a woman I knew could change me for the better.

I gotta admit, making love was a new concept for me. I usually fucked with half-brain hoochies. My skills as a high school varsity basketball player were impressive, but running game on women was what I did best. Hell, I must've been a poet in another life, because the lines I threw at babes had them taking off the thongs. Romance was rarely on my agenda, but tonight was different. Paige had a special place in my heart. She was someone I'd commit to once I got creeping out of my system.

Paige stopped kissing me, her eyes intense. "I want you," she said in a seductive voice.

I smirked as I reached behind me to shut off the shower. "I'm gonna make sure you get what you want."

Paige and I got out of the tub, dried off, and headed straight for the bedroom. We were at my uncle's apartment. He was away for a few days on a trucking job, so I told him I'd look after the place. Paige's mama was working, and my mama was busy keeping watch over my younger sister, Camille. Mama knew I could handle myself. If I said I was chillin' with my boys, she didn't question it. Tonight, Paige and I would enjoy each other with no distractions or worries. I turned off the lights, and then opened the blinds to allow the light from the moon to shine into the room.

Paige smiled. "Makin' love under the stars. That's a switch."

I licked my lips as I scooped her up in my arms. "I told you I could be romantic. Besides, my uncle Charles said if his electric bill is a dollar more than what he paid last month, he gonna beat my ass." We laughed as I laid her down on the bed. I lowered my body on top of hers and kissed the middle of her neck. She moaned as she spread her legs, giving me room to work my magic.

"I'm gonna get you ready for me, ai'ight?" I whispered as I licked her earlobe.

"Yes, baby," she sighed as she ran her hand over my cornrows. "Make me feel good."

I moved to my side as my hands traveled down the curve of her hip to between her thighs. I closed my eyes as her hand stroked my hard manhood.

"Damn, girl," I moaned. "Keep working me like that. I taught you well."

She giggled as my fingers traveled from her thighs to the center of her delicate wet folds. I massaged her on the right spot.

"Darin, give it to me. I can't wait no more," she muffled.

"Let's take our time, sweetheart," I said. I pushed the bedsheet to the floor and headed down to Paige's essence. I licked the flower petals that had turned my girl into an erotic woman. My desire intensified, but I stayed focused on Paige. I was her first love, and we'd only had sex a few times. I wanted her experience to be just as pleasurable as mine. I sucked her potion until her legs clamped around my head.

"Darin, please . . ." she screamed.

I gently inserted my middle finger inside of her. Her cushioned walls tensed for a second, then melted. That's when I knew she was ready for me. I slowly penetrated her. Paige's body received my thickness, and the feeling of our bodies meshed together was beyond belief. Her hands rubbed over the beads of sweat on my back as I thrust deeper into her warmth. Her hips waved to me, rocking her body with my pelvis.

"Paige, I can't get enough of you," I said, breathless. "You makin' me weak." I increased my pace and gazed into Paige's eyes. She had natural beauty, no makeup needed for her smooth ebony skin. Our bodies beat like a drum, sending shockwaves through me. I hollered

Paige's name. She shuddered, satisfied by her own
climax. I caressed her body as she rested her head
against my chest.

"I wish we could be close like this all the time,"
Paige said softly.

My jaw clenched as I held her. I sighed as I leaned
against the headboard. Other babes had said the same
thing, and all I did was lie and tell them, *"Me, too."*
I didn't want to lie to Paige, so I told her what I felt.

"Let's just pretend tonight is forever, and don't
think about tomorrow, Paige," I said as I kissed the
crown of her head.

Midnight came fast, so I had to get Paige home
before her mama got off work. I went back to my
uncle's place and started cleaning up the bedroom. I
happened to look over at his dresser. There was an
old picture of him and his brother . . . my pops when
they were little boys. I picked up the dusty picture
frame and stared at the father who I'd grown to hate.

My mama cleaned hotel toilets so she could provide
for me and my sister. She takes care of a household that
should be handled by my pops. When I was nine years
old, he came home drunk, fussing about some nonsense. Mama was at the stove, stirring gravy as she tried
to keep the peace. My sister Camille was crouched
under the kitchen table, crying. I got in between my
mama and pops in an effort to calm things down. Pops
punched me hard in my chest, sending me to the
ground. That's when Mama lost it. I heard her curse at
him for the first time. Pops got pissed and struck her in
the face. Mama got mad and dumped boiling gravy
on him. He howled as he fell to the ground, calling out
for God. Mama hit Pops in the head with the cast-iron

skillet, asking the Holy Ghost to knock some sense into him. Pops managed to crawl out the front door, like a wounded dog with his tail between his legs. We ain't seen or heard from him since.

I rubbed my nose, blocking out bitter emotions as I placed the picture back down on the dresser. I stared at my image in the mirror. I look like Pops— fair-skinned, tall with a muscular build. People from my town of Goode, Virginia, think I act foul just like him, but haters don't affect me. Ain't nobody better than me other than God, and I haven't even been giving Him the time of day. I see cats on MTV, blingin' all over the damn place. I wanna be just like them. God seems to allow fools to prosper, while plain folk die from battling a financial drought all their lives. I bust my ass playing basketball, hoping one day I'll make the pros. I want basketball to make me rich and erase the struggle I've seen all my life.

Where Is the Love?

Paige

"To fall in love is an opportunity . . . to stay in love is a privilege."

Mrs. Miller, my writing composition teacher, told me to expand on a quote she'd written for my take-home exam. I am flunking this class. She doesn't understand why, but I do. I don't like to make up stories. She said I have writing talent, so I should try a little harder. I like crunching numbers, so why bother? When the school bell blasts, releasing students from full-time boredom, she rides off in her Volkswagen Beetle to Buppyville. I ride home on a funky cheese bus to the sticks. I want to be an entrepreneur, but right now my mind is on something else. I gotta find a way to stay focused, because I didn't get this far to stay stuck in high school.

I rested on a hill in the park, my hips cushioned by plush grass. I twirled one of my braids with a ballpoint pen, trying to decide what to write. Sun rays covered Redmond Lake like a golden blanket. A warm spring breeze crept under the hem of my denim Guess skirt, tickling my thighs. I closed my eyes and inhaled the fresh air. A couple of kids ran by and I turned back to the notebook on my lap.

The music from my headphones had boring lyrics. Somethin' about red roses and a wonderful world . . . whatever. Mrs. Miller had replaced my SWV CD with *The Best of Louis Armstrong*. She assured me that it would set the mood for creativity. All I know is, she better give back my SWV CD when I turn this in tomorrow. Talkin' 'bout she holdin' my music as collateral so I can expand my horizons. Mrs. Miller has no clue about me. I've never seen fairy tales formed from the back roads where I live.

I moved the braids that framed my face behind my ears. I angled my pen on the notebook paper and wrote:

> *I reckon love is really like a little girl's dream. She sees layers of cotton candy and decides to dive into all that sugar. She's falling fast. Soon, the layers close in, and she cannot breathe. She finally wakes up, covered in sweat. The little girl wonders, what went wrong? She grows older, and the dream becomes a bitter reality. She feels trapped inside the arms of the lover she trusted. Her privileged one. He takes every opportunity to cover her with layers of lies. The sugar turns hard from her tears. Sadly, she never looks at cotton candy the same.*

I sighed in frustration as I placed the pen down on my blanket. I wished there were CliffsNotes for students who wanted to write bullshit in twenty minutes or less. I took a sip of my soda. I struggled to fill the pages for this assignment, but I had enough drama to fill up a book.

Everything in my life is flat including the ginger ale
I'm drinking. No bubbles. No relief for my upset
stomach. Just flat.

Goode is a small, blue-collar town bustin' at the
seams with folks who lived for the weekends. The
liquor store and the church were the extent of
Goode's attractions. The sinners who gyrated all night
in the pub to bass-filled beats were the same ones
crying in church for salvation during their five minutes of repentance. Like God would forget the
Monday-through-Saturday partyin', just 'cause they fell
out in the sanctuary on Sunday, spirited up.

I have a business mind that should be focused on
getting into college. There's one glitch. I got it bad
for a baller. I've loved him from the first day I laid
eyes on him. He is my everything. Mama always said
never put a man on a pedestal, 'cause God gonna
crush it. Mama don't know everything. I love Darin
Simms, and I'm holding on to my dream of us being
successful together. Ain't nothing much to hold on to
in Goode, except a slice of hope. My heart wants me
to believe that Darin will take me away from this deadbeat town. My gurgling gut is telling me to get a life,
'cause my little secret might turn my love fantasy into
country dust.

I See Your
True Colors

Paige

Easter Sunday I'd gone to church with Mama. Pastor Frazier gave an uplifting sermon about how Jesus was resurrected. I went home and took a pregnancy test. Fear brought me to my knees in prayer, just in case Mama got the urge to put me six feet under for being careless. Two blue lines on the test stick, and I was positively in deep trouble.

I called Logan Banks, my best friend, who was six years older than me. Originally from Philadelphia, she moved to Goode at the age of fifteen to live with her grandmother after her mother died of an aneurysm. We met at a church social and been tight ever since. Logan is everything I'm not . . . loud, rebellious, bossy, and fit to cuss any fool out that gets on her nerves. She attended St. John's College and was now in studying for her LSATs. I think with her brains and hot temper, she won't be having any problems getting into law school.

"Hello?" she huffed, bothered as usual. She hated to talk on the phone, unless she was the one calling, wasting your time.

I sighed into the cordless receiver. "Logan, it's positive," I said.

She grunted in the middle of smacking her gum. "Damn. Didn't I tell you? Miss Adams know?"

"Naw. I ain't got up the nerve to tell Mama yet. I'm busy wondering how I'm gonna tell Darin. With all he has on his plate right now, this is the last thing he needs."

"Girl, don't be silly. Darin is about to get paid. I overheard him talking to one of them recruiters. I'm almost positive he's going pro. Sounds like he's leaning toward New York, too. This baby ain't gonna have no worries."

I closed my eyes and took a deep breath. I was already fed up with this conversation. "Logan, it's not about the money," I said. I lay against the big fuchsia pillows propped against my bed headboard. "Darin is my heart. I don't want to upset him. He's already on edge. This pregnancy might push him further away from me. I should've been more careful."

Logan smacked her lips. "Wait a minute," she said in a high-pitched tone. "Darin is just as guilty. And as far as the finances, stop lying. You know you my girl and all, but you got the money motive like everybody else chasing after that fool."

I almost choked on the water I was gulping. "How can you say that about me, Logan!" I screamed.

She laughed loud and long, as if she were actually funny. "I said it, and I'll say it again," she said. "Your eyes are on the prize, girlfriend. Don't front. If you was so concerned about Darin's feelings, you would have gone to Pendol Clinic and started taking birth control pills like me. Unfortunately, I don't have a baller like you, so I gotta protect myself from these busters."

I pouted as I folded my arms over my chest. "I'm not trying to get over on Darin," I mumbled. "I thought you knew me better than that."

Logan sighed. "Girl, everybody is trying to get over," she said. "You're no different. You want better for your life than this dry-ass town. That seed in your belly is your way out, and ain't nothing wrong with that. If the tables were turned, I'd be the cheesiest motherfucker in the world. Guaranteed pension for my dedicated pussy service? Chile, please."

"Don't be ignorant," I snapped. "I need to figure out what I'm gonna do."

"What's there to figure out, Paige?" she asked. "You havin' Darin's baby, and he's gonna have to take responsibility for his actions. He was man enough to lay with you. Now he gotta be man enough to be a father to his child."

I bit my lip, nervous about how Darin might react. "Logan, I'm afraid to tell him," I said. "He's gonna be pissed. I know it."

"Who cares!" she yelled. "Paige, get a backbone. Why you always act like you scared of him? I noticed how he's been avoiding you lately. Darin's been treating you like a stepchild. You been whinin', talkin' 'bout you fit to be patient with him and shit. Forget that. The ball's in your court now. It's your body, and you decide the outcome. I know you love Darin, but the question is, does he love you? This is the test."

I held my head as my eyes started to water. "Look, don't tell nobody about this, okay?"

She popped her gum in my ear. "All right chick, I won't. Chill out."

I grabbed a tissue to wipe my face. "Let me tell Darin, then I'll deal with everybody else."

"Just do it, girl," Logan said. "Basketball has Darin's head all messed up. He's in his own little world, but this will wake him up."

"Logan, thanks for listening," I said.

"You my girl," she said. "It'll be all right."

"All right, bye," I said, weary as I placed the cordless phone back into the cradle. Logan was right. It was time for me to be strong, even if I felt like my world with Darin was crumbling. I wanted to be happy about this baby. A child is a gift from God. I didn't know if Darin would feel that way, though. He never did like surprises.

Back in the hospital,
September 12, 2006, late evening

Paige

Darin had drifted to sleep in the middle of us reminiscing. Our teenage years were not the happiest, so I guess it was a good time for him to just block things out and rest. The doctor had come in and checked Darin's vitals. He said Darin did well in surgery, and that the medication was reducing the swelling to his spine. Unfortunately, it was still too early to rule out permanent paralysis, but the doctor said more testing and a full forty-eight hours would yield a more accurate prognosis.

I was beat, so I decided to take a shower in Darin's suite. Luckily, Logan had brought me a ton of clothes in case I had to stay a while. She also bought me a few sandwiches from Panera Bread to keep me away from that terrible hospital food.

The warm water of the shower relaxed my muscles. When I got out, I threw on some beige sweats and my favorite fuzzy purple socks. I lay on the lounge chair, and nibbled on some Kettle potato chips as I opened my chicken sandwich. I glanced out the window, focusing on a maple tree with pretty orange and yellow leaves. While Darin slept peacefully, I continued to think back to all the drama of our youth.

Through the Fire

Spring 1988

Paige

I'd traveled up the squeaky wooden steps of the Simms's bungalow many times, but fear had my legs weighed down like lead. Each step up made me feel as if I would fall under pressure.

I stuffed my hands in my jeans pockets and looked down, frowning at the scuff mark on my new Reebok Classic tennis shoes. I walked in the house, taking caution as I closed the screen door. Even though Miss Maria, Darin's mama, wasn't home, I could still picture her singing gospel by Tramaine Hawkins, all the while fussin' at neighborhood kids for slamming her rickety screen door when they came to visit.

"Uhmm-uhmm," I coughed, vying for my boyfriend's attention. His eyes were glued to the television. "D?" I moved to the living room, hands placed on my waist. I'd caught him in the middle of a yawn. He gave me a seductive smile as he got up from the recliner.

"Hey, sweetheart," he said in a husky voice as he walked over to me.

Darin's caramel baby face could make any woman forget his faults, but he was on my shit list, and I wanted him to know it. I rolled my eyes at him as I walked over and leaned against the sofa arm. Darin bopped toward me, licking his lips like I was hot gravy on top of tender pork chops. He pulled me close to his body. I pulled away, which puzzled him.

His forehead creased. "What's wrong?"

I folded my arms and tapped my foot, trying to release nervous energy. "What's wrong? Darin, did you forget I existed? I never see you anymore."

He exhaled loudly, looking up to the ceiling as he placed his hands behind his head. "Paige, you know I've been tied up with basketball stuff," he mumbled.

I shrugged and kept quiet as I looked over at the family photos on the coffee table.

His soft fingertips lifted my chin. "After the conference tomorrow, we'll be able to make up for lost time. I promise," he whispered.

I moved his hands away and sat down on the couch. "Don't make promises you can't keep. After the conference, you'll be a NBA player not thinking twice about me."

"Who told you I was going pro?" he asked, sitting next to me.

I glanced at the chipped nail polish on my fingernails. "Nobody had to tell me nothin'," I said. "I know what's up."

Realizing his BS wasn't working, he held my hand. "All right, Paige, here's the deal," he said. "I decided to go pro and play for New York. I hired an agent, and contract negotiations are already in progress." He gave me a huge grin as he squeezed my hand against his knee. "Baby, I'm psyched! My dream of playing in the NBA is now a reality. I can't believe it!"

Darin looked like a little boy with a new bike at Christmas. His smile was so wide and bright, he made my soul feel lighter. I smiled and gave him a hug. I needed to remember this moment, because I feared the warmth of our embrace would soon be chilled by my moment of truth.

"Darin, I knew you would make it," I said, rearing back to stare at his beautiful hazel eyes. "This is what you've worked so hard for, and I'm proud of you. All of Goode knew you would make it. You proved us right."

He blushed. "I haven't proved anything yet," he said. "I got a long road ahead of me."

I nudged him. "You'll do fine, boy. Before you know it, you'll be breaking records in the NBA, just like you're doing in high school. You know you'll always have folks supporting you here, so don't forget about us." I slowly released my hands from his, biting my bottom lip as I thought about what I was gonna say next. "I'll always be there for you," I said as I fidgeted with the class ring on my finger. "Me . . . and the baby will always be there for you."

Darin smiled and shook his head in agreement until my words registered. He jumped up like he had been stung.

"Say that again?" he asked, his voice cracking. He pulled up his sagging blue jeans, as if he was suddenly uncomfortable with droopy-drawers fashion.

I tried to smile as I stood up to face him, but my strength was fading fast. "*Baby*, Darin," I said, wringing my hands. "We're gonna have a baby."

He grabbed my shoulders and stared at me, dazed. "Paige, I know I didn't hear what I thought I heard," he said, stressing every word slowly. "Tell me you're joking."

I looked down for a second as I tried to keep my emotions in check. "Darin, I'm not playing. I'm pregnant."

He threw his hands up and started pacing the floor. "You weren't on birth control pills! I thought you . . ."

I was on his heels as he continued to have his toddler tantrum. "You thought, Darin, but you never asked," I yelled. "Correct me if I'm wrong, but I didn't hear your condom sermon before we hit it, neither!"

Darin stopped and turned toward me. "I bet Logan's poppin' those pills," he said. He waved his finger, chastising me. "Y'all in each other's face all the time. You dress alike. Weave each other's hair and shit. The one time when y'all should've been playing Simon Says, you decide to be independent. Ain't that a bitch!" He grabbed a pillow from the couch and threw it on the floor.

His sarcasm wounded my spirit, and I couldn't fight the hurt feelings flowing down my face like a waterfall. "Darin, you act like this is all my fault!" I shouted, leaning against Miss Maria's old console television. "You're just as responsible for this pregnancy!"

He stood in front of me and held my hand. "Look, we should've used protection," he said. "I'm partly to blame." Darin shook his head. "But, Paige, I thought you were smarter than that."

I narrowed my eyes at him. "Oh, so I'm a dumb ass now?" I asked. "Get out of my face!" I pushed him away from me.

He grabbed on to my arm. "No, listen," he said in a calmer voice, wrapping his arms around me. "All I'm saying is, you've been my girl forever. Even before we were a couple, we were close. I thought I could trust you."

I smirked as I peeled his hands from me. "Trust? You got some nerve. You're gonna talk to me about trust when you're screwing half the cheerleading squad? You're real trustworthy," I said as I pulled back my braids and secured them with the pink scrunchy ponytail holder that had been on my wrist.

Darin clasped his hands, closing his eyes briefly before he spoke. "Paige, I admit that I've stepped out on you before. I apologize for that. But you know me like family. You know what I'm trying to accomplish. I didn't think I had to protect myself when it came to being with you."

I got up in his face. "I should be the one worried about protection," I said. "I don't know who you've been with. I need to get checked out, just to make sure I'm disease free. I suggest you do the same. You know, dogs carry ticks." I poked his neck with my index finger, making him grimace. "Your leeches been leavin' passion marks all over your damn neck! I'm not stupid, and I'm not blind." I plopped down on the couch with my arms folded over my snug polo top.

Darin sighed as he sat down beside me. He placed his hand on my thigh. "Paige, did you plan this? Is this your payback for the dirt I've done?"

I brushed his hand away and scooted farther down the sofa. I was sick of him, and irritated by my jeans, which had gotten tighter over the past few days. "Why are you asking me that, Darin?" I asked, adjusting my position on the sofa. "I'm not answering your dumb questions. You think what you wanna think."

"Are you ready to be a mother at seventeen?" he asked.

I shrugged. "It's not an ideal situation, but we gotta make the best of it."

He held his head in his hands. "Paige, you're not

thinking straight," he mumbled. "You are in high school with no job." He looked over at me. "Your mama is working two jobs to support you."

I raised my brow. "Well, it's not just about me," I said, working my neck like I had a supreme attitude. "You're going to have to share the responsibility in this, so stop judging. Start planning to support your child."

He moved closer to me. "Paige, it's not about the money. I will take care of what's mine. I'm just asking you to think this through some more. What about your plans to take business classes after graduation? Don't you want to enjoy life some more before being tied down with a baby?"

I rolled my eyes. "What is there to enjoy in Goode, Darin?" I asked. "Be real."

"Listen to me," he said, reaching out for my hand.

I didn't fight as he threaded his warm fingers between mine. He gave me a soft peck on the lips.

"You and I are together now, but that ain't guaranteed." His expression became intense. "We haven't even figured out why we're not getting along, and now we're gonna bring a baby into the world? Yeah, I'll be a rookie making some decent money, but I'll feel like I'm under a microscope. Rookies catch a lot of flack, and with me coming straight out of high school, critics are gonna try to find anything to bring me down. Despite me being a good baller, I'm still a black man. Team owners want you to fit their little mold. So, entering the league as an eighteen-year-old father is not gonna look right."

I let go of his hand. "Darin, stop thinking about yourself," I said, annoyed. "I'm the one that has to carry this baby, go to school, and try to find a job.

You'll be gone, and I'll be stuck here with folks talkin' 'bout me behind my back."

He grabbed another pillow and mashed it into his hands. "Paige, when these corporations find out I'm a teen father they will look at another player to support their products," he said, his tone rising in frustration. "Anytime an athlete gets into trouble, the companies they endorse drop them like flies. My agent already wants me to start a charitable foundation. I don't want to wear the role model hat, but it's branded on me. If I'm not thriving, then all of us are gonna suffer. You'll still be in Goode, and my ass might be right back here with you."

I wiped traces of tears from my face. His reaction was just what I had expected. "I know it wasn't planned, but I want this baby, Darin," I said, folding my hands over my belly. "You have a promising future. I believe we will be all right."

I could tell Darin was getting pissed again. He got up off the couch and stood in front of the TV. "Paige, don't do this to me," he said. "Things are just starting to go right in my life. You know I care about you. I'll always care for you, but having my baby to get me to stick around is not going to work. We might get married someday. If that happens, we'll have children later when the time is right." He came over and knelt down in front of me. "Paige, I want you to get an abortion," he said softly, clasping his hands on top of my knee.

Darin's expression resembled that of a has-been Romeo, all played out. Desperate to get back in the game. He now looked deep in thought, as if he really believed I would see his point of view. "I know it sounds cruel, but I think it is the best decision for both of us," he said, slowly rising from the floor.

He swallowed hard as he saw my face flush in anger. I jumped up from the couch, swinging at him as he blocked my fists.

"Go to hell, Darin!" I screamed. "You wanna kill your own flesh and blood to save your squeaky-clean image. You're not thinking about our future. Our future ended the day you fucked me. All you can think about is yourself! You better thank God for Miss Maria praying over you all the time, because you don't deserve the good fortune that's getting ready to come to you. You definitely don't know what's best for me. If you did, you wouldn't be trying to talk me into destroying the only joy I have right now!"

My body shook as I cried uncontrollably. Darin tried to hug me, but I moved out of his reach.

"Paige, I don't want to hurt you," he said. He walked over and gently pulled me close to him. "Please try to understand. I don't want anything to mess up this golden opportunity. A lot of people are counting on me."

I cried on his shoulder as he rubbed my back. "I was counting on you, too," I sniffled. "You're worrying about what everybody else thinks, but my feelings don't count. Forget Paige!" I withdrew, feeling like he was patronizing me more than comforting me.

"I don't feel that way, Paige," he said, somewhat choked up on his words. His eyes were red, clouded by tears. "I'm afraid of failure. I'm scared of messing up my life. Mama's health is bad. She can't do day care anymore, and we're getting behind on bills. My pops didn't have the balls to stick around and take care of home, so I had to take over. If I can't do it, then I'm no better than his sorry butt." He wiped his eyes.

I sighed as I took his hand in mine. "Darin, you are

acting just like him by wanting to kill your baby. You're running away from your obligations just like he did."

He rubbed the hair fuzz on his chin. "Paige, I know I'm right about this. We still growing ourselves. We ain't fit to raise no baby. I can't force you to get the abortion, but you need to give it more thought." He patted my braids with his hand, giving me a half-smile. "Come to your senses. I'll borrow the money from my uncle to pay for it. I'll take care of everything."

Darin's words left a sour taste in my mouth and I spit right in his face. He flinched. "I don't need your murder money! I'm keepin' our baby, so deal with it!" I bumped him with my shoulder, clearing the way for me to get the hell out of his house. He tried to grab me, but I yanked my arm away. Tears streamed over my lips as I ran out the front door and down the steps. Darin called out to me from the porch.

"Paige!" he shouted as he pulled his white tank shirt out of his jeans, agitated. "Come back, Paige!"

What Becomes of the Brokenhearted

Paige

Curled up in my bed, my melody of cries finally lulled me to sleep. A loud ringing sound woke me up. I looked over at the clock on the nightstand. It was five PM. I picked up the cordless phone. The call screen showed Logan's number. "Yeah?" I mumbled in a groggy voice.

"How did it go?" she asked.

"Well, he didn't break out the cigars, that's for sure," I said.

"Fuck him!"

"No thanks," I said, stretching. "Been there, done that. Knocked up, pissed off."

She sighed. "I hear you."

I got out of the bed, yawning as I looked at myself in the bureau mirror. I had bags under my eyes. I touched my puffy cheekbones, shaking my head at how fast the pregnancy was changing my appearance. "Logan, he wants me to get rid of it."

"What? Well, what did you say?" she asked.

I glanced at my profile in the mirror. "I told him I was keeping it."

"Good for you!" Logan cheered. "I swear Darin can be an asshole sometimes."

I shook my head as I sat on the edge of the bed. "Tell me about it," I said, toying with one of my braids. "He was pretty angry when I left."

"Whatever. He'll get over it. And if he doesn't, oh, well. As long as he knows how to sign a check, it's all good."

I closed my eyes, massaging my temples. "Logan, I'm sorta tired from all the drama this morning. Can we talk about this later?"

"Yeah, girl. Get some rest."

"All right," I said.

"See ya."

We hung up. The phone rang again. I didn't recognize the number. I picked it up, in case it was Mama calling me from one of the phones at work during her break. "Mama?" I asked.

"No, Paige, it's me," Darin whispered, sounding pitiful.

"Don't call here anymore!" I yelled and hung up the phone. It rang again. I knew it was him. "What!"

"Paige, don't hang up," he said. "I'm sorry. I want to explain my . . ."

I got up from the bed and stomped over to my window. "Darin, you're trifling," I said, closing the miniblinds. "I have nothing else to say to you."

I clicked off the phone and lay back in bed, determined to get a couple more hours of rest before

I had to do homework. His words had caused enough stress for one day.

School was out for spring break, which was fine with me, because I didn't feel like dealing with classes and homework right now. On a Monday morning, I told my mother I was going to the mall with Logan. Instead, I went to a doctor's appointment at the clinic.

The doctor said I was two months along. He told me that I would have to start prenatal care right away.

The next day I called Darin. I was about tell him something I knew I would regret for the rest of my life.

"Hello?" he asked.

"Darin. Be at my house by ten o'clock tonight with four hundred dollars."

"Why? Paige, you gonna get the abortion?" I could hear the relief in his voice.

"Yeah," I said. "Are you happy now?"

"Paige, please let me help you through this," he said. "When is your appointment?"

"Oh, so you're concerned about me all of a sudden? I don't need your help, Darin. You can't even help yourself. I'm sorry I ever loved you."

There was silence for a few seconds. "Paige, let me go with you."

"Shut up. Just be at my house at ten. Don't be late."

When he arrived, I opened the door and snatched the envelope from him.

"Paige, can we talk for a few minutes?" he asked, reaching out for me.

"No," I said, slapping away his hand. "Don't say shit to me. Leave now."

I shut the door in his face. I got emotional again. Part of it was my hormones. Most of it was heartbreak. I had to tell my mama. This would burden her for sure. I felt so alone. I placed my hand on my stomach. The sensation gave me a chill down my spine. "I'm sorry, baby," I said as I looked down at my stomach. "I'm so sorry."

I went upstairs to my bedroom. I got down on my knees and prayed for God's forgiveness . . . and my own.

Lean On Me

Paige

Mama got home from her work shift early this morning. When I walked into her bedroom, she was in her bathrobe, brushing her hair.

"Hi, Mama," I said as I leaned against the door frame. I crossed my ankles. She smiled as she looked over at me. I had on my favorite Hello Kitty nightshirt.

"Hey, baby girl," she said. "I just knew you'd still be asleep." She frowned a little as she looked at my face. "Your eyes are puffy. You been crying?"

I nodded slowly. "Yeah, Mama."

"Paige, sit down beside me," she said, patting the space on the bed. "What's going on? You get into trouble at school?"

I bit my lip. "No, ma'am," I said, looking down at my hands. "Mama, I have something to tell you, but you gotta promise not to get mad."

She folded her arms. "Now, Paige. What do I always say? Make it plain. I'm not up for guessing games this morning. The only thing I will promise is that I won't beat you. Your ass is bigger than me, and I ain't trying to hurt my hand. By the looks of you, I think I know." She sighed. "Let me hear it."

"I'm pregnant, Mama," I cried, my lip trembling.

"I knew it," she said, shaking her head. "You been sleeping all day and slacking on your chores. Paige, how could you let this happen to yourself now?"

"I'm sorry, Mama," I said. "I wasn't thinking."

She held her head. "I blame myself. Me working all the time gave you too much freedom."

I touched her shoulder. "Mama, don't say that," I said. "You've been doing the best you can. Nobody forced me to have sex. Don't blame yourself for my foolishness."

"I had a feeling you and Darin were hot and heavy," she said, tightening the belt on her robe. "Ms. Shay told me she seen you sneak out of the house with him. I wasn't gonna kid myself to think you weren't having sex. You've liked that boy for so long. I knew it was only a matter of time. I just figured you'd protect yourself when it got to that point. We've talked about sex plenty of times. I told you to come to me when you felt you needed contraceptives. What happened?"

I moved a few braids behind my ear. "I don't know, Mama. I was embarrassed, I guess."

"Embarrassed for what?" she asked. She grabbed my hand. "Paige, you're a beautiful young woman. Exploring your sexuality is a part of growing up, but you can't be careless. Getting pregnant is only one issue. There's stuff you can catch out here that you can't get rid off. You gotta look out for yourself." She smiled proudly as she ran her hand over my hair. "I don't care how old you get, you always gonna be my baby. I don't wanna lose you over some mess. You hear me?"

"Yes, Mama," I said in a muffled voice. She held me as I cried into her bosom.

"Paige, I know you feel bad, but mistakes happen. I had you at your age. I guess we're growing up together and learning as we go." She exhaled. "I still ain't figured out what I'm supposed to do with myself. One thing I do know is that I love you. Ain't nothing we can't overcome. We'll do what we have to do to get by. I can work some more overtime."

I straightened up and held her hand. "No, Mama. You work too many hours as it is." I wiped my face. "Mama, I don't know if I'm keeping the baby. I'm thinking about getting an abortion."

She held my face with her warm hands. "What? Did you come up with this solution, or did Darin decide for you?"

"Mama, Darin don't want this baby. He thinks it will mess up his career. He decided to go straight to the NBA."

Mama waved her hand in disgust. "I don't care what Darin wants," she said. "That's Maria's worry. You my child. What do you want to do?"

I rubbed my arms. "I wanted to keep it, but now I'm not sure," I said.

"Well, it's time to think long and hard, baby girl," Mama said, tapping my thigh. "You ain't got to look far to see what single parenthood is all about. It's tough. No more getting your hair and nails done every week. No more hanging out late with Logan. She's your friend, but she gonna be fancy and free. You find out who your true friends are when something like this happens. Nobody wants to hang around you with a screaming kid. Logan likes to show off." Mama chuckled. "You're gonna wreck her flow if you totin' a diaper bag."

I pouted. "Mama, it's not funny."

"I'm just trying to cheer you up, girl," she said, pinching my cheeks. "I've been there. Your father told me the same thing Darin told you. Men can be insensitive, especially when they feel threatened." She folded her hands in her lap. "Baby, you gotta weigh your options on this thing. I'll support you, whatever you decide."

I held up my hands. "Mama, Darin will be making a lot of money soon," I said. "Why wouldn't he want this baby?"

Mama motioned for me to get down on the carpet. She began oiling my scalp with her shea butter hair oil. "Darin's a good boy," she said. "He's taking care of his mother and he's trying to pave a better way for his folks. He just ain't ready to risk his chances of making it big over some puppy love."

"Mama, it's not puppy love," I whined.

She nudged me with her knee. "Paige, most adults don't know what being in love is all about, so what makes you think you know?"

"I know I've never felt this way about anyone else."

"Well, I don't mean to make a comparison, but Darin is in love, too. You love him. He loves basketball. Basketball is his comfort zone. Paige, a man will always choose the path of least resistance in life, especially when it comes to women. You're trying to make him choose between you and this baby, and basketball. Darin wants to be the next Jordan. He's not gonna let anything interfere with that." Mama brushed the baby hair around my temples. "I know Darin disappointed you, but you have to think about your life," she said. "I want better for you. Be a businesswoman like you planned. You got plenty of time for kids."

I looked up at her. "Mama, I just don't want to end this pregnancy and regret it for the rest of my life."

She put down the brush. "Time heals all wounds," she said, placing one of her satin scarves around my head. "That's what prayer is for. Ask the Lord for guidance."

I knew Mama was tired. "Mama, I'm gonna let you get some sleep," I said, rising from the floor.

She wiped her hands on her robe. "All right, baby girl," she said, giving me a kiss on the cheek. "We can talk about this some more tonight."

As I was walking out her door into the hallway she called my name.

"Paige?"

"Yes, ma'am?"

"You gonna be fine," she said. "Just fine."

I had no reason to doubt my mama. She had already walked in my shoes. Now she was willing to carry me despite my wrong. I went back to her doorway.

"Mama?" I asked.

"Yes, baby?" she asked, getting in her bed.

"Can I rest in here with you?"

"Sure, baby, come on."

I got in the bed with Mama and snuggled close to her like I used to when I was little. We both closed our eyes. She understood my pain. I understood her love. It was a morning to remember.

God Bless
the Child

Paige

The discomfort from my headache increased as I sat
in the parking lot of the abortion clinic with Mama. The
more time passed, the more I thought about changing
my mind. Mama was upset because the warehouse had
scheduled her for the morning shift at the last minute.
She'd wanted to stay to make sure I was okay before
she left.

"Look, Paige," she said, gripping the steering wheel
like she was tense. "Are you sure you don't want me to
stay?" She studied the parking lot, apprehensive. "I'm
your mother, I should be with you. I already called my
boss and told her I would be late due to a family
crisis."

"No, Mama," I said as I unbuttoned my denim jacket.
"We need the money. Besides, Logan is gonna meet me.
Her boyfriend let her borrow his car so she should be
pulling up any minute."

"Are you certain you don't want me to stay?"

I nodded. "Yeah. You can't be in the room with me, anyway. I just need you to go in and sign the consent form. They told me to arrive fifteen minutes early to sign all the paperwork."

She sighed as she shook her head. "Well, let's go in," she said.

When we walked in, all eyes were on us. The stuffiness of the room made me anxious. Luckily, there were only a few other people in the waiting area. I'd taken a morning appointment to avoid seeing somebody I knew. Mama and I walked up to the receptionist's window. After we checked in and sat down, Logan walked through the door. A nurse from behind the desk came up and told me I would be seen in a few minutes. She gave me a warm smile, but I started to feel sick. I asked where the bathroom was, just in case I had to make a run for it. Logan sat down beside Mama. They were both teary-eyed, making me feel worse.

"Mama, you don't have to stay any longer," I whispered. "I'll be all right. Logan will call you if there's an emergency."

"All right," she said. "Listen, baby, come outside with me for a second."

"Huh?"

"Come on. They gonna call you soon."

Logan watched my stuff while I went outside.

"Get in the car with me," she said, removing her keys from her purse.

"Why, Mama?"

She quickly opened the door. "Just do it, girl. Hurry up."

We got into the car. Mama stared at me. "Paige, you don't have to do this."

I peered up at the dreary sky. Rain mist covered the windows. "Yes, I do, Mama," I said in a sullen voice. "My mind's made up. Please don't make this harder than it already is."

"Okay," she said, taking my hand. She bowed her head in silence. A tear dropped from her right eye. "Paige, say 'The Lord's Prayer' with me. 'Our Father, Who art in . . .'"

"Mama, please. I don't want to . . ."

"Say it, baby. Say it!" she cried.

I joined Mama as we said the prayer. I held her hand tight, so I could remember the feeling when I would be on that table inside. We finished praying and I gave Mama a kiss good-bye. I walked back into the office. Logan was reading a *Sister 2 Sister* magazine. I sat down next to her.

"How you feelin'?" she asked.

"Nervous," I said. "My stomach's been bubblin' all mornin'."

"Did you eat breakfast?"

"Naw. I was afraid I'd puke if I ate anything." I looked at my hands. "I feel so bare. When I made my appointment they told me to take my acrylics off. No jewelry. I'm ready to get this over with," I said, crossing my legs. "Did they call my name?"

"Nope," she said, putting down her magazine.

A nurse came out the door. "Paige Adams?" she called.

"Yes," I said.

"Would you come with me, please."

I got up, trying to battle a dizzy spell. Logan grabbed my hand.

"It's gonna be all right, girl," she said.

I walked with the nurse into the medical ward.

She asked, "Was that your friend who will be taking you home?"

"Yes, ma'am."

"All right," she said. "I'm going to have you wait in this office right here." We walked into a room that reminded me of somebody's living room. "By law we are required to provide counseling before we perform a procedure of this nature. Were you aware of that?"

I nodded.

She touched my shoulder. "All right. The counselor will be in shortly to talk with you."

Damn. More waiting. The counselor came in and started asking me about my feelings. I was not in the mood to talk about how I felt to a shriveled up, old white lady. She had no clue as to what I was going through. I tuned her out. Finally, she finished talking and asked me if I wanted to proceed with the abortion. I told her, "Yes."

The nurse came and got me. We walked into the examination room. She handed me a gown to change into, and told me to sit on the table when I was done. When she left, I hurried out of my clothes. I started to shiver because my nerves were shot, and I was cold sitting on that table. Although the air conditioner was going full force, I still felt beads of perspiration on my nose. Time seemed to be dragging, but I knew my baby's end was near.

The nurse came back in the room with two doctors. They quickly said hello and told me who would be doing what. Before I knew it, my feet were in the stirrups. The heat from the examination lamp felt like it was burning my vagina. I didn't complain. I just stayed as still as I could, trying to block out what was going on. The doctor who examined me gave the okay to the other doctor who was by my head. The nurse was on the other side of the table holding my hand. I pretended it was Mama's hand and closed my eyes.

The doctor asked me if I was ready. Words formed in my mouth, but nothing came out at first. I opened my eyes and managed to say, "Yes."

The doctor gave me a fake smile and told me to relax. The other doctor put a mask on my mouth for the sleeping gas. He told me to count back from a hundred. I looked up at the ceiling where there was a poster of a beautiful rainbow. Except the more I looked at it, the more I noticed the colors bleeding together, dripping off the paper toward me like the Skittles commercial.

I counted. "One hundred, ninety-nine . . ." I tasted something wet and salty running down my left cheek. Fear, nausea, and regret all bottled up inside of me, I began to shake. A line of saliva came out the edge of my mouth as I cried and counted some more. "Ninety-eight . . . nine . . . ninety-seven, ninety-six, God, please don't hate me . . ."

Recovering

Darin

Two months, another surgery, and intense daily therapy in the hospital had me on my feet. Tired of the nightmares from what had happened on September 11th and at my wedding, I was happy to be back in Maryland at my Woodmoore estate. I walked around the perimeter of my heated pool daily with the assistance of a walker or someone holding my arm. I had a long stint of rehab ahead, and, honestly, I was sour about the process. I'd done my dirt in life, but I never thought I'd be disabled. Basketball with the Washington Warriors was out. The doctors didn't recommend playing professionally again, even if I made a full recovery. The team had promised me an executive office position in their Player Development and Recruitment division. I had mixed emotions about being affiliated with the team but not being able to play, especially since basketball was a lifelong dream. Luckily, I had my wife, my son, and a crazy best friend/former teammate named Harper to help keep up my spirits.

Harper was helping me exercise around the pool while Paige fixed us lunch.

"Man, this shit is getting old already," I said, wincing. Pain shot down the middle of my back and behind my legs as I took each step.

Harper nudged me. "Darin, stop complaining, man. Your body needs time to heal. I'm not trying to downplay what happened, but things could've been a lot worse."

I clenched my jaw. "No lectures, Harp, all right?"

Harper laughed. "All right, how about I throw your ass in this pool? I bet you be calling out to Jesus then!"

I poked him in the side with my elbow. "Be quiet, man," I said, smiling. "Listen, let's sit down on this wicker bench."

"All right," Harper said, helping me down on the cushion. We glanced over at my nine-year-old son, DJ, who was shooting hoops on the custom-made sports court. "Darin, you know basketball ain't no bed a roses. Besides, we're both thirty-six now. It's almost time to retire and focus on reopening our sportswear firm in D.C. You got a good wife in the house cooking us fried chicken for lunch. A healthy little boy. I got two beautiful daughters. At the end of the day, that's all you need."

I nodded. "I know I'm blessed, man. Some days it's just hard to deal with the fact that my life is so different now."

Harper cut his eyes at me. "Yeah, you had to give up your player membership."

"Whatever, man," I said.

Harper grabbed the pitcher from the side table

and poured me some water. "Be glad you're not back in the game of women."

I took a sip of my drink. "What you talkin' about, man? You've never been a player, and you are married, or did you forget?"

Harper frowned. "I wish I had some damn amnesia, 'cause Noelle's ass is driving me crazy."

Harper got himself a tall glass of lemonade from the cabana, which meant we'd be talking for a while about how Noelle baited and hooked him in.

Joe Cool

Harper

I attended Georgetown University. In the fall of my senior year, I remember being toasted from too many Coors Lights, dancing with a buckedtoothed female at a Homecoming party. My roommate, Keith, approached me on the dance floor. He cunningly interrupted my dance partner's salsa and removed me from the scene.

Keith said he had a friend for me to meet. As we headed to the refreshment table, there was a group of young ladies smiling at me and whispering to each other. A gorgeous, petite honey emerged from the middle of the clique. She walked toward me. I nudged Keith and asked for a piece of gum, because I suddenly had all of my faculties, and a strong case of bad breath. She introduced herself. Her name was Noelle Washington, and she was a junior. I'd seen her around campus, but I never paid her much attention. She was always with some other dude. She looked like a darker Selena with cocoa-brown skin, and straight jet-black hair flowing down her back.

Noelle and I exchanged idle chatter about where we were from and our academic majors. She admired how I played for the Hoyas. The usual hype I was accustomed to hearing from females. I liked her style, though. She was articulate, and seemed to have a good head on her shoulders. Noelle was a writer for the school newspaper. I could tell by her unfocused eyes that she was feeling good from a buzz, too, so our conversation was relaxed. We decided to continue our conversation without the distraction of loud music. We left out of the humid campus center, headed to Starbucks a few blocks away. As we walked down the residential streets, Noelle and I became more familiar with each other.

Our backgrounds were similar. She had been adopted by a white couple at four years old. Before that time she had been shuffled between several different foster homes in Delaware. Her adoptive parents met her at a Parents Fair through Social Services. Noelle said that from what she remembers, the way children met prospective parents was tastefully done, but it was difficult for the older children. Most people, whether they were black or white, were looking for infants or toddlers. Noelle was in that age range where the odds of being overlooked were high. She had been subjected to three of those fairs. The thought of strangers staring at a kid's every move like some animal on display was sickening to me. At her last fair, her parents asked her if she wanted to be their daughter. Noelle cried and held on to her mother's hand tightly, knowing that if she let go she may not see her again.

I could relate to Noelle's fear of rejection. I knew my mother, Heather, but she didn't stick around long enough to know me. She got pregnant at sixteen and gave birth to me the summer before her senior year. The only thing I knew about my father was his name. I was told that my mother was very bright. American University had accepted her, offering a partial scholarship. Determined to fulfill her plan of going to college, she worked two jobs to give my grandmother, Priscilla, money to support her and a baby. We lived in my grandmother's three-bedroom house in Oxon Hill, Maryland. Priscilla was not ready to take on the name of Grandma at the age of thirty-nine. She insisted that I call her Peaches. All my friends had their grandmothers baking cookies for them, and I had a grandmother where the only cooking she liked to do was on the gambling table in Atlantic City. She took a bus trip to New Jersey twice a month. She frequented Trump Plaza so often, management used to send her annual birthday and Christmas cards.

Peaches let Heather know from the start that she was not going to be a professional student for five or six years, leaving her to be a nanny. My mother did complete three years of college. I guess trying to be a prelaw student and a single parent got the best of her. One morning, she left a note on my grandmother's bed saying that she had dropped out of school. She was leaving Maryland to go find herself. She must have forgotten to pack me when she took her stuff from her room. I woke up hearing Peaches cursing and crying in the living room, saying that Heather had lost her damn mind leaving me in the house by myself.

Peaches thought Heather's leaving was just an attempt to get attention, but she was sadly mistaken.

Heather left with her closets empty and her hands free of the responsibility of a four-year-old child. She abandoned her family the week before Labor Day. We haven't heard from her since. I used to spend hours looking out the window, hoping she would miss me and come back. Having to raise a grandson alone on a legal secretary's salary was a rude awakening for Peaches. She loved me dearly, but she had always cherished her independence. Freedom liberated Heather but locked Peaches and me into a world of uncertainty. The day my mother deserted me was the day I realized I had to prove to my grandmother that I was worthy of her love. She gave up her way of life to care for me, so I wanted to make her proud. I did well in school and I took an interest in basketball from an early age. I received academic scholarships from several universities, but I accepted a basketball scholarship to Georgetown.

My game continued to improve in college. Playing ball was my way to success. By age nineteen, I was being recruited by the NBA. A year later, there was promise of a contract from the Miami Lightning and the Washington Warriors. I declined to leave school early, but they continued to sweat me. I was that good. My grandmother had to give up her gambling to raise me, but luckily I played my cards right. I knew within a few years I'd be making enough money to ensure that Peaches never longed for her betting days again. She wouldn't have to lose money taking chances. All she had to do was gamble on me, and I was a sure bet. There was no doubt in my mind that I would be drafted. I could not repay Peaches for the sacrifices she made, but I was going to give her the lifestyle she deserved.

That autumn night walk Noelle and I took was sobering. We arrived at Starbucks totally uninterested in purchasing coffee. We turned around and headed back to campus. As the cool wind brushed against our backs and the leaves fell around us, we continued to share our life stories. We strolled back onto campus and into Lee Hall, Noelle's dormitory. Two orphans sympathizing with each other's pain became two lovers enjoying a sex serenade that would create a new saga of life-changing episodes.

Sharp Shooter

Harper

Noelle called me at home during Christmas break to announce that I was going to be a father. I immediately informed her that I would not claim any child until I was indicted by the results of a paternity test. We started dating the night after we met, but our relationship endured numerous breakups, due to my basketball travels and her infidelity. Sex with Noelle was good and she was good-looking, but she was not above an ass abandonment. My boys kept me informed as to who was going down on my woman while I was on the road. I called it quits. She was having fun while I was trying to be some whipped dude, saving my goods for when I was back at school.

Her charms were hard to resist, though. In between scenes with various part-time lovers, we used to reunite for romantic interludes. The last few times we were together I noticed that she had gained weight, but it didn't look bad. It wasn't concentrated in one particular area. She looked thick or, as the brothers would say, "phat." Noelle tried to say she'd gained "the freshman fifteen" about two years late. I thought she just was retaining sugar from all the booze she was consuming.

In the five months that I had known her, she had been cited twice by campus police for drinking in public. She was showing her true self, craving liquor, and it was no longer cute. One of her intoxicated incidents happened at a home basketball game. Security escorted her out for starting a disturbance with one of my lady friends. The drama was highlighted in the school paper that employed her as a writer. Luckily, I was not associated with her in the article. Noelle was not so lucky. She lost her job and a summer internship due to her love of the bottle. I had tapered off my drinking, because the Warriors were prepared to sign me to a contract in early June. I didn't want any alcohol or drug altering my thinking, or my game. Some of the guys I hung out with were into weed, but I wasn't down with that. I had come too close to winning my NBA goal to lose it over savoring illegal substances.

Unfortunately, I let my dick win over logic when it came to women. I was suddenly forced to play the waiting game. The thought of fathering a child brought on anxiety, but it was nothing that I couldn't handle. I had been down that road before. Two other women had accused me of fathering their children my sophomore year of college. One of the two I knew was lying, because I did wear a condom with her and the shit did not break. Both paternity tests found me not guilty, and I was hoping to be acquitted again with Noelle.

New Edition

Harper

Summer madness was in full effect, battling Noelle, but I was drafted into the NBA. Noelle had the baby and named her Holland Ayana Joe. She called me an hour after the delivery. I wanted to make sure I was the daddy before I got emotionally attached. I also didn't appreciate the fact that the child had my last name before the paternity tests were taken.

I had been seeing a nice young lady who I'd met in a history class. Her name was Tyla, and she was a political science major, like me. Tyla was a breath of fresh air compared to the women I'd dated. She wasn't all caught up on having the latest hair styles, or what she needed to wear to get noticed. She respected my career path, but I never felt like she was planning to use my basketball position for personal gain. We dated for most of the spring semester, but the relationship was constantly in jeopardy. Noelle's harassing calls and campus gossip took a toll on Tyla. When the baby came, she respectfully declined to wait around to hear what I was hoping would be good news. I couldn't fault her for wanting out. She was a beautiful and talented woman whose ambition would probably yield her success in some corporate law firm. I needed that kind of woman in my life. A classy woman who was physically and intellectually stimulating.

The day after Holland was born, I got a call from a doctor at the hospital. He said that Noelle had requested a paternity test. I was surprised that she'd initiated the procedure, but I guess she didn't want to delay because she knew she would not be entitled to any cash unless the test gave her the green light to give me grief. The doctor said the test had to be done soon because Noelle was being discharged the next day. I told him I would be there within the hour.

Be a Man About It

Harper

When I arrived at the maternity ward, I saw a woman talking to a doctor right outside Noelle's door. I approached them. "Excuse me. Is this Noelle Washington's room?" I asked.

"Yes," the doctor said. "Are you a visitor?"

The woman that was talking to him said, "He isn't a visitor. He is the child's father. This is Harper Joe." She looked me up and down, disdain all in her face.

The doctor and I both looked at her like she was crazy.

"Miss, I don't know who you are, and you sure as hell don't know me. Don't speak on my behalf, or make assumptions as to the father of Noelle's baby," I snapped.

The anonymous woman tried to speak again, but the doctor cut in. "Uh, let's all keep our voices down. This is a hospital."

I backed off, but the woman kept looking at me like I stole something.

"Mr. Joe, I'm Dr. Roberts," he said, shaking my hand. "We spoke earlier today. Please wait right here. I need to check on another patient and then pick up some paperwork for your testing. I'll be back shortly." Before he walked away he looked at the woman and me. He lowered his voice and said, "Please remember what I said about keeping the peace."

"All right," the woman grunted, adjusting the pocketbook on her shoulder.

I shrugged. "I'm cool, Doc," I said, running my hand down the front of my crisp blue oxford. "I'll be waiting right here." There was a visitors' area right down the hall. I was walking in that direction when I heard the woman's annoying voice again.

"Aren't you going to at least go in and see how Noelle is doing?" she asked.

I stopped dead in my tracks to look at her. "Who are you?"

She came closer. "My name is Mona Taylor. I'm Noelle's assigned psychologist from the university. I was also her labor coach, since you conveniently decided to be absent," she retorted, lips pursed.

Mouth slightly open, I shook my head in disbelief. This woman didn't even know me, but she talked to me like I was scrub. Hell, my mother wasn't even around to talk down to me, so this woman was on crack if she thought she was gonna continue speaking to me like I was one of the chumps she'd obviously belittled in her lifetime.

I folded my arms as I looked down on her badly weaved halo. She wore a curly bob style, caught in a 1988 era. Her overly colorful shorts set and bad personality did nothing to complement her five foot pudgy frame. "I wish I could say I'm pleased to meet you, but I don't take well to women putting their three cents in my business and expecting to get change. My choice to be absent from the birth really doesn't concern you. I'm a grown man. I do what I wanna do."

She scowled with her hands on her hips. "You think you're a man," she said. "I can't believe you would desert Noelle at a time like this. You all are supposed to be friends. These past few months have been torture for her, dealing with a difficult pregnancy and breakup from the man she loves. You knew about her troubled childhood. I would think you'd have some sympathy. Why don't you show Noelle a little consideration, and sit with her for a while?"

I raised my shoulders. "Why?" I asked. "Noelle sure didn't show me any consideration when she lied about being on birth control. Plus, she dated other men while with me. Now she wants to cry monogamy to suit her motherhood plans? Hell no. My no-show role ain't over until your fat ass stops singing sympathy songs for Noelle, and the doctor tells me my swimmers won the race."

"Watch your mouth!" she shouted.

"You watch yours!" I said, my tone two octaves higher than hers. "You're the one trying to preach to somebody!"

I lowered my voice because a couple of visitors from the waiting area peered around the wall. I knew my face had turned red, because I started to sweat. My head throbbed from this busybody asserting her opinions. During one of our civil conversations, Noelle told me she had started seeing a psychologist at the campus counseling center. This woman fit the description of the person Noelle said was helping her with the so-called depression she said I'd inflicted.

"Listen," I said. "I don't appreciate you being

condescending toward me, especially since Noelle is no saint."

She sighed, retreating a few feet away from me. "I just feel like you should be more sensitive to Noelle's situation. She wants to finish school, but she's uncertain about her future."

I looked at my watch. "Well, to be candid with you, I really don't care how you feel. As a counselor, you should be more professional in terms of how you interact with people in stressful situations. Noelle may need your guidance, but I don't. Your input is not wanted here. I'm confident that Noelle and I can resolve this matter maturely and privately."

She held up her hands. "All right," she said in a more relaxed tone. "I will not press the issue. Obviously, my interfering won't change your attitude about this awkward situation."

I let out a dry laugh. "It is only awkward because you are magnifying my mistakes instead of focusing on Noelle's needs." I rubbed my goatee. "If it makes you feel any better, I will visit with Noelle. We would have to associate anyway if the baby is mine."

"I agree," she said.

I pointed to the door. "Is it all right to go in there now?" I asked.

Mona fanned herself, apparently caught in a menopause hot flash. "Yes. I'll let you be."

"You're so kind," I said sarcastically.

She rolled her eyes. "If Noelle asks where I am, please tell her I went to the cafeteria," she said.

"I'll do that." I gently knocked on the door and walked into the room. Noelle was in the bed reading a book. She smiled when she saw me. I gave her a slight grin in order to appear like I was halfway interested in being there. "How are you, Noelle?"

"Better now that I've seen you," she said.

I stuffed my hands in my jeans pockets and rocked on my heels. "Was the delivery all right?" I asked.

She placed the book on her lap. "Yeah. My contractions were painful at first, but after the epidural I didn't feel a thing."

Sorta like when you were hitting the Jack Daniels, huh? I thought. I was determined to keep my cool and be on my best behavior. "I'm glad," I said. I rubbed my hands together. "You look well. You can't tell that you just had a baby. Your hair is not even messed up."

She patted her ponytail. "Thanks, Harper. That means a lot coming from you. I guess I can thank one of my parents out there for giving me the genes for this petite frame," she said as she surveyed her body. "The doctor said I should be back to my prepregnancy weight in no time."

I nodded. "That's cool," I said. I tried to think of topics to discuss, because I didn't want to get into a whole lot of baby talk just yet. Noelle knew I could be sentimental, and she would use any means necessary to push my buttons.

Noelle grabbed the remote to raise her bed higher. "Harper, I know we've had our differences. I'm to blame for a lot of the conflict, but I just got a whole lot of mental baggage I'm trying to work through." She sighed as she moved her book to the hospital tray and reached for my hand. "Please come closer, Harper. I'm not gonna bite."

No, but that venom was poison, I thought. Her bite that night in the dorm room had intoxicated mind and body. I was nervous about the outcome of this soap opera, but I let her take my hand. I stared into her eyes, trying to find the person behind the mask. We were both educated in the school of hard knocks.

I just didn't want to break down my barrier and let her infiltrate my soul. You can only show vulnerability to certain people. Once someone is allowed to experience the deepest part of you, the innocence of your spirit is no longer your own. Your secrets, your fears, and your dreams become susceptible to public forum, similar to playing in the NBA. Still, I held the hand of a woman who could make my heart melt.

I sat down on the edge of the bed. "Noelle, is the baby healthy?"

"Oh, Harper," she exclaimed, beaming. "God blessed us with a perfect little angel! She's a mini me."

Oh, Lord, no. An infusion of Noelle's looks was a good thing, but if the baby had her personality, there was going to be a need for constant prayer.

She folded her hands. "Harper, I know you weren't really around to witness this, but I have started to turn my life around," she said. "I gave up drinking when I was in my first trimester, and I'm determined not to touch another lick of alcohol."

I raised my brow, surprised. "Good," I said. "You needed to tone down the drinking."

"I know. Did you meet Mona?"

My cheeks deflated like I'd bitten into something sour. "Yes. I made her acquaintance," I mumbled.

She took a baby outfit out of a gift bag, admiring the style. "Mona has been really helping me get back on track. I just don't know if I'll be able to stay at Georgetown. Dad's still making good money as a scientist for NASA, but Mom is disabled now. He's going to have to use his salary to provide for the four of us. They are excited about meeting their new granddaughter, though."

"Noelle, your dad won't have to fret about caring for

Holland if she's mine. My child will be loved and taken care of financially."

"I know, Harper," she said, shaking her head. "I just want to get myself together. I want to be the type of mother Holland can depend on. A couple of months ago, I started going to Sunday Mass on campus. I really enjoy it. I want to have Holland baptized in the Catholic faith if that is all right with you?"

I shrugged. "Yeah. That's fine with me, but I should not be deciding things for Holland until I find out whether or not I'm her father."

Noelle started to tear up. "Holland is yours, Harper. I know I stepped out a few times, but I wasn't seeing anyone the night we met. I'm not the slut everybody depicts me to be. School had just started, for goodness sake! You're a smart man, do the math. Holland's birth correlates with the month we got together in the dorm."

I held up my hands. "Let's just see what the test says, all right?" I took a deep breath, narrowing my eyes at Noelle. "Tell me something. Did you ever care about me? I mean, you acted like you did when I was with you, but I'd go away and you would play me. Getting with other guys as if I didn't exist."

She wiped her face. "I never meant to hurt you, Harper."

"Well, you did," I said, getting off of the bed. I walked to the corner of the room, my back turned to Noelle.

"Harper, I do care for you deeply. The alcohol messed my head up. I loved being with you. What we had was special. I just wasn't ready to receive the love you had to offer. I guess I felt like I didn't deserve it."

I felt her hand on my back. I turned to face her.

"I thought you were another baller that wanted to

hit it and run. I never thought you would develop any real feelings for me. With you being pegged to go into the NBA from the minute you stepped on campus, I figured you were too good for me. So, I wanted to enjoy your company while I had the chance."

I trailed my fingertip down her arm. I knew Noelle would never be caught in hospital-issued attire, so it was no surprise to see her radiant in a peach satin nightgown. "NBA players aren't made of steel, you know," I said, my stare intense. "I don't want to be an athlete that people feel they need to worship, especially not my woman. I'm no better than anybody else. I just want to find love with someone I can trust. I'm tired of having my feelings stepped on."

She took my hand and we walked back over to the bed.

"Harper, sit down beside me."

I consented to her request and sat down.

"I was hoping that you would give me another opportunity to love you," she said, squeezing my hand. "Holland needs a good man like you in her life. I need you, too, Harper. I want to make up for my past. I know I could make you happy."

I swallowed hard as I looked down at the floor. "Noelle, I'm not going to give you or anybody else that chance right now," I said. I pulled my hand away. "I got to focus on the league. I have practice and a lot of business affairs to handle. I can't afford to get distracted."

"I understand." She kissed me softly on the cheek. "I'm not going to give up without a fight. Why don't you go see how beautiful Holland is? Come on, I'll show you." Noelle got up and put on her satin robe. She moved toward the door but stopped when she noticed I was still sitting on the bed.

I rubbed my hands against my jeans. "I'm sorry, Noelle, but I can't," I whispered.

Noelle frowned. "You could at least go to the nursery for a quick minute and look at her."

"No. Not until I know for sure."

Noelle started to cry. She went back to the bed and lay down. I gently touched her thigh. "Noelle, I gotta deal with this on my terms," I said. "I don't mean to . . ."

"Mr. Joe?" Dr. Roberts said as he walked in. "I'm sorry to keep you waiting. My patient follow-up ran longer than I anticipated." He looked over at the bed and noticed that Noelle was upset.

"Miss Washington?" he asked. "Are you all right? Is there something I can do for you? Something you need?"

"No," she softly. "I just got a little emotional, that's all."

"Well, if you are experiencing any discomfort, please page the nurses' station," he said.

"I just want to rest now," she said. "I'm sure Mr. Joe doesn't want to delay the testing any longer."

"Certainly," he said. "We will leave you to rest."

"I'll talk to you later, Noelle," I said.

She grabbed her book and began reading. "Yeah, right," she mumbled.

Dr. Roberts and I walked to the lab. I sat down in a chair as he looked at his clipboard. He handed me some papers.

"Please review everything and sign the highlighted areas," he instructed. "Miss Washington has already completed her forms. Five minutes ago I got a call from Dr. Stevens in Pediatrics. The infant blood specimen has already been collected. Do you have any questions?"

I cracked my knuckles, suddenly feeling nervous.

"Yeah," I said. "How long will I have to wait for the results?"

Dr. Roberts leaned against the wall. "Well, it normally takes several hours, but I'm going to speed things up. I can have the results for you in less than two. I can tell you're anxious to find out."

I nodded. "You're right about that. Either way, I'm gonna stay positive. You live and you learn, that's all."

The doctor glanced at his vibrating pager. "Yes, you do. The nurse should be in to draw your blood in a couple of minutes. Do you have any other questions?"

I smiled. "No, Doc. I really appreciate you doing this for me."

He tapped my shoulder. "My pleasure. Are you going to wait around here, or should I call you?"

"I'm not going anywhere. I'll be in the waiting area."

"I'll come get you as soon as I can."

"All right."

Survey Says . . .

Harper

"Mr. Joe? Mr. Joe?" I heard someone whisper.

"Huh?" I asked, hoarse. "Oh. Hey, Dr. Roberts." I sat upright in the chair and stretched my arms. "I guess I must have dozed off."

I saw a look of concern on his face. I stood up and gave him a reassuring pat on the back. "It's all right, Doc," I said. "Are visitors' hours over for the nursery tonight?"

He placed his pen in his lab coat. "No," he said. "Not for parents."

"Okay. Thanks man." I shook his hand.

"Sure," he said. "All the documentation will be coming to you in the mail." He began to walk away. "Between you and me, I'm a big Georgetown fan and heard about the deal on Sports Center. Congratulations on joining the Warriors."

I chuckled. "Looks like that NBA gig came through just in time, huh?"

He gave me a thumbs-up. "Damn right," he said. "You take care."

"You do the same, Dr. Roberts." I was facing an unexpected fate, but I couldn't stop smiling. I believed that I would be equipped to give Holland a good life. She would never be an orphan, or be treated like one by some deadbeat dad. I was ready to hold my daughter on my first Father's Day.

Proud Papa

Harper

"Noelle?" I asked as I walked over to her hospital bed.

"What, Harper?" she snapped.

"I was wondering if you would accompany me to the nursery so we could see our baby."

She looked over her shoulder with a facial expression that displayed a mixture of certainty and relief. She smiled. "See, you had to depend on a test to tell you what I knew all along. Wait until you see your baby girl. Holland is too precious to deny." She got off the bed and I helped her put on her robe.

As she tied her belt, I gently squeezed her shoulder. "Um. Noelle," I said. "I just want to apologize. You know, for not being here earlier."

She waved her hand. "It's all right," she said. "I realized you had reservations from the day I told you I was pregnant. I knew it would take the baby being born for you to start trusting me again. At least, I was hoping that you would."

"I want to trust you, Noelle. I don't know. Maybe as time goes on we can begin to build the kind of friendship we never had in the beginning. Having Holland is definitely going to keep us connected in some way."

She grabbed my hand. "Who knows?" she asked. "Maybe it will be a love connection."

I smiled. "Maybe. Why don't we just focus on respecting each other for right now. Deal?"

"Deal. Well, let's go," she said. "Holland is waiting to say hello to her daddy."

When we got to the nursery window, there were three babies in bassinets. I looked at the name cards but none of them read Joe. Noelle wasn't saying anything, just smiling. Finally, she pointed down the hallway and said, "Go down and look at the window around the corner. I think you'll find what you're searching for."

I walked what seemed to be a mile down the corridor. When I turned the corner and peered through the glass I was mesmerized. An angel was before my eyes. A beautiful blessing that I could not believe came from me. I placed my hands on the glass and bowed my head. Words couldn't describe the joy I felt. I hadn't even touched her yet, but I knew that I would do anything in my power to protect her from harm. I felt like I could stand at that same spot all night, staring at her tiny face. I broke out of my trance when I felt Noelle's hand rub the middle of my back. I grabbed Noelle in a bear hug and kissed the top of her head.

"Uh, Harper?" she asked. "I can't breathe."

I released my arms. "I'm sorry, Noelle," I said, giddy. "Thank you for my daughter. I can't believe how pretty she is."

Noelle placed her hands on her hips. "And why

not? Just look at her parents. You see all that hair on her head? She's got good genes from the both of us." She wrapped her arm around my waist and rested her head on me as we looked at our love child. "She is a sweetie pie, isn't she?"

"She sure is," I said. Holland was moving her legs a little and her eyes were squinting, as if she was trying to see her proud parents.

"You wanna hold her?" she asked.

"Can I?"

"Of course, silly." Noelle led me to the door of the nursery. The nurse picked up Holland and gave her to me. I was so nervous that my big hands were gonna drop her. I had never held a baby before.

"Harper, come sit in this rocking chair so you can bond better," Noelle said.

I walked over and sat down. As I rocked the baby to sleep, a tear ran down my cheek. I looked up and Noelle was by my side, crying as well. I stopped rocking and bent down to give my baby a kiss.

"Daddy loves you, Holland Ayana," I whispered. "And I'm going to live the rest of my life making sure you know that."

I drove Holland and Noelle from the hospital to Mona's house. Mona had offered her home to Noelle for the summer, with the option to rent for the next school year. When we got to Mona's place, Noelle was exhausted. I knew she wanted to rest, so I asked her if I could take the baby to meet Peaches. Despite fierce protests from Mona, Noelle approved. It was a beautiful day to introduce Holland to her greatgrandmother. I promised that I wouldn't keep the baby out long.

After Noelle supervised me snapping the carrier car seat into my Jetta, my little girl and I were on our way.

My key wasn't even in the lock good when I heard the door hardware click. Peaches had opened the door so fast, I almost lost my balance.

"Let me see that greatgrandbaby!" Peaches said, excited like a person who'd just won the lottery. She took the carrier right out of my hand and walked into the living room, totally ignoring me. I laughed as I shut the door. I walked into the room and sat down on the floor beside Peaches. She had decorated the entire first floor with pink streamers and baby girl Mylar balloons. Peaches could make anything an event in five minutes flat.

"She's so pretty, Harper," she said, her face beaming. "All that hair. She looks like a little Indian."

I rubbed Holland's tiny hand. "Yeah, she's my little baby doll," I said. "I can just imagine all the gray hairs I'll have when she becomes a teenager and I'm fighting off sorry dudes who are after her."

"Yes, indeed," Peaches laughed as she rustled my hair with her hand. "How you feel about being a daddy?"

I unbuttoned the top of my oxford and took off my watch. "Scared, but I'm excited too," I said. "I don't want Holland to come up short on anything, especially having a father. I want her to have what I didn't."

Peaches gently placed the baby on her shoulder. "I know," she said, patting Holland's back. "It's a trip when parenthood falls into your lap, though, ain't it?"

"You got that right," I said, getting up and sitting beside Peaches. Holland was sound asleep.

Peaches took my hand and held it as she rocked her latest legacy. "But you know what, Harper?" she asked. "It's a job that only God can give. And this little princess is definitely gonna be your reward for busting your butt in the world. So, you only got one chance to raise her right. You hear me?"

"Yep," I said. I squeezed my grandmother's hand tight. "I hear you, and I'm listening."

Her eyes became weary. "I know your mother broke your heart by leaving you like she did, but Grandma tried to do the best she could," she said.

That was the first time I'd heard Peaches call herself a grandmother. I raised my brow. "Grandma?" I asked. "Oh, so now I can call you that since Holland is here?"

She nudged me. "No," she said. "Peaches will be fine. I'll let Holland start the Grandma trend." She sighed as she leaned against my shoulder. "This aching body says I'm old enough to be called that now. But I'm always gonna be Peaches to you, and you always gonna be my son."

I rested my head on my grandmother's lap as my daughter rested in her arms. Finally, I felt like I belonged.

Good Grief

Harper

A week after my daughter was born, I got a call from my agent, Dean Davis. He had an urgent matter to discuss, so I told him I could be at his office today. I arrived at noon. His secretary, Donna, escorted me in.

"Hey, Dean, what's up?" I asked as we shook hands. "How was Aruba?"

"It was great," he said. "In fact, I wish I was still there." He scratched his head. "A situation came up while I was away." He nodded to his visitors' chairs. "Have a seat, Harper. A call was forwarded to me from an attorney here in D.C."

He sat down in his big leather chair. His hands gripped a Montblanc pen. I took a seat, wondering why Dean had an annoyed look on his face. I tried to think of what I could have done to have him so mad. I joined Dean's sports agency my freshman year of college. I had been in publicity spots for charity events and local commercials since my basketball days in high school. Peaches felt I needed representation early on to handle my career. Dean was a young, straightlaced businessman. He was aggressive when it came to working deals, and he pulled no punches. I felt comfortable having a brotha as my agent, watching my back. There weren't too many black agents around. However, the look in his eyes right now made me wish that I didn't know him.

"Harper, who is Tyla Robinson?" he asked.

I shrugged. "A woman from school that I dated, why?" I asked.

"Well, she's claiming that you got her pregnant."

I jumped up. "What!"

He shook his head. "Her attorney was the one that contacted me in Aruba."

I placed my hands on my head, disgusted, as I walked over to Dean's office window. "I can't believe this crap. How much more does a brotha have to take?"

"The question is, how much longer are you going to keep planting seeds where they don't belong?" he asked, his index finger directing me to sit back down. "Harper, I cannot effectively represent you if you continue being irresponsible. No team wants a jackass jock making babies all over the place."

I held up my hand. "Now hold up," I said, sitting back down. "This woman has to prove paternity. You need to set up a meeting with her attorney, so we can . . ."

Dean interrupted. "That won't be necessary. Her attorney called me this morning. Apparently, she had a miscarriage yesterday."

I exhaled, eyes rolled up to the ceiling. "Thank God," I said, folding my hands. "Somebody must be praying for me."

Dean scowled. "Really? Well, they're not praying hard enough. When are you going to grow up and learn from your mistakes, instead of having your dick history repeat itself like a broken record?"

I pointed at him. "Listen, you are not my father, so cut the lecture, all right?"

Dean rose, hands planted firmly on his desk as he leaned toward me. "No, you listen. In this business, I'm your daddy, your mommy, and every other freakin' relative you have. You think you call the shots, but you better recognize who is pulling teeth trying to get endorsement deals and solidify your contract. Until you start paying me enough money to tolerate your headaches, you are going to do just what you're told."

I waved him off, pretending my ego wasn't deflated. "Dean, go to hell if you're tired of dealing with me. Agents are a dime a dozen."

Dean plunged back into his executive chair, exasperated. "Harper, I've practically worked for free for you, dealing with this baby bull. As I have stressed numerous times before, being a good baller is not the sole key to success in this industry. You have to see the big picture. You are an excellent player, but you are not the only rookie forward around. If the Warriors decide to trade you and capitalize on what they think is a better opportunity, you're screwed. Signing on the dotted line means nothing. You have to start out playing your ass off and attracting a mainstream fan base. The Warriors are expecting a return on their investment."

I rubbed my sweaty palms against my trousers. "I understand the importance of having a good image, but the focus should be about the skills I bring to the court," I said. "My personal life has yet to affect my game."

"Oh, but it will," he said. "When you start to lose sponsorship, and you're not playing the kind of minutes you want, you'll change that self-serving attitude.

Basketball is a game on and off the court. Thinking strategically is crucial. Team owners desire winners in all respects. You're a nice kid, but being a nice ball player in the NBA doesn't cut it if you fail to use discretion in the bedroom. The media has a field day blasting this kind of behavior over the news. Having children out of wedlock is not beneficial for your career. Sex is damn important, but you cannot be reckless."

I rubbed my hand over my face, frustrated. "Look, I'm not perfect, Dean. I don't appreciate you coming down on me like this, but I know you're one of the best agents out there. You've stuck by me. So, I'm not going to take what you're saying lightly."

Dean folded his hands on top of his desk. "Harper, we don't always see eye to eye, but I do have your best interest at heart. I've been working with athletes long enough to know what it takes to survive in the basketball business. I also want both of us to make long cash, so I'm gonna continue to be hard on you. If I wasn't doing my job well, you'd fire me, right?"

I nodded. "Yeah."

"So, understand that if you don't play smart, your livelihood is hindered and so is mine."

I looked over at his Perseverance plaque on the wall. "I hear you," I said. "So, what do you expect me to do?"

Dean twisted a rubber band as he stared at me. "Pick one," he said.

"Excuse me?"

"Pick the best Belle of the Ball and get hitched."

"Are you serious?"

"Dead serious," he said. "I don't care who it is, just do it. Fans like players who are family men."

I threw my head back with a nervous laugh. "Well, you were making sense up until now," I said. "I just had fatherhood thrown into my face, and now you expect me to jump into a marriage?"

Dean raised his shoulders. "It's a business decision. This is your first year in the league, and you need a clean start. By getting married at a young age, you can show the public that you have decent values, and that you're disciplined."

I shook my head. "Dean, that's a shady thing to suggest," I said. "Why would I marry somebody I don't love?"

He pulled a cigar from an ornate oak case. He winked as he offered me one. "Cheers?"

My jaw clenched. "I ain't in the mood for jokes, Dean."

He laughed. "Time and money wait for no one, Harper," he quipped. "You can learn to love later. Right now you have to master the art of the game. I know what I'm talking about. We'll have her commit to a prenuptial contract. You can always dissolve the marriage after a couple of years."

I threw up my hands. "That's easy for you to say. You wouldn't have to live with the person. How is having a shotgun wedding playing smart? Isn't that what you were preaching a few minutes ago? Having a good strategy?"

He leaned back in his chair with his cigar between his lips. "I get paid to make deals happen and make people rich," he said, crossing his legs. "If you want to reap the full benefits of this business, then you better take heed to my advice."

I rose from my seat and told Dean that I would have to ponder on his proposal. As I descended down the steps of the Metro station at Farragut North, I wondered how I allowed myself to get into these predicaments. On the subway ride back home, I thought about what Dean had said in his office. I needed to wise up and make better choices in my life. Holland was counting on me now. It was time to restore the positive image that I had worked so hard at building. But I wasn't sure that marriage was the best way to begin that process. Going through these experiences made me realize that women can be conniving. Never underestimate the power of greed.

I ended up taking my agent's advice. Noelle was the lucky winner of my wife contest. We got married during the fall of my rookie year. When she walked down the aisle, I waited at the front of the church, uneasy, like I was in the Twilight Zone. Today, I still believe that from the moment we said "I do" we'd made a mistake. The only benefits of matrimony were my daughters, Holland, who is fourteen years old, and Hunter Nicole, who is three.

Celebrate Life

June 2007, Disney World, Orlando, Florida

Darin

Never underestimate the power of prayer. After almost a year of rehabilitation, I made a full recovery. To celebrate, the family took a trip to Disney World. As soon as Darin Jr. got to the hotel, he took a nap in his room. All of the hustling we had to do just to get to the flight on time, really wore him out. Paige and I relaxed in our private suite at the Grand Floridian. Butt-naked in the whirlpool tub, we nibbled on chocolate-covered strawberries.

I wrapped my arms around my wife. "It doesn't get any better than this, does it babe?"

Paige leaned her head back on my chest. "Nope," she said, giggling from me tickling her ribs.

I rested my chin on the crown of her head. Her braided hair smelled sweet, like an Apple Jolly Rancher. "Tell me something, Paige. Did you ever think we'd actually get married?"

She shrugged. "Honestly, there were times when I never wanted to see you again. But you and I have been through so much together. We had DJ. We lost Malcolm and Serena on the same day, September 11th. I almost lost you at our wedding . . . But God gave us a second chance to build something beautiful."

I massaged Paige's thigh. "DJ is growing like a weed. Seems like yesterday we were tripping, trying to get him in the car seat for the first time." I kissed her neck. "You remember when he was conceived?"

Paige shook her head, smiling. "How could I forget?" she asked as she handed me a flute of champagne. We toasted and got comfortable in the tub again as we drifted back in time.

Back Down
Memory Lane

August 1996

Paige

Miss Maria's death was devastating for Darin. It was tough on all of us. I still can't accept that she's gone. Miss Maria suffered a heart attack while on the porch. She had been hospitalized once before due to a mild attack. The doctors told her to lose weight, but it was difficult for her. She was used to eating good country cookin'. Darin had the financial resources to hire a chef to prepare her meals, but she refused. She didn't want Darin fussing over her. She didn't even want to move into the nice new house he had built for her on the west side of town. So, he decided to use that as his second home.

Darin had finally convinced his mama to have her house remodeled. She was excited about getting a modern kitchen, so she could cook food for folk. All of the renovations were finished a week before she passed. Darin and I really weren't communicating, but I made sure I was available to help the family in any way I could. I felt like I owed it to Miss Maria, because she treated me like I was family. Practically all of Goode mourned. Maria Simms was well loved. She had the kind of spirit that would make you forget about your troubles. There were plenty of times when she would take care of people's kids for nothin'. That's part of the reason why her family had financial problems back in the day. Even when her family lacked, she loved enough to give what she had. Darin was her heart. She glowed anytime you mentioned his name. She always gave thanks to God for allowing her son to play in the NBA. She didn't care about the material stuff he gave to the family. All that mattered was that her firstborn was happy living out his dream.

I was still bitter toward Darin for not wanting our baby, but I couldn't turn my back on him during this loss. There was too much sadness to have room for anger. The day of the funeral overwhelmed him.

When we got back to the house from the burial, Darin went straight to the attic. His sister, Camille, was on leave from the army. After Camille and I finished serving some of the guests, I fixed a plate of food and took it upstairs to him. He sat on the bed, looking at an old photo album.

"Darin?" I called as I pushed open the door. "I thought you might want something to eat. I figured I'd bring you a plate now before it's all gone. Folks downstairs eatin' like there's no tomorrow."

He looked up from the album, his face streaked with tears. "Thanks, Paige," he whispered, taking the plate. He put it on a crate beside the bed. "How you holdin' up?"

I folded my arms. "I'm okay," I said. "What about you?"

He removed his tie from his shirt collar. "Man, this ain't even real to me yet. Mama gone?" He shook his head in disbelief. "It's like I'm waiting to wake up from a bad dream, you know?"

I swallowed hard, trying not to get emotional. "I know," I said, sitting beside him. "It just happened so suddenly."

He stared at his hands. "I feel like a part of me died with her," he said. "Mama understood me. She never judged. Even when she knew I was doing crazy shit she kept it to herself. Now who am I gonna turn to? I wasn't even home when she needed me."

He sobbed. I rubbed his back while I tried to prevent my own tears from running. "Darin, please. It's not your fault. I guess it was just Miss Maria's time."

Darin dropped the album onto the floor and buried his head on his knees. "I can't accept that. If I had been home, things would have been different. I know it." He looked up at me. "When stuff like this happens, it makes you realize just how insignificant you are. I mean, I throw a ball in a hoop for a living. My mama saved people from being thrown out in the street. Fans sweatin' me, and I ain't done nothin'."

"Don't be so hard on yourself," I said. "You give back. You got your camp, and you started your foundation for at-risk families."

He pulled his handkerchief from his pocket and wiped his face.

"Just give it time, D," I said. "You'll be all right." I squeezed his hand and got up. "I'll get you some water."

I started to walk away, but he pulled my arm to sit with him again.

"Don't go, Paige. I don't need anything right now. Just stay with me and talk."

He gently rubbed his hand down my cocoa-colored face. I looked down to avoid his eyes calling out to me.

"I appreciate all you've done," he said softly.

I patted my freshly styled hairdo, moving a spiral curl behind my ear. "Don't thank me, Darin," I said. "I was blessed to have Miss Maria in my life." Darin stared at me, longing to say something.

"Paige, I know we're not on the best of terms," he said as he looked at the wooden floor. "I'm to blame for that. I just want to apologize again for . . ."

I held up my hand. "Darin, stop," I said, irritated. I got up and walked toward the door.

Darin got up to prevent me from walking out. He positioned himself in front of me. He shut the door with his back, forcing me to look at him.

"Wait, Paige. I know you probably hate me for what I put you through. I just wanna say I miss how things used to be between us. I messed up a good thing." He grabbed my hands. "I'm sorry."

He held me tenderly, snug in an embrace I knew I should've resisted. He rested his head on my shoulder and started to cry again. I tried to pull away, but Darin wouldn't let go. He lifted my head, searching my eyes for forgiveness.

My face was wet from crying. I felt butterflies in my stomach as confusion of the moment escalated. "Darin, please, let me out this door," I pleaded. "I need some air."

His face solemn, he slowly stepped aside, but as I opened the door his hands caressed my waist. I closed my eyes as he pulled me close to the hardness of his body. I felt the warmth of his breath penetrate my bare upper back like a laser. My hand shut the door, and I turned around to face him. His hands cupped my face as he placed his lips on mine. The kiss intensified with every moan. Darin lifted me into his arms and laid me on the bed. He lowered his body on top of me, waiting for clearance to initiate his journey into my threshold. I wrapped my arms around his neck, welcoming his peace offering.

Caught in
Confusion

Darin

An old-school groove by Frankie Beverly & Maze, a little candlelight, and a lot of merlot had me in chill mode at my estate in Maryland. This girl named Kim was giving me serious head. I'd met her at Club Phoenix the other night. I love a woman that don't mind tastin' my syrup. Honey Dip raised up and took off her thong, ready to mount for the Kentucky Derby when the phone rang. *Shit, party over,* I thought, shaking my head at the sound of the ringtone. It was my emergency line.

"Hey, baby," I moaned, fixing my pants. "I'm sorry, but I gotta answer that." She frowned as I got up from under her but didn't say a word. I picked up the cordless and walked out of the bedroom, shutting the door behind me.

When I was home I didn't ignore this phone line,

especially ever since Mama died. I wanted to make sure I was available in case my family needed me.

"Hello?" I asked, annoyed as I rubbed my bare chest. A good blow job was priceless, so whoever this was had better be in dire need of help.

"Hey."

"Paige?" I asked as I adjusted my belt, shaking off the excitement Kim had caused.

"Yeah," she said, her tone shallow as if she'd been crying.

"Why you sound like that? What's goin' on?"

"I'm pregnant."

Dead silence.

"Hello?" she asked. "Darin, you there?"

I held my head. "Yeah," I said as I winced at her breaking news. I might as well go down to the bank and open up another account, because Paige was about to give me serious issues.

"Darin, I know this is a shock, but we need to talk," she said.

I rolled my neck, trying to release tension. "I know. Look, can I call you back first thing in the morning?"

She sucked her teeth. "All right, bye."

"Peace," I said and hung up the phone. I walked back into the bedroom. "Sorry to keep you waiting, Kim."

Kim was fully undressed. I couldn't even remember this girl's last name. Actually, I don't even recall if she told me her last name. Yet, as she got off the bed and sauntered over to me, I felt a familiar rekindling underneath my briefs. The jackhammer between my legs reminded me that I knew her kind very well.

"No problem," she said, pouting her lips seductively. "Now, where were we?"

She put her arms around my neck and gave me a

kiss. My loins were in overdrive, but my mind was not in the mood for this anymore. I gently released myself from her embrace. "Kim, I know this is sorta awkward, but we're gonna have to stop tonight and resume some other time." I moved my hand over the waves of my trimmed hair. "That was an important call from back home. I gotta make a few more calls and tend to some family business in the morning."

Kim's face showed obvious disappointment, but she said she understood. I ain't care if she didn't. I was pretty certain that I would never see this girl again. I mean, she was fine. Her body was tight, but I see that every day. When I met her my intent was never to keep her. That was just the nature of the game. Stick and move.

She got dressed. I put on a shirt, threw on some loafers, and grabbed my keys. We left my house and I drove her home. We didn't say much in the car.

"Is there anything I can do?" she asked, touching my hand.

I shifted my Porsche into third gear, giving her a macho glance. "Naw, I'm straight," I said with extra bass in my voice. Who was I kidding? I was straight-assed out.

Once we got to her apartment in Greenbelt, I apologized a couple more times and said good night. I told her I would call, but that wasn't gonna happen. I gotta slow down and rethink some of my extracurricular activities with these women.

I lay on my bed, restless. I decided to call Paige back even thought it was the middle of the night.

"Hello?" she asked in a raspy voice.

"Paige, it's Darin. I'm sorry to call you so late. I've

been thinking about you since you called earlier. You feel like talkin' right now?"

"We can talk," she said. "There's just one thing I gotta say before you say anything. I'm keeping this baby."

I took a deep breath as I remembered the pain I'd put her through. "Paige I wasn't gonna ask you to terminate the pregnancy. I know it's difficult, but let's try not to dwell on the past. I promise I'll do right by you this time." I got out of bed and walked over to my bedroom sitting area, retrieving a bottled water from the custom minibar. "To be honest, I had a feeling we would conceive again that night in the attic. So, you feelin' all right? You need anything?"

"No," she said. "I'm all right, just a little nauseous."

I smiled as I leaned against my mahogany dresser. "When's my son due?"

"How do you know it's a boy?" she asked.

"I just know. So?"

"The doctor estimated the due date next year, around Mother's Day."

"For real?" I asked. "That's nice. A perfect gift. I know you will be a good mother."

"I hope so. I'm gonna do my best."

"Hey. Why you sound so down? This is what you wanted, right?" I gulped some water.

She sighed. "I wanted the first baby, Darin. I wanted us to be a family. I'm happy about this baby, but it isn't exactly how I envisioned my life right now. It was hard enough dealing with the guilt of getting pregnant the first time. Now I find myself traveling down that road again and I know where it's gonna lead."

I frowned. "Paige, what are you talking about?"

"Darin, where do we go from here?" she asked. "We are not together, and I have a strong feeling that

ain't gonna change." She paused. "You're not in love
with me."

I shook my head as I sat down on the edge of the
bed. "Paige, listen. We just need to take it day by day.
I do love you, but you're right, I guess I don't have
feelings strong enough to commit at this point. I'm
seriously attracted to you, but you and I both know
sex ain't gonna sustain us."

"I know," she said. "Isn't it amazing, though? We
can't have a serious commitment, but we can have a
baby. God help us. If we don't grow up, we're gonna
be some crazy, impulsive fools."

"We're gonna be just fine," I said. "God let this
happen again for a reason. I'm not saying we created
a baby under the best circumstances, but what's done
is done. All I want is for us to be friends. No matter if
we're together or not, we will always have a bond now.
I don't wanna see you in the state you were in eight
years ago. I swear to you, I'm not gonna punk out this
time."

"I want to believe that, Darin," she said. "I'll hold
you to your promise."

Spring Rain, Blessings Bloom

May 1997

Darin

When I saw my son's head emerge from his mother's body I felt a little queasy. The sight of something the size of a football coming out her stuff was overwhelming for me. After twenty-four hours of labor, Paige was out of gas. For some reason, she refused any pain medication. She cried, saying she couldn't push anymore. I told her the baby was almost here, and she had to hold on just a little while longer. The agony showing through the beads of sweat on her face told me the pain was unbearable. I thought she would break my hand, she held it so tight. Paige's legs shook. Just as she belted a deafening scream, the doctor pulled the baby out and placed him on her stomach.

A variety of emotions flooded me. I thanked God

that the baby was healthy, and kissed Paige for giving me this beautiful man-child. One night of passion created life, and one day of pain brought my son, Darin Christopher Simms Jr., into the world. The doctor handed me the scissors and told me to cut the umbilical cord. Camille took a picture as I cut the cord. As I looked at my son I prayed that I would be the kind of man he could depend on.

Once the baby was cleaned off and observed by the staff, the nurse handed him to me. I placed him in Paige's arms. He was so quiet. I guess he was tired from all that screamin' he did during the pediatrician's exam. Darin Jr. opened his eyes.

Paige smiled at me and said, "He's got his daddy's eyes."

Meet
Miss Independent

September 2007

Logan

I spent all day at the mall looking for a new outfit. Big mistake. Montgomery Mall was always crowded on Saturdays. I don't know why I had to put on new clothes for a first date. Maybe subconsciously I felt like I was starting a new phase in life each time. My aunt Gina had set me up with one of her classmates from graduate school at the University of Maryland.

Three years had passed since my last serious relationship. My best friend, Paige, thought I was handling too much emotional baggage. She recommended that I see a psychologist in D.C. Dr. Adu was her name. Trust me, Dr. Adu should have been on the couch and I should have been behind the desk. Sista was strange, clanging cymbals and burning incense. She was extremely philosophical. I had to take personality tests and keep a journal. Like I really had time for that. Once I realized she liked hearing herself talk more than me, I called it quits. I decided self-therapy would be more convenient, and a lot cheaper. I went to Borders and bought all of Iyanla's books. I burned my own aromatherapy candles, put my ass in the tub, and let Calgon take me to Maui anytime some fool worked my nerves.

My fingertips feathered my smooth copper skin, as I applied the finishing touches to my makeup. Satisfied with my freshly cut hair, I walked out of the bathroom. I heard a knock. I tied the belt on my black pantsuit and answered the front door.

I got flushed in the face because the first things I noticed were perfect teeth and deep dimples on a tall, hot-chocolate brotha.

"Good evening, Logan. I'm James Nesbitt," he said in a sexy tenor voice, holding a beautiful bouquet of peach roses.

I ran my fingers through my hair. "Hi, James," I said. "Come on in." I took the bouquet from him. "The flowers are beautiful."

He rubbed his hands together. "I was confident that Gina would match me with a beautiful young woman, so I brought these just to complement the obvious."

I smiled brighter, feeling like a teenager. "Thanks. Have a seat." I showed him to the living room as I took the flowers into the kitchen. I walked back over and sat next to him on the sofa. James had on some jeans, slightly faded. Nice loafers. His white linen shirt gave a hint of his muscular chest.

"Would you like anything to drink?" I asked.

"No thanks. I think I'll wait until we get to the

movie theater. I got tickets for the nine thirty movie. Is that okay?"

I checked my watch. "Perfect. So, James, tell me about yourself. Gina was vague when I drilled her for information."

He touched his silver link bracelet. "Well, I teach history, grades nine through twelve at Wilson High in Laurel. I will finish my master's degree in business administration this fall. I have a brother who's thirteen years younger than me. People always think he's my son. Oh, I'm also a deacon at my dad's church in Odenton. I head up the singles ministry."

I raised my brow. "I'm impressed. So you're a preacher's kid, huh?"

He laughed. "Yeah, and I don't mind. My dad's a great minister. Anytime I can help him do God's work, I don't hesitate. I'm enjoying my spiritual journey. Being active in the church keeps my mind off worldly things that cause chaos to a brotha."

I crossed my legs. "I hope I'm not causing a distraction," I said, being coy.

He shook his head. "No. I like meeting people. I guess I'm just trying to meet someone I can settle down with. This dating process is stressful, especially when you're searching for a spiritual woman." He waved his hand. "Enough about me. Tell me about you."

I shrugged. "I grew up in Philly, but I moved to Virginia when my mother passed. I went to Georgetown for law school. I have my own law firm. Business is good. My best friend, Paige, found me this loft condo that I just love. I like interior decorating. Not much else going on."

"Hopefully, you won't be taking care of a household by yourself for long. God willing."

He winked at me like I was the lucky one he'd

chosen from a lineup of women who had obviously boosted his ego too damn much. He had the audacity to keep rambling.

"I don't mean to sound sexist, but the Bible does say the man is the head of the home."

Was he trying to amuse me, or was he just being an arrogant, opinionated ass?

"That's good in theory, James, but I'm not exactly pressed to have a husband right now," I said. "I'm not disagreeing with you, but until I can find a man to entrust with that responsibility, I'm gonna let God take care of home. We've been doing fine thus far."

He held up his hands. "I didn't mean to offend you," he said. "I just don't understand why women are afraid to let a man take care of them." He looked around the room. "For instance, this is a beautiful condo, but wouldn't you have preferred to be in a single-family home with a loving husband?"

My jaw dropped—mouth open, ready to speak in a tongue he would not like. I took a deep breath, trying to remain composed. "I like to live where I feel safe and comfortable, single or not. A house doesn't make a home. If the people on the inside are in disharmony, the shit . . . I mean, stuff, is gonna tumble down." He scowled at me like I was a heathen. I didn't bat an eye. "Whether it's a hut or a mansion makes no difference," I continued. "By the way, where do you live?"

He cleared his throat. "I'm waiting to find Mrs. Right so I can build her a home. My family owns a construction business in Bowie."

Uh-huh. He was talkin' all that yang, livin' with Mommy and Daddy.

He reached for my hand. "Logan, let's change the subject. I think we've gotten a little too serious for a first date."

"I agree," I said, narrowing my eyes.

He squeezed my hand. "So, what else should I know about Logan Banks?"

I looked him straight in the face. *I don't take nonsense, so don't try me,* I thought to myself. "I'm an assistant dance and cheerleading coach for the Gunpowder Mill Recreation center in Beltsville."

"That's wonderful," he said. "I coach varsity football at Wilson. I had practice tonight, but I was easy on the kids and let them go early. The extra time allowed me to relax a little. I didn't want to be rushed when I met you." He patted me on my knee. "Well, it's nine o'clock. Are you about ready to go?"

"Sure," I said. We got up off the sofa. I grabbed my jacket and we headed out.

He opened the car door to his Mercedes. It was nice, but I purposely didn't give him a compliment. Men love for you to jock their ride. It could be a Hyundai with a gold kit package, and the brotha would think he's smooth. Mercedes . . . Metro. They're all the same. They depreciate, and someone can hit it or steal it at anytime. I got my own damn car. I don't need to be impressed about a man because he got one. Besides, I like Lexus, anyway.

We made good time to the movie theater in Beltsville. James asked if I wanted any refreshments, but I declined. I was still full from the leftover spaghetti I had had earlier. I was enjoying the movie, but I don't think James liked it. He kept grunting every time there was a scene with heavy cursing. During a kissing scene, I thought he was gonna lose his mind. His sanctified antics seemed like overkill to me. He bent over and whispered in my ear, "Why do our movies always have to expose our women?"

Why did he ask me? I didn't write the movie. Send

the director an e-mail or something. I just shrugged my shoulders. He looked back at the screen. I was still staring at him because I couldn't believe this negro. James needed to stop pretending.

After the movie we decided to go to the Silver Dollar Diner in Laurel for dessert. As we drove I noticed a red Kia to my right keeping pace with us. I glanced over and there were two women in the car grittin' on me. The one driving mouthed something. I looked away because I thought she might have been intoxicated. You never know what state people are in these days. James accelerated to switch lanes, so they were left behind. Next thing I knew, the Kia was parallel to our car again. At first he acted like he didn't see them. Then they sped up, switched to our lane, and then switched to the left lane. As our car approached from behind, they maintained a parallel position on James's side. The driver smiled and waved. James gave her a goofy grin and waved back.

"Do you know them?" I asked.

He sniffed and rubbed his nose as if he were trying to conceal something. "No," he mumbled, gripping the steering wheel.

Both cars stopped for a traffic light. The girl in the passenger's seat of the Kia rolled down her window. James rolled down his. The woman driving looked over. She rolled her eyes at me, then said to James, "I thought you had football practice tonight."

"I did," he replied, as he adjusted his position in the seat. Inconvenienced by getting caught. When the light turned green he accelerated ahead. The Kia did not keep pace. No need for girlfriend to give chase anymore. Her mission was accomplished. James looked over at me with puppy dog eyes.

"Logan, I'm sorry about that," he said. "I told you

I didn't know her because I've only met her once. She attended my church one Sunday, and my uncle introduced us. It was so long ago, I only vaguely remembered what she looked like. My uncle thought that he'd made a match, but she is just not my type. She continues to call me to go out. I tell you, it's getting to be quite annoying."

Don't lie, you proper pimp, I thought. "No need to apologize, James," I said, staring out the window. From that moment on, I knew his churchie ass had to go. We definitely didn't click. See, that's why people don't go to church now. Too many hypocrites. James was probably gonna call that heifer in the Kia for a late-night Bible study as soon as he got home.

After we ate our dessert he drove me back to my place. When we got to my front door he said, "I've had a lovely evening, Logan. We must do this again soon. When can I call you?"

My lips were pursed like I had bit into a tart gumball. "Well, you have the number, so feel free to call anytime before ten," I said nonchalantly. "Everything shuts down for me after that, especially during the week." No TV, no phone, and no thinking about jerks like him. "I will be busy in court next week, so it may be difficult to catch me."

He nodded. "Okay. My schedule's pretty hectic next week as well. I have a business trip in New Jersey. Why don't I call you when I return?"

"Fine," I said, hand planted firmly on the door to shut him out. I knew I wouldn't be waiting by the phone.

"Good night, Logan." He kissed me lightly on the cheek and gave me a pseudo hug before leaving.

* * *

Over the next few weeks, needless to say, I avoided this man like the plague. I never returned any of his calls. After a few more unsuccessful attempts to contact me, his calls ceased. I didn't want to be bothered with him. I thanked Aunt Gina for trying, but he was not the one. Bringing liars into my life doesn't agree with me. Gives me heartburn.

I'm Looking
for a New Love

Logan

I rolled my eyes as Paige rambled on the phone. "Paige, I am not a charity case. I wish y'all would stop trying to set me up with jive gigolos." I secured the cordless phone with my shoulder as I cooked my beef stir-fry.

"Come on now," she said. "I have never tried to set you up on a blind date before. Don't blame me for your aunt Gina's fiasco."

I emptied the contents of the wok into a bowl. "Tell me some more about the dude," I said. "He sounds like a buppie."

"No, he's not," she said. "Mallory is down-to-earth. He's a pharmaceutical rep. I was his real estate agent three months ago. He bought a big house in Kensington. Believe me, he's definitely your type. Based on his profession, I'm sure he makes good money. He drives a BMW 7 Series. Isn't that the type of man you're looking for?"

I looked up at the ceiling. "Yeah, yeah," I said. "Tell me what he looks like, and don't front with the details."

She sucked her teeth. "Logan, you are so superficial. He has a pleasant disposition. That's not enough?"

"Hell, no."

"Logan, lighten up," Paige said. "Mallory is nice-looking, girl. He sort of has that Blair Underwood aura."

"Yeah, right," I said, sampling my stir-fry. This guy probably looked like the bottom of my shoe. "All right, I'll let you play Cupid just this once. I guess I have nothing to lose."

"Great!" she said. "This time next year you could be Mrs. Mallory Clark."

"Let's not go there, okay? Mallory sounds just a little too perfect. What's wrong with him? He's got money, movie star looks, no kids, and he's never been married. What's up with that? The man is thirty-seven years old. Something has to be wrong with him. Besides, I'm forty-two. I don't know if I wanna be bothered with a younger man."

"See, that's why your high-expectation butt doesn't have a man now. You're too calculating, Logan. You should have been an accountant, you know that? Always talkin' about how this and that don't add up. Just relax! Live a little."

"Whatever. Look, my food is getting cold. Just go ahead and give him my phone number. Maybe we can get together this weekend."

"Yes! When he saw your picture he practically tried to steal the thing off my desk. You'll like Mallory, Logan. He's a true gentleman."

"Time will tell," I said.

Definitely Delicious

October 2007

Logan

When I arrived at Bonefish Grille in Bowie, I walked in and, surprisingly, there were only three couples waiting to be seated. I approached the hostess and asked if a Mallory Clark had checked in. She said he had opted to wait at the bar for me. When I got to the bar, I didn't see anyone who remotely looked like the man Paige had described. I sighed as I sat down on the leather bar stool. I happened to glance to my right, suddenly blinded by a brotha in a yield sign–yellow rayon pants set. He winked at me. My stomach turned. Just when he looked like he was gonna stroll my way, I felt a tap on my shoulder. I turned to see a bronze Adonis in a Brooks Brothers suit.

"Logan?" he asked.

"Mallory?" I asked, standing.

"Yes," he said, giving me a hug. "It's nice to finally meet you."

"Same here," I said as I savored the scent of his cologne.

He pointed to the dining area. "The hostess saved us a table," he said. "Are you ready to eat?"

I snapped out of my dream of ripping the crap out of his tailored shirt and kissing his chest. "Oh, I'm sorry, Mallory," I said, flustered. "Yes, I'm ready."

He extended his arm. "After you, madame."

"Thank you, sir."

We sat down at the table and the waitress brought us two glasses of water. She introduced herself and asked if we wanted another beverage. I decided to show off and order a glass of Harveys. Mallory ordered wine. Neither one of us was very hungry. When the waitress came back, I ordered a Chicken Caesar salad, and Mallory ordered a half of a turkey club sandwich.

"Logan, you are truly a beautiful woman," he said.

"Well, thank you," I said. "You're not too bad yourself. I was expecting to hear an accent, though. Aren't you from Trinidad?"

He took a sip of wine. "Yes, I am. I normally don't have my accent unless I'm talking with family. Plus, my accent isn't as strong as it used to be. I've been living in the states too long, I guess."

I offered to say grace over the food. Mallory accepted. Afterward I said, "You are very tall. What is your height?"

"I'm six foot five," he said. "You've never been out with a guy as tall as me?"

He caught me chomping on salad greens so I just shook my head no.

"I caught you with your mouth full. I'm sorry."

I nodded. My healthy salad was doused with salad dressing. I asked for it on the side, but I usually didn't send food back for minor stuff. Sending a plate back can spell salmonella or some other cruel act when you piss off a restaurant employee. I felt a trickle of salad dressing on the edge of my mouth. I dabbed it with my napkin.

"You missed a spot," he said. Mallory grabbed his napkin and dabbed the left side of my lower lip.

Great. The saturated salad was low on taste, and I was low on cool points. "Thanks for not letting me hang with food on my face," I said.

"Well, if we were better acquainted, I would have licked it off," he said, smiling.

I blushed. "We wouldn't want to offend anyone by playing licking games in a public place, now, would we?" I asked.

"There's no need to be ashamed when you're as skilled and confident as I am."

I took a sip of my drink. "Oh, really?" I asked.

"Yes, but for right now, let's focus on getting to know each other better."

"Good idea. It's getting a little heated at this table," I said.

"Heat is good at the appropriate time. Please preserve that feeling. Who knows? We may need it down the road."

"Anyway, do you enjoy your job?" I asked. "Paige tells me you're in pharmaceutical sales."

He checked his vibrating Blackberry, then placed it back inside his suit pocket. "The money is good, but most times I work fourteen-hour days, so I rarely get a chance to enjoy what I make." He took a bite of his sandwich.

"Yeah, I can relate. I work crazy hours. Being a lawyer is tough." I ate the chicken out of my salad, leaving the remainder of wilted lettuce.

He clasped his hands. "So, you have your own firm?"

I nodded.

"Wow, that's quite an accomplishment." Mallory finished his meal in five minutes. He neatly placed his paper napkin on top of his plate.

"Yeah, well I have a passion to get paid," I said. "Entrepreneurial stress is a whole lot better than salaried slavery."

Mallory raised his wineglass to me. "A woman who speaks her mind is a woman who will go places in life." We toasted. The waitress brought the bill to the table. "Would you like anything else? Dessert, maybe?" he asked with a sly grin.

I folded my napkin as I admired the thick eyebrows that complemented his dark brown eyes. "No, thank you. Not tonight."

He paid the bill and we exited the restaurant.

"I had a good time tonight, Mallory," I said as I put on my DKNY bolero jacket. I caught Mallory admiring the curves that clung to my knit dress as we walked through the parking lot.

"I'll make it my business to show you a good time," he said. "You feel like seeing a movie?"

My brows creased. "I'm not really up to sitting in a theater tonight. Any other suggestions?" We had arrived at my car and I got out my keys.

"Why don't we stop at Lake Arbor for a night stroll?"

"Great. Let's go."

We gave each other a hug and got into our cars. When I drove off, I turned on my sound system and pressed the button to play the Prince CD. I was in the mood to listen to "Dirty Mind." Mallory was truly mindblowing. Now, I knew for sure we weren't gonna be doin' the wild thang tonight, but if his vibe remained impressive, he would definitely be slotted to get it.

Where's the Beef?

Logan

Mallory and I had been seeing each other for about a month. I'd been having a great time with him. Last week we went to see Boney James and Kim Waters in concert at the Warner Theatre. We went to Zanzibar for fine dining and took walks at the picturesque Mall in D.C.

Mallory was adventurous. He parachuted out of a plane, raced Jet Skis in the ocean, and snowboarded in Vail, Colorado. He invited me to go white-water rafting next summer, but I told him I'd have to think about that. That may be too much water for me.

Tonight, my island man cooked. I was prepared for a candlelight dinner with booty cake for dessert. Mallory made Curried Chicken, Kalaloo—which was similar to collard greens with fish mixed in—and Fungi, a dish similar to cornbread. The food was very good. As we sat at the table across from each other, I couldn't help but let my mind wander. I dreamed about our hot calypso later on. I tuned back to reality when I heard him call my name.

"Logan, is everything all right?" he asked.

"Oh, yeah. I was just thinking about something," I said.

"A penny for your thoughts?" he asked.

"Well, let's just say this delicious food has me thinking of other possibilities with you," I said.

He licked his lips. "Yeah?"

"Absolutely."

Mallory came around to my chair. He bent down and gave me a stimulating kiss on the neck. "I've been waiting for this night," he said.

"Me, too," I said.

He put his hand under my legs and lifted me out of my chair as I held on around his neck.

We were kissing and petting so much, we didn't even make it to the bedroom. He laid me down on the floor. He lifted my red sweater to lick the middle of my cleavage. I reached behind my back to unfasten my bra. When he unzipped my jeans I asked, "Do you have protection?"

"Yes," he said, breathless. "Right here."

He pulled the Trojan out of his jeans pocket and put it down on the coffee table. I finished taking off my clothes. I watched him undress, waiting to be the beneficiary of his body. Then I realized the stereotype about island men being well hung was a big-ass lie. Mallory was missing a few crucial inches. I needed another glass of champagne to dull my senses.

"Are you ready, baby?" he asked as he lay down beside me.

"Yeah, are you?" I asked, narrowing my eyes.

He gave me a goofy grin as he wrapped his arms around my body and lowered me to the carpeted floor. I was surprised to see that the condom could actually cling. He clumsily crawled on top of me and rubbed his penis up and down my clit. If my pussy could, it would have laughed as he burned rubber with his limp dick. Obviously, he had an impotence problem. He tried to use my vagina as a matchbox to strike up an erection. What the hell? I decided to say something.

"Uh, Mallory?" I asked. "I'm sorry to disturb you, but I am not enjoying this."

"Just wait a minute, baby," he said. "I've been under a lot of pressure lately, so my body is a little tense. Give us a few minutes to get adjusted to each other."

I sighed as he continued the pointless poking. *No, that's the problem. Your ass ain't tense enough,* I thought. Finally, the bitch in me climaxed.

"Stop, Mallory!" I yelled. "I'm sorry, but this ain't cuttin' it." He looked defeated as he lifted his weight. I moved from under him.

"Logan, baby, I'm sorry," he said. "I guess I'm just tired tonight. Let me find another way to please you," he said as his head started to go downtown on me. I scooted away.

"No, that's not necessary," I said.

"We just need more time. I can . . ."

"I don't mean to sound crass, but there's not that much time in the world, Mallory."

He clasped his hands in prayer fashion. "Logan, please," he said. "Give me another chance. Sometimes things like this happen to a guy. All I need is a little rest. Stay with me tonight. I promise to be revived and ready to give you satisfaction tomorrow."

Yeah, right, I thought as I put my underwear back on.

I had never experienced this with any other guy, and I knew for damn sure I was not the problem. My stuff always got rave reviews. However, it was late. I decided to take him up on his offer and stay the night. I chalked up the impotence incident to miscommunication of body language. Tomorrow had better bring the promise of penis envy, or I was gonna throw his ass in the sea to get run over by one of them Jet Skis.

The next morning it was the same script, and my leading man was still a no-show. I tried everything I could to arouse Mallory, but all attempts failed. He started asking for more extensions, but I told him hell, no. His clock was punched out on getting any more overtime. The only thing he needed right now was a sex therapist. He lay there, looking baffled as I got dressed. I did a boomerang on his butt and said good-bye.

As I drove home, I said to myself, "Something just don't gel including his dick." I was gonna figure out this mystery no matter what.

Pissed Off

Logan

I was not home five minutes before I picked up the phone and called the practical joker.

"Hello?" Paige asked in a groggy voice.

"Good morning," I said, turning on my coffeemaker.

"Logan?"

"Yes, ma'am," I said.

"Girl, it's six AM on a Saturday. Is everything all right?" she asked.

I pulled some raisin bread out of the refrigerator and popped it in the toaster. "Well, Paige, I'm sorry to disturb your sleep, but I just got back from Mallory's house, and I couldn't wait to tell you thanks."

"Oh, yeah?" she asked, giggling. "All right, let me have it. Spare no details!"

"I'ma let you have it all right," I said. "I got one question for you."

"What?"

"Since you know Mallory so well, does he have a spare dick?"

"What!" she screamed.

I ran my fingers through my hair. "He's a preemie."

She burst out laughing. "Girl, stop playing!" she said.

I leaned against my counter. "You hear me laughing?" I asked.

"Oh, no. He's small like a little boy?"

"Saying the thing was small would be giving him a compliment."

"I'm sorry, girl," Paige said. "You know, he does have a demanding job. Maybe his body is just stressed out."

"Yeah. That's what he said." I took my bread out the toaster and placed it on a butter plate. "Paige, I'm disappointed. I really like this man, you know?"

"What are you going to do?"

I sighed. "I don't know. I told him I'd call him later tonight to wish him a safe trip to Seattle." I took a bite of my toast, totally losing my appetite when I thought of Mallory's cocktail weenie. I threw the rest of the toast in the trash can and headed to the bedroom.

"Maybe Mallory will just have to be one of those guys you have as a friend," she said. "Being friends first gives both people a better understanding of each other and their flaws. Intimacy isn't just about a sex act."

"All that sounds good, but you and I both know how important sex is in a relationship," I said. "If I'm gonna have a drought I don't want it to be because of some limp lover." I fell onto the bed, disgusted. "Damn. Mallory is too fine to have penis issues. Well, I'm tired of talking about this. I'm going to take a cold shower, and I'll let you go back to sleep."

"All right, cheer up, girl," she said.

"I'll try. Give DJ a kiss for me."

"Okay," she said. "I'll talk to you later."

After we hung up, I took a long shower, trying to wash away another bad chapter of my love life.

Fruity Pebbles

December 2007

Logan

Paige and I were in D.C. eating at the Bookstore Café for lunch. Adorned with books and abstract oil paintings on multicolored walls, this was the place for getting good food and listening to jazz.

We didn't have to wait to be seated. The host, who had an abundance of facial piercing, took us up the iron steps to the second floor. He showed us to a table. Our waitress, who looked like Raggedy Ann with a boob job, came over.

"Welcome to Bookstore's," she said. "My name is Sheridan, and I'll be your server. What can I get you ladies to drink?"

"Paige, I know you stopped drinking, but try their Strawberry Daiquiri Sorbet," I said. "Get a virgin one. They put French vanilla ice cream in it, and it is so good!"

"Okay," Paige said, holding the menu. "Hi, Sheridan. I'll try the Daiquiri, no alcohol, please."

"And you, miss?" the waitress asked me.

I moved my menu to the side. "I'll have the same, but with the alcohol. In fact, you can put her portion of rum in mine, because Bacardi is a terrible thing to waste."

The waitress laughed. "I'll be right back with your drinks," she said. "The specials of the day are on the insert page of the menu."

"Thanks," I said as I looked out into the dining area. I noticed the back of a man's head that seemed familiar.

Paige looked over the menu. "Logan, what do you recommend?" she asked.

I was still staring at the man sitting a few tables down from us. The man sitting across from him caught me staring. He looked annoyed and rolled his eyes as he continued his conversation.

Paige touched my hand to get my attention. "Logan, what's the matter? What are you staring at?"

I tilted my head toward the man's table. "Paige, I think that's Mallory sitting back there with that bald-headed guy with the earring," I said.

She casually peered over there, squinting. Paige was nearsighted, and since she had left her glasses in the car, I knew she didn't have a good view.

"Are you sure?" she asked.

I slowly took off my wool blazer, still looking at the man. "Pretty sure."

"Well, go over and speak," she said, putting down the menu. "If Sheridan comes, I'll order for you."

I bit my lip. "No, I need you to come with me. I got bad nerves about this, for some reason." I moved a loose strand of my hair behind my ear.

She shook her head, smiling. "You always try to put me in the middle of some mess."

I waved her off as we got up and walked over to the man's table. The bald-headed guy alerted the other dude. It was Mallory.

"Hey, Mallory," I said. He was sipping on a glass of wine and almost spit it out when he saw me. I kissed him on the cheek. "How are you doing?" I asked. "I haven't talked to you in a while."

He got up and gave me a hug. "Hey, Logan," he said. He seemed jittery. "It's good to see you." He smiled at Paige. "Paige, how's it going?"

"I'm good," she said, patting his arm. As Mallory held me, the other guy sat chisel-faced with his eyes glued to our every move. Feeling claustrophobic in the embrace of one man with another one shooting eye darts at me, I gracefully pulled away.

Mallory cleared his throat, directing his attention to the man. "Logan, this is a good friend of mine, Nigel Monroe," he said.

I extended my hand. "Hi, Nigel," I said. He barely touched my palm as we shook hands.

Mallory's fingers fidgeted with his gold bracelet. "Nigel, I told you about Logan Banks. And this is her friend, and my realtor, Paige Simms."

Paige got the cold handshake from Nigel as well.

Mallory sat back down when he noticed Nigel looking pissed from our intrusion on their lunch.

"It was a pleasure meeting the both of you," Nigel said in a light twang.

He smoothed his hand over his bald head, then looked away from us. I guess that was the cue for Paige and me to go back to the table where we belonged. I decided to talk a little longer because I wanted to see where Mallory's head was at.

"How was the sales conference in Seattle?" I asked, as Paige looked around the room, bored with being beside me in this discussion.

"It was great," Mallory said.

"Uh, Logan, excuse me," Paige said. "I'm going to the ladies' room."

"Okay, girl," I said. "It's downstairs near the back."

Paige waved. "It was nice meeting you, Nigel," she said. "Take care, Mallory."

Mallory said, "You do the same, Paige."

Nigel said nothing, but his dark eyes screamed everything but well wishes. Paige headed down the steps.

I placed my hands on Mallory's right shoulder. "Have you been hiding from me, or what?" I asked.

He rubbed his chin. "Not at all," he said softly. "I've just had a lot of business affairs to tend to."

"Humph," I heard Nigel grunt under his breath.

"Well, I would like for us to talk soon," I said. "I think we sorta left things on a sour note before you went on your business trip."

He nodded. "I agree," he said.

I could tell that Mallory was uncomfortable. He squirmed in his seat. I had disrupted his lunch with Nigel and his relaxed mood.

"Mallory, I'm going to let you get back to your lunch," I said, wringing my hands. "Are we still on for Christmas Eve?"

Nigel started coughing. I rolled my eyes at him, because the brother was rude.

Mallory gave him a slight frown, then looked back at me with a fake smile. "You bet," he said. "I'll see you next week."

"All right, Mallory," I said, touching his back. "Have a good day."

Before I turned to leave his table, I said, "Good-bye Nigel. It was nice meeting you."

Nigel crossed his legs. "Charmed, I'm sure," Nigel said, drawing his cheeks in to match his Pop-Tart personality.

I rolled my eyes and walked away. The waitress had just put down our drinks when I got back to the table. Paige came back from the restroom.

"Are you all ready to order?" the waitress asked.

"Give us a few minutes, please, Sheridan," I said.

Sheridan put the pencil back behind her ear. "Okay. I'll give you a few more minutes," she said.

The noise from the other guests on the second level was loud enough for Paige and me to have a private talk about the scene that went down at Mallory's table. We both looked at each other and shook our heads.

Paige cracked a smile. "What's up?" she asked.

I rolled my eyes. "I'm not sure anymore after our little visit to his table."

"Was it just me, or did you think Nigel was a little light?" she whispered.

I frowned. "A little?" I asked. "If he acted any lighter he would be starring as Tinkerbell in the next production of *Peter Pan*."

She laughed. "Girl, if eyes could burn you'd be burnt to a crisp. Nigel certainly showed you displeasure for whatever reason."

I stirred my Daiquiri with the straw. "How about that? I don't know what's up with Mallory. Right before the night we became intimate, he told me about a friend who was having a lot of personal problems, and how he was trying to help him. One time when I was at his house, he got a call and left me to go talk to this friend for over an hour. I also noticed changes in his behavior. He was edgy and his attention span lessened. Not to mention his pitiful performance in the bedroom. He probably couldn't get it up because he felt guilty about cheating on his boyfriend over there."

Paige put her index finger to her lips. "Logan, keep your voice down, girl," she said. "We don't know for sure that either one of them is gay."

The waitress headed our way. I grabbed the menu. "Paige, let's figure out what we want to eat before the waitress tells us off," I said. "We can finish this conversation later."

This encounter had me perplexed. However, it didn't take a genius, or a trip to Sister Betty's House of Fortune, to see that Nigel was fruity . . . and Mallory was definitely under suspicion.

A Down
Low Shame

Logan

Christmas Eve was here and I was sitting at the dinner table with a full plate of roast beef, red potato wedges, and broccoli florets. The smooth sounds of Eric Benét were playing in the background. I waited an hour and a half for Mallory to show up before I decided to eat. I was about to grab a roll to butter when the phone rang. I ran to the kitchen to answer it.

"Hello?" I asked.

"Did he show up yet?" Paige asked.

I sighed. "No, Paige, I'm still alone," I said as I sat back down in the dining room. "I called him twice, but there was no answer. I left a message on his machine."

"Maybe something came up to cause his delay," she said.

"If anything's up, it's Nigel up in his butt!"

Paige laughed. "You know there are a lot of bisexual

men out here. Especially some of the brothas with the fashion model looks."

"Paige, why is it so hard for me to find a good man? I'm educated, with good looks, and I got a decent job. I'm self-sufficient. What's the problem?"

"Logan, my advice to you is to be yourself," she said. "Follow your own instincts and do what you feel is right. No perfect man is going to fall in your lap, but that doesn't mean you got to settle for second best. Don't lower your standards, girl. You need to continue to date and have fun, figuring out what you want in life. Enjoy the single phase you're in." She paused. "You do need to get checked out, though. If Mallory is walking in and out of the closet, you gotta make sure your health is okay."

"I know. I have a checkup scheduled in April anyway, which would allow for that three-month window to detect HIV, God forbid."

"If you start feeling any usual symptoms, go to the doctor sooner than scheduled," she said.

"I will," I said.

She laughed. "Listen, I have to pick DJ up from his friend's house. You all right?"

I poked a potato wedge with my fork, bored. "Yeah, I'm all right."

"If you get depressed, you can always come over here with us."

"Thanks, girl, but I'm traveling to my soror's house in a few hours. We're going to midnight Mass at her church."

"Well, be careful and say a prayer for peace of mind," Paige said.

"Okay. I'll call you tomorrow to wish you a Merry Christmas," I said.

"I'll leave Santa some extra cookies tonight with a note to bring you Denzel next year!" she quipped.

She made me laugh. "You do that!" I said as I hung up and put the cordless phone beside me on the table.

I bowed my head to bless my meal. I also gave thanks to God for the signs of Mallory's invisible life. I wasn't certain about him being gay, but I was not going to wait around to find out.

New Year Nookie

January 2008

Harper

The weather was unseasonably mild for winter, so Darin and I decided to hang out in the District. We were walking on M Street, doing a little window-shopping when a red sport motorcycle drove onto the sidewalk and breezed past us. I reared back, stunned by how fast the cyclist was moving.

"Damn, I thought shorty was gonna hit us," Darin said as the person applied brakes and parked the bike next to the wall of the ANA Hotel.

I shook my head. "Yeah, man," I said. "Homie needs to be more respectful of pedestrians."

As we walked closer to the hotel, the rider took off his helmet and turned around. It was then that I realized Homie was a fine sista. Copper complexion. Seductive, exotic eyes. Short in stature with short, tightly coiled auburn hair.

"Oh, snap," Darin said, laughing. "That's Logan.

Paige's homegirl. She must have just cut her hair,
'cause I almost didn't recognize her. You remember
her at the wedding?"

"Nah, but honey definitely has my attention now,"
I said, biting my bottom lip as I examined her curves.

Darin nudged me. "Man, she high maintenance.
She can't stand me from stuff that went down with
Paige back in the day. I wouldn't mess with her."

I smirked as I saw Logan flip Darin her middle
finger. I playfully pushed him. "Man, she must really
hate your ass!"

Logan took off her backpack and removed a
manila folder out of it as she talked to the bellman
of the hotel.

"Well, she is your type. Small frame, big booty,"
Darin said. "She's older than us, though."

"Older, but gorgeous," I said. "I wouldn't mind her
teaching me a thing or two, because right now my
type is anything sober."

Logan and I made eye contact. I smiled and waved.
She looked me up and down, then looked away to
continue her conversation.

Darin cracked up. "I guess she ain't feelin' you," he
said. We were in front of HUGO BOSS. "I'm going in
here to check out the suits, man. You comin'?"

Disappointed that she brushed me off, I said,
"Yeah." I was behind Darin as we walked into the store
when I changed my mind.

"You know what?" I asked. "I'm not giving up that
easily. Go on, D. I'll be back in a few minutes."

"More like a few seconds," he said. "Why are you
gonna embarrass yourself? If she was interested, she
would've stepped to you already."

I looked myself over, confident that my appearance

was tight. "Making a fool out of myself is just the chance I'll have to take."

He gave me a pat. "All right, Keith Sweat. Go hit the streets and start beggin'. I'll be in here while you play yourself."

"Whatever, man," I said as I strolled out toward her. She leaned against her bike, talking on her cell phone when I approached. I could tell she'd spotted me in her peripheral vision because she scooted more to her left, with her back turned. I kept a safe distance and waited patiently for her to get off the phone. I only had to wait a minute or two. She closed her phone and turned in my direction. Finally, she cracked a smile, which was my green light to get closer.

"Nice bike," I said, smiling.

"Nice ass," she said, looking behind me. "Now that we've gotten the compliments out of the way, did you stop here to admire my motorcycle or talk to me?"

"You are far more intriguing than the motorcycle. So, yes, I did stop to chat with you. And, this young man does have a name." I extended my hand. "Hi, I'm . . ."

"Harper Joe," she said as she gave me a firm handshake. "I know exactly who you are."

I nodded. "And you are . . ."

She interrupted. "Logan Banks, Esquire."

I folded my arms. "A lawyer, huh?"

"Yes," she said, surveying her bike. "I guess my gear and transportation threw you off, right?"

I fiddled with my Rolex. "A little. I'm sure it's exhilarating, being able to speed down the road with the wind hitting you."

She licked her lips. "It is a thrill," she said. "A good stress reliever. Better than sex, actually."

I smirked as I put my hands in the front pockets of my khakis. "I don't know about that," I said.

Her eyebrows raised. "Have you ever ridden a motorcycle?" she asked.

"No, I haven't."

"Then you have no authority to question my comparison."

I inched closer, inhaling her intoxicating fragrance. "Maybe you haven't been with the right person. I'm sure there's someone out here that can stimulate you better than a machine."

"Maybe." She placed her hands on her hips, moving even closer to me.

If we were at a club, we'd be in perfect bump-and-grind position. I felt the warmth of her X-ray vision at the heart of my crotch. I changed the subject. "So, I take it you follow basketball?" I asked.

Logan backed up. "Yes, and if the Warriors don't find a way to free up some money to get a strong center, then I'll be following you all right back into another season of losing."

I chuckled. "I can't put up too strong of an argument there."

She waved her finger. "You never want to argue with me. I'm too much of a pain in the ass to beat."

"I can tell you're a woman that gets preferential treatment. How did you manage to park your bike here without getting hounded by the meter maid or the police?"

She glanced down the street. "I'm an attorney that has gotten a lot of these D.C. cops out of some serious shit. So, yes, I would say I have clout. They know me, and they know my bike. I'm here to drop off paperwork to a client." She sighed as she looked at her watch. "I didn't think I would be here this long, until you decided to tie me up with chitchat. Where's your wedding band, Mr. Married Man?"

I rocked on my heels, suddenly uncomfortable. "I don't wear it much anymore," I said. "It irritates the hell out of me."

She tilted her head, looking cynical. "I bet it does. Well, I think I've had enough of the small talk, so let me ask you one last question."

"What's that?" I asked.

"You wanna fuck me, don't you?"

I burst out laughing, caught off guard by her frankness. "What gave you that impression?"

Logan's face was stoic. "You simply posed another question instead of giving me an answer. Good thing you're not in my profession."

I rubbed my goatee, slightly offended. "What is that supposed to mean?"

"What I mean is, I think you're fascinated by the fact that I'm not some groupie, trying to get a piece of you," she said.

"No," I said, running my hand over the arm of her soft leather jacket. "I'm fascinated by the fact that your sassiness has taken you to higher heights in life. But I'm not going to lie. Your sex appeal is turning me on."

Logan traced her fingertip over my belt buckle as she looked up at me. "Let's just cut to the chase. You like what you see. You have me curious. Meet me tonight at nine thirty."

I edged my face closer, wanting to kiss her. "Name the place."

"Here. At this hotel."

She's Got A Way

Logan

I was up to my eyeballs in legal briefs, not to mention dictation. To top it off, I was preparing for a trial tomorrow. Fortunately, I perceived it as an easy win. The plaintiff's case against my client had no merit. Once I tossed in a can of whup ass, with favorable witnesses and impressive exhibits, his case would be thrown out.

I guess I deserved to be exhausted and backed up with work. I had been showing off, spending time with Harper every day this past week. When he approached me at the ANA Hotel the other day, all I'd planned to do was sex him. Harper had other plans. We did dinner at Georgia Brown's, danced until the wee hours of the morning at the Ritz, and saw Rachelle Ferrell at the Carter Barron. Then nights, we did it in his Bentley, on my desk at the office, and on his pool table when the Mrs. announced she was taking the kids on a weekend trip to Ski Liberty.

Finally, I told Harper we'd have to chill until I got

through this trial. The bottom line was that I was still about my business. I had a law firm to maintain. I knew at any moment my little fling with the Warriors's power forward could come to an abrupt end. Only young girls dreamed of courtships with ball players. The only dream I had was a wet one, and he had successfully satisfied that. I saw our little cheat sheet for what it was worth.

I was on the phone with the plaintiff's attorney for tomorrow's case when the intercom light illuminated on my phone. I interrupted the attorney in the middle of his whining.

"Excuse me for interrupting, Gregory," I said. "Would you hold for a second?"

"Sure," he said.

"Thanks." I put him on hold and pressed the intercom button. "Yes, Carolyn?"

"Ms. Banks, there's a Mr. Joe here to see you," she said. "I didn't see him on your calendar for today."

I held my head. "That's all right, Carolyn. Send him back."

I had a ton of work and no time for socializing. However, I couldn't help but smile at the thought of his tenacity. What a man wouldn't do to reserve his spot in a woman's panties.

I picked back up on line 1. "I'm sorry, Greg," I said. "Where were we?"

He cleared his throat. "I was asserting the fact that your client, Haines Janitorial, is clearly negligent in this case," he said.

I twirled my fountain pen. "Let me assert the fact that your case has no basis, and your client is full of crap," I snapped.

There was a soft knock on the door as it opened. Carolyn held the door as I motioned for Harper to come in and take a seat. He had his hands full with a beautiful crystal vase of fresh flowers and a large shopping bag from Sutton Gourmet. There was no room on my desk to put down the vase, so Carolyn took it from him and placed it on the wide window ledge behind me. She left out as Harper sat down.

I mouthed, "One minute," as he sat there, grinning at me.

"Logan," Gregory said. "We have lowered our settlement demand to a hundred thousand. Why don't you convince your client to settle, and draw up the release for my client to sign. I think it's time for everyone to move on with their lives."

"Not a chance," I said. "Discovery proved that your client has next to nothing to support his allegations. You and I both know that I have enough evidence to get a summary judgment in a heartbeat. Greg, you are an asshole."

Harper's eyes got wide. I looked at him and smiled.

"Gee, thanks, Logan," Gregory said. "And even after dating you for nine months until you dumped me, I still can't say the same about you."

"You're also an excellent attorney," I said. "Don't waste talent by initiating what will undoubtedly be a lengthy trial. I would seriously consider advising your client to drop this matter."

"No can do," he said, his tone abrupt.

I shrugged. "Well, this conversation is over," I said. "See you in court tomorrow."

"Good luck," he said.

"I won't need it. Oh, one more thing."

"Yes?" he asked.

"Please refrain from wearing those loud ties in the courtroom," I said. "They annoy the hell out of my eyes. Besides, they will give you no power in this case."

He sighed. "As you wish," he said.

"Great, good-bye." I hung up.

Harper and I stood up. I rested my hands on my desk as he leaned over to give me a peck on the lips.

"Damn, Counselor," he said. "You are tough."

I nodded. "That I am," I said, touching his cheek. "Now, as I recall, I believe I told you I was too busy to meet today. As much as I enjoy seeing your handsome face, I have no time for personal visits."

He clasped his hands. "Actually, this is a business visit."

"Oh, really?" I crossed my arms and walked around to his side of the desk as he sat back down.

"I thought maybe you'd consider taking me on as a new client. When I talked to you two hours ago you said you hadn't eaten any lunch, so I figured I'd bring some food to you. We could do a power lunch to discuss my legal matter."

I rubbed my stomach. "I am famished, so thank you for whatever's in that bag, and thanks for the calla lilies. I guess you were listening when I told you they were my favorite."

He winked. "No problem. I just brought us a couple of turkey sandwich platters with a little potato salad on the side. Nothing fancy. Just a sincere ploy to take up a few minutes of your time."

I glanced at my Movado. "And as you know, time is money. So before we eat, let's discuss my retainer fee for this legal matter you have."

Harper chuckled and grabbed my hand to hold. I looked at him, serious and silent.

He got up and wrapped his arms around my waist, holding me close.

"I thought maybe you and I could make a payment-plan arrangement," he said in a husky voice.

He got a smile out of me on that one.

"I see," I said. "Well, my vagina vouchers don't count. So, what kind of an arrangement are we talking?"

He kissed me gently on the forehead. "Can we talk about your fee a little later?" he asked. "You know I'm good for the money."

I turned up my nose. "I know no such thing," I said. "Give me your accountant's phone number and I'll find out." He sighed and squeezed me tight as he looked down at me. I rubbed his back. "All right, Mr. Joe, I'll cut you some slack. What can I help you with?" I released his arms and went back around to my desk. I put on my glasses and sat in my chair. Harper sat back down.

"I need a good divorce lawyer," he said, pounding his hands together.

"You got that right," I said as I leaned back. "Did Mrs. Vanity Fair sign a prenuptial agreement?"

"Yes, she did."

"You may not be in too bad of shape, depending on how smart you and your attorney were when the document was drawn up."

"It's pretty comprehensive. I think I covered all bases."

I moved my legal pad closer to me. "I hope so. What happened to the lawyer that assisted you with the prenup?"

He rubbed his hand over the tuft of thick curls on his head, looking sexy as hell. "He moved out of state," he said.

"Well, I don't practice family law, but I can give you a couple of referrals." I opened my Rolodex to retrieve the information. "You should interview both of these gentlemen to determine who you feel comfortable with.

You may not care for either of them, but I happen to think they're outstanding attorneys."

"Since you're offering high recommendations, they must be qualified."

I finished writing down the numbers on a piece of legal notepaper. "Yes, and when you and I are said and done, at least you can say you got some good sex, and good legal guidance from me," I said.

He held up his hands. "Who says we'll ever be done?"

I rolled my eyes. "That comment reflected your age, sweetheart," I said.

Harper smiled. "I'm a romantic, and thirty-six, so what? I'm not sweatin' the six years between us. Age is nothing but a number."

I put down my pen. "Yeah, well, being a romantic is what got your butt in a rushed marriage, making you miserable. Romance is a good thing, but never let reality take a backseat."

He got up and walked over, kneeling in front of me. "All I'm saying is, don't give up on us before we even get started." He kissed my hand. "Like Lenny Kravitz said, 'It ain't over till it's over.'"

I tapped his nose with my fingertip. "The way I see it, all we have is fucking potential," I said. "With your estranged wife between us, the end is already at the starting line."

Diary of a Drunk Drama Queen

Logan

Tired from a long day, I unbuttoned the top button of my silk blouse as I dictated a deposition summary report in the glass conference room. I was looking out the window, dictating into the portable recorder, when I heard someone shout at my assistant in the reception area. I turned around to see a young black woman wearing a formfitted black knit dress. Her attire was definitely inappropriate for business purposes. I wasn't surprised. I knew exactly who I was dealing with.

Noelle stormed into the conference room with Carolyn behind her. Noelle stood directly across from me, separated by the long mahogany conference table. Her hands were planted on her hips.

Carolyn was flustered. "Ms. Banks, I'm sorry for the interruption," she said. "I informed Mrs. Joe that the office was closed for the day, but she insisted on seeing you."

Noelle jerked her head at Carolyn then grimaced at me. I took a sip of my Perrier water. "That's all right, Carolyn," I said. "I'll take it from here. You can leave us. That typing can wait until the morning."

"Are you certain, Ms. Banks?" she asked. "I don't mind sticking around."

"No. Everything will be fine," I said. "You have a good evening."

Hesitantly, Carolyn backed out of the glass conference door. "You do the same, Ms. Banks," she said.

I cleared my throat and placed the recorder on the table. "Yes, Mrs. Joe?" I asked, trying to sound as professional as I could with this bitch. "How may I help you?"

She flung her weave. "You can stop fucking my husband! That's how you can help me."

I raised a brow as I leaned against the conference table. "And who might your husband be?"

She slammed down her Chanel purse on my table. "Don't play games with me. I found your business card and a funky lace thong in my husband's glove compartment! You know I'm Harper's wife. I know you've been in my house because I've smelled that stinky perfume all over the place. I don't wear Casmir."

I glanced outside the door to the reception area. Carolyn was organizing her desk in slow motion, staring at us.

"Why are you trying to destroy my marriage?" Noelle asked. "Are you so desperate that you have to settle for a married man's sloppy seconds?"

I glanced at my French manicure, uninterested in her questions. "Maybe you should look up the word *desperate* in the dictionary because I'm not the one storming into a law office, looking like a madwoman."

She rolled her neck with a solid attitude as if I

would give a damn. "Don't think just because you're some big shot lawyer Harper is gonna leave his family for you! Underneath that tired suit you are nothing but a slut," she hissed. "You are just the flavor of the month, girlfriend."

I drank some more of my refreshing water as bobblehead simmered from her tirade. "I have no problem being black history if that's what Harper wants," I said. "Unfortunately, I think you've underestimated the situation, and misjudged your husband. He has no intentions of leaving his family. He's just leaving you."

"Oh, yeah? Keep dreaming. My husband is not going to ruin his marriage just to knock the cobwebs out of your ass. His children mean too much to him, and I work too hard to keep this family together!"

I threw my head back, amused. "Noelle, please. You work hard at keeping the wet bar stocked, and seeing what plastic part you can have surgically attached to that body next. Harper wants a career woman. Someone with some ambition. I work. You do nothing."

She switched over to my side of the table and stopped a few feet away from me. "For your information, I am a homemaker, which is more important than this bullshit you're doing," she said. "While Harper is running up and down a basketball court, I am raising his children. Nurturing them. Teaching them to have good morals so they don't end up being a whore like you. And don't call me by my first name. We are far from being on a first-name basis."

I sat down in the leather executive chair, pretending to be deep in thought. I lightly tapped my temple. "A homemaker?" I asked. "Oh, yes, that's right. I forgot about that. I do apologize. And despite the full-time au pair, housekeeper, and chef, I can imagine that your job is still very demanding."

Noelle frowned, trying to look intimidating. "Bitch, you're just jealous," she said.

"You're right," I said. "I spent four years in law school just so I could be a Domestic Goddess like you."

I laughed because this woman was more pathetic than Harper had depicted. She decided to lean her butt on the edge of my table with her arms crossed.

"I don't understand what Harper sees in you," she said, scowling like she smelled something stale. "I caught you two at the Bookstore Café. What kind of woman rides a motorcycle? You have no class whatso-ever. You're probably bisexual. You sure look the part with that butch hairstyle."

I folded my hands. "Oh, so you're an authority on homosexuality?" I asked. "I thought you majored in Ho Economics. Did you finally get your degree?" I looked out the door again. Carolyn was still in the office, pretending to water one of our dead plants. I sighed at Noelle, giving her an annoyed look. She was interfering with my work. My clients would not be happy if they knew their attorney was in the middle of a drama with this wedlock witch. "I'm sorry if my lifestyle doesn't fit your concept of womanhood. As far as my sexual orientation, I think we both know that Harper can confirm my femininity."

Visibly shaken, she got up off the table and started pacing the room. "What do you want from my hus-band?" she asked, tears pouring down her face. "Why don't you just leave us alone!"

I brushed a piece of lint off my suit. "I don't have to explain myself to you," I said. "The way I feel about Harper has nothing to do with you. You're a young girl, so I'm gonna break it down. This pussy is aged to perfection, and Harper loves the taste. He wants more than a Barbie doll on display. Obviously, I'm filling a void in his life, and I'm happy to provide. Maybe if you stopped shopping at Lil' Kim boutiques all day and paid more attention to your man, you'd understand why he's so frustrated."

She wiped her eyes. "You don't love Harper," she sniffled. "You're just going to use him."

I looked at my watch. "All you do is spend his money," I said. "You don't know him, and I suspect that you don't care to know him. Your only concern is the separation from your lazy behind."

She walked toward me and pointed her finger in my face. "Listen. I came here to tell you to stop seeing my husband! I mean it. You've been warned."

I looked away from her. I tried to stay calm, but this fool was testing me. I rolled my chair back a little. "I can't stop what I didn't start," I said. "If you were that concerned about your marriage you'd be seeking professional help, not standing here giving me idle threats. Why don't you have a tantrum on Harper's time? I have clients to contact." She decided to invade my space again. It was on now.

"Harper's dick ain't big enough for the both of us," she snapped.

I folded my hands in my lap. "I agree, and rumor has it our CEO will downsize. You know, summer help is always the first to go. Me? I have no worries. The cleanup woman never gets fired."

Noelle slapped my face, hard. I thought I was going to fall out of my chair. Before I could recover and give her an opportunity to hit me again, I rammed a punch into her stomach. I knocked the wind right out of her. While she was bent over in pain, I jumped on her back and quickly wrestled her to the ground. She moaned as I pinned her down with my knee.

"Noelle, don't you ever bring this bullshit into my place of business again!" I yelled. I released her and we both got up quickly, breathing heavily. I was ready to go another round. She was smoothing her hair and adjusting her dress, which now exposed more fake cleavage. Noelle's eyes looked like they were about to pop out of her head. She was surprised that this forty-two-year-old had kicked her thirty-four-year-old, childish ass.

Carolyn ran into the conference room in sheer panic. "Ms. Banks?" she asked, exasperated. "Should I call Security?"

I swallowed to catch my breath, and brushed off my suit. I regained my professional demeanor. "No, Carolyn," I said, waving her off. "I have everything under control. You can leave for the evening, all right?"

"All right, Ms. Banks," she said and hurried out, finally leaving the office.

Noelle backed up and cut her eyes at me as she grabbed her purse off the table. She traveled to the other side of the room.

"I'm gonna sue your ass for battery!" she cried.

"Go for it," I said. "I like to play hardball. You better make sure your shit is correct, though. I pay my assistant very well. Your little tirade will be portrayed in my favor. I'm an excellent litigator, and I'm from Philly. You don't know who you're messing with, Miss Thang." I walked toward her. She stood at the conference door, fuming. I was cool as a summer breeze. "Let me give you some free advice. You need to get off that pedestal of yours and get a life."

Noelle put her purse strap on her shoulder. "And let me give you some advice, Logan. You better watch your back."

I smiled and turned around to admire the vastness of Rock Creek Park from my 19th-story window.

"I don't think that's necessary," I said. "I'm sure you've got the surveillance covered." I turned my head to acknowledge her for the last time, giving her a sly grin. "But, chile, you should see the view when Harper's committin' a foul!"

Noelle stormed out of the conference room. I looked back out the window and smiled . . . pleased with my closing argument.

Leaving a Diva

Harper

Practice was hard today. My muscles ached, and all I wanted to do was soak in the Jacuzzi. I tensed up even more as I pulled into the driveway of my three-million-dollar home. I was so focused on the impending drunk-diva dialogue from my wife, that I barely noticed that the contractors had finally finished the landscaping work to the front grounds. I couldn't see the fish pond and plantings around the Japanese maple tree, but the floral arrangements along the natural stone foundation were beautiful. After five years of construction, alterations, and additions my house was complete. The family that dwelled inside was falling apart.

I walked through the mudroom off the garage into the kitchen. Surprisingly, Noelle was there, smiling and cooking my kids some dinner for a change. Our housekeeper, Gretchen, must have fainted when Noelle told her she could have the night off.

"Hi, baby," Noelle said as she grabbed me by the waist, expecting a kiss.

"Hey," I said. My facial expression was stone-cold as I looked down at her. I removed her arms from around me and sat down on the counter stool to sort through the mail.

Noelle was wearing a black negligee. I don't know why. We had been living separate lives and sleeping in separate beds for months.

"How was your day?" she asked as she planted a slobbery kiss on my cheek. She reeked of wine.

"Fine," I mumbled, wiping away the wetness on my cheek. I got up and went toward the bedroom to change clothes. The door to my daughters' room was closed, but I could hear them singing to a *High School Musical* tune that was playing on their CD player. I proceeded into my room, with Noelle following me like a dog in heat. For fear of her trying to lounge in the tub with me, I held off on the Jacuzzi. I decided to throw on some casual clothes instead. I opened my dresser drawer and pulled out a Hilfiger sweatshirt and some jeans. As I undressed, Noelle tugged on my pants zipper, trying to be of assistance.

"Let me help you with that," she said, licking her lips. "I thought maybe we could have a little appetizer before dinner."

I pushed her hands away. "No thank you," I said. "I'm not hungry."

Noelle rolled her eyes at me and sat on the edge of the bed with her arms and legs crossed. She was mad because I'd ignored her advances. I ducked into the walk-in closet, slipped on my clothes, and headed out the bedroom door. I went into the family room to watch television.

A few minutes after I'd sat down on the leather

couch, I saw Noelle enter the room. She stood behind me.

"So, how's your geriatric biker babe?" she asked.

I smirked. "Better than you. Last I recall, you're the one that needed a lube job and a gallon of Summer's Eve."

"Fuck you."

"Go back to coach class and learn how."

She decided to be childish and walk right in front of the TV screen. "Why are you doing this to your family!" she cried. "I'm tired of you coming home when it is convenient. We don't deserve this, Harper."

I put down the remote control. "I'm tired of you sitting on your ass all day drinking the bar dry, when you could be working, or going to school to better yourself," I said. "Your drinking is out of control. You either get help, or I am going to take the kids and leave sooner than I'd planned."

She came over to me. "Like hell you are. You are not taking my girls anywhere. And as far as your moving plans, you can get to steppin' if you're so unhappy. You haven't even tried to make this marriage work. I'm doing my best to love you, and all you do is run into someone else's bedroom." She touched my shoulder. "Can't we at least try counseling again? For Holland and Hunter's sake?"

I stood up. She wouldn't move, so I picked up her petite frame like she was a mannequin and placed her to the side. "Our children do not need to see all of this bitterness every day," I said as I headed to the kitchen. "I can tell it's starting to affect them. Teachers are calling me on my cell phone because they can't reach you at home. I know why. You've been creeping with that personal trainer of yours." I leaned against the breakfast bar, scrutinizing her. "Jesse's his name, right?"

Noelle looked away from my eye contact.

I shook my head. "Yeah," I said. "I thought so. Cut the innocent act."

She ran her fingers through her frizzy mane. "I love you, Harper," she said.

I placed my hands behind my head as I stretched. "You love what I represent. From day one it has been about the dollars with you."

"That's not true," she said.

"Yes, it is," I said.

She toyed with the diamond stud in her earlobe. "What does Logan have that I don't?"

I cut my eyes at her. "Common sense, for one," I said as I opened the refrigerator and reached for a soda.

Noelle was right on my tail. "You bastard!" she said.

Accustomed to her outbursts, I swiftly retrieved my beverage and walked toward the guest bedroom suite. Noelle stormed behind me.

"That bitch has messed up your head, Harper!"

I turned in her direction. "Lower your voice," I said, my teeth clenched.

"Don't tell me what to do!" she screamed, poking me in the chest. "You've changed, Harper. I can't believe you're breaking my heart like this."

I shrugged her off. "Kill that noise, Noelle. I opened the guestroom door and shut it in her face.

"Open this damn door, Harper!" she yelled, banging like she would break down the door.

I opened the door, ready to curse her out. She swung at me, hitting me in the chest with her fists. I just stood there. My body was numb.

"Noelle, I'm not a punching bag, so save your energy," I said. "You are not hurting me."

"Mommy, stop! Please, Mommy!"

At that moment we both froze. Holland was in the doorway crying.

"Go back to your room, Holland!" Noelle shouted.

"Don't talk to her like that!" I snapped. I went over and hugged Holland. "Mommy is just upset. I'm all right." I rubbed her back. "Let's go get your sister. I'll take you all to get pizza." We walked out toward her room.

"They need to eat, Harper," Noelle said in a smug tone as she dragged her drunk ass down the hall behind us. "Dinner is ready."

"You eat it," I said. "Nobody wants that processed lasagna you got in the oven. I'll feed my daughters."

Holland and I entered her room. Hunter was in her playhouse. I saw her little head peek out the window. She had a tear on her cheek. When I approached, she huddled down inside.

"Hunny Bear, it's okay," I said. "Come on out. Daddy's gonna take you for a ride."

Hunter slowly crawled out into my arms. I went to the closet to get her shoes. I sat on the edge of the bed putting on Hunter's sneakers. Noelle was standing inside the doorway. "Take their heavy jackets," she said. "It's cold out tonight."

The atmosphere was colder in my house than it was outside. "Girls, go wait for Daddy in the family room," I said. "I'll be right there."

My daughters started to walk out, but grabbed on to their mother for a hug and kiss. Noelle obliged and they left. No matter what crap a mother puts her children through, she still gets much love and respect from them. Especially when they're young and innocent.

Sometimes I wish children came from storks instead of some of these silly women like my wife. Men are quick to be labeled as dogs, or mere sperm donators. I'm not saying that some of us aren't, but most of the women I've encountered ain't far from the tree. Noelle loves our daughters, but if I wasn't the designated daddy, I'm not so sure Holland and Hunter would be on this Earth. I make motherhood easy for Noelle, which leaves her time to make herself top priority.

Agitated, I got up and walked to the master bedroom to get my tennis shoes. Noelle tagged right along. As I put on some socks, I said to Noelle, "When we get back, you had better be calmed down and sobered up."

"This conversation is not over, Harper," she said.

"Yes, it is. This kind of drama is exactly the reason why I'm leaving your butt."

"Get my girls back here at a decent hour."

"You get some class, and stop making a fool out of yourself in front of your children." I walked out to the family room. The girls were sitting on the couch watching the Disney Channel. "Come on, girls, let's go," I said. They got up and ran toward me. I put on their jackets and we headed out.

Before I closed the door to the garage, Hunter waved to her mother and said, "Bye, Mommy."

"Bye, sweetheart," Noelle said. Then she rolled her eyes at me and walked away. There is a fine line between love and hate . . . and I was prepared to cut all ties that bind.

Double Trouble

A week later . . .

Harper

Logan and I were at her condo on Connecticut Avenue, in the bed. We drank wine and fed each other fruit, relaxing after an evening out on the town. She had surprised me with tickets to see the opera singer Denyce Graves at the Kennedy Center. It was my birthday, and I was just about to spread Logan's legs to taste some more of my birthday dessert, when I heard my cell phone fall down from the nightstand, vibrating. Logan sucked her teeth and reached over to pick it up. She didn't even look at the number when she handed it to me.

"Harper, stop ignoring this thing," she said, irritated as she pulled the Luxe linen sheets up to her waist. "Call your wife."

I sighed as I dialed home. I looked over at Logan, who now had her back turned to me.

"Hello!" Noelle shouted.

I closed my eyes as I cracked my neck. "What is it, Noelle?" I asked, frustrated.

"It is your birthday, Harper," Noelle cried. "You couldn't even take an hour away from that slut to celebrate with your children. They've been anxious to see you all day. They even decorated the house. But you, being the selfish bastard you are, have us sitting at the table, staring at this stupid cake!"

I frowned as I held my neck. "Are you talking to me in front of the girls?"

"Why do you care?" Noelle asked. "You're never here, anyway."

I scratched my head as I looked back at Logan. She threw the condom—the one I was just getting ready to open—at me. Logan cursed under her breath as she pulled the covers over her head.

I rubbed my temple. Living with two women had me losing my mind. "Listen, Noelle, I'll leave in a few minutes."

"Don't bother," Noelle said. "You spoiled our appetites." Click. She hung up on me.

This Masquerade

March 2008

Harper

Noelle and I are on the Baltimore-Washington Parkway, driving home from a charity event for the Small Wonders Foundation, hosted by the Warriors. I totally ignored Noelle as she whined in the car. I had my mind on Logan. She was upset that I couldn't attend the symphony at the Meyerhoff with her tonight. I explained that the Warriors's owner made it very clear that players were to bring their spouses, even if it was just for show. This was a family-oriented function, and he wanted everybody to appear happy for the media. Logan wasn't trying to hear it. She did not return any of the calls I'd made to her office before I headed to D.C. I left a voice mail, promising her that this would be the last function I attended with my wife. I wasn't about to spoil a good thing with Logan by putting up a good front with Noelle.

Hunter and Holland were asleep in the backseat.

They had learned to drown out most of Noelle's lectures.

"Harper, you could have at least put your arms around me for the photograph at the arena," she said. She adjusted the collar on her fur coat. "Despite your desire to be a whoremonger, you are still my husband. How could you be so cruel to want to break up your family?"

My jaw clenched as I gripped the steering wheel. "Because, for the hundredth time, Noelle, I don't love you," I said. "Any love I had left when you started drinking again, and sleeping with Mr. Fitness."

She scowled. "Oh, so now it's an eye for an eye?"

I shrugged. "No. I just got my wake-up call, that's all. From day one this marriage has been about you. All you do is reap the benefits of wearing that wife title. I need somebody who's gonna have my back."

"And you think Logan's gonna be there?" she asked.

"Yes, I do," I said, adjusting the heat in my car.

"Well, I wouldn't get your hopes up too high, Harper, because that woman is nothing. She better stay away from my house, or else I'll get her locked up for trespassing."

I chuckled at her silly butt. "Nonsense. You better stay away from her office before she gives you another beat down."

She looked out the window, twirling a piece of her fake hair. "Whatever. If you weren't a professional basketball player, Logan wouldn't be giving you the time of day."

I cut my eyes at her. "Neither would you, so what's your point?"

One-On-One

Logan

Enjoying an Indian summer–type day in late March, Harper and I walked along the Potomac River on a path near the White House. We stopped to look out at the tranquil water. I wore the cream cashmere wrap sweater he'd purchased for me at Tysons Corner. He looked handsome in the ivory Ralph Lauren mock turtleneck I'd given him for Christmas. I grabbed Harper's hands and held them at my chest. I stared up into his almond-shaped brown eyes.

"Harper, make sure you know what you are asking," I said. "You're certain you want to be with me exclusively? You're sure about this?"

"I've never been so sure of anything else in my life," he said. "Logan, I had lost all hope in relationships until you came along. All in love was never fair to me. It's been terrible trying to cope with a taxing career and a bad marriage. My only relief is what I've found in you. Being with Noelle, I couldn't see past the day. I thought

I would just go on living in a failed fairy tale, but you came in and edited my life story."

I was silent for a moment as we walked hand in hand. "Harper, you never cease to amaze me," I said.

"What?" he asked.

I shook my head. "From the first day I met you, I told myself I would not lose control. I had always managed to keep my destiny in the romance department under lock and key. Being with someone was always on my terms, and the relationship was always played by my rules. But you came into my life, and all of a sudden this litigator is lost on how to handle herself."

He squeezed my hand. "When love is right, you can let your guard down," he said.

"Is what we have together right?" I asked. "Harper, you are talking about a long-term commitment with me, but you haven't even legally dissolved what you have with your wife."

"Baby, you know that's in the works," he said. "I've met with my attorney and papers are being drawn up. The divorce could be a lengthy process. Children are involved, and all the material fruit of my hard labor, which Noelle will try to claim as community property. I'm not stalling on the divorce. I just want to proceed in the best way to prevent unnecessary heartache for Holland and Hunter." He kissed the crown of my head. "I love you more than my life, Logan. I know you feel my love, but I don't know if you believe in it like I do."

"I do love you, Harper, but with that love comes reason," I said. "I never expected us to get this close. I thought we'd go out, maybe travel. I never imagined we would evolve into a romance like I've never known. Before I realized what was happening, you had kidnapped my heart and turned my world upside down."

I nudged him. "I probably shouldn't say this, but I was just enjoying you sexin' my brains out. I wanted to savor our moments of lust until you either got bored or started to guilt trip, cheating on Noelle. I saw you as a fine baller whose job was to win championships and womanize. I wasn't thinking about being happy with you. Then, I got to know the person inside, and it made me ashamed of the stereotypes I had allowed to fester in my mind. You have an innocent and sincere heart, Harper. You think Noelle has made you hard and defensive, but that's not true. God blessed you with a pure spirit, one that can't be penetrated by people of ill will or false intentions. You know what you need to be content, and I'm glad I can be a part of that formula. I want this relationship. I just get skeptical sometimes."

He kissed my hand. "I had doubts about us in the beginning," he said. "But we have to stop worrying, and let our faith in this relationship run its course."

I wrapped my arm around his waist as we strolled past a couple jogging. "We definitely have chemistry, Harper, but as much as I love you, I have to keep it real. You're a star athlete that practically lives on the road. I'm an attorney with a thriving law practice. We face a lot of challenges. I want you to know that for me, there are conditions that I will still maintain within this love territory."

"What do you mean?" he asked.

"Your desire is to play the rest of your career in Washington, but nothing is ever guaranteed. You may be offered a better opportunity at some point."

He nodded. "Yeah, I know."

"Well, I know I cannot leave my practice if we got serious to the point where living arrangements would have to be addressed. I'm proud of the firm's success.

I've been lucky to have a flourishing career, and I can't give all of that up to follow you wherever your career leads. It's taken me four short years to build the kind of lucrative clientele that it takes most firms decades to acquire."

We headed toward a bench.

"Let's sit down for a minute," Harper said.

I nuzzled next to him as we sat on the bench.

He lifted my face to plant a soft kiss. "Logan, I appreciate your honesty," he said. "I know where you're coming from. Do you think I would expect you to drop your career to watch me excel at mine?"

I raised my shoulders. "I'm just being candid. My job as a lawyer is very important to me. I will always practice, even at the risk of losing you."

He held my hand. "I understand your ambition. I fell in love with it. I would never ask you to sacrifice all you've built. All I'm asking is that you continue to share my world, and that we mutually support each other in every endeavor. Maryland will always be home for me. So, don't even fret over projecting the future. We're gonna be fine. I'll do whatever it takes to prove that to you, Logan. This is not infatuation, and let me show you by starting out with this." Harper pulled out a long rectangular jewelry case from his tan suede jacket. "Open it," he said.

I took the case and opened it, only to be blinded by the brilliance of diamonds mounted in a gorgeous tennis bracelet.

"Harper, this is beautiful," I said.

He smiled. "No, it's only beautiful when it adorns the wrist of the woman who exemplifies the essence of beauty." He placed the bracelet on my left wrist. "Leave your ring finger bare, too," he said. "The next gift from me will be for eternity. The bracelet is just a keepsake to let you know how much you mean to me. A token to remind you that I've got your back, and your love won't be taken for granted."

I grabbed Harper and held him tight. My eyes were overflowing with tears. "Thank you, baby," I said.

"You're welcome, sweetheart," he said.

I admired the gift. Not the bracelet—Harper. They say diamonds are a girl's best friend. Well, diamonds can make a woman smile, but only God can send a genuine man.

March Madness

Darin and I spotted Noelle's Benz. She was stopped curbside at the intersection of Old Georgetown and Norfolk, out of gas. She was infamous for letting her tank get to empty because she hated pumping gas. According to Noelle, that was my job. Instead of calling roadside service, she called me. Her car was blocking the driveway of a dental office. Since there was no place to park next to her, we pulled into the driveway of Johnny Rockets. Darin and I laughed as we walked toward Noelle.

When we reached the car, steam was coming from under the hood. The radiator must have been running hot. That was nothing compared to the steam coming from my wife's big head. I'm sure she was pissed from breaking down on manicure day. Noelle was so spoiled it was ridiculous.

Darin opened Noelle's door. I stayed put, looking at the car's smoke. I knew good and well I wasn't about to be valiant with Noelle. I could tell from where I was standing that she wasn't injured, so there was no need to act interested. Noelle got out of the car and slammed the door as she walked over to stand in front of me.

"I love you, too, Harper," she said.

I just stood there, grinning.

Darin laughed as he helped Noelle out of the car. "You all right?" he asked.

She nodded. "I'm fine," she said, doing her normal roll of the eyes at me.

Darin pulled out his cell phone. "I'll call AAA. Then we can walk up to the diner and get something to eat while we wait," Darin said.

Noelle folded her arms. "Why bother with towing? Just leave this car on the side of the road. I want a new model, anyway. Harper can afford the loss."

"You better stop sniffing that nail polish remover, Noelle. Any new car you get, you will buy, which means you ain't gettin' a damn thing."

"What?" she asked, narrowing her eyes at me.

I just waved her off. "Noelle, you're just tripping because you missed your spa appointment. Too bad your foot fungus can't be cured today."

Darin cracked up.

"Fuck you, Harper!" Noelle yelled, tearing up.

"Not a chance, Noelle," I said. My stomach started to sour at the thought of having sex with my wife. I knew when we got home I'd have to drown out her crying the blues about being unhappy. My next meeting with the divorce lawyer couldn't come soon enough.

Sweetest Taboo

April Fool's Day

Logan

I was in my office late, burning the midnight oil, as I prepared for a difficult case next week. Suddenly, Harper came busting into the room. His tailored shirt was missing its cuff links, and his dress slacks were somewhat wrinkled. I got up from my desk, ready to get on his case. "Harper, I told you I needed a few days to prepare . . ."

He pulled me into him, caressing my face as he kissed me. "I needed to see you," he said softly.

I pushed him away, annoyed. "I gave you my office key for emergency purposes only. I need to work. When are you going to realize that what I do for a living is extremely important!" I snapped as I headed back to my desk. He grabbed my arm, yanking me back into him.

"Logan, stop walking away from me," he yelled, his breathing heavy. "You're a talented lawyer, but you have mastered the art of destroying anything good that gets close to you. Well, you're not gonna brush me off like I'm a piece of lint. I need you now!"

He pressed his lips against mine, forcing his tongue into my mouth. I conceded, my body simmering from the heat of his tongue. I'd never seen Harper be this forceful. I was shocked.

He stopped kissing me. "Our relationship is more important than that paperwork on your desk. Do you believe that?"

"I . . . uh . . . Harper . . ."

He shook me. "Do you believe that!"

I moved my hand over my head. "Harper, have you forgotten . . ."

He released me and started pacing the room. "You know, I've been a competitor all my life, but I've always tried to be nice. Be a gentleman. But you know what I've learned, Logan? Nice guys don't get results, they get shit on. Manipulated and molded into somebody else's agenda. I'm done with being nice. Fuck nice!"

I gingerly walked over to him as he continued to pace. "Uh Harper . . . did you have a bad day?" I asked, reaching out to him. He brushed my arms away and moved to the other side of the room.

He cut his eyes at me. "I got loving you on my mind, a crazy, alcoholic wife in my house, and two little girls who cry themselves to sleep because their parents fight all the time. So, to answer your question, Counselor, my entire life right now is a fuckin' bad day!" Harper walked up close to me. He seemed to look right through me as if he was searching for something.

I held up my hands. "Look, let's sit down and talk about what's on your mind," I said.

He didn't move, but I saw a vein bulge in his bald head. Initially, I had had a fit when Harper shaved his silky curls off, but seeing him angry right now, his new style was sexy as hell. My wet panties were trying to distract me, but his uproar was indeed costing me precious work time. I glanced at my watch. "Harper, either we can talk about this now, or you come to my place."

He calmly walked over to my leather chair, picked it up, and threw it against the wall, breaking a part of the wooden frame. "That's the one thing I hate about lawyers . . . they talk too much. Like I told you before, I need you. I'm here because this is the only place I want to be."

My mouth was still open, shocked by what he had done to my chair. "Motherfucker, you are gonna pay for that chair. You know that, right?" I asked, walking over to my once-beautiful custom mahogany chair.

"Take your clothes off," he said in a hoarse voice.

I slowly turned back toward him. "You must be outta your mind if you think I'm gonna let you sex me after you have fucked up my chair!"

He stormed over to me. He tugged at my ivory blouse, breaking all of the pearl buttons. "I said, take your damn clothes off!"

I was geared up for him now. I took off my blouse and unlatched my lavender lace bra. He watched it fall to the ground, along with my skirt, lace thong, and panty hose. I rubbed my hands together. "Okay, you tall-ass, Air Jordan wannabe. You wanna play bad, fine. Take your clothes off!"

He swallowed hard as he looked at me, removing his shirt and trousers. At first there seemed to be a tinge of regret showing on his face for the way he'd acted, but then I saw the fire in his eyes again. Once he got naked, he took me in his arms by force, kissing me hard as he backed me against the wall.

I tried to free my arms, but he had them pinned against my chest. "Take what you want, tough man, but you better make it worth my while," I said, grimacing.

His jaw clenched as he looked at me. "Don't worry, I will." He released my arms. "Turn around."

I curled my lip seductively as I followed his instructions. I placed my palms flat against the wall as Harper straddled my legs. I turned to look at him as he licked his fingers. He moved his index and middle fingers through the crevice of my ass, down into the moist membranes of my throbbing vagina.

"Aw, yeah . . . that's what I'm talkin' 'bout. Now, you kneel down and eat my shit," I ordered with my eyes clamped shut. I tried not to cum from him pinching my clitoris the way I liked.

"Stop talking," he said as he knelt under me. He pressed his face into my reservoir, flicking his tongue fast against my folds. When he parted me with his fingers, probing his tongue into my hole, I thought I would climax all over his face. My knees buckled.

"Harper!"

"Shut up," he said, slapping my ass. "You a rough rider, but I wear the pants around here, you got that?"

I smiled as I gripped his head. "Whatever you say, man," I moaned. "Just keep it right there."

He got up abruptly and squeezed my butt cheeks as he pushed his hot wand into me.

Harper had me from behind, trying to fuck my brains out. My eyes rolled up in my head as I savored every inch of him. He plunged harder, sending my body up and down the wall.

"Damn, baby. Don't stop," I cried as he took me closer to my edge of release.

"Logan . . . I . . . need . . . you to know . . . that I . . .

love you." His short breaths of desire tingled the side of my neck. Harper's words got more direct with every thrust. "I want you . . . to fight . . . for us like . . . you fight in that courtroom. Don't give up on me, Logan . . . Fuck . . . you feel good . . . Don't stop fighting for us!"

I winced as he pumped me to the point of no return. "I won't, Harper," I said. "I won't give up. I . . . I love . . ."

"Ohh . . . !" We both screamed, collapsing under the pressure.

We caught our breath as we held each other. "I do love you, Harper."

He kissed my hand. "I feel like you do, but I need to hear it." He took a deep breath. "Now more than ever."

We sat up and leaned against the wall. I touched his sweaty brow. "What's going on?"

He rubbed his chin. "Noelle and I got into an argument about me wanting a divorce. She threatened to take my kids away from me if I ever left her."

I wrapped my arms around him. "Harper, you know there are ways to protect your rights as a father."

He shook his head. "You're not dealing with the average person. Noelle can be vindictive." Tears ran down his face. "She knows that Hunter and Holland are my world. She'd do anything to break me."

I raised his chin. "You'll get through this. You are not gonna lose your girls," I said, wiping his tears.

He bit his lip. "I can't imagine life without them. If I lose any more of my family, I'll die. First, my mother, Heather, left. Now I run the risk of not seeing my kids when I want. I already don't see them enough, being on the road all the time."

I kissed his full lips. "Everything will work out, have faith."

Harper sighed. "You know, Logan, a day doesn't go by where I don't think of my mother. I mean, why hasn't she contacted me? I'm on television. I got a website. She has to know I play ball. How can a mother not give a damn about her child? As much as she hurt me, I'd forgive her in a second if I could see her again. I just want her to be alive and well. I want my daughters to know their grandmother."

"If you want to find her, we'll pool our resources together and try to find her," I said.

He smiled as he ran his finger down my cheek. "You sure you want to help me? I was off the chain a few minutes ago."

I moved on top of him. "Yes, you were," I said, wrapping my arms around his neck. "And I was wondering if we could rewind the tape to where you were going off, saying something about *fuck nice!*"

He laughed as he looked over at my desk. "I thought you had to get back to work."

I winked at him. "Work can wait a few more minutes," I said, massaging his long shaft. I shoved all that stiff tension back inside of me. I arched my back and enjoyed the ride as Harper got mean all over again.

Discovering

Logan

Last week, my law firm sponsored a Breast Cancer Awareness seminar at Washington Hospital Center. I've never really thought about breast cancer much, especially since I didn't know of any women in my family that had it.

The seminar was conducted by some reps from the American Cancer Society. There were plenty of pamphlets available to keep as reference materials. They even gave out mini breast models that helped you learn how to detect lumps. Paige was always preaching about doing breast self-examinations. I hadn't done one in at least six months.

On a whim, I decided to put my practicing on the breast model to the test. I was in my bathroom feeling each breast with my fingertips. The left one seemed fine.

I felt the right one. When my hand reached the side of my breast, I stopped. Damn if I didn't discover a lump.

* * *

    I told Paige about the lump I found. She said it wasn't uncommon for women my age to have lumps in the breast, especially women who took oral contraceptives. Just to be on the safe side, she recommended that my gynecologist investigate it further during my visit next month.

    I went to the gynecologist's office for a checkup. Dr. Torres gave me a Pap smear, and ordered some blood tests including an HIV test. I needed to make sure I wasn't contaminated from Mystery Man Mallory. I told Dr. Torres about the lump. He felt the breast and detected it easily. After his palpitation, he thought it was best that he refer me to a radiologist. At first he thought that maybe it was fibrous tissue. But the lump seemed too stationary to him. So, consulting with a specialist was the next step.

I Need to Know

Logan

I went to the radiologist for a mammogram and ul-trasound. After they had me wait forty-five minutes in a private dressing room, the doctor came and got me. We talked in his office.

"Ms. Banks, the tissue in your right breast is very dense," he said. He put up the film on the lighted view box so I could see. "I'd like to get a few more views of the breast if you have time."

I held my head. "Dr. Weis, I have to have my breast flattened like a pancake again?" I asked.

He took off his eyeglasses, placing them on the desk. "Yes. I know there's some discomfort, but I be-lieve additional X-rays are necessary."

"Some discomfort" was an understatement. Maybe if I was a Double-D cup, it wouldn't be so bad. But I was barely a B, and at the rate this radiology center was probing on me, I'd be left looking like a shriveled raisin. I wrung my hands. "Doctor, are you requesting more tests because you think I have cancer?" I asked.

"No, but due to the size and texture of the lump, we can't rule it out," he said. "I'm going to send you to a breast surgeon. He'll review the X-rays and determine whether some of the tissue needs to be removed for examination."

I closed my eyes. "Surgery."

"Perhaps," he said.

I tried to stay calm. "All right," I said. "Let's do whatever's necessary."

Two weeks after my appointment with the radiologist, I was in the breast surgeon's office with Paige. I had taken off a week to try to relax and undergo a needle biopsy. Dr. Rosen had removed tissue from my breast early yesterday morning. We were waiting for him to come back with the biopsy results.

The doctor came into the room. I held Paige's hand. He looked at her, then at me. I looked at the sweat on his forehead.

"I just got off the phone with the lab," he said. "Logan, the mass we removed was malignant. I'm sorry."

The news hit me like a ton of bricks. I broke down immediately, crying on my best friend's lap.

Running from Reality

Logan

When Paige and I got back to my place, she told me to rest while she fixed lunch. I lay in bed trying to sleep, but I couldn't. I lifted the cross pendant that rested on my chest.

"Is this really my fate, God?" I asked out loud, looking up at the ceiling. I sighed as I let the pendant drop back down on my neck.

"Logan, stop thinking negatively," I said to myself. "You're a survivor. God's not gonna let you die this young."

Building Something Beautiful

Logan

Harper and I went to Takoma Station together to see Maysa sing. Afterward we chilled out at my condo, eating chocolate chip cookies. Harper looked at my sorority scrapbook.

"Damn, you were skinny back then!" he said, leaning back on the sofa. "You're skinny now, but you were sure nuff bare bones in college."

I poked him in the arm. "I was pledging," I said. "Believe me, when you're on line, you choose sleep over food."

He shook his head. "What's that all about, anyway? I couldn't have my peers ordering me around like they got rank. I'd have to hurt somebody."

I shrugged. "I know it doesn't seem that significant, but you'd have to experience it yourself." I laughed. "You really think I'm skinny?"

Harper winked. "You'd be tight with another twenty-five pounds on you."

I pushed him. "What!"

He kissed my cheek. "I'm serious."

I waved him off. "You have lost your mind," I said.

Harper had me laughing so hard I had a cramp in my side. We were working on our second bag of cookies. I had on an old George Benson CD. He and Aretha were singing in the background. We looked through my photo album. "This album is real nice, Logan," he said. "You have good friends in your corner."

I stared at his eyes, mesmerized. My lips made it over to his, and he opened his mouth to let in my tongue. His breath was warm and sweet. I lifted my hand to feel his smooth cinnamon-toned face as I enjoyed the taste of chocolate. When we stopped kissing, he got up off the couch, smiling. He picked up his baseball cap and put it on.

"What are you doing?" I asked.

"I'm going to Giant real quick," he said.

"The grocery store?" I got up and wrapped my arms around him. "You don't have to. My place is prophylactic equipped."

He laughed as his face turned red. "No, it's not that," he said. "We're running low on the cookies. I wanna make sure you get a refill of the ingredients in that cookie, because with a kiss like that, I'm gonna get fat stocking up on the sugar."

Sure enough, Harper went to the store. I told him to add whipped cream to the grocery list.

When he got back, we went straight into the bedroom. We blended on my bed, and our recipe was much better than any cookie ingredient. Afterward, I lay down on the pillow. Harper was propped on his side. We looked dreamily at each other. He rubbed his hand down my back. My mind drifted back to reality. I looked down at my cross pendant.

"Harper," I said. "There's something you should know."

"What?" he asked as he propped himself farther up on the pillow.

I bit my lip. "I have cancer."

He had a look of concern as he held up my chin. "Where?" he asked.

Tears formed in my eyes as I took his hand and placed it on my right breast. "Here," I said.

He sighed as he moved closer and put his arm around me. "Logan, don't be afraid," he said. "You'll beat it. You're gonna be all right."

I shook my head. "Harper, I have to have surgery soon," I said. "I don't know how my body will look from the lumpectomy. I could also get sick from treatment. That's why I'm letting you know now. If you want to stop seeing me, I'll understand."

He rubbed his thumb across my cheek. "I appreciate you giving me the heads-up, but I'm not going anywhere," he said.

I looked down. "I don't want you feeling sorry for me," I said.

"I'm not gonna feel sorry for you," he said. "I'm going to make you feel good." He moved his hand from my waist onto my chest. His fingertips cupped my right breast as he softly kissed my nipple.

"Do you feel sick right now?" he asked.

"No," I whispered.

"Is your breast giving you any discomfort?"

"No."

"All right, then. Get ready for round two," he said as he kissed my lips, resting his body on top of mine.

Be Strong

Logan

I had avoided the inevitable long enough. Fourth of July weekend, I had the lumpectomy. Then, less than two weeks later, my first radiation therapy followed. My surgeon did an excellent job at sparing my breast. Because the cancer was detected at an early stage, she was able to remove the tumor and just a small section of tissue surrounding the area. Dr. Burke also removed the lymph nodes under my arm to be certain that the cancer hadn't spread into my lymphatic system. Now, the next step was making sure the cancer didn't come back. She wanted me to start cycles of chemotherapy. I wasn't happy about the idea, but I was willing to try just about anything if it meant I would live.

The first cycle of chemo went okay. I had bouts of nausea and extreme fatigue, but nothing major. I still felt normal. I was able to work and do pretty much all my regular activities. The second cycle of chemo was a different story. Death felt like it was coming full force at me. I'd hit rock bottom. Nausea turned into projectile vomiting every few hours. I lost my appetite, and I lost fifteen pounds. It had gotten to the point where I would get sick just looking at my frail body. I covered up all the mirrors in my house. I hated myself. I'd yell at God, asking Him why He was letting me waste away like this. If death was my fate, I wanted it to come now.

Don't Give Up

Logan

While I endured my illness, my family and friends endured me. I was bitchy before the cancer, so being sick turned my attitude up several notches. I knew I was a pain in the ass, too. I didn't care, though. I wanted folk to get tired of me. I wanted them to give up and leave me. I was real pissed that the disease had now caused me to miss weeks of work. Sickness will always bring out the worst in you.

I soon realized that the only foe I had was yours truly. I had no fair-weather friends. They stood by me through all of my cursing, crying, and complaining. They cooked for me. Prayed when I didn't want to. Their compassion for me revealed that there were indeed angels on Earth. Paige kept close watch over me on the weekdays. Harper stayed with me on the weekends. He had been extremely supportive. Any man that could stick around after I spit up on him was cool beans with me.

You're Always on My Mind

Logan

During my second round of chemo, Harper thought about canceling his business trip to North Carolina, but I convinced him to go. He'd been my rock these past couple of months. Paige stayed with me while Harper was out of town.

I had just washed my hair. As I combed it, clumps started to come out.

"Paige!" I yelled from the bathroom. She rushed in.

"What's the matter?" she asked.

I was in tears as I held up the comb. She grabbed me and held me tight as I cried.

"Logan, I know this is hard for you," she said. "But you gotta stay strong. The doctor said your hair might fall out while you did your treatment. Logan, it's gonna grow back."

"I want my life back, Paige," I said. "I wanna be well again."

"Well, your body can't begin to heal until you calm your soul. God's with you, Logan, but you have to show Him that you're not bitter about this. It's time to stay positive, and trust in Him to do His will. Your faith is what's gonna make you well."

I pulled away from her and leaned against the bathroom vanity with my head down. "Why did I have to get cancer?"

She rubbed my back. "Why does anybody have to get sick? Disease or not, you have to live your life, Logan. Be encouraged, and thank God for blessing you with another day."

Harper had been gone a week. By the time he came back, my hair had fallen out to the point where I had to shave off the rest of it. I was so embarrassed at my appearance. Harper thought it was sexy. He said I looked like a younger version of Grace Jones, with my high cheekbones. I thought I looked more like Mrs. Peanut. I thought it was cute when he came home with a couple of matching bandannas for us to wear. I liked mine because it kept my head warm. It was late summer, but the chemo treatments made me anemic. I was cold all the time. I was too weak to do much for myself.

One morning after Harper had given me a bath, we rested in my rocking chair. I sat on his lap as he read a passage from Iyanla's book *One Day My Soul Just Opened Up*. When he finished, he gave me a soft kiss on my forehead.

"Why are you so good to me?" I asked.

"Because I thought I would live the rest of my life unhappy, until you showed me it was okay to love again," he said. "You put up a good front, but you're a sweet and sincere woman, Logan. And I'm in love with you."

I laughed. "You still feel that way, after all I've put you through these past months?"

He tapped the tip of my nose. "I'm still here, aren't I?"

"I kissed him. "Yes, and I love you for being man enough to stay."

More Drama

Logan

At seven o'clock early Saturday morning, I decided to ride my motorcycle through Hains Point en route to my office. The doctor gave me clearance to ride again, so I wasted no time getting back on the road. I had a family reunion in Philadelphia later on in the day, so I needed to finish some research on one of my cases for Monday. Harper insisted on seeing me before I left town. I was very premenstrual, but I told him he could come to my office for a quickie. I thought about pulling over and calling him on my cell phone. I had a craving for some chocolate-frosted doughnuts. I decided to call him once I got closer to the west end of the park. Since I saw no other drivers, I picked up speed, feeling like I owned the road.

As I rounded the corner, enjoying the wind whipping against my jacket, I saw a black Grand Am headed in my direction. I decelerated, given that there was another vehicle in sight. Also, the road was wet in spots from the morning rain. I kept a steady speed, but as I got closer to the other vehicle, I was stunned by what I saw ahead. The Grand Am had crossed into my lane, bolting straight for me. This moment was the first time I remembered being scared in a while. The car put on its high beams, which hindered my judgment of the distance between us. I swerved to the left. The car followed me, then screeched to a halt when my motorcycle hydroplaned. As the bike slid, it sent me to the ground. I stopped rolling inches away from a tree. My adrenaline allowed me to raise up a little from the ground, but the pain in my ribs made me pause as I put weight on my hands. The vehicle was still stopped as I cursed at the bastard. I stopped yelling when I saw a smiling face and two little hands waving at me.

Suddenly, the car sped off. Not fast enough. I was able to get the license plate number. I was also able to make out the face in the backseat of the car. It was Hunter, Harper's daughter. I collapsed back onto the ground, crying. I slowly pulled my cell phone out of my jacket. I dialed 911.

My World
Almost Ended

Harper

I rushed to Washington Hospital Center when I got the call that Logan had been injured in a motorcycle accident. I felt a sharp pain in my chest when I opened the door to her room. Her left arm was in a cast, and she had an IV in the right arm. She was lying motionless, with her eyes closed. I walked closer to her. Tears welled in my eyes as I quietly pulled up a chair and sat down. I clasped my hands and bent my head down to pray for her healing. I gave thanks to God for keeping her alive.

"Hey, you," I heard her say softly.

I stood up. I kissed Logan gently on the lips as one of my tears hit her cheek. I felt her hair and stared at the gauze bandage on her temple. "Baby," I said in a hoarse voice. "What happened?"

Logan got teary-eyed and looked away for a second.

She looked back at me. "Harper," she said. "Would you get me some water? I'm thirsty."

"Sure," I said as I hurried to the other side of the bed. I picked up the pitcher and poured the water. I handed her the cup. "You need me to raise the bed a little?"

"No, I'm all right," she said as she winced while bending her head to take a drink. After she finished the water, I took the cup from her and held her hand.

"Logan, did you fall?"

"Yes," she said, slowly nodding her head. "When your wife tried to run me over, I did."

You Better Run

Harper

I opened the front door to my house and slammed it as hard as I could. I walked through the marble foyer like a raging beast looking for its prey.

"Noelle!" I screamed. No answer. I went to the end of the hallway and opened the basement door. "Noelle!"

"I'm down here," she said in a smug tone.

I wanted to run down the steps and wring Noelle's neck, but I walked down to the landing and stopped to take a deep breath. I knew that if I stayed calm, I'd get more cooperation from her. When I walked around the corner I saw her standing at the bar, with one hand on her hip and the other hand holding a tumbler. She pretended to watch TV as I stepped to her and got right up in her face.

"Where are the girls?" she asked.

"I left them with Peaches," I said, my tone sharp. "Why?"

I ignored her question. "Noelle, were you involved in a car accident today?" I asked.

She frowned. "What?" she asked.

I felt a line of sweat trickle down my brow. "You heard me."

"Harper, didn't you park in the garage? Did you see anything wrong with the Mercedes?"

I folded my arms. "Answer my question."

She sighed as she rolled her eyes up in irritation, then looked back at me. "I was in Rockville all day running errands with the girls," she said. "Then I dropped them off at your grandmother's house and came home."

I cracked my knuckles. "Okay, Noelle," I said. "You have two options. Either you tell me the truth, or I take your ass straight to Upper Marlboro so the cops can put you in jail!"

"What are you talking about?" she asked as she casually took a sip from her glass.

I knocked the drink she was nursing out of her hand. The contents emptied onto the Berber carpet. I snatched Noelle up in the air and threw her down on the couch. I had never touched a woman in anger before, but right now my wife was not even human to me.

"Harper!" she said, her eyes wide. "I'm going to call the cops on you if you put your hands on me again!" Her lip started to tremble. "You are scaring me!"

"You should be scared," I said. "Scared about the prison sentence you're about to face."

"For what?"

"Attempted murder! You ran Logan off the road today, didn't you?"

She flung her hair. "What? Don't be ridiculous," she said, avoiding direct eye contact with me.

I paced the floor. I wanted to hit her so bad, but I exercised restraint. "Logan is in the hospital with a fractured arm and rib," I said. "When I left the hospital to get the girls from Peaches's house, Hunter told me something very interesting."

"Wha . . . What did she say?" Noelle asked, half-drunk and shivering like a wet alley cat.

"Hunter ran up to me all excited, talking about how you all took a fast ride, and how you made the red Power Ranger fly."

"Don't believe Hunter! Harper, she's a child!"

I stopped pacing, cutting my eyes at Noelle. "My daughter doesn't lie. Logan's motorcycle is red. She was riding through Hains Point as she normally would to meet me. Her riding gear is red. So, are you going to confess to what you did?"

We both started to cry. My tears were tears of pain. Noelle's were tears of guilt. She had tried to hurt me by hurting Logan.

Noelle put her hands on top of her head. "Harper, it was a mistake. I didn't mean to hurt her."

"Like hell you didn't!" I shouted. I was so mad I picked up one of the soapstone statues from the mantle and threw it across the room, shattering the mirror on the wall behind the bar. Noelle jumped when the glass shattered.

She jumped up. "I was angry!" she yelled. "Angry at Logan for taking you away from me. I was just trying to scare her."

I moved over by the fireplace. "So you decided to get revenge while endangering the lives of your children!" I plopped down onto the floor, closing my eyes and resting my back on the cold fireplace hearth. When I heard Noelle apologize and move toward me, I opened my eyes and gave her a look so intense, the couch became a magnetic field and sucked her butt back down.

"Don't you even think about coming over to me," I snapped. "I have no sympathy for you. I will say this, you better get down on your knees and pray that Logan doesn't press charges. I told her to do it. One way or another, you're gonna pay for what you've done."

Noelle clasped her hands. "Harper, please," she said. "Try to understand."

"Understand what?" I asked. "Understand that you could have killed people today!" I stood up, wiping my face. "Noelle, this was the straw that shattered the camel's back. I want to thank you for giving me the two most precious jewels in the world . . . my babies. But now, I would appreciate it if you would get the fuck out of my house!"

She got up and stood a few feet away from me. "Harper, what are you saying?" she asked. "Where am I supposed to go?"

"I don't care what happens to you," I said. "Until I decide what's best for our kids you are not welcome here. Holland and Hunter will stay with me. Oh, one more thing. Make sure you let me know your location for service of the divorce papers."

"You can't just throw me out and not let me see my children!" she cried.

I stared her down. "Watch me," I said. "Now, do you want to leave peacefully, or do you want to suffer a few broken bones when your ass hits the pavement?"

She placed her hands on her hips. "What about my stuff?" she asked. "What about all of my clothes?"

I frowned. "Well, all of your stuff was courtesy of Harper Express, but since you've been a gold digga forever, I'll give you the privilege of keeping the crap."

She had the nerve to get mad. "I'll be waiting for

the divorce court summons!" she said. "I'm gonna take your ass to the cleaners! Even if it takes the rest of my life, I'm gonna make sure you don't have a pot to piss in when I'm through! No judge will give you sole custody of the children with your lifestyle."

"I know you're not talking about lifestyle," I said. "Threaten me if you like, but I'm not the one behind the eight ball. I suggest that you get a good criminal attorney. In the meantime, go get help. You've earned more than enough frequent flyer miles to the nuthouse."

Divorce Does a Body Good

Harper

Noelle and I were face-to-face in the presence of anger, and in the presence of our attorneys. We all sat along a conference table at the law office of my attorney, Richard Klein. Noelle was served divorce papers promptly after I put her out. I requested a pretrial conference to see if this matter could be settled without court intervention. I wanted out of this marriage like yesterday. Noelle and her counsel agreed to the meeting. I sat beside Rich, getting bubble guts from looking at Noelle's face and from listening to her attorney's bull.

Noelle's attorney, Stuart Dyer, said, "Mr. Klein and Mr. Joe. My client and I are contesting the prenuptial agreement."

"Unbelievable," I said as I shook my head.

Dyer continued. "It is our position that Mrs. Joe was coerced into signing the contract that Mr. Joe and his agent, Dean Davis, had drawn up with counsel," he said.

Rich said, "Mr. Dyer, don't attempt this. Your client was able to comprehend the conditions of the contract. She was fully aware of what she would be entitled to in the event of a divorce."

Dyer tapped his pen on the table. "I'll prove otherwise before a judge," he said. "If satisfactory terms cannot be met, we will proceed with the hearing."

"Noelle, I can't believe you're playing innocent like this!" I shouted.

Rich grabbed my arm. "Harper, please."

I pulled my arm away. "No, Rich, let me say something," I said. "I feel that a court hearing is not necessary. I do not want this process to linger."

"I don't either, Harper, but you're being unfair," Noelle said.

"Unfair about what?" I asked. "Me taking care of my children is a given. So tell me, Noelle, what do you want?"

She turned up her nose. "I want to remain in the house and be able to handle the expenses," she said. "I would like to have the resources to go back to school to finish my degree."

I laughed. "School, huh?" I asked. "You've already mastered being a con artist. What do you need to go back to school for?" I slammed my hands down on the table, scaring the mess out of Noelle and her lawyer. In my chair, I pushed myself closer to the wall behind me. I was tired of this discussion already.

"Harper, calm down," Rich said.

"Let's not be petty here," said Dyer. "My client is entitled to resume the lifestyle she is accustomed to."

"No," I said. "Your client needs to get off of her ass

and get a job! I recommend that you confer with your client again."

I looked at Noelle with a piercing stare as the hate for her in my heart mounted. "Noelle, think long and hard before you start making demands and trial requests," I said.

"Mr. Dyer," Rich said. "Why don't you submit your client's terms of divorce in writing for Mr. Joe and me to review."

"Mrs. Joe, is that acceptable to you?" Dyer asked.

"Yes," she said.

"All right," Dyer said. "I'll have my office forward the documents to your office by the end of the week."

"Fine," Rich said. "We'll be expecting them."

We all got up. Rich and Dyer were making small talk as they gathered up their papers. Noelle looked at me to see if I would say anything else to her. I wasn't going to waste any more energy talking to her today. I told my attorney I would talk to him later, and I headed out.

"Good-bye, Harper," I heard Noelle say as I walked out the door into the hallway.

I pretended like I was deaf and kept moving.

Don't Let Go

Harper

I kissed Logan's neck as I gave her a massage. She was stressed from putting in long hours at the office, trying to get caught up. She had been on extended sick leave due to the accident.

"How did the meeting go today?" Logan asked as she bent her head, yielding to my hands soothing her shoulders.

"Noelle was tripping as usual," I said. "She's contesting the prenup."

"I predicted that. The prenuptial agreement should hold up in court, though. What were her stipulations for settlement?" she asked.

"She wants to stay in the house I paid for, and she wants me to pay to send her back to college," I said.

She sucked her teeth. "Well, she needs all the intelligence she can get," she said.

"Tell me about it. I have a feeling this thing is gonna drag on," I said.

Logan sighed as she raised her right arm to remove my hand massaging her shoulder.

"Am I rubbing too hard, baby?" I asked.

"No, that felt good," she said.

"Then why did you move my hand off?" I asked.

She sighed. "Harper, I've had a lot to think about over these past few weeks. I've been thinking that maybe I should back off. You need time to resolve this separation."

I kissed her cheek. "I don't need space, so that leaves you. You need time off?"

She ran her fingers through her hair. "I didn't think so at first, but now I'm not sure. Ever since I met you, I've been questioning why I got involved with a married man. I fell in love with you, and I prayed that all of my inhibitions about this relationship would fade away. I'm wondering if love is worth all of the worrying. All of the late nights grabbing onto the pillow that you had just left. Watching you leave to make the morning rush back to bed with Noelle, so the children wouldn't suspect foul play."

I grabbed her hand. "Logan, you know I haven't slept in the same room with Noelle in months," I said.

She pulled her hand away. "Do I?" she asked, agitated. "I only know what I see. I don't have a clue as to what goes on behind closed doors between you and that bitch."

I shook my head. "Logan, I have never lied to you. My feelings for Noelle are null and void. It's been like that for a long, long time. I can't blame you for having reservations, especially now. I just don't want you to give up on us. We've come too far to turn back."

She stood up and got her red satin robe. "It's never too late to turn back, especially when it's a matter of life and death," Logan said, tying the robe around her. "Your wife tried to kill me. I'm being the 'good whore,' saving your ass and hers by not going to the police. Now I'm trying to salvage my law practice. All in the name of love. I think I've had just about enough."

I got up off the bed. "What are you saying, Logan?" I asked, walking over to her. "Do you want to leave me?"

She held up her hand. "Harper, I want to leave this drama," she said. "Whether that includes leaving you or not is what I'm still trying to figure out."

I picked up my keys from her dresser and backed away toward the bedroom door. "I'll grant you space if that's what you need, but let me just say this," I said. "I would never leave you, Logan, for anything or anybody," I said as I walked out her door.

I Want You Back

Logan

Dr. Burke stopped chemotherapy after the second cycle. She saw no evidence of cancer left in my body. I would still have to be monitored closely during follow-up exams, but the worst part appeared to be over.

Fall came, and my hair was starting to grow back. I had my stylist keep it cut short. It was easier to manage that way. I felt like my body was healing well from my battle with cancer. I had energy again, and I had returned to work. God had worked a miracle in my life.

Harper left messages on my answering machine every day. I never responded. I wasn't quite sure how to. I was torn between seeing justice served by pressing charges against Noelle, and loving Harper, whose only crime was marrying the wrong woman. I've never been a quitter. Giving up on him just because his wife went loco would have been too easy. That's what Noelle wanted. To break Harper and me up. Well, she should have killed me. Because now, I was gonna love him that much more. Divorce would have been inevitable for them even if I had not come into the picture. Noelle needed to get a grip and have another liposuction surgery, so she could move onto the next gullible guy.

I missed Harper. Once I made the decision not to have Noelle prosecuted, I decided to get in contact with him. He let me know on his messages that he'd been staying over at his grandmother's house. Noelle had threatened to go to the media about her eviction. He let her go back home to avoid baller bashing in the news.

I drove over late one evening to see him. I knocked on the door. His grandmother answered.

"Yes?" she asked.

"Hello, Mrs. Joe, I'm . . ."

"Logan," Harper said as I saw him inside the house, coming down the stairs.

Harper's grandmother folded her arms as she sized me up. "So, this is the Quiet Storm, huh, Harper?" she asked.

"Peaches, please," he said, embarrassed. "Move so Logan can come in."

She mushed him in the back of his head. "This is my house, boy!" she said, rolling her eyes at him. "You the one that got kicked out of Noelle's boot camp for gettin' extra booty."

"Peaches!" Harper said as he pulled me in.

I smiled and shook my head. As I walked farther into the foyer, Peaches squeezed my shoulder.

"Logan, I'm just teasing," she said, laughing. "I'm Priscilla Joe, but feel free to call me Peaches. You seem like family, as much as Harper talks about you."

I gave her a hug. "Thanks, Peaches," I said. "I know

this is sort of an awkward situation, but I do love your grandson."

Harper smiled as he put his arm around my waist. I rested my head on his chest.

She shrugged. "Well, it ain't awkward for me, if it ain't awkward for y'all," she said.

"I never liked my daughter-in-law, anyway." Peaches shook her head as she walked up the stairs. "I wish you two the best. I hope Noelle leaves Harper a little money, so he won't be living here and moving you in with him!"

"Good night, Peaches," Harper said in an annoyed tone.

"Good luck," she said as she got to the top of the stairs and walked into the hallway.

Harper pulled me into him, giving me a warm kiss on the lips.

"Hey, you," he said as he tapped my nose with his index finger.

"Hey, handsome."

"I'm glad you're here," he said.

I wrapped my arms tighter around his waist. "This is where I want to remain," I said. "Always."

Case Closed

Logan

My law practice is doing very well. Clientele expansion and workload demanded that I secure help. I hired two law associates, both graduates of Howard University. Both black women, feisty and ambitious as hell. We're Charlie's Angels in a court of law. No holds barred.

My body healed completely from the accident. God spared my life for a reason. I'm starting to understand why. I used to spend most of my hours trying to win cases, redeeming my clients. Never taking the time to find counsel in Him for my own dilemmas. After falling off that bike, things began to change for me. I joined a church near my home and started a legal ministry. Working pro bono for some members of the church, helping them sort through legal issues.

As for Noelle? The more things change, the more they stay the same. We still can't stand each other. I've been trying to cut a deal with God, to allow me one freebie to hate. He's not negotiating. The woman tried to kill me, so I find it difficult to love her like a good neighbor. I hold my peace with her around Harper and the kids. No sense in being petty. Her vengeance made me victorious. Harper is still the love of my life. We're planning our future together as we build a new home in Cabin John. Noelle got the old house and finally a liberal arts degree. She surprised me by going back to school, but her higher learning and sobriety certificate still haven't earned my respect. In retrospect, I guess it was inappropriate for me to creep in the middle of her marriage. However, her being weak made it fair game.

When will women learn that the battle is never with the other woman? Infidelity is not about sex. Men who say they cheat because their women don't cook, or give them enough intercourse, are liars. I don't cook a damn thing for Harper. Men cheat because they need an outlet from the incompatibility at home. Women cheat because lovers are more loyal than husbands and boyfriends. There's no guarantee that Harper and I won't meet the same fate. I doubt it, though. He adores me. We're a good match up. He knows how to make a pass. I know how to handle the ball well. Good litigators never lose.

Last-Minute Surprise

Harper

Under the haze of a moonlit night, I asked Logan to marry me. We toasted to our future as we stood on the heated platform of the Infinity pool that I designed. Construction on our new home finished just in time for the housewarming. After the festivities were over, Logan and I held each other tight, enjoying the first peaceful moment we'd had in months. Personal drama behind us, we were excited about our journey together. Logan was good with the kids. Grad school, therapy, and a new man seemed to be keeping Noelle content. Things couldn't have been better.

Logan removed the champagne crystal flute from my hand. "Come inside with me for a second," she said, placing our flutes on the nearby bar ledge.

I smiled. "Why, babe?" I wrapped my arms around her. "I thought we might go skinny-dipping in the pool. The weather's nice tonight."

She nudged me. "Maybe I should just push you in the pool, so you can cool off."

I licked my lips. "I can't help myself. You got your hooks in me. Just like that O'Jays song."

She gave me a playful pat on the butt. "What do you know about the O'Jays, Youngblood?"

I smirked, then kissed her neck. "I know you were callin' me Daddy last night."

She ran her fingers through her short curls, blushing. "Listen, don't give me flashbacks, or I might have to surrender to your skinny-dipping offer."

My fingertip feathered her cheek. "Gretchen's got her job covered, doing scrapbooks with the kids down in the rec room. What's the problem?"

Logan looked at her watch. "I'm expecting a delivery any minute. Let's get inside."

I frowned as we walked to the sunroom door. "Gretchen can accept the package. Besides, what kind of delivery are you expecting this late at night? It's ten o'clock."

She winked at me as we sat down in the living room among the housewarming presents from our guests. "I got a housewarming present for you," she said.

I kissed her soft lips. "I have you. No present can compare."

She tapped the tip of my nose. "That's sweet, Harper, but I think you'll be pleasantly surprised." The doorbell rang. "Go get the door while I check on the girls," she said as she got up from the sofa.

"All right." I got up and headed for the door. I looked through the peephole. It was Peaches. I opened the door. She was smiling, but she had tears in her eyes. "Hey," I said, pulling her into the foyer and closing the door. "What's wrong? You lose all your money in Atlantic City?"

She poked me in the chest. "No, boy. I won, so I figured I'd give you a little something for good luck."

I kissed her cheek. "Now you know I don't take money from you."

"I ain't talking about money." She leaned her head toward the door. "I got something better. Open the door."

I looked at Peaches suspiciously as I walked over and opened the door.

"Surprise," the woman said in a soft voice as she came from around the corner of the portico and walked up to the front door.

I stood frozen, blinded by the tears pooling in my eyes. My mother, Heather, stood crying in front of me. She was just as beautiful as I remembered. Long, straight hair with a part down the middle. There were a few specks of gray in her mane that complemented the honey tones of her skin. She walked inside the house, tentatively stretching her petite hand out to touch me. Overwhelmed, I embraced her fully and leaned my head on her shoulder. Her apologies were drowned out by the cries of a little boy lost, trapped inside a man's body.

"I missed you so much, Ma," I said in a muffled voice. I looked at her again.

"Harper, I was young and confused when I left," Heather said, squeezing my hands. "I needed time to get myself together. I've been living in Paris, teaching political science at one of the universities. Two months ago, I decided that if my sabbatical was approved, I'd take the year off, come back to Maryland, and try to reconcile with you. I called Peaches, but the phone number had changed." She looked down. "Writing letters or sending e-mails seemed too impersonal. I wanted to face you, and own up to the pain I'd caused the family." She wiped her face and smiled at me. "The day after the sabbatical was approved, I received the letter from Logan's private investigator. So, here I am."

My mind was racing. The room seemed to spin like a carousel. All the memories of missed good night kisses, lonely birthdays, and bitterness from her not being at my games were a blur. The only thing that mattered was that God had brought Heather back to me. Finally, my nerves settled and I looked around the foyer at my family. Peaches was in the corner wiping tears as Hunter and Holland giggled at her side. Logan held the digital camera with one hand, using her free hand to wipe her tears. Gretchen passed out Kleenex for everybody. I smiled at Logan. "How'd you pull this off?"

Logan shrugged as she came over and gave me a peck on the lips. "I had a good detective handle things."

I glanced at the ceiling. "Thank you, Father," I said as everyone got emotional again.

A few months ago, Logan and I had joined the church and I rededicated myself to Christ. I had been praying for a miracle to make me better. By having Heather, Peaches, my daughters, and Logan in my life, I knew I was headed in the right direction.

Victory Won

Paige

Life can sweep you off your feet in total bliss, or kick you to the curb like discarded trash. Darin and I had had a rocky start, but in time we came to respect one another as friends and support one another as spouses. We promised to take each day as it comes, and battle life's challenges by faith, together.

I was recently honored by the National Association of Realtors as one of the top real estate producers in the Mid-Atlantic region. I am an associate broker, destined to have my own brokerage firm within five years.

During a trip back to Goode to visit family, I made it a point to stop past my old high school. The pleasant elderly secretary was still there, asleep at her desk. I unbuttoned the jacket to my Ann Taylor linen pantsuit and cleared my throat. "Excuse me, Ms. Dowle?"

She slowly opened her eyes, smiling like the dead had arisen. "Hi, sugar," she said. "You need a permission slip to leave early?"

I chuckled, flattered that in her senility I still

looked like a teenager. "No, ma'am. My name is Paige Adams-Simms, and I'm a former student."

Ms. Dowle blushed, putting her hands over her mouth. "Oh, sweetie, I'm sorry. How can I help you today?"

"Does Mrs. Miller still teach here?" I asked.

She nodded. "Yes, she does," she said in a refined Southern drawl. "In fact, she should be on her lunch period right now. Shall I page her?"

I shook my head. "No, that's all right." I pulled an envelope from my camel-colored Coach briefcase. "She may not remember me, but I'd like to give her something."

She extended her pale, thin hand. "Sure, dear. I'll put it in her mailbox."

I held up my index finger. "Would you mind waiting a minute?" I asked, holding on to the envelope. "I'd like to read it over one last time."

Ms. Dowle patted her neat silver bun. "Of course," she said, picking up some manila folders. "Take your time. I'll file these away and be back shortly."

"Thank you, ma'am," I said.

She walked toward the back of the office. I removed the crisp cotton paper from the envelope. I took a deep breath, then read silently:

Mrs. Miller,

Years ago you gave me a quote: "To fall in love is an opportunity . . . to stay in love is a privilege."

The assignment was to elaborate on what was written. At the time, I was seventeen, pregnant, and feeling unloved. Sure, my mama loved me. I knew my best friend, Logan, loved me. Sadly, their love didn't fulfill me. I craved total affection from a man. He shattered my heart into a million pieces. Just when I thought I couldn't be crushed anymore, I almost killed myself when my baby was washed away in a sea of guilt.

Why did I decide to scribe my personal pain now? I wanted to rewrite my response to your quote. Make it better than the C grade you gave me initially. I realize that I am better than average. I am a beautiful woman who has been privileged to fall in love with a God who never saw me as broken and bruised. He took fragments of my heart, sealed them with His grace, and favorably polished my new heart like a rare diamond. I am a precious jewel in His sight, and the greatest miracle is that I now believe what God says I am.

Ironically, I married the man that broke my heart. Life for us is better now. We have a son. When he turns seventeen, I'll give him the quote you gave me. He'll know what to write without reservation, because he'll love like he's never known anything else.

So, where does my story go from here? I don't know. I am not the author of my fate. I do know it won't end like it began. True love catches you when you fall. And like the little girl who enjoys the sweet smell of cotton candy, I am enjoying all of the privileges God's love has to offer.

Thanks for inspiring me to expand my horizons. Hopefully, one day my story will give someone an opportunity to dream.

Sincerely,
Paige Adams
Class of 1988

I smiled as I placed the paper back into the envelope. Ms. Dowle walked back up to the reception desk. "Are you ready for me to take that, dear?" she asked.

I nodded as I handed her the envelope. "I'm ready," I said with confidence.

Game Over

Darin

I am blessed. I have a beautiful wife and son, and God gave me another chance to be a better man to them. Today, I'm at a photo shoot for the cover of *Sports Weekly*. Paige gave me an idea that I had been thinking about for quite some time. A few years ago, the magazine did an article on NBA players who had fathered children out of wedlock. The headline was, "WHERE'S MY DADDY?" I thought the way *Sports Weekly* put us out there was messed up. Drama sells. Exploiting personal turmoil in a professional athlete's life always peaks interest. Private matters become a circus event and the media is the ringleader. The price you pay for stardom. Players need to have media recognition, but on the other hand, your reputation can be on the line at any time. You definitely have to watch what you say in interviews.

When the media airs a baller's dirty laundry it doesn't necessarily bother us as much as it does our families. It can be hurtful. So, when *Sports Weekly* approached me with an article and cover offer, I jumped at the opportunity. They wanted to highlight my career and talk about the success of my sportswear line, Final Game. When my attorney called to advise me of the shoot date, I contacted the editor. I told him I wanted to change the content of the interview. I had a better story.

The magazine agreed to my terms for the interview. The cover headline would be, "HANG TIME: DADDY IS RIGHT HERE." I wanted to talk about family. To acknowledge that most NBA players do take fatherhood seriously. Sure, many of us have made mistakes. Some of us had babies with women out of wedlock. There are a few players who have even denied children. However, most of us have matured and taken responsibility for our actions. You never hear stories about the players who have reconciled with the mothers of their children. Every extended family does not endure "Baby Mama Drama." The media doesn't tell you that some of us have full custody of our children or have adopted our spouse's children. God does grant second chances. I'm a witness. Many players have wives and girlfriends who never gave up on us.

It takes faith to get you through life's struggles. It takes faith to be a good father, a good husband, and a good basketball player. That's what I wanted to focus on . . . the power of faith.

I sat in a director's chair, holding a basketball. My son, Darin Jr., was standing by my side. I couldn't believe he would be a teenager in a couple of years. He was almost six feet tall, breaking records playing basketball for a recreational league. The editor asked if Paige wanted to be on the cover with us. I told him she'd declined. She wanted the cover to reflect what I was going to project in the article—a man's pride and a father's joy. I'm excited that Paige and I are expecting our second child. We're going to name our daughter Avé Maria, after my mother. Rest her soul.

The photographer reloaded the film into his camera. The lighting was adjusted, and the photographer got behind the camera, ready to shoot.

"Darin, look more to your right," he said. "That's it. Chin down a little. Okay. Now move DJ a bit to your left so I can get a good profile. Great. Here we go . . . one, two . . ." Snap, flash.

After it seemed like a hundred pictures were taken, the photographer finally said, "Thanks, Mr. Simms, that's a wrap."

About the Author

Shawan Lewis received her bachelor of science degree in sociology from James Madison University. A native of Baltimore, Maryland, she often highlights historic places from her hometown in her literary projects. After years of working in the insurance industry, Ms. Lewis stepped out on faith to pursue a career in writing. She is also a real estate agent. In her spare time she enjoys reading, collecting Billie Holiday memorabilia, dancing, listening to jazz music, and traveling. Presently, she is working on her third novel and a series of children's books. She resides in Baltimore with her daughter.

Please visit the website *www.shawanlewis.com* for author updates and book information.

THROUGH THE
EVIL DAYS

THROUGH THE
EVIL DAYS

Julia Spencer-Fleming

headline

First published in Great Britain in 2013 by
HEADLINE PUBLISHING GROUP

1

Cataloguing in Publication Data is available from the British Library

ISBN 978 1 4722 0000 6

Typeset in Janson by Avon DataSet Ltd, Bidford-on-Avon, Warwickshire

Printed and bound in Great Britain by Clays Ltd, St Ives plc

Headline's policy is to use papers that are natural, renewable and recyclable products and
made from wood grown in sustainable forests. The logging and manufacturing processes are
expected to conform to the environmental regulations of the country of origin.

HEADLINE PUBLISHING GROUP
A division of Hachette Livre UK Ltd
338 Euston Road
London NW1 3BH

www.headline.co.uk
www.hachette.co.uk

In memory of Ronald C. Tucker (1930–2012)

As for me, I know that my Redeemer lives and that at the last he will stand upon the earth. After my awakening, he will raise me up; and in my body, I shall see God. I myself shall see, and my eyes behold him who is my friend and not a stranger.

—THE BOOK OF COMMON PRAYER

If thou but trust in God to guide thee
And hope in Him through all thy ways,
He'll give thee strength, whate'er betide thee,
And bear thee through the evil days.
Who trusts in God's unchanging love
Builds on the rock that naught can move.

Sing, pray, and keep his ways unswerving,
so do thine own part faithfully,
and trust his Word; though undeserving.
Thou yet shalt find it true for thee.
God never yet forsook at need
the soul that trusted him indeed.

—Georg Neumark (1621–1681)
tr. Catherine Winkworth (1827–1878),
The Hymnal 1982, The Church Pension Fund

LAKE INVERARY

ADIRONDACK MOUNTAINS

Haines Mountain Rd.

Private Drive

NORTH SHORE DRIVE

SOUTH SHORE DRIVE

SOUTH SHORE DRIVE

NORTH SHORE DRIVE

COOPER'S CORNERS

MILLERS KILL (50mi. south)

1 mi.

1 mi.

Friday, 9 January

ONE

The dog's barking woke Mikayla up. Ted and Helen – she was supposed to call them Uncle Ted and Aunt Helen, but she never did inside her own head – had told her Oscar was really a sweet dog. And it was true, he never growled at her. He was so big, though, with his tail going thunk-thunk-thunk and his long pink tongue and his stabby white teeth. Mikayla didn't care how sweet he was, he scared her.

Right now his big deep bark was booming, over and over and over again. Mikayla burrowed beneath her quilts and pulled the pillow over her head. 'Shut up, stupid dog,' she whispered. She waited for the thud of Ted and Helen's bedroom door, footsteps on the stairs. It sounded like Oscar had to go bad. She shivered. What if the MacAllens didn't do anything? She would have to let him out. That was the rule. Then she'd have to stand around in the freezing hallway until he pooped so she could let him back in.

She pushed her pillow away and scooted up. It sounded like the dog was already outside. Maybe Ted had let him out and fallen asleep. Grown-ups could sleep through anything. There had been times Mikayla had to talk to her mom before the bus came in the morning, and she'd shake her and shake her and Mom still didn't do anything but mumble and roll over.

She climbed out of bed and put on her booties and her robe. The MacAllens had given them to her the afternoon she had come out of the hospital. The robe was pink and woolly and the booties had real sheepskin inside, which was good, because the MacAllens' old house was always cold. She missed her mom's apartment. She could spend all Saturday watching TV in her shortie pajamas, it was so warm inside.

Mikayla opened the bedroom door and wrinkled her nose. The hallway stank like a gas station, and the night-light was out. Moonlight streamed from Ted and Helen's open door at the other end of the hall, and for a second she thought about trying to get one of them to let Oscar in. But they might be mad if she woke them up.

She clung to the railing as she walked down the unlit stairs. The stink was even worse in the front hall. She had her hand on the doorknob to let Oscar in when someone said, 'Wait.'

She screamed.

'Shh. Shh. Mikayla. It's me.'

She caught her breath at the familiar voice. 'You scared me!'

There was a clank, like a pail setting on the floor, and then a figure moved out of the deep dark of the living room into the shadowy gray of the hall. 'I'm sorry. I'm here to take you to your mom.'

'My mom?' Her heart was going bumpety-bump. She wasn't sure if it was from her fright or from the idea of seeing her mom. 'Really?'

'Yeah. I was just coming upstairs to get you.'

'But—' She frowned. 'It's the middle of the night. Are you supposed to be here?'

'Look, do you want to stay here with them? Fine by me. I'll just leave.'

'No! Wait!' Mikayla stumbled toward the living room. 'I wanna go. I wanna see Mom.'

'I dunno. Maybe I made a mistake, coming to get you.'

'No! No! Just let me – I have a suitcase. I'll get my clothes, and then we can go.'

'I'll get your clothes. You go get in my car. It's in the driveway. I'll be there in a minute'

It was snowy outside, and she was in her robe and pajamas, but she was afraid if she argued, she'd be left behind. 'Okay.' She turned back to the door. 'Can I take my coat and my book bag? They're right here.'

'Yes, yes, yes. Jesus.'

She snatched them off their hooks and opened the door. Oscar's barking got wilder.

'And don't let the dog in!'

Mikayla shut the door behind her and ran along the narrow shoveled path to the drive. Oscar, standing in the snow, whined as she passed him, but he didn't do anything to stop her. She jumped into the backseat of the waiting car and slammed the door. She sat, shaking from excitement and fear, her arms wrapped around her book bag. She was going to see her mom again. It had been so long.

Then she had an awful thought. Her recorder. She had left it in the bedroom, and Monday was music class. If she forgot it again, Ms Clauson would kill her.

She could run back and get it. She knew right where it was. It wouldn't take more than a couple of minutes. That would be okay. Maybe. She bit her lip and opened the door. Slipped out. She left the door open. That would prove she was coming right back.

She had taken three or four steps toward the house when she heard a whumping noise. Oscar stopped barking and lay in the snow. He whimpered. It sounded almost as bad as the barking. Then there was another whump, and another. In the black, moon-blank windows, she saw something orange-red kindle. It was far back, like something in the kitchen, maybe.

Oscar whined again.

The door slammed, and for a second she thought, *It's Ted, he's running to stop me, he's coming to get me, he's going to save me,* but she could see it wasn't Ted MacAllen at all.

The orange-red glow grew brighter. Oscar sprang up, barking and barking, and Mikayla's whole body shook. She remembered what she learned on Fire Safety Day: *Don't run back into a burning building,* and that was a burning building, and what she had to do was call 911 and the firefighters at the station had been nice and she had gotten a real, hard helmet—

'What the hell are you doing? Get into the car, goddammit!'

She scrambled into the car. The door slammed against the bottom of her boot, like a hard slap. She twisted around to see out the back. The firefighter helmet was up in the bedroom, too, she remembered. With her recorder. She stuck her thumb in her mouth. The car engine firing up almost hid the sound of breaking glass. She sucked her thumb harder. She wasn't going to think about Ted and Helen. She wasn't going to think at all. But she stayed facing backwards looking at the snow and the moonlight and the house and the fire, until they rounded the bend in the road and she was gone.

TWO

In her dream, Clare Fergusson was flying. Fast and low, heeled hard to the Black Hawk's nose, aiming for the drifting gray-brown column of smoke and debris on the horizon. The radio cracked.

'Bravo five-two-five, this is three/first transport. Where the hell are you? We need evac, and we need it now!'

Three/first transport had been forty klicks out of Mosul when they hit the IEDs. Clare's crew had been the closest. They had unceremoniously dumped a load of officers at the nearest Forward Operating Base, and now—

Clare switched on her mic. 'Three/first, our ETA is in five. Hang on.'

She dropped the nose another five degrees. Checked the yaw to make sure she wasn't overcompensating. Then flew on, over flat, hard-baked desert and over coffee-brown, irrigated fields, and over narrow canals and cement villages, but the slowly rising smoke never got any closer. Clare could feel her heart pounding in rhythm with the rotors. 'We need more speed!'

'Roger that.' Beside her, her copilot switched on the remaining fuel tank and increased the oxygen mix.

'Bravo five-two-five, this is three/first. We've got people bleeding out here. For chrissakes, hurry it up.'

Fear turned and kicked in her belly. Clare gasped, sucked in air, tried to control her panicked breathing. 'We'll be there, three/first. Hang on.' The yoke grew slippery in her hands, and her feet felt like lead ingots on the pedals. More desert, more fields, more canals, more villages, and the smoke always ahead, always in sight, always out of reach.

'Help us, Bravo five-two-five. For God's sake, help us!'

'I'm trying!' She blinked away tears of frustration and rage. 'I'm trying!'

6

Her copilot shook her arm. She took her eyes away from the dirty, drifting column to look at him. It was Russ. 'Clare, wake up,' he said. 'Wake up, love, wake up.'

She rolled toward him, bringing the sheets and blankets with her, her heart pounding, her breath coming in short pants. 'Oh, God.' Over his shoulder, she could see the clock glowing. 2:00 A.M.

Russ pulled her close, rubbing her back with a firm hand. 'What was it this time?'

She took a deep breath. 'I was flying a medevac. People were dying, they were calling and calling on the radio, but no matter how fast I flew, I couldn't reach them.' She shivered.

'Can I help?' He chafed her arm. 'Do you want to talk about it?'

'I'm supposed to.' The PTSD counselor she was seeing encouraged her to share each bad memory out loud in order to lessen their power. Like the ancient Hebrews, who knew that to name God was to in some way control Him.

But dammit, Russ was her husband, not her therapist. She laid a hand on his cheek, rough and in need of a razor. 'I'm sorry I woke you.'

'Hey, I have bad dreams about helicopters, too.'

She made a noise. 'Vietnam-era Hueys. *My* nightmare helicopters are much cooler than yours.'

In the darkness, she could hear him smile. 'No doubt.' He slid his hand down her arm, onto her hip. She scooted closer.

'Maybe there is something you can help with.'

'Mmn? And what's that?' He shifted so his leg was beneath the curve of her belly, his knee pressing between her thighs.

'I have a hard time relaxing. So I can fall back asleep.' One by one, she undid the buttons of her flannel nightgown.

'Do you, now?' In his voice, she could hear both amusement and heat. She gasped as his hand closed over her breast. He murmured something deep-throated and inarticulate as he bent his head to her.

From the bedside table, his phone rang. Russ cursed, sighed, then swung away from her, grabbing the phone and curling upward in one smooth movement. As the Millers Kill chief of police, he had long experience with

7

middle-of-the-night calls. 'Van Alstyne here.' There was a long pause. 'Oh, hell. Yeah. Okay.' He snapped on the lamp. 'Give me the address.' He jotted something down on a notepad. Then he looked at her. 'Yeah, she's here.' His eyebrows rose. He handed her the phone. 'John Huggins. He wants to talk to you.'

'Me?' She wrestled herself into a sitting position. 'Is it a missing person?' Huggins, the head of the volunteer Fire Department, had taken her on as a searcher a couple of times, but Clare knew she was at the bottom of his roster. She couldn't imagine he'd want her now. Maybe he didn't know. 'Hello?'

'Fergusson? You're still a reverend, right? I mean, you didn't have to quit or anything, now you're hooked up with the chief?'

She rubbed her face. 'Episcopal priests can get married, John.' She watched Russ haul his heavy winter uniform out of the closet.

'Good. Good. I got a favor to ask. We're on a fire call, and it's a bad one. The folks who lived here didn't make it out.'

'Oh, no.'

'A lot of my guys never worked a fatality before. They're kind of shook up. I was wondering if you could maybe be out here, you know, to talk to any of the guys who need some bucking up.'

She slid out of bed, shivering again as her feet hit the cold floor. 'Of course. I can hitch a ride with Russ.'

'Yeah, that's what I thought. I figured since you were going to get woke up anyway, I'd ask you instead of Dr McFeely or Reverend Inman. See you over here.' He hung up.

Russ tugged his thermal shirt over his head. 'What was that?'

She handed him back his phone. 'Evidently, we're now a twofer.' She picked up yesterday's clerical blouse from where she'd tossed it. 'Huggins asked if I could go over with you and make myself available to anyone who needs to talk.'

Russ paused from buttoning his insulated pants. 'Are you sure that's a good idea?'

'He said it's the first fatal fire for some of the volunteers. If I can help, I will.' She tossed a bra and long johns onto the bed.

8

'I meant – you need your sleep. And I don't think it's a good idea to be standing around all night in minus-ten-degree weather when you're . . . you're . . .'

She pulled her voluminous flannel nightgown over her head, displaying her abdomen, in all its well-rounded, five-and-a-half-months glory. 'Pregnant is the word you're searching for. Expecting. With child. In a family way.'

His face tightened. He turned back to the closet and lifted his gun locker from the shelf. 'Fine. If you're okay with it, I'm okay. Dress warmly.'

'Dress warmly,' she muttered, wiggling into her underwear and long johns. She felt plenty warm already, from the small hot flame of anger that had ignited in her gut. 'Knocked up,' she said to his back. 'A bun in the oven. Enceinte. Preggers.'

He whirled toward her, startling her. 'Are you trying to start a fight?'

Yes. At least a fight would clear the air. 'I just want you to be able to talk about it. We never talk about it.'

'We're having a kid. What is there to talk about?' He picked up his glasses and put them on. 'I'll make us some coffee to go. Hurry up.' He headed downstairs.

'Decaf for me,' she yelled after him. God, how she hated decaf. She layered a heavy wool sweater over her clericals before buttoning on her collar. She fastened her silver cross around her neck and held it tightly in one hand. She closed her eyes and tried to let her anger float away with her breath. *Dear God, please help me to be more understanding of my husband, who's being a monumental jerk* – She started again. *Dear God, please help me to break through my husband's stubbornness* – No. She released the cross and pressed her hands against her abdomen. She knew what the right prayer was. 'Dear God,' she said, 'please help me.'

THREE

Huggins had said the fire was a bad one, and he hadn't been exaggerating. Standing shin-deep in the churned-up snow near the fire chief's vehicle, Russ could feel the heat in waves across his face despite the single-digit temperatures. The MacAllen place was – or had been – an old farmhouse, set uphill and across the road from its barn. The land on either side had probably been cleared in the distant past, but it had been allowed to run wild, so that the blazing structure was boxed in on both sides by trees and brush.

'We're concentrating on keeping it contained at this point.' Huggins had left his oxygen mask dangling beneath his chin, but otherwise was fully suited in his turnout. He pointed to where teams of men were hosing down the foliage on either side of the house. Russ could swear he saw the arcing water freeze as it touched the spindly black branches outlined against the moon-bright sky. 'If it gets past us, these woods could carry it to the neighbors' farther on down the hill.'

Russ nodded. 'Any idea how it started?'

'Smoking in bed? Faulty kerosene heater? You know how it is, this time of year.'

'Oh, yeah.' Winter was always the worst. Christmas lights in overloaded sockets on tinder-dry trees. Candles left burning in empty rooms. This January, with the extreme cold they'd been having, people were lighting fires in unused hearths and running badly wired space heaters next to oil cans in the garage.

'I'll tell you one thing.' Huggins squinted at the structure, as if he could see inside the blackened timber and blinding flame. 'This bastard's spreading a lot faster than your usual house fire. Look at how the fire's boxed the place, both floors, corner to corner.'

'You thinking an accelerant?'

Huggins made a noise. 'Maybe. I'm no expert, but if we can save enough of her, I might be able to tell.'

'You're sure the MacAllens were inside?'

'Are they on your snowbird list?'

The Millers Kill Police Department kept a record of residents who fled to milder climates until spring. Their homes were checked out regularly during patrol; Russ had found fully furnished, empty houses were a magnet for trouble. 'I don't remember ever seeing their names.'

'Well, there you go. Their cars were in the drive.' Huggins pointed again. 'We had to tow 'em back out of the way.'

Between the ladder and the pump trucks crowding the driveway, Russ could glimpse a couple of vehicles wedged into the snow. Beyond them, the EMTs had erected a rest station out of the back of the ambulance, a half-open tent containing a few camp stools and a sports keg of water. They must have had heaters, because Clare, talking to one of the firefighters, had shed her parka. 'Anybody else who might have been in the house?'

'Not that we know of. One of my guys says they were an older retired couple. If they had any kids, they were long gone.'

Clare turned as the firefighter strapped his helmet back on.

'Huh,' Huggins said. 'She's, uh . . .'

'Pregnant. I don't suppose your guy has any contact names? Closest relatives?'

'Nope. That's up to your people.' Huggins was still staring as Clare shouldered on her parka and walked the firefighter out of the tent and through the snow bordering the drive. 'They can do that? Protestant ministers?'

'If they're women they can. Did you see anything else that made you think the fire might have been deliberately set?'

'Nothing offhand. I'll be able to tell you more tomorrow.' He finally tore his gaze from Clare and looked at Russ. 'So you're gonna be a dad.' He whacked Russ's arm. 'Better you 'n me. I have a hard enough time keeping up with my grandkids, and we get to give 'em back at the end of the afternoon. If Debbie told me we were having another kid, I'd shoot myself. Of course, she's already gone through the change, so we don't have to worry about that.' He gave Russ another whack for good measure. 'Guess that's the downside of those younger women, huh?'

'I guess so.' This wasn't the first ribbing he had taken about becoming a father at his age. Clare didn't get it. Sure, she had to deal with telling her congregation and the bishop, but people were excited for her. They congratulated her. But him? It was an ongoing joke. The old guy who couldn't keep his hands off his young wife. Looking forward to a baby when his peers were looking forward to retirement.

He watched as the man Clare had been talking to tapped out one of the guys on the pumper. The newly relieved firefighter raised his hand in greeting as he climbed down, but didn't seem inclined to talk to a priest. Instead, he pointed to the far side of the rig. Clare vanished around the nose of the truck.

A wrenching wooden groan drew Russ's attention away from his wife.

Huggins switched on his radio. 'The roof's gonna go. Everybody back. Everybody back.' The teams staggered away from the farmhouse, clumsy with the snow and their water-whipped hoses. With a roar, the roof collapsed inward, sending sparks and gouts of flame high into the frosty air. Huggins shook his head. 'I take back what I said about telling you tomorrow. It'll be a miracle if there's enough left for us to make out how this monster started. We may need to call in one of the state investigators if we want to rule out arson.'

'I'll do a rundown on the MacAllens from my end.' The noise from the fire and the water was louder now, and Russ almost had to shout to be heard. 'See if there's anything that raises a red flag.'

Clare emerged from the far side of the pump truck and headed toward them, a big, broad-chested dog walking beside her.

'How 'bout that,' Huggins said. 'She got the mutt to come with her.' He looked at Russ. 'The dog was in the front yard when we got here. Ran off when we towed the cars and wouldn't let any of us get near it.'

The dog stopped several yards away and dropped to the snow. Clare bent down, scratching its head and ruffling its fur until it rolled over and allowed her to rub its belly. She stood up and slapped her thigh. 'Come on, Oscar. That's a good dog.'

Oscar obediently rose and accompanied her. As they waded through the snow toward Russ and Huggins, the dog whined and trembled.

Clare stopped a few feet from them. 'I think he's a little shy with men.' She dug her fingers into the dog's fur.

Russ got down on one knee in the snow. 'Hey, boy.' He held out his hand. Oscar sniffed toward him but wouldn't leave Clare's side. Russ looked up toward Clare. 'Did you get his name off his tags?'

She nodded. 'And his address. Fifty-two Crandell Hill Road.'

'That's the MacAllens',' Huggins said. 'Looks like we'll have to get PJ over here.' PJ Adams was the Millers Kill animal control officer.

Clare made a sound of protest.

Russ braced a hand on his knee and pushed himself back up. 'How did he get out of the house?'

Huggins shrugged. 'Must've been kept outside.'

'Did you see a doghouse? Any other outbuildings?'

'Just the barn.'

Russ looked across the road. In the bright bands of moonlight, he could see the barn's double doors shut up tight. 'Maybe.' He could hear the doubt in his own voice.

'So they left him out for the night,' Huggins said.

'Not in this weather.' Clare thumped the dog's side. 'Look at him. His coat's thick enough to keep him comfortable for a while, but he's still a short-hair. He's cold right now.'

She was right. The trembling Russ had taken for fear was the dog's reaction to the deep freeze. 'Could he have escaped from inside the house somehow?'

'Maybe,' Huggins said. 'The front windows blew out before we got here. He would have been pretty scorched and smoky if that were the case.'

Clare squatted down and buried her face in the dog's fur. 'Smells like baby shampoo.' She rubbed briskly over the dog's legs. 'Somebody took good care of you, didn't they?'

'What's the deal about where the dog was?' Huggins asked.

Russ looked at the inferno that had once been a home and was now a funeral pyre. 'If he was an indoor dog, one of the MacAllens had to let him out before the fire started.'

'To do his business. So?'

'So if one of them was up with the dog, how come neither of them made it out alive?'

FOUR

The dog came home with them. Russ hadn't planned on it. Of course, nothing in his life seemed planned at this point – everything rolled over him, one chaotic accident after another.

What little he could do at the MacAllens' was done; he wasn't going to roust any of his people out of bed before the state arson investigator made a ruling, and Huggins assured him that wouldn't happen until midmorning at the earliest.

Clare was kept busier than he was. She sat in the warming tent, the dog at her feet, and passed out Gatorade and talked with the guys. Once in a while she and the dog walked down the road a ways with one or another of them, her head bent, nodding, listening as they told her what they didn't want their buddies to hear.

When Russ was sure every volunteer had cycled through the warming tent at least once, he collected her. The fact that she only put up a token protest told him how tired she was. In his truck, she closed her eyes and let her head fall back, one hand on her stomach and the other on the dog, who had wedged himself between her seat and the glove compartment and sat with his head resting on her thigh.

He called PJ Adams and got a recorded message letting him know she was vacationing for the week and any emergencies should be handled by the Glens Falls Animal Control Department. Their message said they would be open at 8:00 a.m. He got a real live human being when he called Glens Falls dispatch, who assured him that he was free to drop an animal off at the impound, but no, they weren't coming to get it unless it was dangerous. He cursed under his breath as he stowed his phone.

'What's the problem?' Clare asked.

'PJ's frolicking on some beach in the Caribbean, which means we're going to have to take the dog to Glens Falls ourselves.'

Clare scratched the dog's head and let out an unhappy sigh. The dog whimpered and butted against her. They both looked at Russ.

'It's a perfectly good shelter. They take excellent care of the animals.'

Clare nodded.

'Somebody will be by to claim him or adopt him in a few days.'

The dog whined.

'Give me a break, Clare. He's used to living out in the country. We live in town near a busy intersection. And we don't have a fenced yard.'

Clare nodded again.

'Besides, we're supposed to be heading up to the lake this afternoon for our honeymoon. What are we going to do, bring him to the cabin with us?'

The dog looked straight at Russ and perked his ears up.

'Cabin,' Russ said. The dog's ears perked up again. 'Cabin.' This time he got a tongue loll in addition to the ear alert. 'Huh.'

Clare bent over Oscar and scratched beneath his jowls.

'Oh, for chrissakes.' Russ threw the truck into gear. 'Just until we make other arrangements.' He pulled back onto the road. Christ. He didn't want a dog. He shot a glance at his wife. She had leaned back and closed her eyes again. She was smiling faintly. He didn't want a kid, either. They had agreed on that, hadn't they? Before they had gotten married. No kids. Being a priest took too much out of her to leave anything left over for motherhood. And he was for damn sure too old for fatherhood.

She had found out at the beginning of November, a week after the wedding. Some blood work that should have been nothing turned up *something*, and he had been so nauseatingly scared it was going to be bad news that when she hung up the kitchen phone and turned to him and said, 'I'm pregnant,' for a second he had felt nothing except a huge heartbeat of relief. Then the reality settled in.

'Pregnant?'

She nodded.

He collapsed into one of the ladder-back chairs. 'How?' She looked at him incredulously. 'I mean, I thought you had the birth control thing all

16

covered.' He jammed one hand through his hair. 'Jesus, Clare, I would've used condoms if there was a problem.' He squinted up at her. 'You didn't forget to take 'em, did you?' He didn't mean to sound suspicious, but it came out that way.

She stalked across the kitchen and slammed the percolator on the stove. 'I didn't screw up my birth control pills in order to trick you into fatherhood, if that's what you're asking.'

He rose from the chair and went to her. Wrapped his arms around her stiff shoulders. 'I'm sorry.'

'This is as much of a surprise to me as it is to you.' She poured a scoop of her home-ground coffee into the pot.

'You didn't have any idea?'

'No.' She turned to face him. 'I mean, yeah, I suppose I had symptoms. I was exhausted in the run-up to the wedding, but it wasn't like I didn't have other reasons for it. And I had some bouts of nausea, but never in the morning.'

'I don't think it has to be in the morning.'

She pushed him away. 'Well, thanks for updating me, Dr Brazelton.' She twisted the faucet on and filled up the water chamber.

'How far along are you?'

'I don't know!' She sloshed some of the water onto the enamel stovetop. She pressed her palm against her forehead.

He took the container and poured it into the percolator. 'Let's think.' He turned on the element, and the blue gas flame sprang to life. 'We decided to forgo sleeping together about a week before we got engaged—'

'*You* decided.'

He bit his tongue before continuing. 'Which was a week before Labor Day. So, mid-August. Which would make you two and a half months.'

'If that's when we conceived! I got home from my tour of duty at the end of June. I could be over four months pregnant right now!' She yanked her baggy sweater up and stared at her abdomen. 'Can you tell? Do I look different?' She didn't wait for him to answer. 'Oh, good Lord, what am I going to do?' She released the hem of her sweater and put her hands over her mouth. She shook her head. When she looked at him, her eyes were full of tears. 'I've been married for a week and I'm going to start popping out any second. What's my congregation going to think? What's the vestry going to say?' She moaned and covered her eyes. 'Oh my God, what's the bishop going to say?'

He rubbed his hands up and down her arms. 'They don't need to know. We'll get this taken care of quietly. We can find a good clinic somewhere outside the diocese if you're worried about your privacy.' He didn't mention it would be harder if she really was over three months along. Better not to borrow trouble before they knew.

'An abortion?'

'If we get it done as soon as possible, no one will ever know you were pregnant in the first place.'

'I'm not getting an abortion to save myself embarrassment, Russ.' She broke his hold on her and went to the cupboard.

'I'm not implying that's the reason why—'

She banged two mugs onto the counter and yanked the silverware drawer open.

'Look, we agreed. No children. For very good reasons. Your job – your *calling* – takes a huge amount of time and emotional energy. You told me you didn't think you could be a priest and a mother both. Right?'

She took out two spoons and nodded.

'And I'm fifty-two years old, Clare. I'd be sixty-five when the kid's in middle school. I'll probably be dead before we get the last college tuition bill. That's not fair, not to me, not to a kid. Is it?'

She fetched the sugar bowl from the table and shook her head.

'So an abortion is the logical solution. Isn't it?'

'Yes, it is.' She poured out the two mugs and handed him one.

Her ready agreement threw him. He spooned sugar into his coffee, eyeing her. 'Okay. Then the next step is to find a clinic.'

'No.'

'Clare—'

She stirred her sweetened coffee slowly. 'This isn't about logic or rational thought. It's about a child, yes or no.'

'No,' he said.

She looked down at her abdomen with an entirely different expression than she had had only minutes before. His stomach sank. 'Look,' he said, before she could say something that was going to blow up their life together. 'We've just found out. Would you at least take the next twenty-four hours and think about it? Please?'

She picked up her coffee and blew across it. 'Of course.' She was about to take her first swallow when she stopped. She put the mug down. 'I can't drink this.' She sounded as if she'd just discovered it was radioactive. 'It's got caffeine.'

And that was when he knew what her decision was going to be.

He pulled into the rectory driveway and shifted the truck into park. Clare was asleep. He looked at her sharp features and the violet smudges under her eyes. He almost hated to wake her.

The dog's wet nose poking at his hand startled him. Reflexively, he scratched the mutt's head. 'Don't get used to it,' he said. 'In a week, PJ's back and you're gone.' He might not have any control over the rest of his life, but he could by God draw the line at a dog.

FIVE

Officer Kevin Flynn had developed a particular morning routine since he got put on the day shift at the MKPD. He got up at five and ate a bagel with peanut butter. Then he drove from his apartment in Fort Henry to the Millers Kill Community Center to work out. Other departments had their own weight rooms – the Syracuse PD, where he had served six months temporary detached duty, had a whole freaking fitness center on-site – but in Millers Kill, population eight thousand and falling, the best they could do was free memberships to the community center gym, where officers could keep duty-ready next to the Keep On Movin' Arthritis Action class and the Mommy-and-Me yoga.

Showing up at 5:30 A.M. meant Kevin was through before the moms and grandmas got in. He showered, shaved, and swung through the McDonald's drive-through for two bacon-and-egg McMuffins. He tried to finish those off before arriving at the station; if he didn't, the chief or deputy chief always wound up reminiscing about the good old days when they could eat whatever they wanted and stay up all night and walk uphill to school both ways. Kevin got ribbed enough for being the youngest person on the force; he figured he should at least be able to enjoy the benefits of being twenty-six without having to listen to the old guys jaw on about their lost youth.

He always stopped by the call center and said hi to Harlene first. Their dispatcher, who was even older than the chief and the dep, liked to give him a sort of eyeball health check. In the summer, she made sure he had on sunscreen. 'You know,' she'd say, 'fair-skinned redheads burn easier than anybody else.' Since his mother had been telling him so for longer than he could remember, Kevin did, in fact, know this. In the winter, she fed him home-baked goodies. 'You need to put on some weight,' she'd say. 'Skinny people die out in the cold, you know that?' Harlene herself was in no danger of death-by-thinness.

Then he logged in, checked the circ sheets, and booted up his computer. He kept his face to the screen until it was time for the morning briefing, not talking, only answering with a quick 'Morning,' as the rest of the shift arrived in the single large squad room that served as everyone's office.

Getting as much paperwork as he could done in the A.M. meant he got out faster in the afternoon. It also meant he didn't see Officer Hadley Knox until roll call. A great deal of his time at the station was choreographed so as to avoid Hadley Knox.

Today, despite burying himself in a CADEA report, Kevin knew when she arrived. He could smell her. He didn't know if it was perfume, or the shampoo she used on her boy-short hair, or if it was just Hadley, but he could always smell her. He stared at the heading CAPITOL AREA DRUG ENFORCEMENT AGENCY as if it was the most interesting thing he was going to see all day until she had passed by.

Lyle MacAuley, the deputy chief, stuck his head into the bullpen. 'Briefing.' Kevin folded up his laptop, grabbed his notebook and followed the rest of the officers out the door. He always got in last to the briefing, so he could position himself as far away from Hadley as possible. In Syracuse, they had sat by tens in ordered rows while their names were called off, but at the MKPD they had a jumble of wooden chairs and no more than five officers at any one time, so he had to keep flexible. He didn't sit behind her, where he'd be tempted to look at her. To the side was best, where he only caught glimpses of her out of the corner of his eye.

When he got to the briefing room, Kevin was startled to see the chief in his usual place, sitting on the large wooden table, his boots planted on two chairs. At his TDY, Kevin had been bemused to see the sergeant in charge standing, behind a podium, with a laser pointer. In Syracuse, they had PowerPoint. In Millers Kill, they had Lyle MacAuley, with the erasable marker, by the whiteboard.

'What're you doin' here, Chief?' Noble Entwhistle stopped in the middle of the floor while he processed the unexpected sight. 'I thought you was going on vacation for the week.'

The chief gestured for them to take their seats. 'I'm still heading out this afternoon. I had a call last night I wanted to get you up to date on.'

'The fire on Crandell Hill Road?' Kevin had read last night's logs, and the only other activities had been a dead deer on Old Route 100 and a couple of low-level traffic stops for missing lights.

'That's right. Home of Theodore and Helen MacAllen, who did not survive the fire. You all know the drill when there's a fatality. The state fire marshal's office'll send one of their investigators over this morning, and Kevin, I want you to be there.'

'You don't trust 'em to share everything they find out?' Lyle MacAuley raised his bushy gray eyebrows. 'I'm shocked. Shocked, I say.'

'When it comes to state agencies, my motto is "Trust but verify." Kevin, be polite, but make sure we've got a copy of everything and that your signature's on the evidence tags along with the arson investigator's.'

Kevin nodded.

'I don't recall their names ever coming across my desk.' The chief glanced around the room. 'Anybody? Noble?'

The big man shook his head. 'I think they moved here three or four years ago. Retired, maybe? Never been in any trouble that I know.'

If Noble hadn't heard of them, they were clean. He had a prodigious memory for the families and features of their corner of the Adirondacks.

'Okay. Knox, I want you to run down the MacAllens from our end. Was there anything going on that might point toward arson? Pay special attention to their finances – they wouldn't be the first people to wind up killing themselves while trying to collect on their insurance.'

'Yes, sir.'

'Okay. I'll be here until noon. After that, report in to Lyle if you run across anything.' The chief's boots thudded on the floor as he slid off the table. 'Kevin? Can I see you a minute?'

Kevin followed the chief back to his office. 'Have a seat,' the chief said. Since there was only one chair that wasn't piled with manila folders, report forms, and back issues of *Police Digest*, Kevin took it.

The chief sat across the paper-strewn desk from him. 'I got a call first thing this morning from Captain Iacocca in Syracuse. He wanted to let me know he was extending an offer of employment to one of my officers.' He folded his arms over his chest. 'I wish the staties would be so courteous. They just poach my guys with no warning.'

Kevin blinked. 'Employment?'

The chief nodded. 'They'd like to hire you.'

'Me?'

'Don't look so surprised. I got a glowing report of your performance after your six-month TDY.'

'But I haven't gotten anything—' He suddenly realized how this must look. 'I didn't apply to them, Chief. Honest, I didn't.'

'I know. The invitation to join their department's in the mail. It'll probably be waiting for you when you get home.' The chief braced his arms on his desk. 'You're a good cop, Kevin. I'd hate like hell to lose you, but I realize Syracuse can offer you opportunities we'll never be able to match. They've got a detective squad, a fraud unit, tactical response . . .' The chief plucked a hair from his sleeve. 'Hell, even K-9, if you want to work with dogs.'

Kevin gripped his chair. He felt like he might lose his balance. 'I don't know what to say.'

'Think about it. If you have any questions, if you want to bounce anything off me, just drop in and—' The chief frowned. 'No, I'll be away. You can call me on my cell. Captain Iacocca would like to hear from you by next Monday. He's trying to fill his positions before going up for budget review.' The chief stood and held out his hand. Kevin got up, knock-kneed, and shook it. 'You'll be a great asset to whatever department you choose. And wherever you go, you'll always be part of the Millers Kill family.'

Twenty seconds later, Kevin was making his way along the same hallway he'd walked down every working day for the last five years. Possibilities spun in his head like pictures on a slot machine. *SWAT team. Major Crimes. Detective.*

Then he thought about what he'd be giving up. Sunday dinner with the family. Going to basketball games in the same gym he played in as a high schooler. Home.

The door to the ladies' room swung open – it had been the visitors' john before the department had hired a woman – and Hadley charged out. Kevin skidded to a stop, barely avoiding crashing into her. She looked up at him. Way up. She was tiny compared to his six-foot-plus. For a split second her dark eyes met his. 'Sorry.' She dropped her gaze and bolted toward the squad room.

Kevin rubbed his chest as he went to collect his parka. He was putting their nonrelationship behind him. He wasn't still dreaming and hoping and wanting all the time. He – oh, hell, who was he kidding. He wasn't moving on, he was just managing to keep from embarrassing the both of them. If he was going to be completely, brutally honest, he had to admit all those other reasons for not leaving were overshadowed by the fact that if he accepted the offer in Syracuse, he wouldn't be seeing Hadley again.

So the question he had to answer was, would he give up his dream job for the chance to keep bumping into Hadley Knox in the hallway? And if so, how pathetic a loser was he?

SIX

Clare normally kept working – her secretary, Lois, referred to it as 'hiding in her office' – until she was summoned to the monthly vestry meeting. But this wasn't the usual meeting, and it wasn't the usual church business, and so she startled Lois when the secretary, carrying a tray with two pots and a jumble of mugs, entered the meeting room and found Clare standing by the black oak sideboard. 'Am I late?' Lois asked, setting the tray down. 'Or are you early?'

'I'm early.' Clare rubbed her stomach. She didn't want to call attention to her pregnancy, but she couldn't seem to help herself. She had no idea where the impulse came from. She'd never had the slightest urge to touch another expectant mother's abdomen.

'Bearding the lions in the den?' Lois unstacked the mugs and set out the sugar and milk.

'I feel like the politicians you see hanging outside the town hall on voting day. One last chance to shake hands and smile before my fate's decided.' She looked around her at the reproduction linenfold paneling, the diamond-paned windows, the worn Aubusson rug. 'Either that or Anne Boleyn. I can't decide.'

'Cheer up! They're not going to cut your head off with a sword.' Lois handed her a mug. 'Have some tea. It's herbal.'

Clare made a gagging noise but poured herself a cup anyway. 'God, I wish I hadn't agreed to this honeymoon thing. I should be here.'

'Doing what? You met with the bishop. The vestry's met with the bishop. You can be sure Elizabeth de Groot's been meeting with the bishop.'

'She probably has him on speed dial.' Clare's deacon pulled her own weight, no one could fault her on that. Still, her primary job responsibility

25

was to keep a close watch and an even closer rein on Clare.

'The die is cast. What's done is done. You might as well be off relaxing and enjoying that hunky police chief of yours.'

Clare gestured toward her maternity clerical blouse. 'That's the point, isn't it? I've obviously already been enjoying that hunky police chief.'

Lois made a token attempt at schooling her expression, then guffawed. She was a petite woman, but she laughed like Santa Claus on nitrous oxide. Clare began laughing helplessly, too, which was when the first of the vestry entered the room. 'Goodness.' Mr Madsen blinked, making him appear more worried than usual. 'Are we interrupting?'

'I suspect they're just blowing off steam, Norm.' Mrs Henry Marshall released the arm of her gentleman friend and gave Clare a hug. 'How are you doing, dear?'

'I've been better.'

The elderly woman nodded. 'At least your trouble's professional this time, instead of personal. Remember, jobs can be replaced. Husbands cannot.'

Mr Madsen paused while easing off Mrs Marshall's fur-collared coat. He frowned, as if trying to tease out where he fit in that statement.

'Hi, everyone.' Geoffrey Burns, the youngest member of the vestry, strode through the door, shucking off his camel coat. He tossed his briefcase on the black oak table with the disregard that comes from having much finer antiques at home. 'Clare, I want you to know Karen and I support you one hundred per cent.'

'Thanks, Geoff. That—'

'Although I still think you're crazy for taking up with Van Alstyne. Hi, Terry.' The lawyer nodded to the portly banker entering the room. 'I've got plenty of divorced friends I could have introduced you to if I had known you were actually getting serious about the guy.'

'There was that nice fellow from Barkley Investments,' Terry McKellan agreed, shucking off his puffy parka. 'I liked him.'

'He knew wines,' Geoff said.

'Yes, Hugh Parteger was a lovely man. However,' Clare could hear her voice stretching, 'I'm married and expecting, so I think you can say I've well and truly made my bed.'

'And now you have to lie in it?' Sterling Sumner didn't enter the meeting room, he made an entrance, with the rest of them serving as his audience.

'Sterling . . .' Mrs Marshall's usually composed voice sharpened.

'I'm just saying this sort of thing didn't happen back when we only had male clergy. Which is what I told the bishop.'

Oh, wonderful. Clare wasn't just embarrassing her own congregation, she was putting a black mark on every woman in the diocese.

'It seems to me,' Mrs Marshall said, 'male clergy have had their share of scandals.'

'Scandal? For God's sake. We're not living in the nineteenth century.' Geoff Burns thumped his coffee mug on the sideboard. 'Hell, nowadays, the fact a couple actually gets married before bringing a child into the world is enough to earn them a gold star from Miss Manners.'

'Barely exceeding the low expectations of the present day is hardly what we're here for, though, is it?' Sterling took his seat, tugging his cashmere scarf for emphasis.

'Back in our day, there were plenty of girls who walked up the aisle in a tight-waisted dress, Sterling.' Mrs Marshall accepted a cup of tea from Norm Madsen and carried it to the table. 'As long as the niceties were observed, no one commented if they had six-and-a-half-pound premature babies.' She paused. 'Well. No one *nice* would comment.'

Clare felt a weight pressing on her chest. At that moment, she was sure if she tore open her blouse, the letters *PMS* would be emblazoned over her breastbone. Pre-Marital Sex.

'Excuse me. Sorry.' Clare looked up to see Lois sidling through the door past two figures in black clericals. The Reverend Elizabeth de Groot entered, closely followed by the Archdeacon, Willard Aberforth. They made an odd pair; the one petite and composed, the other stiltlike and stooping. One worked closely with Clare as part of the St Alban's family. The other was opposed to women's ordination in general and many of Clare's actions in particular. One would throw her under a bus with a regretful moue. The other would step in front of the bus in her place, lecturing her until the moment he was mown down.

Aberforth had already divested himself of coat and boots, which meant he had stopped at Elizabeth's office before proceeding to the meeting room. Clare tried to gauge his news by the look on de Groot's fine-boned face. The problem was, her deacon only had three basic expressions, as far as Clare could tell. Saintly patience, regret, and *I'm disappointed in you.* No, there was a fourth. Smiling bravely. She was using it right now, crossing the room, looking as if she'd just heard that the rector of St. Alban's had a fatal disease. 'Clare. Oh, Clare. Are you nervous?'

'Archdeacon Aberforth's just here to tell the vestry the next step in the bishop's review.' Clare kept her voice calm. 'I don't think he's going to hand me a bell and send me out to cry, "Unclean".'

'I wish I had your sense of humor. It just makes me sick to think—' Elizabeth touched the silver cross on her chest. 'Well, I suppose that's the benefit of being so impulsive. You never really have to think about the consequences of your acts until it's all too late.'

Clare smiled tightly. 'Shall we sit down?'

She took her usual place at the head of the table. Until and unless the bishop removed her, she was still the rector here. She wasn't so far gone that she didn't see the grim humor in her possessiveness. She'd been wrestling with doubt ever since she became a parish priest. She'd jumped at the chance to recommission in the Guard as if the army were a rescue basket waiting to lift her away from her pastoral failures and a relationship she'd believed was irretrievably broken. She dropped her hand on her abdomen again. The voice of her survival school instructor echoed in her head. *You're not very bright, are you, Fergusson?*

'. . . are you, Ms Fergusson?'

'Hm?' She snapped to attention.

'I asked,' Father Aberforth said, 'if you were waiting for anyone else.'

'Mr Corlew isn't here yet,' Elizabeth said. 'He's our senior warden.'

'We can bring him up to speed when he arrives.' In the tally she kept in her head, Clare suspected he was a no vote. Not that they would be voting today. 'I believe you all know the Reverend Canon Aberforth. Archdeacon? This is your meeting.'

The archdeacon nodded perfunctorily to the rest of the table. The

28

droops and folds of his face made him look like a basset hound – if bassets had shrewd eyes and caustic tongues.

'The bishop first wishes me to thank all of you for the time you've taken to respond to his questions. He knows this is a matter of some delicacy, and he appreciates the vestry's willingness to be perfectly frank with him.'

Clare's gaze slid toward Sterling Sumner. She could just imagine how perfectly frank he must have been.

'As we know, the church's position toward her clergy is that they be either married or celibate.'

'Or in a faithful, monogamous relationship if they're not allowed to marry by the laws of their state.' Clare knew Aberforth had heard her argument before, but she couldn't help repeating it again.

Aberforth blinked at her. 'Yes, Ms Fergusson. I believe we all know your position in that regard. However, there was no legal or moral impediment to *your* marriage.'

'You just jumped the gun,' Sterling said.

'This is ridiculous,' Geoff Burns said. 'Clare and Van Alstyne tied the knot less than five months after she'd gotten back from deployment! When my wife and I got engaged, it took her mother a year and a half to organize the damn ceremony. Frankly, I think starting their family as quickly as possible is smart. It's not like Clare's getting any younger.'

Clare covered her face with one hand.

Aberforth looked at both men quellingly. 'The circumstances surrounding Ms Fergusson's pregnancy are well known to the bishop.'

And boy, hadn't that been a fun conversation.

'Nevertheless, the disciplinary canons are clear. Under Section Four, Title Four, Ms Fergusson could be brought up on charges of sexual misconduct and conduct unbecoming to a priest.' He raised his hand against the room's instant uproar. 'The bishop has no wish to convene a disciplinary panel. He feels the resulting publicity would reflect poorly on St Alban's, the diocese, and the church as a whole.' From across the table, Aberforth pinned her with his black eyes. 'Therefore, he is offering you the chance to quietly resign. If you do so, no actions will be taken, and you will be free to seek a parish in another diocese without the taint of charges following you.'

Resign? Clare swallowed. 'Does he . . . do I have to give you my answer right now?'

'No. I've informed him of your upcoming vacation, and suggested a period of quiet reflection and prayer, away from the press of your day-to-day duties, would be beneficial. You can give us your answer when you return.'

'So . . . a week?'

Aberforth nodded. The vestry erupted into arguments; Geoff threatening, Mrs Marshall high-handed, Mr Madsen pointing out the pros and cons of the plan to anyone who would listen.

The archdeacon continued to look at her intently. What was he trying to say? Should she take the offer? Should she fight? Was the bishop seeing this as a test? Or as an opportunity?

One week. Her hands curled over the edge of the black oak table as if she could anchor herself to it. *One week.*

SEVEN

Kevin Flynn had expected the wreckage of the burned home to be messy. Cinders, charcoal, melted snow refrozen to ice – picking his way around the rubble of the MacAllens' life had already coated his boots with a gray slime and stained his uniform pants up to the knee. What he hadn't expected was the smell.

'God.' He waved his glove beneath his nose in a vain attempt to clear some breathing space. 'Stinks like an industrial accident in New Jersey.'

'Yeah.' Patrick Lent, the state arson investigator, didn't look up from his camera, aimed at a stack of debris the rest of the fire marshal's team was sorting through. 'The crap that gets released when a house burns is crazy. Toxic chemicals, asbestos, lead.' He snapped off a series of photos. 'The insulation, the electrical system, rubber, plastic – that's why we've got my partner here.' Lent made a gesture, and the dog that had been sitting quietly a few feet away rose and trotted to his side. Unlike most K-9 police dogs, the arson dog wasn't in a vest or identifying collar. He could have been someone's mutt, a mix of German shepherd and Lab, maybe, watching the scene.

'What's he do?' Kevin asked.

'Dakota's trained to sniff out accelerants. Somebody could have gone through this house with a bucket of paraffin-oil blend, and you and I couldn't tell. But Dakota catches the smallest trace of a fire-starter and can track it for miles.'

'What about the bodies?' Both men looked to the far corner of the ruined house, where firemen were shifting debris from a towering pile suspected to have been an upstairs bedroom. Part of the second floor had collapsed onto the floor below, making the search a slow excavation rather than a quick retrieval. Nothing had been found yet, but everyone knew it was only a matter of time.

'He hasn't been trained to find corpses. He'll ignore humans, unless they've got accelerant on them.' Lent pointed to the charred and listing timbers framing nonexistent rooms. 'Dakota. Seek.'

The dog trotted toward the ruins. He entered through the shell of the front door and veered to the left, picking his way over the wreckage, nosing in what looked to Kevin like a random pattern. Suddenly, he sat.

'Huh,' Lent said. 'That was fast.' He walked toward where the dog was sitting. 'Show me.' The dog scratched. Lent bent over and placed a marker where his canine partner had indicated. 'I'll take the evidence sample after Dakota's run the rest of the house. Seek.'

The dog sprang up and headed toward what must have been the center hall. Abruptly, he sat again.

'Does he do that every time?' Kevin asked.

'Yeah. He'll only scratch to indicate the spot. Keeps him from injuring himself.' The arson investigator set another marker. 'Seek.'

The dog went a few feet and sat again. Kevin and Lent followed the dog throughout the house, walking, sitting, marking. After forty minutes, they had a trail of fluorescent flags streaming in and out of every room.

'Jesus,' Kevin said. 'Whoever did this wasn't leaving much to chance, was he?'

'Doesn't look like it.' Lent scratched Dakota's head and gave him a treat.

In the heap of charred rubble that had been a bedroom, one of the fire marshal's men straightened. 'Hey. Officers. We got remains.'

Kevin and Lent made their way through the scorched and broken rooms. 'If the owners were inside, chances are good it's not going to be insurance fraud, which is what my first guess would have been.' Lent stepped back while two firemen lifted another timber out of the way. 'The other most usual scenario is a pissed-off husband or boyfriend.'

'They were an older married couple,' Kevin said.

'Then I'd check out the grown kids. Do they have a daughter who broke up with someone? Left an abusive husband?'

Two of the fire marshal's men lifted a ragged panel that might have been attic insulation. 'There they come,' another man said.

Kevin concentrated on keeping his face neutral and his stomach down. He had seen death before, but not like this. The two corpses, blackened, mummylike, were barely identifiable as human. Age, gender, and features had all been burned away. The bodies curled toward one another, as if they had been—' It looks like they were just lying there.'

'We see that a lot,' Lent said. 'The smoke gets them in their sleep. These two probably never even woke up.'

Thank God for that. Kevin stepped closer as the arson investigator picked up his camera again. 'We'll get the shots, and then you can bag the remains,' Lent told the fire marshal's men.

'Wait.' Kevin removed his leather gloves and stuffed them in his parka pocket before tugging on purple evidence gloves in their place. He bent over the two heads. Each skull had charred cracks radiating from a chipped hole. He touched one hole lightly. His finger went all the way through. 'The hell? These look like gunshot wounds.' He glanced up at Lent. 'Is this some sort of natural result of extreme heat?'

'No. It's not.' The arson investigator's voice was grim. 'Better call in your ME.'

Kevin retreated to his squad car, grateful for the chance to warm up. He held one hand out to the vent as he keyed his mic with the other. 'Dispatch, this is fifteen-sixty-three.'

'Fifteen-sixty-three, go ahead.'

'Requesting a medical examiner at 52 Crandell Hill Road. We've found—' He almost said *the MacAllens' remains*, but the chief's rule stopped him. *Never assume.* 'Human remains. Two adults who appear to have been shot in the head.'

'Roger that, fifteen-sixty-three. Please hold.' Kevin unscrewed the lid of his thermos and took a swig. He almost spat the mouthful out. His hot chocolate had gone cold and gritty.

'Kevin?' MacAuley's voice crackled over the radio. 'What's this about the burn vics having GSWs?'

'We found remains,' Kevin repeated. 'Two adults. Both of them with what appeared to be gunshot wounds to the skull.'

'What's the arson guy say?'

Flynn unzipped his parka and let the heat seep inside. 'There was accelerant all over the place. Looks like someone walked around the house with a twenty-five-gallon can of gasoline.'

There was a pause, during which, Kevin knew, MacAuley was swearing. Finally his radio came on again. 'Roger that,' MacAuley said. 'Harlene says the ME's on his way. I'll let the chief know. I got a feeling this is gonna put a cramp in his honeymoon.'

EIGHT

Russ closed his eyes. *God.* 'Okay. Obviously this is top priority.' He opened his eyes again. Lyle was still standing there, a sorry-to-be-the-bearer-of-bad-tidings expression on his face. 'I'm authorizing any overtime necessary. Call me with updates.'

'You're still going off on your vacation?'

'Jesus, Lyle. You take off every other day during hunting season. I can't get a week off for my damn honeymoon?'

'We're looking at a double homicide! Who's gonna run the investigation if you're away? Eric's—' Lyle dropped his voice, even though the only other person in the station was Harlene, and she knew everybody's business already. 'Eric can't take lead on this. He's on night shift right now. He's barely clocking thirty hours with all his . . .' Lyle made a vague gesture. 'Stuff.'

Sergeant Eric McCrea's 'stuff' was two anger-management sessions a week and therapy with his estranged wife. All of which made him pretty much unavailable for an investigation, a temporary arrangement Russ had signed off on.

'I know it's a bad time. And I know if I stay and work the case we won't have as much overtime. But let's face it, there's never a good time.' Russ looked at the corkboard, full to overflowing with circ sheets, alerts, and be-on-lookout faxes. 'There's always going to be some case going on. There's always going to be a good reason to come in early and stay late and drop in on the weekend and postpone the vacation.' He looked at Lyle. 'I screwed up my first marriage because whenever the choice came between Linda and my job, I picked the job. Every. Damn. Time. I'm not going to make the same mistake with Clare.'

'You've got some all-new mistakes to make with her, huh?'

35

Russ snorted. 'No doubt.' He picked up the case file Lyle had thrust into his hands and gave it back it to his deputy. 'You already know you can run this place without me. Put Kevin on as lead investigator with Knox as his support.'

'Kevin? The guy who trips over himself with excitement when we've got a homicide? Paired with Knox, who was working as a California car-show model two years ago.' Lyle stuck out his leg. 'Pull the other one.'

'They're perfectly capable. We sent Kevin off on those TDYs to upgrade his skill set. Time to get our money's worth out of him.' Before he jumped ship for Syracuse. 'And Knox may still be a little green, but she's smart and tough. She wasn't showing off cars on a turntable when she was working for the DOC.' In fact, it had been Hadley's stint as a prison guard that had convinced Russ to hire her.

Lyle made a noise that was a cross between skepticism and surrender. Russ slapped his arm. 'You and I aren't going to be here forever. We've got to give the next generation a chance to step into our shoes once in a while.' He grinned. 'I can just see it now. Chief Flynn and Deputy Chief Knox.'

'The day Kevin Flynn puts on your badge is the day I hole up in my fishing shack on Raquette Lake. Stock the place with a few hundred pounds of that freeze-dried crap and wait for the end of the world.'

'Well, don't plan your retirement yet. You and I—'

'Chief!' Harlene called. 'Better get in here.'

'What?' Russ looked at his watch. 'Is it Clare?'

'No. Get over here.' In times of stress, the dispatcher ignored the convenient fiction that Russ was her boss. He and Lyle crossed the hall into the dispatch room.

Harlene waved them closer, setting her springy gray curls in motion. 'Hold on a sec, Merva,' she said into her headset. She snapped a switch. 'Okay, I've put you on the speaker. The chief's right here.'

'Russell?'

He recognized the voice. Merva was one of his father's cousins, halfway between his parents' generation and his own. She worked in the town clerk's office. 'Yeah, Merva, I'm here. What's up?'

'You need to get over here to the town hall and you need to do it right now. They're talking about the police department.'

Russ frowned. 'Who is?'

'The aldermen. They're going into a closed-door meeting.' Meaning the public hadn't been notified in advance.

'It's okay, Merva. I've put in a request to hire another officer. They're probably in there complaining about the cost.' The only thing they liked to bitch about more than the MKPD was the road department.

'They're not complainin' about hiring a new officer.' Merva dropped her voice. 'They're talking about getting rid of you.'

'Me? What do you mean?' Russ's contract had just been renewed at the start of the fiscal year.

'No, no, not you, personally.' She sounded flustered. 'The department. The whole police department. They're talking about getting the state police to take over patrolling here and Cossayuharie and Fort Henry. There's been other towns done it and saved lots of money.'

Lyle and Harlene stared at him. *What the hell?* Russ took a deep breath. 'I'll be there in five minutes. Thanks, Merva.' He nodded. Harlene switched the call off. 'Christ on a bike. What the hell is Jim Cameron thinking?'

'It might not be the mayor's idea,' Lyle said. 'The aldermen've been pushing hard to shrink the budget.'

'On the backs of our department? Those penny-pinching sons of bitches.' Russ ducked into his office and snatched his parka off its hook. 'Harlene, I'm supposed to meet Clare by three thirty. Will you call her and tell her I'll be late?'

'I'm coming with you.' Lyle, his parka in hand, fell into step as Russ strode down the hall. 'You need somebody to stop you from going in there with guns blazing.'

'Fine. You can be the good cop.' He paused in front of the outside door and tugged his MKPD watch cap on. Lyle opened the door, letting a gust of icy air into the hall. 'Wait a sec.' Russ wheeled around and jogged back up the hall to dispatch. 'Harlene? You got my wife on the line yet?'

'Just about to call her now.'

'Good. Listen. Just tell her I had to respond to a call.' He grimaced. 'She doesn't need one more thing to worry about.'

NINE

Clare was about to head back to the rectory when Lois caught her with the message from Harlene. She checked her watch, looked out the diamond-paned windows of her office at the late-afternoon slant of the sun, and frowned. Russ was the one who had wanted to be on the road by three, so they wouldn't be unloading the truck after dark. It figured. Her earlier hesitation about going had vanished in the wake of the bishop's ultimatum. Questions, decisions, explanations, apologies – suddenly, sitting alone in a cabin staring at a frozen lake for a few days sounded pretty damn good.

She sighed and headed to the undercroft to see if she could lend a hand with the Young Mothers program. At three o'clock, the teens and their children would have just arrived. The young moms would be doing their homework or talking with one of the mentors about job hunting or child rearing, while their kids were cared for next door.

The nursery in St. Alban's undercroft was as cheery as two windowless rooms could be, with lemon-yellow walls and puffy white painted clouds forever floating over a blue painted sky. Sundays, the space sheltered the youngest members of her congregation. The rest of the week, it served as day care, homework spot, and employment center for teen mothers.

Clare opened the playroom door, bumping into a toddler and sending him staggering forward. Another two-year-old, taking advantage of his loss of balance, rammed into him and grabbed the doll he'd been holding. The little boy screeched, the thief laughed, and another child at the play kitchen started banging pots together. 'Oh, Lord.' Clare didn't know which one to deal with first. 'I'm sorry.'

'Clare! What are you doing here?' Karen Burns, one of the volunteers, laid an infant in a playpen and expertly scooped up the red-faced little boy.

'Here you go, Braeden, here's a baby for you.' She wiggled a doll in Braeden's face. He snatched the substitute. When Karen let him down, the avaricious little girl came at him again. 'Uh-uh, Jazmin.' Karen performed a knee block that would have done the New York Rangers proud. She steered Jazmin toward the low table at the other end of the room. 'You and I can change our babies together.' Karen lifted the infant back out of the playpen, then handed the pots-and-pans musician a basket of fake food. 'Kiefer, can you make us all a yummy meal?' The boy accepted the container and began laying plastic pork chops and burgers on wooden skillets. Karen did a sort of shift-and-flip and the baby on her arm was lying on the changing table with its feet waving in the air.

'Oh my God, Karen.' Clare shook her head. 'I'm never going to be able to do this. I mean it. I am so unprepared for motherhood, it's not funny.'

Karen's hands flew as she unsnapped, ripped, folded, and tossed. 'You'll learn. We all do.'

'I don't even know how to change a diaper.'

Karen held out a box of wipes. 'Want to learn?'

Clare wrinkled her nose. 'Not really.'

Karen laughed. 'Trust me, I felt the same way the first time we brought a foster child home. Utterly incompetent in the face of a six-month-old. But I figured if I could make it through law school and pass the New York bar, I could learn how to mash bananas and give baths in the sink.'

'You bathe them in the sink?'

Karen gave her an amused look. 'I have some books I can pass on to you.' She hoisted the now-fresh baby into the air, kissed her terry-covered tummy, and handed her to Clare. 'Here.'

Clare reflexively accepted the bundle.

'So what are you doing here? Aren't you supposed to be off for seven glorious days and six fun-filled nights in an ice-fishing shack?' Karen moved to the sink and turned on the faucet. 'For which, by the way, you earn the saintly wife award. If Geoff had suggested something like that for our honeymoon, our marriage would've ended after the reception.'

'It's a beautiful vacation cabin with eight hundred feet of shoreline. It's the ideal year-round getaway.' At least that's what the Realtor had said.

Russ's description had been more succinct. *No phone, no neighbors, and too far for your parishioners to just drop in.* 'This is our chance to try it before we buy it.'

'In January. In the Adirondacks.' Karen scrubbed her hands. 'No wonder you're hiding out down here.'

'Russ had some last-minute work to do. I figured I could help out.' The infant in her arms began to squirm and fuss.

'With your black-belt child care skills?' Karen took the baby from her.

'I was thinking more along the lines of their mothers.'

'Mae Bristol is in the other room helping with homework, if you want to lend her a hand.'

'How much of a hand does she need? She taught for thirty years before she retired.' Besides – and Clare would never admit this – Mae Bristol intimidated her a little. It was the way she looked at you, like she had caught you without a hall pass.

'Okay, then, Gail's in the other room with the job search and life skills kids. Pop in and see if she needs an assistant.' Karen grinned at her. 'Just don't try to tell them that all-black is an appropriate interview outfit.'

'It worked for me,' Clare said. As she exited the nursery, her smile fell away. Chances were good *she'd* be job hunting with an infant in tow.

Across the hall, in the room they used for the Rite 13 youth group on Sundays, Clare found Gail Jones bent over a table, helping a young woman of eighteen or nineteen decipher a document. Another girl was working on a laptop, while a third frustratedly jabbed buttons on her phone. She wasn't going to get any less frustrated – it was almost impossible to get a signal down here.

'Hey, Clare.' Gail straightened, smiling. 'Here to check out the work in progress?' She turned to the girl on the laptop. 'Reverend Fergusson is *my* supervisor.' The girl stared at Clare. Clearly, there was a work-related backstory Clare was missing.

'Nope. Just dropping by to see if there's anything I can do before I leave.'

'Oh, that's right, you're going out to Lake Inverary! How romantic!' Gail wiggled her eyebrows suggestively. 'A rustic cabin, a bear rug in front of the fire . . .'

The girl with the laptop looked skeptical, though whether that was because of Clare's advanced age or her condition, Clare couldn't tell.

'You're going to Lake Inverary?' The third girl shoved her phone in her pocket. She stuck her hand out. Clare took it automatically. 'I'm Amber Willis. I'm desperate to get to my family's cabin on Lake Inverary. Could I catch a ride with you?' Amber Willis looked like a cheerleader; her hair pulled to the top of her head as if any other style would take too long; her skinny frame jittery with energy.

'Oh,' Clare said. 'Um . . .'

'It's just, my boyfriend came down from Lake Placid, and I was supposed to go up and meet him at the lake, because it was sort of a halfway point, but my mom's taken my car and disappeared with it, and Elijah – that's my boyfriend – he left a message for me that his truck died in Canterville and he got a ride from the tow guy out to the lake, but now I can't reach him because, you know how it is out there, you can never get a signal, which is why this was supposed to be the perfect getaway weekend for us – he's been saving up lots of money from his winter job and I think he might have popped for a ring.'

Amber ran out of air at that point. Or perhaps the ring was the culmination of her saga.

'Ah . . . your father? Can't he give you a ride?'

'No, he's downstate this weekend. That's why I invited Elijah to the cabin.' She looked at Clare like a puppy in its last hours at a kill shelter. 'I've been calling around to see if one of my friends could take me, but I'm not having any luck. Oh, please? I'll pay for gas. I'll be quiet. Or I'll talk, if you want the company.'

'No, it's – my husband is coming with me.' Clare seized on that fact. 'We're going in his pickup truck. I'm afraid there won't be room for you.'

'I'll ride outside in the back.'

In January. For an hour. 'What? No, that's not what I meant. We have a little backseat space.'

'Perfect! I don't take up much room at all.'

'I don't think—'

'I love Jesus!'

Clare blinked. Good Lord. The kid thought she needed to make a profession of belief before she'd get help. Had someone taught her she couldn't rely on Christians unless she parroted bumper-sticker theology and prayed the Sinner's Prayer? That made up Clare's mind for her. 'I love Jesus, too, but you don't need to pass a religious test in order to get help at St Alban's.' She shoved her hands in her skirt pockets and crossed her fingers, knowing she was telling at least half a lie. 'My husband and I will be happy to take you with us to Lake Inverary.'

TEN

Russ's glasses steamed opaque as soon as he entered the overheated foyer of the town hall. He snatched them off and shucked his parka as he headed down the hall to the session room, Lyle close behind him.

Russ shoved the door open with way more force that he'd intended. It creaked and slammed against the wall, silencing all conversation, jerking everyone's attention to his dramatic entrance. Russ couldn't make out individual faces from this far away, but he could tell everyone was looking at him. *Crap*. Probably waiting for him to go postal on them.

'Hi, all.' Lyle's voice, warm and genial, promised shelter from Russ's storm. 'The chief and I heard you were discussing the department, and we wanted to be on hand to help out with any questions you might have.'

'Everyone? You know Deputy Chief Lyle MacAuley.' Jim Cameron's voice was dry. 'And, of course, our chief of police.' Russ put his glasses back on. The room snapped into focus. Five of the six aldermen sat at the long, Formica-covered session table, with the mayor in the moderator's seat at the center. The town secretary's shorthand machine had just fallen still, echoing the awkward silence in the room. Merva had been right – there weren't any members of the public taking up space in the folding chairs. However, the town's attorney was on hand. And there, at the speaker's podium, stood a tall drink of water in a state trooper's uniform. His ol' pal Bob Mongue. *Oh, wonderful*.

'This is a budget meeting,' the mayor went on. 'We have your annual report. We didn't feel we needed any extra information at this time.'

'Then what's Sergeant Mongue doing here?' Like the door, Russ's voice was louder and harsher than he intended.

Cameron hesitated for a second. 'Since we fall within his troop's area, we've asked *Lieutenant* Mongue to give us his thoughts on how the state police might be more . . . of a presence in Millers Kill.'

'And Cossayuharie and Fort Henry,' Harold Collins said. 'Let's face it, they already help out with some of the patrolling and investigating you people do. Duplicatin' resources!' He banged his fist on the table, setting his water glass aquiver. 'That's what we joined up the towns to get away from.'

'Back in the fifties,' Garry Greuling said. 'Times change. Our needs change. Our economy is based on tourism now. I don't think handing local law enforcement over to the state police is the best way to serve our visitors.'

'So we hire seasonal officers to patrol the town in the summer.' Bob Miles leaned forward. 'Straight salary, no benefits. We'll have the coverage we need and still save upwards of a hundred thousand a year.'

Bob Mongue showed no sign of giving up the speaker's podium, so Russ strode forward and took a stand directly in front of the aldermen. 'Let me get this straight. You're considering closing down the Millers Kill Police Department? Thinking that the staties – the state police – will be able to replace us?'

'Town's broke,' Collins said.

'It's not broke,' Cameron said. 'And you're out of order, Russ.'

'I'm out of *order*? My people are out there twenty-four hours a day, seven days a week, fifty-two weeks a year, keeping your kids and your homes and your businesses safe. Do you have any idea how many domestics we stopped last year? How many teens we picked up and returned to their parents before they could get into trouble? How many assaults we shut down because we're right there, in the community, every night and day?'

'And you do a great job. But this economy is squeezing us at both ends. Revenue is down and expenses are way up. Do *you* have any idea how much we spend just on gas for your cruisers? For their insurance and maintenance and upkeep? How much it costs to keep the heat and lights and water on at the station? Forget the personnel costs – the infrastructure alone is killing us.'

'We've applied for a Department of Homeland Security grant,' Lyle said. 'If we get that—'

'You haven't gotten any money from them the past two years you've applied.' Cameron sounded tired. 'I don't like the idea any more than you do. But our buy-in for state police coverage will be half what we're spending to keep our own police force running.'

'This is not a done deal.' Garry Greuling was looking at Russ, but his voice was pitched toward the mayor. 'This is one option that we're weighing.'

'Do we have a voice in this? Or are you just going to hand down your decision from on high?' Russ knew he sounded angry and bitter, but he couldn't help it.

'Your annual report is your voice.' Jim Cameron squared the stack of document folders in front of him. 'We have a written proposal from Lieutenant Mongue and accounts from five other municipalities in the state who've taken the step we're considering. The aldermen and I are going to carefully read and digest this information, and at our meeting next Friday, we'll vote on whether to put it on the ballot or not.'

Russ opened his mouth.

'Thank you,' Lyle said. 'We'll see you then.' His tone closed off any further discussion. 'Chief?' He gestured toward the door.

Russ let himself be frogmarched out of the sessions room. In the hall, he turned to Lyle.

'Not here.' Lyle pointed toward the exterior door. Outside, standing on the concrete steps with cold biting at them, he said, 'Okay.'

'Why the hell did you go belly-up in there? *Thank you?* God.' Russ struggled into his parka. '"Read and digest this information." I'll give him something to digest.'

'I shut you down because you were two minutes away from alienating every single friend we might have on the board.' Lyle tugged his watch cap low over his ears. 'We're not gonna make our case in there, in front of the whole pack of 'em. We're going to make it one on one. With tact. And finesse.'

Russ grunted. 'You sound like a goddamn politician.'

Lyle started down the stairs. 'That's why you keep me around. That, and my natural charm and good looks.'

'I keep you around so I'm not the only old guy on the force.' They fell into step. The sun had already set behind the mountains, and above the bare-branched trees lining Main, the sky was streaked with ice pink and rose and orange. The street and the shops were shaded in blue, their windows warm golden squares of light. Russ felt a squeeze in his chest, the same desperate possessiveness he sometimes felt watching Clare sleeping or cooking or lost in a book. *My wife. My town.* The inevitable echo: *My child.* Jesus. How was he going to take care of a kid when he couldn't even take care of his own officers? 'I've got to cancel the honeymoon.'

'What? Why?'

'We've got seven days to convince a majority of the board that shutting down the department is monumentally stupid. I can't do that if I'm sitting on my ass, ice fishing.'

'No offense, but you're not my first choice as a lobbyist. Or my second or third.'

'Who, then?'

'I'm pulling out the biggest gun I can think of. Kevin Flynn's mother.' Lyle smiled and held the door open for an attractive middle-aged woman entering the bakery. She blushed and smiled back.

'Flynn's *mother*? What's she going to do? Play a sad Irish song about her soon-to-be unemployed son?' Except it wouldn't be Kevin left high and dry. It would be Knox, who had to stay close to town in order to take care of her grandfather. And Noble, who would never find employment in another department. And Tim and Duane, the part-time guys. And Eric, struggling to keep himself and his marriage together.

'Elle Flynn heads up the state Small Business Finance Organization. Before that, she was a policy assistant to the last governor, and before *that*, she was the director of the Municipal Development Foundation. Word is she's going to run for Congress this year. She put together an exploratory committee last month.'

'Kevin Flynn's *mother*?'

'Yep.'

'How come I didn't know any of this?'

'Because for most of the last year the only news you've been interested in came from Iraq. And then when the reverend finally got home, you were a little distracted.'

'You can say that again.' Russ pulled his own cap on. 'Huh. Good job.'

'I keep telling you, I'm more'n just a pretty face.'

'I guess so.' A car rolled past them, and both men automatically stepped to the side to avoid getting slushed. 'Okay. Keep me up to date. I mean vote by vote.' He shook his head. 'Maybe if you sew this up fast enough, I can avoid telling Clare the bad news.'

ELEVEN

Bumping over the poorly plowed road that led to Amber Willis's family's cabin, Clare kept sneaking peeks at Russ. It had been almost dark when he'd gotten home, fully an hour after he had planned on leaving, to be confronted by Clare and Amber and her baby.

Of course there was a baby. Clare had wanted to smack herself in the head at her blank surprise at the sight of Amber emerging from the nursery with a one-year-old. It was, after all, the Young. Mothers. Program. At the rectory, instead of dragging Clare into the kitchen for a heated, whispered argument about strangers and boundaries, Russ had greeted the addition of mother, child, diaper bag, car seat, backpack, and suitcase with a resigned 'Right. Sure. It is on our way.' Clare found it disorienting. During the hour-long ride up to the lake, while Amber chatted and the baby babbled and the dog snored beneath Clare's feet in the passenger well, Russ had been . . . distracted? Depressed? She couldn't tell. It worried her.

Russ swung the truck off the county highway and onto the road that ran along the south shore of Inverary Lake. There were a cluster of winterized houses and a mom-and-pop store near the highway, identifiable by their lit windows and parked cars. They petered out within a half mile, and the road closed in, rutted snow below, dense pines above. In the headlights' halo, Clare could catch glimpses of the summer houses: log cabins, vinyl-clad cottages, angular redwood garrisons. Most of them jostled for space between the trees and the shore.

'Is it this crowded all the way around?' she asked.

He shook his head. 'The north shore, where our place is, is part of a land trust. Nothing's been built on it since the conservation easement. So there's more space, a lot more trees, and you won't see any tear-downs like that.' He pointed toward an incongruously large, many-gabled house that threatened to squash its rackety one-story neighbors. He raised his voice. 'Uh—'

'Amber,' Clare whispered.

'Amber, where's your family's place?'

The girl leaned forward to get a better view out the windshield. 'About a mile more on, maybe? It's a lot closer to the turnoff to North Shore Drive.'

'I didn't think any of the houses out here were winterized.'

'It's not insulated, but my grandpa installed these electric baseboard heaters back when I was a little girl. If anyone wants to stay off-season, all they have to do is turn them on. My dad and my uncle taped the pipes so they won't freeze.'

'Taped the pipes?' Clare had spent – what was it now, three? four? – winters in the North Country, but there was still a lot she didn't know.

'Heat tape, with electrical wires in it,' Russ explained. 'Amber, you're sure your boyfriend is going to be there?'

'Oh, yeah.'

Russ flicked a glance at Clare. She had a sudden vision of arriving at the girl's destination and finding it dark and snowbound like all the other homes they were rolling past. Then what would they do? Host the teen and her baby overnight in their cabin? That would be the cherry on the cake.

'Look. There it is.' Amber pointed past Clare's head to where a light gleamed through the trees.

Thank you, Lord. Russ rolled to a stop. Only the top of the place was visible from the road, but someone had shoveled the steps leading down the embankment to the house. There was no driveway. Why waste the waterfront view on parking? Instead, like several of the homes they had passed, Amber's family had a two-door garage on the opposite side of the road. Russ didn't bother trying to pull alongside it. He yanked the parking brake and switched on his four-ways.

'Okay.' He opened his door to a swirl of icy air. 'Let's get you two down there first.' He tipped his seat forward and helped Amber and the baby out.

'I can help with her bags,' Clare offered.

'You' – he pointed at her – 'stay put. The last thing we need is you slipping and falling down a flight of stairs.' He slammed the door, definitively ending the conversation.

Oscar sat up and pawed at the door.

'Do you have to go out, boy?' Clare reached around him to wrestle a lead – left over from a dog-sitting stint several years back – out of the glove compartment. She shrugged into her parka, clipped on the leash, and opened her door. Oscar bounded down, Clare scrambling to keep up with him. He barked once, then got down to the business of sniffing the tires, the snowbank, the mailbox, and the top of the stairs. Clare could see the lit windows down below, their warmth somehow more lonely for being the only sign of life around. Behind her, the road glimmered white in the reflected glow of the truck's headlights, then disappeared into inky blackness. She tugged on the leash and led Oscar toward the front of the pickup, where the headlights' illumination ensured she wouldn't take a wrong step along the side of the road and end up sliding down the steep embankment. Oscar peed and sniffed, sniffed and peed.

Russ hove back into view and opened the door again to collect the rest of Amber's things. 'Everything okay?' Clare asked.

'Yeah, the boyfriend's there.' He swung a backpack over his shoulder and wedged the car seat under his arm before reaching in for the suitcase. 'Jesus, babies take a lot of stuff. I've gone on deployments with less than this.'

Clare bit back a grin. 'Be careful,' she said. 'The last thing we need is you slipping and falling down a flight of stairs.'

'Smart-ass.' He slammed the door and vanished down the stairs. Clare walked a little farther down the road, pausing so that Oscar could mark two more mailboxes.

'All set,' Russ called. She turned around. He was waiting beside her door, and behind him, in the distance, she saw a pair of headlights.

'Somebody's coming,' she said.

He turned around. 'They can get by us. Come on.'

She tugged the lead and Oscar obediently followed. The lights slowed as they grew closer, until an SUV pulled up alongside them and stopped. The window rolled down. 'You folks lost?' the driver asked. It was hard to make out his details. He was a large man, with a knit cap pulled down low, concealing his hair.

The dog lunged toward the SUV, barking at the man behind the wheel. 'Oscar!' Clare hauled on his leash. 'Bad dog! Bad!'

'Nope.' Russ raised his voice to be heard over Oscar's deep-throated barking. 'Just dropping someone off.'

'Sorry.' Clare tugged the dog back toward the truck.

'You'll be able to get home before the storm, then,' the driver said.

Oscar was bracing himself, stiff-legged, refusing to budge. Clare hauled against the lead. 'We're not going home—'

Russ cut her off. 'Storm?'

'Yep. They don't know if it's going to dump snow or rain or wintry mix. Supposed to be an unchristly mess, through. You staying here at the lake?'

Russ made a noncommittal noise. 'Thanks for the heads-up on the weather.' He opened Clare's door. 'Oscar, come.' The dog gave one more bark, then jumped into the truck. Russ handed Clare up and shut the door behind her. She watched him say something, then wave. The SUV's window rolled up and it drove off, making new tracks in the poorly plowed road.

'What was that?' she asked, as soon as Russ had climbed into his seat.

'I don't like telling strangers my business.' He buckled in but didn't shift the truck into gear. 'We don't know who that guy is.'

'This is a cop thing, isn't it?'

'No, it's a sensible safety measure thing.'

'And we're sitting here instead of driving on because . . . ?'

'I'm giving him lots of space. The road's not good. I don't want to risk skidding into his tailpipe.'

She rolled her eyes. 'I bet you got his license plate, didn't you?'

Russ made another noncommittal noise. He shifted into gear and drove on. After another mile or so, Clare spotted the green of a road sign. 'I think this is it,' she said. Russ slowed the truck. 'Haines Mountain Road and North Shore Drive,' Clare read.

'That's us. North Shore.' The road itself, once they had turned onto it, was barely more than a depression in the snow. Russ shifted into a lower gear. Clare peered into the darkness on either side of them. The mailboxes and shadowy roof lines of the cottages had disappeared. Nothing but thick evergreens and bare, gnarled branches bending beneath the weight of the snow. 'Are we going to get stuck?' she asked.

'If we do, we eat the dog first.'

She whacked his arm. Suddenly, the trees fell away. The darkness lightened, and Clare could see open land rising to her left and the long, empty stretch of the lake to her right. After the claustrophobic tunnel of trees, the vastness of the sky was dizzying. 'Wow,' she said.

'This is where the conservation easement begins. There's a public beach and boat launch down there in the summer, but you won't see any more houses until we come around to the north shore.' She could make out the dark, irregular edges of the shoreline against the ice. A narrow islet rose up in the middle, like a galleon caught in the ice.

The road turned to the east again, and the trees closed around them, blocking off the view. Russ shifted again as the road rose higher. Clare could feel the tires churning through the snow, trying to maintain a grip on the surface. 'They're sure not spending a lot of time plowing out here. You do realize we could be trapped if there is a bad storm.'

'Don't worry. I'm an expert in winter survival.'

'Oh, you are?' She tried to suppress her smile. 'So enlighten me. What are the basics?'

'First, find a hot woman and get her into your bed.'

Clare laughed.

'Second, make sure you've got enough food to keep an entire platoon going for a month.'

'Which we do.' Some women overpacked clothes or beauty items. Clare could go away for a week with just a small overnight bag, but if she was going to be cooking, she brought half the contents of her pantry along.

'Right. Third, you have to have a plan to keep yourself occupied until rescue arrives.'

'And you plan to keep yourself occupied . . .'

'With sex and eating.' Without taking his eyes off the road, he flashed a grin. 'Maybe a little ice fishing, if I can fit it into my busy schedule.'

Despite the darkness and the claustrophobic closeness of the pines and the slow, shaky progression of the truck, Clare felt everything was a little lighter. Whatever had kept Russ quiet and unresponsive, it wasn't bothering him now. Which meant it must have been a work issue, not an I'm-still-pissed-off-that-you're-pregnant issue. Thank God.

'This is it.' A sign announcing PRIVATE DRIVE marked the turn-off from the North Shore Drive. A dozen weather-beaten slats with names like ALTPETER and the ROSENS hung off the pole. The barely discernible lane dipped low, bringing them close to the water again. More trees, more darkness, more barely passable road surface. They passed one snow-mounded, dark cottage, then another, and then— 'Here we are.' Clare craned her neck, but just like at Amber's father's place across the lake, all she could see was a ramshackle one-car garage on one side and a mailbox and the suggestion of a roof line far below the other edge of the road.

'It looks like we're going to have to shovel out the garage door,' Clare said.

'Yeah.' He switched on his four-ways. 'Let's get you inside first.'

'I can help unload the truck, Russ.' She bit off the words *and why do you care, anyway?* She knew why. Whether he disapproved or not, he would take care of her.

'You can help by getting the fires going and lighting the kerosene lamps.' He reached under his seat for the safety box and retrieved his Maglite. Clare opened her door and let Oscar out before climbing to the ground. Snow crunched beneath her boots. When Russ had first proposed a week in an unelectrified cabin, the idea of cooking on an old-fashioned woodstove and evenings by lamplight had seemed cozy and romantic. Now, with the wind blowing stiff and cold off the frozen lake and nothing but a flashlight to show the way down a half-buried flight of steps, it sounded like complete insanity.

'Okay,' she said in her most chipper voice. 'Let's go!'

TWELVE

It was getting close to sunset when the arson investigator said he was ready to wrap up. 'Nothing more I can take away here,' he told Kevin. The ME had left an hour earlier, after confirming that yes, those were gunshot wounds to the cranium. He promised to have the preliminary autopsy results to them tomorrow. Not that it was going to make a big difference in the investigation. Shot and then burned or burned and then shot, some bad guy out there was going up for murder one.

Like the chief had said, Kevin signed off on all the bagged evidence. Now he was back in his squad car, updating his preliminary notes on his laptop and waiting for Patrick Lent, who was in his car updating *his* notes on his laptop. They were going to swap files before leaving the scene.

'Fifteen-sixty-three, this is Dispatch. Respond, fifteen-sixty-three.'

Kevin unhooked his mic. 'Yeah, Harlene, I'm here.' He was too damn tired to use code.

'You still at the MacAllens' place?'

'For about ten more minutes. What's up?'

'Hadley's got something for you. Hold on, I'm connecting you to fifteen-seventy.'

There was a snapping sound, and Hadley's voice came on, thinned out as it always was on the car-to-car band. 'Flynn? You've found remains?'

'Yeah. Two adults with GSWs to the head. Why?'

Even over the bad connection, he could tell she was upset. 'There may be another body in there. It turns out the MacAllens were fostering a little girl.'

* * *

'Her name's Mikayla Johnson.' Hadley wasn't great at doing the unemotional cop voice at the best of times. Now, standing in the squad room reporting on this little girl, she was worse than usual. 'She's eight years old.' Eight. The same age as Genny. Her throat tightened. 'The MacAllens' daughter told me about her when I interviewed her. It took me a while to find anyone at Children and Family Services who could tell me anything, but I finally got a caseworker who knew a few of the details.' She focused on the notes in her hand. 'Mother, Annie Johnson, lost custody a few months ago after she got cranked on meth and drove into a tree. Mikayla was severely injured. She had to have a liver transplant.' She glanced up from her notebook. 'The MacAllens had experience dealing with the post-transplant issues. The daughter I spoke with had had a kidney transplant when she was a kid.'

MacAuley looked at Flynn, sprawled in a chair, his usual immaculate uniform crumpled and filthy. 'Any sign of a third body?'

'No. As soon as I got the call from Hadley – from Officer Knox – the fire marshal's team and I started the search over again. By the time it got too dark to see, we'd sifted through anything we hadn't gotten to during the afternoon. She wasn't in the house when it burned.'

'Thank God,' Hadley said under her breath. Flynn glanced at her.

'Did anybody have overnight visitation privileges?' the dep asked. 'Grandparents? Aunt and uncle?'

Hadley shook her head. 'Supervised visitation only with the family members, according to CFS.'

'Yeah. Probably a whole clan brewing up hillbilly heroin.' MacAuley chewed his lip. 'So this kid was taken. Why kill the MacAllens? Why burn the place down?'

'Patrick Lent, the state investigator, told me lots of first-time arsonists overestimate how much a fire will destroy.' Flynn brushed at his sooty pants almost unconsciously. 'There was accelerant splashed all over the place. Could be whoever set the fire thought everything would be burned down to ashes, with no way to tell who had died in the fire and who had survived.'

'Where's the mother?' The dep's gaze went back to Hadley.

'Out on bail awaiting trial for possession, reckless endangerment, criminal speeding, evading and resisting.'

'Is there a father in the picture?'

Hadley shook her head. 'Not according to the birth certificate CFS had on file. There are grandparents over in Fort Henry. I've got last known addresses.'

'Okay. We start with the mom and the grandparents.' He pointed to her, then to Flynn. 'See what you can find out about the father, or another man in the mom's life who might be involved. You'll want to talk to the girl's teachers and her caseworker. See if she self-reported anything funny going on beforehand. Run up the sex offenders list. It's not likely, but it could be she was marked as a target by a pedophile.'

Hadley glanced at Flynn before looking back at the dep. 'You want *us* to take lead on this?'

Flynn wiped the side of his face, leaving a faint sooty streak along his angular jawline. 'Both of us?'

'Unless you've got something better to do, yes, both of you.' The deputy chief raised his bushy gray eyebrows. 'The chief has confidence that you two can handle this, and so do I.' His jaw tightened, and Hadley could almost hear the unspoken warning: *So don't screw this up.*

'You're going to let the chief know, right?' Flynn was usually gung-ho for any investigation, but right now he sounded a little wavery. Hadley didn't blame him.

''Course I am. I expect he'll head back here right quick. Skipping the murder investigation was bad enough. A missing kid's even more time-sensitive. Not to mention—' MacAuley snapped his mouth shut.

'Dep,' Hadley said, 'about that time sensitivity.'

'What about it?'

'According to the caseworker at CFS, Mikayla's on several daily medications because of her new liver.' She checked her note-pad to get the word right. 'Immunosuppressants.'

'Good. Find her doctor and put out a med alert at all the area pharmacies. If we're lucky, whoever took her will waltz right in and fill the prescription.'

Hadley shook her head. 'No, listen, the caseworker told me. She has to have this stuff or her body will start to reject her transplant. If whoever took her didn't also grab her medication, or doesn't know how important it is, she's going to get very sick, very fast.'

'How fast?' Flynn moved to her side, his head cocked to see her notebook.

She could feel his nearness, a tingle along her skin, a slow deep surge of blood. She stared at her notes and forced herself to concentrate. 'A few days. Maybe seven or eight. After that, no drugs will help. Her body rejects the liver and . . .' Her voice trailed off.

'She dies,' Flynn said.

THIRTEEN

Annie Johnson's address of record was a third-floor walk-up on Causeway that looked like it was one good storm away from collapsing into the old canal that ran behind the street. This part of town, with its weary tenement houses and narrow streets running down to abandoned mills and rotting remnants of wharves, was not a place the shoppers or skiers or leaf peepers would ever see. Johnson's was one of several apartment houses in the neighborhood that were regularly visited by the MKPD. Kevin debated a stealth arrival by parking a block away, but he figured by the time he and Hadley had walked halfway to the building, everybody on the street would be texting each other a warning. They double-parked and got out in front of the apartment house.

In the sickly orange glow of the streetlights, the sagging facade's peeling paint and battered aluminum trim were obvious. Hadley pulled on her watch cap and gloves. 'I'll take the fire escape.'

'In case she runs? You sure?'

'I'd rather hang out in the freezing dark than breathe the air in there. Everybody over the age of seven smokes in that building. You risk lung cancer just walking up a flight of stairs.'

'It can't be worse than the Los Angeles smog.'

'Hey. California was banning indoor smoking while you New Yorkers were still selling kids packs out of cigarette machines.' She started to grin up at him, then looked away. Their bitter words from last November hung in the air.

Look, Flynn, we can still be friends, she had said.

With me slicing myself open every day and you waiting and dreading the next time I break down and beg you to love me? Is that what you really want? No. I guess I don't.

58

He had been so heartsick, he couldn't even face her. *I didn't think so.*

It was his fault she couldn't even smile at him now. God, he was stupid. He cleared his throat. 'I'll give you a squawk if she's not there. No sense waiting around in this cold any longer than you have to.'

She nodded without looking at him and headed to the back of the building. Kevin tried the front door. Locked. He flattened his hands and pressed all eight apartment buttons at the same time. Somebody would buzz him in without bothering to check.

He was right. The door clicked open at the same time a male voice crackled 'Who is it?' over the speaker. Kevin slipped in and jogged up the stairs, figuring speed was more important than silence. At Johnson's apartment, he rapped on the door. Nothing. He rapped a second time, then rang the bell.

'Who is it?' The voice was muffled but definitely female.

'Annie Johnson? Millers Kill police. We'd like to talk to you about your daughter, Mikayla.'

There was no response, except for the thudding of footsteps and a thump.

'Ms Johnson! Millers Kill police. Open the door and put your hands on top of your head!'

His shoulder mic cracked on. 'She's running!' Hadley said. 'She's on the fire escape. She's carrying—' The line went dead. Kevin stepped back and smashed the flat of his boot against the door's lock. The shock of the impact vibrated up to his hip, but the door didn't budge. Dead bolt. Great. He spun around and leaped for the stairs, bouncing down three at a time until he arrived at the phone-booth-sized foyer. He burst through the outer door in time to see Hadley race past, clutching a . . . blanket? Pillow? He didn't waste time asking, just took off after her. He pounded up Causeway, rounding the corner and nearly running into Hadley, who was bent over, panting. 'Lost her,' she gasped.

Kevin scanned the area. 'Did you see if she cut between those buildings? She could have gone through the yards to Beale Street. Or maybe the back alley behind Depot.'

'Didn't see her.' Hadley sucked in air. 'She got too far ahead of me.'

'What the hell happened? I thought you had the fire escape covered?'

'I did! I was drawing my Taser and warning her to stop when she threw *this* over my head.' Hadley thrust the bundle toward him. It was one of those life-sized baby dolls, tied up in a couple of flannel blankets.

'She threatened you with a doll?'

'I thought it was a baby, dumb-ass! I dropped my Taser and dove for it. By the time I saw what it really was, she was off the fire escape and halfway down the street. *Shit!*' Hadley kicked a clump of ice into the street.

'Why are you still carrying it?'

Hadley looked down at the doll. 'I have no idea.' She tucked the decoy baby beneath her arm. 'Let's go see what we can find in her place.'

They went in through the fire escape window. Normally, Kevin was a stickler for observing the proprieties, but he didn't have the patience to track down the landlord or the management company and demand a key. He wanted to get in, get out, and hopefully salvage something from this goat cluster.

Annie Johnson's apartment was a mess – crumpled fast-food wrappers everywhere, garbage piled haphazardly around the trash can, clothes in cardboard boxes and broken laundry baskets. The kitchen smelled like someone had taken a dump in it, and the bathroom mold looked like something out of a horror movie about creeping slime.

Hadley tugged on her evidence gloves. 'Jesus. I am so looking forward to getting home tonight. My place is going to look like the Ritz-Carlton after this.'

Kevin was searching the kitchen cabinets for gasoline or kerosene when Hadley yelled, 'Flynn. C'mere.' He followed her voice into one of the bedrooms. Hadley had snapped on the overhead light. 'Take a look at this.'

The room looked like a pharmaceutical company's loading dock. No furniture, no decorations, just box after box filled with decongestants. 'Pseudoephedrine,' he said.

'All different kinds.' Hadley pointed out three different name brands and two generics in the box nearest them. 'Annie Johnson's been smurfing.'

'Yeah.' Since the Feds had starting restricting access to pseudoephedrine, meth cookers, who needed the drug to create methamphetamine, had gotten creative. The bigger operations switched to hijacking barrels of the stuff off

Chinese cargo ships. The smaller manufacturers hired smurfers, who traveled from pharmacy to pharmacy buying the legal limit with fake IDs. Smurfers usually worked in teams, making their purchases over a half hour or so, then hitting the next store.

'This is a lot for just one person to buy,' Hadley said.

'I was just thinking that.' Kevin gestured toward the narrow hallway. 'Any sign there's someone else living here?'

'One bedroom is set up for a little girl. I'm guessing it was Mikayla's before her mom lost custody. I didn't see any men's things in the other bedroom.'

'She could have a female roommate.'

'Maybe. One way or the other, she's got people helping her with this.' Hadley looked up at Kevin. 'Which means one of them might be holding Mikayla for her.'

She let Flynn make the call to the deputy chief. It was cowardly, but after twelve hours on duty, she just wasn't up to personally hearing what MacAuley thought of her brilliant police work. As it was, she winced every time Flynn said, 'Yes, but—' and 'I know, but—' Clearly, the dep was in rare form. When he hung up, Flynn looked a little green around the gills.

'He's calling in the state CSI van to take pictures and secure the evidence.'

'We're gonna need a bigger van,' she misquoted.

Flynn's face creased into what would have been a grin if they weren't both so tired. 'He wants you to stay here and see they get it all loaded. Then you can clock out.'

'What about you?'

'I'm going to write up the report and put in a records request to Children and Family Services and Johnson's bail bondsman. Eric's already heading over to the grandparents' to get their initial statement. We can follow up tomorrow.' He gave her a sly look. 'After you put in some track practice.'

She wound up staying another hour and a half. Sergeant Morin, their usual CSI tech, brought enough coffee for four. She drank hers and the one meant for Flynn as well, and left, after helping to load the van, with a great deal more energy and a warm glow of appreciation for the staties. She could make it home in time to put Genny to bed and check over Hudson's homework.

Her heart sank when she saw the rental car in Granddad's driveway. She adored her grandfather and was grateful he'd given her a home after her divorce, but at least once a month he had some old navy buddy up to visit. They would stay up until all hours drinking, which was bad for Granddad's diabetes, and smoking, which was bad for his heart. She squared her shoulders as she mounted the kitchen steps, readying herself to play Health Cop.

The door opened before she could grasp the handle. 'Honey!' She stared at the man in the doorway. He opened his arms wide. 'Come on in, babe, let me give you a hug!'

It wasn't a navy buddy. It was much, much worse. It was her ex-husband.

FOURTEEN

'What the hell are you doing here, Dylan?' Hadley stomped past him into the kitchen. She unzipped her MKPD parka and hung it on one of the coat hooks. She kept her back to him, struggling not to explode into a screaming fit. She had left California and moved across the country to get away from Dylan and everything he stood for. Now here he was, in her granddad's kitchen. She chafed at her nose. Maybe she was having a bad dream.

'That's it? Not even a hello? I haven't seen you for two years!'

Hadley took a breath and turned around. 'Exactly. Two years. During which time, the kids have gotten four phone calls, three postcards, and one Christmas package from you.'

'I was broke! You're going to bust my balls because I couldn't afford to shower the kids with presents?'

'I'm busting your balls, as you so sweetly put it, because you only remember you have kids a couple times a year. And the thought of them has never, ever inspired you to get off your ass and do something with them. So I repeat: What are you doing here?'

Dylan shook his head. 'Look at you. What has this cop job done to you? You used to be a beautiful woman. Now you look like an angry dyke in motorcycle boots. You don't even have breasts anymore!'

'I'm wearing a tac vest under the uniform, you—' She cut herself off. God. Two minutes and he already had her justifying herself to him. *Breathe. Breathe.* 'I'll ask you one more time before I throw you out. What. Do. You. Want?'

He looked over his shoulder, his face breaking into that charming, lazy smile she knew all too well. 'Why don't we discuss it after we get these guys to bed?' She turned around. Granddad, Hudson, and Genny were standing in the doorway between the kitchen and the den. Hudson was grinning at his father like he was a week off from school and a trip to Disney World. Genny hung back, sheltering under Granddad's arm.

'Can Dad tuck me in?' Hudson asked. 'Please?'

Hadley glanced at the clock over the sink. It was barely his bedtime. Usually he was bargaining like an assistant DA for five or ten or fifteen more minutes. She closed her hands into fists to keep from snatching him up and carrying him away from his father. 'If he's willing to, sure.'

'Willing? I'd love it! How about you, princess?'

Genny shook her head. 'I want Mommy to tuck me in.'

Dylan squatted down. 'You sure?' Genny nodded her head. 'Okay, then. C'mon, ninja boy!' He swooped down and tossed Hudson over his shoulder. Hudson shrieked with laughter. Hadley felt like she was looking through the wrong end of a telescope. Was this her son, so prickly about his new maturity as a sixth grader? He hadn't let her pick him up in ... at least two years. Of course. He had been nine when he last saw his father. Eight when they still all lived together. All Hudson's memories were from that sweet spot of childhood.

She looked down at her daughter, still holding on to Granddad. She'd been five when Hadley had kicked Dylan out. Hadley took her free hand. 'Do you remember Daddy, sweetheart?'

'Sorta.' Genny looked toward the stairs.

'You know, it's okay if you feel a little shy around your dad. He'll understand. You can take time to get to know him again.' *Unless I get my way and he's headed out of town before midnight.* Hadley had a premonition she wasn't going to be that lucky.

'Okay.'

'I want you to go upstairs and get on your nightie and brush your teeth. I'll be up in a minute to tuck you in.'

Genny frowned up at her. 'No one's going to come into my room, are they?'

'No, sweetheart. Just shut your door. I'll give you our special knock when I get up there.'

'Okay.' Genny kissed Granddad good night and headed upstairs. As soon as Hadley was sure her daughter was out of earshot, she turned on her grandfather. 'What happened?'

'I'm sorry, Honey. That sumbitch showed up at the door smilin' and carryin' on like I was his long-lost granddaddy. I tried to get rid of him, but he started going on about he's dying to see the kids, and how you and him are supposed to be sharing custody.'

Hadley rubbed her forehead with the heel of her hand. 'Yeah, well, that's true as far as it goes. We do have joint custody. He's just never given a damn about exercising his rights.' That phrase from her custody agreement had never seemed so ominous. 'He wants something. That's the only reason I can think he'd come all the way out here.'

'Mebbe he's moving?' Granddad, who had lived all his seventy-six years in Millers Kill, had never understood why someone would want to live anywhere else.

'No. The only reason Dylan leaves LA is to gamble in Vegas or to hang out with fourth-rate celebrities in Mexico.'

'Mebbe he's on the lam.'

'I wish. Then I could arrest him and be done with him. Look, I have to get out of this uniform and tuck Genny in. Will you—'

'I'll keep myself right here in the den,' Granddad said. 'You'll want some privacy, I reckon. You can talk to dipshit in the dining room.'

Hadley smiled a little. 'Thanks, Granddad.' She glanced outside the window, where the lone streetlamp cast an orange glow over the snow drifted up to the top step of the porch. 'Maybe I'll make him stand in the yard and talk to me via cell phone.' She ran upstairs. From Hudson's room, she could hear what sounded like a story being read. In her bedroom, she shut her door, locked it, then stuck a chair against it for good measure. Stupid, probably, but Dylan was never one to underestimate his so-called seductive charm. She secured her sidearm in her lock box, stripped out of her uniform, and was in Genny's room, dressed in jeans and a sweater, in under four minutes.

Dylan was already downstairs when she finished tucking Genny in. Hadley stopped by the fridge, grabbed a beer for herself, put it back, took out a soda instead, and then, in a burst of creative genius, got the beer for Dylan. The only arguments she could ever remember winning were when he was drunk or stoned. Maybe her record would stand.

He was sitting in Granddad's chair, tilted back on two legs. 'Love what you've done to the old place, baby. Early twentieth-century poverty, right?'

She tossed a coaster in front of him and clunked his beer onto it. 'Put the chair down. You're not twelve.'

He rocked forward and twisted the beer open. 'Now this is the way it should be.' He slugged down half the bottle. 'You and me, sitting around the table in the ancestral manse, sharing a drink after a long day.' He cocked his head, an affectation that made his silky dark hair feather across one side of his face, highlighting his jaw and cheekbones. It had made her swoon when she was eighteen. Now, she noticed, it also highlighted a little sagging skin under his chin and an increasing number of lines along his throat.

'I'm ready to talk business,' she said. 'Tell me what you came here for, and I'll let you know what I can do about it.'

'You really don't believe I came here to see my kids, do you?'

Hadley pushed away from the table. 'Fine. Feel free to drop in tomorrow morning. We'll have pancakes, and then the kids and you and Granddad can play board games. They'll really like that. Good night. You can find your way out.' She stood up.

'Wait,' he said.

'I'm tired and I have to work tomorrow. If you're just going to bullshit me, I'm going to bed.'

'Sit down,' he said. She sat. 'Okay, it's like this. I've been offered this really great producing opportunity. It's a reality show about Vegas hookers.'

'Really.'

'It's totally straight, for cable. It'll have celebrities and make overs and all the glamour of the Strip. We're pitching to the Vegas tourism board to see if we can get some funding from them.'

'Let me know when it's playing. I'll make sure to miss it.' Of course, it never would make it that far. Dylan would cross the wrong guys, or try to sell it to Nickelodeon, or put all his partners' money up his nose.

'I just need twenty grand.'

'Oh, for God's sake. Look around you, Dylan. I don't have twenty grand. I don't have two grand. I'm still paying off the Visa balance and the tax bill you stuck me with. I live from paycheck to paycheck, and if I'm lucky, maybe I'll be able to put a little aside in the kids' college fund now and then.'

'How much is in there?'

She was grateful she had locked away her Glock already, because she could have shot him on the spot. 'Do you actually think I'd let you steal your own children's future for one of your crappy pie-in-the-sky projects?'

'Hey! You and I did all right, and neither of us went to college.'

'I don't even want to *think* what you mean by that. The answer is no, Dylan. No cash, no college money, no nothing. You should have called first. I could have told you all this over the phone while you were hanging out at whoever's house you're sponging off of right now, and we both would've been a lot happier.' She stood up.

'Then give me back DHK Productions.'

Their old filmmaking company. She should have known. 'What do you mean? There aren't any assets there.'

'There are the movies.'

She thudded into her chair again. 'There's no way I'm giving you those films.'

'Think about it, Honey—'

'Don't call me that.' She had never liked the ridiculous name her parents had saddled her with. In the context of the movies she had made when she was eighteen and nineteen and twenty, it sounded obscene.

'Okay, okay.' He raised his hands. '*Hadley.* Think about it. Those films were never digitized. They sold like crazy back when we were in business, but they've been unavailable for ten years. You sign 'em back over to me. I'll digitize them. I've got a distributor already lined up. We could take in forty thousand easy, maybe more! I'll split the net with you. Think what that'd do for the kids' college fund.'

'No.'

'What do you mean, no?'

'I mean no. As in no goddamn way I'm releasing those movies. I changed my name and moved three thousand miles so I could get away from that time in my life.' She snapped her mouth shut before she could spill any more. If Dylan knew how desperate she was to keep her past buried, he'd be at the station tomorrow morning, telling the chief all about her former life in porn.

'Goddammit, Honey – Hadley, I mean. It's the answer to both our problems. I could seal my deal, and you wouldn't have to live in this dump of a house with your grandfather. You could pay off the IRS.'

She wrapped her hand tightly around her bottle. 'I'm in debt to the IRS because *you*' – she pointed at him – 'signed over complete ownership of DHK to avoid going to jail for tax fraud. And you know what? I'm glad you did. Because even if I'm still paying off that debt when I'm in adult diapers, I can make sure those movies never go into circulation again.'

'They're still out there!'

She leaned back and took a swallow of her soda. 'Sixteen-year-old videotapes aren't "out there". They're sitting in the bottom of cardboard boxes in basements.'

'Yeah? I've still got my copies. Maybe I'll just digitize 'em and sell them anyway, cut you out of the profits completely.'

'Okay, one? Digital copies of old VHS tapes are going to look like shit. Two, no distributor is going to take your shitty copies if you can't prove you've got legal right to them. And three, stop treating me like I'm still a stupid twenty-year-old. I realize that you thought I was never going to get out from under your thumb when you signed the company over to me. But I did, and now you're stuck with it.'

Dylan leaned back in his chair and looked at her through half-closed eyes while he drank his beer. He put the bottle down, leaned forward, and spread his hands on the table. 'I need that money. You either sign the rights back to me and hand over the master reels or come up with twenty thousand.'

Hadley opened her mouth.

'If you don't, I'm taking the kids back to California with me.'

The air squeezed out of her lungs. She couldn't speak, couldn't breathe, couldn't think.

'You've been in violation of our custody agreement for over two years now. You took my children three thousand miles away. I could get sole custody with one phone call after that.'

She found her breath again. 'You told me it was okay.' Her voice came out in a squeak. She took another breath. 'We discussed it. You said you had no problem with it.'

Dylan shrugged. 'There's nothing in writing. It's going to be your word against mine. And how much weight do you think the judge at the Family Court is going to give to the word of an aging porn star?' He stood up. 'I'm flying back on Thursday, either with my money or my movies or my kids. Your choice. *Honey.*'

Saturday, 10 January

ONE

Clare awoke to sunlight streaming through the windows and Oscar whining to go out.

'Quiet, dog.' Russ's voice was low. Through the French doors separating the bedroom from the rest of the cabin, she heard the creak of the kitchen door opening and the tick-tick of Oscar's nails as he trotted out to do his business.

'Do you think it's okay to let him out without one of us with him?' She raised her voice to be heard.

Russ came around the counter and crossed the open space – Clare wasn't sure if it was meant to be a very small den or a very large extended kitchen – to open the French doors. 'Sorry. I didn't mean to wake you up.'

She took a moment to admire the sight of Russ bare-chested, his jeans riding low on his hips. 'That's okay. It looks like past time I was out of bed, anyway.' She glanced around the bedroom. Across from where Russ stood was another pair of French doors leading, Russ had assured her, to a little flagstone patio, now buried in snow. In front of her, where an old horsehair sofa held a haphazard pile of their luggage, another huge window gave a breathtaking view of the lake. 'Wow,' she said. 'It sure looks better by daylight.'

Russ laughed. 'Told you. Feel like some sausage and eggs?'

'If you're cooking, sure.' She yelped when her feet hit the floor and hustled over to the sofa to dig through her suitcase for her slippers.

'That's one of the things I'd like to do if we buy the place,' Russ said. 'Put in hot water pipes under the flooring. It's basically always-on heat.'

'I could go for that.' She followed him to the kitchen and hoisted herself none too gracefully onto one of the tall stools beneath the counter. The kitchen was a simple U shape, with the cheap laminate counter forming the outer half. It ended in a dry sink and some ramshackle drawers. Russ had stacked a wall of water jugs next to the faucetless sink. The bottom of the U was taken up by an old-fashioned wood-fired cooking stove, currently sending off delicious smells and waves of heat. The door Oscar had just gone through was kitty-corner to the stove, its window letting in the only natural light in the kitchen. Next to it were open shelving and a propane-fueled refrigerator that they hadn't bothered to start up last night.

Russ slid a couple of orange and avocado melamine plates in front of her and handed over a mismatched jumble of flatware. 'Looks like the owners furnished the place with Mother's hand-me-downs,' she said, laying out two places.

'Or Grandma's.' Russ tapped the stove with a spatula before shoveling up a huge bowl of scrambled eggs. 'I hope you're hungry.'

'Are you kidding? When am I not hungry these days?' The eggs were followed onto the counter by a plate full of sausages. Clare didn't even wait for her husband to take a stool before she started chowing down. 'Angkhhs,' she said around a mouthful. 'Ih gugh.'

Russ sat beside her and helped himself to eggs and sausage. 'Here's what I'm thinking about for this area,' he said. 'We can't change the footprint of the house, because of the conservation easement. But we can do anything we want within those limits. I'd like to move the bathroom from there' – he thumbed at the curtain-covered doorway that stood between the counter and the bedroom – 'to where the fridge is now. Move the kitchen into this space, open it up, and convert where it is now to a mudroom-slash-utilities-room.'

Clare swiped a napkin over her mouth. 'Are you planning to upgrade that drafty drop toilet? I thought my ladybits were going to freeze off last night when I went to the bathroom.'

Russ grinned. 'Don't worry, darlin'. I have a vested interest in keeping your ladybits nice and warm. I'll put in a very up-to-date chemical composting john.' He pointed through a wide rectangular archway to the central room and enclosed porch that formed the longest part of the L-shaped cabin.

'Over there will be a family room/dining room/library combination.' It looked like the owners had had a similar multi-usage idea, as the room currently held an armoire, a rectangular table shoved against one wall, and two squishy chairs in front of a small woodstove.

'I'm thinking I could install bookshelves under those pretty clerestory windows and add matching windows to the other side. I could fit another set of French doors in that archway real easy, to match the ones leading to the bedroom on this side.'

'Sounds beautiful.' Clare swallowed a last bite of egg, wiped her mouth, and slid off her stool. She crossed into the center room. 'But where do our guests sleep?' She looked up. There was an unadorned loft space above her, dark and inaccessible.

Russ followed her. 'No guests.'

She gave him a look.

'All right, all right. The loft runs to the end of the kitchen. If we finish it off, it'll be big enough for two bedrooms. Two very small bedrooms. I don't want any visitors getting too comfortable.'

'If one of them is going to be the baby's room, you're going to have to put in stairs. There's no way I'm climbing up and down that thing' – she thumbed toward a wooden ladder wedged into the corner – 'while holding an infant. Or worse, a squirming toddler.'

Russ grunted. She thought, *Please let's talk about this*, but all he said was 'I can build stairs. Don't worry.'

He turned around. The top of the cabin's L had once been its main entrance; it still sported a door and a pair of wide widows. At some point, someone had added on a finished porch. In the summer, it would be perfect – cool breezes and a to-die-for view of the lake. Now, it stood cold and bare of furniture.

'I'd like to winterize the porch,' Russ said. Evidently, the discussion of the baby's room was over. 'Insulation, hypocaust heating – that's the pipes under the floor – and double-paned glass. There's this cool thing I've been wanting to try. Mesh screen that rolls up into the top of the frame. You slide up the winter windows, roll down the screen, and bam, you're ready for summer.'

Clare put her frustration and disappointment away. They would have plenty of time to talk. The thought of time caught at her. 'How long do you think it will take to do all these improvements?'

'Depends on how many weekends we can get away. If we try to get up here regularly, and if we take our vacation time . . . I'd estimate five or six years.'

'Five or six years? That's not a weekend getaway. That's a construction project!'

'It's been on the market for years because nobody's wanted to deal with the challenges. I do.'

'You mean challenges like no electricity, plumbing, or running water?'

'This place could be a showpiece with a little elbow grease and thought.' Russ took the poker off its hanger and opened the woodstove door. 'Solar panels on the cabin and boathouse roofs. Rainwater collection into cisterns. Maybe even a wind-powered pumping system.' He shoved a half-burned log toward the back and tossed in another split. 'Better add on another year or two to my estimate.'

'Seven or eight years.' Clare sat in one of the squishy chairs, tucking her feet up under her flannel nightgown to get them off the cold floor. 'I had no idea you were so green and eco-minded.'

'It's not that.' He dropped into the chair opposite her and stretched out his legs to rest his booted feet on the woodstove's raised brick hearth. 'Taking this on means we can get a lake house we can afford, with great water frontage and lots of privacy. I know it seems like a long time to share the space with sawdust and power tools, but we'll be building something we can enjoy for the rest of our lives.'

She smiled. 'I like the sound of that.'

'Me, too. Maybe it was all those years of army housing, where I couldn't even paint the walls. It left me with the need to leave my mark on my surroundings. "Russ Van Alstyne was here".'

She couldn't resist. She drew her nightgown taut across her rounded belly. 'Russ Van Alstyne was here,' she said.

'Jesus! Not like that.' His cheeks went pink.

'Will we be able to do all this work with a baby underfoot?'

'Underfoot? It's not even born yet!'

'Russ.' They had known about the baby for almost three months now, but he was still refusing to accept the timeline. 'The baby's due by the end of April. By this time next year, we'll have an eight-and-a-half-month-old. When you start working on the house that summer, she'll be over a year, toddling around and getting into things.'

Russ pushed himself out of his chair. 'I don't want to get into it now. Can't we just have a relaxing vacation without rehashing all that stuff? Please?'

'It's getting a little hard to pretend I'm not pregnant, don't you think? I'm starting to blow up like the Pillsbury Doughboy.'

'Don't say that. You look beautiful.' He touched the side of her cheek, feather-light, then stood. 'I'll clean the dishes. You get dressed, and I'll show you what ice fishing is all about.'

'Okay.' She tried not to feel defeated.

He paused in the archway, his back still toward her. 'You said "she". At the last exam, did you—'

'I was just picking a pronoun. I want it to be a surprise.'

His voice was dry. 'You already managed that part, Clare.'

TWO

'This is it,' Hadley said, peering through the squad car's windshield at the mailbox. She double-checked her notebook. 'Fifty-five Canal Street, Fort Henry.'

It was a quiet street, full of small, neat houses that had probably been built after World War II. The sort of neighborhood that had seen several generations of kids grow up and move away. Probably not too many had come back – Hadley saw a lot of meticulously cleared walkways and drives, but no snowmen or sleds left in the yards.

Kevin pulled up to the curb. 'Huh. Just a few blocks away from my place. I wonder if I've seen them before.'

It was the first thing he'd said during the morning ride from Millers Kill that might be considered personal. Of course, seeing as how Hadley had once spent the night at his place just a few blocks away, it might be very personal indeed. She had been stiff and quiet through the morning briefing and hadn't relaxed in the squad car. He hoped it was just nerves about their responsibility for the investigation and not discomfort about working with him.

She flipped over her notebook to an earlier page. 'You want to try the bail bondsman or her lawyer one more time? Before we talk to the grandparents?'

'No. They're just as likely to know where Annie might be and who her associates are. People will confide things to their parents they wouldn't tell anyone else.'

Hadley snorted. 'Not me. I never told anything to my parents if I could avoid it.'

They got out of the cruiser. The sun off the snow was almost blinding, and the air felt softer and warmer than it usually did in early January. Might be due for what his mother called a strawberry spring – a few days' thaw in the midst of the long, cold upstate New York winter. Kevin put his cover on. 'What did the CFS caseworker know about them?'

'They're the mom's parents. They'd applied for custody of Mikayla but got passed over in favor of the MacAllens.'

He gestured for her to precede him up the walk. 'Because of the transplant issue?'

Hadley shrugged. 'Maybe. You know how Children and Family Services are.' Getting info out of CFS was like prying one of Genny's stuffed animals away from her. You could do it, but it was going to cost you no end of grief.

'Oh, yeah.' There was still a cheery Christmas wreath hanging on the front door. Flynn knocked. 'We'll need to get a warrant going ASAP. I can—'

The door swung open before he could say anything else. Kevin got an impression of dark eyes and a deeply creased face before the man holding the door open said, 'Thank God. Come in, please. Come in.' He stepped back so they could enter the living room. 'I'm Lewis Johnson.'

Hadley and Flynn both wiped their feet on the large mat in front of the door. Mr Johnson closed it behind them. Kevin took off his lid and stowed it beneath his arm. 'Mr Johnson. I'm Officer Flynn, and this is Officer Knox.'

Kevin took in Johnson's mahogany skin and the crucifix hanging in the foyer while Hadley shook the older man's hand. Latino? Then he spotted the bead and quill work decorating the walls and revised his opinion to Iroquois. Probably Mohawk, in this part of the state.

A sixty-something woman emerged from the kitchen, still wiping her hands on a dishtowel. 'This is my wife, June,' Johnson said.

'Have you found her? Do you know where she is?'

Hadley glanced at Kevin. 'No, ma'am,' he said. 'We don't know where your daughter or Mikayla are yet.'

'The sergeant who was here last night said they might be together.'

'Sit down, June.' Johnson gestured for them to take two chairs in the tiny living room. 'Let's let these officers ask their questions and see if we can help sort things out.'

Kevin perched awkwardly on the chair, which was a little too short for his legs. 'We went to your daughter's apartment on Causeway Street last night. She fled when I tried to speak with her. She was alone at the time, but there were girl's things in one of the bedrooms.'

'Mikayla's room,' Mrs Johnson said. 'She was hoping to get unsupervised overnight visits, but the court won't allow it.'

'When we searched the apartment, we also found a large amount of over-the-counter pseudoephedrine, which is used in making—'

'Crystal meth,' Mr Johnson said. His voice was deep and heavy. 'We know much too much about what goes into making crystal meth.'

'She used to steal it from us,' his wife said. 'We had to put a combination lock on our medicine cabinet. Then she started stealing money to buy it with. When she started stealing our belongings to sell . . .' Her sigh was the sound of an unhappy nostalgia, looking back to the bad old days that had reared their head again.

'Right now,' Kevin said, 'we're working on the theory that Annie was in some way involved with your granddaughter's kidnapping.' He hoped to God this wasn't going to be one of those cases where an addict mother exchanges her child for her next fix. 'However, since your granddaughter wasn't with Annie last night, we think there must be a person or persons helping her.'

'Not necessarily,' Johnson said. 'She's quite capable of leaving Mikayla alone in a parked car all night. Or in a grocery store. Or at a rest stop.'

'We've already put an AMBER Alert out on Mikayla,' Hadley said. 'If she's in a public place, chances are good someone will find her. In the meantime, we'll be doing everything we can to get her back. Does Annie have any friends who might be involved? Maybe a boyfriend?'

'We don't know any of her friends anymore,' Mrs Johnson said.

'She doesn't have friends,' Mr Johnson said. 'Just fellow users. Any one of them would sell another for the price of a fix.'

Mrs Johnson touched her husband's arm. 'She does have a boyfriend. Travis Roy. They've been together about a year, year and a half.'

'What do you know about him?' Hadley said, writing in her notebook.

'He's bad news,' Mr Johnson said. 'Just like all of her boyfriends. A jailbird with tattoos up one side and down the other and a mean streak.'

Mrs Johnson gave him a look. 'He's a white man, about, I don't know, five-nine? He has dark hair that he keeps very short.'

Mr Johnson stood up. 'I think we have a picture of the two of them somewhere you can have.' He went to a flip-down writing desk and opened a drawer.

'You said he was a jailbird? Do you know what he was in for?'

Mrs Johnson frowned. 'Annie said he'd been in Fishkill for possession. And he was arrested for some sort of firearms violation. Carrying an unregistered weapon?'

Mr Johnson returned to his seat and handed a photograph to Kevin. It showed an attractive if too thin woman with a midnight fall of hair standing next to a rope-muscled guy who looked like he could be a redneck gang enforcer. A little girl in shorts and a Hannah Montana T-shirt stood in front of them, grinning to reveal a missing tooth. 'That's Mikayla,' Johnson said.

Her grandmother smiled a little tearfully. 'She's such a wonderful girl. Despite the chaos in her life and some of the horrible things she's seen. She's smart and creative and funny.'

'We have her with us as much as possible,' Mr Johnson said. 'I mean, before the accident. Sometimes she'd stay with us for weeks at a time while Annie was off doing God-knows-what. Whenever Annie called, wherever she was, we'd drop what we were doing and come get Mikayla.'

'But you didn't get custody of her after the accident.' Kevin handed the photo to Hadley, who tucked it into her pocket.

'We didn't even know where she was. She'd show up for her visits with a caseworker. She'd talk to us about how well Mikayla was doing after her transplant, and all the time looking at us like we might be cooking meth in the kitchen. But you know what? It's not the first time an Indian child's been taken away from her family by white folks. I thought it was bullshit—'

'Lewis!'

'—and we're not going to take it,' he continued. 'June and I are taking classes at the Washington County Hospital for caretakers of transplant recipients. And we're getting qualified as licensed foster parents. As soon as we're done, we're reapplying for custody. I suspect – I hope – that when Annie goes to trial, she'll be locked away for a few years.'

Mrs Johnson took his hand and squeezed it hard. Kevin thought of his own family. He could imagine how his parents would suffer if one of his brothers went down that broken road.

Mr Johnson shook his head. 'And now this.' He let out a sigh that seemed to rumble up from the basement of his soul.

'Why would she take Mikayla? Why?' Mrs Johnson dropped her husband's hand and stood abruptly.

'Is there anyone else you can think of who might have reason to take Mikayla?' Kevin looked from one Johnson to the other. 'Her father, maybe? CFS didn't have a name for him.'

'Hector DeJean.' Mr Johnson looked even more grim than before. 'He was another mean son of a bitch.'

'Lewis . . .'

'Let's call a spade a spade, June. Annie wouldn't put him on the birth certificate because she was afraid what would happen if the state went after him for support money. He used to hit her all the time. She finally left him after she fell pregnant, and he tracked her down and beat the shit out of her. It's a miracle she didn't lose Mikayla. And then she *still* turned around and started in with one of his friends.' He shook his head. 'She doesn't care. So long as he can give her drugs, she doesn't care.'

'What happened to DeJean?' Hadley asked.

Johnson grunted. 'He did four years in Plattsburgh for assault.'

'Has he had any contact with Mikayla since?'

'Oh, yeah. He came back around when he got out three years ago, all changed and reformed.' Johnson's tone left no doubt what he thought about DeJean's alleged reformation.

'He got counseling for domestic abusers in prison,' Mrs Johnson said. 'Anger management, dealing with conflict, that sort of thing.'

'Bunch of crap,' Johnson said. 'Women-beaters never change. They're like pedophiles. Best thing to do would be to put them down like rabid dogs.'

'Lewis!' Mrs Johnson sat back down. 'He doesn't mean that.'

'Yes, I do.'

'Hector sees Mikayla every month or two,' she said. 'Not since she's been in foster care, of course, because he doesn't have any legal claim to her.'

'Has he ever been violent with Mikayla?' Hadley asked. 'Has she ever expressed any fear of him?'

Mrs Johnson shook her head. 'No. He's living with a woman named Dede . . . something or the other.'

'Probably beating that woman, too. She just doesn't have the brains to leave him.'

'Oh, Lewis, for heaven's sake.'

'I'll tell you something.' Johnson raised his finger and looked directly into Kevin's eyes. 'When your sergeant was here last night, telling us what had happened, the first person I thought of was Hector DeJean. I don't care if he's living with the Blessed Virgin and the infant Christ, that man is completely capable of killing two innocent people and burning their house down.'

THREE

Clare lasted an hour ice fishing. In the five years since she'd moved to the southern Adirondacks, she had learned to enjoy certain winter sports. Cross-country skiing. Snowshoeing. Sports that involved activity, and movement, and working up a sweat.

'I've got it all set up for us,' Russ said, as he shouldered a large duffel bag and helped her off the embankment and onto the ice. She was still enough of a native Virginian to get a thrill when she stepped onto a frozen lake. They walked between the cabin's dock and the boathouse, which, she discovered, was basically a garage. If a garage had a floor of solid ice.

'The easement allows us to bump the boathouse ceiling up a few feet, which means I can build a good-sized guest room above the docking part,' Russ said. He went on about the solar panels and heating the place and water reclamation while Clare marveled at the landscape – the waterscape? – unfolding as they walked farther and farther from the embankment. Hemlocks and fir trees and eastern white pine crowded the shore as far as the eye could see, anchoring the glaring white expanse with their dark green solidity. The ice beneath their boots was a pale layering of translucent brightness and cloudy depth, bordered by irregular drifts of snow. It re-minded her, she realized, of the rocky desert plains of Iraq, and she had a sudden prickling sensation between her shoulder blades. They were com-pletely exposed. Completely vulnerable. She must have made some noise, because Russ cut himself off and said, 'Are you okay?'

'Just . . . the space. For a moment, it felt like we were about to get lit up with mortar fire.'

'Do you want to go back?'

She took a firmer grip on his arm. 'No. Just keep talking. How long is Inverary?'

'About nine miles.' He pointed to the east. 'That's where that little cluster of year-round houses and the store are. You can't see them from here because the lake curves slightly.'

'Are you kidding? I can barely see the houses over there.' She nodded toward the opposite shore.

'Well, this is the widest part of the lake. It's a good mile across at this end.'

'Are there any homes on the little island?' Truth to be told, it didn't look that little as they got closer to it. It humped up from the ice like a mythic world-turtle, dark and shaggy green.

'No. That's part of the conservation area. I understand it's a nice place to row out and have a picnic in the summer.'

'It's hard to imagine this place crowded with people and boats and campers. It feels like we're the last two human beings on earth out here.'

'There's always our good friend Amber and her baby daddy. I doubt we'll see them out on the ice, though. And here we are.' He gestured with a flourish at a ragged-edged hole in the ice.

Clare peered down into it. It was about the size of a large dinner plate, its gray-blue edges dropping almost a foot until it met black water. 'I thought it would be larger.'

'You don't need a manhole opening. It just needs to be big enough to get the lines in and the fish out.' He unzipped the duffel and drew out two bath mats and two folding canvas camp chairs. He ceremoniously laid the mats across the hole from each other and set up a chair on each mat. Then he reached back into the duffel and handed Clare a thermos and a wool blanket. 'Hot cocoa.' He put his own thermos on the ice and tossed a second blanket onto his seat. 'Best part of ice fishing. Excepting catching the fish, of course.' He carefully pulled two fishing poles and a Tupperware box of bait out of the duffel.

'Anything else in there? Umbrella? Potted plant?'

'Couple of sandwiches and some of those chemical hand warmers, in case you get cold.'

'You certainly come prepared, Chief Van Alstyne.'

He grinned at her. They baited their hooks with chunks of leftover sausage and dropped them into the hole. 'Now what?' Clare asked, arranging the blanket around her legs.

'Now we fish.'

It turned out when he said 'fish', Russ meant 'wait'. They sat and chatted, and sat and were silent, and sat and drank cocoa, and sat and flexed their fingers, and sat and watched the clouds slowly overcast the sun, so that the sky became the same color as the lake's icy surface.

Clare tried dropping her line low, spooling it high, jiggling it up and down. Finally, she said, 'Russ. I love you.'

He raised his eyebrows. 'Thanks. I love you, too.'

'But this is the most boring thing I've ever done.'

He laughed.

'My brain is going as numb as my feet.'

He reached for her pole. 'Tell you what. Why don't I walk you back and get myself some more hot cocoa, and you can prop your feet up in front of the woodstove and read.'

'Do you mind?'

'Hell, no. You lasted half an hour longer than I thought you would.'

She stood up and stomped her boots to restore circulation. 'This is payback for that helicopter ride I took you on, isn't it?'

He held out his arm. 'There will *never* be enough payback for that trip.'

As they walked away from the fishing hole, Clare felt that sense of exposure and vulnerability rising again. The dock and the boathouse seemed very far away. The trees, rising steeply up from the water, could hide any-thing – a sniper, a mortar unit, a band of Iraqi rebels. *That's utterly ridiculous.* The thought couldn't stop her heart rate from rising, though.

Then she saw it. A glint though the trees, high up where the road would be. Like sunlight off a rifle barrel. 'Gun!' she yelled, then hit the ice, curling around her belly as if she could protect her baby from a .38.

Of course, nothing happened. No shot, no thud of bullets into flesh, no sudden cries.

'Clare?' Russ knelt down next to her.

'Oh, God.' She pushed herself up to her knees and clambered to her feet. 'I'm so sorry. I saw a light or something through the trees and I thought it was a gun.'

Russ put his arms around her and held her tight. 'Don't apologize. It's okay. You're okay, darlin'.'

'Goddammit. I just want to get the war out of my head once and for all.' Her voice was muffled by his parka.

'It takes a long time for those instincts to settle down. And they never really go entirely away. Look at me.'

His own combat service had left scars on Russ's body and mind. 'Yeah. You can't walk through a green forest without watching for snipers, and I can't be out in the open without thinking I'm going to be lit up.' She laughed shakily. 'Are you sure this is going to be the best choice of a vacation home for us?'

'Sure. You stay inside during the winter, and I'll stay inside during the summer. It'll be like a time-share.' She laughed a little more strongly this time. 'C'mon,' he said. 'Let's get you home.'

Back in the cabin, Oscar was thrilled to see them. He quivered and bumped against their legs as Russ stoked up the fires and Clare made more hot cocoa. 'I'll go get the fishing stuff and bring it back up here,' he said when she handed him his thermos.

'You don't need to do that. I'm fine. Go catch us dinner.'

He frowned. 'Hmm. Let me at least trot up to the road and see if I can spot what it is you saw.'

'Oh, Russ. I was probably imagining it.' She hadn't had a flashback in several months – not since she started a new REM therapy with her counselor – but she had had some doozies in the summer and early fall.

'It'll just take me a sec. Hang on.'

She smiled at him, one-sided. 'Hanging on.'

He paused at the kitchen door. 'That's my girl. C'mon, Oscar.'

While they were gone, Clare traded her ski overalls and wool socks for flannel maternity pants and slippers. She picked a mystery from the stack of books she had brought up with them and took it to one of the squishy chairs. The wood stove was radiating heat, and the icebound lake that had seemed so scary while she was walking across its surface looked like a beautiful picture through the porch windows.

God, I want a drink. She could almost taste the bourbon, feel it burning its way down. Three or four glasses and all these stupid feelings would float away. Or maybe a couple of uppers, to set her heart tripping and her mind buzzing, racing ahead so fast the bad things in her head couldn't catch up with her.

Behind her, the kitchen door opened. She started, as if Russ would be able to tell what she had been thinking about. 'You did see something,' he said, wiping his feet on the mat. 'There were fresh tracks. Looks like a vehicle drove past and somebody got out to take a look.' He took the thermos off the counter. 'You probably saw the sun catch his sideview mirror or something.'

Oscar came up and nudged his head beneath her hand. She scratched between his ears. 'Why would someone stop and check out our cabin?'

'Could be somebody nosy, like that guy in the SUV last night. But that's a hard haul through unplowed road to drive all the way down this lane and then back up to the North Shore Drive. My guess is it's a winter caretaker. Some of the places along this stretch are very pricey. It wouldn't surprise me if there's a local guy who swings around on weekends to keep an eye on things. Saw that someone had parked in the garage up there, stopped to make sure we weren't a couple of kids making trouble.' He clomped over to her and dropped a kiss on her hair. 'Will you be okay if I go back fishing?'

'Yes, I will.' She smiled. 'If somebody comes, I'll sic Oscar on 'em.' Oscar perked up at the sound of his name, his tail thumping on the floor.

'Oh, yeah. He's a real killer.' The dog licked Russ's hand. 'Okay. See you soon.'

She did indeed prop her feet up on the hearth. The fire popped and snapped. Oscar circled thrice and thumped to the floor next to her chair. She picked up her book.

Maybe the last renters had left a bottle of something behind in one of the cabinets?

Stop it. She pressed her hands against the hard curve of her belly. *Haven't you done enough damage already?*

FOUR

Sitting in the obstetrician's office on that first visit in November had been one of the most humiliating experiences of Clare's life. She knew – she *knew* – that every other pregnant woman in the waiting room had been taking folic acid six months before conceiving and had stopped drinking as soon as the stick turned blue. The doctor, who looked like someone's kindly grand-mother, laid the sonographer's report on her desk as she indicated the chairs opposite. Clare and Russ sat.

The doctor tapped the sonograms. 'Based on the fetal measurements, I'd estimate you're fifteen weeks along, Ms Fergusson. When was your last period?'

'Well . . . that's part of the problem. I was taking birth control pills. I had several . . . they seemed light but I *thought*—'

'We weren't trying to get pregnant,' Russ said.

The doctor frowned and folded her hands. 'We don't do terminations at our practice, but I can refer you to—'

'No,' Clare said firmly.

Russ cleared his throat. 'There's also an issue of . . .' He glanced at Clare.

'Substance abuse.' She was amazed she could get the words out, her throat was so dry. 'I didn't realize I was pregnant, as I said . . .' Her voice trailed off. She took a deep breath. 'I was taking sleeping pills. And amphetamines.' Her eyes felt hot and prickly. 'And I was drinking pretty heavily.'

Russ took her hand and squeezed tightly. He gave her a look of com-plete and utter understanding. He himself had been dry for over a decade, but his experience as an alcoholic made him uniquely sympathetic to the temptations to drink. 'She just got back from a tour of duty in Iraq five

89

months ago. She was having a hard time readjusting. As soon as she found out she was pregnant, she stopped.'

He didn't want to be here, he disagreed with her decision, and he still leaped to her defense. Even under these excruciating circumstances, it made her heart lift.

'I see. Are you getting any support for your sobriety?'

'I'm seeing a therapist twice a week,' Clare said.

'Is there any way to tell if there's been any damage?' Russ leaned forward. 'At this point, I mean?'

The doctor pursed her lips. 'There's no evidence at this time that amphetamines or sleeping pills are teratogenic – that they cause any birth defects. Although obviously, I don't recommend you take either during pregnancy.' She looked down at the sonograms. 'It looks like the fetus has good spinal closure; there's no evidence of hydrocephaly or any of the other developmental defects we might be able to see at fifteen weeks gestation. We can do amniocentesis in another two weeks – that will enable us to rule out Down's syndrome and a few other genetic problems. The issue is going to be the alcohol. Can you give me an idea of how many drinks per day you were consuming before you knew you were pregnant? And when you stopped?'

Clare swallowed. 'Probably two or three on average. Some days only one. Some days . . . a lot more. I had my last drink around the twentieth of October.'

'So about two weeks.' The doctor nodded. 'That's actually encouraging. While the effects of drinking vary from woman to woman, as you'd expect, I wouldn't expect to see fetal alcohol syndrome resulting from that level of consumption.'

'Really?' Russ asked. He shook his head. 'I thought, you know, they say no drinking at all for pregnant women.'

'That's right. But FAS requires a lot more than your wife was putting away, for a lot longer time.'

Clare felt as if a heavy weight had been lifted off her chest. She looked at Russ.

'However.' The doctor's voice sent her thudding back to earth. 'It is possible the baby will show signs of fetal alcohol effect.'

Russ frowned. 'That doesn't sound good.'

'The symptoms aren't that much different than what we see in certain types of processing spectrum disorders. Learning disabilities, poor impulse control, attention issues – that sort of thing.'

'Can we . . .' Clare reached for a life preserver. 'Can we test for that? So we know in advance?'

The doctor shook her head. 'I'm sorry, no. FAE can only be diagnosed after birth.'

'Is there anything I can do? To ameliorate the effects?' Clare raised her hands, as if she could pluck something hopeful out of the air. 'Eat . . . organic? Take vitamins?'

'No. At this point, *if* there's been any damage – and I reiterate, that's still very much an if – it's irreversible.'

'So you're saying it's a crap shoot?' Russ's voice was rough. 'She goes through the pregnancy, and if she makes it to the end, we may or may not have a kid with brain damage?'

'"Brain damage" is an unnecessarily severe way of thinking about it, Mr Van Alstyne. You may or may not have a child with special needs and challenges, and even those can occur in such varying degrees. An enormous amount can be done with early intervention. I'll put you in touch with our counselor. She can give you all the information you'll need to prepare yourselves. If it proves necessary.'

They left the obstetrician's office under a cloud of silence, Clare clutching a prescription for prenatal vitamins and a date card for her next appointment. She couldn't look at Russ. He had conquered his alcoholism before he could harm anyone but himself. She wasn't sure if he would be able to forgive her for what her drinking might have done to their future child. He opened the truck door for her and shut it behind her after she climbed into the cab. He got in behind the wheel. He sat there, keys in hand, his eyes in the middle distance, doing nothing.

Finally she broke. 'Say something.'

He shut his eyes. 'I've already told you what I think.' The lines of his face stood out.

'I know I've made mistakes, Russ. If I could go back and change what I did—' She swallowed to get her voice under control. 'But I can't. And I can't correct those mistakes by making another one.'

'Oh, Christ, Clare.' He bent his neck until his head rested against the steering wheel. 'Do you have any idea what having a disabled kid can do to a marriage?'

She reached out and touched her fingertips to his back. 'Yes. But I also know what having strong and loving parents can do for a disabled child.'

'And what's this going to do to you, Clare?' He turned toward her. 'You're barely off the drugs. You're seeing two counselors twice a week, and you're *still* having nightmares and flashbacks. Hell, you can't drive to the IGA without drifting into the middle of the road to avoid IEDs. Now you're looking at *more* stress with a special-needs kid?'

'Two weeks ago, you told me that if we just kept holding on, if we didn't let go, you and I could get through anything.'

'I didn't mean we ought to go looking for more problems! Pregnancies are dangerous. You wake up every morning wondering if it's going to last. You can't talk about what-ifs and you can't think about it like there really might be a baby, because then what happens when things don't pan out? So there's nothing but silence and stuff you didn't say and grief and anger . . .' He trailed off.

'Whoa. Why do I get the feeling we're not talking about this pregnancy all of a sudden?'

He leaned against the side window and grunted.

'Is this about what happened to Linda?' She knew Russ's late wife had lost several pregnancies.

'No. Maybe. Some of it.'

'Her sister said she'd had three miscarriages—'

'Five. Two were early, before we'd told anyone she was pregnant.'

'Oh, Russ.' She took his hand in both of hers. His skin was chilled. 'I'm so sorry. That must have been awful. Did she have some sort of uterine condition?' Clare was vague on the details, but she knew there were women whose wombs simply couldn't carry to term.

He shook his head. 'No. That was the hell of it. It was always something

92

different. Infection. Failure to develop. Cord death – Jesus, that was a hard one.'

She put her hand on his cheek and turned his face toward hers. 'There's no reason to think any of that will happen this time.'

'So instead we get to burn ourselves out and risk your mental health taking care of a dependent special-needs kid?'

'It might not—'

'Of course you think it might not, Clare. That's how you operate. You live in a world of belief, and faith, and half-full glasses. I live in a world of bad news and worse outcomes.' He pushed away from her and started the ignition. 'Look, I can't change you. I never wanted to change you. But don't ask me to change, either. I've been on this ride too many times before. I know where it comes out, and I don't want to go there again.' He threw the truck into reverse and backed out of the parking spot. 'I won't say a word against you on this. But don't expect me to pretend to be happy about it.'

FIVE

If you had asked Lyle MacAuley what was the least favorite investigative task he could think of, it would have been visiting men on the sex offenders registry. First off, they were scum. Second, there were way too many of them. There were a few guys who had gotten on for stupid reasons – usually sleeping with their underage high school girlfriends after they'd turned eighteen – and he could eliminate them from his checklist, but that still left dozens of sickos who liked to flash little kids, or molest their stepdaughters, or liquor up twelve-year-old boys and rape them. Lyle had been dealing with criminals for thirty-five years, but nothing got under his skin like these guys.

It didn't help that he was working his way through the list alone. He didn't dare put Eric McCrea on this – the man was a father with anger-management issues. Lyle didn't want to imagine what Eric might do if he snapped while interviewing one of these perverts. He had tried calling Russ twice already to bring him up to date, but the only person he reached was the computer operator, telling him the chief's number was 'unavailable due to network failure'. Kevin and Hadley were trying to track down the little girl's father, in the hopes that might shake something loose.

That left Lyle, ringing bells and looking into slack, panicked faces, asking if he could 'come in out of the cold' so he could listen for the sound of a child somewhere in the house or apartment. He listened to their protestations of how clean they were, how recently they had checked in with their parole officers, how diligent they were about therapy. He wrote down their alibis – he figured Eric could run those down safely enough – and got their numbers and work addresses. Mostly, he looked for the guy who was off. The one who sweated a little too much or smiled too widely or who just smelled wrong.

He found him on his third stop after grabbing a greasy sack lunch out past the Super Kmart. Wendall Sullivan, twenty-seven, last known address 8 Smith Street, Fort Henry, a listing two-story house with asphalt shingles flaking off the exterior. Lyle parked on the street in front, marched up to the front door, which was flaking paint, and rang the bell. It was answered by a guy flaking dandruff, making the place a perfect trifecta of neglect.

'Yeah?' Flaky Shoulders said. He was too bored at the sight of a cop to be the guy Lyle was after.

'I'm looking for Wendall Sullivan.'

'He's at work.'

Lyle waited a beat. Nothing else was forthcoming. 'Which is where, exactly?'

'Huh? Oh. Maid for You. They're over on River Street, by the Italian bakery and the comic book shop.'

Lyle thanked the roommate and got back into his cruiser, resisting the urge to brush off his uniform. He found Maid for You right where the guy said it would be, housed in a small storefront with a sign featuring a pin-up-style drawing of a girl in a saucy French maid's costume. Lyle guessed it was either a cleaning service or a kinky escort business, and since he couldn't picture a two-time con in high heels and a frilly black skirt, he was betting on the cleaning service.

Inside was bare – just two benches, industrial-strength carpeting, and a receptionist behind a desk. Sadly, she looked more like someone's chain-smoking granny than a naughty maid. She was on the phone when he came in, so he stood at parade rest while she went over the sanitary wonder that could be the client's home for the low, low price of two hundred dollars.

Evidently, that wasn't low enough, because she hung up with a disgusted look on her face. 'Damn economy,' she said. 'People'd rather live in a damn pigsty than break out their checkbooks.' She took a drag on her smoldering cigarette. 'Help you, Officer?'

'Yes, ma'am. I understand you've got an employee named Wendall Sullivan.'

'Yep. Good worker. Came with a great recommendation. Punctual, too.' She exhaled a stream of smoke. 'Please don't tell me he's in trouble, because I'm having a bitch of a time finding cleaners. Everybody's too damn good to scrub a toilet these days.'

'I just need to ask him a few questions, ma'am. Do you know where I can find him?'

'Of course I do. He's with the B crew, out on a job. You need to talk with him now? I hate to interrupt a team when they've got the process going.'

'It sure would make my life a lot easier.' Lyle smiled at her. The old MacAuley charm worked its magic, because she tore a piece of paper off her pad and scribbled down an address.

'Here you go.' She took another drag. 'If it turns out you have to arrest him, will you for God's sake wait until he's done steam-cleaning the carpets?'

The B team was working in the Mountain View Park development, which was the sort of place Lyle would have expected to have maid service. Houses the size of barns, with those giant half-moon windows and brick driveways. Four bedrooms but six baths, and granite-and-copper kitchens with five-thousand-dollar ovens for people who always grabbed takeout on their way home from Albany.

There were several beater cars and a Maid for You van on the street. Lyle parked in the drive and headed for the front door across a walk that had been snowblowered with a surveyor's precision. The door was opened by a forty-something woman before he had a chance to knock. 'Hello,' she said. 'Can I help you?'

Since she was wearing an expensive-looking sweater and a diamond the size of a .22 cartridge, Lyle figured she wasn't here to mop the floors. 'Ma'am.' He doffed his lid and gave her his most reassuring smile. 'I'm Deputy Chief MacAuley of the MKPD. I just need to speak with the supervisor of your cleaning crew.'

'Oh. Are they – is there some trouble?'

'Just looking for some information, ma'am. May I come in?'

'Oh! Of course.' She stood aside, then closed the door behind him. 'I think Bea's the supervisor. At least, she's the one I always give instructions to. She's in the family room right now.' She led Lyle across an acre of wall-to-wall, giving him a chance to appreciate her tight little tush. Probably did Pilates. Something about those exercises always gave women a nice, high—

'Bea!' They stepped down a few steps into the family room. A solidly built woman in jeans and a Maid for You shirt was wiping down an enormous window that showed the promised mountain view. 'This officer wants to ask you a few questions. I'm going to give you some privacy. When you're done, will you meet me in the kitchen, please?'

'Sure will, Mrs Moore.' The homeowner vanished into what Lyle presumed was the kitchen.

'I'm Deputy Chief MacAuley of the MKPD,' he started.

Bea stuffed her cloth into a many-pocketed bucket and nodded. 'Yeah, Jackie called me to let me know a cop would be coming around. You want to see Wendall, right?'

'That's right. Does he expect me, too?'

'Nah. Everybody on the crew except the supervisor has to keep their cell off. Clients don't want to pay to see somebody standing around yapping to a boyfriend or bookie. Wendall's doing the power wash in the master bedroom. Follow me.' They went up a wide, glossy set of stairs, past another woman in a Maid for You shirt polishing the banister. 'Please don't touch anything,' Bea said as they turned on the landing. 'Our guarantee is "No Fingerprint Left Behind".'

As they walked along the upstairs hall, Lyle caught a glimpse of another Maid for You employee scrubbing a bathroom and a teenager sitting with a laptop in one of the bedrooms. 'Do you usually work while the owners are at home?' he asked.

'Depends. Some clients' – Bea's exaggerated emphasis on the words let Lyle know what she thought of them – 'don't trust us to be here on our own. We're fully bonded, but, you know.'

'Ah-hah.'

'A couple of the older clients, I swear they just hire us so they got someone to talk to once a week. Follow the crew around while we're trying to clean. Kinda sweet, but it can drive you batty, you know? Here he is.'

The door at the end of the hall was open, and Lyle could hear a low, deep roar, like a vacuum. Except for the bed and some dressers, the master bedroom looked just like the family room – same giant windows, same acre of carpet, same wide-screen TV. Sullivan was running one of those rug-shampooing machines, wearing noise-canceling headphones. Bea walked over and tapped his shoulder.

Lyle watched as Sullivan caught sight of a police uniform. His eyes went round, and he started blinking fast. He switched off the shampoo machine and removed his headphones.

'Wendall, this officer wants to talk with you. Jackie says go ahead, tell him what he needs to know, you'll still get your usual break time.' She turned back toward the door. 'I'll be downstairs if you need me. Remember' – she pointed at Lyle – 'no fingerprints.'

When they were alone, Lyle smiled. 'Hi, Wendall. I'm Lyle MacAuley, deputy chief over at the MKPD. Do you know why I wanted to talk with you?'

Sullivan swallowed. 'I haven't done anything.' He was a medium-sized guy who looked younger than twenty-seven: pink cheeks, smooth skin. Curly hair. He smiled nervously and a dimple popped in his cheek. Kids would trust him.

'Really? That's not what I hear.'

Sullivan kept the smile pinned in place. Lyle could see the shine of sweat on his upper lip. 'Somebody's been trash-talking me? They're full of it. I go to work, I pick up a few DVDs at the library, and I go home. I don't go near no schools, or playgrounds, or nothing like that. I keep my nose clean.'

Lyle tugged on his lower lip. 'Now that surprises me. It's not like that last girl was a one-time deal, was it? You did four years federal time for taking a girl into Massachusetts.'

Sullivan flushed. 'That's my juvie record. That's supposed to be sealed.'

'Then a year after your release, you reoffended. What was the second one? Seven? Eight?'

'Nobody proved I did anything to that girl. I was in for kidnapping, not for rape.'

'Yeah? Did they put you in general, then?' The general population of a prison – garden-variety dealers and thieves and killers – would tear apart child molesters. Special population offered safety, but also mind-numbing segregation and a complete lack of freedom. A prison within a prison. 'The way I see it, you been out more'n a year now. You gotta see them everywhere, even if you are staying away from schools. Girls in the supermarket with their moms, riding their bikes, checking out books in the library. Must get pretty lonely after a while. Hard to resist.'

Sullivan wrapped his hands around the handle of the shampooing machine. His knuckles were white. 'I don't do that no more. I did a nickel in Fishkill, stuck in Special the whole time. I'm not going back there. I don't care if I have to whack off for the rest of my life. I'm not going back.'

'Mikayla Johnson,' Lyle said.

Sullivan blinked rapidly. 'Who?'

'Cute little girl. Eight. Used to live with her mother, Annie Johnson, until about six months ago. Since then she's been in foster care with Ted and Helen MacAllen.'

Sullivan looked at the carpet. 'Don't know her.'

'Sorry?'

Sullivan raised his head. His mouth was flat and hard. 'I don't know her. I didn't have nothing to do with her. I didn't have nothing to do with nobody. If you think you got something, go ahead and take me in. Otherwise, I gotta get back to work.' He jammed the earphones on and started up the rug shampooer. This close, the machine sounded like a jet engine running up on a tarmac.

Lyle retreated. He didn't have anything yet, but there was something there; sweating, twitching, then shutting down cold. Lyle clattered down the stairs, not touching anything as instructed, and found Bea dusting a shelf of golf trophies in what looked like a home office. 'Everything okay?' she asked.

'Oh, yeah,' he said. 'One question. Have you ever cleaned for a couple named Ted and Helen MacAllen? Big old house out on Crandell Hill Road in Millers Kill?'

She frowned. 'Nope. Not that I can recall. But different people switch around on different teams. It depends on the days available and how many hours you want to work. You should check with Jackie. She could tell you if we take care of them.'

After two tries and getting nothing but a busy signal, Lyle decided it would be quicker to run back to Maid for You and talk to Jackie in person. On the way to Fort Henry, Lyle radioed the station and asked Noble Entwhistle to get started on the paperwork for a warrant to search Sullivan's apartment. If he turned up something, he wanted to move fast. Sullivan had looked dead serious when he said he wasn't going back to prison. If he had Mikayla Johnson, Lyle didn't want to give the scumbag a chance to crawl back to whatever hidey-hole he was using and make sure the girl could never testify against him.

The owner of Maid for You was still holding a smoldering cigarette, still on the phone trying to sell someone on cleanliness being next to godliness. This time, Lyle leaned over her desk and said, 'I need to speak with you right now.'

Her face pruned up. 'Can I put you on hold for just a sec?' she said into the phone. 'I have another client on the other line. Thanks.' She jabbed a button. 'What?'

'Have you ever cleaned for Ted and Helen MacAllen? At 52 Crandell Hill Road?'

'Yeah. They're once-monthly clients. Why?'

'Has Wendall Sullivan ever been on the team assigned to their house?'

'He is in trouble, isn't he? Crap.' She turned to her computer screen. She clicked, scrolled, clicked again. 'Yeah. Yeah, he was on D team the last three times they were there. Goddammit. Did he steal something? Because we're fully—'

Lyle was out the door and in his unit before she could finish. He raised Harlene this time. 'Sullivan cleaned house for the MacAllens.' He flipped on his red lights. 'I'm going to bring him in. He might spill if we lean on him, but I wouldn't count on it. Tell Noble I want that warrant request ready to take to Judge Ryswick when I get there.'

He drove a bit above the speed limit, without sirens. It had just started snowing – not heavy, but enough to make the road slick. He was thinking about the search, and where Sullivan might have stashed the kid, and realizing they just might be able to wrap the whole thing up without having to drag Russ away from his honeymoon. Back at Mountain View, he swung in behind the van and its line of cars.

'You again.' The lady of the house didn't look very happy to see him.

'Yes, ma'am. May I . . . ?' He strode past her, through the football-field living room.

'I have to say this is disrupting our Saturday routine!' She trotted after him.

'Bea?' he called. The supervisor popped out of the kitchen.

'And it's making me have second thoughts about the reliability of your cleaning service!'

Bea gave him a look that said *See what I have to put up with?*

'Where's Sullivan?'

Bea pointed toward the door. The line of beater cars, he realized. One of them was— 'He told me he was too shaken up to work,' the supervisor said. 'He's gone.'

SIX

Hector DeJean hadn't been home that morning. Hadley and Flynn had found his address easily enough, a double-wide on a country road in Cossayuharie. What would have been the attached garage had been converted into a business, with two cars parked out front and enough room for at least three more. The sign overhead read DEDE'S DO AND DYE. Next to the beauty shop, a good-sized cruiser was cradled in a boat trailer, its lines obscured by winter shrink-wrap. 'Huh,' Flynn said. 'He's gone from a junkie to a successful businesswoman. Maybe he has reformed.'

'Men don't reform.' Hadley was in no mood to give any guy the benefit of the doubt after last night's disaster. 'They just get better at covering their tracks.'

Flynn gave her a look but didn't respond. When they entered the shop, the bell tinkled. It looked a lot like the salon Hadley went to – shampoo sink, three chairs, posters of edgy hairstyles that no one in Millers Kill would ever wear.

'Be right with you!' A slim woman with fire-engine red hair was bent over an old lady, winding perm rods into her silver hair. She gave a last squirt and twist, stripped off her gloves, and turned around. She frowned when she saw them. She patted her customer on the shoulder. 'I'm setting the timer, Mrs Bain,' she yelled. 'You just sit here and relax.' She handed the woman a magazine and walked over to Flynn and Hadley. 'Deaf as a post,' she said in a normal tone of voice. 'Nice lady, though. Good tipper.'

'We're looking for Hector DeJean,' Flynn said.

'Of course you are. Who's complaining this time? His meth-head ex? Her parents?'

'Is he here?' Flynn said.

'No, he's not here. He's at work. He's a driver for DHS Deliveries. He leaves before dawn every morning and works hard all day making a better life for us.' She braced her fists against her hips. 'He'll be home by four. You can come back and talk with him then, but whatever they told you, you're barking up the wrong tree.'

Hadley was about to ask about Mikayla, but Flynn cut her off. 'Thanks very much, Ms . . .'

'It's Mrs. Mrs DeJean.' The redhead held up her left hand to display a gold band. 'This is a God-fearing Christian home. We're not living together like animals, thank you very much.'

'Okay. Mrs DeJean. We'll be back at four.'

'That was not what I expected,' Hadley said as they walked back to the squad car.

'I guess he found Jesus as well as anger management in the pen.' Flynn sounded bemused. 'Let's track down some less God-fearing associates of Johnson and see what we can shake loose.'

They didn't shake loose much. They found a small-scale dealer who lived on Depot Street who said Annie Johnson used to come around once in a while, but he hadn't seen her in months. They canvassed her apartment house, got a few names or descriptions of people who had been seen with her, and followed up on as many of them as they could find. One skinny, hollow-eyed girl told them Annie had stopped hanging out and had gotten serious about finding money in the past year. They found one guy with a prison-gym body working behind the counter at Stewart's who had heard she'd gotten in with a pretty heavy crowd.

'What's your impression?' Flynn asked. They had picked up a couple of coffees while they were at the Stewart's, and they were parked in a turnout on the Cossayuharie Road.

'Why are you asking me? You're the one with the drug squad experience.' Flynn had been the MKPD officer detailed to the Capital Area Drug Enforcement Agency.

He blew on his coffee. 'I want to know what you think.'

'Ugh. You sound like the chief.'

He grinned.

'Okay. Most junkies or meth heads, from what I understand, are just small-time dealers if they're also using. Eventually, they give up on the dealing altogether, because they use their own stuff faster than they can sell it.'

'Uh-huh.'

'Annie Johnson seems to have gone in a different direction. From what her folks said, she's been using for years. But she's not hanging around with the small fry. It doesn't look like she's turning tricks or stealing to pay for her next hit.'

'Right. Instead, she's smurfing in a big way.'

'It's got to take a lot of money up front to buy that much pseudoephedrine. I mean, have you priced that stuff lately? I had to get some generic kid's decongestant for Genny last month and it cost me like nine bucks.'

'We don't know if it's all been paid for. When the state lab finishes running down the bar codes, they'll be able to tell us.'

'Yeah, but even so.' She took a drink of her coffee. The first snowflakes of the predicted dump were starting to fall. 'I think she's hooked up with a much bigger fish. Somebody who's running a commercial lab, not home brew. He supplies her with the money and just enough product to keep her hanging around.'

Kevin nodded. 'Did you notice in that picture her parents showed us? She doesn't look like a meth abuser yet. She's still got some flesh on her bones. Her teeth are still good.'

'Yeah. She'd be a good front person while it lasts.' She turned in her seat to look at him. 'Especially with a cute little girl in tow.'

'Uh-huh.' He wedged his cup between the radio mount and his laptop. 'It's four o'clock. Let's go see if the ex has anything he can tell us.'

By the time they got back to the DeJean residence, the snow was falling in earnest, wet, sticky flakes that went down the back of Hadley's neck as she crossed the parking area toward the front door. Lousy driving later tonight. Maybe it would be enough to keep Dylan holed up in whatever hotel he was staying at. Maybe he'd drive off the road, get stuck in a drift, and freeze to death. No – get eaten by wolves. Get partially eaten by wolves, *then* freeze to death.

'Why are you smiling?' Flynn asked.

'Sorry.' She schooled her expression into a good cop face. Flynn knocked on the door. The guy who answered it was big, as tall as Flynn and sixty pounds heavier. He looked like a professional cage fighter – rawboned, thick-skulled, his hair shaved to a shadow. 'Hector DeJean?' Flynn asked.

'That's me.' He opened the door and stepped back so they could come in. Hadley barely came up to his breastbone. Jesus. No wonder the Johnsons thought he could do some real damage. He could take Flynn out with one punch and finish her off with the backstroke.

Dede came out of the tiny hallway. 'So my wife tells me you came around this morning,' DeJean said. 'Why don't you tell me what you want, and then she and I can get on with dinner.'

'Why don't you and Mrs DeJean sit down,' Flynn said.

'I don't want to—'

'S'okay, Dede.' DeJean laid a massive paw on his wife's shoulder. 'You sit down, they stand up. It's a way to intimidate the people they're talking to.' He gave Hadley an amused look as he sat on the couch, as if pointing out that even down on the floor in cuffs, he wouldn't be intimidated by a woman a foot shorter than he was.

Flynn spotted it. He gave her a subtle nod. *Go ahead. You take lead.*

'Mr DeJean, what can you tell us about your relationship with Annie Johnson?' Hadley asked.

'I don't have a relationship with Annie Johnson. I got an arrangement. Once a month, if she doesn't get stoned and forget or wander off, I come by and collect my daughter from her. We visit for a day or two, then I bring her back. I don't talk with Annie, and she for sure don't talk to me.'

'You don't have any legal right to custody of Mikayla, is that right?'

'Yeah, that's right.'

'It's not fair.' Dede picked up a pillow and punched it into shape. 'That woman abuses drugs, she deals, she hangs out with the worst lowlifes in Washington County, and then she nearly killed Mikayla—'

'My daughter was in a bad car accident last summer,' DeJean said. 'Annie was high and drove into a tree. *She* was fine, but Mikayla needed a liver transplant.'

Dede nodded. 'Which Hector gave to her.'

'What?' Hadley looked at Flynn. DeJean pulled his shirt up to his armpits, revealing several tattoos and a crescent-shaped scar on one side. 'How is that even possible?'

'She's a little kid. They just carved off a piece of mine. I guess grown-ups have more liver than we need. The doctors say it'll grow along with her.'

Hadley blinked. 'Mr DeJean, I'll be honest. I'm having a hard time reconciling the guy who would give up part of his own liver for his daughter with the guy who put her mother in the hospital while she was pregnant.'

'I was a sorry sack of shit back then,' he said. 'I grew up with my mom beating on me and my dad beating on my mom, and I thought life was either screwing or getting screwed. I was doing meth and angel dust and heroin. I thank God I got caught and sent to Plattsburgh. I thank God for it. I was the most miserable sinner alive, but Jesus led me into that hole and I found healing there.' He took Dede's hand. 'When I got out, this lady was waiting for me.'

'I was a volunteer for the prison ministry,' Dede said.

'The church helped me find a job, get my life together – now look at me. I got a home, I got a straight job, I got respect without having to beat anybody down for it.'

Okay. It sounded good. Hadley tried to rein in her skepticism. 'Where does Mikayla fit in with this new life?'

'After the accident, we looked into trying to get custody of her,' Dede said.

'I talked to a lawyer about doing a paternity test, getting my name on her birth certificate. He said I could do that, but with my record, there was no way the court would grant me custody.'

'Our big worry is that Annie's parents will get custody of her.' A timer buzzed. Dede stood and went to the kitchenette.

'They'll never let me see her. Not without a court order. Maybe not even then. The lawyer said I'm in a bad position, since I've waited until she was eight to go on the record as her dad.'

Hadley glanced at Flynn. 'Mr DeJean, where were you last Thursday night and early Friday morning?'

DeJean closed his eyes. 'Our church has a summer camp up by a place called Cooper's Corners, about an hour north of here. One of the neighbors called our pastor, said it looked like there was a water leak coming out the main building. I had Thursday and Friday off, so I took my tools and my welding kit and headed up there. It was a couple burst pipes. I fixed 'em, cleaned up, spent the night, came back Friday morning.'

'Is there anyone who can vouch for your whereabouts?' Flynn asked.

'I can.' Dede straightened from where she was checking something in the oven. 'I was right here when he took the call from our pastor!'

DeJean shook his head. 'Nobody went with me, if that's what you mean.'

Flynn nodded. 'Mr DeJean, sometime between Thursday and Friday, someone went to the foster home where Mikayla was staying and took her. They set fire to the house, presumably to cover the fact that Mikayla was missing, killing the foster parents in the process.' They had decided to keep mum about the gunshot wounds. 'Do you have any idea who might have wanted to take your daughter? Or where she might be?'

'What?' DeJean stared at them for an endless moment. 'What?' Then his face grew red. He let out a strangled noise like the sound of a bull about to charge. 'What the hell?' he roared. 'My daughter's been kidnapped and you wait until after we're discussing the damn *custody arrangements* before you tell me?' He stood up. Flynn and Hadley both took a step back. 'Since Friday morning? She's been missing a day and a half and you assholes didn't think to *tell* me?'

'Look, Mr DeJean,' Flynn started.

'Don't "look Mr DeJean me", you little punk-ass pig. Where's my daughter? What have you done to find her?' DeJean balled his hands into fists.

'Sit down *now*.' Flynn's voice cracked with authority. 'You do *not* want me to cuff you and haul you out of here in front of your wife.'

DeJean let out another noise, like hot steam venting, but he sat down. 'The MKPD is pursuing any and every lead we have. There's been a regional AMBER Alert issued. Annie Johnson fled from us when we tried to question her, but she did not have your daughter with her at that time. We're looking for her.'

DeJean slapped his hand over his mouth and mumbled something into his palm.

'I'm going to give you the station number, and my cell number.' Flynn took out one of his cards. 'I want you to give me the name and phone number of your pastor, and the address of the camp you say you were at Thursday night.'

Dede stepped toward them. Her eyes were huge and wet. 'Hector would never put Mikayla in danger. Never. He loves her. We both do.'

'Ma'am,' Hadley said, 'we have to look into every possibility. The quicker we can cross off the negatives, the more time we can spend on the likely suspects.'

'Give it to them, Dede. Just give it to them.'

She stalked back to the kitchenette and scribbled furiously on a piece of paper. 'Here.' She thrust the note at Hadley. 'Take it.' The tears in her eyes were spilling over her cheeks now.

'If you think of anything that might be helpful, if you hear of anything, if anyone tries to contact you, call us. Anytime, day or night.' Flynn settled his hat on his head.

'I'll do better than that.' DeJean stood again. Looking just as dangerous as he had before. 'You guys don't come up with something in the next twenty-four hours, I'm going looking for her myself. And when I find her, I'm not leaving anything behind for the cops to have to deal with. You understand what I'm saying? I find whoever did this thing, that person's never walking this earth again.'

SEVEN

Russ decided the closest spot where he could hope to get cell reception was the Cooper's Corners general store at the head of the lake. It would've been better if he could have waited to call after the five o'clock end-of-shift reports, but there was no way he was going to try to make it around the bottom of the lake, up South Shore Drive and back again in the dark. Not with the snow coming down like it was. Anyway, if they were going to be snowed in, he wanted to buy a couple more gallons of water and milk.

Clare insisted on riding along, of course. 'What if the truck gets stuck in the snow?' he asked.

'Then I can help you get it out.'

'Not like that, you can't!'

She rolled her eyes. 'Russ, just because I'm pregnant doesn't mean the rest of my body's stopped working. Hang on a sec, I'll get into outdoor clothes.'

He watched her from behind the kitchen counter while she tossed her jeans and sweater on the chair in front of the woodstove and peeled off her pajamas. In the firelight, she glowed like the first peach of summer. She was right; so far, she was as strong and healthy as she had ever been. In fact, being pregnant seemed to make her . . . more. Her color higher, her skin warmer, everywhere, when he touched her, more responsive. Everything curvy and rosy and luscious. He felt like the worst goddamn hypocrite in the world, but seeing his wife ripe and round made him incredibly hot. There were times making love when he was so swamped by a tidal wave of lust and possessiveness and pleasure he'd bite her neck and shoulders in a frenzy of *mine, mine, mine*. He shivered. *Russ Van Alstyne was here*. She was closer to the mark than she knew.

'You all set?' she asked.

He adjusted his jeans. 'Oh, yeah. Ready to go.' *Hypocrite.*

The entrance of the narrow garage was still clear enough for him to back the truck out unimpeded. He tossed the shovel in the bed, though, because he didn't think he'd be so lucky by the time they got home. The snow was falling thick and fast, fat wet flakes that covered the windshield between swipes of the wipers, so that his eyes seemed to be blinking in and out of focus: tire tracks, white spatter, mailboxes, white spatter, hemlocks, white spatter, carports, white spatter.

Clare was quiet, letting him concentrate on driving. He negotiated the turn onto South Shore Drive, slipping and sliding in the ruts left by other drivers headed past the lake onto Haines Mountain Road. He kept his speed slow and steady, riding the crest of the road until they finally reached the short stretch of year-round houses that led to the county highway. No one drove past him, but the parking lot of the Cooper's Corners general store was jammed with trucks and cars.

'Wow,' Clare said. 'It's a convention.'

'Everybody stocking up before the storm. Water, TP, batteries.' He wedged the pickup in next to a snowbank and turned the engine off.

'I've never understood that. Even if the storm is bad, how long will it be that you're stuck inside? A day? Two at the most?'

'Usually, yeah.' He hitched himself off the seat to retrieve his cell phone. 'To be fair, though, out here it could be a lot longer. The lake is probably pretty far down on the county road crew's list.' He pointed to the truck next to them, which had a snowplow mounted on its front. 'Unless you do it yourself.'

'Do you want me to do the shopping while you talk with Lyle?'

He grinned. 'Giving me privacy? Thanks, but you might as well stay. That way I won't have to repeat the whole conversation when you grill me about what's going on.'

He reached Lyle on the second ring. 'Thank God,' his deputy chief said as a greeting. 'I didn't think I was ever going to get to talk to you.'

'I told you the reception out at the cabin is bad. I'm out here at Cooper's Corners. Give me the rundown. Any movement on the murder investigation?'

'The homicide's been put on hold.'

'What? What does that mean?'

'Let me finish. Turns out the MacAllens were fostering an eight-year-old girl. Mikayla Johnson. She's missing.'

Russ's stomach pinched. 'You mean you can't find the body?'

'I mean there is no body. The state arson guy and the fire marshal's team sifted the wreckage with teaspoons. The girl was taken before the fire was lit.'

'Oh, shit.' Clare looked at him inquiringly. He held up his hand.

'Yeah. We're working off the theory that the fire was supposed to hide the kidnapping.'

'AMBER Alert?'

'Already done. The kid's mother, one Annie Johnson, lost custody after nearly killing her in a car accident a few months back. She had to get a liver transplant, which means—'

'She has to be on immunosuppressants. Where's the mom?'

'She ran when Kevin and Hadley went to question her. Turns out her apartment had enough pseudoephedrine in it to stock every drugstore in New York.'

'She's a smurfer?'

'Big-time. Her rap sheet's five pages long. Possession, distribution, assault, misdemeanor theft, DUI, you name it, this chick's done it.'

'What about the father?'

'Not listed on the BC. Frick and Frack are running down Annie Johnson's parents, her parole officer, associates – you know the list. I haven't heard anything from them yet.'

It was getting cold in the truck. Russ switched on the ignition, and the heater kicked in. 'You need to work the smurfing angle. If she's really got that much clear in her apartment, she's probably working with a team.'

'Noble's on it. We expect to get the retail locations from the state crime lab by tonight or tomorrow. He'll hit the stores and run down their name-and-license list. However, there's another possibility.'

'What?' *Mother snatched kid* would be the usual story. Even with the mom being a druggie, chances that one of her contacts took the kid for leverage were slim to none. Users couldn't muster the long-range planning for something as organized as kidnapping, and dealers cut off the supply before their customers could run up a tab.

'The MacAllens had a home-cleaning service come in regularly. One of the guys on the crew is on the sexual offenders registry for first-degree rape of an eleven-year-old.'

'I don't like where this is going, Lyle.'

'Yeah? You'll like this less. When I went to bring him in, he rabbited.'

'Oh, that's just . . .' Russ pinched the bridge of his nose. 'Two POIs and you lose both of them?'

'If you think you can do better, by all means—'

'Okay. Okay. I'm sorry. It's not your fault. You're understaffed for something like this.'

'No shit. I'm about to call in the staties just to get a few more boots on the ground.'

Russ took off his glasses and rubbed his eyes. 'The girl. Mikayla. What do we know about her medical condition?'

'Hadley got hooked up with her doctor through CFS. He said she's got seven or eight days after her last dose before her body shuts down.'

'Jesus Christ.' He looked at Clare and mouthed *sorry*. She shook her head. 'Okay. I'm heading home. Let me pick up a few things at the store and get Clare back to the cabin – no, wait, I don't want her out here all alone with a storm coming on.' He glanced at her. She spread her hands and mouthed *I'm fine*. 'I'll have to pack our things up—'

'Stop,' Lyle said. 'It's almost dark and the snow's picking up. You're not going to be any help tonight. Go on back to your honeymoon suite, hunker down, and you can make the trip tomorrow. The temperature's on the way up, so I'm guessing the storm's gonna be a bust. By Sunday afternoon, the roads'll be clear.'

Russ breathed deeply. 'Yeah. You're right.'

'Course I am. We'll see you sometime tomorrow.'

'Lyle, wait. What about' – he glanced at Clare – 'that other thing?'

'What other thing?'

'The town thing.'

'Oh! Yeah. I'm going to ask Kevin to hook me up with his mother when he gets back in tonight.'

'Great. Don't tell him or Hadley what it's about. I don't want anyone worrying until we know . . . well, until we know.'

'Roger that. See you tomorrow.'

Clare was giving him a particularly piercing look as he hung up. 'What's the town thing Lyle can't tell Kevin and Hadley about?'

'Uh.' He hadn't meant to sit on the aldermen's threat. He was just waiting for the right time to discuss it. Which wasn't parked in front of the Cooper's Corners general store. 'It's complicated. I'll tell you later.'

'Mmm. And the investigation?'

He went over what Lyle had told him. Clare looked paler and paler as he spoke. 'That poor little girl,' she said when he had finished.

'Look, I know this sucks, but—'

'No. Of course you need to go. Don't even think about it.'

He squeezed her hand. 'Thank you.'

'I'd like to stay, though.'

'What? Alone? That's crazy.'

'Russ. If you're serious about the cabin being our weekend and vacation home, there are going to be times in the future, just like now, when you'll be called away. If being out here alone drives me crazy, I'd like to know now, before we sink hundreds of thousands of dollars into buying the place.'

'No. Absolutely not.'

'Besides.' She unlatched her door and slid out. 'I'm not alone. I have Oscar to keep me company.'

He got out of the cab and followed her toward the store. 'Clare—'

'Russ.' Her face was half-lit by a neon Bud Light sign. 'I'll be fine. I need some time away from the church and the rectory to think about things.'

'What things?' He opened the door for her. A blast of warm, moist air fogged his glasses. He snatched them off.

'It's complicated. I'll tell you when we get back to the cabin.' She picked up a plastic basket and started down the first narrow aisle. 'What do we need besides milk and water?'

He shouldered past a woman pulling disposable diapers off a shelf. 'You won't even have a vehicle. What if something happens?' He lowered his voice. 'With the baby?'

She looked at him. 'Does that worry you?'

'Oh, for God's sake, Clare. Of course it does. I don't – Jesus. It's not like I want something to go wrong.'

They had reached the meat and deli counter at the rear of the store. An old guy in a trucker's cap and the woman at the counter both stared curiously at him. 'Batteries,' he said tightly. 'Double A's and D's.'

She headed up another aisle. 'I'm sorry. That wasn't fair.'

'No, it damn well wasn't.' He pulled a couple of packages of Energizers off the shelf and tossed them into her basket.

'Let's not argue. You go. Find that little girl. Then you can come back and get me and Oscar. Maybe we'll even have a little vacation time left.' She picked up a package of toilet paper and peered at the back. 'Do we need something specially biodegradable for the privy?'

He knew he wasn't going to win this one. Clare had this thing she did; she wouldn't fight, she'd listen to all his arguments, but in the end she'd get exactly what she wanted. Emotional jujitsu. He walked to the cooler in the corner of the store and got one of the last remaining gallons of milk. They were already out of water. He and Clare joined the line of folks at the checkout waiting for the one teenaged clerk – probably the owner's daughter. Several people turned around to look, first at Clare, then at him, then back to Clare. Coming from Millers Kill, Russ didn't often feel like a sophisticated urbanite, but out here he might as well have been from New York City.

'Hi,' Clare said to the sixty-something woman in front of them who was still examining them. 'That looks like a smart idea.' She nodded toward the bag of de-icer resting on the woman's hip. 'Do we need some of that, Russ?'

'Already got it in the truck.'

'You're not from around here,' the woman observed.

'We're from Millers Kill. We might be buying a place on the lake, though.' Clare smiled brightly.

'No, I mean your accent. It's ... southern.' She sounded like a suspicious villager in an old Hammer horror film. Russ half expected the next thing out of her mouth to be a warning not to go up to Count Dracula's castle.

'Yes, I'm originally from Virginia. You know what they say. You can take a girl out of the South ...'

'I know you.' The man next in line nudged his neighbor. 'Ed. Take a look at this guy. Didn't we see him on the TV?' The two men stared at Russ.

'Yeah,' Ed said. 'You're, um, you're—'

Clare looked at him, bemused.

'That police chief,' his friend said. 'Who got shot a couple years back.' The rest of the line and the cashier all stared at Russ.

'From Millers Kill,' the woman added.

'It was all over the news for a while.' Ed leaned forward as if he were scanning Russ's parka for bullet holes.

The woman with the bag of de-icer nodded. 'He and his—' She paused, looking at Clare.

'Wife,' Clare said firmly.

'—wife are getting a house lakeside.' There was a murmur of approval from the people in line.

'That's wonderful.' At the head of the line, the disposable-diaper woman was handing the cashier a twenty. 'It's about time we had some law enforcement around here.'

'We got the state police,' Ed said.

'They only show up after there's trouble. Having an officer living here might keep trouble from happening.' She got her change and picked up her bag but showed no signs of leaving the store.

'Not an officer,' Ed's friend said. 'The *chief* of police.'

'And his wife!' The older woman beamed at Clare. 'When are you due, dear?'

'Late April.'

The diaper lady smiled up at Russ. 'Do you know if you're having a girl or a boy?'

'Ah . . . one of them. Yeah.' Beside him, Russ could feel Clare shaking with barely suppressed laughter. They got through the checkout and escaped the store amid a barrage of questions, advice, and welcome.

'My husband, the celebrity,' Clare said as they walked through the heavily falling snow to the truck.

'So much for keeping a low profile.' Russ slung their bags into the narrow backseat. 'We might as well have taken out an ad in the local *Pennysaver.*'

Clare grinned at him as they got into the cab. 'Think of it this way. If I get into trouble, I'll have lots of people I can call on for help.'

'Oh, yeah. If you can make it twelve miles around the lake.' Russ started up the truck and backed it out of the parking lot. The snow was still falling straight and fast. They'd have six inches before morning. At least. He was half-tempted to just head for Millers Kill right now. But there was that damn dog back at the cabin. And Lyle was right – it would be safer in daylight, after the roads were plowed.

Driving past the place where they had dropped Amber off the night before, Russ could see lights in the house below the road. 'Should we stop?' Clare wiped the condensation off her window. 'Make sure she and the baby are okay?'

He slowed down. 'How come you'll be fine but I should worry about her?'

Clare's voice was dry. 'For one, she's a teenager, not a combat vet with survival training. For another, I won't be affected if the power goes out. She will be. They heat the place with electricity. What happens if the power cuts out?'

He made a noise. 'I'll drop by tomorrow.' After he spent the night kicking himself for coming up with this lake house plan in the first place. What had he been thinking of? What?

EIGHT

Kevin found his gaze drifting toward the squad room clock during the end-of-shift briefing. Not that he was impatient to get off duty and get home, although he was already anticipating the pleasures of a hot shower, a cold beer, and a good book. He simply couldn't believe it had only been two days since Mikayla Johnson had gone missing. Two days since the homicide. Two days since he had gotten to his apartment to discover the chief had been right, there was an offer waiting for him from the Syracuse police. He felt the pressure of time hanging low on his horizon, like threatening storm clouds ready to burst.

'So that's where we are so far.' The deputy chief turned away from where he'd been scrawling notes on the whiteboard. 'Tonight, Eric's going to continue to track down the pharmacies involved in pseudoephedrine buys, and Paul will get out there and beat the trees for known associates of Annie Johnson.'

Hadley looked up from the desk where she'd been rereading her notes. 'Paul? You really think he's going to do any, you know, *investigating*?' Paul Urquhart was the kind of cop who did the absolute minimum in any situation.

The dep's bushy gray eyebrows knit together in a scowl. 'You volunteering to take his shift?' She slid deeper into her chair and shook her head. 'Didn't think so. Look, we don't have enough men, that's a fact.' Kevin could see Hadley roll her eyes at MacAuley's unconscious sexism. 'The chief will try to get here by tomorrow afternoon, but that's iffy, with the weather and all.'

Noble stood up, frowning in thought. 'Dep, why'n't we call in the staties? They've helped us before when we've been shorthanded.'

'No.' MacAuley's voice was absolute. 'The state Sexual Offenders Task Force is already helping out by running down those of Wendall Sullivan's nearest and dearest in other jurisdictions. Mikayla Johnson's face is in every law enforcement database in a ten-state radius. The rest we can do ourselves.'

Kevin prepared to kiss Sunday dinner at his folks' goodbye. 'Are we pulling another shift tomorrow?'

'I can come in if you need me.' Hadley sounded positively eager to work, which was weird. She was a good, conscientious cop, but she didn't like to take any more time away from her kids than she could help. Maybe she needed the overtime.

'Half shift. All the part-time guys will be in to handle traffic, so you can concentrate on finding this kid.' MacAuley splayed his hands on the big worktable and leaned toward them. 'I'm going to remind you all that this isn't just a kid-down-the-well situation. It's a kid-down-the-well-and-the-water's-rising-fast situation. Dismissed.'

Kevin and Hadley got to their feet as the dep left the room. Noble cracked his back and yawned. 'Good night,' he said. 'See you in the morning. Sorry you're gonna miss church, Hadley.'

'Thanks, Noble. I'll live.'

MacAuley stuck his head back into the room. 'Kevin, I almost forgot. I need to speak to your mother.'

'What?' Kevin could feel his cheeks pinking up. Hadley was looking at him, amused.

'I mean professionally. As a politician.'

'Oh. Okay.' Kevin was so relieved that the dep didn't have some bizarre checking-up-on-him thing going on, he didn't bother to ask what professional reason MacAuley might have to talk to his mom. 'I'm seeing her tomorrow for Sunday dinner. I'll have her call you.'

'Do. It's important.'

That was enough to ignite Kevin's curiosity, but the dep disappeared again, to be replaced by Harlene in the doorway. 'Hadley, you got a call while you were out. Your granddad said somebody named Dylan was taking your kids to the Chuck E. Cheese in Glens Falls, and you could meet 'em there. Noble, are you headed home right now? Will you help me shovel out my car? The plow boxed me in.'

Noble shambled after Harlene, leaving Kevin alone with a no-longer-smiling Hadley.

'Who's Dylan?' He kicked himself the second the words were out. It wasn't any of his business if she was dating someone.

Her face worked. 'My ex,' she finally said.

'Your ex-husband?'

'Yep.'

'From California?'

Her mouth twisted in a bitter smile. 'Come to spend a little time with his dearly beloved children.'

Kevin paused. 'You didn't mention anything about the kids' dad visiting.'

'It was unexpected. Like the asteroid that killed off the dinosaurs.'

Wow. Okay. She was obviously unhappy about this. Kevin had no idea what to say in response. This was the most intimate conversation they'd had since the night of the chief's wedding, when he and Hadley had done their best to destroy their relationship. Friendship. Whatever. 'How do Hudson and Genny feel about it? Seeing their father again?'

Hadley hitched one hip against a desk. 'Hudson thinks it's great. All he remembers are the fun times. "Dad took us to the beach. Dad took us to Disneyland."' She looked at Kevin. 'Dylan used to drag the kids places when they were little and cute and pretend to be a divorced dad to pick up women. *I* paid for the trip to Disneyland.'

Kevin slid his Taser from its holster. 'Let's go tase him.' She laughed. 'Seriously. We'll sneak up behind him. You hit one side and I'll hit the other. I bet if we juice him a few times we can give him convulsions.'

Hadley laughed until she had to wipe her eyes. 'Oh, man. What I wouldn't give to see that.'

'It'd make you feel better.' He stated it as a fact.

She sighed. 'Yeah. It would.' She looked at him again. 'You make me feel better. Thank you.'

He waved her gratitude away. 'Are you going to be okay?'

119

'Yeah.' She picked up her parka from where she had slung it over a chair. 'He's scared shitless of driving in snow, so he's probably already on his way back to Granddad's. I'll terrify him about the road conditions and he'll split for his hotel.'

'He's not staying with you?'

She took her car keys out of her pocket. 'God, no. There's no way I'd let him, and Granddad's house is much too downscale. Nothing but the best for Dylan Knox.' Her voice had gone bitter again.

'Where's he staying?'

'The Algonquin, of course. What other five-star hotel is there around here?'

Kevin stroked his Taser theatrically. 'Good to know.'

She laughed. 'Good night, Flynn. See you tomorrow.' She vanished down the hall, still laughing.

He picked up his own parka. Stuffed his notebook into the pocket. The homicide. The missing girl. Sunday dinner. Syracuse. *Hadley*.

The clock ticked.

NINE

Mikayla woke up shivering with cold. She rooted around in the darkness, tugging her bedding into place. She had a heavy wool blanket to keep her warm, but it was scratchy, so she laid it on top of the quilt, and it liked to slide off the narrow cot onto the floor.

Everything was quiet. There had been somebody new here today, after dinner, with arguing and loud shouts and long quiet times. Mikayla had stayed in the little room and didn't hear anything. She was good at not hearing. Sometimes Mom had people over at her apartment that Mikayla wasn't supposed to see or hear. She would curl up in her bed and read really hard, until the only thing in her head was Amelia Bedelia or Junie B. Jones.

She had books here, too, and even though they were really old – like her Meme could have read them when she was a girl – they were okay. She was reading a funny one called *Mr Popper's Penguins*. She read it when she ate and when she heard weird noises coming from the other bedroom and even in the bathroom, because if she read and read and read she could forget there was someone standing there right in the doorway. He said he wasn't watching, but it still made her feel all shivery and cold inside.

She slid out from beneath the sheets and crossed to the window. It was blacker than black outside, but she could just see the snow piling up on the window ledge. She thought, for a moment, about leaving. She could sneak out now when the whole wide world was quiet. She was a Mohawk, her Pepe was always saying, and she could do anything. He had taught her to find the mossy side of a tree and to make a shelter of pine branches and leaves and how to orient by the North Star if she forgot her compass at home. But mostly he said if she was ever lost to stay put and stay warm and the park wardens would find her.

She climbed back into bed. Besides, if she left, she wouldn't see Mom. The police were keeping Mom away from her because they liked to boss people around and make themselves feel important. Except the lady police who had visited her in the hospital with Mrs Schmidt the social worker. She was nice. She had given Mikayla a bear with a little badge sewn right in his shoulder. Mikayla had put her fire helmet on the bear after her class had visited the station. She had left the bear in her bedroom at Ted and Helen's house.

Her eyes went watery and she blinked a lot. She didn't want to think about Ted and Helen's house. Maybe if she read some more? She was reaching for the lamp when she heard a creak outside. She slid way down and tugged the covers up until they were nearly over her head. *Go away*, she thought. *Go away, go away, go away*.

The door opened.

Sunday, 11 January

ONE

The first thing Russ registered when he woke was *warm*. The heavy quilt was rucked up to his ears and he was wrapped around his wife, their legs tangled, one hand splayed over her rounded abdomen. The second thing was *cold*; his nose and brows and the top of his head twinging from the bite of the air. He should have put more wood in the stoves last night, but when they arrived back at the cabin it was as if an unspoken agreement lay between them to pack in at least one more night of honeymooning. They ate the stew that Clare had simmered on the stove all day and then made love with a desperate, grasping abandon that left them panting and sheened with sweat, the quilt and blankets kicked to the floor. The sex had wrung all the guilt and frustration out of Russ, and he had dropped into sleep as quickly and quietly as the snow falling outside.

Beneath his hand, Clare's belly bunched and moved in a muscular wave. *Holy shit.* He was torn between yanking his hand away and leaving it in place. Then the kicking started. He had never imagined what feet *inside* someone's body might feel like, but there was no mistaking the sensation, light as it was, against his palm. The kid was jumping against Clare like she was a trampoline.

Her hand covered his. 'Mmm. Feel that?' Her voice was sleepy.

'Yeah,' he whispered. 'It's . . . a little creepy. I mean, there's something alive inside of you.'

She laughed low. 'Saw *Alien* a few too many times, did you?'

'I guess so.' He paused, trying to articulate what was in his head. 'You're not going to have a miscarriage, are you?'

'No. I don't think so.'

'I guess I figured that. You're already farther along than . . .' He took a

125

deep breath. 'This . . . is really going to happen. The baby.'

'Yes, it is. On or about April twentieth.' She rubbed her hand along his forearm. 'Does that make you feel any differently? About becoming a father?'

Becoming a father. He thought of his own dad, and his grandfathers. His bum knee and his bullet scars. The kids he'd seen in the line of duty, scared or beaten or abused or old too soon. All the stuff he didn't know – Christ, he had never even changed a diaper. The question was too big. 'I don't know,' he said. 'I don't know how it makes me feel.'

'Let me know when you figure it out, okay?'

He buried his face in her hair instead of answering. They lay together in a not entirely comfortable silence until Clare said, 'What's that?'

'What?'

'That tick-ticking noise.'

Now she mentioned it, he could hear it, too. Pinging and ticking and rattling. 'Oh, crap.' He sat up and tossed off the covers. 'It's hailing.' Goose-bumps swept over his skin. He shrugged on his robe and walked to the bed-room's French doors. The small deck outside, which he had shoveled clear yesterday afternoon, was covered in a gravelly mix of slush and hailstones. More was falling from a leaden sky, thick wet flakes and hard icy pellets.

'What's it look like?' Clare asked, still burrowed beneath the quilts.

'It's slushing. And hailing. The temperature must be rising.' He crossed the freezing floor to where he had left the weather radio on the kitchen counter. 'Probably going to turn into rain soon.'

'Will you try to leave before then?'

He started cranking the radio to power it up. 'No. Safer to let the rain and the road crews clear the way first.'

'In that case . . .' Her tone of voice made him turn around. She was half sitting, half sprawled against the pillows, the covers fallen around her thighs. 'Why don't you come back to bed and get warm?' The cold that was making his bare feet ache was doing wonderful things to her nipples. 'Mmm?'

Jesus. 'Warm,' he said thickly. 'Yeah.' He dropped the radio back onto the counter. Ice. Hail. *Warm.*

TWO

Ice and hail. 'Frigging wintry mix,' Kevin said, slowing the cruiser to a stop behind a line of cars cautiously creeping across the avenue into the Super Kmart parking lot. 'We should've just taken my Aztek. It has four-wheel drive.'

'Quit bitching.' Hadley had the laptop tilted toward her and was scrolling through the list of names and addresses Noble had uploaded this morning. 'It's not that bad.'

'For a Californian, you're awfully confident about driving in upstate New York weather.'

'I didn't grow up in California. I moved there after I left high school.' She paused. 'Dropped out.'

Kevin smiled a little. That was Hadley. Brutally honest, even when she was on the receiving end. Evidently, she misunderstood his expression, because she said, 'I got my GED. Later.'

'I'm not judging you.' The Buick in front of him finally decided it was safe to cross the intersection. Kevin made a slow left, trying to get a feel for the road surface. 'My father never finished high school. State school, it was called in Ireland.'

'Two streets and then a right,' she said, her eyes on the laptop. 'Your dad is Irish? I mean, really Irish?'

'Yep. He came to Boston with a bunch of friends back in the sixties. Great pay doing construction back then. My mom was going to college at St Mary's. They met and bam! Love at first sight.' He signaled and made the turn Hadley had indicated. 'Well, love at first sight for him. She took a little longer to get on board.'

'Okay, this is it. Here.'

Kevin wedged the cruiser into the foot of the driveway and turned off the engine. 'This looks too nice.' The house was a large two-story with a shoveled walk that was rapidly filling with slush and hailstones. Neatly trimmed yew bushes gaped open under the accumulating weight of the wet snow.

Hadley sighed. 'Probably another fake.' They had hit six homes already this morning, going off the license information Noble was collecting from various drugstore registries. Every one so far had turned out to be faked, the real ID copied with its picture replaced and birth dates fudged. All they had to show for a morning's work was a bunch of worried civilians who now knew a lot more about identity theft. Hadley grabbed the pile of license printouts anyway. They put on their plastic-wrapped hats and parkas and trudged up to the door.

The young man who opened the door was in T-shirt and sweats, his hair still rumpled from bed despite the fact that it was close to ten. Hadley looked at the papers in her hand. 'Samuel McKenna?'

The guy went white.

'We have a few questions for you, Mr McKenna. May we come in?' Kevin already had his hand on the door and was stepping over the threshold. The guy backed away. His eyes were huge. Hadley held up the printout so Kevin could see the photo. This was him, all right. Young guy. Barely twenty. 'You are Samuel McKenna?'

The kid jerked his head up and down. Hadley shut the door behind her. In the sudden hush, Kevin could hear the drip-drip-drip of melting snow sliding off their covers. He took his off, and Hadley followed suit.

'What . . .' The kid seemed unable to get the rest of the sentence out.

'Mr McKenna, your driver's license was used as ID in multiple pharmacies around the area to purchase pseudoephedrine.'

'Oh, *shit!*' The kid bent over. 'Oh, shit, oh, shit, oh, shit. I knew this was going to happen. I knew it.'

Hadley looked at him, one eyebrow lifted.

'I swear to God, I'm not a user. I never touch drugs. I don't even drink. Oh, shit. Oh, shit.'

Kevin looked back at her. No, this one wasn't going to require their ace interrogation skills. 'Mr McKenna, is there a place we can sit down and talk?'

The kid made a despairing noise and led them down a hallway lined with years of family photos. In the kitchen, he pulled out a chair and collapsed at the table. A half-eaten bowl of Cheerios sat on a place mat. Kevin sat. Hadley stood, blocking the doorway. 'Mr McKenna. Samuel.' Kevin hardened his voice enough to get the kid to look up at him. 'Tell me about what you did.' He didn't usually ask such open-ended questions, but he had a feeling this kid would spill his guts if Kevin said, 'Boo.'

'I was just trying to earn tuition money,' Samuel said. 'I'm not a criminal. I just needed money for college. I'm already maxed out on federal loans, and I kept hearing horror stories about graduates becoming like indentured serfs to the private bank loans.' He waved his hand at the walls around them. 'I couldn't ask my parents, they're stretched enough as it is—'

'Samuel. How did you get started smurfing? Were you recruited? Who did you work with?'

Samuel blinked. 'My buddy Jason. His older brother was in high school with this girl – woman – who was running a group.'

'Annie Johnson?'

Samuel moaned. 'Yes. Oh, shit, you already have her? Oh, shit.'

'They hooked you up with Annie?'

Samuel nodded. He looked as if he were about to cry. 'She had the van and the money and everything. It was just buying cold medicine. It wasn't going to hurt anyone!'

Hadley broke in. 'Samuel, did you ever hear Annie Johnson talk about her daughter?'

He nodded. 'Yeah, I guess. A couple times. There was some problem. The kid wasn't living with her.'

'Her daughter was kidnapped from her foster home Friday.'

Samuel's eyes widened. 'I don't know anything about that!'

'She's just eight years old,' Hadley went on. It amazed Kevin how utterly pitiless she could sound without ever raising her voice. 'A little girl. She has a medical condition that can kill her if she's not found and given treatment.'

'Oh my God.' Samuel did start to cry. 'I didn't know. All I did was ride around from store to store and buy the stuff. It wasn't going to hurt anyone!'

'Do you know where Annie Johnson might be if she were hiding her daughter?'

'Uh,' he sniffled. 'Her place. Her boyfriend's place.'

Kevin looked at Hadley. They had already ascertained that Travis Roy, who was also missing, had no fixed residence. 'Where else?'

'I don't know!' Samuel paused. 'Maybe the house in the country.'

'The house in the country?'

'That's what Annie called it. She only mentioned it a few times. She had to make a delivery to the place in the country, she'd say.'

'That was where they manufactured the meth?'

The kid flinched away at the word. 'I don't know. Nobody told me what happened to the stuff after we bought it.'

'Where is this house, Samuel?'

'I don't know. Someplace north or west of here, I think. Nobody told me anything. I didn't want to know anything.'

Hadley held up her sheaf of printouts and looked questioningly at Kevin. He nodded. 'Samuel. Officer Knox here is going to show you a bunch of driver's licenses. You're going to tell us the real names of everyone pictured. Got that?' He stood up and let Hadley take his seat.

As she went over each suspected smurfer, Kevin weighed the possibility of the meth house being Annie Johnson's bolt-hole. Meth manufacturing was a smelly, dangerous business, prone to toxic chemical spills and explosions. Would Annie be careless enough to take her daughter there? Maybe. She wasn't about to win any mother-of-the-year awards. On the other hand, the meth house wasn't hers. It probably wasn't her boyfriend's, either. They were both working for someone else – someone financing the operation. Someone who wouldn't want the attention a child's kidnapping brought to his business. He couldn't just cut Annie loose, though. If – *when* – she was caught, the first thing she'd do was roll over. Give the DA a bigger fish to fry. If her boss was smart, he'd realize this. So maybe he was keeping her and Mikayla under wraps.

'Samuel. Who was Annie working for?'

The kid looked up at him, puzzled. 'What do you mean?'

'I don't think she was cooking meth herself. And she sure wasn't able to afford the money for your shopping trips on her own. So who was behind her?'

'She never said outright, but she mentioned one guy's name a few times. Tim LaMar.'

Hadley glanced up at Kevin, a pleased expression flashing across her face.

'But he's in jail,' Samuel said.

'What?' Hadley asked.

'If it's the same guy Annie mentioned, he's in jail,' Samuel said. 'Down, I don't know, somewhere around Poughkeepsie. It was in the papers.' He frowned at them. 'Didn't you know? I figured . . . that's where you got my name, right? He's telling the cops about the rest of us to get his charges reduced. Right?'

THREE

The weather wasn't letting up. No matter how many times he checked it, Russ's hand-cranked radio kept giving them the same forecast: wintry mix and freezing rain from Albany to Montreal. As the morning progressed, Clare watched her husband go from boneless satisfaction to busily packing and prepping the cabin for his absence to stalking back and forth across the space, glaring at the unchanging vista of wet snow and dripping ice. 'I just want to know what's going on,' he said for the tenth time.

She was tempted to ask him if this was changing his mind about their little no-one-can-reach-us hideaway, but she knew he was on edge about the missing child and the problems the department would be having with the worsening roads.

The next time he paced past her to stare accusingly at the lake — now invisible through a scrim of snow and icy rain — Clare set her book in her lap and said, 'What about the radio in your truck?'

'What do you mean?'

'The police band radio. Why don't you use that to contact Lyle?'

'I'd never reach our signal from here.'

'Of course not. But there must be *some* emergency bandwidth out here, right? They do have nine-one-one?'

Russ stopped in his tracks. 'Yeah. Yeah, they do.'

'Can't they relay your signal?'

He grinned at her. 'Yes. They can.' He ruffled her hair. 'Smart girl. I knew there was a reason I kept you around.'

'Mmm.' She went back to reading as he wrestled on his outdoor gear.

'Be right back,' he said. 'C'mon, Oscar. You might as well get out, too.' As the door shut behind them, Clare put her book down. She really did want some alone time this week. She never realized how much sheer energy her pastoral work took out of her until she was away from it. These past three months had been like working under a Laundromat's steam presser. Nothing but scorching heat and pressure and every last wrinkle ironed out of her. She smiled a little. Except for the being-married-to-Russ part. Despite the huge issue that lay – literally – between them, marriage was turning out to be good for her. A bulwark against her PTSD-induced cravings for alcohol and amphetamines. A guarding line between her personal life and her ministry. The place where she wasn't the Reverend Fergusson or Major Fergusson or even – as strange and spiky as it sounded – Mrs Van Alstyne. Just herself.

Oh, hell, she couldn't stay here alone. She sat up and tossed her book on the rickety end table. She didn't need solitude to figure out what to do about the bishop's ultimatum. She needed Russ.

The kitchen door slammed open. Oscar bounded in, shedding snow and ice. 'Good Lord,' Clare said.

Russ was on the dog's heels. 'Get a towel before he—'

Oscar shook himself hard enough to make his short red-gold coat stand to attention. Clare flung up her arms to protect herself from the shower.

'—shakes off,' Russ concluded.

'Thanks for the tip.' Clare grabbed one of the towels hanging on the wall next to the bathroom. She rubbed Oscar down as he wiggled and twisted and tried to lick her face. 'Did it work?'

'Sure did. The state police barracks relayed my call to Harlene, who patched me through to Lyle. It wasn't the best connection, but we could communicate.'

'What did he say?'

'Kevin Flynn and Hadley Knox turned up an interesting lead yesterday evening. Seems the missing girl's father – an ex-con named Hector DeJean – was up here at Cooper's Corners overnight Thursday. Allegedly fixing up a sprung pipe at a church camp. Lyle asked me to check it out.'

'Good thing you didn't leave first thing this morning, then.'

He slanted her a smile. 'Good thing.'

'Listen.' She caught his arm. 'You were right. About me staying. I should go back with you.'

'Thank God. Okay, we can—' He glanced around the cabin. 'No, wait. I don't want to take the time to pack the rest of our stuff up right now. I need to get up to Cooper's Corners.'

'Fine. We go and come back after you've cleared the place.'

'What we, kemosabe?'

'You know, you shouldn't keep saying that. I think it may be racist.'

He held out his hand and made a beckoning motion. *Spill it.*

'The thermostat's turned down to fifty at the rectory, and the driveway is probably completely impassable at this point.'

'Yeah. So?'

'So is that what you want to come home to after a long, stressful drive through bad weather? After dark? Geoff Burns said he'd turn the heat back on and arrange to have us plowed out the day we were getting home. I'm going to ask him to do it this evening, before we get in.'

Russ made a face. He wasn't terribly fond of lawyers, and in Geoff Burns's case it was an actual antipathy.

'You don't need to come all the way up to Cooper's Corners for that.'

She scooped her cell phone off the kitchen counter and slapped it into his hand. 'Okay. *You* call Geoff and ask him to do it.'

Russ looked at her phone as if it were a giant cockroach. Which was close to how he saw Geoffrey Burns. 'Okay,' he finally said. 'But you stay in the truck.'

'All right.'

'With the doors locked.'

'Okay.'

'If – and it's a long shot – but if the little girl is there—'

'We head straight for the nearest hospital.' She hugged him. 'Come on, love. We're burning daylight.'

He looked over her head to where the windows showed their unchanging view of pelting snow and ice. 'Such as it is,' he said.

FOUR

Lyle finally caught a break just before noon. The warrant to search Wendall Sullivan's miserable rental house came through around nine, and he had spent a good chunk of the morning going through Sullivan's room, examining each and every paper, leafing through the books, taking apart the bed, and searching the drawers inside and out. He had pulled the dresser and nightstand away from the wall to see if Sullivan had concealed something, anything, along their hidden surfaces. Nothing.

He was digging into the pockets of the clothing hanging in the closet when he found it. An old peacoat with nothing in its pockets jingled when he slid it out of the way. Lyle shook it again. Another jingle. He traced the stitching of the pockets again, more carefully.

There. A rip in the lining. Lyle pulled the coat off its hanger and fished his nonregulation Swiss Army knife out of his pants. He slid the tip of the knife in at one end of the coat and slashed the lining open. A shower of small change, paper clips, lint, and crumpled receipts fell to the floor. Lyle got down on his knees and started in on the receipts. McDonald's. Dunkin' Donuts. Gas. Gas. Bob's Self Storage Units.

He smoothed the small paper out, trying to read the details. It was dated last March. Two months after Sullivan had gotten out of Fishkill. One hundred twenty dollars charged to his card. No other details. No indication that it was a unit rental. Bob's sold cardboard boxes and rented trucks and those pod things people used when they moved. Lyle trusted his nose, though, and right now it was telling him Sullivan hadn't needed any U-Seal-It packing tape last March. He pulled his cell phone from his pocket and placed a call.

'This better be pretty goddamn important.' Eric McCrea's voice was rusty with sleep.

'Get your gear on,' Lyle said. 'You're coming in early today.'

FIVE

The church camp was empty. Russ searched the main building first, a deep-eaved shingle-sided structure that was basically one football-field-sized room with a kitchen in the middle and toilets on each end. He could see where a leak had indeed sprung; if it was Mikayla's father who had fixed it, he tidied up well after himself, but the floorboards and wall were stained with a film of ice. Clare met him on the wide porch as he came out. 'Can I call from here?' She thumbed back toward the truck. 'I can't hear myself think with the rain on the cab roof.'

The snow and hail was thinning out, replaced with icy rain that pounded on every surface like a pellet-gun attack. 'Sure,' he said. 'It's clear. Don't touch anything, just in case.'

'I won't.' She went into the meeting-house. Russ tightened his hood around his head and waded through the slop of slush and snow to search the individual cabins scattered among the thick pine trees framing the central building. They were small and spare, just empty bunk frames and hooks along the walls and a tiny water closet squeezed into one corner. They were empty, too, and, given the smell of damp and disuse, had been since last September. Russ stepped out of the last cabin, latched it tight, and turned just in time to hear a crack overhead. He slammed himself flat against the door. A thick, ice-encrusted pine branch crashed to the ground, so close he could feel the whiskery brush of needles as it fell.

He looked up. The tree's other branches yawed toward the ground, the weight of the accumulating ice spreading over every needle and twig. The stump left by the breaking branch stood out jagged and white against the near-black bark. *Shit.*

He stomped back to the meeting hall, registering for the first time how his boots were breaking through a crust of ice before sinking into the slurry below.

He kicked the rest of the snow off against the meeting-house porch and went inside. 'Clare—'

She held up one finger. 'No,' she said to her cell phone. 'I haven't decided yet.' She turned away from him. 'No, thanks, Karen, I don't need to be represented yet. And if I do, it'll be under canon law, not civil.' She was standing in the middle of the empty space, not touching anything, like she promised. 'Thanks. I'll keep that in mind. And thank Geoff for us again.' There was a pause. 'Yeah, I figure' – she checked her watch – 'about four hours from now.' She turned back around and smiled tentatively at Russ. 'I will. Bye.' She folded her phone and slipped it into her pocket.

'What was that about?' he asked.

'We're all set. Geoff is going over to turn up the heat, and the man who plows for the Burnses will clear out our driveway.'

'I don't mean that. What's this about a decision and needing a lawyer?'

She looked up at the old-fashioned tin light fixture overhead. 'Russ—'

'Clare . . .'

She threw up her hands. 'I was looking for the right time to tell you.'

'Tell me what, exactly?' His voice was harsh. He tried to bring it under control. 'Are you in trouble? Over a church thing? That's what canon law is, right? Church law?'

She nodded. 'The bishop—' She sighed. 'The bishop's given me an ultimatum. Either I resign my cure quietly, or I face a possible disciplinary hearing for sexual misconduct.'

'Sexual—!' He stared. Then he got it. Her bishop had put two and two together and gotten three, just like everyone else. 'Because you're pregnant.'

'Because I was pregnant before we got married. Yes.'

'But—' He tried to shove his hand into his hair but hit the furred edge of his hood instead. He yanked it down. 'You talked to him. Right? I thought you had to confess and repent.' Goddamn ridiculous church rules. This was why he wasn't religious.

'I confessed.' Her lips curved up. 'I didn't repent. I don't think what we did was a sin. Was it conduct unbefitting a priest?' She shrugged. 'That's the question.'

Russ sat down heavily on one of the long benches lining the walls. 'Sounds like the damn army.'

Her boots thunked across the floor as she walked toward him. 'Actually, that's what the Rules are based on. The Uniform Code of Military Justice.' She sat down next to him.

'When did you find this out?'

'Friday.' She gave him a regretful half-smile. 'I should have told you right away, but there was Amber in the car, and then all the hustle of moving into the cabin, and then I just wanted to enjoy some time alone with you that wasn't . . .'

'I know.' He took her hand. 'So. What are you going to do?'

'I have no idea.' She tilted her head back until it hit the pine-sheathed wall. 'If I'm tried and convicted, it'll be a huge black mark on my record. I may never get another parish again.'

He wanted to say, *You see? This baby is screwing up everything.* He wasn't that much of an idiot, however. And it sure as hell wouldn't make Clare feel any better.

'If I resign, I'll never have another parish in the Diocese of Albany again. I could possibly look elsewhere, but you're committed to staying in Millers Kill as long as the police department needs you.'

'Uh. About that.' He shifted on the hard wooden bench. 'Remember when you asked me what I was talking to Lyle about?'

'Yes . . .' Her voice was wary.

'He and I barged in on an aldermen's meeting on Friday. One we hadn't been invited to. They're considering shutting down the department. To save money.'

'What?' She sat bolt upright.

'Doing away with the whole thing. Having the state police cover the three towns instead.'

'Good God! That's a terrible idea! Why didn't you tell me about this before?'

He smiled a little. 'I just wanted to enjoy some time alone with you that wasn't . . .'

She sagged back against the wall. 'Good Lord. We're a sorry pair, aren't we? If it falls out for the worst, we'll have no jobs, no home, and a baby on the way.'

'Look on the bright side. At least there won't be anything keeping us from moving to a better climate.'

She sat up again, twisting toward him. 'Russ, you've got to fight this. I mean, besides it being the wrong thing for Millers Kill, think of everyone in the department without their jobs. Without health insurance. Harlene. Hadley Knox. All the part-timers who make ends meet with their traffic work. It would be a disaster for them.'

'I know. Believe me, I know.'

They sat side by side for a moment in the cold, empty room. Through the slatted shutters protecting the windows, Russ could see it growing dimmer outside. 'C'mon,' he finally said, standing up and pulling Clare with him. 'We've got to get back to the cabin and start packing before we lose the light completely.'

'Some honeymoon.' She pulled her hood up. 'We might as well have booked a cabin on the *Titanic*.'

He turned off the lights as she opened the door. The outdoors was a glistening rectangle of gray. 'Could be worse,' he said. 'It could always be worse.'

SIX

In the past two years, Hadley had never once wanted to keep working when her shift was over, so arguing with Lyle MacAuley over the radio was a novelty.

'You two are already in overtime. One more hour and you go to triple time, and we can. Not. Afford that. Over.'

She keyed the mic. 'Look, we still haven't hit everyone on the smurfing list. Somebody's got to know something about Annie Johnson's location. Or the meth house. Over.'

'A team from the FBI is going in to talk to this LaMar guy.'

The radio squealed as Hadley signaled at the same time. 'The Feds? What are they doing in this case?'

There was a pause. Either MacAuley was waiting for her to signal 'over', or he was thinking up new ways to rip a strip off her. Finally the radio crackled on again. 'The Feds are involved because racketeering is a federal crime. We don't have all the pieces yet, but it looks like LaMar is into something a lot bigger than cooking up ice in Washington County. He's being held in federal custody without bail at Fishkill.' His voice took on a solicitous tone, as if he were working customer service. 'As to the rest of your concerns, Officer Knox, Eric can complete the interviews after he's done helping me, and the chief's coming home this evening. Does that make you feel better, Officer Knox? Do you approve of those arrangements? Over.'

She looked at Flynn. He was struggling not to smile. She keyed the mic. 'Yes, sir. Over.'

'Good! Now let me remind you that running the department is above your pay grade, Officer Knox! Log out and go home. Do not pass Go and do *not* collect two hundred dollars. MacAuley out.'

She slammed the mic into its holder. It fell out. She slammed it in again and held it there. 'Goddammit.'

Flynn slanted a sideways glance at her. 'You're pretty invested in this, huh?'

'Don't you think you should pay attention to your driving? And how come you're always the one behind the wheel, anyway?' Which was stupid, because she didn't want to drive in this slop.

Flynn being Flynn, he didn't take offense. 'I want to find her, too.'

Hadley's temper deflated. 'God. She's only eight years old. I keep picturing Genny in the same situation. Taken away someplace. Scared. Sick.'

'If LaMar's being held without bail, he's got some powerful motivation for cooperating. And if he's really the one running the operation, chances are good he'll know where we can find Annie Johnson.'

'*If* the Feds cut him a deal. *If* Annie really works for him. *If* she's the one who took Mikayla.'

Ahead of them, a Camry took the right onto Veterans Bridge too fast and slid across both lanes. Flynn slowed and reached for the light-bar switch, but the little car spun up a shower of slush from its rear wheels and righted itself. Flynn relaxed. 'I'm glad we're not on call this afternoon.' He downshifted and held the cruiser steady at thirty. 'It's gonna be nothing but fender benders and off-road skids. People ought to stay off the roads if they don't have a heavy vehicle with four-wheel drive.'

'Some us aren't that lucky, Flynn.' Hadley slouched in her seat. 'With my car, I figure I'm doing well if I can get out of the station's parking lot.' She owned a twelve-year-old Escort with enough miles on it to have gone to the moon and back.

'Why don't you let me drop you at your house? We're going right past Burgoyne.'

She waved her hand. 'That would be great, but how do I get to work tomorrow?' She thought about the lousy roads. Thought about the likelihood of her getting stuck between the station and her house. 'Actually, you know, that *would* be great. Granddad can drop me at the station tomorrow. He's got this ancient Pontiac that weighs as much as a tank.'

He hummed in agreement. It wasn't until he was turning into Burgoyne Street that she realized Flynn had offered to help her out and she hadn't turned him down flat for fear things might get personal. It was working with him the past three days, she supposed. Somewhere between getting caught rescuing a doll and running down fake licenses, she had gotten . . . comfortable with him again. This morning, he had gone into the Stewart's while she tanked up the cruiser, and she hadn't thought twice about accepting the coffee he bought her. It was nice.

'You've got a visitor,' he said.

Hadley sat upright again. Dylan's rental car sat in Granddad's driveway. 'Oh, for chrissakes,' she said. Flynn pulled the squad car as close to the curb as he could get, given the lousy plow job the road crew had done. As she slid open the plexi divider to get the parka she'd tossed in the backseat, Flynn said, 'Hadley . . .' His voice was alert. Tense.

She dropped back into her seat. The front door was open, and Dylan was shepherding the kids onto the porch. They were carrying their sleepover backpacks.

'Oh, no. Oh, that son of a bitch—' She was out of the cruiser and across the lawn in five strides, heedless of the wet snow spattering her uniform blouse and soaking the bottom of her trousers. 'Dylan! What do you think you're doing?' She pounded up the porch steps. 'Kids, get inside.' Granddad was standing in the doorway, looking miserable. She shot him a glare before turning to her ex. 'Where do you think you're taking my children?'

Dylan gave her a patronizing smile. 'We're going to have a sleepover at my hotel.' He beckoned to Hudson and Geneva, who were looking at their father, then their mother, then back to their father.

'Oh, no, you're not.'

'The Weather Channel was saying there's a major storm front stalling out right over upstate New York. Snow and freezing rain. Lots of power outages expected.' He squatted down, bracing his hands on his knees. 'What do you guys think? Do you want to be here when the power goes out? Or at my hotel? They've got generators to keep things going no matter how bad it gets outside. Plus, they have a pool . . .'

Hadley felt the situation sliding away from her, like that Camry losing control on the bridge. 'Tomorrow's a school day. No sleepovers on a school night.'

'But Mom, it's probably gonna be a snow day!' Hudson complained. 'Dad's got cable TV at his hotel! And you can play video games right on it!'

'Tell you what, Honey – if the weather's good enough, I can bring them back tonight. Surely you can spare them for the rest of the day.'

'No, I can't!' A gust of wind sliced through her uniform blouse, and she shivered convulsively.

Dylan laid his hand on Hudson's shoulder. He kept his smile pleasant, but his eyes narrowed as he looked at her. 'Why not? What could be more important than letting Hudson and Genny spend time with their dad?'

'Actually, they're coming to my folks' house for Sunday dinner.' Flynn walked up the porch steps and handed Hadley her parka. 'You ought to get changed, if we don't want to be late.'

'Yes,' she said, grasping the lifeline he'd thrown her. 'Everybody inside so Mom can get changed.' She took Genny's hand and dragged her into the house, trusting Flynn would have her back.

And he did, because a second later, Hudson and Dylan followed her, with Flynn bringing up the rear. Granddad slammed the door shut, and there they all were, a knot of surprise and suspicion and relief all clustered together in the living room.

'I'll be right back.' Hadley looked into Flynn's eyes, hoping he could read her message. *Don't let him leave with the kids.* Flynn nodded, a motion so small she would have missed it if she hadn't been so intent on his face. She pounded up the stairs and into her bedroom, leaving her door wide open so she wouldn't miss what was going on downstairs.

'Who are you?' Dylan asked.

'He's Kevin Flynn,' Hudson answered. 'He helps coach my cross-country team.'

'Minutemen for the win,' Flynn said. She heard something that sounded like slapping hands as she locked her gun and belt away.

'Well, Kevin, I'm Dylan Knox. Hudson and Geneva's *father.*'

'Are we really going to your house for dinner?' Genny asked.

'It's my mom and dad's house, but, yes, you are, sweetheart.'

'But I want to go to Dad's hotel.' Hudson hadn't whined like that since he was three. Hadley had forgotten how obnoxious it was. Flynn said something – she missed his words as she pulled a sweater over her head, but his tone was drier than before. Hudson mumbled a reply.

'Look, *Officer*.' Dylan was doing his do-you-know-who-I-am act. 'I'm sure visiting *Mom* and *Dad* for *Sunday dinner* is a breathtaking, once-in-a-lifetime experience, but I've come all the way from LA to spend time with my children—'

'That's great, man. Spending time with your kids is hugely important.' Flynn sounded cheerfully oblivious to Dylan's condescension. He went on as Hadley wriggled into her jeans. 'Have you guys been having fun with your dad? What have you been doing?'

She couldn't hear how Hudson answered, but Genny piped up loud and clear. 'We watched TV.'

'Tomorrow – or Tuesday, if the storm doesn't clear out tonight – you three should go on the Audubon Society winter nature walk. It's a super-easy trail, and you can see all sorts of animal tracks and birds and sometimes animals themselves. Last time I went, I saw a gray fox and an owl.'

Hadley, sitting on the bed wiggling her socks on, almost laughed aloud at the thought of her ex on a nature walk.

'We're going to spend some quality time at the Algonquin Waters.' Dylan's social superiority sounded even more strained than usual. 'You're probably not familiar with it. I imagine a cop's salary doesn't stretch to luxury resorts.'

Hadley stepped back into her wet boots, grimaced, then tossed another pair of socks and her sneakers into a tote bag.

'Nope. Never stayed there. But I did take part in a sting operation there last fall. It wound up in a standoff with an army SWAT team. Our guns were out, their guns were out, we're all shouting, "Put your weapons down!"'

Hadley ran downstairs. Hudson was hanging on Flynn's every word. Dylan looked like a toddler who had been forced to share a toy. 'Then what happened?' Hudson asked.

'He'll tell you the rest of the story in the car.' Hadley gave Hudson and Genny a little push. 'Scoot. We don't want to make the Flynns wait.'

Granddad opened the door so fast it sent a swirl of cold air through the room. 'S'long! Use your good manners!'

'Do we get to ride in the police car?' Genny was already headed for the porch.

'Until we get to the station.' Flynn followed her. 'Nice meeting you, Dylan!'

Hudson dug in his heels. 'But I want to go with Dad! I want to play video games!'

'You can see your dad again tomorrow. He can come over and help you with your homework.' Hadley leveled her best laser-eye gaze at her son. 'Now go get in the car.'

He sulked out the door.

'I have a right to see my kids,' Dylan said.

'You don't have the right to disrupt our plans and take them off without consulting me.' Hadley picked up her parka from where she had tossed it over a chair. 'What, were you hoping to be gone with them before I got home?'

His eyes shifted to where Flynn had just walked out the door. 'What's with the police escort? He looks like a walking carrot. Is that the best you can do around here?' He shook his head. 'Jesus, your tastes have gone downhill.'

'He's a co-worker. And a friend.'

Dylan laughed. 'You're telling me you never slept with him? That'll be a first.'

She clenched her teeth. 'I'm not telling you anything. Because my life is none of your goddamn business anymore.' She thrust her arms into her coat and zipped it to her chin. 'Next time, talk to me in advance if you want the kids with you.'

'Oh, I will. How about I let you know *right now* that they'll be coming with me back to California unless you give me my property back!'

She stiffened her spine and walked out the door. Dylan followed her onto the porch. 'And don't think you and your boy toy can stop me. You're the one violating our custody agreement, Honey!' The cold wind brought tears to her eyes. She blinked them away and kept walking. 'The law's on my side,' Dylan yelled. 'There's nothing you can do about it! The law's on my side!'

SEVEN

The trip back up the South Shore Drive was bad. As near as Russ could tell, no one had plowed since they had first driven through on Friday night. The truck kept slipping and shuddering as it fell in and out of ice-hardened tire ruts. The drumming of icy rain fought the roar of the heaters and the thwap-thwap-thwap of the wipers. Clare was quiet, letting him focus on keeping them on the narrow road. He was almost startled when she said, 'I think we ought to check in on Amber and her baby.'

He grunted. 'We still have to get the dog and our stuff and make it back out through this mess without getting stuck.' He was already thinking of taking North Shore to get out to the highway. It wasn't plowed at all after their cabin, but with everything icing over, it might be easier to break virgin snow than to try to recross the increasingly slick churned-over surfaces of this road.

'Oh. Well, if you think they'll be okay . . .'

He sighed. 'No, you're right. We should look in on them.'

'I know.'

He risked taking his eyes off the road long enough to toss her a smile. 'And by *we*, I mean *me*. You stay in the truck.'

'I'm not going to argue with you on that one.'

'Look at that. Miracles do happen.'

She was laughing as he pulled on the parking brake and set the four-ways flashing. He clambered out of the cab, hunching his shoulders against the sodden shower. Someone had scraped the flight of stairs leading to the lake house bare, which Russ took as a good sign. They were already starting to ice over again, however, so he went down slowly and carefully. A busted

146

tailbone would be just the souvenir he'd bring home from this train wreck of a honeymoon.

He knocked hard on the door to be heard over the icy rain. It was opened by a man in his late twenties with a goatee and long hair in a ponytail. Russ had seen Amber's boyfriend when he'd dropped her off, and this guy wasn't him. 'Hey,' the man said.

'Hi. I'm Russ Van Alstyne. My wife and I dropped Amber off on Friday.' He tried to see around the guy, but all he caught was a sliver of the kitchen. 'I thought I'd check in on her. Make sure she and the baby were okay with the storm coming on.'

'Oh, yeah. The cop. She mentioned you. No, she and the baby left this morning with her boyfriend. They didn't want to take the chance and get stuck out here.'

'Really? I guess he got his car fixed up a lot faster than he thought.'

'Yeah, I drove them up to the garage to pick it up.' The man was bright-eyed and pink-cheeked, as if he had a fever. His face was hollowed out, his arm, where he held the door against further opening, all ropy muscle.

Whoever he was, he was on something. Speed, maybe, or coke or crank. Russ smiled. 'And you didn't have any trouble on the roads?'

'Nah. I got a two-ton with serious snow tires. I can get through anything.'

'She said this was a family cabin. You must be related.'

The man stopped smiling. 'I'm her uncle. My brother and I own the place.'

'Then do you have a number for her?' Russ casually braced his forearm against the door frame. 'My wife is going to want to know how she and the baby are getting on.' He let his voice drop into a you-know-how-women-are tone.

The man paused. 'I don't, no. Not that I can lay hold of right away.' He paused again. His eyes flicked right for a split second. 'Why don't you come by later? I can dig something up for you.'

Russ had spent the worst year of his life in a jungle in Vietnam, waiting and listening for the faintest sound of sandals walking on grass or a rifle stock being steadied against a branch. Which is why he heard, from somewhere behind the half-closed door, the almost inaudible snick of the action releasing on a semiautomatic.

He smiled. 'No need to bother. Clare and I are on our way back home right this minute. We didn't want to leave Amber in the lurch, but since that's not a problem, we'll be on our way now.' He held up a hand in farewell.

'Bye,' the bearded man said. 'Drive safe.' He shut the door. Russ could hear the lock click.

He walked back up the slippery stairs, the spot between his shoulder blades burning. He climbed back into the cabin and released the parking brake.

'Everything okay?'

He glanced toward the lake house. Only the roof was visible from the road. Which meant they couldn't see the truck. He slipped his gun-locker key off the key ring and handed it to Clare. 'I want you to reach over the backseat and get my rifle and a couple boxes of cartridges out of the locker.'

'Russ? What's going on?' Even as she questioned him, she was unlatching her belt and turning around.

He shifted into gear and slowly rolled away. 'Some guy who says he's her uncle answered the door. Claims he drove Amber and the baby to the garage to pick up the boyfriend's ride this morning.'

The locker lid banged as Clare tossed it open. 'I thought his car was in the shop until Monday.'

'So did I. Here's the thing: There was someone else in the house with him, hiding behind the door. Someone with a firearm.'

He heard her check the safety. Then she thudded back into her seat. 'Ooof.' She rubbed her stomach. 'Surely that's not unusual in this neck of the woods.'

'I heard him chambering a round after I asked for Amber's number.'

Clare sucked in a breath, but all she said was 'Where do you want the rifle?'

'Your side. But within reach.'

She laid it between her seat and the gearshift mount. 'We can turn around once we reach the cut-across.'

'I know. But I'm not going to drive us past that house again if I can help it.'

'What about Amber and the baby? Was he lying, or are they really gone?'

'I didn't see or hear anything to indicate they were still there.' He slowed down and carefully turned onto the road leading to Inverary's north shore. 'We're going to drive to the cabin and get Oscar and whatever we can grab in five minutes. Then we'll keep on going around the lake until we reach the county highway on the other end. Once we've got reception, we can call the state troopers and report it. Somebody can check and see if Amber and the boyfriend were at the garage.'

She twisted in her seat to look behind them. 'Do you think they'll come after us?'

'I'm hoping they're just a couple addicts who freaked out when a cop knocked at the door. If that's all, they'll want to lay low.'

'But . . .' she prompted.

'*But* what the uncle said about Amber worries me. If he and his buddy just came for the weekend to hang out and get high, why did she leave? And if she hasn't left, why is he lying about it?'

'Shouldn't we—'

'No.'

'But Amber—'

'My first concern is making sure *you're* safe.' He goosed the gas a little and made himself finish his sentence honestly. 'You and the baby.'

The deer came out of nowhere. One second the road was clear, and the next Russ was swearing, pumping the brakes, skidding to avoid a collision. They sailed over the ice, no control, sliding, sliding, sliding up over the roadside berm of crusted snow thrown up by the last plow, headed straight for the trees. Russ flung his arm in front of Clare, a useless gesture, and braced for impact.

Nothing happened. They came to a stop five feet in front of the nearest pine. The deer bounded off the road and disappeared into the woods.

'Good God almighty.' Clare sounded breathless.

'You okay?' Russ touched her neck, her shoulder, her leg, his mind already racing ahead to what they were going to do, stuck in the snow halfway between an armed meth head and their cabin, night coming on fast.

'I'm fine.' She laid a hand on his arm, squeezed. 'Just shaken up.'

Russ opened his door and sank into snow up to his knees. He waded around the truck. Clare opened her door. 'What's it look like?'

'No damage. All we have to do is get a tow truck out here to winch it out of the snow, and away we go.' His voice rose in frustration.

She bit her lip. 'We can't shovel it out ourselves?'

'Not unless by "shovel" you mean "backhoe", no.' He looked up toward the road leading from the cabin. 'Oh, shit.'

'What?'

'Someone's coming.'

EIGHT

Lyle was worried he was going to have to get yet another warrant executed for searching the storage unit, but he caught a break. The owner was on-site, helping a couple back their moving pod into place. 'Yeah,' he said when Lyle and Eric McCrea approached him. 'Sundays and Fridays. Busiest days of the week for me. Everybody moves over the weekend. Do-it-yourselfers, anyway.' He thumbed toward the couple, now getting into their car. Their plates read WYOMING. 'C'mon in the office, let me look that up for you.'

The office was banged up out of plywood, every surface covered with rolls of bubble wrap and tape dispensers and flattened cardboard boxes. The owner went behind the counter and sat in a squeaky rolling chair, pulling a long metal filing box toward him.

'You're not computerized?' Eric asked.

'Paper's good enough for me. I can find what I want when I want it, and nothing's gonna go poof if I press the wrong button.' His thick fingers made a rustling noise as he worked his way through the tightly packed yellow papers. 'Besides, I pay enough for the damn credit card machine. Used to be able to take cash for rentals, but that changed after 9/11. Now it's credit cards or nothing.'

'Any of these units heated?' Lyle asked.

'Nah. People don't hardly ever ask for heat. They got electric, though. Each unit's got a light goes on and off with the door. The renters can see their stuff when they go in and out, and I don't pay a fortune in electricity. Here it is.' He eased a paper out of the file. 'What was the name of the guy?'

'Wendall Sullivan.'

The owner shook his head. 'Nope. Sorry. This unit's rented out to Jonathan Davies.' He peered at the credit card receipt Lyle had given him, then back at the form. 'Numbers match up, though.'

Eric leaned on the counter. 'Do you check ID with all your renters?'

The owner shrugged. 'Gotta admit, I don't got any way of verifying what they give me. Somebody's card goes through, I take it on faith it's theirs.'

'The guy we're looking for is a possible suspect in a little girl's kidnapping.' Lyle dropped his voice. 'Can you help us out? Let us take a peek into the unit. Just to see if it might be his.'

The owner frowned. 'Yeah, I guess so. If it's a mix-up, I guess there's no harm done. You're not gonna touch anything, right?'

'We just want a look.'

'Okay, then.' He crossed to a pegboard filled with tagged keys and unhooked number 68. 'Let's go.'

They followed a few steps behind the owner, their boots splashing in the slush. 'None of this is going to be admissible,' Eric said quietly.

'If we see anything likely, you're going to get a warrant. Finding the little girl's got to be our first priority.'

Eric's face pinched. 'You think she's in there?'

'I sure as hell hope not. But it wouldn't be the first time. Sullivan found a place with no computer records to trace and power in the units. That means—'

'Yeah. He could have a refrigerator in there.'

The owner paused in front of a square storage unit, identical to the others stretching out in a row in either direction. They were all twelve-by-twelve, about the size of a room, and old, made of painted metal instead of the more modern plastic compound. The owner bent down and unlocked the front. He rolled it up like a garage door, leaving most of one side open to the weather. Lyle and Eric stepped inside.

No body. No captive child, either, and no innocuous-looking chest freezer that might turn out to have a nasty surprise inside. In fact, the unit didn't have much in it at all. A big recliner piled with blankets. A plastic cooler big enough to hold a six-pack. A few boxes along the walls. A card table with an older-model computer on it and a folding chair drawn up against it.

'All right, this ain't allowed.' The owner had his hand on an outdoor power cord running from the overhead light to a surge protector on the floor. The computer was plugged into it. Three unplugged cords led to three electric space heaters.

'Dep,' Eric said. 'The boxes.' He was reaching inside one.

'Eric, we can't—'

'This one was open.' The sergeant held up a handful of glossy magazines. *Little Cuties*, read the one on top. He handed another to Lyle. *Lollipop Girls*. Lyle flipped it open and then slapped it shut, his gut churning.

'What'n the name of Christ is that?' The owner's voice was outraged. 'Kiddie porn? Jesus Christ!'

'This was like his rec room,' Eric said. He looked at the computer monitor as if it were a huge, hairy spider waiting to strike. 'What do you think's on that hard drive?'

'Nothing I ever want to see,' Lyle said. He turned around in a slow circle. 'Is there anything that might tip us off where the girl is?'

'He could've kept her in here,' Eric said. 'With the heaters running. A couple sleeping bags on the floor, some water in the little cooler . . .'

'Jesus Christ,' the owner repeated.

'Have you heard anything out here since Friday?' Lyle asked. 'Noises? Or seen anyone coming or going?'

The man shook his head. 'Once they got their keys, the renters come and go on their own. I mean, if I hadda *thought* . . . but Christ, who'd've thought of *this*?'

'Okay. Eric, the first thing we have to do is to find out who Jonathan Davies is. Did Sullivan have a fake ID? Or is Davies another pervert he met up with while he was doing time? Once we've gotten that down, we need a warrant and a forensic team. I want to know if the girl was in here at some point in the last three days.'

Eric nodded. 'If she was, where do you think he or they moved her?'

Lyle crossed his arms and stared at the concrete floor. 'My gut's saying he – or they – went to ground. There's an AMBER Alert out, which makes it a lot more dangerous for him to be in a car. Hard to hide a kid in a car.' It would be a lot easier to hide a body, but he didn't need to tell Eric that.

'Not a lot of motels open this time of year.'

'Yeah, and they have people around. Maids. Managers.'

'Someplace private,' Eric said. 'Preferably away from the towns. Maybe Davies has a house out in the country.'

'Let's hope so.' Lyle took off his hat and banged it against his leg. 'Because all anyone has to do is keep her tucked away long enough for her body to reject that liver. She dies of natural causes and we've got nothing to say who's responsible.'

NINE

Grab the rifle and the cartridges,' Russ said. Clare stuffed the boxes in one parka pocket and slid out of the truck. She leaned in, flipped open the glove box, and removed Russ's heavy Maglite.

'Clare. Into the trees. Now.' She bumped the door shut with her elbow. Russ was breaking the trail for her – literally, as the freezing rain was creating a hard crystalline crust over the deep snow beneath. She floundered, trying to catch up to him. He reached out, and she passed him the rifle. She shoved the flashlight into her other pocket and took his proffered hand.

The pines were dense, sheltering them from the incessant rain. Russ tugged her deeper and deeper into the trees, the ground sloping more steeply as they descended toward the lake. They pressed on until even the yellow shine of their headlights had disappeared from view. Russ stopped and cracked open the rifle's magazine.

'Maybe it's a good Samaritan,' she said in an undertone.

He held out his hand for the cartridges. She passed him a box. 'I hope it is.' His voice was as quiet as hers had been. 'I hope I'm being a paranoid fool.' He thumbed the cartridges in and safetied the rifle. 'Listen.' He took her hand. 'I'm going up there to see what's going on. If you hear anything – any gunfire, any yelling – I want you to keep walking downslope until you reach the lake. It's only about a quarter, half mile from here.'

'Russ—' she said.

He went on as if she hadn't spoken. 'Follow the lake until you get to our place. You can hole up there until daylight. You can stoke the fire in the woodstove, but don't turn on any of the lamps. As soon as it's light enough to move, head up the north shore toward the county highway. Stay off the road.'

'I won't leave you.'

He leaned his forehead against hers for a moment. 'I'm not planning on being left behind. This is just in case.'

'Be careful,' she whispered.

'Always.' He turned and headed back upslope, swinging wide of the trail they had broken, cutting through virgin snow. She wanted to go after him, to offer to do something, but she knew that pregnant and unarmed she'd be more of a distraction than a help. She felt useless, useless and afraid. *Oh, God, please protect him. Please keep him safe. Please, God, please, God, please.*

She waited. And waited. And waited. She heard nothing. Oh, God, what if someone took Russ without a shot being fired? How would she know? She could follow him. She might be bulky, but she could still move quietly. And she had the Maglite, long and heavy, like a club. She would follow Russ and see what they had done with him and then . . . then . . . she would figure something out. She always worked best when she was improvising, anyway.

A movement in the trees ahead of her sent her down into the snow – a less-than-useful camouflage when she discovered she couldn't get as flat as she used to. She raised her head to see her husband threading his way between the hemlocks.

'Is that your attempt at hiding?' Russ was still speaking in an almost-whisper. Her hopes that the oncoming vehicle had been friendly drizzled away.

'I figured standing behind a tree wouldn't work.' He reached down and helped her to her feet. 'What's going on?'

'Two guys in an SUV. Both of 'em armed. They got out of the vehicle and walked up and down the road.'

'Our tracks.'

Russ nodded. 'They found them. Followed our trail to the trees. They got close enough for me to ID one of them. It was the guy in the cabin.'

'So.' Clare swallowed. 'Not good Samaritans, then.' Not when they went looking for lost motorists with their rifles locked and loaded.

'They opened up the truck and rifled through the glove compartment.' Russ shook his head. 'I'm worried, Clare. Real worried. This is exactly the kind of country you're likely to find meth houses or pot barns. If these guys are up here on serious business, we could be in a world of trouble.'

She leaned against him. 'I'm so sorry. This is all my fault. I knew Amber Willis for exactly four minutes before I offered her a ride out here.'

Russ put his arm around her and hugged her as close as they could get in two bulky parkas. 'Whatever's going on in that house, I don't think Amber knew about it ahead of time.'

'Still. It might have been useful if I knew her uncle was, I don't know, a convicted felon. Or that her boyfriend was on the terrorist watch list.'

Russ let out a huff of a laugh. 'That one, I think I can give you a pass on.'

'Now what? The truck is still stuck in the snow. Do you want to change your mind about shoveling it out?'

'No. What I want to do is go down the road a ways and take shelter someplace where I can see if they decide to come back. While I'm keeping watch, you're going to get on the radio and see if you can get through on the emergency band.'

'How about I keep watch and you make the call? If I can raise a dispatcher, she'll take you more seriously.'

'Because if anyone *does* come back up the road, my plan is to shoot out one of their tires and then run like hell.' He pressed one gloved hand against the bulk of her abdomen. 'Running like hell through snow isn't your strong suit right now.'

'Sadly true. Okay, let's—' A screeching, whirring noise split the cathedral quiet of the pines.

'The hell?' Russ turned and jogged upslope, twisting through birch and hemlock and pines, his legs churning up more snow in his already-broken path. Clare ran after him as well as she could. In the best of circumstances, the pregnancy threw her balance off; now, in irregularly compacted snow over hidden roots and slumbering plants, she had to fling her arms wide just to keep from toppling over.

She lost Russ altogether for a moment, then rediscovered him at the edge of the wood, where the mature trees began to thin into saplings and brush. He was sprawled in the snow in a classic sniper's position. He gestured for her to get down. She dropped to her hands and knees, then curled sideways into the lowest silhouette she could manage.

The whirring sound was coming from a winch motor bolted to the front of a heavy work truck, one of the two-ton jacks-of-all-trades she was used to seeing all over Cossayuharie's farm country. As she watched, a snowsuited man carried the unspooling tow wire to the rear of Russ's pickup. He bent down and vanished from their sight for a minute.

'Was that one of the men you saw?' she whispered.

Russ was peering through his rifle scope. 'Yeah. Amber's alleged uncle.' Russ's voice was low and tense. 'I didn't see whoever it was behind the door, but the driver's got to be the other guy. The uncle told me he owned a two-ton. The other guy's got the SUV. That means there are likely only the two—' He broke off as the pickup shuddered. The winch engine roared, whined, and then their truck was rolling back up through the deep ruts they had gashed in the snow. It tilted crazily for a moment getting over the snow berm, and then it was back on the solid surface of the road. The man who had hooked up the winch wire climbed into the passenger side of the heavy-duty truck. The vehicle slowly backed down the road, towing their pickup with it.

'Well, that's that.' Russ rolled over and sat up. 'Christ, what a goat cluster.'

Clare clambered to her feet. 'Come on.'

'Come on?' He looked up at her. 'Where?'

'It's time to put your just-in-case plan into action. We walk along the lake edge to our cabin. We can hole up there for the night.'

Russ handed her the rifle before standing up and brushing the snow off himself. 'You do realize they probably know where we're staying, right?'

'I thought your idea was sound. No lights. There's no way anyone will be able to see any chimney smoke at night in this miserable weather.' She reached up and pulled a clot of frozen snow off the fur trim of his hood. 'This ice storm isn't stopping anytime soon. We need shelter. And heat.' *Or we'll die.* She didn't have to add that last. She could read it in Russ's eyes.

'We'll have to sleep in watches.'

'I can do that.' She turned downslope, toward the lake. It was going to be a long, miserable march, and they would both be soaked by the time they got to the cabin. Better to get started sooner rather than later.

'You're a hell of a woman. Have I told you that lately?'

She tossed a smile over her shoulder to disguise how scared she was. 'Next vacation? Caribbean beach. And *no one* knows where we're going.'

TEN

If Hadley had thought about it – and okay, yes, she had – she would have pictured Kevin Flynn's family as Flynn in duplicate; a bunch of bright-eyed, optimistic redheads in a dumpy house with lots of books. As it was, they did seem to be a cheerful crew, but Kevin's brothers, ranging from their early thirties to college age, all had sandy blond or brown hair, and his parents' house was big and modern and in a ritzy development outside of Saratoga.

Flynn ushered her and the kids in – she hissed a last-minute warning to Hudson, who had been complaining during most of the ride there – and she was immediately overwhelmed by what seemed to be hundreds of Flynns. They resolved into two older brothers with wives and small children, two younger brothers, unattached, and Flynn's – *Kevin's* – parents. His dad resembled one of the stevedores she used to see at Long Beach, buttoned into a good shirt and ordered to stay clean. His mother looked to be the one buttoning and ordering; she had expensively cut and colored hair and a puff of a sweater that had to be cashmere. Hadley, in jeans and a turtleneck, felt a twinge of self-consciousness, but the daughters-in-law weren't done up any fancier than she was, so she supposed she would do.

Flynn – *Kevin* – did a rapid-fire introduction of his relations, of which Sean and Elle, his parents, were the only names that lodged in her memory. He finished with 'Everybody, this is Hadley Knox, and her kids, Hudson and Geneva.'

'Hadley Knox?' One of the daughters-in-law smiled.

'The one who works with Kevin?' the youngest Flynn asked.

'That would be *Officer* Knox to you, frog-face,' an older brother said.

Elle Flynn parted the crowd to take Hadley's hand. 'You're even more lovely than Kevin's description.'

Hadley's wash of embarrassment was mollified by the sight of Flynn's face turning bright red. 'Mom . . .' he protested.

Elle ignored her son. 'We're so glad you could join us for Sunday dinner.'

'About time you finally brought a girl, Kev. We were starting to wonder.' The oldest brother punched Flynn in the arm.

Flynn smiled tightly. 'It'd be a shame if I had to ticket you for a busted tail-light, Connor.'

'My tail-light isn't – hey!'

'Boys.' Sean Flynn's voice cut through the catcalls and jeers rising from his sons. 'Leave Kevin alone, or he'll never be like to bring another girl for Sunday.' He turned and beamed at Hadley, and she could see where Kevin had gotten his breathtakingly sweet smile. 'And what a waste and a shame that would be.'

'Oh, Lord help us, he's breaking out the blarney and we haven't even poured the wine yet.' Elle Flynn linked her arm through Hadley's. 'You come in the kitchen with me and the girls. It's a testosterone-free zone.'

Flynn had told her his mother did something for the governor's office, but Hadley figured the woman's training was in law, because in the half hour before they sat down, Elle Flynn deposed Hadley like a master. She got Hadley's life story – at least the expurgated version – her kids' grades, sports, and interests, the Hadley family history, and her religious affiliation. 'Oh. You're not Catholic?' Elle waved one oven-mitt-clad hand. 'Well, never mind. Sadie wasn't Catholic, either.'

The dark-haired daughter-in-law tossing salad rolled her eyes. 'I'm *still* not Catholic, Elle.'

'Jewish is practically Catholic,' Elle said. 'You have the guilt, you adore your mothers, and you own good silver candlesticks.'

'Don't let Elle throw you,' Sadie said as she and Hadley toted steaming dishes out to the dining room table. 'She loves her sons, but she always sides with the girls against the boys.'

'Flynn and I aren't . . . we just work together.' Hadley plunked her bowl of stuffing on a hot pad. The lace-covered table was larger than her first West Hollywood flat. 'I mean, we're friends, but we're not, you know . . .'

She shut up at the amused expression on Sadie's face. God. She sounded like a high schooler justifying accepting a ride from a boy at school.

She excused herself to find her kids. Hudson and Flynn were playing Wii tennis in the family room, with Flynn's brothers encouraging Hudson to wipe the floor with Kevin. Genny was upstairs, playing dress-up with a curly-headed girl of about six who had to be Sadie's daughter. Hadley hustled both of them off to wash their hands and got back down just in time to be seated.

Sean Flynn led them in a prayer that included blessing the food, the grandchildren, and all the souls of the faithfully departed. Hadley half-expected to see the men lunge for the heaping platters of roast chicken and lasagna, but either Elle or Sean had trained them up well, and the dishes passed around the table in an orderly fashion.

'This is amazing,' Hadley said to Flynn, who was seated to her left. 'In my family, we didn't have meals like this at Thanksgiving, let alone every day.'

Flynn shook his head. 'We didn't eat like this every day, believe me. Mom went back to work for the Small Business Administration full-time after Ian started kindergarten.' He nodded toward his youngest brother. 'I was raised on microwave dinners and takeout from Amato's Italian Diner.' He grinned. 'Which is probably why we're the only Irish American family that eats pasta alfredo on St Paddy's Day instead of corned beef.'

'What's that you're saying about the blessed saint?' Sean asked from the head of the table.

'I was explaining we didn't have dinners like this seven nights a week when we were growing up.'

'God, no.' Sean took a sip of his wine. 'We'd none of us be able to fit out the door. We were both of us working long hours when the boys were young,' he said to Hadley.

'Dad owns his own construction company,' Kevin explained. 'Connor works with him.'

'But Elle had the brave idea that we should all sit down as a family once a week. So we started, and so we continue. Our table keeps getting bigger, with daughters and grandchildren and' – Sean raised his glass to

Hadley – 'the occasional charming guest. But we'll keep the Sabbath together so long as we fit into this dining room.'

'That's not going to stop him,' Connor said. 'He's already got plans to expand out through the back porch.' He grinned. 'Once Kevin gets off his duff and starts contributing to "the grandchild shortage around here".' He said the last words in a perfect imitation of his father's accent.

Flynn threw a roll at his brother's head.

'Boys!' Elle set her fork down and glared at them.

'They're getting their Irish up now,' Sadie said.

Hadley could imagine what it would be like, coming here every Sunday, wrapped in the warm and easy affection of the Flynns. Watching the children grow up, watching the grandparents grow old, with Flynn always beside her, steady and rooted as the Adirondack mountains. She could be one of them. Part of the family. Right up until the moment when they found out about her unlovely past.

She laid her fork on her plate and took a stab at rejoining the conversation. 'How about you, Elle? Are you Irish, too? Your name's French, isn't it?'

The table erupted in laughter.

'What?' Hadley turned toward Flynn. 'What did I say?'

Elle folded her hands and smiled. 'I am Irish, yes. Although my family came to America about a century before my husband finally made it.'

'Always save the best for last,' Sean said.

'I changed my name when I married Sean. To my initial. My Christian name was' – she sighed – 'Lynn.'

Hadley paused for a moment. Then she got it. 'Oh!' Up and down the table, Elle's sons were snickering. 'I changed my first name, too.' She didn't normally advertise the fact, but she felt a kindred spirit with Flynn's mother. 'My parents called me Honey.'

'A little too sweet for an officer of the law, then.' Sean took another drink of wine. 'Honey Knox.'

'No, Knox is from my former husband.' That and the children were the only good things he had ever given her. 'My, um, birth name was Potts.'

There was a moment of silence at the table. Then the room rocked with laughter. Hadley couldn't help it. She began to laugh as well – the first time she had been able to join in on the amusement engendered by that awful, awful name. Sean raised his glass. The rest of the table followed suit. 'Ladies and gentlemen,' he said, 'a toast. To Honey Potts and Lynn Flynn. May their names be a blessing.'

Flynn drove them home. The wintry mix had turned to a remorseless icy rain that hit the roof of the Aztek like bird shot from a 20-gauge. The big plows were out on the Northway, in a futile battle to keep the interstate ice-free. Flynn kept his SUV at a steady thirty-five, and that felt just about right. 'Do you think we'll get called back out tonight?' Hadley asked.

'Not unless aliens invade. I think MacAuley would rather close up the streets with barricades than pay us triple time.'

She laughed softly. 'Yeah.' She twisted around to check the kids. They were both sound asleep, Hudson leaning against Flynn's rolled-up emergency blanket, Genny clutching a giant pillow buddy Elle and Sean had insisted she take. Hadley faced front again. 'I like your family.'

Flynn smiled. 'I like them, too.' Something passed over his face, outlined in the dim glow from his dashboard.

'What?'

'I have to—' He stopped.

'What?'

He let out a breath. 'I've gotten a job offer. From the Syracuse Police Department.'

Hadley blinked. What did he mean? 'A job offer, like another TDY for a few months?'

'No, a permanent position. As an officer on the force, full-time.'

'You mean, you might leave Millers Kill for good?' Hadley couldn't help herself, her voice cracked on the last word. She couldn't fit her head around the idea of the MKPD without Flynn.

'I don't know. It's a great opportunity. Get off of patrol, move into investigations. In a few more years, I could make detective.'

'You investigate here. We're running a missing persons case right now.' She forced her voice into a less panicked tone. 'They're not going to let you do that in Syracuse.'

'We're running one part of the case because there literally isn't anyone else to do the work. That's a long way from actually being a detective.' He shook his head. 'There *are* no detectives on the MKPD. The town won't authorize that pay grade.'

'You could be a sergeant. Like Eric.'

'I'm not going to make sergeant until MacAuley retires and Eric steps into his shoes.'

'But still. Do you really want to leave Millers Kill?' Cripes. Now she sounded like her grandfather. She didn't know why she was arguing with Flynn. He was right. Syracuse would offer him more. More money, more opportunities—

Don't go. Please don't go.

She shifted in her seat.

'I don't know. I've never been the kind of guy who had the big urge to go out and see the world. My family is all within an hour's drive. My friends from high school.'

'Did you like working at the Syracuse department? When you were there on TDY?'

'Yeah, I did. It was ... lively. It's a big city, and there was always something going down. The guys I worked with were good cops.' He paused. 'It was nice not being "the kid", you know? I mean, the chief and MacAuley are great, but they still look at me like I just got out of the academy. There were a lot of young guys in Syracuse, so I wasn't the junior boy detective there.' A car pulled into the lane ahead of him, splattering ice and salt over the Aztek's windshield. Flynn slowed down.

'I guess ... Syracuse would be a good place for you. Careerwise, I mean.'

'Yeah. I just have to figure out if it's what I want.'

He didn't seem to want to say anything more about the job, so Hadley let him focus on his driving. Moving on would be a sensible choice for him to make. She leaned forward and adjusted the dash vent. So why did the idea make her so miserable? It wasn't like she was going to have a personal relationship with him. Dylan's arrival had just underlined why that would be impossible. Was it because they made a good team? She let her eyes half-shut. She had been glad when MacAuley assigned them to this case. It had gotten them past the awkwardness of rejected romance and back into the groove of working together. Flynn was pretty close to the perfect partner for her. Even though she was eight years his senior, they had similar tastes in food and music and movies. They *got* each other. He was smart and intuitive and hardworking. And he had this way of defusing situations, of calming people down that was a good balance to her more confrontational approach.

And he was amazing in bed.

Jesus H. Christ, what was wrong with her?

'What?' Flynn asked.

'What do you mean, what?'

'You just made a noise.'

She touched her heated throat, grateful he couldn't see her flush in the dim light from the dashboard. 'Nothing. Just thinking.'

'About your ex?'

She grasped the conversational lifeline. 'Yeah.'

'Let me know if he tries anything, okay?'

'Yeah, I will.'

He took one hand off the steering wheel and touched her arm just above her wrist. 'I mean it. You're not alone, Hadley. You can ask for help.' He dropped his hand. 'And if you're, you know, uncomfortable talking to me, go to one of the other guys. We're family. We look out for one another.'

She swallowed. 'Thank you.' He returned his attention to the road. She looked at his profile: high cheekbones, bumped nose – he had broken it in a high school basketball game – his forehead, where his regulation-short hair threatened to flop forward within a week after he visited the barber. Who he was shone out of his features, good and kind and honest. Flynn was a clear river running by; no darkness, no hidden snags or treacherous rapids. Compared to him, she felt like the Swamp Thing.

Granddad had left the porch and kitchen lights on, but his window was dark; he had already gone to bed. There was no sign of Dylan's car. Hadley steered her sleepy son into the kitchen and straight upstairs. Flynn carried Genny. For once, Hadley gave a pass on toothbrushing, and she got the kids into their pajamas and bedded down within minutes.

Flynn was waiting for her at the bottom of the stairs. 'Everything okay?'

'Oh, yeah. Thanks for taking Genny to her room.'

His smile was outlined in the half-light spilling from the kitchen. 'I had no idea there were that many Hello Kitty posters in the world.'

'Yeah. When she gets into her Hello Kitty nightgown, I can't spot her unless she moves.'

They both laughed a little. They were standing in the shadows near the door. Everyone else in the house was asleep behind closed doors. He looked down at her and she saw that clear river running, felt the whole-body shock of diving in.

She had made the move on him, that first summer she was on the force. Then again at the chief's wedding. It had been good, why not do it again? It had frustrated her – no, she'd been pissed off – that he kept shoving emotions into what should have been a simple, mindless, physical release.

But looking into his eyes in the half-light, Hadley realized she couldn't do it anymore, despite the hour and the darkness and her bed just a stair flight away. Not because he might say no again. Not because she didn't want to hurt his feelings afterward. But because she was so close to falling for him that even sliding her arms around his neck and stretching up for a kiss might send her over the edge.

She broke her gaze and stared at her stockinged feet. 'Good night, Flynn. Thanks for everything.'

She heard him breathe. 'Good night, Hadley.' He paused at the door. 'It was my pleasure.'

ELEVEN

Mikayla tossed fitfully in her narrow bed. She was so hot. She had kicked off the blankets earlier, but that hadn't helped. Aspirin hadn't helped – awful, grown-up aspirin that she had choked on until it turned to powder in her mouth because there wasn't any of the chewable pills or bubblegum-flavored stuff her mom gave her.

She wanted to open the window even though the rain was still coming down, but she had been told to keep the window locked and the curtains closed. She wanted her mom. Or her Meme. Or even Helen, who made a game out of all the medicines Mikayla had to take. She wanted someone to change her sweaty sheets and bring her a fresh clean nightie and lay a cool washcloth on her head. She didn't want to be here. She wanted to go home, even if she wasn't sure where home was.

Mikayla pressed her face into her pillow and began to cry.

Monday, 12 January

ONE

The wail of a siren woke Clare up. She had taken the first watch, after they had finally gotten to the cabin and dried off. It had been a nightmarish slog through the dark and the pelting rain, the flashlight angled down so that they could only just see where their boots would fall, the crack and boom of branches snapping under the steadily accumulating layers of ice. By the time they reached the cabin, Clare felt like one exposed nerve, numb with cold and scraped raw by the artillery-like barrage of exploding wood. She had been drop-jawed when she checked her watch and found their hike had lasted less than two hours.

Russ had toweled dry, wolfed down two bowls of the stew she had made that morning, and was asleep before she had finished hanging their wet clothing over an old drying rack she had found in the bathroom. Even the thud of small branches falling on the roof hadn't awakened him. Clare had roamed from window to window, watching for the telltale gleam of head-lights or flashlights, certain she would never be able to sleep in the face of the noise of the storm and her own sick dread of what might be out there in the darkness. But after she shook her husband awake and took his place under the covers – the bed already warm and smelling of Russ – she fell into a dreamless sleep.

Until the siren. She pushed herself into a sitting position, groggy and disoriented. The light through the windows was gray and watery. 'Russ?' Her voice was dry. She scrubbed the sleep out of her eyes.

The stoves were stoked, but Russ and the dog were gone. As was the rifle. Clare struggled into her clothes and was just tying on her boots when the siren ceased. The sudden lack of noise enabled her to hear the spatter-ping of the falling ice. The storm was still going on.

She shrugged on her parka – the clothing from yesterday was board stiff and bone dry, hanging next to the woodstove – and went out the door. She couldn't see the road from where she stood, but she thought she heard the thrum of an engine up there. The steep stairs they had used just yesterday were so coated with ice they could have served as a luge run. Next to the steps, however, she could see where Russ's boots had stomped an irregular path through the ice-crusted snow. She followed in his footsteps. Despite the hill's angle, her footing was sound; beneath the thick layer of ice, the snow was firm, catching and crunching beneath her boot treads. She popped over the lip of the hill, panting and hot, to find Russ and another cop sitting inside a state police cruiser.

The passenger door swung open, and Russ stepped out. 'I'm sorry, darlin'. You didn't have to come all the way up here.'

'What's . . .' She waved at the car while catching her breath '. . . going on?'

The trooper stepped out of his vehicle. He was as tall as Russ, but leaner, bald with a laurel wreath of gray hair clipped down to a shadow at the back of his skull. 'You remember Bob Mongue, don't you?' Russ said.

'Sergeant Mongue. Of course.' Every time Russ's path had crossed with Bob Mongue's, it was like watching two dogs snarling over the same bone. She had never really gotten the story why.

'It's lieutenant now, Mrs Van Alstyne. Why don't you get into the car where we can all stay dry?'

Clare ducked into the rear seat. Oscar was already there, his nose making smears against the Plexiglas shield that separated cops from criminals. Russ and Bob Mongue climbed back into their places. Mongue slid the partition open, leaving a grated screen they could talk through.

'Lyle and the Burnses both reported us missing,' Russ said, before she could ask what had brought the state police to their door. 'I've told Bob what happened yesterday.'

'We've called in the license number of the truck that towed your vehicle.' Mongue tapped the elaborate radio and computer mount on his dashboard. 'We're waiting to hear back on the owner.'

'You just . . . drove right past there, without any trouble?' Clare glanced at Russ. Had his concerns about the danger been overblown?

Mongue laughed a little. 'Well, I do have chains on the tires. I'm not going to take a nosedive off the road like Russ's truck did.'

Her husband's lips tightened.

'I meant, no interference from anyone,' Clare said. She checked her watch. It was almost eight o'clock. 'Did you use your siren the whole way?'

'I certainly did. It could have been an officer down. We all remember what happened that other time Russ went walking through icy woods.' He grinned. 'Although that was more like officer falling down.'

'I don't think one broken leg in ten years as chief actually sets a precedent,' Russ said.

'Still, we're glad you came.' Clare wanted to get the subject away from 'officer down', before they started showing each other their bullet scars. 'I'd expect a trooper, not a lieutenant.'

'Oh, Mrs Van Alstyne. I wouldn't have missed this for the world.'

Russ opened his mouth, but at that moment the radio crackled to life. 'State delta oh-four-nine.' The voice was washed with static.

Mongue unhitched the mic. 'This is state delta oh-four-nine. Go ahead.'

'The owner of record is Travis Roy. He has one arrest one conviction possession, one arrest one conviction—' The voice was drowned in a surge of static.

Mongue twisted the dial. 'Dispatch? Can you copy that?'

'—possible ten-fifty.'

Russ and Mongue both sat up straight. Russ gestured to Mongue. The lieutenant keyed the mic again. 'Dispatch, ten-twenty-one.'

'Travis Roy is BOLO from the Millers Kill Police Department in connection to a possible juvenile ten-fifty.'

Russ sucked in his breath.

'What's a ten-fifty?' Clare asked.

The grating cast a shadow over Russ's face. 'Missing person,' he said.

TWO

'Dep?' Noble Entwhistle peered around the door, waving a sheaf of papers in his hand. Lyle was spending the morning working the phones in the chief's office, split between worry over Russ and annoyance that the man had gone on his benighted honeymoon in the first place. Lyle knew what honeymoons were supposed to be for, and as far as he was concerned, you could do it at home in the comfort of your own bed. But no, Russ had wanted ice fishing, and as a result they were shorthanded during what was bidding fair to be the ice storm of the goddamn century.

He beckoned Noble in, still talking into the receiver. 'Then turn your search and rescue guys out. If they can find idiot hikers in the mountains, they should be able to throw up a few barricades and help direct traffic.' John Huggins had called him up complaining about not having enough emergency roadway volunteers. Lyle, who already had a bad taste in his mouth after having to go hat in hand to the state police for help in finding Russ, wasn't inclined to baby the fire chief.

'I can't ask those guys to—'

Lyle cut him off. 'I don't care if you ask the Girl Scouts to do the job. We're getting calls about fallen tree limbs and downed lines and all the National Grid guys can tell me is we're on their list and they're responding to reports in order of importance. So you get someone out there before somebody drives over a goddamn live wire and fries himself!' He slammed the phone down. He'd pay for it later, but it sure made him feel better right now.

'I got the circ sheet info for Travis Roy.' Noble frowned at the stack of papers in his hand. 'There's more than one.'

'There usually is.' Lyle took the papers and began thumbing through them.

'Dep?'

'Yeah?' Lyle pulled out one of the circ sheets as a possible.

'You know you asked me to run a check on the MacAllens? Just in case?'

'Yeah.' Here was a good one, he thought, glancing over the sheet in hand. Guy had been arrested for soliciting for prostitution – pimping. Maybe he had branched out into little girls.

'There was something kind of funny.'

Lyle finally focused on Noble. 'What?'

'Mr MacAllen was retired FBI. And, uh, as near as I can tell, they never took in any foster kids before they got sent Mikayla.'

THREE

Mongue wanted to head over there right away. 'There are two of them,' he said, leaning over the kitchen counter. 'There are two of us.'

'Two is the minimum number. There may be more.' Russ stuffed his flannel-lined jeans and a heavy sweater into his fishing duffel. 'Plus hostages. If he is the kidnapper, he's got our missing girl. Plus there's a chance Amber Willis and her baby are still in the house.'

'All the more reason to hit 'em now.' Mongue crossed to the enclosed porch and peered out to where, on a clear day, they would have seen the morning sun. 'Before they get moved to another location.'

Clare looked up from where she was filling her day pack. 'Is it possible Roy has the girl? It sounded like the mother had taken her when you told me about it.'

'Yes, it's possible.' Russ swung his rifle's magazine cover open and let the cartridges fall into his hand. He locked the safety and slid the gun into the duffel. 'But whoever took Mikayla Johnson left two bodies behind. They're dangerous. Which is why you're not getting anywhere near them.'

'You could leave her here,' Mongue suggested.

Russ rounded on him. 'I'm not leaving my pregnant wife alone in the middle of an ice storm so you can get another commendation letter in your file!'

Mongue's jaw set. 'Fine. Have it your way.' He picked up Clare's pack. 'I'll carry this up for you, Mrs Van Alstyne.'

'Please, call me—' But Mongue was already out the door. She turned on Russ.

'I'm not going to just drop this lead,' he said. 'But I want to get you somewhere safe first. Then we'll get proper reinforcements, and *then* we can hit that house and question Travis Roy.'

She shook her head. 'What *is* it with you two? Every time I've seen you together you've been at it like . . . like he stole your lollipop or something.'

'More like I stole his.' Russ picked up his duffel. 'When Chief Gardiner retired from the MKPD, Bob was one of the applicants to replace him. He got far enough in the process so that it was down to him or me. The board of aldermen chose me.'

'Ah. That explains a lot.'

'Yeah, well. I thought it was mostly water under the bridge, until this last meeting that I crashed. Turns out Bob's been the guy presenting the evidence the staties should take over the MKPD.'

Clare nodded. 'And you think he's doing this out of animus toward you?' Her voice was neutral.

'Oh, hell.' He jammed his fingers in his hair. 'No. Probably not. It was the aldermen's idea. He's just the highest-ranking investigator who's done a lot of work with us.' He frowned down at her. 'But he definitely took this job because he wanted to lord it over me. "Bob Mongue has to rescue Russ Van Alstyne after he drives his truck off the road".'

'Really?' She slapped her leg and Oscar leaped off the floor. 'Because I was thinking the road conditions must be so bad after twenty-four hours of icing that the state police are forced to use investigators to do the jobs their patrol officers would normally handle.' She opened the door and Oscar shot out. 'Coming?'

Russ followed her. Damn woman. She wouldn't even allow him the pleasure of his irrational irritations.

Mongue had set his parka and Clare's day pack in the passenger seat. Fine. If he wanted to be petty, Russ wasn't going to argue. He piled his duffel bag and a grocery sack of perishables on the seat and slid into the back. Unfortunately, instead of his wife, he found Oscar, ears pricked and tail thumping. Clare got in on the other side, leaving the dog between them. She shot Russ a glance. 'Thank you again for coming to our rescue, Lieutenant Mongue. Is it as bad out there as I imagine?'

'Depends on how good your imagination is, ma'am. We're up to our neck in accidents, but the real trouble is the electrical grid.' Mongue put the cruiser into first and began a slow, churning drive through the unplowed stretch of their access lane. 'Phone lines and power lines are coming down all over the place. I heard there was a cell tower up by Lake George that went down under the weight of ice alone.' Beneath them, the chains thunked and clanked against the tires.

Clare looked at Russ. 'Is that even possible?'

He nodded. 'If there's enough area. It's the cumulative weight. You take one twig and coat it with ice, it's not much. You take a thousand twigs, and the weight can split a tree right in two.'

The cruiser crested the lane at a steady pace and was on the North Shore Drive. The road was only visible as a flat, pale stretch through a thick forest of oak and hemlock, birch and white pine. The unbroken, ice-smooth surface was littered with twigs and branches. Russ leaned forward. 'Are you going to have a problem getting a team together? For moving in on Travis Roy?'

'Hell, yeah, I'm going to have a problem. We've got plainclothes behind the wheel because so many of our officers are dealing with accidents. We're diverting more men to help evacuate people to shelters because of the power outages. We'll be lucky if we can find a crossing guard and one of those old guys who does the cold cases to back us up.'

'If you'll waive the jurisdiction, I can get a couple of my – shit, Bob, look out!' There was an impossibly loud crack. At the same moment, a massive tree fell directly into the path of their car. Russ twisted and flung his arms around Clare, getting a face full of dog fur. The car slid as Bob made a futile effort to stop them from colliding with the enormous trunk. Russ heard the wrench-pop of the parking brake, and then the cruiser crumpled into the tree, its front end wedging itself into the pine and wood. Metal shrieked and the engine ground to a stop. They slammed forward convulsively. The air bag exploded with an acrid-tasting bang. Clare cried out, the dog yelped, and from the front, Bob was swearing in a voice shaking with pain and adrenaline. 'God damn fucking *shit* that hurts!'

Russ's face was inches from Clare's. 'You okay?'

She was pale and wide-eyed, but she nodded. 'He needs help.'

Bob was alternating between panting breaths and loud cursing. Russ unbuckled and tried to open the back door, but something had jammed in the crash. He swiveled sideways and, bracing himself between the front and rear seats, kicked the door until it creaked open. He slid out, Oscar and Clare fast on his heels.

'Oh my God, Russ.' Clare was staring at the tree. It was an ancient white pine, the trunk at least three feet in diameter. Its jagged stump stood twenty feet from the road, and its full, bushy crown was another thirty feet toward the lake. The monster had smashed another, smaller pine into splinters beneath it and had lopped off a quarter of a maple as it fell. 'If we had gone a couple of feet farther . . .'

Clare, trapped in the car as that monster relentlessly fell . . . Russ's gorge rose.

Bob's continued railing snapped him out of his sick horror. He waded around the car, breaking the thick crust of ice where the tires hadn't already done the job. He hauled the driver's door open. He could see what had happened. Bob had stood on the brakes in his hopeless effort to avoid the tree. He hadn't gotten his foot out in time.

Clare peered around his shoulder. 'Can we slide him out?'

'Bob, I'm going to get down there and take a look,' Russ said. 'Try not to move.'

'Move?' Bob gritted his teeth. 'It feels like my goddamn leg's been cut off.'

The metal had pinched down, snapping his leg. 'It's broken, all right. I can't tell if it's a compound fracture.' Russ backed out of the well. 'We'll get you out of there and splint you up tight.'

'How the hell are you going to get me out? You got a Jaws of Life in that bag of yours?'

'The jack.' Clare was using her pilot's voice, calm, assured, in control.

'The jack won't lift that tree,' Russ said.

'It doesn't have to. All it has to do is force an inch of space up into the engine block.'

'Yeah. Okay. Let's do it.'

It took them twenty minutes, alternating on either side of Bob's swollen leg, Russ stretched out across the passenger seat, ratcheting against the metal, then Clare kneeling in the door, throwing all her weight behind the jack's lever. Bob let out a moan when they finally released the pressure against his shin. Clare tipped the seat back as far as it could go, and together they hauled Bob out of the wrecked interior. Russ tried to keep him as steady as possible, but even the slightest jolt caused the other cop to gasp with pain.

They laid him on the broken snow next to the cruiser and bent to get a closer look at the damage. Russ sucked in a breath. 'Jesus, that looks bad.' He glanced at his wife. 'Sorry.'

'There are ACE bandages back at the cabin,' she said. 'And I was thinking – one of the chairs has skinny slats in the back. If you could break it apart—'

He nodded. 'Yeah.' He straightened. 'Bob, we're going to take you back to the cabin and do what we can to stabilize your leg.'

'Then what?' Bob's words were bitten off, brief syllables he could spare from fighting the pain.

'If you could get through the South Shore Drive, so can an ambulance.' Russ reached inside and unhooked the mic. It was dead. He flicked the on-off toggle and tried the computer. Nothing. He traced the wiring dangling from beneath the radio mount to where it ended in a shorn-off tangle. 'Shit,' he said under his breath.

Clare laid her hand on his shoulder. 'No radio?'

'The battery connection's been severed.' Russ looked the opposite direction, down North Shore Drive, a narrow tunnel piercing the woods ahead of him. 'We're not going out that road. Even if the two of us could carry him over this tree trunk we're risking the same thing happening again. Except without a car to shelter us.'

'Let's get back to the cabin. It's a mile's hike in hard snow, but at least we'll be out of this' – Clare's mouth worked – 'ice, we'll be warm, and we can make him as comfortable as possible. Then we'll plan our next move.' Another artillery-shell blast went off in the forest. She flinched. Another tree down.

'I'm sorry,' Russ said, in a voice that stuck in his throat. 'I'm so sorry I dragged you here.'

She shook her head. 'No. I'm fine. And the only person you're going to be dragging is Lieutenant Mongue.'

FOUR

'What do you mean, we can't speak to LaMar?' Kevin was trying to keep things calm and professional, but the attitude of the FBI agents he and Hadley were dealing with was starting to piss him off.

They had taken off this morning, driving south through utter crap – the speed limit on the Northway still forty-five, and what should have been a two-and-a-half-hour drive had taken three and a half hours. That hadn't stopped other idiots from driving too fast, of course. They had passed three cars off the Northway, one of which looked to have done a complete three-sixty while plunging into the median. They shouldn't have gone; there was going to be more work than the department could handle even without the investigation. But the Department of Corrections officer Hadley had spoken with that morning assured them they would be able to question Tim LaMar face to face. All they had to do was check in with the agents in charge first.

'Look, son, I'm sorry whoever put you on this detail didn't think to call us first.' Tom O'Day was about the chief's age, tall, graying, and dressed in an expensive suit that still managed to look completely forgettable.

'We don't want to step on any toes,' Hadley said, 'but the girl could die within a matter of days if she doesn't get her medication. Her mother and her mother's boyfriend are the prime suspects at this point. We're looking for their possible whereabouts. That's all.'

They were in the agents' office in the Albany Federal Building, a modern brick construct with no distinguishing features. Industrial carpeting below, fluorescent light panels above, the furniture straight out of an office supply catalog. Everything had a bland, move-along-nothing-to-see-here feel to it. Which was the vibe Kevin was getting from this conversation.

The other agent working the LaMar case was Marie O'Day. Same name, same age, same lanky frame, same suit – although hers fit a lot differently.

Husband and wife. When they had introduced themselves, Kevin had thought, *Partners and lovers. It is possible.* He had inadvertently flashed a look at Hadley – which Marie O'Day had noticed. Her red glasses were the only thing in the office that didn't look as if it had been government issued. She had watched them with her sharp eyes, silent, while her husband handled the preliminary runaround. Now she pushed back from her desk and stood. 'How do you know the girl doesn't have her medication?'

Hadley looked at her as if she had grown a second head. 'That's your response? Really? Somebody kidnapped an eight-year-old and killed her foster parents, and you think it'll be *okay* if she's got her *medicine?*'

The agents looked at one another. It was the same kind of look Kevin sometimes saw the chief and the dep sharing. 'This isn't a surprise to you, is it?' he asked.

Hadley turned to stare at him.

Tom O'Day sighed. 'No, this isn't a surprise. Let me give you some background. Timothy LaMar is not your typical upstate meth head, not by a long shot. He used to be a major player with the Salt Warriors – you've heard of them?'

Kevin nodded. 'A bike gang. They ran drugs and guns in and out of central New York. They got shut down in a federal sting a few years ago.'

'We assisted the Syracuse office with that investigation. LaMar was indicted with the rest of the gang, but the attorney general's office couldn't get any witnesses to the stand to testify against him.'

'Couldn't get witnesses to the stand?' Hadley asked.

Marie O'Day's lips twisted. 'They had a way of dying before they could testify.'

'LaMar had contact with dozens of mom-and-pop meth cookers in Canada, eastern New York, and western Vermont and Massachusetts. He relocated to Poughkeepsie last year and started taking them over one by one. If they cooperated, they became part of his organization. Got funding and protection. Professionalized, if you will. If they didn't . . .' He folded his hand into the shape of a gun. 'Bam.'

Kevin frowned. 'Okay. Where does our missing girl come in?'

'We've been trying to get something on LaMar since he started up operations,' Marie O'Day said. 'It's been . . . difficult. He keeps his meth labs spread out from rural Quebec to Dutchess County. He uses word-of-mouth communications and proxies to pass on his orders.'

'We think he headquartered in Poughkeepsie because he's using convicts and their family members as messengers.'

Kevin could see that. There were no fewer than four state prisons in the area, ranging from a tiny women's work farm to the maximum security Fishkill. Plus nearby Albany was where two interstates linked up. Ideal for any drug lord's transportation needs.

'If people get out of line,' Marie O'Day said, 'they wind up dead. If they say anything, they wind up dead.'

'And nobody's been able to pin anything on him?' Hadley sounded skeptical.

'They're hard-core criminal scumbags.' Hadley glanced at Kevin. Her expression said, *Tell us what you really think, Marie.* 'Nobody cares if they live or die, and if someone does? They're not talking.'

'Six months ago,' her husband said, 'Poughkeepsie police found a pair of bodies double tapped and dumped in Fallkill Park. No prints, no casings, nothing to tie their executions to anyone. Then we caught a piece of amazing luck. A highway patrol officer stopped LaMar for a tail-light.'

'Were they following him?' Kevin asked.

'No. It really was just dumb luck. LaMar had a gun in his possession. Unregistered, of course.'

'Let me guess,' Hadley said. 'Ballistics matched.'

The tall agent smiled faintly and tapped his nose. 'But we had a problem. His lawyer copped to the illegal weapons charge, but he claimed the gun had been taken from LaMar's house and that LaMar found it again tossed in the bushes outside.' The O'Days exchanged identical cynical looks.

'Without a witness to tie LaMar to the murder scene, we had nothing,' Marie O'Day said.

'We ran pictures of LaMar on local TV stations asking for help,' her partner said. 'And lo and behold, someone came forward.'

'Annie Johnson.' Hadley shook her head in disbelief.

'No. A man named Lewis Johnson. Her father.'

FIVE

Russ made a travois out of two long branches, two short branches, his duffel bag, and Clare's polar-plus jacket. They piled the rest of the clothing over Lieutenant Mongue, who couldn't stop shaking – Clare thought from shock. She carried Mongue's duty belt, his ammo clips, and as much food as she could fit in her day pack. She cradled the rifle beneath one arm, ready to hand it over if Russ needed it.

They followed the deep tracks the cruiser's chain-belted tires had dug into the snow before it had crashed. The ends of the travois straddled Russ's track on either side, scraping over the ice and giving Mongue as smooth a ride as possible – which, if his muffled exclamations were any indication, wasn't very. They turned off the North Shore Drive and, with slow steps, crept downhill on the access road that would lead them to their cabin, unfortunately situated at the farthest point from where they were. As they passed one and then another cabin on their way, trudging ever downward, Clare's exhaustion got the better of her. At the next snow-mounded mailbox they came to, she pleaded, 'Should we just stop here? Break in?'

Russ shook his head. 'I don't know if any other houses are winterized out here. You and I could maybe take the cold, but we've got to keep Bob warm.' He shut his mouth over anything else he was going to say. Clare didn't have to hear the rest. Lieutenant Mongue's broken leg called for a fast ride to the emergency room and immediate attention. None of which he was going to get.

Clare concentrated on keeping her boots inside her track for a while. The enormity of their situation felt like another layer of ice, weighing her down, chilling her to the core. They had no ride. They had no way to contact anyone. Behind them was a badly injured man and ahead of them were a pair of armed men who might be holding a child hostage. To her right, a stand of birches bowed down into a series of ghostly arches. A crow, its feathers ruffled against the downpour, roosted at the top of one inverted U. It cawed at them as they passed. *One for sorrow. Two for joy.* They needed to find a second crow quick.

Then a thought occurred to her. 'Won't the state police send someone after Lieutenant Mongue? When he fails to report in?'

'Eventually. The trouble is, he's an investigator. He doesn't have to report in like a patrol officer.'

'But he came out here to find us. *Someone* will notice we're not home and he hasn't been heard from.'

'Yeah. I'm sure Lyle will start kicking and screaming sooner or later. We'll just have to hope it's sooner rather than later.'

The fur edging on his hood kept most of his face from her view. 'Russ. What aren't you telling me?'

He sighed. 'It's this damn weather. I've lived in the Adirondacks a lot of years and I've never seen an ice storm last like this. That tree—' He shook himself. 'I'm afraid it's not going to be just a case of every cop and firefighter in the region responding to accidents. With ice like this, we're going to *be* the accidents. Once you've got cruisers and ambulances going off the road, it's not going to take long for the situation to become a complete . . .'

'Charlie Foxtrot?'

'Yeah. And if that story about the cell tower going down wasn't just a piece of gossip passed along on the radio, communications are going to be screwed.'

'I thought Homeland Security paid to harden the emergency comm networks.'

'Oh, they did. And every police and sheriff's department, every firehouse, every hospital, and every ambulance will be trying to use the same network at the same time.'

'Oh, God.' Clare thought of some of the communications snafus she'd experienced in Iraq. Once you couldn't move troops on the ground or talk to your people – 'We're screwed.'

As if to underline her conclusion, there was another ear-splitting boom

185

from their left. She had just enough time to register the high-pitched whistle of a thousand pine needles whipping through the air when it was cut off by crunching and clattering and shattering glass.

She waded across the road toward the sound, Oscar gamely plowing through the crusted snow beside her.

'Clare, be careful,' Russ called.

She only had to go to the lip of the road to see what had happened. Another huge white pine had toppled over, this time square onto the roof of a modern redwood-and-glass house. Thirty seconds ago, it had been someone's expensive vacation home. Now it was a disaster site. If anyone had been in there . . .

She turned and waded her way back to the tire track. She envisioned their little cabin. Their safety. Their refuge. Surrounded on three sides by woods. They were in a conservation area. The trees were old, well protected. Very large.

'We don't have a cellar, do we?' She bit her lip.

'No.'

'The cabin's not going to be any safer than driving through the woods, is it?'

'No.'

'We're not just going to be able to sit tight and wait to be rescued, are we?'

'No.'

She nodded. Pressed a mittened hand against the side of her belly. *I'm sorry I brought you here, baby. I've been a pretty crappy mother all the way around, and you haven't even been born yet.* 'Okay then.' Up ahead, she saw the now-familiar shape of their mailbox. Almost there. Almost there. Almost there.

SIX

Hadley used her phone to contact the deputy chief on the drive home. There was no way she and Flynn were going to use the radio after what the FBI agents had told them about the conveniently dying witness in the last LaMar case.

'Johnson agreed to testify,' Tom O'Day had said. 'We figured since he was living quietly upstate in East Jesus—'

'Fort Henry,' Flynn said.

The agent tilted his head, conceding the point. 'As you say. It was far enough away that we thought if we kept his identity locked down, it would be more effective than spotty police protection.'

'Why wasn't the MKPD notified of this?' Hadley asked. 'It's our jurisdiction.'

'Only the attorneys working the case in the attorney general's office knew. *No one* was notified.' Marie O'Day tucked a strand of chestnut hair behind one ear. 'You understand the need for security.'

'Everything seemed to be fine,' her husband said. 'Then, a week after Mr Johnson had contacted us, Annie Johnson drove her car into a light pole.'

Hadley tapped one finger on the desk. 'Don't forget her daughter. Who was inside the car as well.'

Flynn frowned. 'Are you saying that wasn't an accident?'

Tom O'Day shrugged. 'Maybe it was. Maybe LaMar got word that there was a witness and targeted the wrong Johnson.'

Hadley didn't ask how a man locked up in Fishkill could be finding out witnesses' identities and ordering hits. She had worked in the California DOC for a couple of years, and she knew the only currency more valuable than drugs inside was information.

187

'When the little girl got out of the hospital, we pulled a few strings at CFS and got her fostered with a retired federal agent and his wife.'

'The MacAllens?'

The tall agent nodded. 'Yes. CFS agreed to supervise visits with the family. Her school was notified there was a danger of a noncustodial relative snatching her. Since the mother was up on child endangerment charges, it was an easy sell. The number of people who knew where she was living was extremely small. The idea was to make her secure without being obvious about it.'

'Like you did with Lewis Johnson,' Flynn said.

'Right.'

Hadley turned to Flynn. 'Why didn't Mr Johnson mention any of this to us?'

Flynn frowned. When he spoke, his voice was grim. 'Maybe because whoever took Mikayla got to him first.'

Now she was on the line with Lyle MacAuley, trying to bring him up to date as the connection dropped in and out. 'So we need phone records,' she said for the third time. 'We need to know who's been calling Lewis Johnson.'

'Noble's out at Powell's Corners with a four-car pileup. I'll see if—' MacAuley's voice blurred into static.

'Goddammit.' She held her phone away from her and squinted at the bars. 'Why am I not getting a signal?'

'Cell towers might be overloading.' Flynn was leaning forward slightly in his seat, as if getting closer to the windshield would enable him to better see the icy road. 'Or they're out of juice. Power goes out, generator fails, goodbye cell signals.' The ice was accumulating on the wipers now, leaving streaks of granular white across their view.

'—anything out.' MacAuley's voice was barely audible over the roar of the hot air from the vents.

Hadley put the phone back to her ear. 'Come back on that?'

'I said, let's not be too quick to rule anything out. I don't want you ignoring other possibilities just because—' The phone fell silent again.

Hadley slapped it shut. 'I can't believe this.' She looked out her window. In the distance, she could see a stretch of power lines, the cables sagging close to the ground, the poles teetering toward one another. She knew Granddad had probably lived through hundreds of ice storms in his life, but she still didn't like the idea of him and the children alone. 'How long do you think it'll take us to get back?'

'Another three hours, easy.'

'Oh my God.' She banged her head against the seat. 'We're going to waste an entire day because those jerks didn't call us with their story as soon as they saw Mikayla's name on the AMBER Alert. *Feds*. Making their case so they can rise to special agent in charge is more important than saving a life. Meanwhile, God knows what that poor girl's going through.'

'Maybe they were right. When they said whoever took her might have brought the medicine.'

'Oh, sure. Because enforcers for drug gangs are always so health conscious. Maybe they packed her special blankie and some nutritious snacks, too.'

'Hey.' Flynn's voice was gentle. 'I'm not the enemy here.'

She grunted. They drove without speaking for several miles, the roar of the overworked blower and the dull chatter of call after call after call on the radio filling the space between them.

'There's another one,' Flynn said. Ahead of them, she could see a whirl of red and blue lights at the side of the road, cop cars and emergency vehicles. They crept past the accident in a line of vehicles, the orange-jacketed state trooper giving them a wave as they went by.

'I'm worried about my kids,' she admitted.

'School's canceled, right? Aren't they at home with your grandfather? The worst that could happen is they lose power for a few hours and have to play board games instead of watch TV.'

'I guess.'

'Or are you worried your ex will try to take them to his hotel again?'

'I don't know. Maybe.' The threat hanging over her head and the terrible sense of time running out for Mikayla Johnson had coalesced into a lump of anxiety stuck at the bottom of her throat. 'Maybe we should send a car to Mr Johnson's house. Bring him in for safekeeping.'

Flynn shook his head without taking his attention from the road. 'If he *has* been contacted, he's undoubtedly been told to stay away from law enforcement. We're better off keeping it on the down low as much as we can. At least for now.'

She thought about that for a few seconds. 'Maybe we should change into our civvies before we go see him, then. Use your Aztek instead of one of the Crown Vics.'

He flashed her a look. 'That's not a bad idea.'

She snorted a laugh. 'Don't sound so surprised, Flynn.' She stretched her booted feet out and flexed. 'Maybe we'll get lucky. Maybe he knows where she is and didn't tell us because he was afraid she'd get hurt. Then all we have to do is swoop in, rescue the girl, and go home and watch this storm blow over.'

'Yeah,' Flynn said doubtfully. 'That would be nice.'

SEVEN

Rest. Ice. Compression. Elevation. The holy quartet of first aid. Russ and Clare got Bob Mongue up on the bed as gently as they could. Clare stepped outside and came back with a dish towel full of ice chunks while Russ scissored away the sides of Bob's uniform pants.

When he exposed the break, he was almost relieved. Bob's leg was swollen and mottled with plum-colored bruises the size of Russ's hands, but the bone hadn't pierced the surface, so they didn't have to deal with controlling bleeding or the risk of infection. On the other hand, there was no telling what sort of damage there was inside the leg.

They piled bed and sofa pillows into a ramp shape and together lifted Bob's legs into place. Clare carefully laid the improvised ice bag over the break and then fed him four Tylenol. 'I don't know if more is better,' she admitted after they had retreated to the kitchen area, 'but let's give it a try.'

Russ jammed his hand in his hair. There ought to be more they could do. 'I wish we had some alcohol in the house.'

'I could definitely use a drink right now,' Clare said.

He almost laughed. 'At least we can say our honeymoon was even more exciting than we had hoped it would be.'

She pulled the kettle off the shelf and unscrewed the cap from one of the water jugs. 'I keep wishing I could rewind the past few days and make them not have happened.'

Russ snorted. 'I keep wishing I could rewind the past few months and make them not have happened.'

'Oh.' Clare poured the water into the kettle without looking at him. *Oh, shit.* 'I mean – God, not the marrying-you part. Not—'

She glanced at him, and in her eyes he saw a world of hurt. She put down the water jug. 'I need to get more wood for the stove.'

'Clare, I didn't mean it like that. Clare—' But she was out the door, without even stopping to take her parka. 'Goddammit.' He lunged for the door handle.

'Better leave her for now.' Bob's voice was thin, but not pain-racked as it had been during their hike back to the cabin.

'Oh, for chrissakes. What are you, eavesdropping?'

'I broke my leg, not my ears.'

'Yeah, well . . .' Russ turned to check on the other cop. Bob's face had regained its normal color, and he had stopped shaking. Maybe Clare's ministrations had done the trick. Or maybe it was letting the poor bastard lie still instead of jouncing him all over the road.

'I hope your people skills are better with your officers than with your wife.'

Russ crossed the floor to look out the window. If he pressed his cheek against the cold glass, he could just see Clare out by the woodpile. 'My people skills are fine.' She hurled a split log into the carrier with so much force it bounced out again.

'You've been married, what, half a year?'

'Three months.' And then, for no reason he could think of, he added, 'Three months at the end of next week.'

There was a pause. Russ could feel Mongue comparing the time to Clare's obvious pregnancy. 'And you told her you'd like to make the last few months not have happened. Jesus, Van Alstyne, you're a bigger idiot than I took you for.'

'Did I ask for your opinion?'

'What, you think you *weren't* an idiot right now?'

Russ turned around again, ready to rip Mongue a new one, but he deflated at the sight of the man's injury. Christ, that's all he needed, to harangue a guy who was lying there with his leg in two pieces. 'You don't understand,' he said.

'I understand she's a new bride, she's got a baby on the way – and I'm thinking this is the first time for both of those for her, right?'

Russ grunted.

'Now she's stuck out here in a complete shitstorm of bad, on what was supposed to be her honeymoon, probably scared out of her mind, and you tell her—'

Russ raised his hand. 'You're right. You're right. I need to apologize.'

'You need to figure out why you'd say a dumb-ass thing like that and fix it, that's what you need to do.'

'Do you do marriage counseling professionally? Or is it just a hobby?'

'Did she turn all moody and weepy once she got pregnant? You know that's temporary, right? You can't ask a woman to have your kid for you and then sulk because she's not the fun-loving—'

'I didn't ask her to have a kid, all right? I didn't want this, and now I'm stuck with it, and there's nothing I can do about it.' He turned away from the window and stalked toward where Mongue lay. Talking about it felt like he was ripping a bandage off an unhealed wound. 'We had an agreement. No kids. Then she gets pregnant because she screwed up her pills and suddenly I'm supposed to be all happy that I'm going to become a father.' His voice was getting louder and louder. 'I'm fifty-three years old! I finally, *finally* had my life exactly the way I wanted it and now it's all upended again. I'm *tired* of having my feet knocked out from under me. Which is what's been happening since the day I met her.'

A loud thunk shut him up. The sound of the full log carrier being dropped on the floor. Russ spun around. Too late, he felt the wave of cold air as the kitchen door swung shut. Clare knelt in front of the woodstove, her face set and white. She opened the door and began loading the woodbox. 'Clare—' he began.

She held up one hand, still not looking at him. 'Lieutenant Mongue, do you think you could drink some chicken broth if I made it? Or tea?'

'Yes, ma'am, I could.'

Russ could almost hear the undercurrent in Mongue's tone. *You dickhead.*

Oh, God. He hadn't said word one about all this except to Clare. And that had only been at the beginning, when he still thought he might have a chance of getting her to change her mind. Since then, he'd kept his damn mouth shut. No one, *no one* knew how he felt. Hell, even *he* hadn't known how he felt until it all came roaring out of him. And to Bob-freaking-Mongue of all people. Jesus Christ, what was wrong with him? 'Clare—' he began again.

'Don't. Just don't.' She got herself up off the floor and went to the cupboard. 'We've got to figure out how we're getting out of here.' She took down a box of instant soup. 'We have to figure out if we're bringing Lieutenant Mongue with us or if we're leaving him in the cabin.' She tore open a packet and dumped it into a large mug. 'And most importantly, we have to figure out what we're going to do about the man who may have taken Mikayla Johnson.' She finally looked at him. 'It's not like you haven't made your feelings plain before this.'

She turned away from him to wrap the edge of a dish towel around the kettle's handle. He would have thought she was as cool and controlled as her voice, except he saw her hand shaking. 'I'm sorry,' he said, his voice low. 'I'm sorry.'

'That's fine.' She poured the heated water into the mug. 'Lieutenant Mongue? If you're feeling up to it, we need to discuss strategy.'

EIGHT

Lyle MacAuley was pissed off. He was pissed at Russ for leaving him shorthanded during what the radio was calling 'the ice storm of the century'. He was pissed that his call to the state police had obviously been tossed in the circular bin. He was pissed that two of his officers were out of commission for half a day because a couple assholes down in Albany didn't know how to share nice with the other kids. And he was really pissed with Jonathan Davies.

For a guy who casually left a credit card trail to a pedophile's bolt-hole, he was hard to track down. No phone number, not on the tax rolls anywhere, a driver's license with an address that turned out to be a Methodist church. No arrest record.

It was Eric who finally found Davies's Albany apartment. He had gone on about lifestyle marketing lists and the crime database subscription and Google search, making Lyle wish it was still 1972, when you could just go out and lean on a guy until he told you what you wanted to know.

'Give me the short strokes. How did you find him?'

Eric grinned. 'He gets his college alumni magazine delivered to his place.'

Lyle slapped him on the shoulder. 'Good job.' He tried to phone his contact at the Albany cop shop, but he couldn't get through, not on the landline, not on his cell, which flashed him a NOT PERMITTED screen instead of Vince Patten's number. He passed a message through the dispatcher for Patten to meet him and headed for the Northway, cursing the weather every mile between Millers Kill and Albany.

Davies's apartment was in one of the grand old buildings that had gotten gentrified up the wazoo in the nineties. Patten was waiting for him right in front, his swarthy complexion and fur-collared coat making him look like a retired mafioso who had gotten lost on the way to Miami. His unmarked was the only car on what should have been a crowded street.

'Parking emergency, Vince?' Lyle gestured at the long line of empty spaces.

'Yep. Everyone else is in one of the municipal garages. Nice not to have to circle the block looking for a space, hah?'

'Until a plow comes through and totals your vehicle.'

'Always looking on the dark side, Lyle.' Patten held the building's carved door open. 'That's what I love about you.' The lobby was tiny but ornate, busy with plaster moldings and gilt and a tiled floor with an elaborate pattern that was almost invisible beneath a layer of winter grime. Patten stabbed the elevator button. The doors opened and they got in. 'When you gonna leave that Podunk force up in Mayberry and come back to work at a real police department?'

The elevator bell dinged and its door opened. 'You're assuming I actually want to *work*,' Lyle said. They walked down the hall.

Patten rang the bell. They waited. The peephole went dark for a second. 'Yes?' a voice said from behind the door.

'Detective Patten of the Albany Police Department and Deputy Chief MacAuley of the Millers Kill Police Department. We'd like to talk with you, Mr Davies.'

The door opened. 'In that case, come on in.' Jonathan Davies ushered them past the tiny foyer into a wide, windowed living room. The place looked like Davies himself – expensive, snooty, and just a little too cute for its own good. 'How can I help you, Detective?'

'You're Jonathan Davies?' The man nodded. Lyle held out Sullivan's mug shot. 'Do you recognize this man, Mr Davies?'

Davies took the picture. 'I think so. Wendall Sullivan?' He looked up at them. 'One of the released convicts that I've worked with over the years.'

Patten's eyebrow went up. 'Released convicts?'

'That's right. I head a small charity that tries to get felons who have served their time back on their feet.' Davies smiled. Lyle could have sworn the guy's teeth actually twinkled.

'How about these people? Know any of them?' He handed Davies a copy of the photo of Mikayla Johnson, her mother, and the mom's boyfriend that Knox and Flynn had gotten from the Johnsons.

Davies's face remained bland, but his chest moved, as if he had taken a quick, quiet breath. 'No. Sorry.' He handed the picture back to Lyle.

'You rented a storage unit for Wendall Sullivan several months ago,' Lyle said.

'I did?' Davies looked confused. Then he flashed his teeth again. 'Oh. Wendall probably had one of the charity's debit cards. I keep several of them, with small amounts on them, for our clients to use.'

'Really?' Patten held out his hand for the copy of the receipt. Lyle gave it to him. 'If this is the charity's card, why's your name on it?'

'Less red tape. And if one goes missing – which does happen on occasion, sadly – it's easier to cancel.'

'Mmm.' Lyle nodded. 'Did you know that Sullivan was using his space to store child pornography?'

Davies recoiled. 'God, no! That's terrible.'

'Mr Davies.' Patten gave Lyle a sidelong glance that said, *Time to turn up the heat*. 'I think you did know. I think you gave Sullivan that card to set up a safe spot where you and he can enjoy your sicko hobby. And I think we need to get a team in here to secure your computer, search your apartment, and see what other perverted porn you've got stashed around.'

Lyle was surprised. Davies didn't even blink at Patten's threat. 'You can do that if you deem it necessary, Detective.' Patten stepped to one side and made a sweeping gesture. 'In fact, you can start right now. But I can assure you, I *am* registered as the head of a state-licensed charitable organization, I've *never* been to any self-storage unit, and my bank will testify that I do indeed provide debit cards for my clients' use, as I have told you.'

Patten looked at Lyle. *Now what?*

NINE

They left the cabin – Russ and Clare, and Oscar tagging along – without Lieutenant Mongue. It took them an hour of arguing to decide, a process that wasn't helped by the fact Clare was mad enough at Russ to consider locking him in the woodshed and throwing away the key.

'I should go alone,' Russ said. 'I'll get help and come back for you.'

'And what happens if you slip on the ice and break something? Or a branch falls and knocks you unconscious?' Clare tried to keep her pleasure at the prospect out of her voice. 'Lieutenant Mongue and I are stuck here with no reliable form of communication.'

'Nothing's going to happen to me. And I can move a lot faster without you.'

'Oh, yes,' she hissed. 'You've made that clear.'

'What about the missing girl?' Mongue's voice was thinning out again.

A tide of shame washed over Clare. She had almost forgotten about Mikayla Johnson, not to mention Amber and her baby.

'I'll do a recon on the cabin,' Russ said. 'See what's going on.'

'Then you'll absolutely need backup,' Clare said.

Mongue nodded. 'She's right. I've been thinking. If you splint me nice and tight and then lace my boot around the splint—'

'No.' Russ's tone was final. 'We'll splint you up so you can move if absolutely necessary, but you're not leaving the cabin.'

'You already have torn-up blood vessels and tissue in there,' Clare said. 'If you walk on it, even if you limp on it, you could cause permanent damage.' Or death. She had flown the medevac for a marine who thought he could keep on going just like Mongue did. The internal hemorrhaging crashed his system. By the time Clare had reached a Forward Surgical Unit, the medics in the back of the bird had called it. 'I'll do the recon with him.'

Mongue looked at her belly. 'You, ma'am?' Clare suspected it was only his innate politeness that kept him from laughing at her.

'Clare is a combat veteran who spent eighteen months in Iraq. She knows how to handle herself.'

A tiny warm glow kindled beneath her breastbone. She had to remind herself that Russ was also a monumental jerk.

They finally settled on Mongue staying and Russ and Clare going. 'And Oscar,' Clare said.

Russ looked up from where he was dismantling the slatted chair to make Mongue's splint. 'The dog? Why the hell do we need to bring the dog?'

'Because I don't think Lieutenant Mongue is going to want to let him in and out. It's going to be hard enough for him to get to the privy himself.'

Russ unscrewed the chair's back and slammed it against the kitchen counter. 'Just leave the dog outside. He can take care of himself.' He held up the still-intact back and frowned.

'Give it to me,' Clare said tightly. She ripped the back out of his hands without waiting for a reply and brought it down with enough force to send a nerve shock into her shoulder. *Wham! Wham! Wham!* The horizontal braces splintered, cracked, and fell apart. She swept the remaining slats across the counter toward Russ. 'There.' She was out of breath. 'We take the dog.'

Russ eyed her warily. 'Okay. We take the dog.'

They dragged the bed to the center of the cabin, where it would be most protected under strong beams, should a tree fall. They left Lieutenant Mongue there with two jugs of water, Clare's bottle of Tylenol, and enough bread and cold cuts to keep him going for a week. There was another debate about his service weapon. He had wanted Russ to take it.

'I'd rather keep my rifle in this situation,' Russ said. 'Give it to Clare.'

She held up her hands. 'I won't use it.'

'Oh, for . . .' Russ jerked the straps of her day pack to fit it to his larger shoulders. They were taking water and some sandwiches, a change of clothing, and the Maglite. He glared at her, but he didn't try to argue. A sidearm was only useful if you were willing to kill someone with it, and Clare wasn't.

'You keep it.' She laid it on the bedside table, next to the kerosene lamp. 'Just in case.'

Mongue looked at her skeptically. 'Save one bullet for myself?'

She squeezed his hand and turned away. She knew they had made the only sensible decision, but the image of the enormous pine crushing the redwood house kept playing and replaying in her head.

Clare moved to the door and slapped her leg. She had wrapped her waterproof windbreaker around Oscar's midsection, tying it on with remainders from the ACE bandage Russ had used on Mongue's splint. The dog now looked like the cover canine for *Outdoor Adventure* magazine, but at least he wouldn't freeze in the icy rain.

Russ and Lieutenant Mongue were talking together in low tones. The fires were crackling, casting warm light throughout the cabin. For a moment, she thought, *Let's just stay right here.* They had everything they needed. They could be safe and dry until help came. The state police knew Mongue had come out to the lake. They'd send someone to investigate. Eventually.

Eventually.

Russ straightened. Shook Mongue's hand. Adjusted his straps one more time as he crossed the floor. He put his hand on the doorknob. 'Ready?'

'Ready,' she said.

TEN

'No. I keep telling you, no one's contacted me.' Lewis Johnson's gravelly voice was frustrated, but it didn't sound like he was lying. Of course, Kevin admitted, he wasn't always the best judge of someone's truthfulness.

'Mr Johnson, we can provide protection for you.' Hadley scooted forward in her armchair. 'If anyone's told you to back off from your testimony in exchange for Mikayla—'

'Look, Officer Knox, if someone had contacted me and offered Mikayla in exchange for me keeping my mouth shut, I'd say yes and be grateful for it. What's one more drug dealer in prison? The moment he's locked away, someone else will take his place. None of this – what you do, what I do, the whole stupid War on Drugs – none of it makes any difference.'

Mrs Johnson walked in from the kitchen, her fingers threaded through four mugs of hot cocoa. Normally Kevin didn't accept any refreshments, but he had been so beaten down by the white-knuckle drive north from the capital area he had leaped on the offer of hot chocolate.

'You should have told them about your being a witness before.' Mrs Johnson handed around the mugs. Kevin took a long swallow. It was hot and sweet and plugged into the pleasure centers of his brain like a controlled substance.

'I wasn't supposed to tell *anyone*, June. Those were the instructions from the FBI. That was the whole point. Besides, we thought Annie had taken Mikayla. Hell, these officers thought Annie had taken Mikayla!'

'Tell me about what you saw, Mr Johnson.' Hadley unbent enough to pick up her own mug. 'What were you planning to testify to when LaMar's case went to trial?'

Johnson sighed. 'Six months ago, I got a panicky call from Annie. That's

201

not unusual – she finds herself in deeper water than she planned on and hollers for me to get her out.' His wife reached over and took his hand. 'But this time she'd been stupid enough to bring Mikayla along for some reason. She asked me to come and get her.'

'This was down in Poughkeepsie?'

'Yeah, they were in this park north of the city. Annie told me to leave my car outside the gate and walk in and get Mikayla from her car. So that's what I did.'

'You went all by yourself?'

Johnson nodded. 'I walked in, no problem. Just as I got to Annie's car, I heard—' He shook his head. 'Begging. Somebody crying and pleading. I had a clear view of them over the roof of the car, through a gap in the bushes. Two men on their knees. He just shot them. Right in the center of their foreheads. I didn't know it was LaMar then, of course. I got his name later when I saw his picture on TV.'

'What about your daughter?' Hadley asked.

'I didn't see Annie anywhere. I woke Mikayla up as quietly as I could and carried her back to where I'd parked. Then I drove home twenty miles over the speed limit the whole way. All I could think about was getting Mikayla out of there as quick as possible. I left and never looked back.'

Kevin glanced at Hadley. Johnson's story matched what the Poughkeepsie detectives had told them.

'Okay, Mr Johnson.' Hadley stood up. Kevin followed suit. 'Call us if anyone contacts you about your granddaughter. Even if it sounds innocent.'

'You two call me, and tell me you've found her. Please.'

Outside, they hurried to Kevin's Aztek. A thin shell of ice had encased the SUV while they had been inside. They had to beat at the doors, breaking the ice, before they could get into the vehicle. Kevin started it up and cranked the blowers. 'Noble's running the phone records now. That'll at least give us an idea of whether he's shining us or not.'

'I dunno. I believed him. I don't think anyone's been in touch with him.'

Kevin shifted the Aztek into gear. 'Yeah. Me, too.'

'The Feds assumed Mikayla was snatched to put the pressure on her grandfather,' Hadley said.

'Yeah.'

'But . . . I don't know, maybe LaMar has an informer in the Poughkeepsie department. Or in the AG's office. But it sounded to me like he'd be thinking *Mikayla* was the witness.'

Kevin nodded. 'I hope there is a leak.' Because if LaMar had Mikayla Johnson taken to keep her from testifying, chances were good she was already dead.

ELEVEN

Now what? Damned if Lyle knew. The guy was dirty; he was sure of it. That involuntary breath of recognition . . . but the storage unit was obviously a dead end. Nobody gave cops a blank check to search their place unless it was already sanitized. He tried a different tack.

'Mr Davies, last Friday, a little girl was taken out of her foster home in Millers Kill. Whoever took her torched the house, killing the foster parents in the process.' They had decided to sit on the fact the MacAllens had been shot. 'The girl recently had a liver transplant. She needs medicine to keep her body from rejecting her new liver. If she misses more than a week's dosage, she could die.' Lyle held up the picture of Annie, her boyfriend, and Mikayla again. 'Sullivan is a person of interest in her disappearance. So are these folks. Do you have any idea where any of these people might be?'

'I'm sorry. No.'

A short answer. Like the way defendants are coached to testify by their lawyers. *Answer the question and nothing more. Don't offer anything.* Lyle pressed on. 'What is it you do, Mr Davies?'

The man blinked. 'I'm a broker.'

'What brokerage do you work at?' Patten asked.

'I work from home.'

'Yeah?' Lyle looked around. There was nothing in the living room, at any rate, that looked like the guy was trading from here. 'Can we see your setup? What do you have, the modern version of ticker tape? What is that?'

'I think it's Bloomberg,' Patten said. 'That's how the mayor made all his dough.'

Davies sighed. 'I don't sell stocks. I'm more of . . . an information broker.'

'Information.' Lyle kept his voice flat.

'Information, introductions . . . you might say I bring people together so they can meet each other's needs.'

'Sounds like pimping to me,' Patten said. He turned to Lyle. 'Lemme check with Vice to see if anyone there's heard of this guy.'

Davies started to look flustered. 'This is harassment. I haven't done anything wrong, and I don't know anything about a missing girl.'

Lyle thought about the information from the Feds Hadley had managed to pass on between cell phone failures. 'Sullivan did his time in Fishkill.'

Davies nodded warily.

'Your charity. You get other clients' – Lyle air-quoted the word – 'out of Fishkill?'

'Of course. It's the closest maximum security prison to Albany.'

'You know what?' Lyle continued. 'I bet all your clients come from Fishkill. I bet if Detective Patten and I got a warrant for your charity's records, we'd find nothing but Fishkill alums.'

Patten gave Lyle his trademarked so-what frown but didn't say anything. 'The Feds have a major meth trader on ice, name of Tim LaMar,' Lyle explained. 'Big network all over the northeast part of the state. They think he does most of his communicating by messengers, everything face-to-face, no electronic trails or phone records to worry about.'

'Hey!' Patten said excitedly. He gave Davies a bright and knowing grin. 'That sounds like bringing people together so they can meet each other's needs!'

Davies's color was up. His gaze kept bouncing around the room, and he was a little damp around the edges.

Lyle nodded conspiratorially. 'That's what I thought, Vince. Poughkeepsie thinks LaMar uses Fishkill cons and their family members as his mouthpieces. Now I figure, if you've got an organization like that, you need somebody to help keep track of your employees.'

'You mean, like a human resources manager?'

'Yeah. Like that. I think Mr Davies here is that guy. Tim LaMar's human resources manager.'

'I don't know anything. I run a legitimate charity, and I think you gentlemen had better go now.' Davies still looked twitchy, but his voice was calm. 'If you want to talk to me again, make an appointment, and my lawyer will come with me.'

Patten glanced at Lyle. 'Okay, Mr Davies. Tell you what I'm going to do. I know a reporter at the *Times-Union* who would love to get an exclusive about the upcoming Tim LaMar trial. So I'm going back to my office and I'm going to call her and let her know – I'll be the unnamed source in the story – that the investigation has been greatly helped by police informant Jonathan Davies, who is expected to be a major witness for the prosecution.'

Davies went white. 'You can't do that.'

'Sure I can,' Patten said cheerfully.

'You can't do that!' Davies grabbed Patten by his coat sleeves. 'He'll kill me! He'll fucking kill me! I won't live twenty-four hours after that story gets out!'

Patten removed Davies's hands. 'And why would he do that, Mr Davies? If he's never heard of you before?'

'Shit. Screw it. I'll tell what you want to know, but nobody gets my name. I mean, it's not even in your reports. We never had this conversation.'

'Why don't you sit down and tell us what really happened with Sullivan. Did he snatch the little girl?'

Davies collapsed onto his sofa. 'Sullivan's nobody. I throw him a few hundred here and there. He runs errands once in a while.' He bent over and buried his head in his hands. 'After he got arrested, LaMar was looking for Annie Johnson's kid. She was a loose end, he said. Annie didn't know where she was – CFS wasn't giving her any visits. Then about a week ago, Sullivan came to me. Said he'd been cleaning in some house up in Cossayuharie and got talking to the little girl there.' He looked up at them. 'I mean, of course he would, the guy's a fucking child molester. He got her to tell him her name.'

'Mikayla Johnson.' Lyle didn't like where this was going.

'Yeah. Meanwhile, I got a visit from one of LaMar's enforcers, a guy who helps run the North Country operation. He tells me to let him know when information surfaces about the kid, because he knows her, and he can take care of the problem discreetly. Not that that's the word he used. The guy's got the mental capacity of a fucking four-year-old.'

'So when Sullivan came to you, you set up a meeting.'

Davies spread his hands. 'I trusted the guy to perform according to his assurances. I mean, he was way ahead of the curve, otherwise. He knew about the kid before LaMar got the word out. How was I to know he'd get totally tweaked on meth and set a fucking house on fire? Discreet, my ass.'

'Who was it, Davies?' Lyle tried not to let his disgust for the man show in his voice. 'Who was the enforcer you sent Sullivan to?'

'I set up the meet with Annie Johnson's boyfriend. Travis Roy.'

TWELVE

Walking on water. Clare kept that phrase centered in her mind, even though their trek across the lake was more like slogging over broken glass. She trusted Russ to navigate, keeping her eyes on her next footfall.

Clare was in the zone, all movement, no thought, so she almost yipped in surprise when Russ stopped. 'What is it?'

'We're getting close enough to worry about someone spotting us. We're going to hug the shore from here on in.'

It was even harder going close to the land. Snow had accumulated on the edge of the ice, and the surface was littered with twigs.

She couldn't see anything past the screen of evergreens blocking the next property. Russ stopped again. 'Now what?' she asked.

Russ glanced up at the lowering sky. 'Now we wait. I don't want to make our move until well after dark.'

'Wait where?'

He turned and grinned wolfishly at her. 'In there.' He pointed toward the house in front of them, abutting the lake.

'Are you sure?' She floundered through the snow after him, breaking holes with her boots, then kicking free. Russ was already up on the front porch. 'How are you going to—'

He lifted one leg and smashed the heel of his boot into the door. It popped open as if it had been on an automatic timer. 'Like that,' he said.

'Oh.' She climbed up the steps and followed him inside. They were in a large cathedral-ceilinged room, with a galley kitchen toward the rear and a loft overhead. Chairs, sofas, and a large table were all swathed with mismatched sheets – someone's third-best bedding demoted to dust covers. It was as cold inside as it had been out.

'I'm going to see if they left any comforters or quilts behind.' Russ headed upstairs to the loft. 'The electricity may still be on. Check the stove.'

The fact that the burners began to glow when Clare cranked their controls felt like the best thing that had happened to her since the start of her honeymoon. Her happiness was complete when Russ returned with several heavy blankets. They were itchy and smelled of mildew, but she didn't care. They sat in front of the open oven door, tented in wool, Oscar collapsed in front of them.

For a while they sat in silence, soaking up the warmth. Clare's legs felt twitchy, as if they were still shifting and balancing as she moved over the pockmarked surface of the lake. Ice legs, instead of sea legs. She stretched and flexed.

Russ unzipped the day pack and handed her a bottle of water and a sandwich. 'Don't say I never take you out for dinner.' His tone was light. Beneath it, she heard *Please let's just forget what I said earlier.*

She made her voice playful. 'Where's my linen napkin?' *Okay. Let's move forward.*

He stood up. 'I don't know about that, but there may be a roll of paper towels left behind.' There was a tall, narrow cupboard next to the refrigerator.

'I was just kidding. I don't need—'

He opened it. Inside, she could see spice jars, mustard, breadcrumbs – the everlasting cooking condiments people always had in their pantries. And booze. A shelf of booze. Gin, vodka, spiced rum, Jaeger – she was still counting when Russ shut the door.

'Sorry.' His voice was gentle. 'Nothing there we can use.'

She swallowed. Stared at the glowing orange elements inside the oven. Weighed her next words. 'Do you ever stop wanting a drink?' she finally asked.

He sat down again. 'Yeah. After a time, it's not even the memory of a habit anymore, so you don't think about it all that much. You can see a bottle or be around other people drinking and it doesn't affect you. It's just something you don't do.'

'Do *you* ever want a drink?'

'Oh, yeah. Sometimes I've had a real good day, and there's a game

I'm looking forward to on the tube, and I'm kicked back in my chair and I'll think, *Man, I wish I had a cold beer.*' He slanted a look at her. 'But I can't have *a* beer. With me, it's twelve or nothing. So far, I keep choosing nothing.'

She had the uneasy feeling she wasn't choosing not to drink so much as making sure she didn't have a choice.

'Clare, about what I said—'

'It's okay, Russ. We've gone from a honeymoon to a scene out of *Deliverance* in the past four days. You were stressed. People say things.'

'I'm sorry. I shouldn't have – you know I'd rather stab myself with a fork than make you feel bad.'

She reached out from beneath her blanket and took his hand. She noticed he didn't say anything about being wrong, or it not being true. She felt a kick inside. Then another. The baby, lulled to sleep during their hike, had awakened. She didn't mention it to Russ. For the first time, she was scared. Not for her safety or her employment prospects, not even for the baby's health. Scared that she had broken something between the two of them and she wouldn't be able to fix it.

THIRTEEN

They left their unknown benefactor's house well after dark. The plan was simple: Clare would pass Roy's cabin, staying on the lake side. She and Oscar would keep on past the next three houses, then climb up to the road and wait for Russ. If anything happened to him, she was to get off the road and keep traveling toward Cooper's Corners until she got a cell phone signal or found help.

Meanwhile, Russ would circumnavigate the other three sides, using his rifle's sight to peer into the windows. If the truck was nearby, he'd take it, picking up Clare on the fly. If not, they would hike out together.

Clare had argued against that last part. Why tip Roy off with the sound of a truck leaving when they could walk to the nearest inhabited home without him knowing?

'Because we don't know where the nearest inhabited home is,' Russ said, wedging a shim beneath the door he had kicked open. 'We know things were bad this morning when Bob got here. It's got to be much worse by now. If the power's gone at Cooper's Corners, the people living there may already have cleared out. Better we're able to drive for help.' He tested the door to see if it would stay shut. 'I'm not as good at hot-wiring cars as I am with breaking and entering.'

He had insisted she take the Maglite, and she accepted. It was pitch black outside; the heavy clouds dropping their load of icy misery blocked out any trace of moon or starlight. Without the flashlight, she probably would have stumbled and fallen a dozen times before drawing even with Roy's house. She couldn't imagine how Russ was making out among all the trees.

She could easily see which house was inhabited. The windows shone bright and cheerful, a promise of warmth and safety that wasn't true. She

211

kept close to the edge of the shore as she passed, ready to douse the flashlight and freeze if she saw any movement in one of the windows.

And there it was. She stopped where she was, switching off the light and sliding it into her pocket. She held herself still. Someone inside, with light-adapted vision, would notice movement if they saw anything in the rainy dark. She thought she heard a scraping noise coming from the house, but that might have been an ice-laden branch, ready to fall. The shape at the window moved – ducked, maybe? – and then Clare could see what the noise had been. Someone had slid the sash up, opening the window to the freezing night.

Clare waited, unmoving, her hand wrapped around the flashlight. Was this an escape attempt? Had the inhabitants of the house heard Russ somehow? Or was it just a smoker, clearing out the room?

The figure in the window vanished. Clare stood there, counting in her head. Ten. Twenty. Thirty. No shots, no shouts, and no one making an unauthorized exit. She shifted her weight and walked on slowly, taking each step with care. She had gone only a few feet before she realized Oscar was no longer at her side. She spun around.

In the faint glow of the window's light, Clare could see the dog galloping up the incline toward the house. He bucked through the crusted snow, the sound of cracking ice and scrabbling nails half-hidden by the rain's percussion. 'Oscar!' she hissed. 'Oscar! No!'

Reaching the open window, the dog reared up on his hind legs. His head was just below the ledge. He began barking, a booming, full-throated bark that could have been heard all the way across the lake.

'Oscar!' Clare yelled. 'Oscar, come!' He ignored her, barking and scratching at the house's shingles. She took one step toward the house, then another. For a second, she struggled with the urge to run up and retrieve him. Except there wouldn't be any fast-and-out through the heavy snow and its icy cover. She would have to leave him behind. She opened her mouth to try one last time—

'Oscar!' Even over the dog's excited barking, Clare could hear the little-girl voice. There was another figure in the window, small, reaching out with one hand. 'Oscar!'

Mikayla Johnson. Clare was headed up the slope before she could think about it. She floundered through the ice and snow, threatening to pitch forward with every stride, boots sinking and catching, breath sawing, heart pounding. She lurched into the side of the house, slapping the window ledge. 'Mikayla! Mikayla Johnson!'

A small pinched face leaned out. The girl had a tangle of black hair and huge eyes. Even with her face in shadow from the lights inside, Clare could see the bright red of fever.

'Did you bring Oscar?' As if Clare's arrival was what he'd been clamoring for, the dog stopped barking. He sat in the snow, his tail wagging.

'I did. Honey, we have to get you out of there. Quickly.'

'Did Ted and Helen send you?'

Oh, God. Clare wasn't going to start by lying. 'I'm helping the police. Climb through the window, Mikayla. You need your medicine.'

The girl shook her head. 'The police are bad.'

'No, honey, I promise they're not. Let me help you so you don't feel sick. Climb through the window.'

'I don't have a coat.'

Clare unzipped her parka and pulled it off. 'I'll give you mine. Hurry, honey, hurry.'

The girl pressed her lips together. Then, decision made, she hoisted herself over the window ledge. Clare reached up. 'I'll catch you.' Mikayla let go. Clare's knees nearly buckled – eight-year-olds were a lot heavier than she had assumed – but she wrapped her coat tightly around the girl and reeled backward. She could feel Mikayla's feverish heat despite the thickness of her sweater. She turned and staggered downslope, Oscar bounding alongside her.

For a moment, she thought the shot was another tree splitting. Then her mind registered the high-pitched echo of a gun, and she broke into a clumsy run. *Get into the trees. Hide in the dark. Just a few more yards.*

'Stop right there!' Another shot cracked and whined. 'Next one goes in your back!'

She stopped. Mikayla clung to her like a lost hope, arms and legs cinched around Clare's neck and waist. For a second, she thought, *Drop her and run.*

They wanted Mikayla, not her. She could escape, get help – then she realized that if the girl was out of harm's way, the kidnappers would have no reason not to shoot her. She had no illusions about her ability to dodge a bullet.

She turned around. 'I'm unarmed,' she said loudly. 'Please don't hurt us.'

She couldn't make out the features of the man wading through the snow toward them, but he was big and broad-shouldered and armed with a rifle. Just like – Russ. *Oh, God, love, keep on going. Keep on going and get help. Don't come closer.*

'I'm not going to hurt her.' The man's voice sounded disgusted. 'Mikayla, what do you—'

Another man rounded the corner of the house, barely visible as a silhouette against the window light. 'What the hell's going on back here? Can't you—'

Beside Clare, Oscar let out a growl that sounded more wolf than dog. He sprang through the snow and broken ice, snarling. Mikayla screamed. The man who had just been speaking let out a choked cry.

'Oscar, no! No, Oscar, no!' Clare reflexively reached toward the dog careening through the snow. If this other guy was armed—

Clare couldn't see him raise his gun, but she heard the loud report, the echo, another report. Oscar yelped, twisted, veered away toward the direction of the unseen road.

'Run, Oscar! Run!' Clare had no idea if he knew what the command meant, but she couldn't keep from shouting it over and over again. The man Oscar had attacked fired one more round into the shadowy trees, but even from a distance Clare could tell that he hadn't brought the dog down. 'Thank God,' she whispered. 'Thank God.'

Mikayla was crying, her face buried in Clare's sweater. 'It's okay, sweetheart. Oscar's okay.'

'That was scary!' Mikayla said tearfully.

'Yes it was.'

Then the big guy plucked the girl out of Clare's arms and settled her on his hip. He pointed the rifle at Clare with his other hand. 'Don't get any ideas.' He was coatless and hatless, his head shaved, with full-sleeve tattoos visible beneath the rolled-up sleeves of his flannel shirt.

The other man floundered downslope and joined them. He had taken the time to put on a parka and toque before leaving the house. Slighter than the man holding Mikayla, but still not anyone Clare would like to tackle in her ungainly state. The dark mustache and chin beard circling his mouth made him look like Evil Mr Spock. 'Missed the bastard.' He had sounded incongruously laid-back, like a surfer lost in the Adirondacks. 'Shoulda shot him back at the foster home.'

'Shut up.' The tattooed man nodded toward Clare. 'What are we going to do about her?'

The bearded man stepped closer. 'She must be the one who brought Amber. Her and the cop.' He waved his semiautomatic at her. 'Where is he?'

'Cooper's Corners,' she lied. 'I was supposed to stay in the cottage next door and let him know which way you went if you left.'

'Shit.' The bearded man half-turned away from her. 'We're in it now.'

'We were in it the minute you decided to go off-script at the damn foster house.'

'That's not going to be a problem. There's no evidence left. Having the po-po running around in our backyard, that's a problem. You shoulda shot him when you had the chance.'

Mikayla made a whimpering sound. 'Shut up.' The tattooed man glared at the other guy and hoisted the girl higher against his chest. 'You're scaring Mikayla.'

'She's sick,' Clare said. 'She needs her immunosuppressant drugs. Please, let me get her help.'

The man turned on her. 'I know she's sick, lady. I'm going to get her medicine as soon as I can.'

'How? Do you think a doctor's going to hand over a bunch of prescriptions to her kidnapper?'

The bearded man barked a laugh. '*You're* ballsy.' He looked at the tattooed man, still smiling. 'Want me to do her?'

'No. Jesus, will you think first for once? What good would that do?'

The bearded man shrugged. 'She won't be annoying you.'

215

'Let's just get her into the house, okay? Before I turn into a goddamn Popsicle out here?'

'All right. All right.' The bearded man gestured with his gun. 'Up you go.'

The men flanked her, one on each side. It was bad strategically, because if they had to fire, they were more likely to cross each other's line. It was fine in practice, though, because she knew she couldn't get more than a couple of yards away in this snow. She was trying to figure out a way to avoid going into the cabin, and drawing a blank. She wished she knew what Russ would do when she didn't show up at the rendezvous point on the road. They hadn't discussed that possibility. Stupid. *Every backup plan needs its own backup plan,* her survival school instructor, 'Hardball' Wright, drawled in her ear.

As with their cabin, the door opened onto a roomy kitchen. Inside, the bearded man gestured with his gun. 'Take off your boots. And your coat.'

'I'm cold,' she lied. She could hear the furnace blowing, keeping the house toasty warm. The overhead light seemed almost too bright after the kerosene lanterns at her cabin.

'Do I look like I care? You're not getting the chance to split out the door first thing my back's turned. Take 'em off.'

'Wait.' The big guy kicked the door closed and set Mikayla down. 'Go back to your room, baby. And shut that window.'

'But I'm hot,' Mikayla said.

'Shut the window. I'll bring you an ice pack for your head.' He gave her a swat on the bottom that straddled the line between playful and threatening. Mikayla left the room. He turned toward the bearded man. 'I been thinking. What if the cop hasn't cleared out for the Corners?'

'What do you mean?'

'I mean, would you leave your pregnant wife behind all alone in a freezing lake house?'

The bearded guy looked baffled. 'I dunno. Maybe?'

The big guy shook his head. 'He's onto us.' He jerked his thumb toward Clare. 'She said she was supposed to keep an eye on us. That means she already knew something.'

'Dude, you threatened to shoot her. Maybe that tipped her off.'

'No. She knew. Which means he knew. And I'm betting' – he turned toward Clare – 'he's still out there. Which means we got a chance to stop him before he gets to the Corners and calls in.'

'He's already called in. He's been in touch with the state police.' Clare threw out a bomb, hoping it wouldn't explode in her face. 'They're the ones who ran your license number, Travis.'

The bearded man winced. 'Shit.'

The big guy looked skeptical. 'Then why hasn't there been any action? One state cop car this morning? And nothing since? Unless you're a cop.'

Travis shook his head. 'Amber said she was some kind of minister. That girl was in a huge hurry or something to leave with that boyfriend of hers. I didn't ask her too much.'

'Good.' The big guy grabbed Clare's arm and yanked her toward him. 'C'mon.' He nodded toward Travis. 'This is the best chance we've got. If we can make her and her husband disappear, the only thing they've got is your truck out here. Mikayla and I can be long gone before anybody shows up asking questions.' He stripped Clare's coat off and tossed it on the kitchen table. 'Switch with me.' He held his rifle out to Travis, who swapped his automatic. Clare had time to see the muzzle and think *.45* before the big guy twisted her hair in his fist and brought it to her temple. 'Are you gonna be a good girl?'

She tried to nod, but her head was immobilized. 'Yes,' she said.

'Good. Travis, tape her hands behind her back.' Travis opened a drawer and held up a roll of duct tape. He wound the sticky stuff around and around her wrists in a figure eight.

'That's good,' the big guy said. 'Open the door.' They walked outside awkwardly, Clare's head tilted back, her belly thrown forward, the man tight behind her, using her as a shield. He pushed her to the edge of the low front porch. She could hear the creak and groan of ice-heavy branches, the spattering of rain on the roof overhead, the click as Travis shut the door behind them. He stepped to the side and raised the rifle.

'What was his name?' the big guy asked.

Clare thought he was addressing her until Travis said, 'Van Alstyne. Russ Van Alstyne.'

217

'Van Alstyne!' The big guy's yell nearly deafened Clare. 'We know you're out there! We got your wife!' He poked her with the gun. 'Say something.'

'He's not there.' She was praying it was true. Or if not, that he'd ignore her captors and keep going for help. They would keep her alive as bait. She hoped. But once they had Russ ...

'Did you hear me, Van Alstyne? We've got your wife! Come on over and check it out! You can see her from the road!'

That was true. The lamps bracketing the front door clearly illuminated Clare and her captors. She swallowed. Breathed in. Breathed out. Tried to calm her thudding heart. *Please, God, no flashbacks right now.* She just had to keep it together. They weren't going to hurt her. Not until they got what they wanted.

'Dude. What if he just waits us out?'

'He's not going to sit on his ass out there and watch us waste his wife.'

Travis made an impatient noise. 'So say we waste her. What then? He calls the po-po down on us.'

'He's not going to let her die.'

'Dude, you don't get it. We can't off her. If we do, we got no hold on him. But if we can't off her, we got no hold on him anyway.'

'But ...' The big guy sounded like his brain was screwed around that conundrum.

'If I can figure that out, I'm guessing he can figure it out, too.'

'That's great. So what does your genius tell us is the solution?'

'We rape her.'

Oh my God. Clare's mouth went dry. Her heart slammed against her ribs.

'I'm a married man.' The big guy sounded outraged. 'I'm not gonna cheat on my wife.' If she hadn't been so terrified, she would have laughed.

'I'll do her,' Travis said. 'I've always wanted to try a pregnant chick.' He stepped next to Clare. Grinning, he raised her sweater. She heaved, trying to break the duct tape binding her wrists. He ran his hand up her belly and fondled her breast. 'Nice tits. Yeah, I'll do her.' She kicked, lashing sideways with her foot, but she couldn't connect.

The big guy yanked her hair. 'Do that again and we'll hit your stomach. We can hurt the baby without killing you, you know.'

There was a roaring in her ears. Bright spots shot upward across her field of vision. *You're hyperventilating,* a part of her brain said. *Get it under control or you'll pass out.*

'Move her on back, dude. I don't want my ass to get iced.'

'Van Alstyne!' The big guy bellowed even louder as he dragged her toward the door. 'You out there, Van Alstyne?'

'That's good.' Travis leaned the rifle against the door. He unbuttoned and unzipped his jeans.

'You better show yourself, Van Alstyne! My buddy here's fixing to fuck your wife!'

Travis closed in on her again, blocking her vision. He grinned. 'Just relax, sweet thing. You might even enjoy it.' She twisted her head, but the big guy's grip in her hair held her fast. She squeezed her eyes shut as Travis reached for her pants.

FOURTEEN

After leaving their unsuspecting host's house, Russ had gone up to the road. If there had been any tracks to tell him where the tow had taken off to, they were gone now, erased beneath a steadily thickening layer of ice. Russ had broken through the trees and walked down South Shore Drive till he was near Travis Roy's house. Across the road was its small garage, just a window-less box, large enough to shelter a couple of cars from the rain. He'd figured one way or another, there were vehicles inside. He'd just begun breaking into the garage when he heard the rifle shot.

Oh, hell no. He should have insisted Clare stay in the cabin with Bob Mongue. He should have told her to wait in the house they broke into. He never should have suggested splitting up so he could surveil Roy's lake house. Plodding down the forested, snow-swamped slope as fast as he could, Russ made his way toward the house. The only good thing about the storm was that the constant spatter of freezing rain and the groan and snap of overburdened timber hid any noise he might make.

He got as close to the cabin's side as he dared. He rested the barrel of his rifle in the crotch of a sapling that would likely never make it to spring and peered through the scope. Kitchen. No one there. Two windows down, a roomy living room, and there was a man sprawled out in a way that suggested watching a TV. Russ could see the back of his head and the tops of his shoulders over the edge of the chair he was sitting in. Buzzed hair, almost bald – not the one he had met at the door. Then the bearded man walked past the window, headed for the kitchen. So, two. At least. He breathed a sigh of relief when there was no sign of Clare in danger. But there was no sign of the little girl, either. She could be in one of the bedrooms on the other side of the house. Or she might be someplace else entirely, along with the tow rig or his truck.

The thought of the truck reaffirmed his plan. He unhitched his rifle and slogged back uphill toward the road back to the garage. Russ figured he could break his pickup – or Roy's SUV – out of the garage, get it going, and be down the road at the rendezvous point without the cabin's inhabitants knowing. He needed backup. The two men weren't the problem, exactly. It was the presence of Mikayla Johnson that was the unknown quantity. Was she there? Did they know where she was? Either way, he wanted enough manpower to shut the house down utterly when they moved in, without a shot being fired.

The garage door was just like the one at their cabin – with the very same lousy lock built into the handle. Russ leaned against the door, centered his boot over the top of the handle, then stomped hard. The cheap metal snapped off. He bent down and hooked his gloved fingers in the circular opening left by his vandalism. He yanked the door up. *Yes!* His truck was parked nose-in, snug against the SUV.

Another rifle shot cracked, metallic and unforgiving. Russ dropped to the road, flinging his arms over his head against splinters from the garage door. Then Oscar, barking and barking. Another shot. This time, he could hear its echo, which was too far away to be from the front of the house, and realized with cold certainty that he wasn't the target. Which meant—

Clare. He scrambled up. He sprinted down the road, skidding and flailing to keep on his feet. When he reached the thicket of trees standing between Roy's house and the darkened cabin next door, he plunged downslope, heedless of the branches whipping across his face and torso. He heard another shot, differently pitched – a sidearm? – and a sharp canine yelp.

He almost missed the glint of the flashlight. He stopped his headlong flight by thudding whole-body into a birch, the shock radiating along his bones.

Clare. Thank God. He could make out her silhouette, along with two men, one of them carrying . . . Russ raised his rifle and scoped again. The light was lousy, but he was pretty sure one of them was carrying a little girl. He began to squeeze the trigger, then released it. No. He was a good marksman, but he wasn't going to risk this shot, not with the rain and the darkness and his wife right there between the two of them.

221

He tamped down the part of him that wanted to tear across the open land and knock the bastards down. If he was going to help Clare, he needed to think, not react. He could use his truck radio to call for assistance, but given the weather emergency, God knew how many hours it would be before help arrived. Roll DeJean's SUV down the hill and hope it smashed into the house? Draw them away from Clare and the house somehow?

Yeah. Make him the one they should worry about, not a pregnant woman. He could call down to them, claim he'd broken his leg, offer to turn himself in. Use his truck as cover and pick them off when they popped over the top of the stairs and stepped onto the road. He was already headed back upslope, churning through the trail he had broken minutes before, as the plan took shape in his head. It wasn't, he admitted, a very good plan. But he had run out of good yesterday. Maybe the day before. Now all his options were crap and crappier.

'Van Alstyne!' A shout he could easily hear over the freezing rain. 'We know you're out there! We got your wife!'

Russ shivered involuntarily but kept going. Forget the truck. No time. His only hope of luring them close would be if they thought he had no chance and no cover. Sprawled out on the frozen road with a 'broken leg' fit the bill.

'Did you hear me, Van Alstyne? We've got your wife! Come on over and check it out! You can see her from the road!'

Clare. Hold on, darlin'. Hold on. He focused on reaching the road. Only on reaching the road. If he gave in to the fear urging him to break cover and charge, they could both die.

'Van Alstyne!' Russ topped the hill and skidded onto the icy surface of the road. Careful now. He didn't want to bust a bone for real. 'You out there, Van Alstyne?'

Russ half ran, half slid back up the road. Scanning for the spot to lay his trap. Back by the garage, as far away from the light at the top of the stairs as possible.

'You better show yourself, Van Alstyne! My buddy here's fixing to fuck your wife!'

Russ's brain whited out. He whirled and staggered to the lip of the hill.

They were framed by the door lights, Clare bound and struggling, one man tight behind her with a gun at her temple, another man yanking—

He raised his rifle. At the last split second a sliver of rationality pierced his mind-wiping rage. *You can't reach the other guy. If you shoot his partner, he'll shoot Clare.* He swung the bore away and blasted the door lights, one, two, exploding in a shower of sparks and glass. He galloped down the hill, ignoring the ice-covered stairs, slipping, falling, rolling back onto his feet. He reached the front of the house while the men were still shouting at each other. He raised his rifle again.

'Police!' he roared. 'Drop your weapons and step away from the woman!' In the faint ambient light from the side windows, Russ could see Clare's would-be rapist raise his hands and shuffle backward.

'Oh, for fuck's sake.' His partner sounded disgusted. 'He's not going to shoot us while we have her.'

Russ fired at the other man. The bullet thudded into the side of the house, showering him with splinters. The man yipped.

'Van Alstyne.' Behind Clare, her captor shifted. 'This is your wife, right? So I'm guessing this is your kid in here.' He removed the automatic from Clare's temple. Pressed it against the side of her straining abdomen. 'I could shoot her right through here. Wouldn't kill her right away. Might even survive if she got to the hospital in time.'

'Please.' Clare's voice was a gasp. 'Please, don't hurt my baby. Please.'

'Put the rifle down, Daddy.'

'Listen—'

'I'm not negotiating with you. Put the rifle down or she has a very messy abortion.'

Russ squatted and laid the rifle on the snow.

'Kick it away.'

He kicked the stock. The rifle slid across the ice-crusted snow.

'Travis, get his gun.'

The other man crossed behind Russ and picked the rifle up. He heard the crunch of the guy's boots. His pause. The swish of something swinging through the rain. Russ only had time to register the stunning pain before he pitched forward into blackness.

Tuesday, 13 January

ONE

Russ was underwater. It was cold, a deep surrounding cold that left no space to be warm, and he could hear the pulsing of a motorboat engine as it throttled its way across the surface of the lake, far overhead. *Thrum. Thrum. Thrum. Thrum.* Every pulse sent an answering throb of pain through his head. He wanted to sink to the bottom of the lake, curl up, and go back to sleep, but he had to get out of here. Had to swim up, up, up as flashes of memory and emotion slid past him, closer, the motorboat so much closer now, and then he broke the surface and opened his eyes.

He was lying on a wooden floor with his head in Clare's lap. It was dark, and there was a heavy, rough blanket over him. For a moment, he saw the faint glow of the electric oven and thought, *I fell asleep. We need to leave this place to get past Roy's before morning.* Then the glow resolved itself into a thread of light beneath a closed door. The motor roar was louder than ever, and his head was pounding. He groaned.

'Russ?' Her voice was low. 'Oh, thank God.'

'You' – his voice was rusty – 'okay?'

'Yeah.' She sounded shaky.

The last minutes before he had been clubbed into unconsciousness reassembled themselves in his brain. 'Are you . . . did they—'

'No. No. He didn't.' She paused. 'Although I may have competition with my helicopter nightmares from now on.'

'Sorry. So sorry, love. Shouldn't have . . .' He trailed off. The list of shouldn't-haves was too long to enumerate. He realized his head was pillowed against her belly. 'Baby? Okay?'

'Yes, thank God.'

'Where . . . we?' He winced. He could form the sentences perfectly in his

227

pounding head, but they weren't coming out right. 'Concussed,' he said raggedly.

'I think you're right. You've been unconscious for hours. I was so – oh, God, I wish I could put my arms around you.' She took a breath, and when she spoke again, her voice was firmer. 'We're in a kind of attached storage shed.' He could feel a slight movement – Clare looking around. 'There's a canoe, life vests, lawn chairs. That sort of stuff.'

'Noise . . .'

'It's the generator. The power went out about an hour or so after you . . . after you were hurt. That's when they stuffed us in here.' He could hear a grim satisfaction in her voice. 'When the lights went out, I head-butted Travis into the next room and took off. Didn't get any farther than the front door. But I thought it was worth a try.'

'That's . . . girl.' He flexed his shoulders. His arms were stretched behind his back, something unyielding around his wrists.

'It's duct tape. I didn't find anything sharp enough to cut through in here.'

'How long . . .'

'I don't know. I've dozed on and off. I stopped hearing people moving around some time ago. I'm pretty sure everyone's in bed.'

Well, he and Clare hadn't been shot outright. That was good. 'How many?'

'The little girl is here. I tried to get her away. That's how they . . .' She breathed in. 'There are two men, Travis Roy is the one with the beard. The other is Mikayla's father.'

'Hector . . . DeJean.'

'Listen. I've been thinking. The whole place is being heated by electric heaters right now. Travis and Hector set them up after the power went out.'

Russ made a go-on noise.

'If we could sabotage the generator, this house would become unlivable pretty quickly. They'd have to pack their things and pull up stakes. Maybe bring us with them.'

'How . . . help us?'

'I'm not sure. But my SERE instructor used to say, "Sow confusion, reap opportunity." Anyway, I figured that would sow confusion. To be honest,

228

we may be reaping the opportunity to freeze to death. If they leave with us still locked in here.'

'Without them . . . hear . . . escape.'

'Without them around to hear us, we can escape?' He heard the smile in her voice. 'You have a lot of confidence for a man with his brains scrambled.'

'Still . . . smarter . . . them. Let me look . . . generator. Let me look . . . it.' He curled his knees toward his chest and rolled until he was kneeling with his head bowed against Clare's legs. It felt like someone was playing tympani inside his skull. He took a deep breath and knelt upright, the blanket crumpling around him.

'Here. Let's see if I can help.' Clare, he saw, had been leaning against a wall. Now she braced her shoulders and wiggled her way up to standing.

'Impressed.' He followed her lead, walking on his knees to the wall and tumbling himself into a seated position. His flannel shirt snagged over the rough timber as he slid to his feet. Uninsulated walls. The heat from the house bleeding through the door and the warmth thrown off by the generator were the only things keeping them from slipping below freezing.

He turned around slowly, careful to keep his head from falling off. The storage shed was maybe eight by ten. A collection of oars and mildewed life vests hung against the wall opposite them, along with a few deflated floaties and a badminton set wrapped in netting. Two canoes rested on the overhead rafters. There were vents installed along the eaves, which was why they weren't choking in fumes right now.

The generator itself sat on cinder blocks near the rear corner. Russ took a shaky step closer and saw that the break in the back wall was a door.

'I tried it. It's locked from the outside.'

That explained the snow shovel, broom, ice melt, and sand leaning against the rear wall. No tracking messy stuff through the house. He walked to the door and threw himself against it. Then again. The third time, he staggered back, almost retching from the pain in his head.

'I *told* you it was locked, you idiot.' Clare pressed against him, letting him rest his head on her shoulder. She leaned her cheek against his hair, stroking him without hands. 'Why don't you sit back down?'

He forced himself upright. His ears were ringing. 'Generator.'

'Tell me how it works.'

'Internal combustion. Needs gas.' In the corner, past the bags of ice melt and sand, he saw two five-gallon canisters of gasoline and a container of oil. Now *that* could sow confusion. Unfortunately, they'd both be fried in the process.

'Is that all? I thought it was some complicated electrical thing.' She pointed to the bag of sand with her chin. 'If you can help me move that, I think we can pour some into the fuel tank.'

It was awkward and painful, but they managed to squat down back-to-back and grasp the open bag with their bound hands. They heaved it up and rested it atop the oval five-gallon fuel tank. Clare's fingers were a lot more agile than his, so she butted up against the edge and slowly unscrewed the cap. Then he tipped the bag over. The sand spilled, of course – on the fuel tank, on the generator, over the floor – but it also ran into the opening.

'I think that's good.' Clare pinched the lip of the now-lightened bag and brought it upright. 'Can you put it back while I get the cap on?'

Russ shuffled the bag over to its spot beside the ice melt and managed to wrap his hands around the broom handle. 'My mom . . . job's not done . . . clean up.'

Clare's smile didn't conceal her worry. 'Okay. I'll blow, you sweep.' They got most of the incriminating evidence off the fuel tank and under the generator. Hopefully, Roy and his buddy wouldn't spend too much time trying to pinpoint what went wrong with the machine. When he backed up to replace the broom next to the shovel, he saw Clare head-butting life vests off their nails. She got two on the floor and kicked them over to where his blanket lay. 'It's gonna be a long night. We should try to rest,' she said. She hunkered down and let herself fall into a seated position.

Russ grunted assent and joined her. They kneed and kicked the blanket over themselves and laid their heads on the life vests. The nostalgic smell of mildew and lake water mingled with wool made him feel, against all reason, safe. Clare's belly was a warm bulwark between them. He looked at her face, blurred and beloved in the shadowy dimness. *You're the most courageous person I've ever known,* he wanted to say. Clare lived like a banner on a battlefield, never looking back, refusing to be set aside or left behind. People thought he was brave because he strapped on a gun when he went to work every day, but he didn't have half her guts.

He wanted to tell her, wanted to say what he felt, but all he could get out was '. . . love you.'

Her voice was somber when she said, 'I love you, too.'

TWO

Hadley hadn't even tried to drive to the station this morning. She'd been awakened at 5:30 A.M. by her cell phone: the school district's auto-call telling her the schools were closed due to the weather emergency. *Weather emergency.* That was a new one. Poor Granddad. She hoped he could manage another day riding herd on Hudson and Genny. The kids were already suffering from cabin fever.

When she rolled over to turn on the light, nothing happened. *Oh, no. Not the power.* She sat up, realizing for the first time that her bedroom was silent. No hot air blowing in from the furnace. She threw back the covers and crossed to the window. No lights in any of the houses on Burgoyne. No streetlights at all. As far as she could see, Millers Kill was blacked out.

She dressed in the dark and used the light from her cell to get herself downstairs. She took the flashlights out of the kitchen drawer, switched one on, and went upstairs to wake Granddad. She knew about the generator in the barn, but she had no idea how to use it. This was her third winter in the Adirondacks since leaving California, but this was the first time she'd seen anything more than a temporary brownout. Recalling the sagging power lines and tilting poles she had seen yesterday, Hadley didn't think the lights would be coming back on in an hour this time.

Granddad met her in the kitchen once he'd gotten his overalls on. Together, they broke a trail through the heavily iced-over snow from the back porch to the barn. Granddad fired up the generator and ran the wrist-thick cable from the barn through one of the cellar windows, attaching it to the circuit board. Hadley closed her eyes with relief when she heard the furnace kick in. Upstairs, she flipped on the kitchen overhead. It flickered.

'Better turn that off,' Granddad said.

'Why? We've got power now.'

'That generator's not rated for a heavy load. It'll keep the furnace on and the icebox running, that's about it. Only turn a light on if'n you absolutely need one.'

'You're kidding. What about TV?'

'No need for it. I got one of them hand-cranked radios. Picks up the news and weather just fine.'

No lights. No TV. 'What are the kids going to do?'

'I got a few kerosene lamps around here. We'll fire 'em up and play Parcheesi. They'll have a good time.'

'Ohhh-kay. If you say so.' On the other hand, what could she do? Between the weather and the investigation she'd undoubtedly be pulling a double shift today. 'Maybe you can bundle them up and send them outside to play.' In the freezing rain.

'I'd feel better if'n you didn't drive yourself to work today. Your car's got jack-all traction. Can you call that friend of yours and get a ride in his all-wheel?'

'Flynn?' She glanced out the window. The driveway looked like a skating rink. 'Yeah, I guess so.' She pulled her phone from her pocket. 'I'll call him after I take my shower.'

'Well, you can take one, but it won't be much fun without no water heater.'

'You're kidding me.'

Granddad shrugged. 'Furnace and fridge. Everything else is – whaddaya say – expendable.'

She sat on her bed in her unlit room and called Flynn. His voice, when he answered, was thick with sleep. 'Mm. Kevin here.'

'Do you have power over there in Fort Henry?'

'Hadley? What the hell time is it?'

'I don't know. Six, six fifteen.'

He groaned.

'I thought you always get up at the crack of dawn.'

'To work out. The community center's closed. There's this ice storm on? Have you heard about that?'

'Yeah. And it looks like the town is blacked out. How about you?'

She heard a faint creak as he rolled over. 'Nope. M'light's on.'

'Lucky. Will you come and get me on your way? I don't want to try my Escort on these roads.'

'Yeah, sure.' He yawned. 'Just lemme shower and get dressed. I'll be there in forty minutes.'

'I'm so jealous. We're out of hot water. Think of me while you're enjoying your shower, will you?'

It wasn't until after she hung up that she realized why he had laughed so hard.

Apparently the police department generator was rated for a much higher load than Granddad's, because it was business as usual at MacAuley's morning briefing: The lights were on, the temperature was warm, and Harlene's board was lit up like normal. What was different was the crowd. Noble and Ed were already out handling storm-related problems, along with the two part-timers, Tim and Duane. The entire Fire and Rescue traffic crew was at the station, its members picking up the state accident report kits. 'Nobody gets any tickets,' MacAuley told them. 'Just fill out the form and make sure they get the paperwork for their insurance companies.'

'What if there's injuries?' one of the crew asked.

'Just get 'em into an ambulance unless there's more'n one vehicle involved. Harlene'll let you know if you need an officer. If you see a downed line, get a barricade up first, then call National Grid. You close a street, call it in to Harlene. She'll update everybody.'

By the time he got the road crew briefed and out the door, MacAuley was steaming. 'Goddammit. I swear to God, I'm gonna kick Russ's ass from here to Buffalo and back for ditching us. Who takes a goddamn honeymoon in January?'

Hadley figured that to be a rhetorical question.

'You haven't heard from him yet?' Flynn asked.

MacAuley hiked up onto the table where the chief always sat. 'No, goddammit.' He glanced around, noticed where he was, and hopped off again. He kept his mouth in a fierce frown, but Hadley could see the worry in his eyes. 'Frigging staties can't help. They got one of their own missing. Not to mention they're more shorthanded than we are.'

Flynn glanced at Hadley before looking at the dep. 'Chances are good he and the reverend are just stuck up there, you know. It's a pretty remote location. Hard to get to once the roads ice over.'

'I know that, goddammit.' MacAuley's snarl did not disguise his growing concern over the chief and Clare. He flopped open the increasingly thick Johnson kidnapping file. 'Okay. Let's get a sense of where we are.'

Hadley spread her hands. 'The pedophile gave Mikayla's location away to Travis Roy.'

'Troop G upstate reported they had a request to run Roy's license plate, but they haven't been able to ascertain which of their troopers made the request. All of the staties are on the lookout at this point, we still have leads, okay?' Lyle said to them.

'Find Roy, we'll find the girl. They're probably with Annie Johnson,' Hadley said.

'If he hasn't already killed her.' Flynn's assessment made Hadley frown. 'Don't look at me like that,' he said. 'LaMar thinks her testimony can put him away. He's probably offering enough money to make her *mother* consider doing the deed.'

MacAuley crossed to his usual spot by the whiteboard and picked up a marker. 'Delighted as I am that you two have already cracked the case, indulge me.' He started scribbling on the board. 'Back in July, Lewis Johnson went down to Poughkeepsie to pick up his granddaughter and saw Tim LaMar capping two guys.'

'The Feds think they were two of his lieutenants who'd been dipping into the profits,' Flynn said.

'They're worried about Johnson getting hit before he can testify. They decide the best defense is to hide him in plain sight. Without letting us know.' MacAuley turned toward them. 'There are some guys down there who'll be getting a personal visit from the chief and me once all this is in the can. Friggin' feebs.' He turned back to the board. 'In August, Mikayla's mom – Annie – has an accident that might not be an accident. She gets cranked

235

on meth and drives her car into a tree. She's okay, but her kid's liver is damaged enough to need a transplant.'

'Which she gets from Mikayla's father,' Hadley said.

MacAuley tapped the old circ sheets he had pulled on Hector DeJean. 'The dad's got a record going back to juvie. Assault, assault with a deadly weapon, dealing, possession, weapons charges – he's been inside more'n he's been out. Then he gets out of Plattsburgh and suddenly he's a choirboy. Not so much as a traffic ticket in the past three years. I'm not sure if I buy that.'

'His alibi—' Flynn began.

'Has holes in it. I'm a little more convinced by the fact he's got a wife and a job. Did that check out?'

Hadley looked at her notes. 'The delivery company confirmed DeJean was their employee. Mikayla's doctor confirmed that Hector DeJean was, in fact, the liver donor.'

'Any financial stress going on? Anything that might tempt him to take LaMar up on his offer?'

Hadley looked at Flynn. 'We haven't checked out that angle,' he admitted.

'He had that big boat parked at the side of the drive,' Hadley said. 'And the monster SUV to pull it. But if the guy went through surgery to save his daughter's life, why would he turn around just to sell her to LaMar?'

Flynn thwapped a pen against his note-pad. 'It sounds like LaMar is big and getting bigger. Somebody who helps him beat a federal murder rap is going to be in a position to reap a lot of benefit.'

'So he's still in play as a POI,' MacAuley said. 'The Feds get one of their own, who's retired up here, to take Mikayla on as a foster kid. Everything is humming along according to plan until Maid for You sends Sullivan to their house.'

'I still don't understand why they had the cleaners in when they were trying to keep Mikayla's location a secret,' Flynn said.

MacAuley shrugged. 'The MacAllens were concentrating on security at the girl's school and with her supervised visits. It was just sheer dumb luck one of their cleaning crew had a connection to LaMar.'

'Mmm.' Flynn sounded unconvinced.

MacAuley jotted on the board. 'So Sullivan brings his news to LaMar's fixer, Jonathan Davies. Davies puts a few feelers out to get a sense of which one of LaMar's enforcers he wants to sell the info to.'

'I thought it was whoever dropped the most money in his hand,' Hadley said. 'Travis Roy.'

MacAuley tapped the whiteboard. 'Well, that's where it gets interesting. Roy isn't even on the Feds' radar. As far as anyone can tell, he's cheap muscle, protecting some of the shipments around this area. And he's a user. That's amateur. You can bet none of the high-ranking guys in LaMar's organization touch the stuff they're moving.'

'Maybe he's got ambitions,' Flynn said.

'Yeah. Let's look at it from Davies's point of view. He has the key to Mikayla Johnson's whereabouts. He's a smart man. He knows there are two ways this can go down. Either the guy he sells the info to is successful in keeping the witness quiet, or he's not. If he's successful, Davies keeps his business with LaMar and also has another grateful officer in the organization. If the guy fails to keep LaMar out of prison, both he and Davies risk getting whacked. We know LaMar has a low tolerance for screw-ups.'

'It doesn't matter in the end, though.' Flynn stood up and headed for the coffee machine. 'Mikayla isn't the one who's going to testify.'

Hadley, who was about to ask him to pour her a cup, jerked in her seat. 'What if Travis knows that?' *Why didn't I see that before?* 'Travis and Annie are sleeping together. Annie tells him the story of her dad coming to rescue Mikayla the night LaMar popped those guys. Travis puts two and two together and realizes that LaMar's got his information wrong. Lewis Johnson is the one who can put him away, not Mikayla.'

MacAuley tapped the side of his nose.

Flynn paused, the half-pint carton of creamer in his hand. 'So what does that mean? Roy kidnaps the girl in order to blackmail Lewis Johnson into not testifying? Weren't we already running with that assumption?'

'That's one possibility,' Hadley said. 'Another is that he *wants* Lewis Johnson to testify. Maybe he's got plans to go into business for himself.' She looked at MacAuley. 'He already knows Davies, so he has someone who can hook him up with the retail dealers. And his girlfriend is running the smurfing gang.'

'That's stupid. Not your idea, Hadley – I mean if Roy is thinking that, he's stupid.' Flynn walked back to his chair holding a mug in each hand. He handed one to her. Strong and black, just the way she liked it. 'How long do you think it'll take Tim LaMar to figure out he's been double-crossed when Roy's *girlfriend's father* puts him away?'

'I may not have been a cop for very long, but one thing I've learned is that most criminals *are* stupid.'

'You got that right.' MacAuley held out his hand toward Flynn. 'Where's mine?'

'Uh . . .' Flynn looked down at his own mug.

'Here's a tip, Kevin. If you want to rise in the ranks, suck up to your superiors, not your partner. She has to put up with you. I don't.'

Flynn sighed and surrendered his coffee to the dep. Hadley picked up the thread. 'Okay, say Travis thinks he can put one over on his boss. Where does that leave Mikayla Johnson? Is she dead? Alive? Wouldn't LaMar want some sort of proof that she's been taken care of?'

Back at the machine, Flynn was pouring himself another mug. 'That was the reason for the arson.'

'What?'

'The arson. Why kill the MacAllens? Why burn the whole house down?' He blew on his coffee. 'Maybe that was going to be the proof for LaMar. The foster parents killed, the house burned down with Mikayla supposedly in it.'

'But it was obvious her body wasn't there.' Hadley took a sip of hot coffee and had a momentary flash of guilt. At home, her kids were stuck drinking Kool-Aid and eating cold cuts. Maybe she could slip away at noon with a couple of Happy Meals.

'Obvious to trained investigators. Patrick Lent, the state arson guy, told me amateur firebugs often misjudge what a fire's going to do. That's why so many of them wind up accidentally killing themselves. It's not a stretch to imagine Travis thought the fire wouldn't leave any human remains behind. In which case, he could simply pack Mikayla off to her mother's apartment. They keep her there until LaMar's trial is done and then—'

'And then one of LaMar's enforcers takes 'em all out on the boss's order,' MacAuley said.

'Not necessarily,' Hadley said. 'Hanging on to power inside requires money, loyalty, and the prospect of getting out someday.' MacAuley cocked one of his bushy gray eyebrows at her as if to say, *Look who's gettin' smart!* 'I was in the Department of Corrections for two years, Dep. I know what I'm talking about. LaMar's looking at a federal charge. That means mandatory sentencing, no parole, and he'll be doing time in one of the federal high-security prisons in Pennsylvania, away from all his homies in the New York system. It's not – what did you say, Flynn? Not a stretch to think his organization could fall into pieces. Travis could get away with it. Especially if Davies is willing to side with him.'

Flynn joined them, cradling his mug possessively. 'Great. We have a good working theory of what happened and how. But we're still in exactly the same place we were Friday: looking for Annie and Travis, trying to figure out where they're keeping Mikayla. Meanwhile, she's gone five days without her immunosuppressant drugs.'

'We've already hit every known meth head in the area,' Hadley said. 'They all just pointed to each other when we asked who Annie Johnson might be staying with.'

MacAuley studied the whiteboard for a long moment. Then he circled Jonathan Davies's name. 'Here's where we go. This guy says he doesn't know what goes on in LaMar's organization, but he knows names. You're gonna head down to Albany and squeeze him until he gives up someone. Then we're gonna squeeze that guy, and so on until somebody gives up Roy and Johnson.'

'Us?' Flynn said.

'We're going to Albany *again?*'

'I'll hook you up with Detective Patten,' MacAuley said. 'I'd go myself, but I can't risk getting stuck down there in this storm.' He frowned at them. 'You got civvies? Change into them. Davies won't take you seriously when he sees a couple uniforms. And bring a toothbrush, in case. If the weather keeps on crapping on us like this, stay in Albany.' He pushed away from the whiteboard. 'I'll go set things up with Vince Patten. Check in with me after you're changed.' He picked up his mug. 'Next time, Flynn? Not so much creamer.'

After MacAuley had left the squad room, Hadley went to one of the tall, old-fashioned windows that overlooked Main Street. The place looked like a frozen-over ghost town; no lights, no cars, no movement except for the unrelenting rain, encasing everything in ice drop by drop. 'He wants us to go to Albany in *this*?'

Flynn snorted. 'What movie title does this put you in mind of?'

'*Lost in the Andes?*'

He shook his head. '*They Were Expendable.*'

THREE

The sound of cursing woke Clare up a second before the latch rattled and the storage room door opened. She hadn't believed she would actually fall asleep on a wooden floor with her hands duct-taped behind her back, but the cool gray light spilling through the vents proved she had been wrong.

The tattooed man – Hector DeJean – stalked past them, headed for the generator. The incessant roar of the machine was gone. Except for the big guy's angry muttering, it was silent.

Silent and cold. *It worked.* Beside her, Russ stirred, opened his eyes. He blinked at her sleepily. 'Whuzzat?'

Hector grabbed one of the canisters of gasoline and unscrewed the nozzle. He upended it into the fuel tank. Clare could hear the glug-glug-glug as the tank filled. He flipped the starter and yanked the cord. He did it again. Then again. Nothing happened. 'God-fucking-dammit!'

'What's the matter?' Travis hung in the doorway. 'We can't be outta gas.'

'No, we're not out of gas. Jesus.' Hector unscrewed a spark plug. 'It's not the plug. The hoses are tight.' He looked at the shelves. 'You got a tool kit around here? I might be able to figure out what's wrong if I open 'er up.'

'Lemme see what I can find in the kitchen.' Travis gave Clare a lingering look that made her flinch involuntarily before he pushed back from the door and disappeared.

Russ nudged her beneath the blanket. *You okay?* he mouthed.

She nodded, relieved to see his eyes were clear and alert. *Sit up?* she asked.

He shook his head once, then shivered exaggeratedly. She got that. *It's cold.* Might as well stay under the wool blanket while they could.

241

Travis returned with one of those ten-piece-in-one plastic-framed tool kits.

'That's it?' Hector asked.

'Dude, one of my cousins is the mechanical guy. If you want, you can call him and ask to borrow his tools. Except, oh, the phones aren't working.' Travis dropped the plastic kit on top of the fuel tank. He turned and kicked at Clare's backside.

Russ rolled to his back and reared up into a sitting position. 'You touch my wife again and I'll cut your goddamn leg off.'

Oh, good. He's talking in complete sentences. The thought floated over her terror that Travis was going to finish what he started last night.

Travis squatted down, grinning. 'Hate to tell you, dude, but you're not in any position to stop me. If I want to take your wife into the bedroom and play hunt the sausage with her, you can't do jack shit about it.'

Russ rocked forward in a scramble of knees and blanket and lurched to his feet, a chest-deep growl that Clare had never heard coming from between his clenched teeth.

Travis jumped back. 'Shit!'

'Oh, for chrissakes.' Hector grabbed Travis's shirt and yanked him backward. At the same time, he rammed Russ with his shoulder. Russ staggered back, thudding into the wall. Hector pointed a wrench at him. 'Cool it. No one's going to diddle with your woman.'

'Sorry,' Travis said. 'It's just so much fun to play whack-a-cop.'

Clare got herself into a seated position and scooted back until she was pressed against the wall. She leaned against Russ's leg, knowing it made her look weak, knowing Travis knew she was afraid of him. But – she realized as she watched him glancing warily at Russ between offering spurious suggestions for fixing the engine – Travis was now afraid of Russ.

'This isn't happening.' Hector threw the wrench down in disgust. 'At least not with this crap set of tools.'

'So whadda we do? It's like fifty-something degrees in the house.'

Hector crossed his arms and looked at the canoes hanging over his head. 'Shit if I know. The church camp's not heated, either.'

The missing girl's father was up here at Cooper's Corners, Russ had said. *Fixing up a sprung pipe at a church camp.* He must have had Mikayla with him the whole time.

'What about' – Travis glanced at them, then turned away – 'the other place?'

'I don't want to take Mikayla there.'

'Dude, we're not going to get much farther. The roads are gonna be nothing but ice.'

'Our place has heat.' All three men in the storage room turned to stare at Clare. 'We have two woodstoves. No electricity needed. Plenty of wood.' She looked up at them. 'You can go to our place.'

Travis and Hector looked at each other. Travis jerked his head toward the door. They both went back into the house, kicking the door shut behind them.

Russ bent over, squatting until his head was near hers. 'What the hell was that all about?' He kept his voice low. 'Sending them to our cabin? With Bob Mongue holed up there, helpless? How's that going to make things better?'

'Lieutenant Mongue has a gun and the use of both his arms. We're stuck here in a slowly freezing storeroom with our hands duct-taped behind our backs. I don't see how it could make things *worse*. I'm buying you time to come up with a solution.'

They had the realization at the same moment. 'The tool kit,' he whispered, as she hissed, 'The screwdriver!' Russ was at the generator lifting the screwdriver out of the jumble of cheap tools by the time she had struggled to her feet.

'Turn around,' he said. 'Let's get you loose first.'

'No. Give it to me.' She turned around. 'We won't have much time. You have the upper-body strength to pull it apart if we get a few holes into it.'

He didn't argue. She felt the brush of his fingers, cold and swollen like hers, and then the screwdriver was in her grip. She pressed it backward, feeling the resistance of the tape.

'Harder,' he whispered.

'I don't want to hurt you,' she said and then shook her head, because what kind of stupid thing to say was that? This time she jabbed, hard, pushed and kept pushing, and then she was through. She jerked it back out and did it again. Then again. The fourth time, she felt something firmer, and Russ hissed in pain. She pulled the screwdriver out. 'Sorry,' she whispered.

'Keep going,' he said, his voice low. She managed three more holes and one more stab into his hand before they heard the footsteps headed toward their room. Clare dropped the screwdriver back onto the generator and let Russ push her back against the wall. When Travis and Hector opened the door, he was facing them, shielding his wife protectively and – not coincidentally – keeping his wrists out of sight.

The two men seized Russ by the upper arms and marched him toward the door. He braced his boots against the floor, struggling to resist the two-sided pull. The men yanked, hard, and Russ stumbled forward.

'Wait!' Clare lunged toward the men. 'What are you doing with him?' Travis kicked his leg across hers and, overbalanced, she thudded face-first onto the floor. She shrieked, rolling sideways too late to save the baby from the blow.

'Clare!' Russ twisted violently, breaking Travis's hold, knocking into him shoulder-first, sending the man stumbling against the wall.

There was a loud click. Mikayla's father pressed a .44 semiautomatic to Russ's head. Clare lay where she had fallen, pain radiating from her mid-section, a scream, a moan, a plea for mercy locked behind her teeth. Russ stared at her, wild-eyed, absolutely still except for his chest, heaving for air.

'I'm going to check out this place of yours, Van Alstyne. If you cooperate, your wife'll be fine except for a little bump. If you don't . . .' He gestured toward Travis, who looked at Russ with loathing. 'I think it's a good idea to have a hostage in our back pocket. Just in case. But a hostage who makes trouble is worse than none at all. You don't want us to have no hostages at all, do you?'

'No.'

'Good. Now say goodbye to your woman. If you behave, you'll get to see her again.'

No he won't. Clare could see the despairing truth echoing in her husband's eyes. Once DeJean made sure the offer of the cabin wasn't a trap, he would kill Russ. He was too dangerous to keep around.

His gaze dropped to her abdomen. 'The baby—'

'Is fine.' She forced herself to believe it. 'We'll be fine.'

His voice dropped almost too low for her to hear. 'I'm sorry. I'm so sorry, love.'

'I know.' She looked straight at him. 'Hold on.'

He nodded. 'Don't let go.'

Travis grabbed Russ's arm again. 'I like "see you later, honey," myself, but whatever. Let's go.'

FOUR

Kevin had a baggy rollneck sweater and a pair of jeans he kept stashed in his locker for emergencies. He drew a Smith & Wesson .40 from the Weapons Locker – his usual service piece wouldn't fit under anything but a trench coat. Hadley's Glock 19 was small enough for concealed carry, but she hadn't replaced her backup civvies the last time she had changed at the station, so they had to swing by her house before heading for Albany.

It was their fourth day at home, and her kids were so desperate for novelty they swarmed Kevin as soon as he stepped inside. He had to explain that his clothing didn't mean he was off duty. The dining room table was littered with board games, cards, watercolor sets, and drying artist's paper. It looked as if Mr Hadley had moved them on to building bird-houses, if Kevin was reading the half-assembled pieces of wood right.

When Hadley descended the stairs in a curve-hugging turtleneck and low-waisted jeans, Kevin did a double take. God, she looked hot. The blazer she shrugged on hid her gun but not her figure. *Friends*, he reminded himself. *Don't get greedy.*

The kids blocked them from the front door. 'Can't we go with you?' Hudson begged.

'We'll be good,' Genny added.

'No.' Hadley frowned at them. 'Absolutely not. If you're getting bored, Hudson, you can get to work on your social studies project, and Genny, you have to make a book box for Reading.'

They made sounds like deflating bagpipes.

'And stop whining.'

Time to unveil his backup plan. 'Tell you what,' Kevin said. 'I've got a portable DVD player that runs on batteries. I'll let you guys use it, *but* you have to get your school work done first. Deal?'

'Deal! Deal!'

Hadley looked at him like he was crazy. 'We don't have time to swing by your place and come back here. We'll be late meeting up with Detective Patten.'

He opened the door. 'It's okay. It's in the back of my Aztek.' He jogged down their porch steps – it looked like Mr Hadley was salting regularly – and grabbed the grocery sack he had filled with DVDs and the player. Hadley was still staring at him when he got inside and handed the goodies over to her grandfather. She didn't say anything until they were buckled in themselves and rolling – slowly – down the street.

'You already had it in your SUV.'

He shrugged. 'I threw it in the car this morning. You told me your power was out. I remember what it was like being stuck at home with my brothers, screaming with boredom. I figured Hudson and Genny could try the DVD player instead of re-creating Iroquois torture techniques, which is what my family did.'

She laughed. 'Good call.' She let the smile on her face die down to a softer kind of look than usual. 'Thanks, Flynn.'

Despite the worsening conditions, the ride down to Albany was a little more relaxed than last time. Kevin had weighted the four-wheel-drive vehicle down with cinder blocks in the back, which was lousy for fuel economy but good for the traction. They talked about his mother considering a run for Congress, and how Hudson was doing in middle school. They debated the merits of superhero movies, and recommended DVDs, and wondered if Eric McCrea was going to be able to patch up his marriage and if Harlene's husband was going to get her to retire. They did not talk about Syracuse, or her ex, or the sense of cool dread that seemed to be slowly glazing over the department with every day the girl remained missing and the chief stayed out of touch.

The city itself was a mess – traffic lights out along with the rest of the power grid, drainage grates dammed with ice that spread in thickening floes across the streets, a constant wail of police and fire sirens.

'Look at this place.' Hadley rubbed condensation from her window as Kevin slowed to a halt for a firefighter signaling a downed line across the road. 'It looks like that postapocalyptic flick where everything froze.'

'*The Day After Tomorrow*.' He backed up until he could turn around. Plows had been trying to keep up with the freezing rain on the Northway, but here in Albany they seemed to have ceded the roads to the storm. He hadn't seen a Public Works truck since getting off 787. He could feel his tires floating over the ice, searching for traction. 'Let's hope we don't get eaten by wolves while we're here.'

They eventually found the Albany PD's South Station, a graceful hundred-something-year-old brick building that looked like a larger version of the MKPD shop. Two uniforms were trying to push a squad car out of its ice-and-slush-covered parking spot, so Kevin took the time to back his Aztek in to the curb, trusting that would help him get his vehicle free when it was time to go.

Detective Vince Patten met them at reception. Patten was about as opposite from Lyle MacAuley as a man could be – barrel-chested, bald, and swarthy where the deputy chief was lean, thick-haired, and pale. 'Call me Vinnie,' Patten said, signing them in. 'All my friends call me Vinnie!' He steered them toward the stairs. 'Good to meet you. MacAuley treating you all right? Let me tell you about your deputy chief back in the day. We were partners, did he tell you that? Two upstate boys in the big, bad city – and lemme tell ya, New York in the sixties and seventies was mighty bad.' He led them to a desk and handed a file to Hadley. 'Here, hold that, will you, sweetheart? Take a look at this.' He picked up a photo cube and rotated it. 'We both made detective at the same time. This was our first day outta uniform.'

Kevin stared in a kind of fascinated horror at the wide-lapeled leather coat and flared perma-press pants on a shaggy-haired MacAuley. Patten had an Afro – an Italiafro? – and wore a corduroy suit.

'They looked like Starsky and Hutch,' Hadley whispered as they headed toward the interrogation rooms.

'What has been seen cannot be unseen,' Kevin intoned.

'Think we'll look that weird in thirty years?'

'Kind of an incentive to stay in uniform, isn't it?'

Jonathan Davies and his lawyer were waiting for them. Kevin would have pegged Davies as a smarmy frat boy even if he hadn't been briefed on the guy. He definitely had money to throw around – his attorney was an older woman in a severely conservative hairstyle and a thousand-dollar suit.

She cut right to the chase as soon as Patten had introduced them. 'My client has agreed to come in and assist in your investigation despite the fact that Detective Patten threatened him yesterday.'

Patten spread his hands. 'What, with a newspaper story?'

'Linking my client to a drug kingpin being held without bail on a double homicide charge.' She focused on Kevin and Hadley. 'Here are the ground rules. My client has immunity for anything he says in this room. My client's name will be replaced in your reports by a pseudonym.'

'Look,' Kevin began, 'we can't—'

The lawyer rolled on as if he hadn't spoken. 'My client will not testify against Tim LaMar or any of his associates. You, as proxy for the DA of Washington County, will agree to keep his name off any witness lists that have been or may be developed during this investigation.' She slid papers toward them and tossed a pen on top. 'Sign here.'

Kevin looked at Hadley. *Now what?* She gave him a how-the-hell-do-I-know look.

'You agree to our terms or we walk.' She glanced up at Patten. 'You can see if you can find a judge still at work to issue an arrest warrant. It may take a few days, though. I understand they're closing the courts down due to the weather.'

Kevin picked up the papers and the pen. Three copies of the terms. 'Are you sure?' Hadley asked.

He clicked the pen open. 'Mikayla Johnson doesn't have a few days.' He signed each copy and passed the papers to Detective Patten, who signed and returned them to the lawyer. She glanced at them, then nodded.

'Okay, Mr Davies.' Kevin sat down. 'Let's talk.'

FIVE

Russ twisted to catch one more glimpse of Clare's face, pinched with pain and stiff with determination, as they marched him out of the storage room and through the kitchen. *Oh, love.*

He wasn't under any illusions. When Hector DeJean started talking about a 'good' hostage, Russ knew it sure as hell wasn't him. These guys didn't think much of women, and a scared, pregnant female probably seemed like a present wrapped up in a bow to them. They underestimated Clare – lots of men did – and she would use that. No matter what happened to him, she would find a way to save herself and the baby. He held to that thought like the last remaining ember in a dying fire.

'You sure you don't want me to come along?' Travis said.

'I don't want Mikayla left alone.' DeJean steered Russ toward the door. He shrugged on his own parka but left Russ's hanging off the back of a chair. Why bother putting a coat on a man who's going to be dead soon? DeJean nodded toward Travis. 'If I'm not back in an hour, kill the woman.' He looked at Russ. 'I don't want any trouble from you. You understand?'

Russ nodded, dry-mouthed.

Outside, the freezing rain continued. His captor gestured toward the snow-and-ice-covered slope. The stairs were completely impassable now, and would stay that way until the next thaw. Russ broke the trail, the ice so thick he had to stomp each time he put his boot down. It didn't help that his arms were stretched behind his back. He clasped his hands together to keep DeJean from noticing the holes Clare had stabbed into the duct tape, grateful that the hard slog up the hill and the constant freezing spatter provided distraction. Of course, keeping his bonds hidden wasn't going to matter if he couldn't break free before DeJean decided to cap him.

250

The sixty-minute deadline yawned beneath him like a chasm.

The garage door was still standing open, as Russ had left it, its broken lock hanging. Inside, the hood and windshield of the SUV were coated with an inch or more of ice. Noticing this, his captor frowned. 'You were busy last night.' He opened the back door and gestured at Russ with the .44. 'Get in. Climb into the far back and lie down. If I so much as see your head over the seat, we're gonna stop until an hour has passed. Got it?'

Russ obediently climbed into the SUV. The wells below the middle seat were packed with plastic containers for gas or kerosene. The accelerants for the MacAllen house fire. He braced his feet and heaved himself over the seat into the storage area, rolling against two twenty-pound bags of sand and a compact shovel. As soon as DeJean fired up the engine and turned the blowers on high, Russ got to work on his restraints, flexing, tugging, stretching, twisting.

The SUV bumped over the edge of the garage door and they were outside. Instantly, Russ could hear the tattoo of rain on the roof and the hood. At least there would be plenty of noise to cover him. He felt one of the holes catch and widen. He strained his arms apart, gritting his teeth to keep from grunting in his effort.

DeJean turned on the radio and began scanning up the dial. Twenty-second blasts of music and talking sliced through the vehicle: hip-hop, sports, an ad for a local auto dealership, a song that had been popular when Russ was in high school. The SUV crept into the turn onto the crossroad. Russ felt another part of the duct tape give way. Despite the chill in the far back he was sweating freely.

'—breaks all records, Stacy,' a voice from the radio said. DeJean locked in the station. 'The combination of high and low systems locked into place is giving us the third straight day of icy rain, with no end immediately in sight.'

The tape was fraying in earnest now. Russ twisted his torso. If he could wedge something between his arms, give himself a little leverage ... he thumped and jounced against the hard plastic well liner.

The radio snapped off. 'Hey!' DeJean's voice was hard. 'Settle down back there.'

251

'The shovel was poking me,' Russ said.

'Just remember what I said. Your wife's life is in your hands, not mine.'

What was DeJean's plan? Would he haul him out of the SUV and shoot him in the road? Truss him up and leave him to die of hypothermia? Was DeJean going to do him before he checked out the cabin? Or after? Russ pictured Bob Mongue lying there, alone, in pain and feverish. Clare at least knew what was coming. Bob didn't have a clue. But Russ was gambling that he could escape and stop Roy before DeJean found the wounded trooper.

When the duct tape finally gave way, it was with an audible tear. Russ froze, holding his breath, but the beat of the windshield wipers and the roar of the heater covered the sound.

He almost cried out when he spread his arms. It felt like he was being tased. His muscles burned and his joints sizzled with electric shocks. He tried to lift his hand off the floor, but all it did was twitch. He clenched his teeth together and forced himself to relax. He needed time. His abused shoulders and biceps would work again. He just needed a little more time ...

The SUV came to a stop.

He heard the jingle of keys being pocketed. 'Okay, Van Alstyne. I'm gonna check your place out. If it's all good, I'll come and get you.'

I just bet you will.

The door thudded shut. Russ counted to three, then sat up. Through the windows, he could see the back of DeJean's head as he descended from the road to the cabin. Avoiding the iced-over stairs here, just like they had at the other lake house.

He needed to get those keys. He needed to stop DeJean, to put him down for good, and to get back to Clare. And he needed to do it in the next forty minutes. DeJean's head disappeared from view. Getting close to the cabin now. In a minute or two, he'd be walking in on the unsuspecting and unprepared Mongue. Under normal circumstances, Russ had no doubt the statie could more than hold his own against one bad guy with a .44. But flat on his back with a busted leg? Mongue was dead meat unless Russ did something.

He rolled into the middle seat and carefully opened the door. The wrenching pain in his shoulders brought tears to his eyes. He staggered to the rear of the vehicle and cupped his hands around his mouth. He sucked in enough air to make himself heard across the lake.

'Bob Mongue!' he roared. 'One man, armed, approaching kitchen door!'

He heard DeJean's scream of rage from downslope. He was going to shout another warning when a gun went off, its bullet biting into a pine branch above Russ's head. *Warning enough.* He took off up the road, running hard, head down, his boots crunching and catching where the tires had roughed up the ice. He counted on the steep slope and the difficulty of moving fast through the crusted snow to give him an extra few seconds before DeJean had a clear line of fire.

Another shot. Russ hurled himself over the mounded snow banking the edge of the road. He hit with an ice-cracking thud and let himself roll, arms and legs flung out, like a kid playing on a grassy hillside. He hit a tree, slid sideways, ricocheted off another. Shouting and swearing above him. No gunfire yet. DeJean would wait until he had Russ in his sights. He tucked his hands over his head and somersaulted down the slope, thudding into tree trunks, whipped by saplings, torn by bramble.

He slowed as the slope evened out. He uncurled and came to his feet, scrambling toward the lake's edge. The trees and brush he had pinballed through screened him utterly from the road. If DeJean wanted him, he'd have to come down the same way Russ had.

Two shots, one, two bullets tearing away ice-encased branches, the echoes falling away fast in the rain-thick air. 'Van Alstyne!' It was DeJean. 'You come up here right now and I won't take it out on your wife! You make me come after you, we'll peel her skin and carve that kid right outta her.'

Russ squeezed his eyes shut against his visceral reaction to DeJean's threat. The best chance for Clare – the best chance for all of them – was his freedom. He gritted his teeth against his rising gorge and leaned into the hemlock sheltering him.

'I know you can hear me, Van Alstyne! I'll give her to Travis first!' There was another long pause. 'You ain't gonna make it anyways! You got no gun and no truck and no place to go!'

Another shot, then another, and another, closely grouped, professional. Mongue. He wasn't out for the count yet. Thank God.

Take advantage of confusion, Clare had said, and he did so, slogging down the rest of the way to the lake and stepping onto the frozen surface. He half ran, half shuffled along the shore, moving fast without trees and brush and deep snow to trip him up. Then he was past the heavy wood beside the cabin. He dropped to the ice and elbow-crawled along the embankment until he could see up the clear slope to the glassed-in porch and the windows where Clare had sat and read and looked at the lake about a million years ago.

There was no sign of DeJean. Which didn't mean he wasn't flat on his stomach in the brush at the edge of the clearing, ready to blow Russ's head off the minute he came into view.

He forced himself to breathe, to slow his racing heart and mind. What did DeJean know? What did he want? And what was he going to do to get it? He knew there was at least one armed man in the cabin. He didn't know Bob was injured, his mobility severely impaired. He didn't know the sum total of their weaponry was limited to one service piece and whatever clips Bob had had in his duty belt. So right now, the cabin must look like a hard and potentially dangerous nut to crack.

DeJean wanted the cabin, though. Or at least a safe, warm place for his daughter. Russ stopped at that thought. Why was DeJean still here? He and Roy had snatched the girl in the wee hours of Friday, well before the ice storm had begun. He could be in Texas by now, headed over the border to Mexico or Honduras, leaving Roy to take the fall for the MacAllens' murder.

He shook his head. The *why* was irrelevant. He wasn't investigating here, he was trying to save Clare's life. And Mongue's. And Mikayla Johnson's.

The rain, freezing, then melting at the heat of his skin, had plastered his hair against his scalp until his forehead and ears ached with cold. His unprotected hands were raw, stiffening with every minute he stayed out in the open. *Think. Think.* It would only get harder as he got colder. He had to get the SUV away from DeJean or stop the man permanently. Either way, he needed to be back at Travis Roy's house – he checked his watch – in twenty minutes. His heart sank. It had taken DeJean that long to drive around the end of the lake to get here.

Get into the cabin. Get Mongue's weapon. Find DeJean. Simple. He hadn't heard anything from either DeJean or Mongue in several minutes. He'd like to think it was because Mongue had nailed the bastard, but it was more likely DeJean had retreated to a better position to avoid the state trooper's line of fire. Which would mean taking the high ground up at the road, facing the side of the house with only one tiny window. From there, he could cut off any attempt to escape out the kitchen door or through the French doors in the bedroom.

But he wouldn't be able to spot a man headed straight up the middle. Russ looked at the twenty yards of open ground between the lake's edge and the cabin's back door. Not so much as a sapling to shelter behind. He had a sudden, head-jerking vision of himself at nineteen, charging a nameless hill in Lao Du, avoiding the bullets that were chewing up half his platoon by sheer random luck. He took a deep breath. Then another. He had lost a lot of speed in the intervening thirty-four years. He hoped he hadn't lost the luck.

He launched himself uphill before he could reconsider. He pumped and flailed and stomped and swung, horrified at the noise he was making but helpless to stop it. He ran toward the cabin the way his younger self had raced to the top of that hill, putting every last fast-twitch muscle in play, leaving nothing behind.

He slammed against the porch, chest heaving, thighs burning. Instantly, a shot rang out, spiderwebbing the window next to Russ. He raised his hands, waving frantically, praying Bob wouldn't drop him where he stood.

Nothing happened. Hands still raised, he climbed the stairs and cracked the porch door. Crossed the porch and opened the interior door. Bob Mongue was straddling a chair, ammo pouch between his legs, his service piece pointed straight at Russ's chest. 'It's me,' Russ said, his voice hoarse.

Mongue lifted his gun away. 'I see. What the hell's going on?' His voice was strained with pain and fatigue.

'A shitstorm of epic proportions.' Russ surveyed the cabin. Mongue had taken up position at the edge of the kitchen, where he had a line of sight through both sides and the porch. One of the windowpanes in the bedroom was shattered, as was the glass set in the kitchen door. 'Did you hit him?'

Mongue shook his head. 'No. I scared him off, though.'

'Did you hear his SUV leaving?'

'Hell, I didn't hear it arriving. First warning I got was you screaming at me.'

Russ pointed to Mongue's weapon. 'How much ammo do you have?'

Mongue picked up the pouch. 'Three clips.'

Thirty shots. 'Okay. I'll take 'em.'

'What exactly are you planning to do?' Mongue's doubtful look changed to something sharper. 'Where's your wife?'

'Back at Roy's cabin, with Roy and the missing girl. That's the girl's father out there. Hector DeJean. He gave Roy orders about Clare. If he's not back in an hour . . .' He couldn't finish the sentence.

'What can I do?'

'Keep watch. Yell if you spot him. I'm going to go out there and kill him.' He was surprised at how matter-of-fact he sounded. His entire career as a cop was predicated on the idea of force as the last resort, but he had no intention of capturing DeJean. He was going to put him in the ground, and if he got a clean line of fire on Roy before Clare could object, he was going to kill him, too.

Mongue didn't blink at his statement. 'Okay. Better get something on over that sweater. And I've got shooting gloves in the inside pocket of my coat.'

Russ retrieved his waterproof anorak from the pile he had left on the floor when he dumped his ice-fishing duffel. He had turned to get Mongue's parka off its hook when he caught the acrid scent of smoke. 'You smell that? Did you throw something into the woodstove?'

'Nope.' Mongue sniffed. 'Smells oily.'

'Oh, *shit*.' Russ bolted for the kitchen door. He could tell, by the heat radiating through it, that it was too dangerous to open. Then he spotted the bright orange lick of flame through the tiny kitchen window. The mingled odor of gas and kerosene was heavy in the air. 'That sonofabitch is trying to burn us out.'

SIX

Tracking down meth dealers in the Albany area during what the National Weather Service was calling 'the ice storm of the century' was marginally better than a root canal without anesthetic. But it was a slim margin. The third time her feet flew out from beneath her and she landed ass-first on the sidewalk, Hadley began to reconsider her decision to move from California. The third time they came up empty, she began to reconsider her decision to become a cop.

Davies had given up four names. All active dealers, all potential snitches. All of them lived in parts of Albany that legislators, lobbyists, and school kids on state capital tours would never get to see.

They couldn't find the first guy. His entire block, a row of sagging two-story houses that looked like they should have been condemned years ago, had emptied out when the grid went down. A city employee, seeing them huddled by the perp's door, leaned out of a Bobcat he was using to scrape out the drainage grates. 'Disbursed to shelters,' he yelled. 'Without electricity, these dumps are like walk-in freezers.'

'Should we search shelters?' Hadley asked.

Patten shook his head. 'Not unless we get desperate. He could be in any one of a dozen schools or churches at this point. Better try number two.'

They found perp number two. Or rather, they found his girlfriend, leading a lights-out party at his row house. She answered the door bundled up in a puffy coverlet, the odor of alcohol rising off her in waves. 'He dead,' she told them.

'Dead?' Flynn peered past her shoulder, where similarly swaddled people were reeling through the room, laughing and waving candles.

'Yeah, this like a wake.' She turned away from the door and snatched a frame off a table. She showed it to them. Instead of a photograph, it held a neatly clipped obituary. 'He dead.' She suddenly burst into tears. 'Oh, my poor Levi! My baby! What I gonna do without you?' One of her friends staggered up and slung an arm around her.

'Okay. Um.' Flynn took off his hat. 'Sorry to disturb you, ma'am. Sorry for your loss.'

'If they don't set that place on fire from the fumes alone, I'll be amazed,' Hadley said, as they crept across the ice to where the Aztek was parked.

'I like a nice wake,' Patten said. 'Cry and drink, drink and cry, until you pass out clutching the dearly departed's mass cards. What more fitting way to see somebody into the afterlife?'

Lunch was sandwiches, cold, from a local bodega, eaten in Flynn's Aztek. Hadley tried to raise Granddad on her cell but couldn't get through. She prayed Flynn's DVD player was holding up. Or that Granddad was. The kids hadn't been in school since last Friday, and if tomorrow was a snow day again – as looked likely – she was going to hook up with some other moms and arrange a playdate. God knew when she'd be able to reciprocate, but Hudson and Genny had to get out of the house.

The third could-be informant had evidently been seeing one of his buddies into the next world, because he was stoned into incoherence. They found him in a heatless, lightless SRO that was in the process of being evacuated. 'I's tell ya sure,' he mumbled, when Flynn pulled him out of the bus line. They frogmarched him to the Aztek and sat him in the back. Flynn insisted on keeping both rear doors open to dissipate the smell.

'We're looking for the location of LaMar's meth factory,' Patten said.

'Ya sure L'mar.' The snitch listed sideways.

'If he looks like he's going to throw up, haul him out of there,' Flynn said.

Patten shook the man. 'That's right, LaMar. C'mon, buddy, stay with me here. Tell me about LaMar.'

'Ya L'mar.' The guy's eyelids fluttered. 'Wha?'

'LaMar's meth cooker. We heard you know something.'

'Oh ya sure.' He tipped his head back. A noise came out of the back of his throat.

'Is he snoring?' Hadley said.

Patten shook him again, harder.

'Hey!' The guy looked at them, wounded. 'Doan be mean.'

'Tell us where LaMar's meth house is.' Kevin leaned in past Patten and held the man's face between his hands. 'Or give us the name of someone who knows.'

'Know wha?'

'This is useless!' Hadley kicked the Aztek's tire.

Patten nodded. 'I gotta agree with you on that. Let's find out what shelter the buses are taking these folks to. If the fourth name turns up nothing, we can come back to Sleeping Beauty here.'

Davies hadn't given them an address for the fourth man, but they had his place of business, such as it was. It was LaMar's favorite haunt when he was in the capital.

'D'Oiron's.' Patten looked up at the dead neon sign sporting the bar's name and a huge cluster of grapes. 'This place was around when my dad was a kid. The whole neighborhood used to be crawling with Francos, come down from Quebec to work in construction and the mills. St Denis Parish was just around the corner there. The diocese shut it down two years ago.' He sighed. 'Nice to see a mobster who appreciates his heritage.'

Hadley stamped her feet on the ice-slick sidewalk. 'We better get moving before we freeze where we stand.'

'Is it open?' Flynn peered in the single dark window fronting the street.

'Oh, sure. They'll have a generator. Probably doing record business with all the guys who haven't had to show up to work today.'

Hadley was going to protest that nobody would go for a beer in a citywide weather emergency, but Patten opened the door and sure enough, the bar was crowded. She and Flynn stepped down into the dim interior, following the detective as he threaded his way past round tables, men in twos and threes looking up at her with undisguised disapproval. She wasn't sure if she was made as a cop or if it was simply because she was a woman.

She leaned against the bar next to Patten, while Flynn stood a couple of feet away, trying and failing not to look like he was casing the room. The slab of wood was scarred with generations of condensation rings and cigarette burns. The bartender was professionally bland, coming over as soon as Patten crooked his fingers. 'What can I get for you folks?' He was reaching for glasses as he spoke.

'I'm looking for a guy named Boileau. A mutual friend told me I might find him at your fine establishment.'

The bartender's expression didn't change. Without taking his eyes away from Patten, he said, 'Hey! Boileau! These cops want to talk with you!'

Oh, shit. Hadley shifted. Before she could turn around, a thickset, chin-bearded man leaped up and smashed a chair into Flynn's chest. Her partner went down with a grunt of pain, skidding across the floor, ramming into the corner of the bar.

'Flynn!' Hadley lunged toward him, her hand reaching for the shoulder radio that wasn't there. Out of the corner of her eye, she saw Boileau shoving men and chairs out of the way. Vince Patten was drawing his gun, shouting, 'Police! Stop! Get down!' Boileau pounded out the door, leaving the detective swearing.

'Flynn?' She dropped to her knees, one hand going to his neck, the other to his chest. White-faced, he tried to rise off the floor. 'Don't move,' she ordered. 'You might have broken a rib.'

He waved her off. ''M okay,' he rasped. 'Go.' At her doubtful look, he pushed her. 'Go!'

She rose and sprinted through the doorway. Patten was a few yards ahead of her, slipping and sliding as he tried to run in his old-fashioned galoshes. Boileau was a shrinking form already halfway up the block, moving fast for a guy carrying a couple of spare tires. She might never make up the difference running on the iced-over sidewalk. *If you had caught Annie Johnson then and there, none of this would be happening right now. Do whatever it takes.*

She clambered over the filthy wall of cement-hard snow past the sidewalk and leaped into the street. There was ice and slush enough to send a car into a spin, but there were also spots of clear asphalt and salt and sand, gritty and firm beneath her boots.

A minivan, undeterred by the fact that half the city was closed down, swept past her, showering her with slush, blaring its horn. Hadley clawed her badge out of her pocket and dropped it over her head, wishing it was a reflective POLICE vest instead. She was gaining on Boileau. 'Police!' Her yell was lost in the spatter and whoosh of another vehicle passing her. 'Police!' She was only a few yards away, but she and Boileau were still separated by that three-foot-high snowbank. Climb over? No. Intersection. If she could reach it before he did—

She gulped air and sprinted. She could see his face now, blotchy red from exertion, mouth open, stringy hair plastered to his forehead. She angled toward the crossroad, dodging cobblestone-sized chunks of snow, bounding over deadly patches of black ice. Boileau saw her, reached behind his back, going for his weapon. She had hers out and was shouting something, hearing nothing but the drumbeat of blood in her ears, and Boileau turned – to reverse course? to shoot? – and suddenly he shrieked and disappeared.

Hadley rounded the snowbank, her Glock ready, and almost discharged it accidentally as Boileau slid, bare-handed, straight into her. She went down on top of him, knocking out what was left of her breath, but he was even more winded than she was and disoriented from smacking the back of his skull on the ice. Hadley wrestled him onto his front and zip-strapped him. She sat on his back, heaving for air, until Vince Patten jogged up, galoshes still flapping, to do the honors on behalf of the city of Albany.

While Patten Mirandized Boileau, Hadley frisked him. No other weapon. She was unsurprised to find a pipe and a section of the *Albany Times-Union* that, unfolded, revealed a dozen glassine envelopes, each containing several grams of what looked to be crystal meth. The envelopes were all stamped with the same design. 'Branding,' Patten said, when she showed him. 'Even with drug dealers, it's all about the branding.'

The sidewalk in front of d'Oiron's was crowded with rubberneckers by the time she and Patten perp-marched Boileau back up to Flynn's Aztek. Flynn was standing there, still pale, and Hadley knew she looked like she had gotten into a fight with a Zamboni. They exchanged a kind of wordless check with one another – *You okay? Yeah, you?* – before he clamped one large hand over Boileau's head and guided him into the backseat. The door made a satisfying thunk as it closed. Patten climbed into the seat next to Boileau, and Hadley took shotgun, tossing the evidence in the glove compartment until they had a chance to label it properly. She turned around when Flynn fired up the SUV. 'Mr Boileau,' she began, 'it looks like you were carrying over ten grams of methamphetamine. That's a felony-level offense.'

'You can cut the act,' Boileau said. 'Nobody on the street can see inside with the tinting on those windows.' He looked around. 'Jesus. They gave you an Aztek? That's like the Chevy Nova of SUVs. Who'd you manage to piss off?'

'What?'

He nodded toward Patten and leaned forward. 'You can take these off now, old man.'

Patten smiled at the perp. 'Kevin, you got any problem if I open the door back here and let this guy's head bounce along the road for a couple yards?'

Boileau stared at him. Then he looked at Hadley. His eyes narrowed. 'You guys aren't from Narcotics, are you?' He laughed. 'Jesus, you have no idea, do you?'

Hadley gritted her teeth and tried to sound patient. 'No idea about what, Mr Boileau?'

'It's Agent Boileau. Special Agent Mike Boileau of the DEA.' He glanced around the vehicle. 'You three stooges want to tell me why you're blundering around in the middle of our investigation?'

SEVEN

Clare was trying to talk her way into the bathroom. 'Look,' she said to Travis, 'I really have to go. Just cut me free for a minute. You can retape me when I'm through.'

She had gotten him to let her out of the locked shed by pleading the cold. The rest of the house wasn't exactly warm – around fifty-five and cooling fast – but sitting on a chair in the kitchen was a damn sight better than stretching out on that frigid floor.

Travis turned to her from where he'd been looking out the window. It had been at least half an hour since his partner had left, and he was jangly and jittery. He kept banging a pipe that Clare was sure wasn't meant for tobacco against his thigh. 'How stupid do you think I am?'

Pretty damn stupid. 'Come on. You can't possibly think I'm a threat to you.' She wiggled her stockinged feet, emphasizing her lack of boots.

'I didn't say—'

'I'm one pregnant woman. You're a strong man with a gun. Your boss is holding my husband hostage. Do you think I'd do anything to jeopardize him?' Travis narrowed his eyes like a bull who didn't understand why someone was annoying him by waving a cape around. 'Put him in danger,' she clarified. 'Please. Just long enough to go to the bathroom. You can stand guard outside.' She was trying very hard to believe that Russ and Lieutenant Mongue would be able to take care of Hector. *Please, God, please let them be safe.* But it wouldn't do any good if she and Mikayla were still here, to be used as human shields.

'Hows about I pull down your pants for you. You won't need your hands then.'

263

'You want to wipe up after me?' She looked doubtful. 'That's . . . well, I guess you could. You probably already know about a pregnant woman's' – she dropped her voice – 'discharge.'

Travis recoiled. 'Discharge?'

'You know. The mucus and the um, meconium and perinium.' She was whispering now, as if the fictional leakage were simply too disgusting to be spoken about aloud.

Travis looked horrified. 'No way. God.' He dropped his pipe on the table and opened a drawer for a pair of scissors. 'Turn around.' She did so. He cut the duct tape around each wrist and pulled it away. 'Okay. There you go. Into the bathroom.' He gestured toward the door with his gun.

The agony of her newly freed shoulders immobilized her. She breathed slowly and silently, her mouth open, blinking back tears.

'Go on.' Travis sounded impatient.

Clare crossed the kitchen floor. The bathroom was centered between the kitchen and the living room, at the head of a short hallway interrupted by three closed doors. Bedrooms. 'How is Mikayla doing?' She managed to keep her voice close to normal.

'You don't need to worry about her.' Travis gestured with the gun. 'Get in there and do, you know, whatever.' Clare did what he said. 'Don't lock it,' he said as she shut the door. Not that the cheap push-tab lock would have stopped him.

Clare examined the space while she did her business. Tub and shower on one side, counter and sink on the other. There was a window high on the wall behind the toilet, but even if she hadn't been five and a half months pregnant, she couldn't have fit through it. Finished, she stood up and stretched, rolling and flexing her arms. The pain was abating to fiery prickles in her shoulders and a dull ache in her elbows and wrists.

'Hurry it up,' Travis shouted through the door.

'Sorry.' She turned on the water, but without electricity to fuel the well pump, only a trickle came through the faucet. She pulled out the console drawers as silently as she could, scanning each one for something, anything, she could use as a weapon. Nothing but toothpaste and over-the-counter medicines and three-quarters-gone bottles of sunscreen.

She flushed the toilet, letting the sound mask the click-click as she opened the doors beneath the sink. Scouring powder and tub-and-tile cleaner and extra-strength mildew spray. A package of toilet paper. Maybe she could bean Travis with a roll of TP, then polish and shine him. Behind the cleaning supplies was a scrub brush and, lying on its side – she felt a surge of hope. An old-fashioned, wood-handled plumber's helper. She eased it around the sink pipe and pulled it free. Two feet of solid hardwood and a thick rubber plunger that must have weighed five pounds. Produced in the forties or fifties, she guessed, designed to last a lifetime. She hefted it in her hand. *Yes.* She could use this.

She picked up the mildew spray. *Warning: Contains bleach. Keep away from nose and eyes.* Okay. She took a breath. 'Travis? Do you have any talcum powder?'

'Talcum powder?'

'The duct tape irritates my skin. I wanted to sprinkle some on before you tape me up again. But I can't find any.'

'Oh, for chrissake—'

Clare didn't find out if he stormed into the bathroom to help her or to haul her out. He was still swinging the door open when she squirted the mildew cleaner in his eyes, once, twice, three times, until the liquid was dripping off his chin and he was screaming and flailing, trying to find her blind. She swung the plunger in a full backward arc and smashed the wooden shaft against his forearm. He screamed again. The gun flew out of his nerveless hand. She dropped the spray bottle and grabbed the plumber's helper with both hands, ramming it into his stomach, putting her whole weight behind it.

Travis folded over, retching. She bashed the door into him and he staggered. She did it again, and again, until he slipped and fell to the floor, and she fell heavily onto his back and bared her teeth and grabbed his long hair and smashed his head into the floor, smashed it and smashed it until her body registered his limp stillness and her mind caught up and she let go, trembling, her blood roaring in her ears.

She tipped back and staggered to her feet. She was shaking so violently it took her two tries to step past his prone body into the kitchen. Her breath was coming in short, hard pants, and it took a minute for her to realize she was crying. She wiped at her face and bent over, letting her head hang down. She stayed that way for a long moment, trying to gain her bearings, trying to find a thought, a plan, to anchor herself to.

The attached shed. It had a real lock on the door. She returned to the bathroom, bent, and grabbed Travis by the ankles. She dragged him across the floor and into the shed. She crouched over him, taking in his bloody nose and mouth. 'I'm so sorry,' she whispered. Pray God she hadn't given him a concussion.

There was enough water in the kitchen faucet to wet some paper towels. She cleaned the blood from Travis's face, then retrieved a pair of sofa pillows and several woolly throws from the living room. She laid him against the pillows, elevating his head and hopefully maintaining a clear airway. She tucked the throws over and around the unconscious man. That should keep him warm enough. She retreated to the doorway. There wasn't anything more she could do.

You could stay around and make sure you haven't given him a life-threatening injury.

She pushed the thought away and locked the door. Her first duty was to Russ. Her baby. Mikayla Johnson.

Testing Jesus, the lawyer asked, 'Who is my neighbor?'

She pressed her hands against her face. 'Dear Lord,' she whispered, 'please forgive me for hurting this man. There was no mercy or justice in what I did. But if I don't help Mikayla, she's going to die. Please keep me strong. Amen.'

The voice in her head fell silent. Her adrenaline rush had ebbed, leaving her tired and discouraged. She found her boots by the door and slipped them on. Shrugged on her parka. Then she went to find Mikayla.

The first bedroom was empty. The second had two sets of bunk beds, a wall of shelves filled with battered old books and thrice-hand-me-down toys, and two large windows overlooking the lake. Clare could see the exact spot where she and Oscar had stopped the night before.

Mikayla was huddled in one of the bottom bunks, hidden in a puffy down comforter, her eyes closed, her face flushed. 'Mikayla?' Clare laid a hand on the girl's forehead. She was throwing off heat like a woodstove. 'Mikayla? It's me, Clare. From last night. Do you remember?'

The girl nodded. Her lips were puffy, almost cracked. Clare picked up the bottle of water on the floor next to the bunk and slid her arm around Mikayla's shoulders, lifting her into a seated position. 'Drink some water, honey. That's a good girl. That's better.'

Mikayla finished off the bottle and sank back onto her pillow. 'I'm going to get you some medicine to bring down your fever, okay, sweetheart? Then after you've taken that, we're going to get you to a doctor. I'll be right back.' Mikayla never opened her eyes.

EIGHT

It was getting very warm in the cabin.

'How long do you think it'll take before the fire breaks through that timber?' Bob Mongue was facing away from the burning wall, keeping guard on the lakeside front.

'Damned if I know.' Russ pawed through the pile of stuff on the floor. He tossed the chemical heaters, his fishing knife, and the insulated blankets into his empty duffel. A couple of heavy sweaters and some socks went in next. 'The cabin's made of whole logs, and they're treated with something to make 'em bug resistant.'

'Does that make them fire resistant as well?'

'I have no idea.' Russ grabbed the bottle of acetaminophen – now seriously depleted – and threw it into the duffel. 'I'm more worried about the roof.' He looked up at the ceiling. Smoke was hanging in a thickening pall, shrouding the loft where Clare had wanted the baby's room. His gut churned.

'Your roof's covered in four inches of ice. It'll be the last to go.'

'We're not going to stay long enough to find out.' Russ set the duffel next to Mongue's chair. He crossed to the bedroom, dropping to the floor and belly-crawling around the bed until he had a clear view of the tiny patio and the narrow stretch of cleared land and the woods. He lay there for several minutes, scanning the area in slow degrees, south to north.

'Anything?' Mongue called.

'No.' The cabin had been carefully planned so that its windows and French doors opened onto pleasing views of the lake and the thick woods, and right now Russ would have paid double the asking price for one lousy look at the road.

'What's the plan? Besides "walk outside, get shot", I mean.'

Russ backed away from the bedroom and got to his feet. 'He's one guy. He can only cover one side.'

'Unless he gets down to the lake. He'll have a clear view of everything from there. Drill us right through the porch windows if he has a decent rifle.'

'Yeah. I'm betting he isn't going to want to get too much distance between him and his vehicle. He doesn't know how many people are in here or how well we're armed. He's got to consider that somebody could stay inside laying down cover fire while one of us hikes up the hill and gets control of the SUV.'

Mongue gave him a smile thinned by pain. 'I like that idea. Why don't we do that?'

'If he starts shooting at us from lakeside, we will.' Russ backtracked to the kitchen. Waves of heat were rolling off the rear wall, and the cabinet, when he bent to open it, was almost too hot to touch. He grabbed the box of thirty-gallon trash bags and brandished it to Mongue.

'Triple ply,' the trooper said. 'Probably also not fire resistant.'

Russ settled the duffel across his back. 'This is your way out of here.' He ducked down next to Mongue. The other man slung his arm around Russ's neck and they stood together. Mongue held his Glock out. 'Keep it,' Russ said. 'You're covering us.' They limp-walked together to the screened-in porch. Russ took a deep breath. 'Okay. I open the door. The trash bag goes down. You go on the trash bag. I drag you as fast as I can down to the lake's edge. We'll be screened by the embankment there.'

'You're completely insane, you know that? The odds of him hitting at least one of us are ten to one. In his favor.'

'You have a better idea?'

There was a whistling sound, like steam in a kettle, and a second later the fire finally broke through the far wall, licking and leaping along the rounded logs. One of the cupboards burst into flames. 'Shit,' Mongue said. 'Okay, Van Alstyne. Your plan is looking better. Let's do it.'

Russ opened the door, expecting the whine and thud of a bullet at any moment. Nothing. He snapped the trash bag out. Nothing. It floated to the snow. Holding the door open with his hip, he hoisted Mongue, stepped off the porch, and swung him onto the heavy plastic. Russ paused at the trooper's sharp breath and grunt of pain. 'I'm okay,' Mongue whispered, although he clearly was not. 'Go.'

Russ bunched the end of the bag in his fist and, crouching, began his downslope run. He tried to keep an eye out for DeJean, but the ice, slipping and breaking beneath his boots, demanded most of his attention. He staggered forward, half running, half falling, jouncing and tipping Mongue, his thighs bunching and burning, his shoulder, still aching from his confinement, cramping and spasming. The repressed sounds of pain behind him stopped about three-quarters of the way down the slope, and when Russ finally reached the lake – jumping and sliding on his ass down the last drop onto the ice – he saw why. The trooper had fainted.

Russ considered taking the gun from Mongue's lap but decided he'd be safer using both hands to stay low and out of sight beneath the embankment. His destination was maybe fifty feet away. He wiggled the duffel off his back and laid it atop Mongue before gathering the end of the trash bag again and beginning an arm-and-two-knees crawl across the ice.

Halfway there, he felt Mongue rolling his head back and forth. The bag rustled with a sudden whole-body twitch, and then Mongue let out a hiss like a deflating tire.

'You fainted.' Russ tried not to sound as exhausted and out of breath as he felt.

'The hell I did,' Mongue said weakly.

Russ didn't waste energy arguing. The wide square door of the boathouse loomed larger and larger and then they were slipping inside, out of the steady, dripping rain and out of sight to anyone not lined up straight across from the boathouse's entrance. Every muscle in his body screamed in relief and protest as he stood up.

The boathouse was the size of a large garage, and about as plain on the inside. A wooden walkway ran around three sides of the structure. Two kayaks rested in wall-mounted cradles, and a battered old wooden canoe hung just beneath the rafters, suspended on a rope-and-pulleys mount. Russ dragged Mongue to the edge of the walkway and lifted him from the now-shredded trash bag. Between the two of them, they managed to wrestle the trooper off the ice and up onto the planks.

''S'not a bad shelter,' Mongue wheezed. 'Little cold.'

'I have a plan for that.' Russ climbed off the ice and walked to where the ropes holding the canoe were cleated to the wall. He tried to unwind one of the ropes from its cleat, but it was frozen.

'Always a plan.' Mongue was trying for his usual sardonic tone but could only manage sounding exhausted. 'Must drive you nuts when things go wrong.'

Russ banged on it with his fist until it started to give. Once loosened, the rope unwound quickly. The canoe's stern lurched toward the ice as if it were re-creating the sinking of the *Titanic*.

'Tough character trait for a law enforcement officer.' Mongue sighed. 'Pain pills?'

'In the duffel.' Russ went to the second cleat and began hammering at the rope. He turned back to the rope, twisting and yanking it into flexibility.

Mongue unzipped the duffel and dug inside. The plastic bottle rattled as he shook out a handful of Tylenol. He dry swallowed the pills, then spat. 'Law enforcement, the plan never lasts. Too much crap coming at you.'

Russ unhitched the rope from the cleat. The bow of the canoe jerked down. Russ dropped it until it was hanging parallel to and a foot below the walkway.

'Your private life, though. That you can keep just the way you like it. Settled. Predictable. No big surprises. Everything the way it was the day before.'

Russ cleated off the two ropes. 'You got a point, Bob? 'Cause I'm a little busy here to take time out for psychoanalysis.'

'That's what you came back to Millers Kill for, wasn't it? So you'd know what to expect for the rest of your life?'

Russ sat on the walkway and slid himself back onto the ice. 'Look. I'm sorry you're still pissed about me getting the chief's job. No, I didn't come home so I could start my march to the grave. I was only forty-three when I left the army, for chrissake.' He pushed against the side of the canoe, moving

271

it forward until its side bumped against the walkway. 'But yeah, I do like to know what to expect. Jesus, I don't think that's too much to ask.'

Mongue watched as he shoved the canoe into position on the walkway. 'Then why the hell'd you marry Reverend Knock-your-feet-out-from-under-you? Seems like she'd be the one woman to drive you absolutely batshit crazy.'

Russ snorted. 'I married her *because* she drives me absolutely batshit crazy.' He had been chief of police five years when Clare arrived in Millers Kill. There had been ups and downs, but basically, yeah, Bob was right. Until Clare walked into his life, each day *had* been like the day before. The way he liked it. Except he had thrown over every shred of sanity and certainty he had for the chance to be with Clare.

He paused on the ladder up to the walkway. *That's what I wanted. I had my life built as sturdy and square as that cabin and I set the whole thing on fire.*

He swung onto the walkway. 'I have to go. I have to get DeJean's SUV and get the hell back to my wife.' He pulled one of the blankets out of the open duffel and laid it in the bottom of the canoe. Then he squatted beside Mongue, knees going snap-crackle-pop, and picked him up. He lugged him over to the canoe and settled the trooper amidships. Russ passed him the duffel. 'If you wrap yourself up in the other blankets, you should stay warm enough inside there.'

Mongue nodded. He handed Russ his Glock and the ammo pouch.

'I'll come back as soon as I can.'

The trooper nodded. 'I know you will.'

Russ rounded the corner of the boathouse and struck off toward the unseen road on a diagonal, climbing through the woods on the far side of the cabin. Or what used to be the cabin. The bright red-orange of the fire lit up the surrounding woods; the birch bark glowed golden, the rain showers of sparks. The steady downpour suppressed some of the smoke, but he caught whiffs of charcoal and creosote as he toiled up the slope, headed for Mongue's squad car. He didn't try to move quietly; the roar of the fire drowned out the crack of snow crust and the snap of branches from his passage.

He emerged from the woods – carefully, slowly – by a cylindrical snowman that turned out to be the next-door-neighbor's mailbox. He was well ahead of where DeJean had parked the SUV, and, sticking to the edge of the road where snow provided some traction beneath the ice, he began to jog toward the squad car.

He looked backward once toward the column of smoke – the phrase *Lot's wife* came into his head – but otherwise pressed hard for the unit. The tracks where he and Clare had walked, dragging Mongue behind them, were still visible beneath a clear, thick coating of fresh ice.

The same layer of ice had entombed the state police car as it was, hood flattened and driver's door open, giving it the look of some ancient relic abandoned in a disaster and never reclaimed. Russ brushed the ice off the steering column and retrieved the keys. A few hard kicks to the back of the car cleared the lock. It took two hands to lift the trunk against the weight of the ice, but once he did, he had his weapon.

The Remington 870 was the standard state police shotgun, powerful enough to blow a hole through a barn door. Russ loaded his pockets with shells and took three emergency road flares for good measure. Bob had also left his rain poncho, which Russ gratefully donned. It wouldn't keep him warm, but it would stop his wool sweater from getting soaked.

He jogged back down toward the cabin on the other side of the road this time. His plan was to circle up above the road, using the trees and the small garage as cover. If he was lucky, he'd get a clear line of sight on DeJean before the bastard even knew he was there. His only real worry was that DeJean had left the high ground and gone hunting for him and Mongue. If anyone found him, the trooper would be as defenseless as a turtle on its back.

When he had climbed through the woods to a good vantage site, though, Russ discovered that his fear was groundless. He had an uninterrupted view of the fire, the cabin, the roiling smoke, and the perfectly empty road, no SUV in sight.

DeJean had gone back to the lake house.

NINE

Clare returned to the bathroom, averting her gaze from the droplets of blood spattered across the floor. She got the children's ibuprofen from the second drawer, then, reluctantly, picked up Travis's gun. She checked it, ejected the magazine, and put the gun in one pocket and the ammo in another.

She grabbed another bottle of water from the kitchen and went back to the bedroom. She coaxed the medicine down Mikayla's throat with a generous amount of water, then helped the girl lie back against her pillow. 'Okay, sweetheart, I'm going to get my truck out of the garage. Then I'm coming back here for you.' Clare pressed her lips against Mikayla's forehead. It was like kissing an oven. 'I know you're feeling awfully sick, but it won't be long now. Once we've gotten you to a hospital, the doctors will make you all better.' *Please God that we're not too late.*

Russ's parka was still hanging on a hook by the kitchen door. She searched through the pockets. No key. She took a deep breath and searched again, forcing herself to go slowly and methodically. Nothing. Either it had been lost in the snow when Russ fell, or Hector had taken it.

Fortunately, Russ, being Russ, had a backup. She had never used it before, but there was a spare key in a magnetic box, stuck to the truck's chassis behind the driver's-side wheel well. As she opened the kitchen door, Clare heard a kind of angry groan from the locked shed. Travis. She was going to have to get Mikayla out as stealthily as possible. If she and the girl were pursued, she didn't want Travis knowing exactly how much – or how little – a lead they had.

Russ's truck was parked inside the garage, nose-in, tight against the far wall. Almost too tight, given her expanded girth.

There was enough of a gap for her to wedge herself in face-forward, so she stripped off her parka and squeezed between the truck bed and the wall, dropped her coat onto the cement, and maneuvered herself like an arthritic camel into a kneeling position.

She pressed her chest as close to the frigid floor as possible, then, gritting her teeth, began sweeping her fingers along the truck's underside, hoping to find the box by feel.

She was about to rear up and scoot forward another foot when her palm hit something sharp-cornered. A rectangle of metal. She sat back on her haunches and pried the box open. The car key, the beautiful key, was inside. Her surge of victory was squelched by the odd squeak of tires on ice. The dim gray daylight in the garage was blocked out and the SUV backed into the space next to Russ's truck. Inches from Clare's hidden body.

She had no place to go. She slid down and lay sideways on her parka, tucking her knees against the bulk of her stomach. If Hector stood between the truck and the far wall, or if he lay on the garage floor and looked beneath the carriage, he would see her. She heard the thud of Hector's boots, the thunk as the door closed, then his footsteps leaving the garage. When she figured he was out of sight and earshot, she uncurled and struggled to her feet, bracing herself between the truck and the wall.

She crossed the opening of the garage and peered into the SUV. For a moment, she went limp with relief. She had been dreading the sight of Russ's body, injured or worse. Then her brain caught up with her emotions. The fact that her husband wasn't in Hector DeJean's car didn't mean he was safe. Far from it.

Be safe, love. Please, please be safe.

Across the street, she heard the front door to the cabin slam. She heard their voices, Hector furious, Travis whining, although she couldn't discern their words. She had perhaps five seconds to make it outside and behind the garage, the only place where she had a hope of not being spotted. She was about to take a step toward the road but then pictured the smooth, virgin snow on either side of the garage. Her boot prints would stand out like bright lights in night-vision glasses.

She scurried back to her hidey-hole. '—already said I'm sorry.' She could make out what Travis was saying. 'Jesus Christ, you said it yourself. She was a pregnant woman. I didn't expect her to go all Rambo on me.' The voice was closer now. 'Don't make a goddamn federal case about it.'

'Y'know, if it was just the one thing, Travis, I wouldn't. But you have managed to screw up every. Single. Fucking. Part. Of the plan up to now. So tell me why I shouldn't just cap you and leave your body in the woods?'

The scrape of boots on concrete. Clare closed her eyes and willed herself as small as possible.

'Dude! I didn't screw up that—'

'Get Mikayla out of the house. That's all you were supposed to do, Travis. Get an eight-year-old out of a dark house where a couple oldsters were sleeping and let the grease take care of the rest.' Hector's voice changed. 'Hang on, sweetheart, let's tuck you in nice and comfy in the back.' One of the doors opened.

Mikayla. Clare felt sick to her stomach. She had promised to get the girl away. Promised her help. Now all she could do was huddle on a cold and dirty cement floor while a pair of killers took her.

'You know, dude, I'm the one who cut you in on this. I'm the one who had the contacts to get you outta the country. The way I see it, you owe me.'

The car door slammed. 'I owe you nothing. You're a fucking idiot. If you hadn't been so tweaked when we went to pick up Mikayla—' Hector's voice sharpened. 'Were you smoking? Is that how she got away?'

'No, man! I said I would stay off it until we straighten everything out.'

'Straighten out.' Hector spat on the floor. 'You're gonna be lucky if your *contacts* don't decide to leave your ass hanging in the wind. Somebody's gonna have to take the fall for offing a goddamn federal agent, and it ain't gonna be me.'

'We can fix this.' Travis's voice was halfway between soothing and pleading. 'Don't worry, man, we can fix this. Just tell me what you want to do, and I'll do it. You want to give me the rifle? I'll go after her right now. She's probably headed back across the lake to her husband.'

'Let her. I took care of the cop and the other guy. Right now, I want to get Mikayla to the factory and see about getting her medicine. If any of 'em make it through the night—' There was a pause, as if Hector shrugged.

'Me and Mikayla are outta here as soon as the weather breaks.' A door opened, then thunked.

Another car door opened. 'What about me? Dude, the grease can't keep me clean if another cop—' Travis closed his door over the rest of his sentence, and the engine fired up. The SUV pulled out of the garage, then stopped. Clare held her breath as one of the men got back out of the vehicle. Then she heard the high-pitched squeaking and rumbling of the garage door, and the tiny building was closed up into near-darkness.

She pushed herself up like a dairy cow exiting a stall and squatted under the crack between the garage door and the cold concrete floor in time to see the vehicle turn to the left. Not headed back out to the highway, then.

She clambered to her feet one last time and pulled on her parka. Should she follow after Mikayla? Or go back to their cabin one more time in the hopes of finding Russ? Was he even—

I took care of the cop and the other guy.

No. He was still alive. The first thing she had to do was reach him. She considered the truck for a moment – there was the police band radio. She climbed in through the passenger door, turned the auxiliary power on, and switched on the radio. She was greeted with a blast of static. She picked up the mic. 'Emergency personnel on this channel, I have an officer down.' She released the mic to more static. 'Emergency personnel on this channel, I have an officer down.' She glared at the unresponsive box. Could the garage be interfering with the signal? No, she had seen Russ use it in an underground parking lot once. 'If anyone can hear me, Chief Russ Van Alstyne and Lieutenant Bob Mongue are injured and in need of assistance on North Shore Drive, Inverary Lake.' She repeated herself two more times, knowing it was useless but having to make the effort.

With no help from outside, she was on her own.

Clare opened the garage door with a heave and a fling and, in a furor, stepped out into the icy rain to find her husband.

TEN

Clare was halfway to the tiny island when she realized the cabin was on fire. The air, gray from the clouds and veiled by the rain, had revealed nothing when she first clambered off the shore and onto the ice. As she made her way across the strange desert, she had noticed a darker patch in the sky, but she had been concentrating on keeping up her pace, crossing the ice as quickly as she could without risking a fall.

It wasn't until she had paused to knock the skim of ice off Russ's parka – she had draped it over her head like a portable tent – that she lifted her head and saw the fat column of oily gray smoke rising past the island's green-black hemlocks. Her heart clogged in her throat.

She took off at a clumsy sprint, no care for footing now, slipping and pitching as she ran toward the western tip of the island. There were other houses along the northern shore, oh, yes, but she knew with a cold certainty it was their cabin aflame. The image of the MacAllens' house – burned black bones and roaring, sky-licking inferno – was so real she could have been running toward it.

I took care of the cop and the other guy.

She rounded the rocky spur marking the farthest point of the island and there it was, the cabin, and the fire, and the smoke, and the figure of a man, crossing the ice.

The rain blurred his details, but she could grasp his outline even from half a mile away: tall, broad-shouldered in a poncho or cloak, carrying some sort of long-arm. Clare seized in place. Russ didn't have any sort of poncho, and his rifle was in Hector's hands. Had there been a third? Was the 'factory' right here along the shore somewhere?

Then the figure paused, swept his arm up and over as if he were signaling a ship, and broke into a run.

Russ. She ran toward him, clumsy and swaybacked. She yanked his parka off her shoulders and held it in one fist, flapping behind her. *Alive. Alive. I knew he was all right.*

Then he disappeared.

'What the hell?' Clare skidded to a stop. He had been there. Right there. She hadn't imagined him. Beneath her coat she was sweaty and out of breath. She sucked in a lungful of air. 'Russ!' Maybe Hector or Travis could hear her. She didn't care. 'Russ!'

That wide-armed wave again, this time from the ice itself. There was a dark shape, flat against the silver-gray, and she realized he had fallen. She exhaled a prayer of thanks and jogged toward him. Why wasn't he getting up? Oh, God, what if he had broken a leg, like Lieutenant Mongue? What if he had hit his head again? What if he'd broken his *spine*?

She got closer and closer, could see him stretched out and scrabbling for a hold on the ice, could see his leg twisted awkwardly behind him – wait. One leg. He looked up at her, his face strained. 'Clare.' He said her name like an answered prayer. 'Thank God you're okay.'

All the declarations of love and concern flew out of her head, and all she could say was 'How on *earth* did you fall into your own ice-fishing hole?'

ELEVEN

They were back in the Federal Building. Even a once-every-hundred-years ice storm couldn't stop the Feds: The place was humming with life and electricity when Agent Boileau escorted them up to the same office they had sat in yesterday. Kevin had managed to get through using the radio in his SUV, so Agents O'Day and O'Day were waiting for them. One look at their grim expressions and he found himself wishing they'd been caught off guard. Screwing up a DEA-FBI investigation. He had a sick feeling the chief would have him and Hadley on traffic duty for the next five years for this.

Marie O'Day studied the three of them while drumming her fingers on her faux-wood desktop. 'Detective Patten,' she said. 'I'd have thought you knew better than to interject yourself into a federal-level inquiry.'

Patten dropped into one of the plastic chairs and crossed his hands over his stomach. 'You gotta let me know about 'em first, Marie.' He nodded toward her husband, who stood flanking the desk. 'Tom.'

She turned on Kevin and Hadley. 'Officers Flynn and Knox. I thought you understood we were taking care of this. Perhaps I should have made myself more clear.'

Boileau, who had been slouching against the closed door, straightened. 'What a minute. *Officers?* You two clowns aren't even detectives?' He threw up his hands and muttered something under his breath in French.

'Listen, fat boy.' Hadley's voice shook. 'We may be lowly uniforms, but we were good enough to take you down. As for you, lady' – she turned on Marie O'Day – 'the only thing you're taking care of is covering your ass. I know your kind. You want the big, showy bust with your name at the top of the headlines and you don't care who you have to step on to get it. Well, not. This. Time. I'll be damned if you think I'm going to let my – that little girl get hurt just so you can tie up LaMar's organization in a pretty bow and hand it to the federal prosecutor!'

Kevin wished he could take her hand or put his arm around her – something to let her know he understood her embarrassment and anger. But all he could do to support her was stand shoulder to shoulder.

'Sit down, Officer Knox.' Tom O'Day's voice was like a whip. Uniformed cops did not tear a strip off the Feds. They just didn't. Hadley took one of the molded plastic chairs, not looking at the agents. Kevin sat next to her. 'I don't know what they teach you about jurisdiction at the state police academy—'

'Mikayla Johnson was kidnapped in Millers Kill. The MacAllens were murdered in Millers Kill.' Detective Patten's tone was easy. 'I'd say that gives them plenty of jurisdiction.'

'Both of those crimes were intimately related to a federal drug investigation.'

'Then why aren't you investigating them? Why?' Hadley kept her seat, but she glared up at Tom O'Day. 'Because you don't want anyone in LaMar's organization knowing you have an interest in the Johnsons. Because making your case is more important than Mikayla Johnson. What the hell, she's just some junkie's kid, right? Who cares about trash like that?'

'One more word, Officer Knox, and you're going on report.' Tom O'Day jabbed his finger at Hadley. 'Believe me when I say you do *not* want us on your tail.'

Hadley's mouth pinched in a tight line.

Boileau lurched upright from his slouch. 'How'd you know to come looking for me?'

'Jonathan Davies fingered you' – Kevin nodded toward the DEA agent – 'and three other guys as possible informants. Said we might be able to flip you for information on Travis Roy's whereabouts.'

'Travis Roy? Annie Johnson's boyfriend?'

Tom O'Day gave Boileau a quiet-down wave. He looked at Kevin. 'You spoke with Davies?'

Patten wiggled his fingers. 'We sat down with him and his suit just a few hours ago.'

O'Day frowned. 'We were holding off on approaching Jonathan Davies until the time was right—'

His wife cut him off. 'You're telling us he's in negotiations with the Albany Police Department?' Her tone implied sitting down with the Albany PD was one step lower than selling stolen kidneys on the black market.

'Davies brokered a meet between Roy and Wendall Sullivan, one of Davies's charity-case ex-cons,' Patten said. 'He found out the little girl was at the MacAllens'.'

'Did he say how?' Marie O'Day glanced up at her husband.

'You don't have a leak, if that's what you're worried about,' Patten said. 'It looks like pure dumb luck. The guy worked for the same cleaning service your foster couple had been using for the past few years. He was on the crew over at their house and got the little girl to tell him her name.'

'Mmm.' Tom O'Day rubbed his knuckles over his chin, frowning. 'Okay. Any chance he also found out about Lewis Johnson?'

'Oh, for Christ's sake!' Hadley twisted in her chair. 'Not everything is about making your case!'

Tom O'Day hitched up onto the desk and crossed his arms. It reminded Kevin of the chief, and it underlined just how junior he and Hadley were, in this room full of agents and detectives. But there wasn't anybody else to represent the MKPD. If they wanted to deal with the FBI and the DEA, it was Flynn and Knox, or it was nobody.

'We have LaMar,' Tom went on, 'and if we can get him to trial without the primary witness folding, we'll have seriously compromised his organization.'

'Compromised,' his wife said. 'Not destroyed. That's where we paired up with the DEA.' She thumbed toward Boileau. 'Agent Boileau has been working undercover for the better part of a year, getting everything he can about LaMar's production and distribution. When the time is right, we're going to move on the middle management – the enforcers and the regional distributors and the heads of the smurfing teams.'

Patten rubbed his hand over his bald scalp. 'I can't help but notice you haven't let any of the local cop shops in on this grand plan, Marie. Despite the fact that the smurfers and the enforcers and all them are, you know, active in those jurisdictions.'

Boileau cracked his fingers. 'We tell the locals when we're ready to move. No need to risk blowing operational security till then.'

Kevin narrowed his eyes. Boileau had a pretty grandiose opinion of himself for someone who looked like he spent his days playing World of Warcraft and munching on Cheetos.

'Locals?' Hadley crossed her arms over her chest. 'You mean those of us who are doing day-to-day, street-level law enforcement? You know, it's not like we're sitting on the porch plucking our banjos until the moment when the mighty alphabet agencies deign to clue us in to what's going on.'

Tom O'Day frowned. 'You need to curb your temper, Officer Knox.'

'Or what? You won't let us in on your investigation? Oh, no!'

Kevin squeezed her arm, trying to picture the issue the way the deputy chief would have. MacAuley was a master negotiator, and part of his strength was that he always found a win-win situation to present. 'The MKPD is going to find Mikayla Johnson. It's our chief's top priority, and that's not going to change.' He looked at the O'Days, then at Boileau. 'We'd like to be able to do it without creating problems for your investigation. For that, we're going to need your help.'

There was a long pause. Finally, Boileau said, 'What do you need?'

'Travis Roy.' Kevin resisted the urge to sigh with relief. 'We don't know if he's trying to curry favor with LaMar by taking out an alleged witness, or if he's preparing to make a move after LaMar is put away. But we're pretty sure he has Mikayla Johnson.'

'I have no idea where he is.' Boileau looked up at the FBI agents. 'You two?'

Marie O'Day shook her head. 'He was background noise before this.'

Boileau pressed his hands together as if praying and pressed them against his lips. After a moment he said, 'I can get the word out that LaMar wants to talk with him.' He tilted his head toward Vince Patten. 'If you can get Davies to act as your mouthpiece, it'll spread farther and faster. Doesn't matter what game Roy is playing, he'll show up for LaMar.'

'There's not enough time,' Hadley said. 'If Mikayla doesn't get her immunosuppressant drugs in the next few days, she'll be dead.'

'And the lines are going down because of the storm,' Kevin added. 'Maybe not here in Albany, not yet, but it's already almost impossible to get a cell phone call through in Washington and Saratoga counties.'

'We need a location.' Hadley glanced at Kevin. 'We need the North Country cooking house. He lives in Millers Kill. It can't be more than an hour or two away.'

Boileau shook his head. 'I don't know where it is.' Hadley opened her mouth, but he went on. 'I do know a couple guys I can lean on. I can get the location to you by this evening.'

Kevin nodded. 'The most efficient thing for us to do would be to drop a net on the meth house. We can either find Roy or squeeze whatever lowlife we do catch.' He looked at the FBI agents. 'How would that affect your investigation?'

'We can live with that,' Tom O'Day said. 'In fact . . .' He examined the ceiling as if he might find a message in the soundproofed tiles. 'Maybe this is the time to make the move.'

'During the ice storm of the century?' Boileau laughed. 'Trust me when I say we don't want any agents running around out there. They'll only end up flat on their asses.'

Hadley smirked.

Marie O'Day glanced at her husband. 'We'll talk about it later.' She walked over to the door and opened it. 'Officers, I'm sure you're eager to get started home. With the weather and all.'

'We are. Thank you so very much for all your consideration.' Hadley used the same fake-polite voice the federal agent had. The two women stood opposite one another, smiling in what Kevin assumed was the female version of 'show me yours'.

Tom O'Day caught his eye. The man gave him a half-rueful, half-proud look that said, *Women. What are you going to do?* Kevin realized O'Day assumed he and Hadley were also a couple. Kevin opened his mouth to set the man straight, then changed his mind. 'Thank you both,' he said. 'Detective Patten?'

He drove back to South Station going twenty miles an hour the whole way. 'What do you think of the O'Days? Will they come through for us?'

Hadley made a rude noise. 'I wouldn't count on it. I'm sure they have a nice plum promotion waiting for them if they can bring down LaMar. Mikayla will just be an unfortunate loss. Too bad. Better luck next time.'

'I disagree.' Patten leaned forward from the backseat. 'Tom and Marie have been in the same office, at the same level, for a lot of years now. The only thing waiting for them is a federal pension check.' He snorted. 'And maybe a job as a greeter in Walmart, if the Feds are as stingy as the state is.'

Kevin pulled into the station's parking lot, wobbling across the ice. 'Are you sure you two won't stay the night?' Patten asked. 'When Lyle called me, he said to keep you here if the weather got too bad. It's gonna be a skating rink once you get off the Northway.'

'Thanks,' Hadley said, 'but I've got children at home.'

'You sure? We got lots of room at my house now the kids are gone. Plus Vince's famous sausage patties for breakfast.'

'We'll be fine. I trust Flynn's driving.'

'All right, then.' The Albany detective sounded doubtful. 'At least let me set you up with a couple travel mugs of coffee and a visit to the restroom. 'Course, you two are young. Maybe you can make it all the way back to Washington County, even in this weather. Me, I gotta stop twice between here and Saratoga to drain the snake. It's hell gettin' old, lemme tell you.'

Kevin and Hadley managed to make it inside without too many more of Patten's pithy tales. They accepted the coffee, turned down the stale Danishes, and were headed out the door again when one of the civilian employees jogged down the hallway to stop them. The headset still tucked over her ears identified her job.

'Officer Knox?' She held out a folded piece of paper to Hadley. 'We got a squawk from your dispatcher while you and Detective Patten were out. She said they tried to call you, but your cell phone's not working.' The woman looked harried. 'First the landlines, then the cell network breaks down from too many calls and too few towers. Keep your fingers crossed we don't overload the emergency system, too.' She waved and jogged back to the communications room.

Hadley unfolded the paper. 'What is it?' Kevin asked. 'Has the chief finally shown up?'

She looked up at him, her face white. She held the message out for him to read. *Call from Glenn Hadley via MKPD. Officer Knox's ex-husband has her children. Please advise.*

TWELVE

As camps went, a half-burned cabin with a working woodstove wasn't the worst Russ had ever slept in. He was a hell of a lot warmer and drier than he had ever been, say, sleeping in mud in 'Nam. On the other hand, as a honeymoon, the whole experience was sucking hard.

When Clare had reached him on the lake, pink-cheeked and out of breath and gloriously alive, he had felt as if joy alone could levitate him out of the trap he had gotten stuck in. Then she had propped her hands on her hips. 'How on *earth* did you fall into your own ice-fishing hole?' She didn't sound overpleased to see him.

'It was an accident! I wasn't looking where I was going.'

'Five square miles of ice and you manage to step into one eighteen-inch-diameter hole.' She squatted, stripping off her gloves. 'I'll lift you.'

He almost told her not to bother, but he hadn't been able to leverage himself yet, and his right leg had gone completely numb. He took her hands and she stood, grunting. He slid from the fishing hole. Clare dragged him free, then dropped him on the ice like an oversized arctic char. Water dribbled out of his boot. He groaned.

She frowned at the sight of his sopping clothing. 'We need to get those pants off and your leg warmed up, or you're going to get frostbite.' She held out her hands again, and he let her help him up without protest. She looked toward the cabin. From this angle, they couldn't see the fire, only the heavy smoke trying to rise against the rain. 'It should be plenty warm up there. Where's Lieutenant Mongue?'

'In the boathouse. I stuck him in a canoe with blankets and a bunch of hand warmers. He should be okay for a while.'

She picked up the shotgun and handed it to him. 'You should have stayed with him. I was coming to find you.'

He slung an arm across her shoulder. They started across the ice, Clare balancing, Russ limping. 'I didn't know that, did I? I thought I was racing to save you from a fate worse than death.'

'I can take care of myself. You ought to know that by now.'

'You weren't doing such a good job of it the other night, when they had you hogtied on the front porch.' He had no idea how he had gone from ecstatic to annoyed in less than fifteen minutes. 'Never mind. How did you get away? And where's the little girl?'

As they walked to the shore, she gave him a rundown of her morning that sounded like the sort of heavily edited report he used to give to officious superiors. Before he could press her to tell him the real meat of the matter, she asked, 'What do you think he meant by "the factory"?'

'Factory implies they're making something, as opposed to storing drugs for transport. Unless they're repackaging smuggled cigarettes, it's probably a meth house. I'm guessing Roy and DeJean didn't drive along the Shore Road. They probably went past the turnoff, into the hills. Nothing up that way but a few old farms. Lots and lots of space, no neighbors. Remember, I told you, perfect country for cooking meth.' They reached land. Stepping into the snow, his right foot twinged. 'I think I'm getting feeling back.'

'Good. Let's get you as close to the fire as we can.'

'You know, a burning house isn't the safest place to hang about getting toasty.'

'If you have a better suggestion, I'm all ears.' Clare set her mouth in a line and continued upslope. In fact, the fire looked to be dying down. Russ could still feel the heat yards away, but the flames no longer roared and reared into the sky. As they drew closer, he could see why. The entire wall facing the road had burned away, and the loft, unbalanced and unsupported, had cracked and fallen at an angle. Fire was trying to chew its way farther down the side of the house, but without DeJean's accelerant, the logs were proving a tough match. Clare led him to the woodshed, which was, ironically, untouched. Roofed and enclosed on three sides, it had trapped heat from the cabin fire. He pulled off his dripping poncho and began untying his boots.

'There you go. Take off those pants and have a seat.'

'Here?' It was warm and protected from the rain, but being so close to the cabin fire made him antsy. 'What if something explodes and the whole place goes up?'

'There isn't anything in there to explode, except maybe what was in the composting toilet, and that's already gone.' She took a few steps toward the remains of the cabin, scooped up a handful of snow, and tossed it against a strip of fire eating its way across a log. The flames sizzled and wavered. 'Maybe we can put it out.'

'Don't get too close,' he warned, working his jeans off. Painful prickles replaced the numbness in his leg. He was warm, and his wife was safe, and he just wanted to rest for one goddamn minute.

When he opened his eyes again, he had a wool blanket thrown over him and the pale gray sky had dimmed into twilight. He rose, stretching and snapping his spine, which screamed at him for falling asleep on a pile of timber. His parka fell, which was when he realized his jeans, boxers, socks, and boots were gone. Clare had left him a pair of thick wool socks last seen in the duffel he had left with Bob. He tugged them on, flexing and testing his leg as he did so. Apparently, his ice-water plunge hadn't done him any harm. He wrapped the blanket around his waist and went around to the back of the cabin.

The canoe, empty and overturned, was set in front of the porch door. He angled past it and walked inside, part of him amazed that the structure was untouched. The rest of him was amazed to see his wife and Mongue, draped in blankets and sprawled in front of the woodstove, talking. Clare had turned over the sofa and chairs and dragged them into a rough curve, capturing the stove's heat and blocking the draft from the blackened ruins of the kitchen and bedroom.

She looked up as he opened the inner door. 'You're awake!'

'I am now.' He stared at where the loft floor had become a lean-to. 'Clare, what were you thinking?' To his left, the bedroom's French doors had split and shattered. Cold air sucked through the half-collapsed hole where the outside windows had been. 'This place isn't safe. The whole thing could come down any second.'

Mongue twirled his hand above his head. ''S fine.'

'I tested it before we set up camp,' Clare said. 'I jumped and pulled and stomped on things. We're okay in this corner.'

She had a roaring fire going in the woodstove. He shook his head in disbelief. 'What were you going to do if the loft had dropped on you while you were jumping and stomping? Jesus, Clare, if you can't stop to think of yourself, at least think of the baby.'

'Gotta take care of the baby,' Mongue agreed.

'I'm sorry to have alarmed you.' Clare's voice sharpened and her Virginia accent increased. Never a good sign. 'In your absence, I had to trust in my *girlish* intuition and my pilot's survival training and the experience I gained from tours of duty in two war zones!'

'You tell 'im, Clare.'

Her frown edged into a half-smile. 'Thanks, Bob.'

So it was Clare and Bob now, was it? Russ picked his way between Mongue and the open duffel bag to sit next to his wife. His wet clothing had been hung on one of the rickety porch chairs. 'It's dry,' Clare said, following his gaze.

He peeled off the damp ragg socks and laid them on the hearthstone. 'You should have woken me up. We could have crossed the lake, gotten the truck, and be gone by now.'

'Bob and I discussed it. The ice storm's been going on for two and a half days now. Even supposing we could drive out on the South Shore Drive without running into another fallen tree or downed power line, there's no telling what condition the highway's in. We could wind up off the road, trapped, with no help coming and no place to take refuge.'

'We could have called for help!'

'I *tried* that. The radio is dead. No signal. Bob and I decided the safer thing to do was to stay put for the night.'

'In a half-destroyed cabin that could fall in on us at any moment. A pregnant woman and a guy with a broken leg.'

''M feeling better.'

Russ peered at the trooper. 'What the hell, Bob? Are you high?'

'Yep.'

'I grabbed a first aid kit from Travis's place before I left.' Clare pointed to a white plastic box with a familiar red cross sitting next to Mongue. 'It turned out it had a different kind of aid than I was thinking.'

Bob rattled the box. 'Oxys.'

Russ stared at Clare. 'You took Travis Roy's OxyContin stash?'

'Well, I didn't know it contained narcotics. But yes.'

'And gave some to Bob?'

''S good stuff,' the trooper said.

'It *is* pain medication.'

Russ hesitated, not wanting to sound suspicious. Something in his expression must have given him away, though, because Clare set her hand on his arm. 'I didn't sample any.' She kept her voice low.

He was equally quiet. 'I didn't think—'

She gave him a look. 'Russ. I have a problem. I understand if you worry.' She looked around the ruins of their cabin. 'Somehow, this didn't seem like the time to fall off the wagon.'

He snorted. 'I have to confess something.'

'You've come to the right person, then.'

'I didn't want to go to a resort for our honeymoon because I thought this would be easier on you.' He gestured toward the darkness through the still-intact porch windows. 'No temptations to resist.'

She looked into the fire for a moment before nodding. 'I think we've managed to go beyond "no temptation". But that reminds me!' She scooted across the floor and retrieved a box from behind one of the tipped-over chairs. 'Animal crackers.' She handed the box to him. 'Hungry?'

In response, his stomach growled. Clare shook the box toward the state trooper. 'Bob? Are you ready for dinner?'

'No steak and potatoes, huh? Damn.'

Clare laid a scarf on the floor and portioned out the tiny cookies into three piles. 'You should have more,' Russ said. 'You're eating for two.'

'You can both split my share,' Mongue said. ''S not like I'm burning up calories running around.'

'Yeah, but you need to keep your strength up. You know, to fight off infection.'

'Enough.' Clare used her Officer Voice. 'We all get an equal share.'

Russ sketched a salute, smiling. 'Ma'am, yes, ma'am.'

'Bossy, i'n't she?' Bob said.

'You don't know the half of it.' They ate the animal crackers slowly, washing them down with water melted atop the woodstove. Clare was exhausted, her eyes smudged with deep shadows, her shoulders rolled forward as if the weight of her head were too much to carry. And poor Bob – Russ glanced toward the trooper. He was feeling no pain, thank God, but the Oxys would just mask the symptoms of the various problems they courted by not getting him to a hospital. 'Tomorrow, we're getting out of here,' he said.

'We need to find Mikayla first.' Clare picked up the water. 'She's gone, what, five days now without her immunosuppressants? She doesn't have much time.'

'I agree,' Mongue said.

'Look, you need medical attention,' Russ said, turning to him. 'And Clare—'

Mongue rapped on the first aid box. 'I can manage for a while longer now I've got these. The little girl's gonna die. We gotta help her.'

Russ pinched the bridge of his nose. 'We'll discuss it tomorrow. First I have to get my truck and see if I can—'

'No more splitting up,' Clare said.

'I agree. Concur. Agree.'

Russ glared at Mongue.

'We should stick together,' Clare went on. 'If there are three of us, it'll increase our chances of being able to get Mikayla away from her father.'

'These are seriously bad people, Clare—'

'You don't have to tell me that.' Her voice was sharp.

He tried another tack. 'With Bob's broken leg—'

'I can still shoot better than you can, Van Alstyne.' Mongue grinned. 'Hell, you can stick me back in the canoe and strap me to the roof rack.'

Clare laughed.

'Okay. Okay.' Russ held up his hands. 'We go together. But we go slow. *If* we can find the meth house, I'll scout it out, and if I say it's too dangerous, that's it. And if either of you two give me any grief, I'm tossing you into the back of the truck and driving out of here. I don't care if the highway's closed down all the way to Lake George, with or without Mikayla Johnson, we're leaving tomorrow.'

THIRTEEN

Hadley had never been afraid before. She thought she had, when she was broke and homeless in LA, when she went through the containment room on her first day as a prison guard, when she had been crouched beside her squad car while shots exploded around her. But those moments weren't fear. This was, standing in the hallway of the Albany PD South Station, holding a paper that said her children had been taken.

'The airport,' she rasped. 'We have to get to the airport.'

'Dylan can't fly out tonight.' Flynn took the message and read it again. 'The Albany airport's closed down.'

'Closed down,' she repeated. 'The airport's closed down.' She nodded jerkily. Then started. 'What if he's taken them to another airport? What if he's taken the train to New York? Is the train running? Would he know where to catch it?'

Flynn caught her hand and held it tight. 'Hadley.' He was using his cop voice on her, the same voice she had used with distracted accident victims and frightened parents. 'Chances are good he's taken them back to his hotel. Let's call there and see if he's checked out or not.'

She nodded again – up, down, *Yes, let's do that*, and followed him to the comm room, screaming inside her head the whole while. The dispatcher who had handed over the message looked at her carefully and agreed to call the Algonquin. After the third failure, she shook her head. 'Sorry, Officers. The landlines are well and truly down. The only places I'm getting through to are other emergency systems, and those are getting spotty because we're all trying to use the same broadband at the same time.'

'Okay.' Flynn exhaled. 'Can you reach the MKPD dispatcher? Tell her we need a unit at the Algonquin Waters Resort. Officer Knox's ex-husband is violating their custody—'

'No!' Hadley grabbed his arm. 'No, don't send that,' she said to the dispatcher. She dragged Flynn back out into the hallway.

'What?'

'You can't send—' She took a deep breath. 'Dylan's not in violation of the custody agreement. I am.'

Flynn looked at her steadily. 'Go on.'

'The decree gave us joint custody, and neither of us was supposed to move more than a hundred miles away from the other unless the agreement was modified by the court.' She had thought herself lucky at the time. The judge handling their divorce had openly doubted her ability to give the children a 'normal, stable' home. 'After the divorce was finalized, I . . . I realized I wanted to start fresh. Granddad offered me a place to stay as long as I needed one. So I went to Dylan and asked him if it was all right if I took the kids to New York. He said he was fine with it as long as I didn't expect any money from him.' She coughed up a bitter laugh. 'I figured since he agreed, I could save myself the cost of getting the custody agreement changed. I never thought to get anything in writing from him. So now he's here, and he's going to be able to get full custody because I've been in violation for two years!' She hung her head, squeezing her eyes against tears she wouldn't let fall. 'Oh, God. How could I have been so stupid?'

Flynn pulled her toward him and she came, letting herself lean against him, pressing her face into his sweater. She was being weak and needy and she hated it, but she couldn't help herself. He wrapped his long arms around her and she felt better, even though she knew it was an illusion.

'Why did he come here?' Flynn's voice was quiet. 'What does he want from you?'

She gave it up, just like any suspect in the interrogation room. 'Money. He wants me to give him twenty thousand for one of his stupid business schemes. If I don't, he's going to take Hudson and Genny back to LA.'

Flynn breathed in and out, her head rising and falling with his chest. 'Do you have it?'

'No. I own' – she caught herself – 'the assets of a business he ran. He'll take that instead of cash.'

'Can you give it to him?'

She thought of those tapes, made digital, images that anyone with a computer and a credit card could download forever and ever, amen. How old would Hudson and Genny be before they saw them? How long before one of their friends' fathers recognized her and the crude suggestions started up again? How long before the mothers found out and the invitations to playdates and sleepovers vanished? The kids had been too young to notice their ostracism back in California. Here, now, they were fully old enough to understand every slight and slur that would come their way. But she had no choice. She couldn't lose her children. 'Yes.' She pushed herself away and Flynn's tight embrace instantly loosened. 'Yes, I can surrender the business assets.'

'Then the first thing to do is retrieve Hudson and Genny.' He searched her face. 'Are you okay to go?'

She swiped away her tears. 'I'm sorry. I'm just . . . I think with the storm and my ex and the little girl missing . . . I'm just on edge.'

He nodded. 'We can still get a call relayed through to the MKPD. The dep would send someone over to the hotel, no questions asked.'

She shook her head. 'I don't want to involve anyone from work if I can help it.' She took a deep breath. 'The kids aren't in any danger from Dylan. He's a cheating, lying jerk, but he's never raised a hand against any of us.'

'Okay. Let me tell the dispatcher we're all set.'

Getting out of Albany was a nightmare. Traffic lights were non-existent, streets were blocked off, and the roads were so bad Flynn's weighted-down four-wheel-drive SUV slid every time they turned a corner. The Northway lights were on, their orange sodium glow wavering in the rain-thick air, but huge swathes of land beyond the confines of the roadway were dark. No billboards, no gas signs, no lights brightening the windows of distant houses.

'It's the end of the world,' Hadley said, staring out the ice-streaked side window.

'No,' Flynn said. 'But it is one hell of a mess.'

'Like my life.'

She could hear him hesitate. 'Hadley. Have you thought about what's going to happen after you give your ex what he wants?'

'He'll go back to California.'

'Is he reliable with money?'

'Oh, God, no.' Hadley twisted in her seat and adjusted one of the vents to blow more hot air her way. 'Hudson's got more common sense than his father.'

'Then what's going to happen the next time he's stuck and he wants cash?'

'Nothing. I'll have a lawyer draw up a custody modification. Once we get it filed with the court, that's it.'

'What if he doesn't agree?'

'Of course he'll agree. Dylan doesn't really care about having the kids close, believe me.'

'Hand me my coffee, will you?' Flynn held out his hand, not taking his eyes away from the road. She gave him his go-cup – *two creams, two sugars* – and watched while he drank. He handed it back to her. 'Do you have any way to *make* your ex sign a custody modification?'

'I'll tell him if he doesn't, I'm not signing over those business assets.'

'But if you don't hand those over, he's taking Hudson and Genny to California with him. Right?'

She opened her mouth. Shut it again. 'Oh, shit.' She dropped her head against the seat back. 'Oh, shit. He's got no reason to sign a modification now. I'm going to become his piggy bank, aren't I? He's going to threaten to haul the kids back to California every time he needs money.'

'Is there anything your lawyer can pin on him? Is he behind in child support?'

She rocked her head back and forth. 'Nothing. He wouldn't owe any child support unless I legally became the primary custodian. Which is just one more reason not to sign a modification.' The rain flashed gold and silver in the headlight beams. 'I'm going to have to move back to California.' The truth of her situation was a dull weight on her chest.

'Let's not jump the gun. Let me think about what we can do.'

Flynn's voice was warm and reassuring. And Hadley wanted to be warm and reassured. She wished she could believe there was a way out. 'You always read about cases where some guy is holding custody over his ex-wife's head, and you think, *Why don't you just let him have them? After two months he'll be begging you to take them back.* Then you're the ex-wife in the story, and you realize you can't. You just can't.' She looked at Flynn. 'I can't have Hudson and Genny thinking I'd abandon them.' Her eyes burned. Flynn laid his hand, open, on the console between them and she took it without hesitation. She linked her fingers through his, for once not weighing or worrying what it meant.

'You're not going to give up the kids. And you're not going to have to move back to California. I promise you, we won't let it happen.'

Once they had taken the Millers Kill exit, the drive became two-handed and white-knuckled again. Route 9 was a pair of ruts dug through ice so thick the rest of the road was pale gray. Flynn hunched forward, his eyes fixed on the narrow tracks, all his attention focused on keeping them in line. Hadley knew if they bumped over the edges and onto the ice, they'd keep on sliding until they lodged in the thick snow at the side of the highway, and they wouldn't be getting out.

Sacandaga Road was even worse, an expanse of icy wasteland so unmarked by plows she couldn't tell where the road ended and the fields on either side began. 'There it is.' Flynn sounded like a swimmer almost out of strength spotting the shore. Hadley hadn't seen the resort's sign until he mentioned it. The lights that normally illuminated its tasteful carved wooden face were out. She finally registered the time. 'Are we going to be able to make it up there?' The driveway – it was really more of a road – snaked two miles up the mountain before reaching the hotel complex.

'We're going to try.' Flynn inched the Aztek onto the drive and downshifted. The engine grumbled with a vibration that went up Hadley's spine. The SUV lurched forward and began climbing the hill. 'Hah!' Flynn grinned, showing his eyeteeth. 'Gravel over the ice. Thank you, Algonquin Waters.'

'Gravel? Like . . . part of a roadbed?'

'Yep. One or two dump-truck loads, I'll bet. Very expensive, but you gotta make sure the rich people can drive in and out.'

As they drove higher and deeper into the mountain, Hadley's heart began racing. It had taken them so long to get here, the normally twenty-minute drive eating up nearly two hours. If she and Flynn had misjudged, if Dylan had already gone to the airport or the train station with the kids, they would never reach him in time.

The drive leading to the grand entrance was designed so that the heavy forest fell away at the last S-curve, and the resort spread out to be viewed in all its glory. Tonight, though, Hadley could barely make it out. Flynn rolled into the lower parking lot and killed the engine. He leaned back, shook out his hands and rolled his neck, then twisted to look at her. 'Are we going in as cops? Or as civilians?'

'Oh. That's a tough question.' She glanced to his plastic lock box, where they had stored their weapons for the drive. Tempting, but . . . 'Civilians,' she said. 'I don't want there to be any hint of police coercion. Even though having the extra authority is nice.'

'You already have authority.' He smiled a little, his blue eyes warm. 'You don't need the suit and badge to make it work.'

She ducked her head.

'Who's the man?'

'Oh, God, Flynn.'

'C'mon. Who's the man?'

'I'm the man,' she mumbled.

'I can't hear you, Officer Knox! Who's the man?'

'I'm the man! I am the Man! I am *the* Man!' She laughed for the first time in what felt like days and threw her arms around Flynn, easy, just like taking his hand had been, no second guesses, no regrets. 'Thank you, Flynn. You didn't have to do any of this. Thank you.'

'Hey, now. Hey.' He patted her back awkwardly. 'We're partners.' He pulled away to look into her face. 'That means I've got your back. Always.'

The interior of the SUV felt close and hot. She didn't know what to say, so she nodded.

'Why don't you grab the Maglite and see if you can spot his rental while I get my parka on?'

She nodded again, thankful for a moment alone to get her bearings. The cars in the lot were anonymous in their icy shrouds, identifiable only as shapes: sedan, SUV, station wagon. She trained the flashlight's powerful beam on the bumpers instead. Rental companies' in-and-out bar codes were brightly reflective. She saw one – an SUV – and then another, a four-door that on closer inspection was a Ford. The third car with a Hertz sticker was a Lexus. She beat against the windows, shattering ice until she could illuminate the interior. When she saw the Dragon Ball manga, she bent over, light-headed with relief.

'Hadley? Are you okay?'

She straightened. 'This is Dylan's rental car. Hudson left one of his comic books in the backseat.'

'Good.' In the scatter from the flashlight, Flynn looked grim. Purposeful. 'Let's go get your kids back.'

FOURTEEN

The young man who popped out of the office in response to Hadley's bell ring looked at the two of them with dismay. 'Oh.' He glanced at the door. 'Um. We're not accepting any new guests tonight.'

'We're not—' Flynn began.

Hadley cut him off. 'You've got to be kidding. On a night like this? People could die out there on those roads.' The receptionist sounded guilty, which was just the way she wanted him. She figured she'd have a better chance of getting what she wanted if he was off-kilter and apologetic.

'I'm sorry, ma'am, really I am. It's just that we're running on generator power, and the manager was worried we wouldn't have enough if we let more . . .' He seemed to realize this was going to sound bad however he phrased it.

'My friend here gave me a ride all the way from Albany so I could meet up with my husband and children. I was going to stand him a night. Are you telling me he's going to have to go back out into that mess?' From the corner of her eye, she could see Flynn arching a brow.

'Um . . . if it were up to me, ma'am . . .'

'I can't believe this. You're going to throw my friend out into the teeth of the storm just to ensure some spoiled brat on a ski trip has enough juice to blow-dry her hair? I promise you my family will *never* vacation here again.' She turned to Flynn. 'I am so sorry, Kevin. So very sorry.'

'It's all right, Hadley. It's not that far to Millers Kill.' He looked toward the door and paused for a second, as if contemplating the likely fate he would meet out in the storm. Then he squared his shoulders, bravely overcoming his fears. 'If I could just use the bathroom and maybe get a hot cup of coffee before I go . . .'

'Of course you can, Kevin. My God, it's the very least I can do.' She pulled her wallet out of her pocket, slanting it so her badge remained hidden. She tugged out her ID and slapped it on the counter. 'My husband is Dylan Knox. Please give me a room key and tell me you have enough electricity so the coffee machines work.'

'Yes, ma'am.' The receptionist peeped at her driver's license, then slid it back to her. He looked regretfully at his computer – another victim of their energy problem, she guessed – then opened a file drawer. He speed-shuffled through some papers before pulling out a form. Hadley held her breath. She could feel Flynn tensing beside her. 'Um . . . Mr Knox is registered for one adult?'

She hit the desk with the flat of her hand. 'The fact that you screwed up our reservation isn't my fault! Or my concern! I've been traveling all day and I want to get to my family!'

'Yes, ma'am. I'll just . . . have to adjust the room rate?'

She leaned across the counter and spoke through gritted teeth. 'I'll discuss adjusting our room rate with your manager tomorrow. Along with your less-than-adequate performance' – she read his name tag – 'Justin. Now give me my room key.'

'Yes, ma'am,' the receptionist squeaked. He fumbled a plastic card and some stiff pieces of paper into a sleeve and handed it to her. 'I've put in four coupons for free admission to the breakfast buffet?'

Hadley plucked the sleeve out of his fingers. 'Thank you.' She started across the expanse of the lobby, Flynn following.

'Ma'am?'

She paused. *Shit.* If he decided to call Dylan for verification . . .

'The elevators are out. I'm afraid you'll have to use the stairs.'

She nodded without turning. She and Flynn mounted the wide carpeted staircase with its ornate wood-and-antler banister in silence. They didn't speak until they had passed through the heavy fireproof door to the second-floor stairs. Then Hadley stopped and leaned against the wall. 'Jesus.'

'You were amazing. I had no idea you were such a great actress. You ought to be doing undercover work. Vice or Narco or something.'

She pressed her hand against her chest. 'I don't think my heart could take it.' She opened the paper sleeve and read the room number. 'Third floor.'

They climbed the next flight of stairs and pushed the door open. The long hallway was dim, lit only by emergency lights. 'What's the plan?' Flynn said quietly.

'We get in, we collect Hudson and Genny, and we get out again.' She started toward Dylan's room. Her boots sank into the plush carpet.

Flynn trod close behind her. 'What if he starts to get heavy?'

'We keep things as calm as possible and don't scare the kids.' She glanced up at him, her mouth twisted. 'Just like any other domestic.' She was at the door. She took a deep breath and inserted the key card. The light blinked green. She opened the door and walked in.

Hudson was sprawled on the far bed, chin in hands, watching a wide-screen TV. Past him, Genny sat with her feet crossed in one of a pair of high-backed chairs flanking a small table, her nose in a book. One of Dylan's garment bags was lying unzipped and open on the near bed. *Two, he had gotten a room with two beds, he was preparing for this all along.* Dylan was nowhere in sight, but the bathroom door to her left was closed, the fan whirring.

'Mom!'

'Mom!'

She strode across the room and grabbed them both in a too-tight embrace. Behind her, she heard Flynn's hands on the garment bag, unzipping, rustling through clothes. Search and secure possible weapons, the first rule when responding to a domestic.

'What are you doing here?' Hudson asked. He backed away and sat on the bed. Genny was still twined around her legs.

'I'm here to take you home, babies. Get your things.'

Flynn had moved on to the closet. She heard the ting and scrape of hangers sliding across the bar. She looked back toward him. He nodded. *All clear.* He held up a Hello Kitty suitcase. 'Genny, did you borrow this from your mom?'

Genny ducked her head and giggled. The bathroom door opened. For a moment, they all stood in a tableau: Hadley with the children, Flynn holding the pink and white suitcase, Dylan staring at them, his dark eyes wide, his mouth working.

'What the fuck do you think you're doing?' Dylan finally asked. He advanced a step toward Flynn. 'Get the fuck out of my room!'

Hudson's mouth hung open. Genny dug her fists into Hadley's legs. Flynn shifted, blocking Dylan's path. 'Mr Knox, you're scaring your children.'

Dylan looked past Flynn. 'You bitch. You think you can just waltz in here and take my kids away from me? After you denied me access to them for two years?'

'Mr Knox.' Flynn's voice was an iron bar.

'I never denied you access to the kids! I begged you to stay in contact with them!' She gulped. *Domestic.* She sounded like one of those pitiful women they pulled away from their husbands on Saturday nights. If she didn't stay in cop mode, she was going to lose it completely. 'Hudson, Genny, I want you to get your things back into your suitcases.'

'Hudson, Genny, stay right where you are,' Dylan ordered.

Flynn tossed the Hello Kitty bag onto the far bed, following it with Genny's pink parka. 'I didn't unpack,' Genny whispered. 'Just my blanket and my book.'

'I'm calling my lawyer right now.' Dylan pawed his cell phone out of his pocket and held it out as if it were a gun. 'I'll have a custody order by tomorrow, you bitch, and when I do we'll see who has to come crawling and playing pretty just to spend an afternoon with her children.'

It was ridiculous. Stagey and overplayed. It made her realize just how much of Dylan's threats had been bluff and bluster. He had relied on the old patterns of their marriage – that she would agree to anything for the sake of the children. Well, not this time. 'I don't think you will,' she said, her voice steady. 'I think you'll have to find a judge in California willing to write you an ex parte order. Then your lawyer will have to hire a New York lawyer, who will have to bring the whole thing to a New York judge, who will be hearing from *my* lawyer. The whole process will drag and drag and you'll be paying out of pocket for every second of it.'

Dylan's jaw hinged open. He stared at her with angry, frustrated incredulity. He had threatened her, and she hadn't buckled under. *That's right, you bastard. I'm not that easy-to-push-around girl you married. I'm a real live grown-up now.*

Flynn bent down to retrieve Hudson's duffel bag. Dylan let out an incoherent snarl and slammed into him, kicking and punching. Genny screamed. Flynn fell against the closet wall. Dylan swung his leg back for another kick, but Flynn lurched upright and rushed him, closing the space, making it impossible for Dylan to carry through. He flailed with his fists instead. Flynn blocked one blow, blocked another, and with a quick turn-turn-push he had Dylan pinned against the wall, straining upward on tiptoe, his arms drawn up tight behind his back. 'Hadley, can you get Hudson's things?' His voice was a little short of breath but calm.

'You son of a bitch,' Dylan snarled. 'I'm going to sue you for police brutality! I'm going to have your badge for this!'

'I don't even have my badge on me, Mr Knox. I'm not here on business.' Flynn smiled tightly. 'This is pure pleasure.'

Hadley grabbed the duffel, Hudson's coat, both the kids' boots. Genny was crying. Hadley unzipped the duffel. 'Where are your clothes, honey?' Hudson pointed to one of the drawers with a shaking finger. She opened it and began tossing things into the bag as quickly as possible.

'What did she do?' Dylan asked. 'Open her legs for you? Believe me, that's nothing special. She's like a bitch in he—' His words were cut off as Flynn slammed him into the wall. Flynn put his face next to Dylan's ear and said something Hadley couldn't hear. Dylan shut up.

'Is there anything else?' Hadley's voice sounded weird in her own ears, as if someone else were saying her words. Hudson shook his head. 'Okay, then. Grab your boots and your coats.' She picked up the bags and herded the kids, stocking-footed, across the room. They slipped past Dylan and Flynn like skaters easing around a hole in the ice, Genny still weeping, Hudson with his head down, refusing to look at his father. She opened the door, ushered them out, then closed it again.

'All right, babies. Get those boots on.' Through the door, she could hear Dylan, not his words, just his tone, snarling and hateful. Probably giving Flynn a detailed description of her former career. Flynn, with his wholesome family and Catholic upbringing and Eagle Scout badges. Flynn, who had been a virgin until she had come along. She bent down to help Genny tie one of her boots. Later. She'd deal with it later.

The door opened as she straightened. 'Let's go,' Flynn said. She nodded. He picked up the suitcase and the duffel bag. She held out her hands. Genny hung on for dear life, and Hudson, who was almost twelve and too old for such things, squeezed her hand tight and didn't let go.

Down the stairs. Across the lobby, past the receptionist, who stared at them as if they were insane. Out the door, into the cold air and buffeting wind and freezing rain. They slipped and slid across the parking lot until they reached the Aztek. They all tumbled in, and Flynn started the engine and cranked the blower. 'Help me get the ice off?' he asked Hadley.

'Buckle up,' she told the kids, before tugging on her hood and hopping back out into the rain. She and Flynn met at the rear of the vehicle. 'What did he say?'

Flynn chiseled a plastic scraper across the rear window. 'He threatened me. Said he was going to get me fired, screw me up good, etcetera, etcetera.'

'You don't sound too worried.'

'I'm not.' He bent down and rapped at the ice caked over the brake lights.

She bit her lip. He didn't sound too happy, either. 'Did he say anything about me?'

Flynn straightened. 'I thought he said quite enough in front of Hudson and Genny. God! I wanted to—' He shoved the scraper into his parka pocket and took her shoulders. 'Please tell me he didn't treat you like that when you were married to him.'

Dylan didn't tell him. He doesn't know. She hadn't realized the weight of dread she had carried out of the hotel until it was gone. 'No,' she managed to say. 'Not usually.' She smiled up at him. 'Can we go home now?'

FIFTEEN

Could they go home, that was the question. Kevin inched down the mountain in second gear, zigzagging across the road for maximum traction. Twice the tires lost contact despite the gravel spread along the drive. Both times the Aztek slid in a slow free fall downhill, gathering speed, until they caught a patch of still-rough stone and Kevin could wrestle the SUV back under control. After the second skid, he said, 'Maybe we ought to rethink this.' He kept his voice low, hopeful the kids couldn't hear him. 'We could ditch the truck and hike back up to the hotel—'

'No.' Hadley shook her head.

'If we showed our IDs—'

'No.' There was an edge to her voice, the sound of someone pushed to the brink and left teetering there.

'Okay.' He downshifted to make another curve, holding his breath until he had swung the SUV through without slipping. 'What about the Stuyvesant Inn?'

'You mean, stop there?'

'It's just a couple miles up the road.'

'I dunno. Maybe.' She scrubbed at her face. 'I really just want to get home. I think the kids need things to be as normal as possible.' She looked at him closely. 'What about you? Are you too tired to go on?'

He was exhausted from the long fruitless day in Albany, and from the teeth-gritting intensity of the drive, and from everything that had happened at the Algonquin. But after all she had been through, he didn't want to hand Hadley one more disappointment. 'I can make it,' he said.

He lost control of the Aztek again when they hit Sacandaga Road. They bottomed out at the foot of the drive and slid across both lanes, stopping only when they wedged the right front quarter into the snowbank. 'Are we stuck?' Genny asked. It was the first thing she had said since leaving the Algonquin.

'I don't think so, sweetheart.' Kevin turned on the four-ways and reached for his parka. 'I think your mom and I can push it out.'

They waded through the snow and braced against the front grille. 'Ready?' Kevin said. Hadley nodded. 'Okay, on my count. One, two, three—' They shoved back, rocked forward, shoved back, rocked forward, shoved back, and the Aztek rolled free. He held out his hand to help Hadley clamber out of the snow.

She stood in the light of the headlamps, shaking her head. 'That was close.'

He rubbed his boot back and forth. 'There's nothing here. It's like driving across a frozen lake.'

She climbed back into the Aztek. He beat the glaze of ice off his coat and followed her. 'Have you ever driven across a frozen lake?' Hadley asked.

'Oh, yeah. My first car was this ancient crew cab that my dad had used for business.' He shifted into gear and gently accelerated. 'Some of my friends and I used to get together for ice races on Summit Lake.'

'Wasn't that dangerous?' Hudson asked. Kevin caught Hadley's eye. *Another country heard from.*

'The most dangerous part was not letting my mom find out. Don't tell her I told you about ice racing. She'll probably ground me.'

Hudson snorted. 'You're a grown-up. She can't ground you.'

'Yeah, but who's going to tell *her* that? You?'

Hudson giggled. Hadley pressed her hands to her mouth and looked down at her lap. Kevin suddenly felt like he could drive the lot of them to Canada, if he had to.

'What's that?' Hudson asked. There was a light up ahead. Not moving, too close to the road to be a farmhouse. 'Is it a car?'

'I think it is. Good eyes, buddy.' Kevin could see the four-ways as they got closer, then a figure that resolved itself into a human shape, standing at the edge of the road, waving both arms. Kevin let the Aztek coast to a halt and put on his own emergency lights again.

'Do you want to get strapped?' Hadley said quietly. It was a natural impulse. Traffic stops were always potentially dangerous, and no sane cop went into one unarmed.

Kevin nodded toward the man walking toward them. He was sixtyish, in a puffy down coat and what had to be a hand-knit-for-Christmas pom-pom hat. 'I don't think he's going to be a problem. You stay here, though, just in case.'

'Okay.'

Kevin shrugged on his parka and got out.

'Thank God somebody came along!' The older man raised his arms as if he were going to hug Kevin. 'We tried calling Triple A, then nine-one-one, but the phone's not letting any calls through. I thought we were going to be trapped here all night.'

Kevin looked to where the man's SUV was planted in the nearby field, at least three car lengths away and perpendicular to the road. 'What happened?'

'Well, according to my wife, I was going too fast for the conditions.'

'I have to side with your wife on that, sir.'

The passenger door opened and the aforementioned wife got out and waded through the snow toward them. 'Hello! Do you think you might be able to pull us out?'

Kevin heard a door thunk behind him. Hadley must have decided he didn't need armed backup in the car. He shook his head. 'There's not enough traction on the road, ma'am. I'd just spin my tires. I'm sorry, folks,' Kevin said. 'You're going to need a tow truck for this one.'

'You can come with us,' Hadley said. 'There's an inn less than two miles down the road. We were planning on stopping there ourselves.'

The couple got their things from the vehicle and followed Kevin and Hadley back to the Aztek, sitting on the road like a lonely lighthouse. 'We were planning on stopping there ourselves?' Kevin asked.

'You were right. What if this happened to us and the kids? I don't want to be sitting in the dark, waiting for the gas to run out, hoping somebody else is stupid enough to be out on the road in this storm.'

They stomped off the worst of the snow when they reached the road. Kevin opened the back door for the older woman. 'Genny, Hudson, we're giving these folks a ride. I want you to climb over the seat and get in the rear.'

The kids scrambled into the rear well, and the elderly couple got in. 'We're so sorry to put you out like this,' the wife said.

Kevin climbed behind the wheel. 'You're not putting us out.' He shifted and began rolling very slowly down the road.

'Where were you headed?' Hadley asked.

'Lake George,' the husband said.

'We retired up there just last summer,' the wife said.

'You're going the long way around.' Kevin glanced into the rear-view mirror. 'The Northway's a lot quicker than routing through Millers Kill.'

'They've closed the Northway,' the husband said. 'No traffic allowed except emergency vehicles.'

Hadley twisted around in her seat. 'You're kidding. I didn't know they did that.' She looked at Kevin. 'Have you ever heard of that?'

He shook his head. 'No.' He didn't want to think what that meant for area law enforcement. The rest of the MKPD must be flat out, everybody working on double overtime to handle the weather emergency.

The older folks chatted with Hadley and the kids, freeing Kevin to focus on getting everyone safely to the Stuyvesant Inn. By the time the rambling Victorian came into view, his shoulders were stiff with tension and a headache was building behind his eyes.

Like the one at Algonquin Waters, the inn's sign was dark, but the many-paned windows glowed with warm, soft light. There were several cars jammed into the side yard; either the inn was having a midweek boom in skiers or they weren't the first travelers to seek shelter from the storm.

The front door opened before their little band had reached the wide front porch. The older of the two innkeepers raised a kerosene lamp. 'Welcome! Welcome!' Kevin plodded up the stairs, Hudson and Genny's bags in hand. 'Officer Flynn! This is a surprise. I take it this isn't an official visit.' He stepped back to allow them to enter. 'Come in, come in.' They crowded into the front hall. The hall, as big as the living-dining room in Kevin's apartment, wasn't much warmer than the outside. Candles in wall sconces threw flickering shadows over spindly side tables and layered oriental carpets. The mahogany stairs led up to darkness. The innkeeper shook the husband's hand as he shut the door behind them. 'Stephen Obrowski. Welcome to the Stuyvesant Inn.'

Kevin blessed the man for introducing himself, because at this stage he could barely remember his own name. 'Mr Obrowski. Do you have rooms available for these folks and for Hadley and the kids?'

Hadley turned on him. 'What about you?'

'I need to report to the department. They've got to be stretched to the breaking point.'

'So are you. You've spent the last four hours driving in this mess. You're going off duty as of now, Flynn.'

He couldn't help but crack a smile. 'Didn't the dep say running the department was above your pay grade?'

'Maybe, but running you isn't.' She looked at Obrowski. 'We all need rooms.'

'Well, there's the rub, as they say. We've got one double room left. No fireplace, but we're wrapping up warm bricks to heat the beds, just like they used to do.'

'How much?' the husband asked.

'Harvey! Give it to this nice couple!' She turned to Hadley. 'I'm so sorry. He just doesn't think.'

'We're not charging,' Obrowski said. 'Didn't seem right, with people stranded by the storm.'

'You take the room,' Hadley said. 'We can camp out in the parlor, if it's okay with Mr Obrowski.'

'Ron!' Obrowski yelled. A younger man appeared at the top of the stairs. 'Will you show these guests to the Clinton Room? Head right on up, folks, Ron will show you where everything is.'

Harvey-the-husband shook Kevin's hand. His wife hugged him. 'Your wife and children are so sweet. Thank you again for rescuing us.' She mounted the stairs before Kevin could correct her. At least, that's what he told himself.

Obrowski beckoned to him and Hadley. 'We can do better for you than the parlor. Lord knows I love our Empire and Renaissance Revival furniture, but it's lousy to sit on for more'n ten minutes.'

He picked up his lantern and led the way down the hall and into the cavernous kitchen, lit only by the glow from the professional-sized wood-fired oven. He opened a door at the far end of the room. 'Taa-daa.' Obrowski opened another door. 'Ron and I renovated part of the original barn for our private quarters.'

The room they were in was small and warm, with a deep sofa facing a tiny woodstove and a pair of plump chairs with matching ottomans. 'Your boy and girl can take the chairs, and you can have the sofa.' He smiled at Kevin. 'I'm afraid it's the floor for you, Stretch. Don't worry, though. We have enough sheets, blankets, and down comforters to bed down the Fifth Regiment.'

'Thank you. Thank you so much.' Hadley's voice shook. 'It's more than generous of you.' She leaned against Kevin, and for a moment he thought, *This is what it would be like.* If she really were his wife. If those really were his children.

Obrowski left to retrieve bedding for them. Hudson and Genny each climbed into a chair. Hudson bounced. 'That old lady thought you were my dad,' he said.

'It was a natural mistake,' Hadley said. She shucked off her parka and draped it over the arm of the sofa.

'Kevin doesn't even look like me. Dad does.'

'Give me your coat, Genny.' Hadley took the pink parka. 'Hudson, hand me yours, too.'

Hudson stood up. 'We should have stayed with Dad. They had the lights on there and the TV worked. Everything was fine until you messed it up.'

'Hudson!'

'Dad said bad words!' Genny looked up at Kevin. 'We're not supposed to use bad words.'

'He didn't say them to us! He just said them because Mom came to take us away!' The boy glared at Kevin. 'You hurt him! I saw you! You pushed him into the wall and twisted his arm!'

'For God's sake, Hudson!' Hadley took hold of his coat sleeves. 'Kevin was helping us.'

'Helping *you*.' Hudson wrenched his arms out of his parka and twisted away from his mother. 'I wanted to stay with Dad!'

'Hudson!'

'Why did you make him stay away? He never came to see us because of you! I hate it here in New York! If we were back in California, I'd see Dad all the time!' The boy's voice was clotted with rage and tears.

Hadley sank to her knees. 'Oh, baby, no.' She was close to crying as well. 'No. I would never keep your dad from visiting you.'

Hudson wiped his sleeve across his eyes. 'Then why did you take us away? How come we're here instead of at Dad's hotel?'

'Because Dad was going to take you away to California, and I can't allow that.' Hadley took a deep breath. 'It may sound nice, but we're better off here in Millers Kill. You're better off. I promise you that whatever decisions I make, they're always about what's best for you and Genny. You may not like them, you may not like me, but I am always and ever looking out for what's best for you.' Genny came to her mother's side and leaned against her. Hadley wrapped her arm around her daughter's waist.

Hudson's jaw jutted out, a barricade against more tears. He glared up at Kevin. 'Why did you have to fight with him? You made him so mad! He wouldn't have said those things if you hadn't made him mad!'

Kevin squatted down so he was face to face with the boy. 'Your dad got overwhelmed by his feelings, so overwhelmed that he lost control. I stopped him from doing something he'd feel terrible about later. I know it looked like I was rough with him, but your mom and I were trained to safely stop people from being a danger to themselves or others. I didn't hurt him, and he didn't hurt anyone else.'

'Dad wouldn't hurt us!'

'Not usually, no. But sometimes people do and say things they're sorry for later. Take you, for instance. I'm pretty sure you didn't really want to make your mother cry.' He glanced over at Hadley, and Hudson followed his gaze, taking in her red-rimmed eyes and blotchy cheeks.

'No-o-o-o . . .' Hudson's jaw loosened and he began to cry, the weeping of a small child exhausted beyond his limits.

'Oh, my sweet boy.' Hadley opened her other arm and Hudson lurched into her embrace.

Kevin met Steve Obrowski at the door and quietly explained the scene. The innkeeper handed him the stack of sheets, pillows, blankets, and comforters – he had been right, the pile could have comfortably slept a small army – and told him he and Ron would give them time to settle the kids down before retiring themselves. Kevin made up the sofa and chairs while Hadley got the kids into their pajamas and supervised their toothbrushing. Hudson and Genny emerged from the bathroom staggering and blinking like a pair of bear cubs in a midwinter den. Hadley steered them toward the chairs.

'Where's your bedroll?' she asked him.

'I'm going to sleep in the kitchen. It'll be plenty warm enough in front of that stove.'

'Flynn, you don't need to do that.' She touched the backs of the children's heads. 'Crawl under the covers now.' She looked up, straight into his eyes. 'Stay with us,' she said, her voice low.

He shook his head. 'I don't think it's a good idea.'

She glanced toward where Hudson was already curled up in one of the chairs, nothing but his ear and hair visible beyond the quilt covering him. 'Is it because . . . ?'

'Yeah.' Then – he didn't know if it was the bone-deep weariness, or the long, hard day they had spent together, or just that he was tired of holding it in – he let her see what he was feeling, what he always felt when he was around her. 'And other things.'

She ducked her head. 'Oh.'

He bent and picked up his share of the bedding. 'Good night, Genny. Good night, Hudson.' He ghosted a smile at Hadley. 'Better get some sleep. We're back on duty as of oh-seven-hundred. And I don't think tomorrow is going to be the cakewalk we've had today.'

SIXTEEN

Mikayla drifted in and out of dreams, hot and always thirsty. Daddy carried her to the bathroom, where she had bad, tummy-pinching poops, and then back to the room they were using. Mikayla hated it – everything stunk and people never stopped talking loud and excited. Nobody bothered her in her room, though, except Daddy and Travis, who sat on one of the other beds and argued in whispers. It got late and later and finally it got quiet, as everyone fell asleep.

It was hard to sleep with all her bones hurting, and she was so tired of feeling sick. She wanted to go home. She wanted to see Meme and Pepe. She wanted to be better, like she was at Ted and Helen's house, when she could play outside.

Far off in the darkness, she heard a dog barking. *Oscar.* Ted had been right, he was a good dog. She remembered he had scared her, but it was hard to feel the feeling, because now she felt safe, knowing he was out there, protecting her. *Good dog, Oscar,* she thought, and then she slid into sleep.

Wednesday, 14 January

ONE

It was a wave of cold air that woke him up. Kevin shivered, snugged the fat down comforter more closely around his shoulders, and muzzily thought, *Time for more wood.* He had woken up once already around midnight, just long enough to load the stove's firebox and then drop back into a profound slumber. Now he tried to rouse himself enough to crawl out of his warm cocoon and brave the chilly drafts by the wood rack.

He heard a clunk, then another. The creak of the stove door. He opened his eyes. Firelight on the wood-plank floor, and the orange-red glow of coals deep in the firebox, and the shiny trim and toggles on the stove glinting. Bare feet beside the black slate tiles. Bare ankles beneath another down comforter. There was a thunk and thud – wood tossed into the box – then the door closed again. The bare feet turned and the down collapsed in a fat puff and Hadley was sitting next to him.

'Hey.' Her voice was low and sweet. She reached out and stroked the hair off his forehead. 'Hey.'

'Mmm.' He smiled and closed his eyes. This was one of those dreams. He loved these.

'Move over,' she said, and he scooted back, leaving a warm place on the folded quilts beneath him. She threw her comforter half over his and slid in next to him. He sighed regretfully. Usually, she was gloriously nude. This time, for some reason, she was wearing panties and a T-shirt.

Then she put her feet on his legs.

'Christ, that's cold!' Kevin's eyes flew open. Hadley was lying next to him, looking at him uncertainly. He stared. *Holy shit.* It wasn't one of those dreams. 'It's you.'

'Yes, it's me. Who did you think it was?'

'I . . .' His head refused to help his mouth out. Finally he blurted, 'What time is it?'

'About three.'

'Oh.' His skin was relaying messages like *warm* and *soft* and *touch*. He had to stop himself from pressing against her. His thermal tee and boxers felt ridiculously inadequate. 'Hadley.' His voice was too breathy. He coughed. 'What are you doing here?'

She bit her lower lip. Her lips were chapped, and he could imagine what they would feel like, a little roughness over the sinking soft. He scooted back another inch. He waited for her to say something. When she remained silent, he asked, 'Is it one of the kids?'

'No.' She shook her head. 'God, this is hard.'

No kidding.

'I'm not very good at relationships, Flynn. You met the guy I married. And he was a prince, compared to some of the men I fell in with. So when you came along, all sunshine and puppy dogs, I just . . . I couldn't believe you were for real. Then I got to know you, and it got kind of switched around in my head, and I saw that I was the one who wasn't real. The stuff you like about me, the stuff you say you . . . love, that's not me. I mean, it is, but it's just the surface me.' She looked at him sadly. 'I'm not a very good person, Flynn.'

He laid his hand on her cheek and stroked his thumb beneath her eye. 'That's not true.'

'I've been . . . cruel to you. There's no other way to put it.'

He shook his head. 'Hadley—'

'It's true. I've been like Hudson was tonight, afraid and . . . disappointed, lashing out at you because I knew it was safe.' She swallowed. 'I want to stop reacting like a hurt child. I want to be a grown-up. I want to be able to say that was my old life, this is my new one, and it's okay to try trusting someone again.' She turned her head and kissed his palm. He shivered. 'To try trusting you.' She licked her lips. 'If, you know, you still . . .' Her voice trailed off.

'Want you.' He could barely hear himself. She nodded. He thought about the first time they had made love, after a long, stressful day full of fear and sorrow. 'I do. Want you, I mean. God, I want you.'

Before he could get out his 'but' she nudged closer. 'Do you?' Then her hand closed over him, stroking, and all he could manage was a groan. 'Flynn,' she whispered. She pushed him onto his back and slid his thermal tee up. His brain was trying to formulate a way to say she was just running away from her emotions again, but his hands went down and yanked his shirt off. She rose over him and bent her head to the blue Celtic knot circling his left nipple. His eyes fluttered shut as she licked his tattoo, licked and bit and sucked until he was panting and jerking beneath her.

'Hadley.' His voice was a wreck. He couldn't push her away, so he patted his hands over her hair, her bare shoulder – when had she gotten rid of her T-shirt? – her soft, smooth back. 'If this is another "have a bad day, screw Flynn to forget" scene—'

'No.' She moved down. Hooked his boxers and pulled and he was kicking them off even while he was trying to talk her out of it.

'Hadley.' He caught at her arms. 'Don't play me. I can't survive it. Don't play me.'

'Oh, Flynn.' She stretched up and slid her arms around his neck. Then he was holding her, drowning in her kiss, and he didn't care, didn't care that he was flayed open to her, heart and soul hers for the taking. 'I'm sorry,' she whispered into his neck. 'I'm so sorry I hurt you.'

He couldn't tell if it was sweat or tears on his skin. They rolled together, under and over, touching, tasting, pressing, testing until she was astride him again, sliding over the length of him all wet and slick and he thought he would die if he couldn't bury himself inside her.

Then he remembered. 'Shit!' He could barely get the words out. 'Stop. Hadley, stop. I don't have any protection.'

She gave him a wild, reckless smile. 'My sweet Flynn.' She rode him, up, down. He moaned. 'Have you slept with anyone else? Since me?'

'No,' he gasped. 'No.'

'I'm clean. I got tested regularly before I left California.' She leaned forward, pushing the damp hair away from his face. 'You're the only lover I've had since I moved to Millers Kill.'

His heart did a thump-turn. 'Hadley. Oh, God.'

'You can't get me pregnant. I had my tubes tied after Genny.' That information skittered and stung across his brain before he buried it for another time. 'It's up to you. But I want this. And I trust you.' Her face was grave, her eyes clear and bright.

'I love you,' he whispered.

'That's why I trust you,' she whispered back.

He took her then, skin on skin, such intense pleasure it felt like his entire nervous system had short-circuited. He kept his eyes on hers as he drove her up, as she whimpered and thrashed and clenched, as she gasped out her climax. When he came, it felt like a dam bursting, and as the floodwaters receded he opened, too, and found himself sobbing against her breast while she stroked his hair as she might have done with one of her children.

'God, I'm sorry,' he said, once he had gotten himself under control.

'It just means you trust me, too.' She kissed his hair. He could hear her smiling. 'Don't worry, I won't tell the other guys.'

The other guys. The department. The chief. The Johnson case. So much they had to talk about . . . then he dropped out of the world.

TWO

Lyle MacAuley was starting to worry. Well, to be honest, he'd been worrying the past three days, what with Russ stranded up at Inverary Lake and the rest of the force stretched thinner than a poor man's undershirt trying to cover the storm.

Now, parked in his squad car on the corner of Burgoyne Street, watching snow pelting down – and wasn't that just what they goddamn needed? – he had a new and exciting problem gnawing at his guts. Where the hell were Knox and Flynn?

He had confirmation from Harlene, who had it from the Albany dispatcher, that they had left the capital at the tail end of the afternoon. There had been some noise about her ex taking the kids, but Tim had stopped by Glenn Hadley's house last night and the old man had told him they were only going as far as the Algonquin. The Northway had shut down, making an unchristly mess; travelers stranded, cars taking 'shortcuts' along impassable roads, folks crowding into shelters at the elementary school and the Baptist church. But again, Flynn's SUV had its emergency lights. He'd have just gotten waved on by the staties.

Ignoring his doctor's orders to cut back on his caffeine intake, Lyle took a swig from the go-cup steaming in his holder. He'd gotten maybe five hours of sleep in one of the cots downstairs in the old cell block. With another eighteen-hour shift staring him in the face, it wasn't going to be the damn coffee that killed him.

When Knox and Flynn hadn't shown up this morning, he'd driven himself over to the Hadley house. Knox's grandfather was doing okay, the gas holding out in his generator, but he hadn't seen or heard from his granddaughter since the morning before.

So where were they? With the emergency channels already stressed to the breaking point, Lyle didn't want to piss off every other law enforcement agency by passing along a BOLO on two officers who had probably stopped at the Days Inn to wait out the storm. He swallowed some more coffee. He hadn't gotten a squawk himself yet, miracle of miracles. Maybe he was going to get a full hour without a car accident or fire or somebody triggering their carbon monoxide alarm.

If so, he was going to take advantage of it. He wedged his coffee into the plastic cup holder and shifted into gear. The chains on his tires clanked as he ground out of the parking spot. Goddamn ice and snow. He had half a mind to retire to Sarasota, spend the winters sport fishing.

He made pretty good time into Fort Henry, considering he got stuck behind a plow and then had to detour around a street where a tree had taken out an entire stretch of power line. He stopped to check, but Huggins had gotten his Fire and Rescue guys there already, and they didn't need his help.

He rolled to a stop in front of the Johnson house. Seeing the driveway bare, he could admit he had been hoping Knox and Flynn had come here to fill the Johnsons in on whatever new information they had dug up in Albany. Not like he knew what it was. Nobody was giving up bandwidth for an extended chat.

A woman answered the door, her face alight with hope and fear. 'Mrs Johnson? I'm Deputy Chief MacAuley. No news, I'm afraid.'

'Oh.' She stepped back, letting him into the foyer. 'Dear. Well, I guess that no news is good news. Isn't that what they say?'

A man around Lyle's age met them in the living room and introduced himself as Lewis Johnson.

'Mr Johnson.' Lyle tucked his cover under his arm to shake hands. 'I'm sorry that I don't have anything to tell you. I just wanted to check in since the phones aren't working. I don't suppose you two have heard from—'

'Nobody's dropped by to threaten me to keep my mouth shut, if that's what you're getting at.' Johnson sounded bone-tired. 'They don't have to. As soon as they clear up the roads again I'm headed to Fishkill. I'm going to talk to this Tim LaMar and tell him he doesn't have anything to fear from me. I'm not testifying.'

'What?' Lyle turned to Mrs Johnson. She looked resigned. 'That's crazy. You might as well put out a contract on yourself. If Tim LaMar knows who you are, you'll be dead before you make it back home to Fort Henry.'

'Do you think I don't know that?' Johnson settled his arm around his wife's shoulders. 'If it saves Mikayla, it's worth it.'

'Look, we still don't know for sure that LaMar is behind her kidnapping. Right now we're concentrating on finding your daughter.'

Mrs Johnson shook her head. 'Annie isn't organized enough to keep Mikayla hidden away for this long. Either she handed her over to someone else' – she glanced at her husband – 'or she never had Mikayla in the first place.'

Lyle jettisoned the argument he had been about to make. If these folks knew what they proposed was deadly and didn't care, his bleating wouldn't make much of a difference. He decided to try another tack. 'I realize it seems hopeless right now, but I assure you, we've got law enforcement all over the state looking for your granddaughter. I have absolute confidence she'll be found and returned to you *without* dragging Tim LaMar into it.'

'*If* she's getting her medicine, *if* she has proper medical attention, *if* you find her before her liver fails—' Johnson broke off. He took a shaky breath. 'We never should have agreed to let her stay with the MacAllens.'

His wife squeezed his waist. 'The FBI agents—'

'We should have told that pair to go stuff themselves. If she had been with us, she'd be safe right now.'

Lyle shook his head. 'I understand you folks are feeling desperate right now. All I ask is that before you go tearing off to Fishkill, you talk with us. Hmn?' He looked at Mrs Johnson. He figured she'd do about anything to get her granddaughter back, but she'd rather it didn't involve her husband painting a target on his back.

'Okay,' she said. 'Yes.'

'We're gonna do everything we can to get your little girl back for you. You have my word on that.'

Johnson sighed. 'We know you're trying. And we thank you for that. It's just . . .' He trailed off, but MacAuley could hear the rest of the sentence.

It's just not enough.

THREE

'Mommy?'

Hadley grunted and burrowed deeper under the covers.

'Mommy?'

'Is she awake?'

'I dunno.'

Something tickled her forehead. 'Go watch cartoons,' she mumbled.

'We can't! The TVs don't work 'cause the power's still out!'

Hadley cracked an eye open. Genny was almost nose-to-nose, her hair falling onto Hadley's face. 'Kevin told us we couldn't bother you until you were awake.'

It all came back to her in a flood – Dylan, the white-knuckled drive, lying awake in the wee hours weighing her bad decisions. *Flynn.* Hadley was suddenly aware of her body; the ache of unused muscles, the tender dampness between her legs, the faint sting of beard burn along her chest.

'She's awake!' Genny bounced on the sofa bed. 'Can we go help Ron with the chickens?'

'What?' Her head was still spinning.

'They got real chickens in the barn,' Hudson explained. 'Ron said we could help feed them and pick up the eggs, but Steve said you had to say it was okay first.'

'Yes,' Hadley croaked. 'Sure. Go. Wait! Are you dressed?'

'Mo-om. We've been up for *hours.*' Hudson and Genny ran out, slamming the door behind them.

She waited until she was sure they wouldn't come bursting back in for some desperately important item, then swung her legs out of bed. She smelled like sex, she had no clean underwear, and she was going to have to wash Steve Obrowski's T-shirt before she could give it back. She scooped up her clothes and fled into the tiny bathroom.

Door safely locked behind her, she stared at herself in the mirror. Her lips were still swollen, and there was a rosy streak along the side of her throat where Flynn had – she shuddered. Good God. She had had sex while her children were practically next door. What had gotten into her?

Wetness on her leg told her exactly what. *Unprotected* sex. She shook her head in disbelief. She hadn't done that since she set out to get pregnant with Genny.

Steve and Ron had left a jug of water on the counter, and she splashed some into a washcloth and scrubbed herself down. She toweled off and got into her clothes, all the while planning her next moves; collect the children, thank the innkeepers, get the kids back to Granddad's—

Don't play me. I can't survive it. Don't play me.

She stopped. Leaned against the counter and hung her head. She was planning on running away. She took a deep breath. Her heart was pounding, and she realized she was terrified.

This thing with Flynn wasn't just sex, it wasn't just for fun – it was something new, so new she felt raw-pink and tender, blind and utterly vulnerable. She had set aside all her shields and defenses, and right now, staring at her almost unrecognizable face in the mirror, she knew Flynn could break her with a word.

But he won't. He loves you, too.

He loves you, too.

I love him, she mouthed to the mirror, not daring to say it aloud. *I love him.* She held the thought close against her still-thudding heart. Terrifying, yes. But there she was.

Back in the living room, she stripped the sheets and blankets from where she and the kids had slept, packed up the rest of their things, and, squaring her shoulders, walked down the freezing hallway to the kitchen.

Flynn wasn't there. Ron Handler was whisking something in a stainless steel bowl and Steve was frying an entire hog's worth of bacon atop the enormous iron range. An old-fashioned pendulum clock – no electricity needed – told her it was nine o'clock. She winced. Lyle MacAuley probably thought she and Flynn were dead, and when they made it in three hours late for their shift, they would be.

The kids – *her* kids – were setting napkins and silverware around the big butcher's block island. 'Who are you and what have you done with Hudson and Genny?' she asked.

'Good morning!' Steve Obrowski smiled at her as if oversleeping were a personal compliment. 'These two are great little helpers.'

'Steve says we're gonna eat in here because it's the warmest place in the inn,' Hudson explained.

'I got to use the feather duster.' Genny almost dropped a napkin onto the butter dish. 'It has real ostrich feathers.'

'And I got to help Steve fix the loose sconches—'

'Sconces.'

'Sconces in the hall. I got to use the hammer and everything.'

'My God,' Hadley said.

'I know.' Ron crossed to the stove and poured what looked like a gallon of scrambled eggs into two skillets. 'Child labor. The Victorians were really onto something.'

The door swung open and Hadley's heart surged, only to drop back down in disappointment as a couple in their seventies and the woman they had rescued last night pushed into the kitchen. 'They've gotten the Smiths' car out,' the woman said. 'They'll be in in a minute.'

'Great timing,' Ron said. 'Everybody pull up a stool for breakfast.'

'Officer Knox.' The woman smiled brightly at Hadley. 'Your – I mean, Officer Flynn explained we had been saved by the Millers Kill Police Department. Thank you again.'

She and the couple hitched themselves up onto stools at the far end of the island, chatting as if they were old friends. 'Officer Flynn and Mr Keene are shoveling out the drive,' Steve said, handing her a jug of orange juice. 'The Smiths are doctors; they couldn't wait any longer to head home.' He glanced out the window. 'Although maybe the snow will help the driving.'

'What?' Hadley set the pitcher on the table and went to the window. It *was* snowing. She had been so distracted, she hadn't noticed the cessation of the rain drumming on the roof. After three days, the temperature had finally fallen far enough to turn the precipitation into snow.

The kitchen door swung open again. The husband from last night – Mr Keene – stomped in, brushing snow from his jacket and shaking off his pom-pom hat. Hard on his heels, Flynn.

She met his eyes and he blushed, which would have been funny, except she could feel her face heating as well. She tried to look away, tried to look casual, but there was an invisible wire humming between them.

'How's it look out there?' Steve Obrowski's bluff voice broke the spell. Hadley crossed back to the island, taking the first stool she bumped into.

'We got the cars relatively clear of ice and shoveled from the parking area to the road,' Flynn said. 'It should be enough to get anyone else out who needs to go.' He stripped off his snow-spattered parka and hung it on a hook near the door.

'Is it safe to travel?' the seventyish woman asked.

Flynn shook his head. 'I wouldn't recommend it, ma'am. At least, not until the plow gets through.'

Mr Keene slapped him on the back. 'Well, there are certainly worse places to get stuck!' He hopped up next to his wife.

'Frittatas are up!' Ron Handler wheeled away from the stove and deposited the two skillets onto iron trivets on the island. 'You're all welcome to stay as long as you like.' He winked at Hadley as he took one of the stools at the near end of the island. 'It's the dead time of year for us.'

'I'm afraid Officer Knox and I need to leave as soon as possible.' Flynn sat next to Hadley. She knew she must be imagining it, but she could swear she could feel the heat of his body all along her side.

The kids let out wails of disappointment.

'Do you have to go?' Steve asked, setting a wooden tray piled with bacon on the center of the island. 'I mean, how much crime could be going on in weather like this?'

Flynn glanced at Hadley. 'They're going to need us for traffic control and accidents.'

'The department needs everyone with—' She stopped herself before blurting out *the chief missing*. 'With the chief away on his honeymoon.'

'Oh. Well, then . . .' Steve sounded disappointed. Maybe that was what made someone an innkeeper – actually *wanting* people hanging around.

Ron sliced the frittatas into wedges, and the noise level rose as people handed over plates, poured themselves orange juice, passed the bacon – 'Might as well eat it before it spoils,' Steve said – and exchanged stories of storms and strandings. Hadley ate silently, unable to slip back into her role as Flynn's partner, unwilling to act more intimate in front of a crowd of near-strangers and her kids.

Flynn didn't seem to have any problems, handing out advice on the most likely routes to travel, telling funny stories about his run-ins with Lyle MacAuley. It irked her, because dammit, she was the one with all the experience. She ought to be calm and collected instead of sitting next to him like a Catholic schoolgirl on her first date.

'—right, Hadley?'

She blanked. Flynn was looking at her so normally, waiting for her to say something. 'Oh. Yeah. Our deputy chief is a bear. We're going to have to do some fast explaining for being late as it is.' She laughed. It didn't sound quite right to her ears.

By the time they had finished breakfast, she was desperate for just a couple of minutes alone with him. When Flynn said he was going to start up his truck, she said she'd go with him, but then Genny barreled back into the kitchen looking for help gravity-flushing the toilet. By the time they had finished, Flynn had come back inside to pick up the bags and thank the innkeepers for their generosity.

They loaded the suitcases and the kids and set off for town. Flynn drove at a conservative ten miles an hour, which made Hadley want to screech, except she knew he was only playing it safe. He remained focused on the almost invisible road ahead, his face set, his hands tight on the wheel.

Route 57 had been plowed at some point, and the road into town was a patchwork of bare asphalt, ice slicks, and packed snow. When they finally reached the house, there was just enough space to park. Flynn snugged his Aztek nose-to-nose with her granddad's old Dodge and grabbed the kids' luggage while Hadley steered them inside.

Hudson and Genny rampaged over Granddad as if they'd been gone a week, while Hadley excused herself to go upstairs and change. When she got back down, Granddad was supervising the children donning their outdoor gear. 'I'm off to snowblow the church,' he said. 'These two can slide down the hill on t'other side while I'm working.' Past the parish hall, St. Alban's lawn sloped downhill toward Route 57 and the river. A century-old iron fence kept sledders from disaster.

'It's still coming down pretty hard,' Flynn observed. 'You sure you want to snowblow now?'

'Got to get ahead of it, don't you?' He held the door open for them. Everyone trooped out onto the porch. There wasn't going to be any chance for a private moment or a quiet word, Hadley saw.

They made it back to the station house and pulled into the parking lot without having said a word, Flynn killed the engine, and Hadley finally opened her mouth. She didn't know what she was going to say – something reassuring, or funny, anything except what she was thinking: *Are you having second thoughts?*

'Are you having second thoughts?' His lips were drawn into a line. 'Because if you are, you know—'

'No!' She blinked at him. 'Are you?'

'Are you kidding? Of course not. It's just you didn't say anything—'

'*You* didn't say anything!'

'The kids were in the car!'

'I thought maybe, I don't know . . .' She turned away to look out her window. 'Some guys, once they've caught your heart, they get scared.' She glanced back toward Flynn.

A slow smile curved his mouth. 'Have I caught your heart?'

'Oh, God.' She pushed at him. 'You know what I mean.' For some reason, she kept her hand resting against his chest.

His gaze dropped to her lips. 'I want to kiss you.'

Her breath caught. 'I think we ought to keep it under wraps at work.'

'Yeah. I agree.' He did not, however, stop leaning closer and closer, looking at her as if he were going to lay her out in the backseat and—

A siren blurped behind them.

'Shit!' Flynn jerked away so quickly his head smacked his window.

In the side mirror, Hadley could see MacAuley getting out of his unit. 'It's the dep,' she hissed.

'Okay. We play it cool. Like nothing's changed.'

'Like nothing's changed. Got it.'

'Once we feel comfortable with it, we talk to the chief.'

'I'm going to need some time to – shit, Flynn, what about your job offer? Syracuse?'

'Hadley.' He laughed. 'I'm not going to move half the state away when we've finally gotten together.'

MacAuley rapped on the driver's window. 'You two having a nice chat in there? Maybe I could bring you out some coffee and doughnuts?'

Flynn opened his door. 'Sorry, Dep.'

'Well, don't let me rush you. Just 'cause it's after ten o'clock and the rest of the department's been on twelve-hour shifts.'

Hadley slid out of the truck. 'We helped some tourists on the Sacandaga Road and then decided to stay at the Stuyvesant Inn until the weather broke.' That sounded good. Professional, even.

'Shoulda stayed in Albany like I suggested.' MacAuley snorted. 'Can't imagine they have any power at the Stuyvesant Inn.'

'Well, I did have to keep feeding the woodstove.' Flynn's expression was bland as they walked toward the station entrance.

'See? You were probably up half the night.' Over the dep's head, Flynn shot Hadley a wicked grin. 'Don't think you can pull over behind a billboard and take a nap, either,' MacAuley continued. 'We're all gonna be busting our balls today. I just got the heads-up from Harlene. Your federal agents are driving up here.'

Hadley stopped, one foot on the granite steps. 'They are?'

'Ayep. Don't know what you said to light a fire under their butts, but they're scraping together a task force. They want to take this meth house we've all been looking for, and they want our help to do it.'

FOUR

Tom and Marie O'Day arrived at lunchtime. Lyle had long since sent Knox and Flynn out on patrol, so he had Harlene reel them back in for the briefing. The FBI agents looked around the Millers Kill station, with its layers of past law enforcement architecture dating back to the 1880s, and managed to avoid sniffing. Lyle, in turn, kept from rolling his eyes. He knew how the Feds worked. If it wasn't the latest high-tech gadget or glass-walled building, they didn't want it.

He had run into the O'Days before, on an interstate domestic that had lit up Millers Kill because the perp, a New Hampshire guy who had killed his wife, briefly squatted with a cousin in town before fleeing farther west. That had been before Russ became chief, so more than ten years now. Which meant, despite their nose-up attitude toward the local yokels, they weren't any different from him. They had peaked in their careers and they weren't going up or out until the Albany office threw their retirement party.

Fortunately, he didn't have to do much entertaining. As soon as they'd gotten coffees – more proof that law enforcement runs on caffeine – they'd hunkered down with Harlene, who was fighting her way through a jam-packed bandwidth so they could pick up what sounded like an ongoing argument with a sergeant from NYSP Troop G. 'We don't need an entire SWAT team,' Tom O'Day was saying. 'We just need a couple of guys.'

'Call the Essex County Sheriff's Department.'

'They're flat out with traffic, and they don't have a Special Forces team.'

'What about your own shooters?' the statie asked. 'You Feds spend more on your teams than we get for the whole damn troop.'

'We need to keep this as quiet as possible. And with this weather, it'll take our team the rest of the day just to get into place. Your station's thirty miles away.'

'In case you didn't know, we're a little busy with the weather as well. We got accidents, downed live power lines, and stranded civilians from here to Ogdensburg, and one of Troop B's men has gone missing in the park. These are the Adirondack Mountains, Agent. We usually do our drug busts in the summer, when you can get up the damn roads.'

Tom O'Day looked at his wife and made a *now what?* gesture. She leaned toward the mic. 'Sergeant, we'd like to speak with your supervisor.'

'I'll be sure to have her call you back, ma'am.' Even over the uncertain radio signal, Lyle could hear the statie's kiss-off-and-die tone. 'She should be back within a few hours.' The sergeant signed off.

Marie O'Day handed the mic back to Harlene. 'You know if we go up there into their jurisdiction without at least some NYSP support, we'll never hear the end of it.'

'The Essex County Drug Task Force?' Lyle suggested.

She waved her hand. 'Would be great, if we had three or four days to coordinate. Your Officer Knox kept yapping about how the missing girl is going to die at any second without medical care.'

Lyle decided to ignore the agent's poke at Knox. They were here, after all, which meant however Hadley nettled them, she did it right. 'Where's LaMar's meth house located?' Maybe he could call in a few favors, if it wasn't too far off the beaten path.

Tom O'Day stood, towering over Lyle. 'Do you have an area map?' Lyle led the agents into the squad room, where a New York State map shared wall space with a window-sized map of Washington County. O'Day went to the smaller map.

'Here.' O'Day pointed to the tip of a lake. 'There aren't any actual towns around. See this spot on County Highway 16? There's a road that branches off here. You follow it all the way up past the lake—'

'Lake Inverary.'

'Yes. As I was saying—'

Lyle didn't wait to hear the rest. He bolted back to the dispatch center. 'Harlene, get that sergeant from Crown Point back on the line.'

Harlene bent to the task of routing her signal across the depleted network. The O'Days followed him, both wearing identical frowns. Marie O'Day crossed her arms. 'What's going on? That place isn't anywhere near your jurisdiction.'

Lyle held up a hand as the state troopers' station came on the line. 'Sergeant, this is Deputy Chief MacAuley of the Millers Kill Police Department.'

'Deputy Chief, I already told those feebs they were barking up the wrong tree. We're busting our nuts up here. We don't have time to send a squad on a wild goose chase.'

'Sergeant, is the missing trooper Lieutenant Bob Mongue? From Troop B?'

There was a pause. Then a suspicious 'Ye-es.'

Lyle grinned at the agents. 'Then Sergeant, this is your lucky day. I know where he is.'

FIVE

'Ready?' Russ looked at Clare. She nodded. 'Count of three. One, two, *three.*' They lifted the blanket beneath Bob Mongue. Russ, who was kneeling in the narrow rear well of the Ford, grunted as he scootched backward. Clare strained to get her end of the blanket higher than her chest.

They were trying to transfer Bob from his berth in the canoe to the backseat of the pickup, which they had moved from the garage onto the road in front of Roy's house. She and Russ had dragged Bob across the ice in the canoe, which he hailed as the only civilized way to travel. Of course, he was hopped up on Oxy again, so his opinion was a little suspect.

When Clare had awakened midmorning, after an uncomfortable night plagued with dreams she thankfully couldn't remember, Russ tried to persuade her to stay with the lieutenant while he retrieved the truck and went hunting for Travis and Hector, where they were hoping Mikayla would also be. She countered by offering to go get the Ford while *he* stayed with Bob, on the grounds that he would be a more effective protector if the bad guys came back. They bickered about it for a while until Bob declared them both ready for martyrdom and pointed out that splitting up that last time hadn't worked well for anyone.

Russ had reached the point where they could hoist Bob onto the seat. 'Can you get him a couple inches higher?'

Clare gritted her teeth and heaved. Bob and the blanket slid onto the backseat. Clare handed up the duffel bag. Russ stuffed it behind the lieutenant, then settled a blanket over his injured leg, stretched out along the seat. Bob leaned back against the duffel, brushing snow off himself.

'How is it?' Russ asked.

''S fine. I'll probably want to brace my good foot on the floor when we're moving, though.'

'Be grateful you're such a string bean. I can barely squeeze in back there.' Russ shut the narrow crew door. 'Clare, I'm going to want you to drive. Climb on in and let the heater blast, will you? I'm going to check the house to see if there's anything else useful for us.'

Clare got behind the wheel. The cab had already started to heat up while they were parked, and for a moment, she simply lay back against the seat, soaking up the sensation of warmth. She unzipped her coat so as to heat up her inner layers, then rubbed her belly as the baby began to roll and kick inside her.

'Acting up, is he?'

She laughed a little. 'Yeah. Lately, it seems as if as soon as I stop moving, he starts.'

'He?'

'Or she.'

'You'll pardon me for sticking my oar in, but you two seem more than usually nerved up for first-time parents.'

Clare adjusted the blowers to send more heat into the back. 'Well. The baby was unplanned.'

'Hell, our first three were unplanned. After that, my wife and I just decided to expect she'd get pregnant. That way, we weren't shocked when it happened.'

Clare laughed. 'How many children do you have?'

'Five. Including one with Down's syndrome.'

Clare's smile died away.

'So I know what it's like to be facing ... ell, let's say a different outcome than you had hoped.'

She turned around in her seat. 'How did you know?'

'Heard you two last night. Him asking you if you'd dipped into the Oxys. You talking about your problem.'

Her voice stuck in her throat. 'I was ... it's not really the pills. I was drinking. A lot. After I finished my tour of duty in Iraq.' She wiped her hand over her eyes. 'I don't usually talk about this.'

'Yeah, I can see why. Your husband's kind of an asshole about it.'

'No! He's not! He's just feeling out of control. It's not his fault. Before we married, we agreed—'

'Not to have kids. Yeah, he told me.'

Unwillingly, Clare's mouth quirked up. 'Do you always get people to open up about their deep, dark secrets?'

'It's a useful trait for a cop. Or, I'm guessing, a minister.' He shifted, bringing his good leg down. 'For what it's worth, I think you're good for him. He used to be stodgy.'

'Stodgy?'

'Like a superannuated Eagle Scout. He needed some shaking up. You know what they call him over at the Troop B barracks?'

'What?'

'Russ Van All-shine.'

She was giggling when Russ opened the passenger door. 'I see you two are getting along.' He tossed a plastic grocery sack into her lap and brushed the snow off before climbing in. He unzipped his parka and held his hands next to the vents. 'Colder'n a witch's tit out there.' He nodded toward the sack. 'Peanut butter and crackers and some of those pudding cups. As soon as they thaw out we can eat 'em.' He reached for the mic and switched on the radio. 'Might as well try this one more time.' He scanned up the dial, then down. Nothing but static. He set it to the emergency frequency. 'Troop G Dispatch, this is Russ Van Alstyne of the MKPD, do you copy?' He paused. Nothing. 'Any emergency service on this channel, this is Chief Russ Van Alstyne of the MKPD. Officer in need of assistance.' Nothing.

'The tower's down,' Bob said. 'Up here, with all the mountains around, they need those physical relays to get through.'

'Yeah.' Russ balanced the mic in his hand for a second, then hung it up again. He turned toward the back. 'Bob, hand me the shotgun.' The trooper complied.

'What are you planning to do?' Clare tried to keep her voice level.

'You're going to drive up South Shore and keep going up Haines Mountain Road. Slowly. Walking pace.' She nodded. 'I'm going to be in the back.'

'With Bob?'

'No. In the bed. I want a clear line of sight in case we come under fire.'

'Do you think that's likely?'

'I hope not. My idea is to drive until we spot some sign of life – parked cars, smoke from a chimney, the sound of a generator. Then we'll stop and I'll go forward on foot to check it out and hopefully find Mikayla.'

Clare looked out the windshield at the steadily falling snow. 'Are you going to be able to see smoke or cars from a safe-enough distance? In this?'

'Our other alternative is for you two to head for help while I reconnoiter on my own.'

'No.' She took his hand. 'We stick together.'

He twined his fingers through hers for a moment before twisting to the rear again. 'Bob, you have the Glock and the Taurus Clare took from Roy. Don't hesitate to shoot out the windows if you need to.'

Bob etched a salute. 'It'd be my pleasure.'

Russ snorted. 'I bet.' He pressed his lips to hers, the briefest of kisses, and opened the door. Clare waited until she could see him in the rearview mirror. He thumped twice on the cab roof. She took a deep breath, shifted into gear, and drove forward.

SIX

In the end, it was one Essex County deputy, two guys from the Troop G tactical team, the Feds, and him and Hadley.

'Us?' Kevin asked the dep.

'You,' MacAuley said. 'You've been working the case all along.'

'But . . .' Hadley's hands twitched. The dep had dragged them into the chief's office as soon as they had gotten into the station. 'Shouldn't you be there, too?'

'Somebody's got to run this insane asylum until the chief gets back. It's getting worse out there, not better.'

MacAuley was right. Snow on top of the ice was bringing down even more trees and lines. National Grid crews were out replacing utility poles for the second time. Near Plattsburgh, an entire substation had crumpled beneath the weight, and Kevin had heard they were bringing in linemen from as far away as the Carolinas to help. The governor had declared a state of emergency.

'You two will only be backup,' the dep went on. 'The Feds and the tac team will take lead. All you have to do is take custody of Annie Johnson, if, please Jesus, she's there, and find out where her daughter is. We'll plan our next move on her information.'

'And if Mikayla is there?' Hadley asked.

'Get her medical attention ASAP. There's the Moses-Ludington up in Ticonderoga, that'll be the closest hospital. At some point, if you can manage it, see if you can get to the chief's cabin. A statie named Bob Mongue drove up to check on him and Reverend Fergusson, and I suspect they're all stuck out there in the woods. Take a set of chains and your SUV. That oughta do you.'

Harlene gave him a yell about the Essex County sheriff's office on the line, and MacAuley took off for her dispatch board. Hadley looked at Kevin. 'We're going to get stuck, you know. Inverary Lake is practically in the High Peaks. They probably already had five feet of snow before the ice hit.'

He couldn't put an arm around her, not in the chief's office, so he settled for a shoulder bump. 'It'll be fine. Turned out pretty good the last time, didn't it?'

SEVEN

It wasn't a column of smoke or the noise of a generator that tipped Russ off. It was the smell. A combination of rotten egg and scorched oil and vinegar, it cut through the clean scent of the snow and the pines, pinching his nose, making his eyes water. He rapped on the roof of the cab.

Clare slowed to a stop, then rolled her window down. 'Want a break?' In the hour that they had been creeping up Haines Mountain Road, he had called three stops to warm himself up in the cab, eat some peanut butter and pudding, and slug back some of the slowly melting water.

Russ swung himself off the bed. 'No.'

Clare sniffed. 'What is that god-awful smell?'

From the backseat, Bob said, 'That, Mrs Van Alstyne, is the smell of crystal methamphetamine.'

Clare wrinkled her nose. 'And people *ingest* it? It must give an unbelievable high. I mean, to get past that.'

Russ hung his arm in her window. 'It doesn't smell once it's cooked.' He gestured for the box of shells. She handed it to him. 'I'm going to walk from here.'

'Let me come with you. You won't have any way to let us know if you get in trouble.'

'If I get into real trouble, I'll fire two blasts. If you hear that, I want you to head for the county highway as fast as you can without putting 'er in a snowbank.'

'I won't leave you.'

'Clare.' He laid one gloved hand on her arm. 'The best thing you can do is be here, in the truck, waiting to make a getaway if I come running. The second-best thing you can do is find help as quick as you can if I don't come running.' He looked toward the backseat. 'Bob? Make sure she doesn't come after me.'

'I should what, shoot her in the leg?'

'Just remind her that you're completely helpless without her at the wheel, and that if she gets hurt or captured, you could die here.' He glanced at Clare.

'Oh, that is utterly not fair!'

'Fair or not, darlin', it's the truth. I'll see you soon.'

She kissed him, hard. 'Be careful.'

'Always.' He loaded the shells and checked the safety, cradled the gun in his arm, and set off up the hill. The road ahead was trackless but not bad underfoot; enough snow had fallen to compact beneath his boots. He thought about approaching through the woods crowding in on either side but figured the benefit of hiding his path was outweighed by the cost in time of working his way through the forest.

The road curved and he left the truck behind. His biggest fear wasn't running into DeJean or Roy – he knew he could take care of himself – but that some other meth brewer might come along behind Clare and Bob. It wouldn't be hard for a large-scale vehicle like an SUV or pickup to block their escape route.

He walked on, alert and straining for something out of the ordinary, but except for the foul odor, there was nothing to trigger his alarm. He didn't see any signs of life; not that he'd expect to with trees all around and the air thick with snow. He didn't hear anything except flakes settling on pine and hemlock needles, a sound that was almost, but not quite, silence.

He had been walking steadily uphill the whole time, so when he reached the next curve and discovered it was a summit, he wasn't surprised. Beneath him, the road dropped steeply down to a single-lane bridge that crossed a frozen stream before rising up through open pasturage to the top of the next hill. Russ stopped. There was no way any vehicle could have made it down that stretch and threaded the bridge during the ice storm. He had been wrong. DeJean and Roy must have gone some other way. He turned to head back to Clare, and that was when he saw DeJean's SUV, covered in snow and wedged in between hemlocks that had screened it from his view.

The vehicle was back a good two car lengths from the road, and Russ could see what looked at first glance to be a natural gap in the trees was actually cleared space. Which made sense, given the dangerous slope of the road. It made sense – if there was a house close enough to walk to.

Russ walked into the trees and brushed the snow off the rear window. There was nothing inside except the bags of sand and the compact shovel he had shared the space with yesterday. He went back to the road. Had they walked down the hill? Or was there a path through the woods to the farmhouse Russ was now sure sat in one of the fields below?

He opted for the road. He descended slowly, occasionally skidding, once slipping and hitting ass-first. When he was three-quarters of the way down, he took to the verge. The going, through deep snow crusted with patchy ice, was much slower, but he wanted to be in a position to see what was past the woods without anyone spotting him first.

He got closer and closer to the bridge. The snow was letting up, giving him better visibility. Across the road to his right, he could see more and more open land, blanketed in white and bounded with a sagging wire fence made beautiful by ice. He stopped near the edge of the stream. Through a thin screen of trees, he could make out a dilapidated farmhouse, shutters dangling off the hinges, painted clapboards scoured away to raw gray wood. It was square in the middle of its sloping field, a good quarter mile past the woods where Russ stood. A long drive that showed signs of having been plowed within the past few days ran down to the road. Russ couldn't hear any generators, but there was smoke coming from the house's two chimneys.

Behind the farmhouse, barely visible from this angle, was a large barn. It looked to be in better repair, with fresh white paint and a solid black door. The wind had changed and the odor of cooking meth was fainter.

He was going to have to get closer. He started working his way through the trees, keeping back far enough so that he would be invisible to any watchers in the house. He churned and floundered through the snow until the lightbulb went on and he realized the stream bed was deep enough to hide him if he crouched while walking. He made his way back to the edge of the trees, dropping to his belly and combat-crawling the last ten feet. He slid over the bank and landed with a thud on the ice. Not even a creak or crack – the stream was probably so shallow it was frozen right down to the ground. He brushed himself off and realized it had stopped snowing.

His goal was to get at a right angle to the buildings so he could see what approach was like from front, side, and rear. Getting across the open ground to the house was going to be a bear of a job. No cover and – he looked up at the sky, which was finally clearing after four days – a good chance of a moonlit night.

He had gone a few yards upstream when he caught a flash of movement in the woods above him. *Shit.* Russ flattened himself against the bank, twisting so he could see upward. He raised the shotgun into ready position, barrel against the side of his face, stock tight against his chest. He heard a scrabbling sound and thought for a second *fox,* but then a branch snapped under the weight of something much heavier than a fox. His heart kicked into high gear. He tried to steady his breathing. There was a high sharp keening noise and then something dropped on top of him and he swung the shotgun out to shoot and was nearly knocked down by Oscar, yipping, dancing, jumping up in excitement. The relief almost knocked Russ down.

'Shh. Shh, boy. Good boy. Get down.' He stripped off his gloves and knelt on the ice. He ran his hands over the dog, checking for injuries, while Oscar tried to climb over him, licking his fingers and face. He yipped again when Russ passed a hand over his flank, and pulling the dog around, Russ could see a streak of rusty red.

'Where have you been, big guy?' Russ gave Oscar's head a fierce scratching, and the dog sighed and leaned whole-body against him. 'Did you find a barn to hide in? Hmm? Clare's gonna be mighty glad to see you.'

When he straightened to continue up the stream, Oscar fell in beside him. Russ feared the dog might draw unwelcome attention by barking, but Oscar seemed content to walk close by, occasionally butting himself against Russ's leg.

They were getting close enough to the house for Russ to start scanning the bank for a likely place to climb up and enter the woods. He got a different idea when he saw an eastern pine that had split and was half-hanging over the stream. He snapped a needle-heavy branch off the tree, packed some snow atop it, and strapped it over his knit hat with his belt – the cold-weather version of the branches-in-helmet camo he had used in Vietnam. Sticking close to the tree's brushy foliage, he pressed himself against the bank closest to the field and rose until he could see over the edge.

At his feet, Oscar whined fretfully. The back door to the house opened, and a man emerged. Even bundled against the cold, Russ could see he wasn't DeJean or Roy. The ease with which he crossed the backyard indicated a shoveled path to the barn. Instead of going to the tractor-sized entrance, he veered toward a narrow door on the left edge of the barn. He pressed against a buzzer. A moment later, the door opened from inside and he entered.

No sign of a window. Maybe the door had a peephole. This wasn't a couple of rednecks brewing up a little crystal for fun and profit. Whoever was running this had put some money and muscle into it. It was going to take more than one middle-aged cop, a pregnant priest, and a statie with a busted leg to liberate Mikayla Johnson.

Russ let himself slide back until his boots were on the ice again. He unlatched his belt and tossed the pine branch onto the snow. 'Come on, boy.' He let Oscar lick his fingers again. 'Let's go give Clare the bad news.'

EIGHT

They had their briefing huddled in the lee side of a mom-and-pop store just off County Highway 16 while waiting for a promised plow truck to open South Shore Drive for them. The snow, having dumped a good foot in the past twelve hours, was finally tapering off. Hadley didn't take it as a sign their weather woes were over. The way this storm had played out, she wouldn't be surprised if they got hit with a hurricane next.

'Our DEA informant tells us there are two structures on site: a barn, where the meth is processed, and a freestanding house, where the workers stay.' Tom O'Day stripped off a glove to hand around several papers.

'How come Agent – your DEA informant didn't come with us?' The question had been bugging Hadley. The O'Days were after Tim LaMar for murder. The meth ring was Boileau's case.

'This isn't a drug bust. The informant' – O'Day gave her a glare, warning her to watch her mouth – 'will remain undercover until the rest of the dealers are ready to be taken down.' He turned toward the others. 'First and foremost, we're looking for Annie Johnson. Secondary to that, her daughter, Mikayla Johnson.'

The Essex County deputy held up a copy of the picture of Annie, Mikayla, and Travis Roy that Hadley and Flynn had taken from the Johnsons. 'This is the girl who's been missing from Millers Kill?'

'That's right,' Flynn said. 'If she's there, she's likely to be very sick, possibly nonresponsive.'

'Shouldn't we have an EMT on board, then?'

Marie O'Day answered the deputy. 'We're lucky to get this group, considering the emergency situation.' She glanced toward the highway, where there was still a conspicuous lack of a plow.

The senior state sharpshooter was looking at the photo. 'This her boyfriend?'

'Yes.' Hadley pulled out the next page in the file. 'This is a mug shot of Hector DeJean, Mikayla's father. Like Roy and Johnson, he's also missing, also presumed to be a suspect.'

Tom O'Day pointed at the photo. 'This is a few years old. He's completely bald now, so keep that in mind.' He held up a hand-drawn map that roughed in house, barn, road, and fields. 'According to our source, the place was chosen both for its remoteness and its position. As you can see, it's in the middle of a cleared acre, giving it a good view in all directions. This area across the road is also cleared.'

'Trees back here?' the second tac guy asked.

'Yes.'

'Okay.' He pulled off his glove. 'We can cross where there's cover. Trooper Burton and I can take the rear corners' – he pointed on the map – 'which will give us a good line of sight for the back of the barn and the flank of the house.' He traced along the cleared area running between the buildings and the trees. 'That leaves five of you to enter the house.'

Hadley stamped her boots to keep her feet warm. 'I thought you tac guys did that.'

'When we've got the squad, yeah. In a situation like this, with just two of us, we're more effective providing suppressing fire.'

'Cover,' Flynn translated in a whisper.

'We won't need everyone to approach,' Tom said. 'Agent O'Day and I will enter the house.'

'What?' Flynn straightened. 'That's crazy. We had a hostage situation a couple years back with two perps in an old farmhouse. We went in with four officers and it still wasn't enough to keep our chief from getting shot.'

'Well, of course.' Marie O'Day gave him a knowing look. 'You're not trained FBI agents, are you?'

'Ma'am, I *am* trained for hostage situations, and I agree with the officer.' The senior tac man handed the briefing sheets back to Tom O'Day. 'There's no telling how many people might be in there and how hostile they are. If they're using meth as well as cooking it, you could be facing some extremely aggressive bad guys, not to mention chemical hazards.'

'We appreciate your professional judgment,' Tom O'Day said. 'But our goal is to retrieve Annie Johnson and, hopefully, her child, without appearing as if we know about the meth production going on in the barn. We'll be very happy if the meth cookers remain completely undisturbed.'

'Uh . . . I don't think my captain will be very happy with that,' the deputy said.

'Do you honestly think you can waltz up to the front door and ask for Annie Johnson as if you were sorting out some custody dispute?' Hadley shook her head. 'Whoever has her is on the hook for felony arson and a double homicide! Do you think they won't realize that?'

'I think you need to leave the strategy to us.' Marie O'Day's tone left no room for argument.

A rumble and clank announced the arrival of the snowplow. It stopped on the road next to their collection of squad cars and trucks. The driver pushed open his door and leaned out. 'You the folks needed to get up this road?'

'That's us.' The Essex County deputy shouted to be heard over the plow's heavy engine.

'Who the hell you goin' after up there? Osama bin Laden?'

'Just plow the road,' Tom O'Day yelled. He and Marie headed for their anonymous black SUV. Flynn jogged over and said something to the driver, who waved in agreement before shifting into gear and lurching forward. His huge steel plow lowered, and the snow and ice that had rendered the road impassable began to roll like water off a tanker's bow, piling up at the side of the road in a frozen tidal wave.

Hadley paused, one hand on the Aztek's door, waiting for Flynn. 'What did you say to him?'

'Asked him to keep going around the lake to where the chief's cabin is.' Flynn swung into his seat.

She climbed in and buckled up. 'What do you think of the Feds' plan?'

'I think it's balls.' He started the engine and looked at her, frowning. 'And I think we're going to have to be ready to move in right after them, because I think this whole thing is set to go south.'

349

NINE

'I think I should go after him.' Tented beneath her parka, Clare tucked her hands inside her sweater to stay warm. They had decided to conserve gas by turning the truck's engine off. She would turn it on again when it got cold enough to see her breath.

'He didn't say I *couldn't* shoot you in the leg,' Bob said.

'It's ridiculous. He's been gone way too long.'

'We haven't heard any alarm shots.'

'What if he wasn't able to fire? What if they got the jump on him?'

Bob laughed. 'Got the jump on him?'

'You know what I mean.' She slammed her boots against the floorboard and growled out her frustration. 'God! I hate this waiting.'

'You're a cop's wife now, Clare. Waiting is what you do.'

She smiled a little. 'Patience has never been my strong suit.' She twisted around to look at him. 'How are you doing? Are you warm enough?' She had folded all their blankets around Bob and layered the extra sweaters over him.

'I'm good. I may have to take this first aid box home with me, though.'

'I don't know if your doctor will approve of those magic pills.' She kept her voice light, but she was concerned. Not over Bob popping Oxys since they had first opened the box – it took longer than twenty-four hours to make an addict, even with a powerful narcotic – but over the damage his leg might be sustaining, masked by the powerful painkiller.

He nodded past her shoulder. 'Take a look.'

She spun around, and there, coming around the bend of the road, was Russ, and beside him—

'Oscar!' Clare leaped from the car, her parka forgotten on her seat.

'Oscar!' The dog bounded toward her and nearly bowled her over with his ecstatic greeting. Clare dropped to her knees and hugged him, ruffling his fur all over until she saw the streak of dried blood on his flank. She looked up at Russ.

'I think it was just a graze,' he said. 'He's moving fine, and he's not acting like he's in pain. He's probably pretty hungry and thirsty, though.' He reached down to help her stand.

'Are you all right? Did you find anything?'

He put his arm around her. 'Let's get in the car. I think Oscar and I both need to warm up some.'

They emptied the Oxys into Bob's coat pocket and poured the contents of one of the water bottles into the first aid box. Oscar drank it all, then most of a second bottle, before settling in the passenger-side well between Clare's legs to dine on the remaining pudding cups. Russ described the scene – the setback for cars, the stream, the wide, cleared fields, and the tightly closed barn.

'There's no way you're getting in there alone,' Bob said.

'That was my take.' Russ looked at Clare. 'I know you wanted to bring Mikayla out with us, Clare, but at this point, the best thing we can do is try to make it to civilization and find help.'

Clare knuckled the top of Oscar's head. The dog sighed and leaned against her leg. 'There has to be ten inches of snow on top of the ice the storm laid down. What if we just get stuck?'

'Then you and Bob will stay with the truck and I'll hike out. Once I get to the county highway, I'll flag down the first vehicle I see and hitch a ride.'

She looked out the window. 'It'll be dark in an hour or so. And the temperature's going to drop like a stone now the skies are clearing.'

'I know.'

Her lips twisted. 'Just once in a while, you could pretty it up for me.' She sighed. 'All right. I don't like it, but we can't sit here and do nothing.'

He took her hand. 'Good girl.' He shifted into gear and began a slow, careful back-and-forth, turning them around until they were pointed back toward the county highway, some twelve miles distant. Clare stroked Oscar's head and tried to settle into a prayer; that they would make it through the snow, that Russ wouldn't be forced to trek miles through the freezing dark, that they could find help for Mikayla Johnson before it was too late. Her eyes were half-closed, but they snapped open again when Russ said, 'The hell?'

They were almost at the intersection of Haines Mountain Road and the South Shore Drive, and there was a full-sized snowplow coming straight at them. It swerved, as if the driver hadn't expected to see anyone in his path, and behind the plow she caught a slice of a black SUV and a patrol car and—

'Clare,' Russ said, 'isn't that Kevin Flynn's Aztek?'

TEN

Ahead of them, the O'Days' SUV stopped and the brake lights lit on the deputy's Prowler. The plow veered to one side, then back, then angled toward what must be another road. Hadley looked down at the map. 'We're not supposed to turn off.'

Kevin feathered his brakes to alert the staties behind them. The SUV's doors swung open and the agents emerged, drawing their weapons. 'What?' Hadley twisted sideways, as if she could see past the plow by force of will. 'Is that them up ahead? Do you think Mikayla's with them?'

Kevin was already unbuckling. 'C'mon.' They jumped out of the Aztek and jogged forward, slipping and sliding in the frozen muck. The O'Days were shouting at the man advancing toward them, telling him to get on the ground, and as they swung their weapons into position the man emerged from the tree shadow into the waning light and it was the chief.

'Oh, shit!' Hadley tore off up the road. 'Stop! Put down your weapons! Put down your weapons!' The Essex County deputy had emerged from his car and was heading toward the Feds as well, his sidearm out.

'It's our chief!' Kevin bellowed as he ran by the deputy. The man stared at him. Hadley barreled right through the Feds – Kevin saw Marie O'Day jerk back with surprise – and skidded to a stop between them and the chief.

'Put your weapons *down*!' She pointed behind her. 'He's a *cop*!'

'Chief!' Kevin raced past Hadley to meet up with Van Alstyne. 'Are you okay?'

The chief looked bemused. 'I'm fine. Did someone hear our radio signal?'

'What? No, we thought you and Reverend Clare were snowbound. We're here after Travis Roy. We think he might be hiding—'

'In a meth house up the road from here? Yeah, I know.' He frowned at the Feds, who had holstered their weapons but were looking at him suspiciously. 'Why don't you introduce me to your friends?'

They walked over to the O'Days and the deputy. The state police tac guys caught up with them about halfway through the chief's account of a couple of days of pure horror show.

'—so we decided to scope out the place and see if it'd be possible to get in and get Mikayla out.' He paused to shake hands with the staties. 'We've got one of your officers back there in my truck. Bob Mongue. He has a broken leg.'

'Then who's that?' the senior tac officer asked.

The chief turned to see who was walking toward them. Kevin saw that flash of expression he always got around the reverend, like he was smiling inside where no one could see. 'Ah. That's my wife.'

Tom O'Day frowned. 'Is she . . . also law enforcement?' He sounded as if he wouldn't have been surprised if the chief marched the entire graduating class of the state police academy out of the woods.

'No. She's an Episcopal priest.'

Hadley hugged Reverend Clare when she joined the group. 'I'm so glad to see you,' she whispered. 'It sounds like you guys had a rough time.'

'That's one way to put it.' Clare raised her voice. 'Do y'all have an EMT with you? Lieutenant Mongue needs medical attention as soon as possible.'

'I'm sorry, no.' Marie O'Day looked at Van Alstyne. 'Our plan was to get in, get Travis Roy, and get whatever information he might have about the missing girl.'

'They're both there,' the chief said. 'Along with her father, Hector DeJean. DeJean's plan is evidently to get out of the country. He's just waiting for the weather to break.' He glanced up at the sky, where the clouds were parting. Long rays of orange and rose lit up the forest and the distant mountains.

'Tonight, then,' Kevin said.

'Most likely.' The chief returned his attention to the Feds. 'If we're going to surround the place, we'd better get into position soon. There's only a short time between twilight and moonrise.' He looked at the tac officers.

'Darkness is the only cover we're going to have over that ground. Somebody have a vest they can spare me?'

'I do, chief.' The deputy headed back to his unit.

Tom O'Day stepped forward. 'Maybe you'd better sit this one out, Chief Van Alstyne. As your officer said, you've had a rough few days. Surely you want to see your wife to a place of safety.'

The chief made a noise in the back of his throat. 'Oh, no. I have a personal bone to pick with Roy and DeJean.' He looked down at Reverend Clare. 'And my wife can take care of herself.'

She let a tiny smile escape before her expression sobered. 'I'll take Lieutenant Mongue to the hospital, then. Now the road is plowed, I shouldn't have any difficulties.'

'Go slow,' Kevin warned. 'Even plowed, the surfaces are still pretty treacherous.'

'I will. Thank you, Officer Flynn. Russ? A moment?'

They stepped aside to exchange a few words. Kevin couldn't help it – he glanced at Hadley. She was looking at him. He expected his face probably looked like the chief's did. Hadley dropped her gaze. Kevin tried to school his expression. If he didn't keep it under control, it wouldn't take more than forty-eight hours for the rest of the department to figure out what was going on.

The chief bent his head and kissed Reverend Clare goodbye. He rejoined their circle in time to accept the ballistics vest from the deputy. 'Nearest hospital is in Ticonderoga,' the deputy said. 'I'll give your wife directions.'

'Thank you.' The chief turned to the others. 'We can get fairly close to the spread before we have to ditch the vehicles. I can show you. Kevin, can I get a ride?'

In the Aztek, Hadley surrendered the front seat to the chief. As Kevin started the engine and pulled out in front of the Feds' SUV, she leaned forward. 'Chief? What did Reverend Clare say to you?'

He crooked half a smile. 'What I always say to my officers. "Don't be a hero".'

ELEVEN

The chief didn't think much of the Feds' plan of attack, either. He paused from checking the SIG Sauer the state police lieutenant had given him and looked at the O'Days. 'That's bullshit.'

Tom O'Day tugged his thermal watch cap over his ears. He and his wife were both kitted out in some sort of sleek performance-fabric version of assault gear. Hadley was jealous. Even in long johns and flannel-lined uniform pants, she was chilly.

'This is our operation, Chief Van Alstyne. Your officers are here as a courtesy, not as part of the tactical team.'

Flynn shot Hadley a look. She rolled her eyes.

'There are at least three men in that house. Maybe more. How are you going to keep from getting shot in the back?'

They were standing on the crest of the road, giving the state tac guys time to get into position before the rest of them took cover around the perimeter of the field. They had all synchronized their watches and said check, something Hadley had thought was reserved for the movies. They all had walkie-talkies, except the chief, but they were maintaining operational silence unless absolutely necessary. Sound traveled a long way on a winter night.

'Our way in is through DeJean.' Marie O'Day strapped her night-vision goggles into place over her watch cap. 'By your account, he's attempting to care for his daughter. We'll give him a way to get her out of the house safely and we'll offer her immediate medical care.'

'Travis Roy is the primary suspect in the arson-murder.' Tom checked the chambers in his pump-action riot gun. 'Once we have DeJean and, more importantly, the child, you and the sheriff's office' – he nodded toward the deputy – 'can close in and arrest him.'

'Roy's and DeJean's needs no longer align. We exploit that. Divide and conquer.' Marie looked at her watch. 'It's time.'

Her husband nodded. They took off down the steep road, the large letters FBI on their backs almost glowing in the deep blue twilight.

'Feds.' The chief shook his head. 'There are so many ways this thing can go bad, I don't even want to think about it.' He dropped the SIG P226 in his pocket and hefted his shotgun. 'Our default is going to be front' – he pointed to himself and the deputy – 'and back.' He pointed to Hadley and Flynn. 'There was at least one person in the barn, and there may well be more, but the entrance is a pretty effective bottleneck. Just don't any of you let youself get picked off by the staties, okay?'

The deputy grinned. 'They can try.'

They headed down the road in a pack, slipping and skidding until they reached the stream the chief had told them about. 'Flares?' he whispered.

They were carrying road flares from the deputy's unit. Hadley and Flynn gave the thumbs-up. 'Got it,' whispered the deputy.

'Mine is the signal. I don't care what you hear coming from the house, you don't go until you see me. Understood?' They all nodded.

'Chief? Are you sure you don't want my walkie-talkie?' Flynn held it out.

'No. You're moving around. I'm going to be in a static position until we advance.' He looked at them. 'Don't just rely on the walkie-talkies. You get into trouble, you light your flare.' They nodded again. 'Okay. Let's go.'

Van Alstyne and the deputy had the unenviable job of belly-crawling along the edge of the road in front of the house. Hadley had to admit, the O'Days had gotten their timing down right. In the indigo end of the day, the two men merged into the gloom and disappeared.

She and Flynn headed up the stream, a much easier route to get into position. Flynn had to bend over, but she was short enough to walk upright. The chief had described the spot with the fallen pine as the perfect vantage point, and it was. She switched off her walkie-talkie so it couldn't cause feedback and harnessed it. They wedged themselves against the near bank and looked over the edge. Across the field, the house's many-paned windows shone with the light from kerosene lanterns, and the snow enclosing it, lit in geometric patterns, cast enough of a glow to let them make out the details of porch, corners, barn.

'Looks like a Currier and Ives picture,' Flynn said, his voice low.

'Grandmother's Meth House.'

Over the river and through the woods, he hummed. She pressed her face into her shoulder to keep from laughing.

He made a noise to direct her attention. The O'Days had emerged from the darkness and were approaching the back porch. Hadley drew her Glock and swept away enough of the snow in front of her to brace her arms and take aim.

The Feds entered the back of the house without a sound. Hadley found herself holding her breath, straining to hear a shout, a scream, or, God forbid, gunfire. There was nothing. The deep winter silence of a cold night pressed down on them unbroken. The minutes crawled by. The chill was stinging her cheeks and forehead, seeping through her pants and parka into her bones. She flexed her toes and tensed her muscles, but she was afraid to move any more than that, balanced as she was against the slippery slope of the bank.

'What the hell's going on in there?' Flynn hissed, and at the same moment, the back door opened. One, two, three people came out, one of them carrying a large bundle. In silhouette, it looked like the O'Days and DeJean, but she couldn't be sure. Unlike the Feds and the state tac duo, MKPD officers weren't issued night-vision glasses.

DeJean was a big man, but the two agents were tall, too, and these three, side by side, gave her no measuring point. They crossed the side yard and continued toward the road. As they walked past the front corner of the house, the ambient lantern light and the angle of their backs met and the letters FBI blazed out at her.

'It's them,' she whispered. Beneath a knit cap, she could make out a bit of DeJean's shaved bald skull. The edge of a quilt, wrapped around the bundle in his arms, flopped over his burly shoulder.

'Easy to recognize,' Flynn agreed. 'Once you've met Hector DeJean, you're not likely to forget him.'

It came to her, just like that, the thing she had heard an hour or two ago and dismissed. 'Flynn. Remember what Tom O'Day said when we were passing around the briefing sheets? He told the staties DeJean didn't look like his mug shot anymore because he was bald.'

'Yeah, sure.'

'That was the most recent mug shot on record. There aren't any new pictures of him in VICAP.' The massive New York database of criminal offenders.

'Yeah . . .'

She looked at him. 'If there aren't any current photos of DeJean on file, how did Tom O'Day know he was bald?'

TWELVE

Lyle was standing in the parking lot of Napoli's Liquor, cuffing a perp, when Harlene called him. It had been as crazy a day as the past two, despite the snow easing up. The volunteer fire company was run ragged with overburdened chimneys bursting into flame and kerosene heaters igniting. Folks stuck in their houses for the past three days decided the break in the weather was just the time to stock back up on water and milk, with a corresponding rise in fender benders as they slid into each other on the way to the store. And a few geniuses, like the guy Lyle was steering into the backseat, realized the massive power outages meant a lot of security systems weren't working. He probably would have gotten away with cleaning out Napoli's till and carting off a trunkful of booze if he hadn't decided to load up on coffee brandy while on the job.

Lyle slid into the driver's seat and picked up the mic. 'Dispatch, this is fifteen-thirty, come back.'

'Fifteen-thirty, message from fifteen-twenty-five, over.' Usually, Harlene would have just patched Eric through, but there wasn't enough bandwidth to manage car-to-car right now.

'Dispatch, go ahead, over.'

'Officer has custody of Wendall Sullivan, wanted for questioning on ten-fifty, over.'

Lyle's eyebrows shot up. 'How'd he manage that? Over.'

Even through the staticky connection, he could hear Harlene's smirk. 'Auto accident. What else?'

Wendall Sullivan looked like he'd been dragged through the bushes backward since Lyle had seen him last. He sat slumped over in the interrogation room, his clothes filthy, his hair greasy.

'Jesus.' Lyle turned away from the window. 'Where's he been hiding? The town dump?'

'Close. I thought we might have squatters back in those condemned buildings on Beale Avenue when I saw him.' Eric handed Lyle the accident paperwork. 'He was at the incineration plant outside Glens Falls. Warm, and nobody around.'

'If you can stand the smell. Has he lawyered up?'

'Not yet.'

Lyle looked in the window again. He could almost see the waves rolling off Sullivan. 'You sure you don't want to handle his questioning?'

Eric slapped Lyle on the shoulder. 'Oh, no. He's all yours, Dep.'

'I do not get paid enough for this job.' Lyle opened the door and was assaulted by the scent of decaying garbage. He waved it away as he sat opposite Sullivan. 'Wendall. Long time no see.'

Sullivan looked up at him. 'Can I get something to eat? I'm starving.'

'We've got a meal coming in for you from the diner. You're going to have to wait until you're at the county lockup for a shower, though.'

Sullivan sniffed at himself. 'Is it bad? I kind of got used to the smell.'

'The ability of the human brain to adjust to things is a marvel, that's a fact. For instance, you adjusting to being back in prison.'

'I didn't touch that girl! I didn't do nothing to her!'

Lyle decided to skip over the storage-locker porn nest for the time being. 'Here's what we're gonna do, Wendall. You tell me everything you know about what happened to Mikayla Johnson. And I'll personally testify as to your assistance and cooperation at your sentencing hearing.'

Sullivan spread his hands against the surface of the table. 'I swear, I wasn't looking for her or nothing. I talked with her some, on the job, that's all. It was when I found out her name that I realized she was somebody. I had heard it before, I mean. This guy I owed a few favors to, he'd put it out wanting to know where this girl was. There was gonna be money for anyone who knew anything. So I got in touch with him.'

'Jonathan Davies.'

Sullivan's eyes went wide. 'You know about him?'

'Yeah. Did you tell anyone else about Mikayla?'

'Jonathan, he sent me to this other guy. His name was Roy something. I told him what I knew, and that was it. I went home and I never saw him or the girl again. I just wanted some extra cash.'

'And you owed Davies a favor. Do you know who he works for?'

Sullivan nodded. 'Yeah. But I don't get into any of that stuff. Davies found a guy inside to keep me safe when this crew from downstate wouldn't leave me alone. That's all.'

Lyle ran over the timeline in his head. Mikayla was released to the MacAllens' custody in September. 'When did you start working for Maid for You?'

'Huh? September. Why? I swear, I been keeping clean. I hardly ever even talk to kids if I see them on the job.'

Something that had been percolating in the back of his mind since Saturday finally bubbled up. The crew leader of the cleaning team. *We're fully bonded, but, you know.* 'Wendall, how did you get past the criminal background check for the job?'

'It wasn't nothing illegal. It was the Feds who arrested me back when I was a teenager. They kinda took an interest in me after I got out, I guess. They told me I oughta apply for the job. Said they'd make sure my record showed up clean.'

Lyle sat very still. 'Who were these Feds?'

Wendall shook his head. 'I'm not supposed to say. They cut me a break. Not many people'll do that for . . . someone on the list.'

Lyle leaned forward. 'Wendall.' He kept his voice steady. 'Who are the federal agents who told you to apply for the job at Maid for You?'

Sullivan flopped his hands. 'Whatever. You can get it from my old arrest record sooner or later, right? They were a married couple. Tom and Marie O'Day.'

THIRTEEN

Clare had been driving forty minutes when the call came through on Russ's radio. Despite the roads, which were, as Kevin Flynn had promised, treacherous, it was a pleasant enough trip. Oscar was curled up in the passenger seat, filling it to overflowing, while Bob had actually nodded off in the back.

The real reason for her peace of mind was the fact she was finally doing something useful. And unlike earlier, when taking Bob to the hospital would have meant abandoning Mikayla, she had confidence that the law enforcement professionals would be able to shut down the meth house and get the girl out safely.

Once she had Bob seen to, she was going to get an ambulance and EMTs and head back up to Inverary Lake. She might meet Russ with Mikayla on the way, but she couldn't help but think that minutes counted at this point.

'Chief Van Alstyne, Millers Kill Police, this is State Police Dispatch Troop G, come in. Chief Van Alstyne, Millers Kill Police, this is State Police Dispatch Troop G, come in.'

The voice was shocking after the long radio silence. Clare almost shimmied across the yellow line. She corrected with a jerk and grabbed the mic. 'State Police Dispatch Troop G, this is Chief Van Alstyne's, uh, vehicle. Over.'

There was a pause. 'Who is this?'

'I'm his wife. He's, um—'

'Tell them he's responding to a possible hostage situation near Inverary Lake,' Bob said. 'Tell them he's out of radio contact.'

Clare repeated the message.

There was another pause. 'Please hold for further information.'

Clare laid the mic in her lap so she could keep both hands on the wheel. 'What do you think they want with Russ?'

'Dunno. Where are we?'

She glanced at the odometer. 'About halfway to Ticonderoga. The Essex County deputy said it was usually a forty-minute trip, but I'm afraid in this weather . . .'

'Not to worry. I've got my happy pills. Take all the time you need.'

The radio squawked to life again. 'Mrs Van Alstyne, the deputy chief of the MKPD wants to speak with you. I'm patching him through.'

A moment later, she heard a rough voice, so small and far away it could have been broadcasting from the moon. 'Reverend?'

'Lyle? What is it?'

'Where are you?'

'On Route 8, heading from Inverary to Ticonderoga. I'm taking Lieutenant Mongue to the hospital.'

'What? Oh, Christ, was he shot?'

'I didn't know he cared,' Bob murmured from the backseat.

Clare keyed the mic again. 'He has a broken leg. Lyle, what is this about?'

'Did Russ meet up with Knox and Flynn?'

'Yes. And a couple of federal agents and a deputy. I told the Troop G dispatcher—'

The radio squealed as Lyle overrode her signal. 'Those federal agents are dirty. They arranged for Mikayla Johnson's kidnapping.'

'What?' She was so surprised she forgot to key the mic.

Lyle went on. 'I need you to turn around, Clare, right now, and get to Russ and warn him.'

'Are you sure?' Oh, *that* was a smart question.

'I'm sure every witness against Tim LaMar has either died or won't talk. I'm sure the O'Days have been working on the LaMar case for years. I'm sure they put an informant in the MacAllens' house to cover their tracks. I *believe* they're on LaMar's payroll.'

'Grease.' Bob sounded disgusted.

Clare let the mic dangle. 'That's what Travis said in the garage, when he was getting into their car. He said something about the grease keeping him clean. I didn't know – honestly, I thought he was talking about something mechanical.'

'Grease is a dirty cop who fixes things for a mobster. Greases the skids.'

'Clare? Have I lost you?'

She had left Lyle hanging. She picked up the mic again. 'Just a second, Lyle.' She glanced in the rearview mirror. 'Bob, I can't take you to the hospital and warn the rest of them in time. Do you—'

'Turn around,' he said. 'Another couple hours isn't going to make a difference with my leg. If MacAuley's right, those agents aren't just trying to clean up this LaMar guy's messes. They'll have to protect themselves now.'

'But – surely they wouldn't harm fellow law enforcement. Would they?'

'If Russ or his people make the connection, it means disgrace and ruin and the rest of their lives in federal custody in Otisville. I wouldn't gamble on what they'd be willing to do to prevent that.'

She keyed the mic. 'Lyle, I'm turning around. Please send help if you can.'

'I'm working on it. Good luck. MacAuley out.'

FOURTEEN

When Russ saw the Feds walk past the side of the house with Hector DeJean, he thought, *Son of a gun. They did it.* He was frankly amazed. He'd done his share of negotiations, but he'd never just waltzed into a hostage situation and come out with the perp tied up in a big bow. They must have been right about the medical angle. DeJean must have figured it was better to see his kid to safety than risk her life in a standoff.

DeJean was carrying Mikayla, wrapped up in a quilt, which meant the O'Days hadn't restrained him yet. He frowned. Better to have cuffed DeJean and had one of the agents carry the child. Of course, that meant they had to stick together; one to hold the girl and the other to be ready in case DeJean got violent. And the plan, once they reached the bridge, was for Marie O'Day to come to his position and brief him on what they saw in the house. The plan, he was realizing, wasn't well thought out. He should have taken Kevin's walkie-talkie when offered. In his defense, he had expected to be storming the house in order to rescue the Feds by now.

He was going to have to go back up the road and meet them instead. He wondered if the emerging stars gave enough light for anyone to spot him from the house. He couldn't see where the Feds were, but he knew his night vision wasn't what it used to be. Better not to chance that one of the meth brewers had younger, more light-sensitive eyes. He shifted out of the snow hollow he had dug for himself and began combat-crawling toward the bridge.

The first hint of something going wrong was when Marie O'Day failed to intercept him. With the benefit of infrared goggles, she ought to have seen him coming up the edge of the road. Stretched out against the ice and snow, his heat signature would look like a blowtorch. He didn't expect to run into her right off the bat; allowing both agents to stick close to DeJean was the point, after all. But he was well over halfway between his surveillance position and the bridge, and he had heard nothing from either agent. His opinion of the pair was going down quicker than the temperature.

He was almost to the bridge itself when he heard a whispered 'Chief! Is that you?'

'Kevin? Where are you?'

'Down in the stream bed.'

Russ hit the corner of the tiny bridge and let himself roll over the side to slide down the bank. He landed on his ass with an audible thud. Hands reached to help him up. 'Knox?'

'Here, Chief.'

He stood up. He could see his two officers well enough, which meant he should have been able to see the federal agents and DeJean. If they had been somewhere around where they were supposed to be.

'Where the hell are the Feds? Have they contacted you?' Like them, he kept his voice low.

'We have a problem,' Kevin said. 'Hadley, tell him.'

'When we briefed earlier this afternoon, Agent O'Day made a comment about Hector DeJean's mug shot. He told the tac guys it was an old picture, that DeJean is bald now.'

'Go on.'

'Chief, I can't think of any way he'd know that. DeJean hasn't been arrested since he got out of jail three years ago. He's got no known connection to LaMar. When could O'Day have seen him?'

'Visiting the Johnsons? Or maybe the MacAllens?'

'The O'Days never had any direct contact with Mikayla,' Kevin said. 'And believe me, the Johnsons wouldn't have had a picture of Hector DeJean around.'

'Well? I take it you two have a theory?'

'I think O'Day knew what DeJean looked like because the two have met. Recently.'

'When we found out about the connection between the Johnsons and the

LaMar case, we thought Mikayla had been taken to pressure Mr Johnson.' Knox blew into her gloves. 'What if we were right?'

'Think about it, Chief. You're a bad guy who wants to keep Johnson from testifying—'

'I'd have him capped. Plain and simple. This isn't a game of Clue, guys.'

'Testifying against *you*,' Kevin went on. 'You want him to stand up in court and say yes, he was there, and he saw someone else hit those two drug dealers.'

'Mr Johnson wouldn't budge if anyone threatened his daughter,' Hadley said. 'I think he's pretty much given up on her. But he loves Mikayla. If LaMar has Mikayla, he can call the shots, as long as she stays alive.'

Kevin stamped his feet. 'That's where DeJean comes in. Mikayla has a complicated schedule of medication she needs to take. The average meth head or muscle LaMar could call on wouldn't be able to keep her alive past a week. But her father was motivated.'

'He and his wife had already taken a course in how to care for a post-transplant child,' Knox said.

'We think' – Kevin looked to Knox, who nodded – 'the plan was for DeJean to snatch his daughter, lay low for a couple days, then get out of the area with the help of LaMar's pet agents.'

'Let me get this straight.' Russ stripped off his glove and rubbed the feeling back into his face. 'You're accusing two veteran FBI agents of conspiracy in kidnapping, arson, and murder? Based on the fact that one of them knew Hector DeJean is bald?'

'Vince Patten had it right,' Kevin said. 'The Albany detective who worked with us. He told us the O'Days had been there forever. They weren't ever going to rise further in the ranks. Maybe they got tired of chasing bad guys who always got away. Maybe they decided they deserved a cut of the pie, too.'

'Kevin—' the Chief began.

'Where are they right now? Did they brief you on the situation inside?' Before Kevin could stop her, Knox had switched on her flashlight. She played it over the surface of the bridge, the bottom of the road, the trees crowding in on either side. There was no one there.

'They could have decided to secure DeJean and the girl in their vehicle and then come back.'

'Without notifying any of us? How did they just walk in and take DeJean without raising any sort of alarm? If Mikayla is the key to putting away LaMar, how come there are only six of us here?' Knox switched off the light and turned toward him. In the renewed darkness, her face was a pale oval. 'Chief, you always tell us to trust our instincts. Would you, unarmed, get into their car right now?'

He weighed his answer a long moment. 'No.'

FIFTEEN

Clare would have kept going right past the spot where she and Lieutenant Mongue had waited that afternoon if Bob hadn't prevented her. 'If there really is trouble, driving into the middle of it and then leaping out of the truck is a good way to get yourself killed.'

'You're right.' She downshifted and let the pickup roll to the side of the road. In the darkness, the headlights tunneling through the woods made her feel claustrophobic. 'I just keep thinking about how absolutely cops trust each other. And how vulnerable they all are if that trust is betrayed.'

'Park the truck crossways, straddling the road.'

She twisted around in her seat.

'There's only one cleared way out of here, right? I may not be good for much right now, but I can be the last line of defense.'

'Bob, if they rammed you, you could be seriously hurt.'

He waved a hand. 'Not as hurt as Russ would be if his truck gets wrecked.' He dug the Taurus she had taken from Travis Roy out of the duffel bag. He held it out to her, grip first. 'Take this.'

She shook her head. 'I won't use it.'

He raised an eyebrow. 'I thought Russ said you were in the army.'

'National Guard. I had my fill and then some in Iraq. I'm done with guns. I'm switching over to the chaplaincy corps. If they let me,' she added to be honest.

'Huh. You're just a bundle of contradictions, aren't you, Reverend.'

'Aren't we all.'

As he asked, she used the truck to barricade the road. She left it running, lights on, to give fair warning to anyone coming over the hill above. She took Russ's Maglite, the warmest hat, and Oscar.

370

'The dog?' Bob asked.

'I said I wouldn't use a gun. I didn't say I'd forgo protection.' She ruffled Oscar's fur. 'Usually, I'm the one who gets asked this, but—'

'I'll pray for you.' He grinned. 'Probably better this way. Everyone knows Catholics' prayers count more.'

Clare was still smiling when she closed the door.

She held the Maglite in front of her until she made the first rise. She didn't see any vehicles at the side of the road up ahead, but she couldn't recall what Russ had said about the distance, and she didn't want to stumble across the FBI agents lit up like a circus. She shoved the flashlight up her sleeve, letting the lens rest against her gloved fingers. It gave a subdued glow, enough so she wouldn't trip over her own feet, but not so much as to draw unwanted attention.

Just as he had when he traveled across the ice with her and Russ, Oscar stuck close and stayed quiet. She reached a second hill and still couldn't see the squad cars and SUVs they had met this afternoon. At the third crest, she turned off the Maglite. She stood a few moments, letting her eyes adjust until the blackness around her lightened into shades of gray: pale snow, ashen trees, charcoal forest. Stars burned hot in the narrow sky between the pines. Oscar nudged her leg, and they went forward again, a little more slowly.

Her hearing sharpened in the dark; she could make out the creak and snap of branches, the shiver of pine needles, the far-off tu-whut of an owl, hunting early after so many nights of frozen rain. And, fainter than the owl, a voice.

No, two voices. The road curved ahead, but she saw no light or movement, so she kept to the open. The road wasn't in good shape – frozen over, then churned by the vehicles that had followed Russ up here – but it offered faster travel than the deep snow between the trees would. When she reached the curve, she left the path, sinking into knee-deep snow. Oscar wanted to stay where it was easy to walk, and it took her two attempts before he joined her. She scratched his head in lieu of spoken praise.

The noise of an engine starting. She waded between birch and hemlock, keeping the road in sight. She could see something now. The glow of headlights, facing away from her, shining brilliantly against Kevin Flynn's yellow Aztek. The voices continued, less audibly. A man and a woman. Clare pushed forward, needing to identify the speakers, thinking she was going to feel a complete idiot if she was sneaking up snow-ninja-style on Kevin and Hadley Knox.

Suddenly, the voices were louder. The people talking were walking away from a black SUV, its engine running, toward the Essex County squad car parked a few lengths behind it. Clare froze in place behind a burly maple, her hand clutched in Oscar's coat to keep him still.

'—handle Roy,' the male voice was saying. 'I've eaten dinners that were smarter than he is. We can keep him quiet until he's locked up. Then he can have an accident.'

'Fine. Fine.' The woman sounded agitated. 'But what about Johnson? What's going to prevent him from testifying once the girl is dead?'

Mikayla.

'LaMar's going to have to take care of that.'

'Goddammit! I hate this!' Even angry, the woman kept her voice down. 'Nobody was supposed to get hurt, Tom. That was the whole point. That we could take care of it better.'

'No, the point was to keep LaMar from getting convicted. We can still accomplish that.'

'Over a pile of bodies!'

'Do you want to march back down and surrender to the locals? We'll spend the rest of our very short lives behind bars before "accidentally" getting shivved in the laundry.'

'No, of course not.'

'Then screw your courage to the sticking point, my dear. Hector DeJean, at least, won't be a loss to anyone.'

Clare couldn't hear it, but she could imagine the woman's defeated sigh. 'All right. Let's do it.'

Oh, dear Lord, no.

They walked back toward the SUV. Clare followed, struggling through the snow, trying to keep up without being seen or heard.

She couldn't see the passenger side of the vehicle from where she was wallowing in the drifts, but she could hear the clunk as the door opened. The interior light sprang on, and she caught a glimpse of DeJean's head.

'It's time for your escape, Hector.' The man stepped back as DeJean got out of the SUV. She could see him clearly in the wash from the headlights now, the tall FBI agent. *You called it, Lyle.*

'I gave her the shots, but I can't get the pills into her.' Hector's voice was a mixture of anger and fright. 'She won't swallow. She's sick. She's really sick.'

'Give it some time. We brought enough in the bag to treat her for a month.' The female agent sounded soothing.

'It won't matter if she can't take it. How am I gonna get her professional help? If I show up in an emergency room I'll get arrested.'

'Pick up your daughter and get into your truck, Hector.' The man's impatience was showing.

Don't do it, Hector! Clare squeezed Oscar's fur more tightly. Maybe if DeJean kept talking, there'd be time for one of the MKPD officers to get here.

'We'll find the name and address of a doctor who will help you,' the male agent went on. 'We'll put it in the e-mail drop box.'

'How soon?'

'Soon,' the man snapped. 'But first you have to escape.'

'Okay, okay, goddammit. How is this gonna work? Do I gotta hit one of you?'

'We're going to give you a few minutes' head start. Then I'm going to fire my gun, and then we're getting into our car to "chase" you. When we return to meet up with the rest of the group here, we'll report you went south, headed for Albany.'

'Okay. Sure. Fine.' The interior lights sprang on again, and Hector ducked. Clare could see him lifting a quilt-wrapped Mikayla and a small satchel. He shouldered his daughter and shut the door. He took a step toward the other side of the road.

Clare plunged across the few yards between her and the road, shaking branches and smashing ice as she ran. She burst out of the cover. 'They're going to shoot you and Mikayla!' she yelled.

The male agent spun toward her, his gun out. She ducked behind the SUV at the same moment the report from his weapon sounded. Oscar began barking furiously. She heard a second shot fired and had time for the thought *Mikayla* before DeJean crashed into the snow beside her. Mikayla let out a weak cry of alarm.

Clare grabbed the back of his coat and dragged them up. 'We're okay,' he gasped.

'Who the hell was that?' the male agent demanded.

'I didn't see!' the woman yelled. 'Come *on*.'

'Into the trees,' Clare said. She pushed DeJean to go first. They broke cover and ran in the path created by Clare's bootprints. Another shot thudded into a birch, showering Clare in ice. It echoed, and then she heard another, more distant report. 'Go,' she breathed, 'go, go!'

'Daddy, don't grab so hard. It hurts.'

'Get the goggles and turn off those damn lights.' The man was in professional mode now, barking out orders.

DeJean pressed deeper and deeper into the woods, breaking fresh trail. Clare, following, grabbed at him. 'Goggles?'

'Night vision,' he gasped.

'Stop!' He plunged on, heedless. 'Hector, stop! Think!' He paused and turned, panting. 'We can't outrun infrared vision. It picks up body heat, yours, mine' – she looked down at Oscar, quivering beside her – 'the dog's. We have to hide. Dig into the snow behind a big tree.'

'They'll find us!' Mikayla wiggled and pushed against her wrapping. DeJean cradled her head with one hand. 'Quiet, baby. Be still.'

'Russ will have heard the shots. He's on his way right now.' *Please, God, let that be true.*

Hector thrust Mikayla at her. Startled, she grabbed the quilt-wrapped girl. 'I got a better idea.' He squatted in front of Oscar. 'Hey, good dog.' Oscar let DeJean hoist him up without complaint.

'Wait, what—'

'Keep her safe till your man gets here.' He kissed the side of Mikayla's head. 'Love you, baby.' He bounded off, Oscar in his arms.

Clare stood there, stunned, until the distant slam of a car door. Ambient light she hadn't noticed disappeared. *Behind a tree*, she thought. *In the snow.* There was a gnarled, thick-trunked oak a couple of yards ahead. She walked in a straight line, praying that the pine she had been sheltering against would keep her out of the agents' line of sight. She sidled around the oak and dropped to the ground, leaning Mikayla against the base of the trunk. The girl whimpered a complaint. 'I know, honey.' Clare cracked the ice crust and scooped out armful after armful of snow. 'Just for a moment.' She dug until she had a long trench just wide enough for – *a coffin* – her body.

She stripped off her parka, hoisted Mikayla and stretched out, her back to the frozen ground, the quilt-wrapped girl atop her. 'We're going to play a hiding game,' she whispered. Clare flung her parka over the two of them, tugged part of the quilt over her face, then reached out from beneath her coat and awkwardly tossed as much of the piled snow as she could over them. She kicked her feet, dislodging more snow on top of her boots and shins.

Mikayla made a noise of protest. 'Shh,' Clare whispered. 'Shh. Just rest on me.' She couldn't stroke the girl's back for fear of knocking the snow off them, so she settled for kissing her hot forehead. They made an ungainly mound of woman, baby, and girl, but shielded by a heavily insulated coat and partially covered with snow, she figured their heat signature was dampened enough to be invisible unless the agents were practically on top of her. Of course, if they did get that close, she and Mikayla were defenseless.

Russ, she thought. *Remember how I said I didn't need you to rescue me? Well, I do now.*

SIXTEEN

At the sound of gunshots, they all swung their heads toward the single-lane bridge ahead, where they had last seen the O'Days headed up the hill. Like pointers sighting a bird, they remained transfixed. 'Damn,' the chief said under his breath. 'Let's go.'

Kevin's walkie-talkie switched on. 'Tac Team One to Team. Anybody know what that was?'

He answered. 'Millers Kill One to Team. Shots fired up the hill where we parked.' He opened his mouth, but the chief shook his head no. 'We're going to check it out.'

The chief put his hand out. Kevin surrendered the walkie-talkie. 'Chief Van Alstyne here. I want everyone to maintain position until you hear otherwise.' He handed the unit back. It emitted clicks of acknowledgment as Kevin holstered it.

The chief clambered up the bank with Hadley behind him and Kevin, as usual, bringing up the rear.

'Okay,' he said when they were standing on the road. 'This is what—'

'Tac Team One to Team. We have movement. One suspect, two, no, three suspects exiting the rear of the house. Suspects are headed for the barn.'

They all swung again, this time toward the barn. *Not pointers*, Kevin thought. *Weather vanes.* He could see what looked like shadows moving toward the narrow barn door.

'Suspects are armed. Millers Kill chief, please advise.'

Van Alstyne grabbed the walkie-talkie. 'Maintain position.'

From above the hill line, another shot rang out. Immediately, the crack of a tactical rifle answered. The shadows separated, sped up, flattened against the barn.

'Goddammit, I said maintain position. That shot came from up the hill, not from the house.' The chief glanced up toward where the Feds had presumably disappeared.

'Go on, Chief.' Hadley pushed him. 'We can keep a lid on things here.'

'You're right. Kevin, mind if I take this?' He held up the walkie-talkie.

'No, Chief.'

'I'm going to see what the hell is going on with those two. Be ready to move when I call you. I may need backup.' He gestured with his chin toward the barn. 'They've got no place to escape to. We can pick our time to round 'em up.' He turned and jogged away, headed up the steep road.

'That sounds exactly like something someone says in a movie before disaster strikes.' Hadley unharnessed her walkie-talkie and turned it back on. 'Should we get closer to the barn?'

Kevin shook his head. 'We stay right here. If the chief needs us, we don't want to lose any time.' He squinted. The shadows were moving. Then there was a crack of light, and one-two-three figures slipped into the barn. He could hear the door slam shut from where he stood.

Hadley toggled the walkie-talkie. 'Millers Kill Two to Tac Team. Can you confirm suspects have entered the barn?'

'That's a confirmation, Millers Kill Two. We should just board the place up and call it a night.'

Hadley let out a huff of amusement. She looked up to where Van Alstyne had disappeared, then at Kevin. In the dim light, he could see her nose and cheeks were red. 'I don't like the chief going after them all by himself.'

'Neither do I.' He chafed his arms and stamped his boots. 'But he knows the situation down here if he's got the walkie-talkie on. He'll tell us when he wants us to move.'

'Also? I'm freezing.'

He laughed softly. 'Not the ideal first date, huh?'

She slapped her holster. 'I don't usually go out with guys carrying and dressed in tactical gear.'

Somehow, he was a lot closer to her face than he had been. 'I know this great way to keep warm.'

She laughed. 'Oh, like I haven't heard that one before.' Still, she tilted her head back. 'What about keeping it cool on the job?'

'It's dark. And we're all alone. Just you, me, and a barn full of meth manufacturers.'

'So romantic.' She was laughing softly as his lips closed over hers. They couldn't really get close, not in vests and parkas, and they couldn't let their attention stray too far, but it was so sweet to be here with her like this, her mouth yielding to his, a hum of approval in the back of her throat. Sweeter, maybe, because it couldn't be about sex or arousal. It was simply affection.

Her walkie-talkie cracked on. 'Tac Team One to Millers Kill officers. You know we have night scopes, guys. Keep it clean.'

'Oh my God!' Hadley jerked away from him, her glove slapped over her mouth.

Kevin laughed. Then the wide barn doors rumbled open, light spilling across the snow, and there was a deep-pitched roar, and three snowmobiles burst out of the building.

SEVENTEEN

It was a good thing Clare wasn't claustrophobic. She lay still, her arms around Mikayla, packed in with snow, listening to the hoarse rasp of the girl's breathing. She wondered if the child was dying, if DeJean had gotten away, if the voices she heard – far away, like a radio playing in another house – were getting closer.

Her jeans and wool sweater were no proof against the frozen ground, and her entire back was aching with cold. That would be good. Lowering her body temperature would make it that much harder for them to see her. Until she got too cold. *They call hypothermia the happy death*, 'Hardball' Wright, her SERE instructor, said. She didn't feel very happy.

A gun cracked, so close she flinched, which set her to shivering. She tried to relax her muscles, but her body wanted to warm up, and she began to shake uncontrollably. Another shot, and then they were shouting something and she heard the high-pitched yelp of a dog in pain. 'Oscar.' Mikayla's voice was a bare wisp. 'Daddy.'

Oh, God. Hector. Clare squeezed her eyes shut.

She could picture the scene: the flare in their goggles, a man carrying a warm, living bundle. Shooting them down, then hurrying over to the bodies. They'd have to put a gun in Hector's hand to justify their shooting. And then discovering Oscar, instead of the girl.

More yelling. No words, just shrieks of rage and frustration. *God, protect us*, she prayed. She thought, for a moment, about leaving Mikayla under the snow, wrapped in her coat and the quilt. She could draw their pursuers away. But if she was killed – her shivering intensified – Mikayla could die of exposure before she was found. She felt a feather-light kick inside her, then another. Mikayla wasn't the only child she had to protect.

Then she heard him, a loud, commanding bellow that sent hope surging through her, as good as a blast of heat against the cold. *Russ.*

Then nothing. She strained to hear. Should she dig herself out? What if the agents were still in the woods? They could easily bring her down before she reached the road. Excuse it as another 'accident'. Were they hiding from Russ? Talking with him? The chill rushed back into her veins. He didn't know what they were. What if they persuaded him DeJean had escaped? All they would have to do would be to get him into the woods in pursuit of DeJean. It would be easy, then, to silence Russ permanently. The gun with Hector's fingerprints would be the one that killed him. No doubt.

She pushed herself out of her hiding place and lurched to her feet. 'Hang on, sweetheart.' She slung Mikayla over her shoulder in a fireman's carry, her parka draped over the girl for extra warmth. The girl grunted in protest. Clare saw a movement, and heard the sound of breaking ice, and turned, terrified that she had just killed them all, and nearly fell down when Oscar thudded into her legs, whining and shaking and very much alive.

'It's Oscar,' she whispered. 'He's okay.'

Mikayla's voice was thin and sleepy. 'Where's Daddy?'

I'm very afraid your father is dead, she wanted to say. *Dead because he drew the killers away from us.* DeJean had been a monster, but his last act had saved her life, and Mikayla's, and her unborn child's.

She took off for the road, the dog by her side. Wading through the deep snow was like moving in a nightmare, sweating, straining, never getting anywhere, until she suddenly realized she could see the glow of headlights again. She still heard nothing except her own rough breath and the crunch of snow and the creak of the forest. Were the agents standing on the road, telling Russ lies? Or were they in among the trees somewhere? Would shouting out save her? Or get her shot?

She took a deep breath. Then another. 'Russ!' She shouted loud enough to hear her own voice echoing back to her. 'I have Mikayla! Don't trust them!'

Still nothing. She staggered forward, panting beneath the weight, closer to the light, closer, until she could see his head, above the black SUV. His hands were over his hat, his fingers laced together. *Too late.*

'Keep going, Mrs Van Alstyne.' The voice came from close beside her. The man was standing in the snow a few yards away, his automatic trained on Clare. She almost turned to flee into the forest, but what was the use? She waded through the last few feet of deep snow and stumbled onto the road next to the SUV.

Russ kept his eyes locked on hers. 'Clare. Oh, love. What are you *doing* back here?' He started to turn toward her, only to be brought up short by the gun pointed toward his head. Marie O'Day stood out of reach, but close enough so that a shot to Russ's skull couldn't miss. Clare wondered, absurdly, how many more times she was going to see her husband held at gunpoint on their honeymoon. She was still shaking, and a more sober part of her brain diagnosed *shock.*

'Stay right there,' Tom O'Day said. Clare, who had been walking toward Russ, stopped. 'We just want the girl.'

'And then what?' Russ said. 'You kill us, too? And then kill my officers and the sheriff's deputy who're coming up behind me? How many deaths do you think you can pin on a guy who's probably already getting rigor mortis out there in the woods?'

'Shut up,' Marie said. 'Tom, get the girl.'

Tom O'Day reached for them with his free hand. Clare clutched at Mikayla, half turning away, and Oscar, who had been leaning against her leg, let out a wolflike snarl and launched himself at the agent. The dog sank his fangs deep into O'Day's forearm. The man screamed and thrashed, beating at Oscar's body, as the dog scrabbled and clawed and hung on as if his jaws were locked.

Marie O'Day shrieked and swung her automatic toward the dog. Russ threw himself at the woman like a linebacker on a goal-line stand. The agent went down beneath him, her gun spinning across the road.

Clare shouldered Mikayla and dashed for the weapon. Tom O'Day, howling and sobbing, fell to his knees. His blood spread over the ice, steaming in the cold air. Clare scooped the automatic from the road and slapped it into Russ's outstretched hand. 'Sit on her,' he said, and Clare complied, dropping onto the agent's shoulders with a thud. She would have worried she was cutting off the woman's oxygen, but Marie O'Day had enough air to curse at her, Russ, and the dog in a steady stream of invective.

'Get him off me! Get him off me!'

Russ strode to Tom O'Day's side and retrieved his weapon. Dropping the gun in his pocket, he slapped his thigh. 'Come, Oscar. Come.' The dog released the agent's arm and backed away, whining. The man collapsed onto the ice. Russ reached down and scratched Oscar's head fiercely as the dog butted against his leg. 'Good dog, Oscar. That's a *good* dog.'

EIGHTEEN

One of the state police snipers put a bullet right through the engine of the middle sled. Hadley saw the shower of sparks, and the snowmobile, which had been building up speed, suddenly slowed. Its driver, anonymous in a cold suit and helmet, leaped off, waving to the other drivers to rescue him. They blasted past, intent on escaping.

Hadley took off for the barn, only to be nearly yanked off her feet by Flynn. 'They have to head for the bridge,' he shouted. 'We can stop them here!'

'How? We can't even identify ourselves!' Unless the fleeing men fired on her and Flynn, they had no justification for using deadly force. Out here in the dark on a freezing bridge, they had no riot gun capable of stopping the sleds, and no beanbag gun that could knock a driver off without causing him harm.

Flynn looked at the remaining two snowmobiles. They were curving around the front, preparing to hit the road near its end and get up to full speed before they rushed the hill. 'Give me your flashlight.'

She handed over her Maglite, hefty enough to be a club. 'You're going to shine a big light at them?'

Flynn unwound the scarf from his neck. He pulled out his own flashlight and wrapped both of them in the end of the scarf.

'No,' he said. 'I'm going to try and knock one of them off his seat. You take aim. If they fire on us, shoot.'

She tugged her Glock from her holster while Flynn secured the flashlights to the scarf with a zip-strap. Grabbing the other end of the scarf with both hands, he hoisted it over one shoulder and began swinging it in a circle above his head.

Julia Spencer-Fleming

The snowmobiles turned onto the road. In the headlights, she could see the silhouette of the Essex County deputy, struggling with the same dilemma they had. She couldn't hear anything over the roar of the engines, but his body language read *Stop! Police!* The sleds blew past him, headed straight for them.

Hadley yanked off her gloves and went down on one knee next to Flynn. She steadied her hand and sighted toward where she thought the driver would be. Above her, Flynn continued whipping the makeshift weapon around, whup-whup-whup until the air hummed. She prayed he wouldn't wrap the thing around his neck or knock himself out. The snowmobiles drew nearer, nearer, and she could see the bubble-headed helmets gleaming in the backwash of the headlights and the noise of the engines was all around them.

In one motion, Flynn *heaved*, whipping the Maglites into the head of the driver nearest him as the snowmobiles blew past. He made contact, and the driver flipped backward off his seat like a circus tumbler, landing full-body on the icy road. His snowmobile, riderless, slowed and veered to the right until it wedged its front runners under the bridge guardrail.

The last snowmobile was escaping over the ridge. *Someone else's work.* She stood, reaching for her cuffs, only to stop at the sight of Flynn with his head thrown back and his arms spread wide above him, in victory. '*Freedom!*' he howled, in his best Braveheart impression.

Then the barn blew up.

384

NINETEEN

Russ guided Marie O'Day into the backseat of the Essex County cruiser so she wouldn't bump her head. He slammed the door on her torrent of abuse and walked back to the black SUV. He glanced inside where Tom O'Day sat, one hand cuffed to the safety bar, the other wrapped in Clare's turtleneck, a makeshift bandage. His wife was waiting for him outside Flynn's Aztek. 'I got it running so she can warm up,' she said.

He didn't answer, just held his arms open. She stepped into his embrace and they rocked together. 'It's okay,' she whispered. 'We're okay.'

Something in that phrase – repentance? love? acceptance? – felled him. He slid to his knees before her and pressed his face into her rounded belly. 'I'm sorry,' he said, his voice cracking. 'I'm so sorry.'

Her hands on his hair were a benediction.

'Hector DeJean died for that little girl.'

'I know.'

'He was scum. I wanted to shoot him. If I had gotten to him while we were at the lake, I would have.'

Her hands stroked his forehead, cupped the back of his skull.

'How can a guy like that turn around and sacrifice his life for his kid?'

'Oh, love. You know how.'

'Yeah.' He let the side of his head drop against her bulk, as if he could hear the future inside her. 'I was wrong. I was angry at you, and at me, and I acted like a spoiled kid because I couldn't have everything just the way I wanted it.'

'It's not your fault. I didn't give you any space for compromise.'

'The thing is, sometimes marriage isn't about compromise. Sometimes it's about giving everything and seeing where it takes you. I'm not . . . very good with that.' He looked up at her. 'But I'm trying.'

She bent over him. 'I love you.'

'I know.' He stood up, his knees creaking. He took her hands. 'I figure if Hector DeJean can die for his child, I can live for mine.' Her eyes were wet, but she smiled at him. He kissed her. 'I have to get back down there.'

'I know. I'll be okay.'

'The rest of the team's got the meth cookers bottled up in the barn—' He paused. There was an engine noise, rising, loud and getting louder, headed up the hill toward them. He had just enough time to push Clare against the Aztek, covering her with his body, before the snowmobile lofted into the air at the hill's crest and slammed onto the road, blasting past them in a shower of ice crystals.

'What was that?'

Russ yanked the walkie-talkie from his pocket and switched it on. 'Kevin? Knox? We just nearly got run over by a sled doing sixty. Something you want to tell me?'

'We got the other two, Chief! We got the other two!' Knox's voice was garbled by some unidentifiable noise.

'Russ, look there. Over the trees.' Clare's tone made him lift his gaze to where she was pointing. The sky above where the meth factory should be was glowing.

He triggered the walkie-talkie. 'Knox, what's going on down there?'

'The barn's on fire, Chief! It just went up in a huge whoosh!' He could hear another voice, saying something. Then Kevin replaced Knox. 'You didn't manage to stop the third guy, did you, Chief?'

'Sorry, Kevin. We'll have to wait until he reaches the highway.' Clare's eyes grew huge. He dropped the walkie-talkie into his pocket. 'What? Is it the baby?'

She shook her head. 'Lieutenant Mongue. I left him in your truck. Blocking the access to South Shore Drive.'

He had a sudden image of that sled slamming into his pickup at sixty miles an hour. 'Kevin's car,' he said. They piled in, and he swung the Aztek in a circle, ignoring the skid as he turned, accelerating down the series of hills.

'Careful.' Clare looked into the backseat, where Mikayla lay drowsing, Oscar beneath her on the floor. 'You don't want to make matters worse by running into him yourself.'

He slowed, then slowed some more as he came around the bend to the final descent. The first thing he saw was his truck, intact and gleaming. The snowmobile was halfway up the trunk of an eastern pine that was now partly uprooted and listing away from the road. He could see the skid marks in his headlights. He slowed to a stop and climbed out of Kevin's SUV.

Bob Mongue was leaning out of the passenger-side window, the Taurus Clare had taken away from Travis Roy trained on the sled's driver, who was sprawled on the ground near the afflicted pine.

'Bob,' Russ said.

'Russ.'

Russ crossed to the driver. 'Keep those hands up,' Bob warned. Russ tugged off his helmet. Travis Roy blinked up at him, his nose bloody, his eyes purpling.

Russ walked back to his truck. 'I've got a pair of cuffs in the glove compartment, if you can reach it.' Bob handed them out. 'Nice collar for a man with a broken leg.'

'I told you I could outpolice you with one hand tied behind my back.' He gestured toward Kevin's SUV. 'Everything okay with your wife?'

Russ found himself smiling. 'Everything's okay. Everything's fine.'

Thursday, 15 January

ONE

We're not sure if the fire was caused by a stray bullet from one of the state police shooters, or if the place was rigged to blow in case of a raid.' Lyle perched on the edge of his seat. There was no way to be comfortable doing this, even if the Johnsons had given him hot chocolate and their best living room chair. 'Because of the chemicals involved in cooking methamphetamine, the fire burned very hot. Everything was destroyed. The men who had been producing the meth said your daughter wasn't there, but I'm afraid there's no way to know for sure.'

Lewis Johnson nodded. 'We have Mikayla legally now. That's all that matters. We're registering her with the tribe so her right to stay with us will be protected. When enough time passes, we'll have Annie declared dead and get permanent guardianship.'

'How's the little girl doing?'

'She'll be in the hospital for a while. But the doctors are hopeful none of her liver function will be compromised.'

'Good. Good.' Lyle didn't know what else to say. Johnson was looking very . . . Mohawk, if Lyle let himself use the stereotype in the privacy of his own head. Stoic. Not giving away an ounce of emotion, despite the fact that his daughter was almost certainly gone.

'You know, there is the possibility that she's still hiding somewhere.'

Johnson shook his head. 'Where would she go?' He looked toward the credenza at the side of the room. It was covered in family photographs. All the other adult Johnson children, happy, living their lives . . . and Annie. 'It's better this way. In New York, grandparents can't sue for custody of grandchildren unless their child is dead. Annie could be so . . .' He paused, weighing his words. 'Pleasing. Always headed for rehab, always just about to get clean, but never quite managing. The social workers would have given Mikayla back to her, you know. After she had finished her sentence.'

Lyle nodded. The man was probably right. He had seen too many kids kept in 'intact' homes until it was too late. 'Still, I wish she had come to you for help after our officers frightened her off.'

Johnson rose, and Lyle rose with him. He shrugged his parka back on and picked up his lid. He and Johnson shook hands. 'If at any time you want to access the files, or know how the investigation is going, Mr Johnson, please give us a call. Your daughter will remain a missing person until we find otherwise.'

'That fire . . .' Johnson had a faraway look in his eyes, as if he could see the meth lab burning. 'You won't find her body.' He focused on Lyle again. 'And there comes a time when a parent has to let go of the child he cannot save, and take up the child he can.'

In his cruiser, Lyle cranked up the heat and let it blow a minute or two before pulling out and headed back to Millers Kill. They would keep Annie Johnson as an open case, but he didn't have much hope. If she had just run to her father like she always had when she was in trouble—

When enough time passes, we'll have Annie declared dead and get permanent guardianship.

The social workers would have given Mikayla back to her, you know.

There comes a time when a parent has to let go of the child he cannot save, and take up the child he can.

'No,' Lyle said emphatically. 'No.' He stopped at a red light. Jesus, he had a chill like someone walked over his grave.

You won't find her body.

'No,' he repeated. He shook himself, hard, then drove on.

Friday, 16 January

ONE

'Well, Ms Fergusson?'

Across the black oak table, Archdeacon Willard Aberforth looked at her piercingly. She glanced around at the faces of her vestry. Mrs Marshall smiled encouragingly.

'I decline,' Clare said.

'Could you clarify?'

'I decline to quietly resign my cure. I have the confidence and the backing of this vestry, and I believe I have the confidence and support of my parishioners. Furthermore, I'm not going to burden my husband with the knowledge that I resigned a position I love and feel called to because we started our family before the wedding could take place. So.' She paused for a moment to make sure her voice was steady. 'If the bishop wishes to convene a disciplinary board and bring up charges, he may.'

Father Aberforth's eyes shone like dark stones. 'Very well.'

'Very well, what?' Geoff Burns asked. 'What's the bishop going to do?'

The archdeacon looked down at the papers before him. 'The bishop gave me my instructions in advance of this meeting. In the event that Ms Fergusson failed to resign . . .' He paused, and she could see it coming before he got it out. *You old drama queen, you.* 'The bishop is willing to let the matter drop.'

Afterward, over a cup of tea in her office, she had her chance to grill him. 'Why did he back down?'

Aberforth tilted his head. 'As you say, you did have the support of the vestry.'

She snorted.

'There was also the matter of the phone calls from members of your

395

congregation.' Oscar roused himself from his makeshift bed beside the bookcase and walked to Aberforth's side. He nudged the archdeacon's hand, and Aberforth began scratching the top of the dog's head. 'While you were away on your adventuresome honeymoon, someone suggested a sort of phone-a-thon on your behalf. Which in and of itself might not sway the bishop, but many of the phone calls also mentioned the matter of money, as in, ceasing to give it if you were brought before a disciplinary board.'

'Wow.' She sipped her tea, trying to pretend it was coffee.

'In addition, I had a conversation with the bishop.' He picked up his cup again. Oscar, deprived of attention, whuffed at him.

'Oscar. Go lie down.' Clare turned back to Aberforth. 'I can just imagine what that went like.'

'No,' he said, quellingly, 'you cannot. I am not entirely in favor of the . . . direction this diocese has taken in the past years. I believe that having just one type of priest, thinking the same thoughts and behaving in the same fashion as everyone else, is detrimental to the church of God. We must have a variety of priests, that we may minster to a variety of people. You, Ms Fergusson, are the spice of life in this diocese.'

She set her cup down and crossed to his chair. She bent over and kissed his head. 'You great big old softy.' She knelt beside him. 'How can I thank you for all you've done for me?'

'Perhaps you might consider naming the child after me.' His tone was desert dry.

She laughed. 'Russ's father's name was Walter. Shall I see if he'll go for Walter Willard?'

TWO

Hadley should have been at the station already. Her shift had ended a half hour ago, but the three drivers involved in the accident near the Super Kmart kept changing their stories, and she had had to keep two tow trucks waiting while she tried to sort out who did what to whom. Now she was on her way back to Millers Kill. She hoped she'd be in time to catch Flynn. They weren't going out tonight, but she was going to join him for his family's Sunday dinner again. They were still trying to keep it on the down low at work, but she could feel herself lighting up every time he walked into the squad room. It was the damnedest thing. She was getting to be as starry-eyed as he was, as if all the crap in her life had never happened.

Her cell rang. She answered. 'Officer Hadley Knox?' The woman on the other end of the line wasn't any dispatcher she knew.

'This is Hadley Knox.'

'Officer, this is a courtesy call from the Albany Airport Police.'

Hadley signaled a turn and brought her cruiser to the side of the road. She turned on her light bar to steer other drivers clear. 'Yes?'

'Your husband, Dylan Knox—'

'My ex-husband. We've been divorced three years.'

'Ah.' The voice on the other end of the line sounded relieved. 'That explains it. Okay. I'm afraid your ex was arrested at the airport earlier this afternoon. A security check of his bag turned up nine ounces of methamphetamine.'

Hadley's body went numb.

'Because it's under the felony possession level, he's going to be processed, bailed, and released, probably by next Monday. He'll be free to leave for California pending his trial.'

'He lives in California.' She had no idea why she said that.

'He got . . .' The officer paused, as if choosing her words. 'Very vocal about his arrest. He blamed you for the meth being in his bag. I'm guessing you don't have the most amicable divorce?'

'No.'

'Yeah. I'm sure you know this, but we ran his record and he has multiple possession charges in his past. So I don't think you're going to have to worry about anyone taking his accusations seriously. I just wanted to give you the heads-up, officer to officer.'

'Thank you.'

'And a piece of advice? Divorcée to divorcée? Make sure your lawyer knows about this. You never know when you'll need some ammunition.'

'Yes. I will. Thank you.'

She sat there after she had hung up, remembering that night when they had gotten the kids from Dylan's hotel room. Flynn staying behind in his car for a minute while she searched for Dylan's rental. Flynn searching through Dylan's luggage. And earlier, that Baggie of meth they had taken from Mike Boileau. She remembered tossing it into the glove compartment to keep until they could enter it in the evidence locker at the Albany PD South Station. But they never did that, did they? Boileau had turned out to be DEA and they all went straight to the Federal Building. She couldn't recall seeing it again after the glove compartment. You were supposed to keep close track of evidence.

Evidence. There was a name for cops who planted evidence.

Flynn's voice, solid and determined. *You're not going to give up the kids. And you're not going to have to move back to California. I promise you, we won't let it happen.*

She didn't think that Baggie of glassine envelopes was in his car anymore. She laid her head against the steering wheel. 'Oh, God, Flynn,' she whispered. 'What have you done?'

THREE

Flynn decided to change in the locker room, so he missed the earlier hub-bub. It was a big package, he knew that, because Harlene and Noble had argued about whether or not it ought to be X-rayed, and then Duane and Tim, who were there to clock in their hours, weighed in that it might be a bomb, until finally Harlene threw up her hands and said she didn't think al Qaeda was targeting Millers Kill, New York, and she tore off the wrapping.

He got back upstairs, having decided to shower and then change. MacAuley would rib him if he noticed, but what the hell. He wandered into Harlene's dispatch. 'Hey. Hadley gotten back yet?'

'No, she called in. Sounds like a bear of an accident. Bunch of idiots all trying to shift the blame on each other.'

'Ah. Okay.' He didn't want it to sound like Hadley was the only thing he was interested in. 'Anything else happening?'

'Eric finally got ahold of that Amber Willis girl. The one who went up to the lake with the chief? Not very bright, if you ask me. Didn't think twice about her uncle showing up with his girlfriend's daughter, and she thought they loaned Hector DeJean's truck to her and her baby daddy out of the goodness of their heart.'

'Huh.' He couldn't even fake being interested in Amber Willis. There was a roar of approval from the squad room. 'What was in the package?'

Harlene snorted. 'Movies. With a nice card, said thanks to all the men of the MKPD for their fine work.'

He shook his head. 'What, nothing for you and Hadley? Sexism rears its ugly head again.'

'Hah. I'm not interested in *those* kind of movies. And that lot in there better have 'em off the TV and into the box before the chief gets back or there'll be hell to pay.'

He walked toward the squad room. Paul and Noble and Duane and Tim had pulled chairs up in a semicircle around the combination TV/DVD/VCR they used for filmed evidence. What they were looking at was definitely not evidence, unless they had had a case involving illegal group sex he hadn't heard about.

The box was open on the briefing table. Some of the videotapes were in boxes, but most were just the plastic cassettes with stickers on them. He picked up one. BARELY LEGAL 3: BACKDOOR. Another one read CHICKS WITH STICKS: HIGH SCHOOL HOCKEY HONEYS.

'Good God.' He put the video down. 'If any of these feature underage performers, you guys will be seriously violating the law.'

'Siddown, Dudley Do-Right.' Paul Urquhart slapped the chair next to him without turning his head away from the screen. 'They're "barely legal". That means they use eighteen-year-olds and put 'em in pigtails and stuff.'

Kevin glanced over their heads. The cheesy music was fading beneath theatrical moans and groans. The sound of flesh slapping against flesh replaced the synthesizer. He rolled his eyes. 'What's this gem?'

'*Girl's College Go-Down,*' Duane said. 'The box says they used real college girls, but I kind of doubt it.'

The camera swung to one heavily made-up brunette who really did look barely legal. She dropped her book bag and said, 'Can anybody join this party?'

Her voice reminded him of Hadley, saying, *You're the only lover I've had since I moved to Millers Kill.* He squirmed uncomfortably. The girl onscreen dropped her book bag and stripped off her dress.

'Now see,' Paul said, 'this is how you know it's an older film. The girls got natural tits. Nowadays, they're all fake. And they all got piercings.'

The girl slowly mounted one of two muscular men lying on a bed.

'I don't get piercings,' Tim said. 'I mean, who wants to rub up against metal?'

The other man moved behind her. The shot cut to a close-up, so there would be no doubt as to what was going where. 'Your wife let you do that?' Tim asked Duane.

'Are you kidding? I'm lucky if my wife gives it to me once a month missionary style.'

The threesome began moving. The rhythmic groaning was accompanied by more throbbing cocktail-lounge music.

'Well. This is certainly a morale lifter to come back to.' MacAuley tossed his lid on a desk and walked up to the group.

'Oh, hell.' Paul lurched to his feet. 'Is the chief with you?'

'No.' MacAuley's voice was odd, but Kevin was too intent on the screen to pay attention. 'You've got another half hour or so.' He pulled up a chair. 'Where'd this come from?'

'A gift from a grateful citizen,' Paul said.

'You guys must be better out there than I think.' MacAuley picked up the box. 'Real college girls, huh? Now I'm starting to regret I never got a degree.'

The camera swung around the trio. Another girl entered the picture. She kissed the brunette and began to go to work on her as well.

'See, that's probably more like what they've got going on in girls' schools.' Tim sounded thoughtful.

The movement picked up. 'Geez. Look at that.' Paul sounded like he wanted to be alone in the room with the tape.

'Mm-hm. That's a nice piece of ass.' Duane slid down in his chair.

The man behind the brunette gathered up her long, heavy locks and twisted them, pulling her head back, giving her the sleek look of short hair. Everyone in the squad room froze.

'Hey,' Noble said. 'That looks like Hadley.'

The camera lingered on the girl's look of ecstasy. Kevin felt – he didn't know what he felt. It was if all his senses had suddenly decoupled from his body. Everything was distant. Fuzzy.

The girl smiled.

'Holy shit,' Paul said. 'It *is* Hadley.'

MacAuley stood abruptly and snapped the TV off. 'Get that thing out of the machine and back into the box. Noble, I want you to take custody of this.' He pointed at the large carton full of tapes. 'Take it out to the dump and leave it there.' He turned to leave, then turned back. 'Break the cassettes into pieces, then leave them there.' He left the room.

'Holy shit,' Duane said.

'Lemme see the box.' Paul stood up, the movie in hand, and began rummaging through the carton.

'Hey.' Noble frowned. 'Dep said don't.'

'I'm just looking to see if they have the same actress, that's all.' He picked one of the boxed cassettes. 'Honey Potts,' he said. He looked at the one in his hand. 'Honey Potts.' He dropped them onto the desk and dug up another one. 'Honey Potts. I'll be damned. Looks like our Officer Knox was a busy, busy girl back in California.'

Duane told Paul to cut it out, and they started arguing, but it slipped past Kevin like conversation in a passing car. He walked across the hall. He walked down the stairs. He walked through the locker room. He walked into the showers. He turned on two, twisting the knobs until they threatened to snap off. And then, when the water thundered down so no one could hear, he pressed himself into a corner and sank to the floor and sobbed.

FOUR

'The town appreciates the yeoman's service given by the police department during the recent weather emergency.' Mayor Cameron leaned against the council table. 'I don't think anyone here would gainsay that.'

'The weather emergency is hardly over,' Russ said. 'There are still large areas of the three towns without power. Which means homes without inhabitants and stores without security. Exactly the sort of situation you need in-community policing for.'

'Neighborhood watch,' Harold Collins said.

'And we're all impressed and pleased that you managed to find the kidnapped girl and the arsonist in such short order.'

'With the help of the FBI, the state police, and the Essex County Sheriff's Department.'

Jim Cameron gave Collins the side-eye. 'You're out of order, Harold.'

Harold made a noise.

'Did you get the statement from Lieutenant Mongue?' Russ was afraid he sounded desperate. He was regretting sending Lyle back to the station, but the board of aldermen had kept them cooling their heels for almost forty-five minutes, and somebody had to sign off on the hour sheets.

'Lieutenant Mongue's letter was quite expressive, yes.'

'And Elle Flynn's recommendation?'

Jim Cameron nodded.

'Hardly a neutral party, is she?' Collins asked.

Russ took a breath. 'I'd just like to say—'

Jim cut him off. 'We really have all we need, Russ. I'm going to call for a vote. All those in favor of putting a measure on the ballot to allow for the disbandment of the town police department and the assumption of their duties by the state police, say aye.'

Russ counted the hands. Bob Miles, Ed Palmer, and Harold Collins.

'All those not in favor, say nay.' Garry Greuling and Ron Tucker raised their hands.

Jim sighed. 'And the mayor votes aye.' At least he wasn't smiling, like Collins. 'I'm sorry, Russ, but the citizens of the three towns have the right to make this decision. It's their tax monies keeping you afloat.'

Russ walked back to the station slowly. He admired the solid granite face of it, the graceful arches and the stone columns framing the huge windows. It was old and out of date and he loved it. He climbed the steps to the front door, something he had done hundreds and hundreds of times in the last decade. The sigh from the door's hydraulic hinge could have come from him.

There was talk going on in the squad room, but he didn't stick his head in. Soon enough time to tell everyone their jobs might be gone. He ducked around the corner so Harlene couldn't see him and drew up short at the sight of Kevin, standing in his office.

'Kevin,' Russ said. He looked more closely. The kid was in civvies. His face was pale, and his eyes were red-rimmed. 'Is everything all right? Family okay?'

Kevin nodded. 'Yes. Thank you.' His voice was tight and low. He swallowed. 'I just wanted you to know. I'm tendering my resignation. I'm taking the job in Syracuse.'

ACKNOWLEDGMENTS

I always thank the ever-supportive folks at Minotaur and Thomas Dunne Books, but this time, I'd like to particularly remember the late Matthew Shear. Everything about Matthew was large – his heart, his laugh, his appetite, his capacity for drink, and, most important, his love of books. Making, selling, writing, and reading them, Matthew knew more about the ins and outs of the publishing business than anyone else I knew, and he was always happy to share his knowledge and enthusiasm. He will be missed.

Thank you, Sally Richardson, Tom Dunne, Andy Martin, Matt Baldacci, Pete Wolverton, and all the terrific talent in the Art department. Thanks to my hardworking editor, Katie Gilligan; her equally hardworking assistant, Melanie Fried; and my very good-natured publicist, Hector DeJean. As ever, Meg Ruley and the good ship Jane Rotrosen Agency had my back.

Thanks to James Taylor, of Taylor Made Design, for my Web site, and to Joan Emerson, who keeps Julia Spencer-Fleming's Reader Space running. Thanks to all the real-life people who let me use their names as characters (you know who you are). Thanks to all my friends at MaineCrimeWriters.com, and to my sister-bloggers at Jungle Red Writers: Rhys Bowen, Jan Brogan, Lucy Burdett, Deborah Crombie, Hallie Ephron, Rosemary Harris, and Hank Phillippi Ryan.

And many thanks to the people in my life who keep me going: Ross, Victoria, Spencer, Virginia, Pat and Julia, Barb and Dan, John and Lois, Rachael and the boys, Les, Tracy, Mary L. Allen, and everyone at the Cathedral Church of St. Luke in Portland.